SPEAK UP!

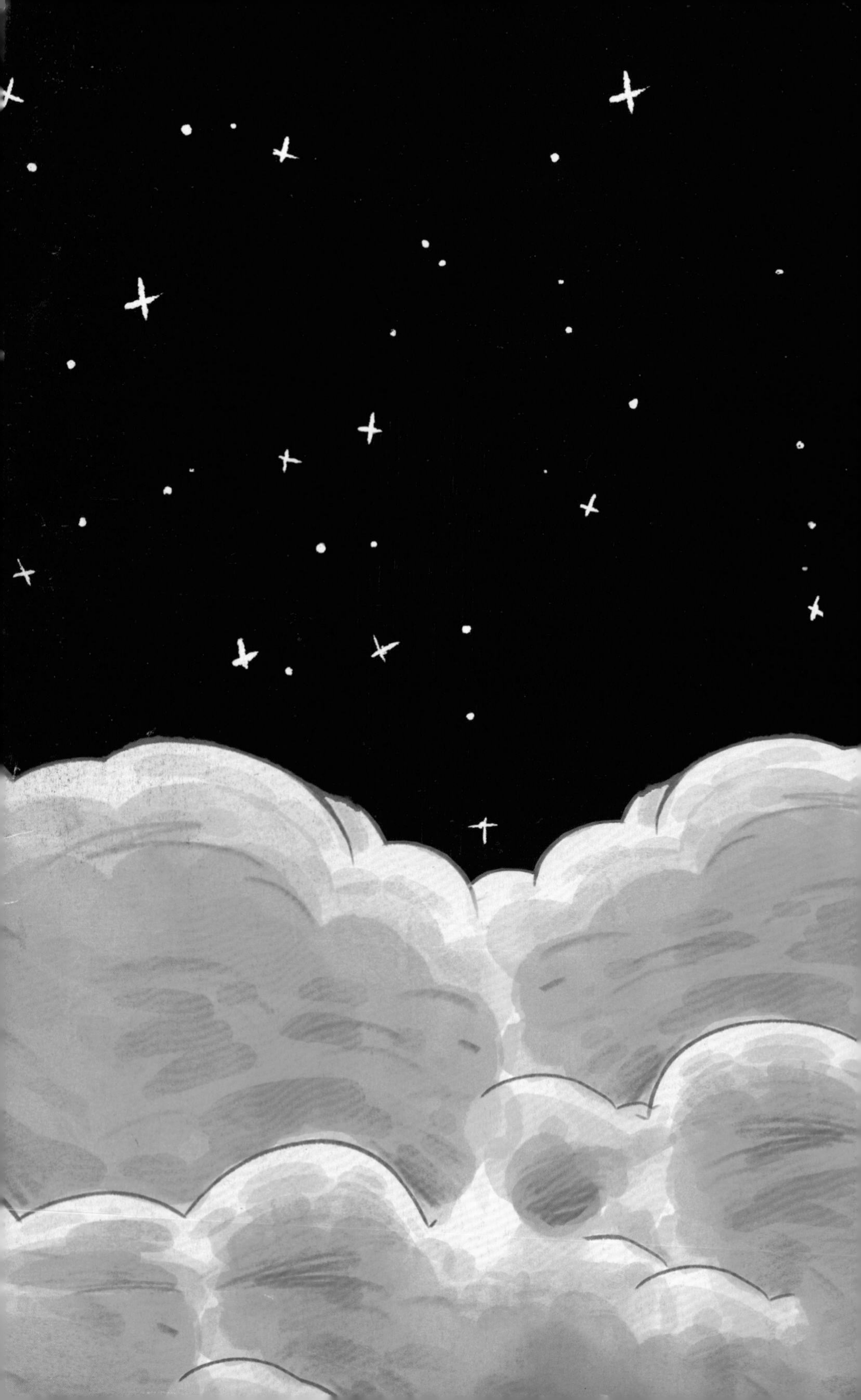

SPEAK UP!

REBECCA BURGESS

Quill Tree Books

Imprints of HarperCollinsPublishers

Quill Tree Books is an imprint of HarperCollins Publishers.
HarperAlley is an imprint of HarperCollins Publishers.

Speak Up!

For information address HarperCollins Children's Books, a division of HarperCollins Publishers, 195 Broadway, New York, NY 10007.
www.harperalley.com

Library of Congress Control Number: 2022934043
ISBN 978-0-06-308119-2 (paperback)
ISBN 978-0-06-308120-8 (hardcover)

The artist used Photoshop to create the illustrations for this book.
22 23 24 25 26 RTLO 10 9 8 7 6 5 4 3 2 1
❖
First Edition

FOR AMANDA, LAURA, KATE, AND MOTH—
AS WE'VE GROWN UP TOGETHER, I'VE SEEN
YOU ALL FIND YOUR VOICES TOO!

CHAPTER ONE

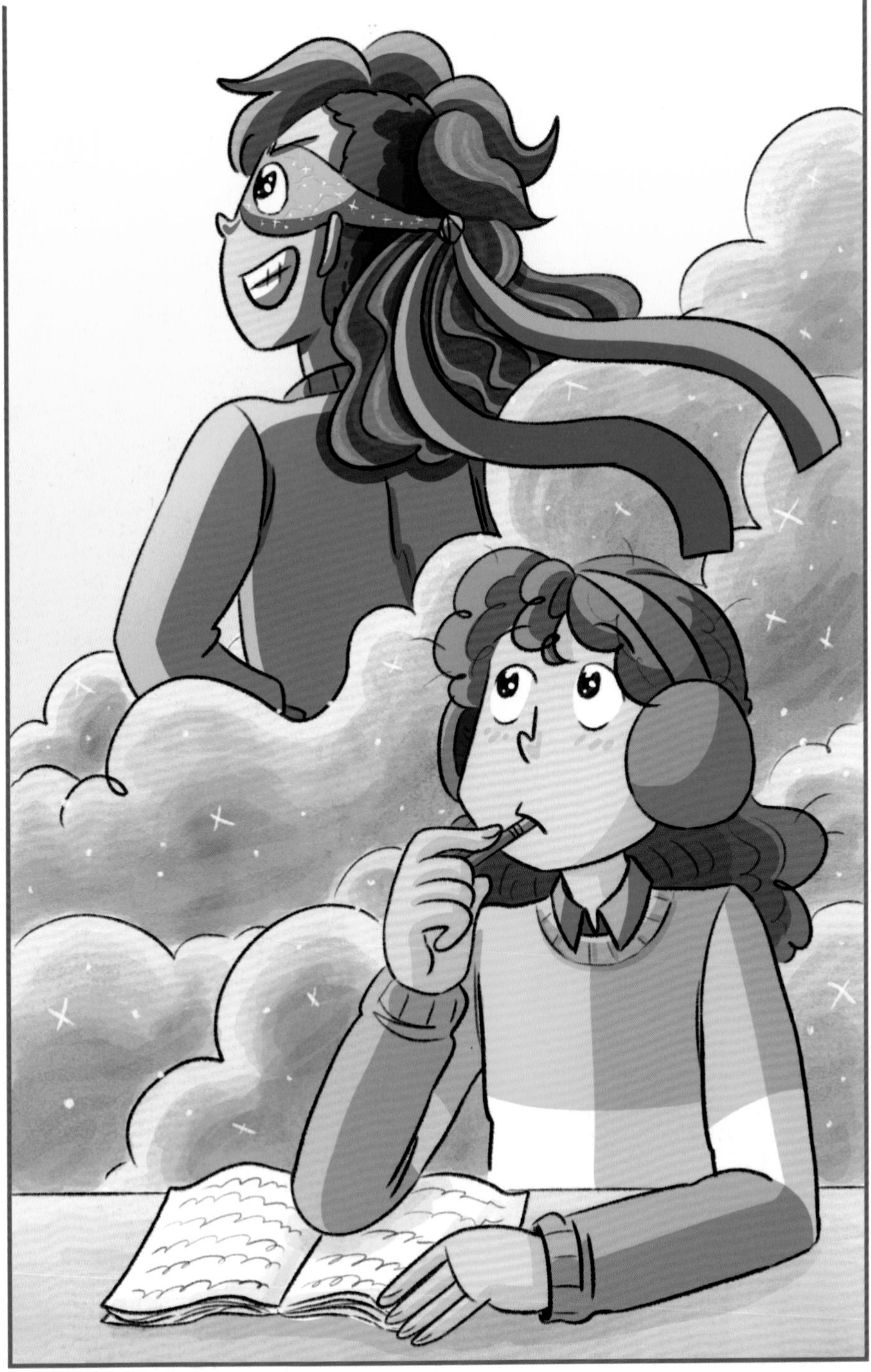

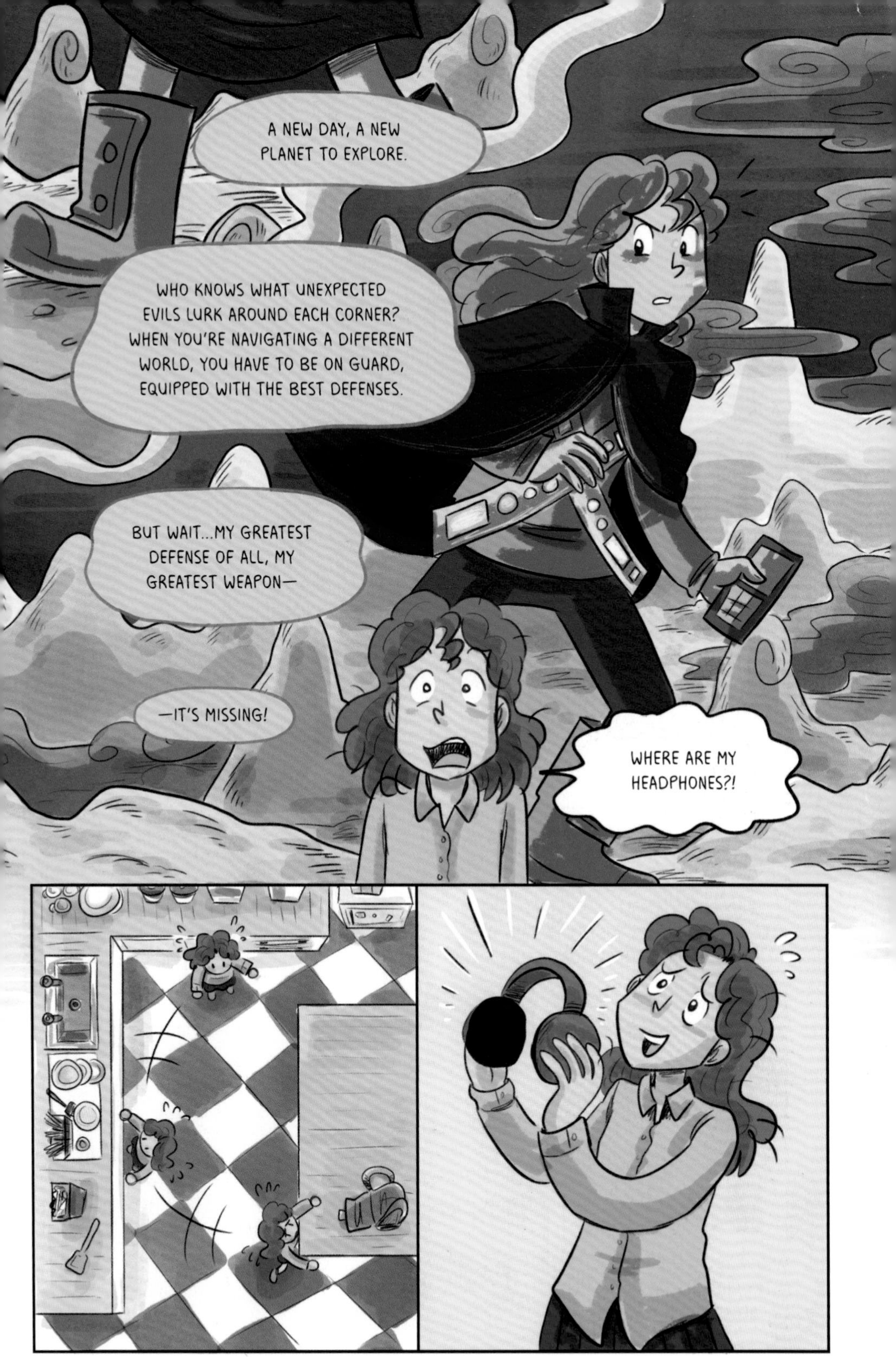
A NEW DAY, A NEW PLANET TO EXPLORE.
WHO KNOWS WHAT UNEXPECTED EVILS LURK AROUND EACH CORNER? WHEN YOU'RE NAVIGATING A DIFFERENT WORLD, YOU HAVE TO BE ON GUARD, EQUIPPED WITH THE BEST DEFENSES.
BUT WAIT...MY GREATEST DEFENSE OF ALL, MY GREATEST WEAPON—
—IT'S MISSING!
WHERE ARE MY HEADPHONES?!

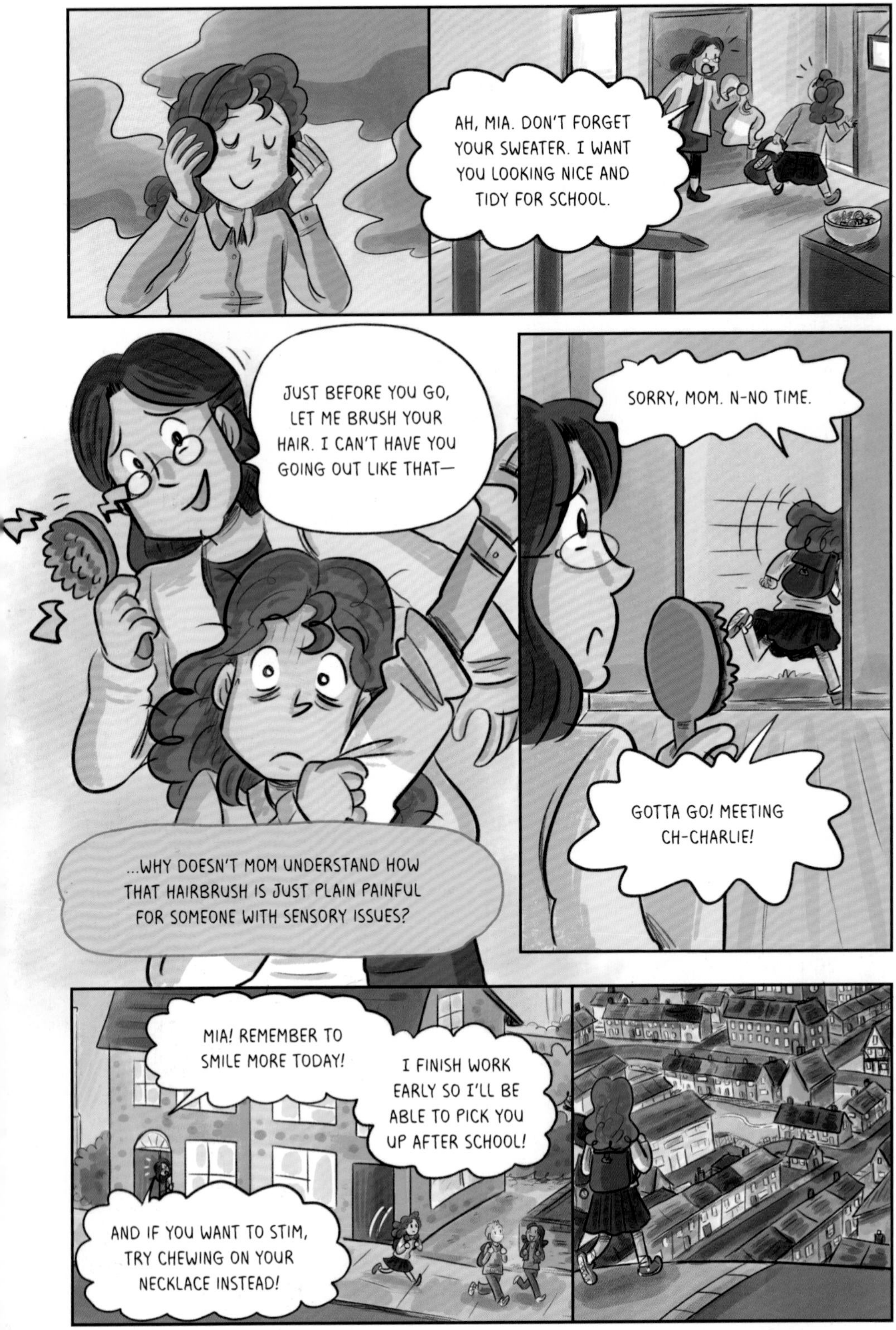
AH, MIA. DON'T FORGET YOUR SWEATER. I WANT YOU LOOKING NICE AND TIDY FOR SCHOOL.
JUST BEFORE YOU GO, LET ME BRUSH YOUR HAIR. I CAN'T HAVE YOU GOING OUT LIKE THAT—
...WHY DOESN'T MOM UNDERSTAND HOW THAT HAIRBRUSH IS JUST PLAIN PAINFUL FOR SOMEONE WITH SENSORY ISSUES?
SORRY, MOM. N-NO TIME.
GOTTA GO! MEETING CH-CHARLIE!
MIA! REMEMBER TO SMILE MORE TODAY!
I FINISH WORK EARLY SO I'LL BE ABLE TO PICK YOU UP AFTER SCHOOL!
AND IF YOU WANT TO STIM, TRY CHEWING ON YOUR NECKLACE INSTEAD!

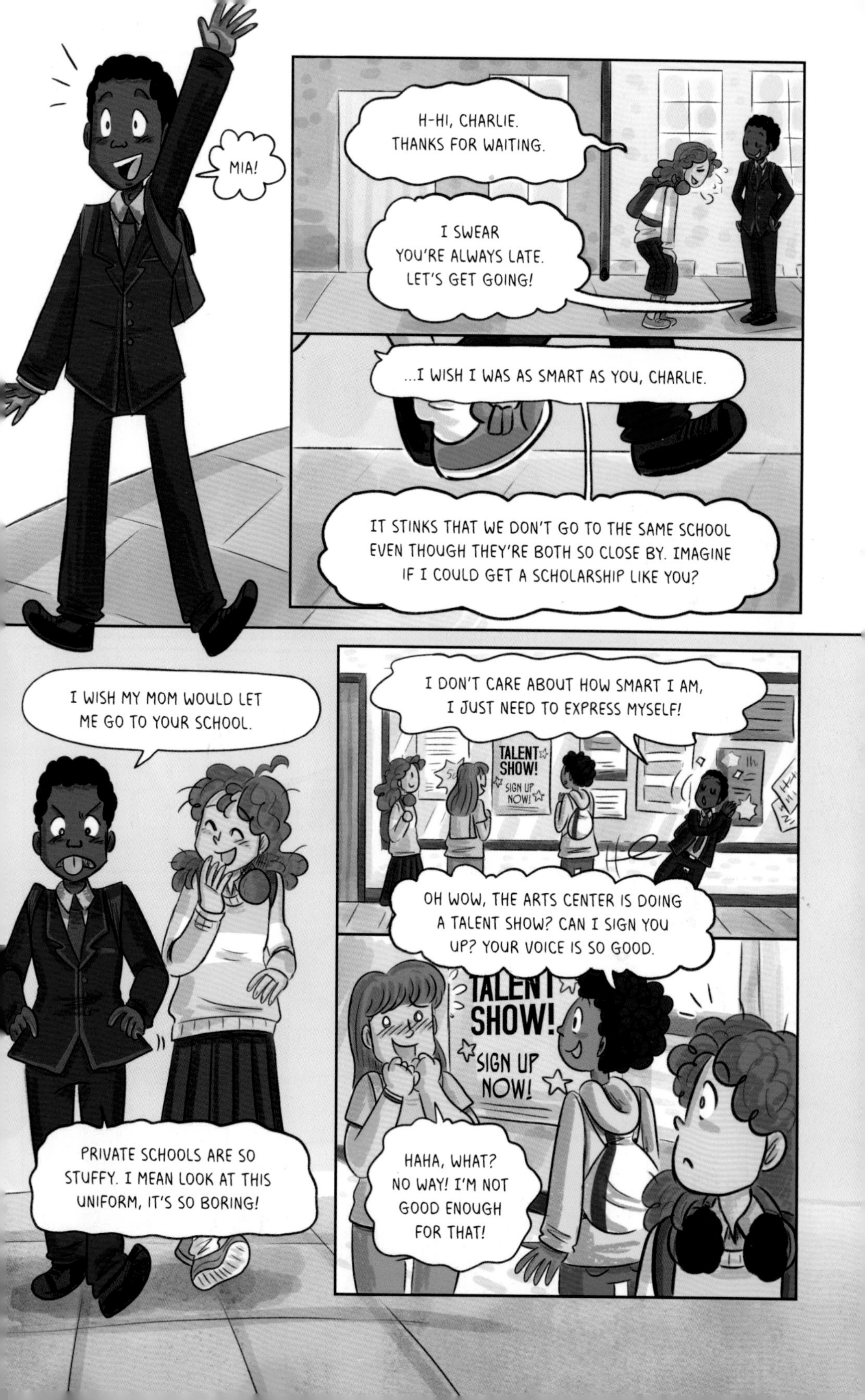
MIA!
H-HI, CHARLIE. THANKS FOR WAITING.
I SWEAR YOU'RE ALWAYS LATE. LET'S GET GOING!
...I WISH I WAS AS SMART AS YOU, CHARLIE.
IT STINKS THAT WE DON'T GO TO THE SAME SCHOOL EVEN THOUGH THEY'RE BOTH SO CLOSE BY. IMAGINE IF I COULD GET A SCHOLARSHIP LIKE YOU?
I WISH MY MOM WOULD LET ME GO TO YOUR SCHOOL.
PRIVATE SCHOOLS ARE SO STUFFY. I MEAN LOOK AT THIS UNIFORM, IT'S SO BORING!
I DON'T CARE ABOUT HOW SMART I AM, I JUST NEED TO EXPRESS MYSELF!
TALENT SHOW! SIGN UP NOW!
OH WOW, THE ARTS CENTER IS DOING A TALENT SHOW? CAN I SIGN YOU UP? YOUR VOICE IS SO GOOD.
TALENT SHOW! SIGN UP NOW!
HAHA, WHAT? NO WAY! I'M NOT GOOD ENOUGH FOR THAT!

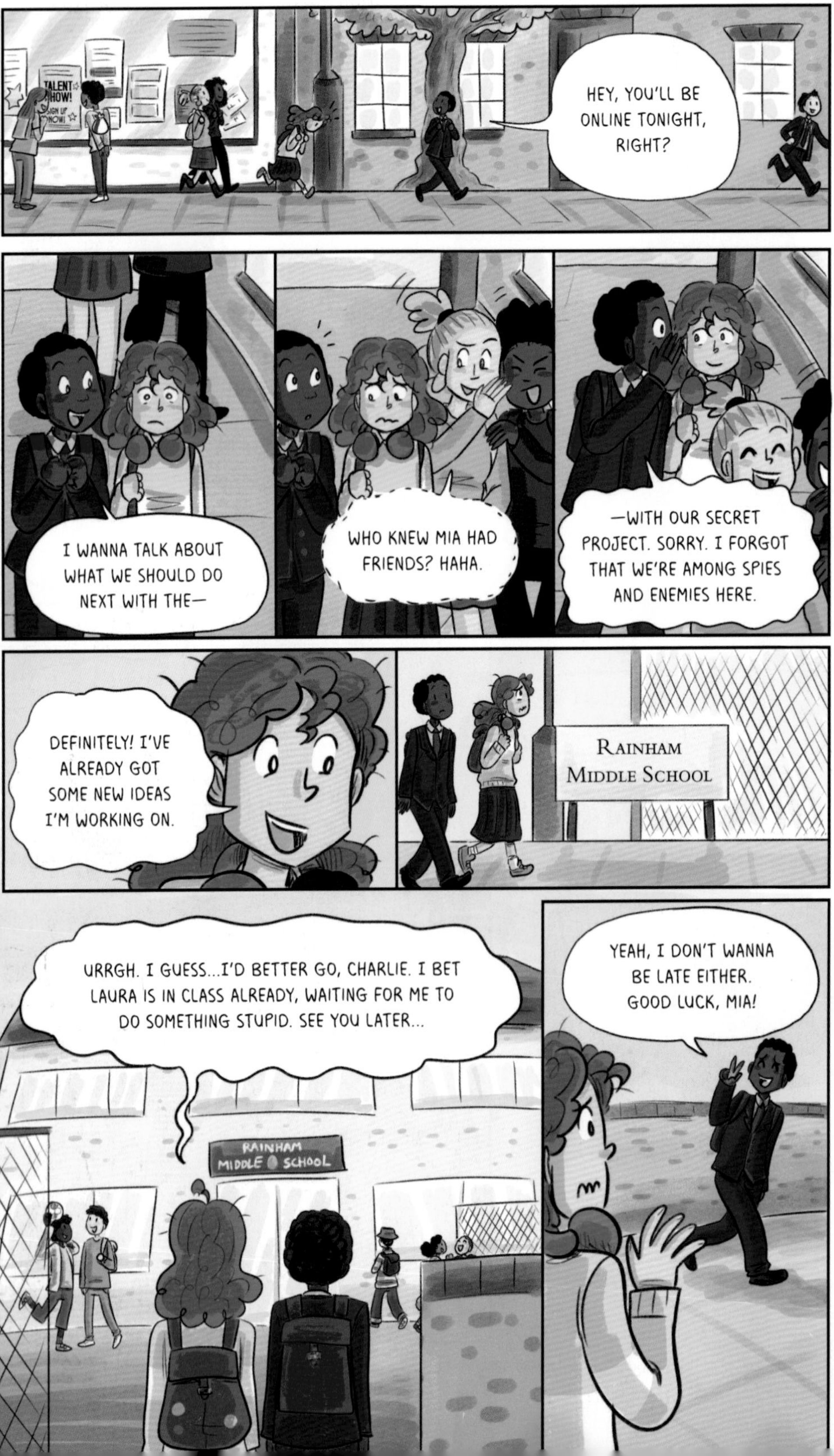
TALENT SHOW!
SIGN UP NOW!
HEY, YOU'LL BE ONLINE TONIGHT, RIGHT?
I WANNA TALK ABOUT WHAT WE SHOULD DO NEXT WITH THE—
WHO KNEW MIA HAD FRIENDS? HAHA.
—WITH OUR SECRET PROJECT. SORRY. I FORGOT THAT WE'RE AMONG SPIES AND ENEMIES HERE.
DEFINITELY! I'VE ALREADY GOT SOME NEW IDEAS I'M WORKING ON.
RAINHAM MIDDLE SCHOOL
URRGH. I GUESS...I'D BETTER GO, CHARLIE. I BET LAURA IS IN CLASS ALREADY, WAITING FOR ME TO DO SOMETHING STUPID. SEE YOU LATER...
RAINHAM MIDDLE SCHOOL
YEAH, I DON'T WANNA BE LATE EITHER. GOOD LUCK, MIA!

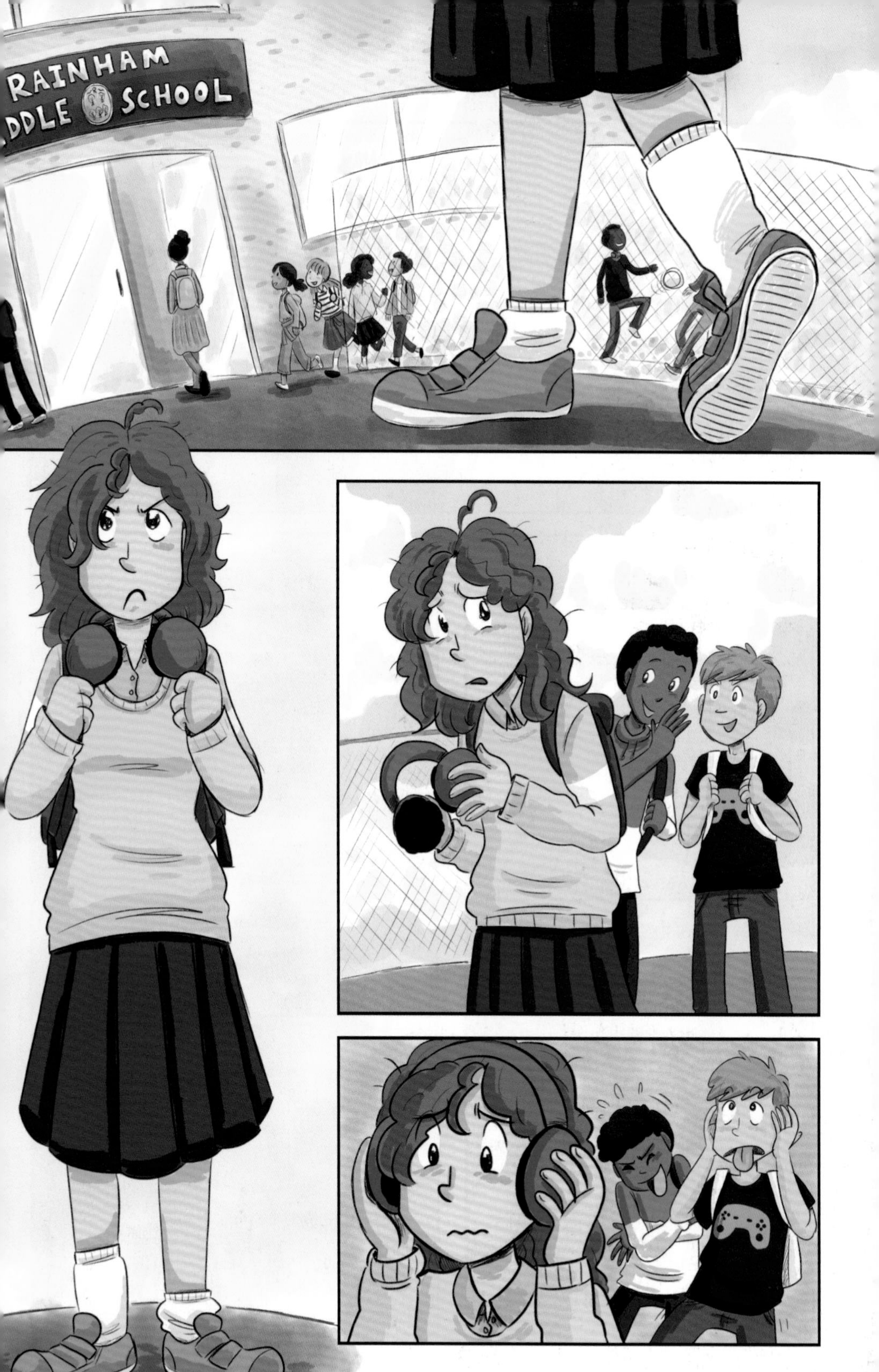
RAINHAM
DDLE SCHOOL

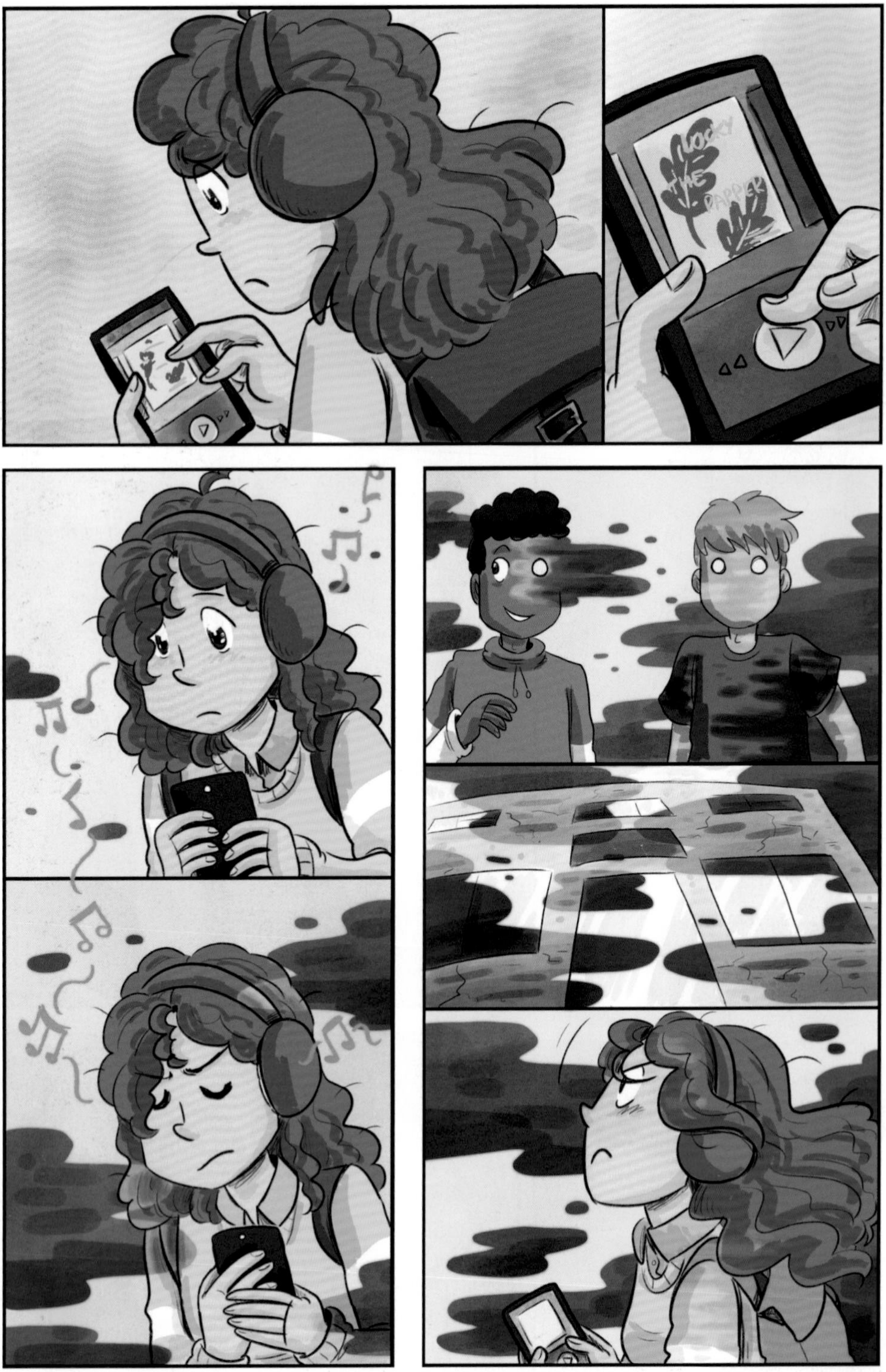

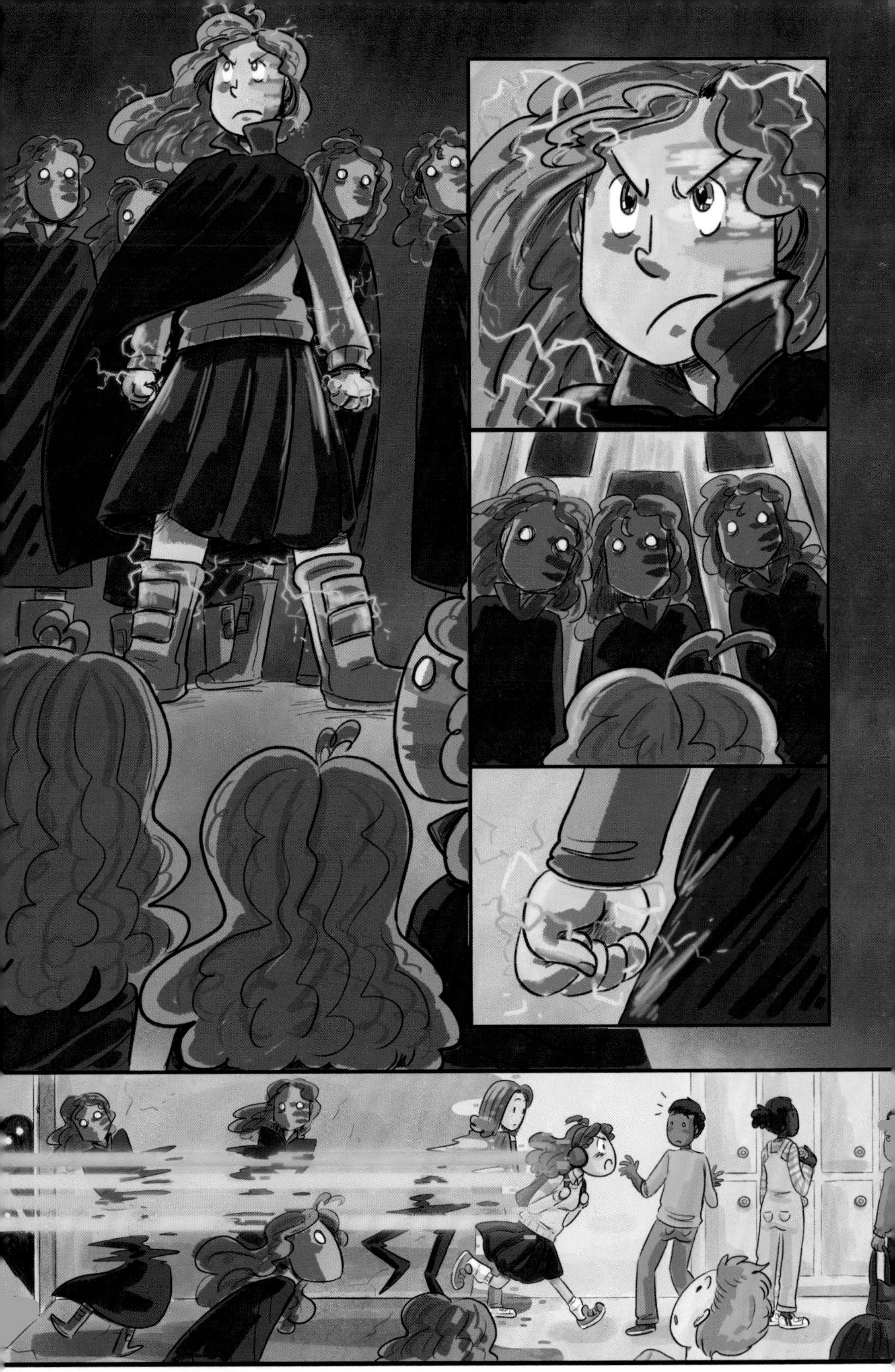

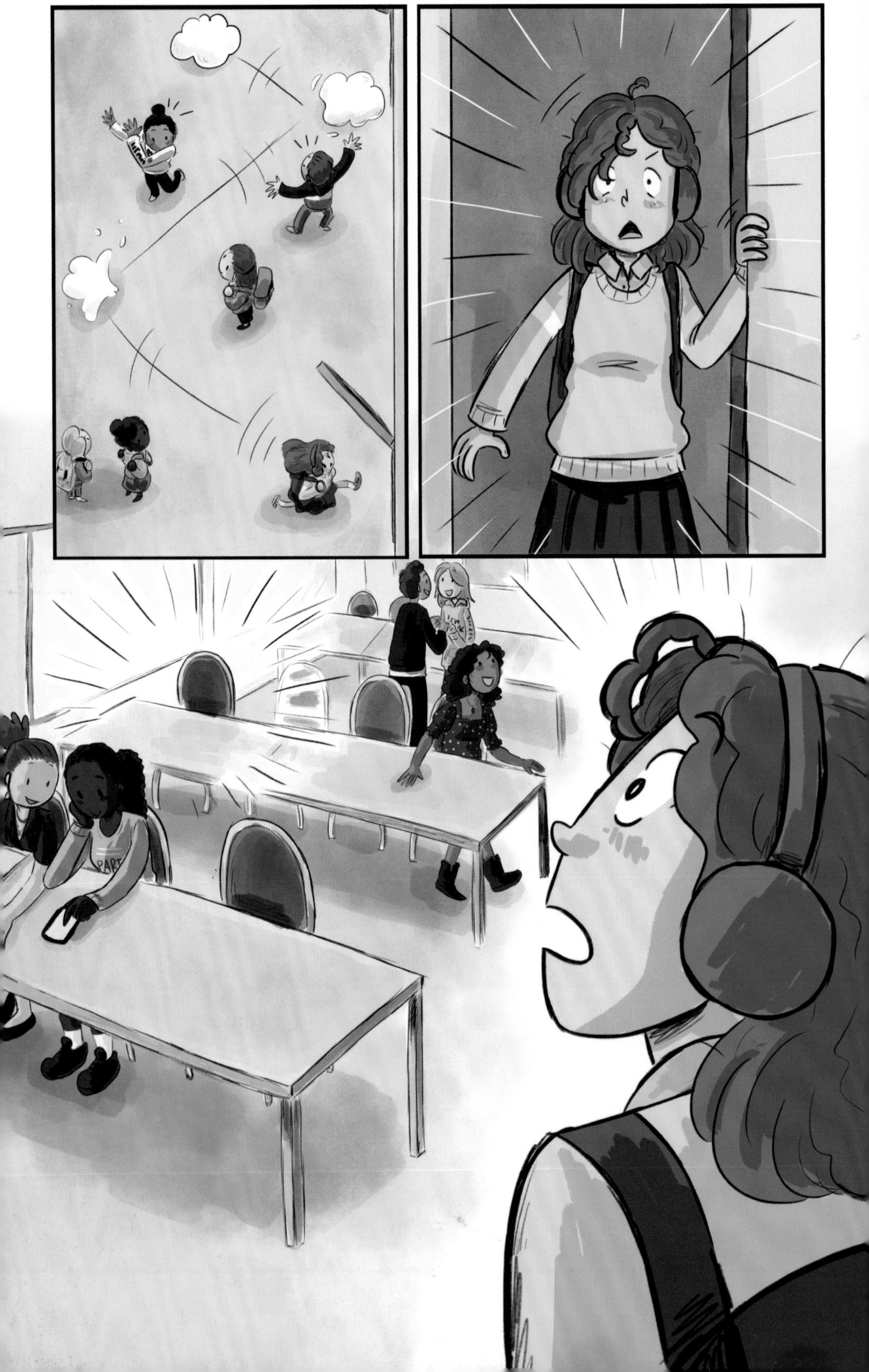
PART

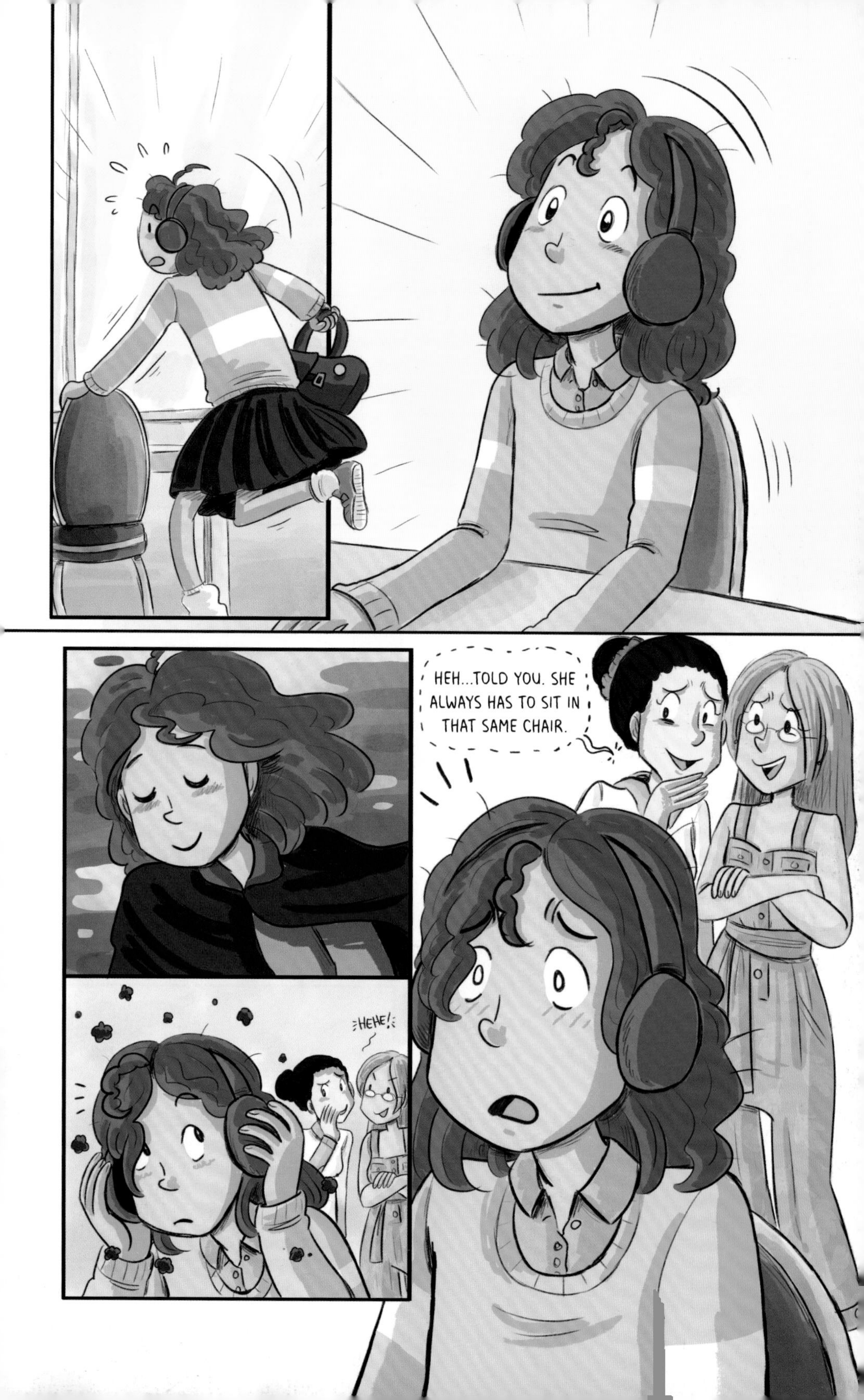
HEH...TOLD YOU. SHE ALWAYS HAS TO SIT IN THAT SAME CHAIR.
HEHE!

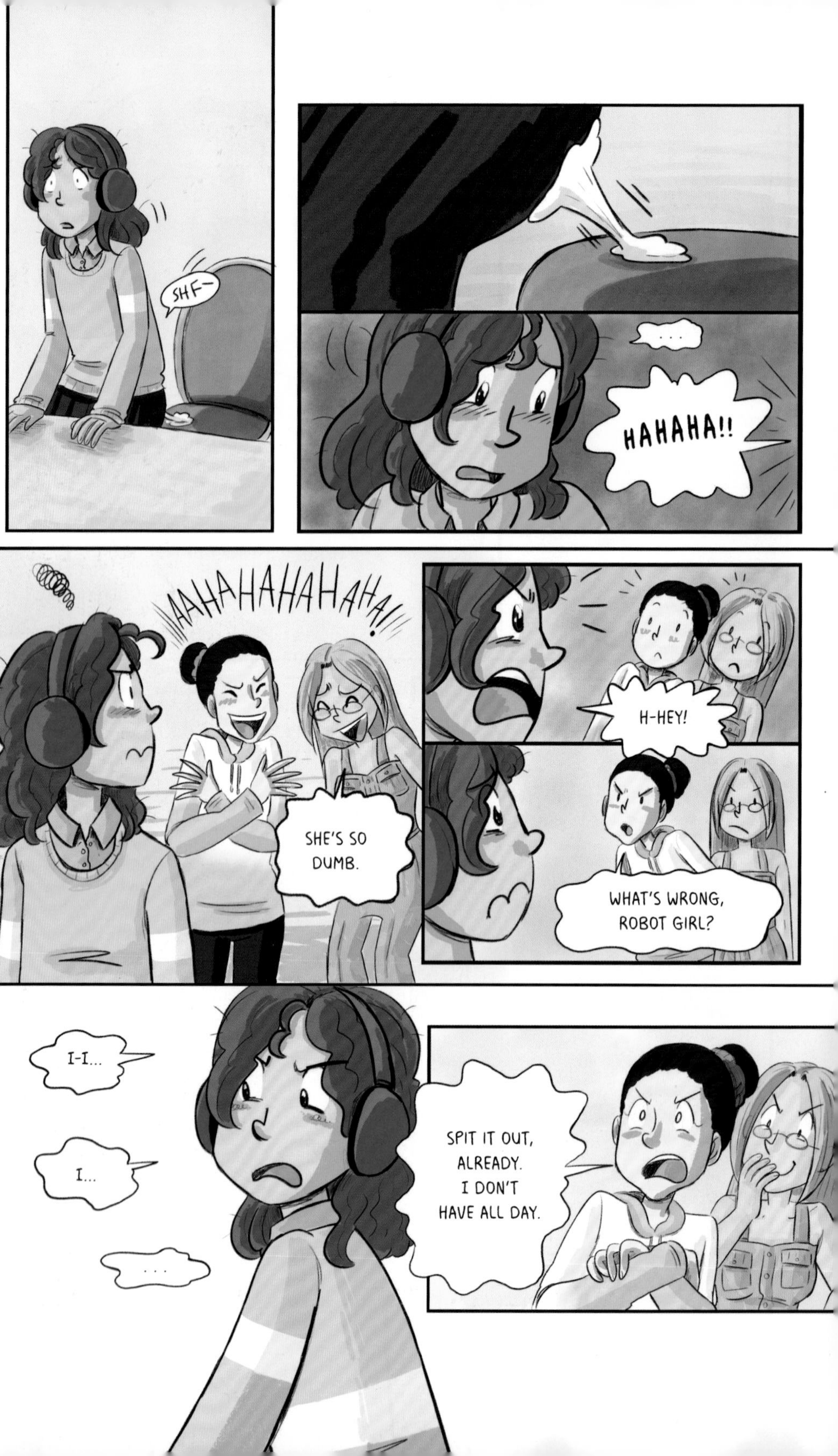
SHF–
. . .
HAHAHA!!
AAHAHAHAHAHAHA!
SHE'S SO DUMB.
H-HEY!
WHAT'S WRONG, ROBOT GIRL?
I-I...
I...
. . .
SPIT IT OUT, ALREADY. I DON'T HAVE ALL DAY.

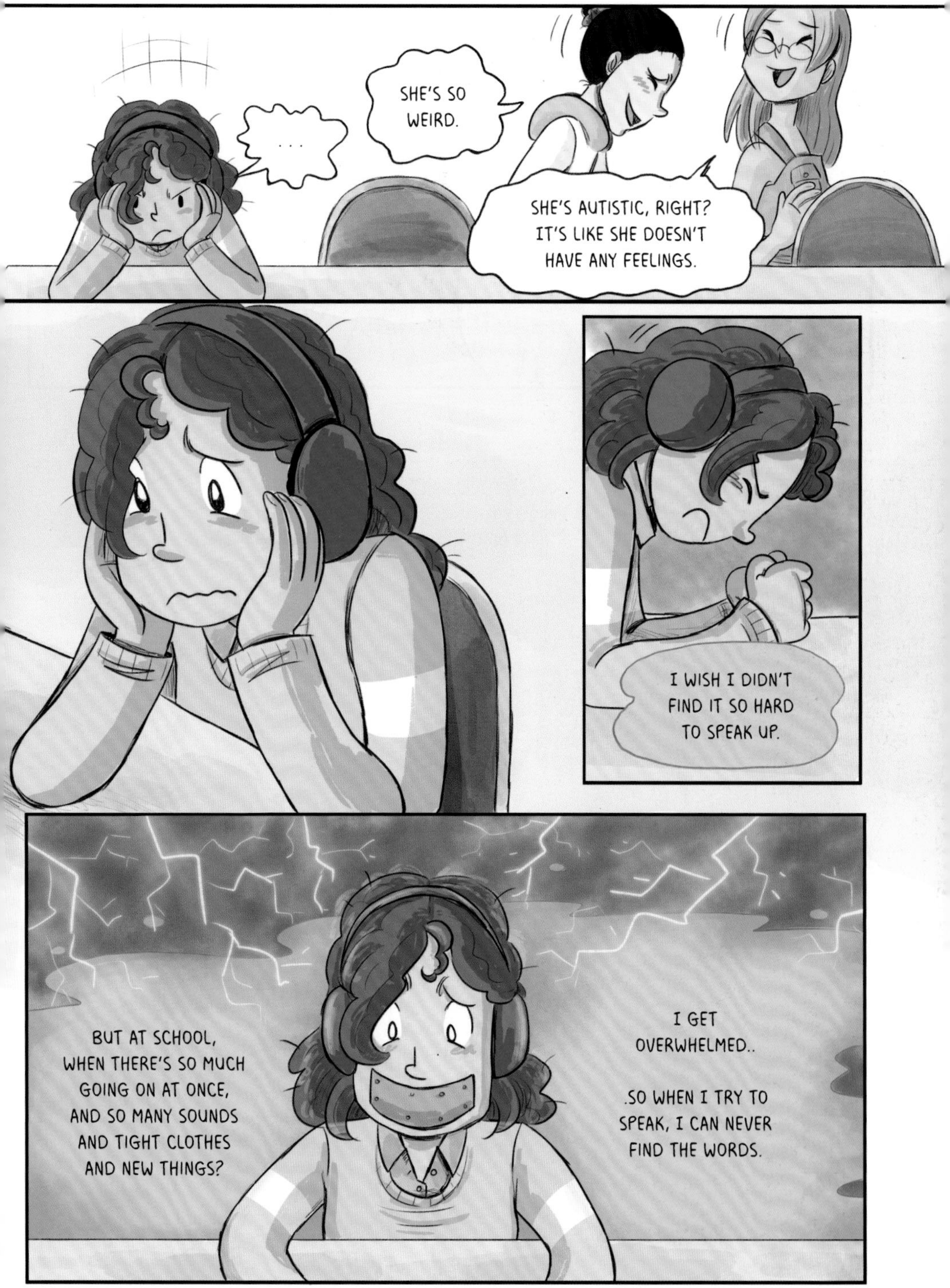
...
SHE'S SO WEIRD.
SHE'S AUTISTIC, RIGHT? IT'S LIKE SHE DOESN'T HAVE ANY FEELINGS.
I WISH I DIDN'T FIND IT SO HARD TO SPEAK UP.
BUT AT SCHOOL, WHEN THERE'S SO MUCH GOING ON AT ONCE, AND SO MANY SOUNDS AND TIGHT CLOTHES AND NEW THINGS?
I GET OVERWHELMED..
.SO WHEN I TRY TO SPEAK, I CAN NEVER FIND THE WORDS.

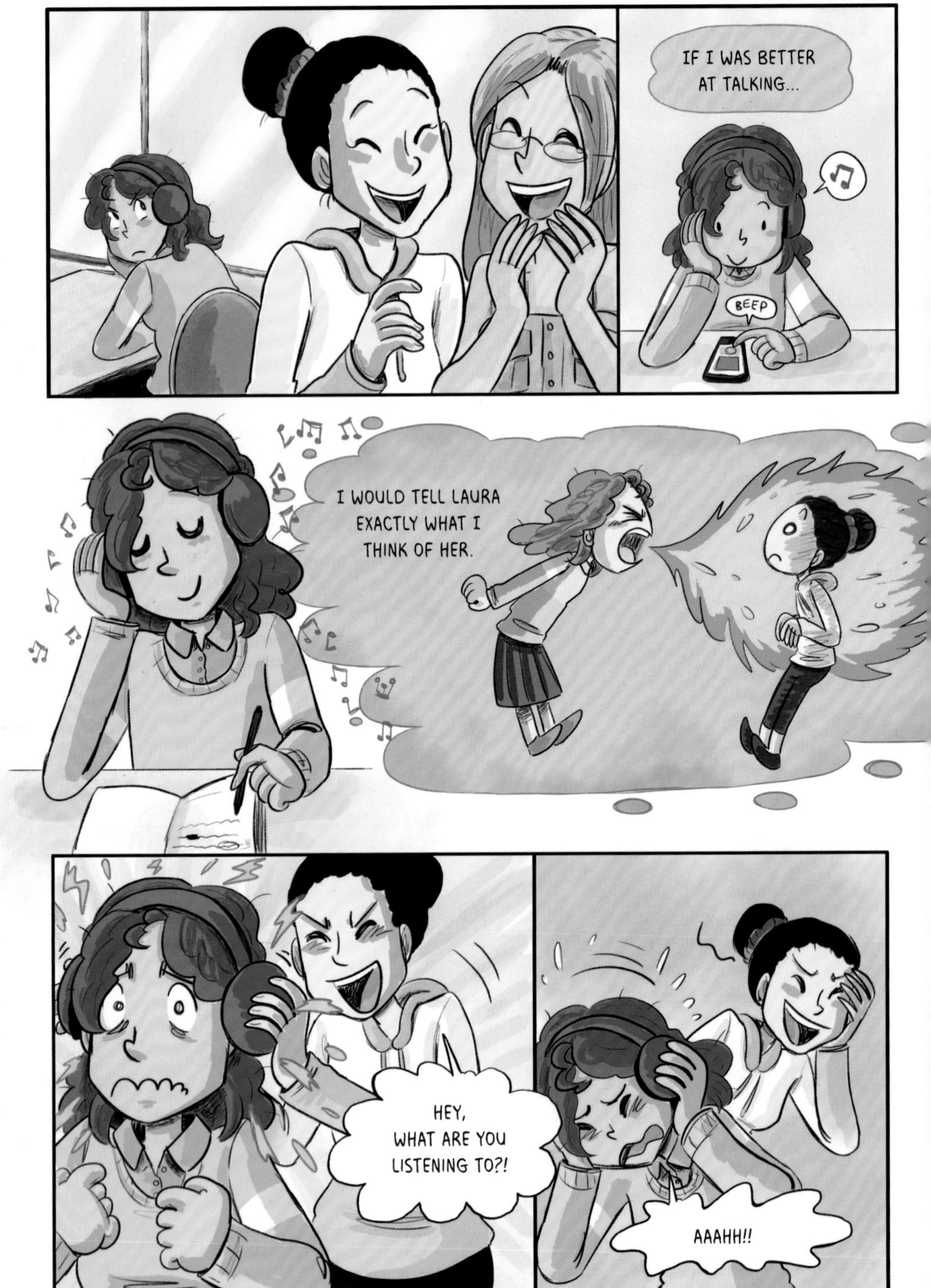
IF I WAS BETTER AT TALKING...
BEEP
I WOULD TELL LAURA EXACTLY WHAT I THINK OF HER.
HEY, WHAT ARE YOU LISTENING TO?!
AAAHH!!

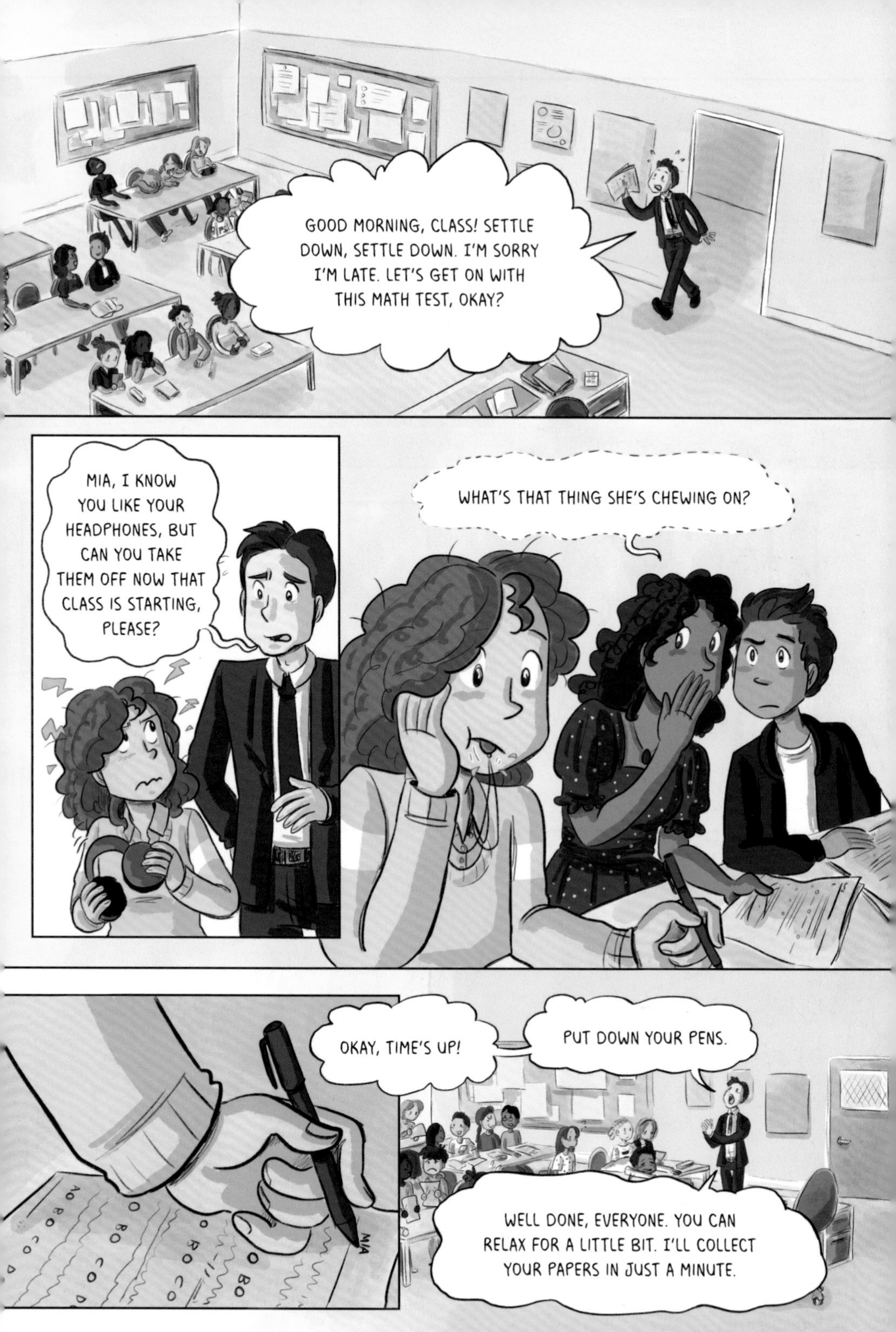
GOOD MORNING, CLASS! SETTLE DOWN, SETTLE DOWN. I'M SORRY I'M LATE. LET'S GET ON WITH THIS MATH TEST, OKAY?
MIA, I KNOW YOU LIKE YOUR HEADPHONES, BUT CAN YOU TAKE THEM OFF NOW THAT CLASS IS STARTING, PLEASE?
WHAT'S THAT THING SHE'S CHEWING ON?
MIA
OKAY, TIME'S UP!
PUT DOWN YOUR PENS.
WELL DONE, EVERYONE. YOU CAN RELAX FOR A LITTLE BIT. I'LL COLLECT YOUR PAPERS IN JUST A MINUTE.

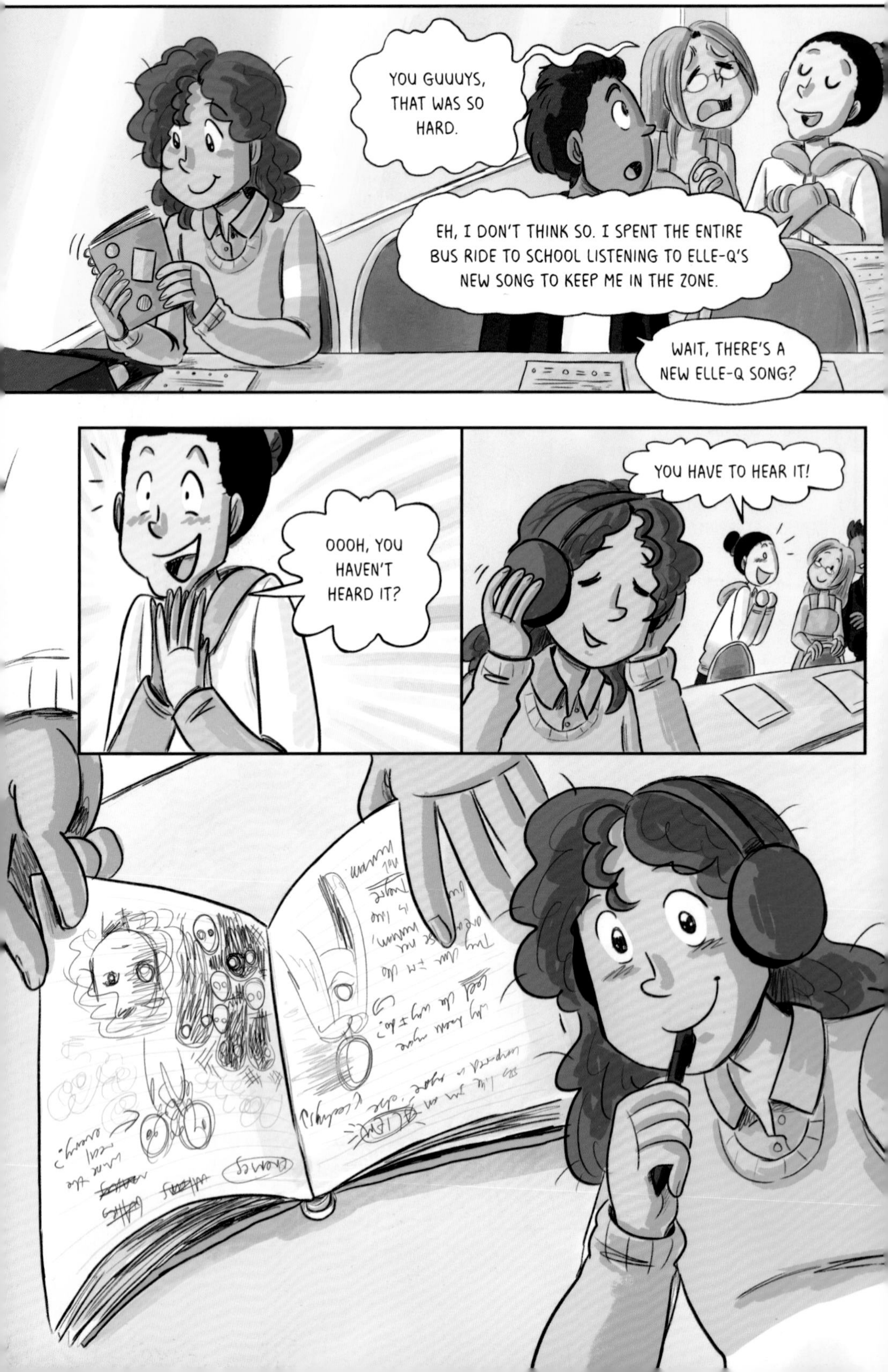
YOU GUUUYS, THAT WAS SO HARD.
EH, I DON'T THINK SO. I SPENT THE ENTIRE BUS RIDE TO SCHOOL LISTENING TO ELLE-Q'S NEW SONG TO KEEP ME IN THE ZONE.
WAIT, THERE'S A NEW ELLE-Q SONG?
OOOH, YOU HAVEN'T HEARD IT?
YOU HAVE TO HEAR IT!

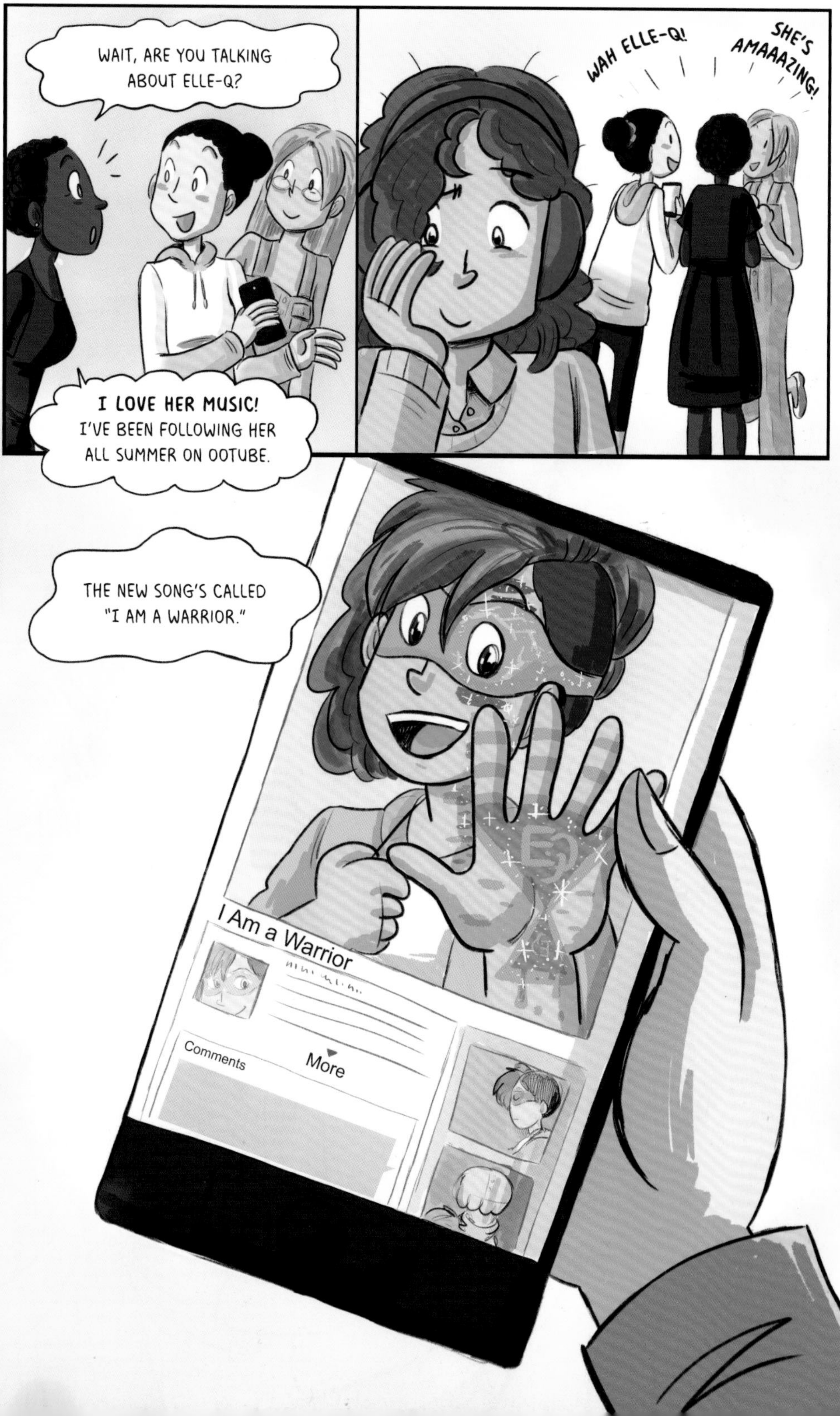
WAIT, ARE YOU TALKING ABOUT ELLE-Q?
I LOVE HER MUSIC! I'VE BEEN FOLLOWING HER ALL SUMMER ON OOTUBE.
WAH ELLE-Q!
SHE'S AMAAAZING!
THE NEW SONG'S CALLED "I AM A WARRIOR."
I Am a Warrior
Comments
More

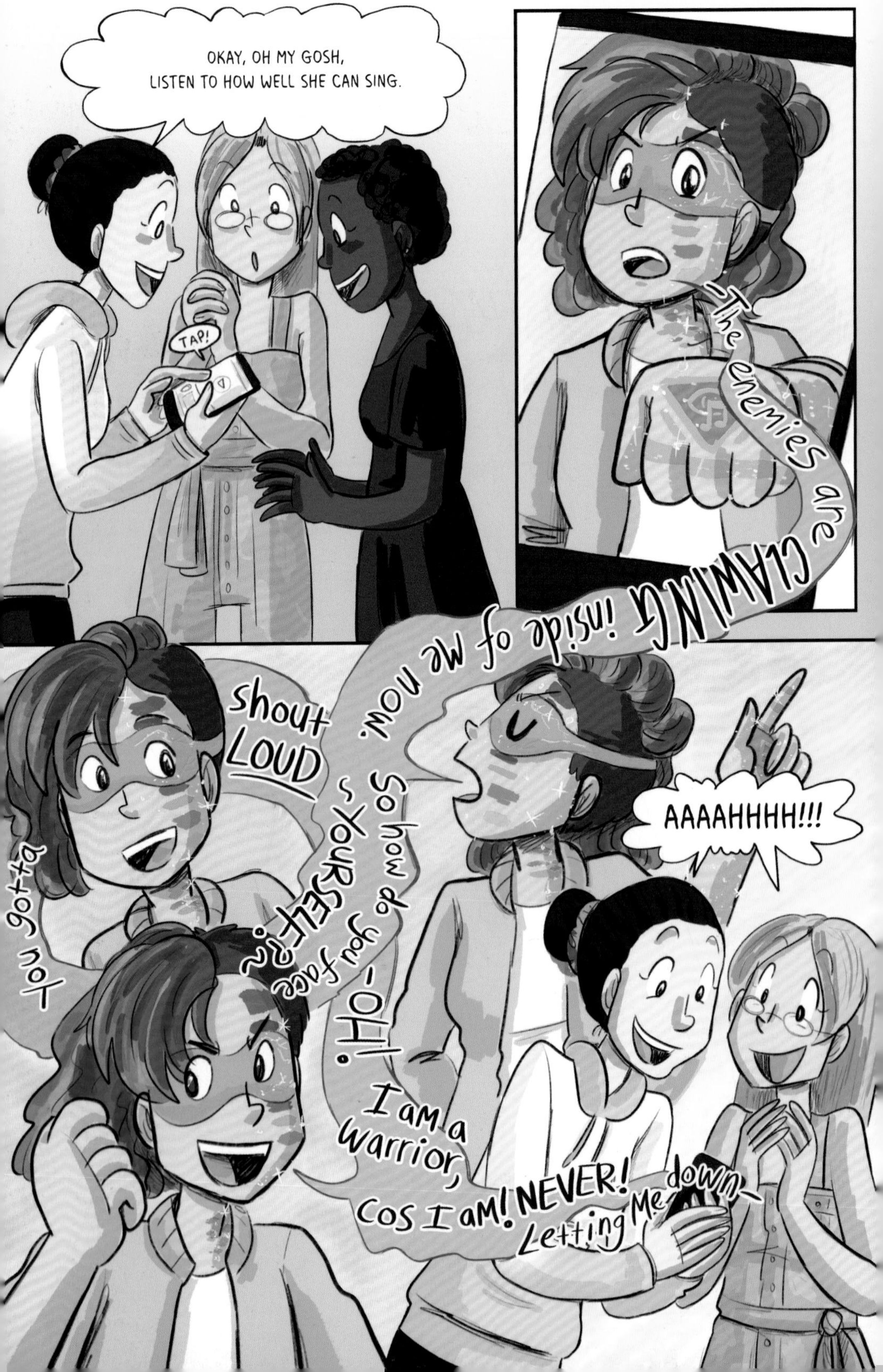
OKAY, OH MY GOSH, LISTEN TO HOW WELL SHE CAN SING.
TAP!
The enemies are CLAWING inside of me now.
So how do you face ~YOURSELF?~
you gotta shout LOUD
-OH!
AAAAHHHH!!!
I am a warrior, cos I am! NEVER! Letting me down-

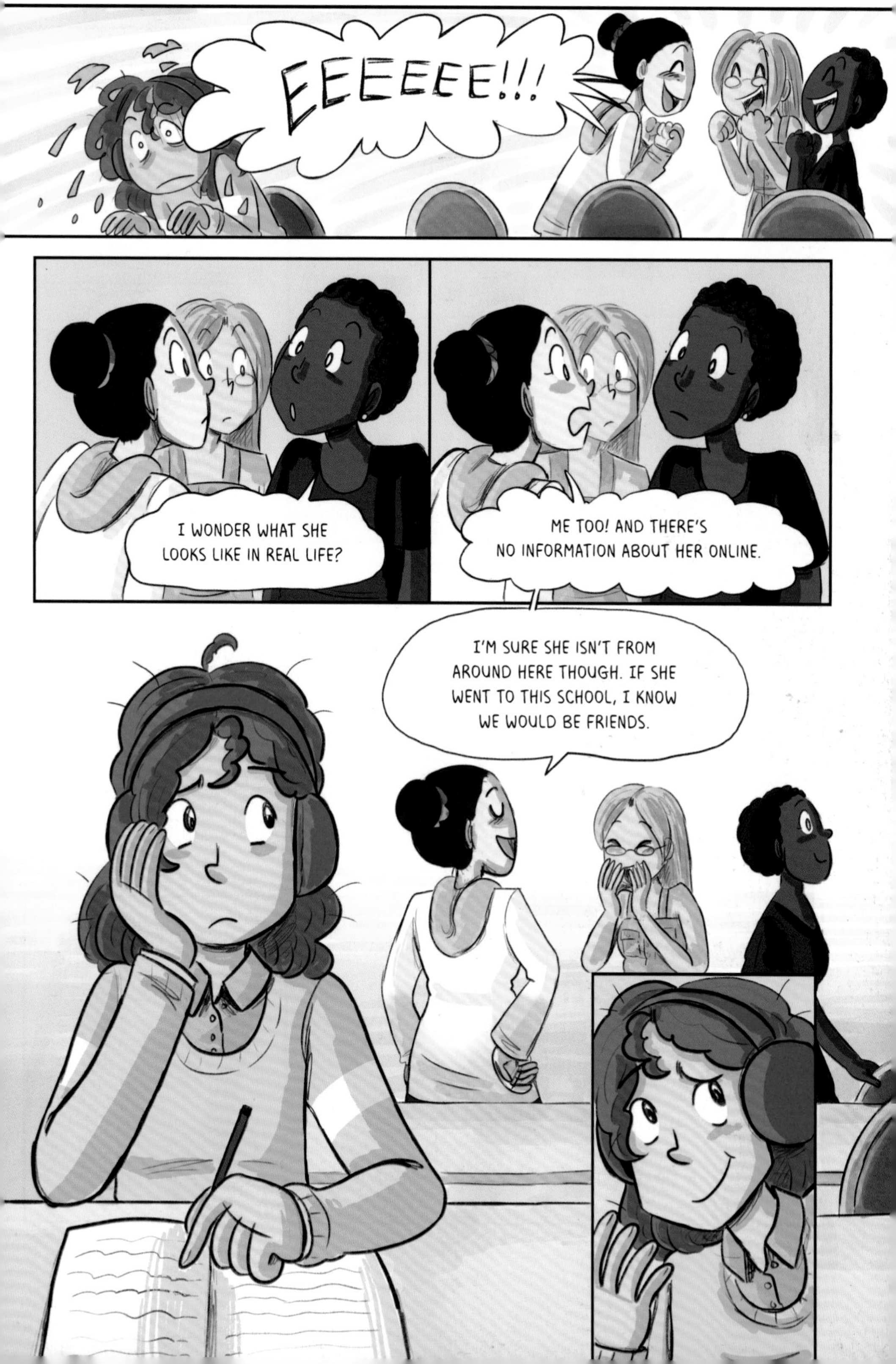
EEEEEE!!!
I WONDER WHAT SHE LOOKS LIKE IN REAL LIFE?
ME TOO! AND THERE'S NO INFORMATION ABOUT HER ONLINE.
I'M SURE SHE ISN'T FROM AROUND HERE THOUGH. IF SHE WENT TO THIS SCHOOL, I KNOW WE WOULD BE FRIENDS.

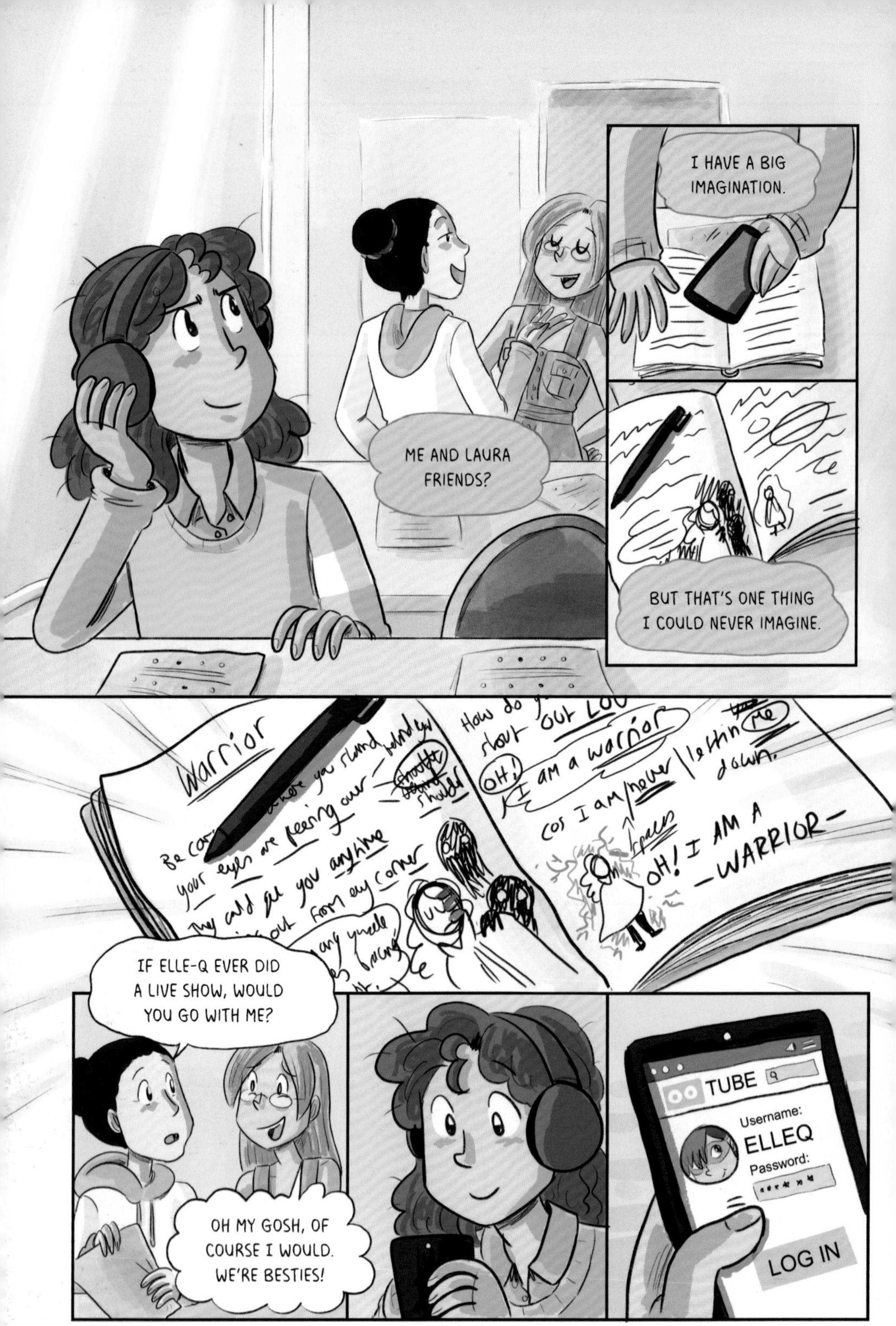
ME AND LAURA FRIENDS?
I HAVE A BIG IMAGINATION.
BUT THAT'S ONE THING I COULD NEVER IMAGINE.
Warrior
OH! I AM A WARRIOR
IF ELLE-Q EVER DID A LIVE SHOW, WOULD YOU GO WITH ME?
OH MY GOSH, OF COURSE I WOULD. WE'RE BESTIES!
TUBE
Username:
ELLEQ
Password:
LOG IN

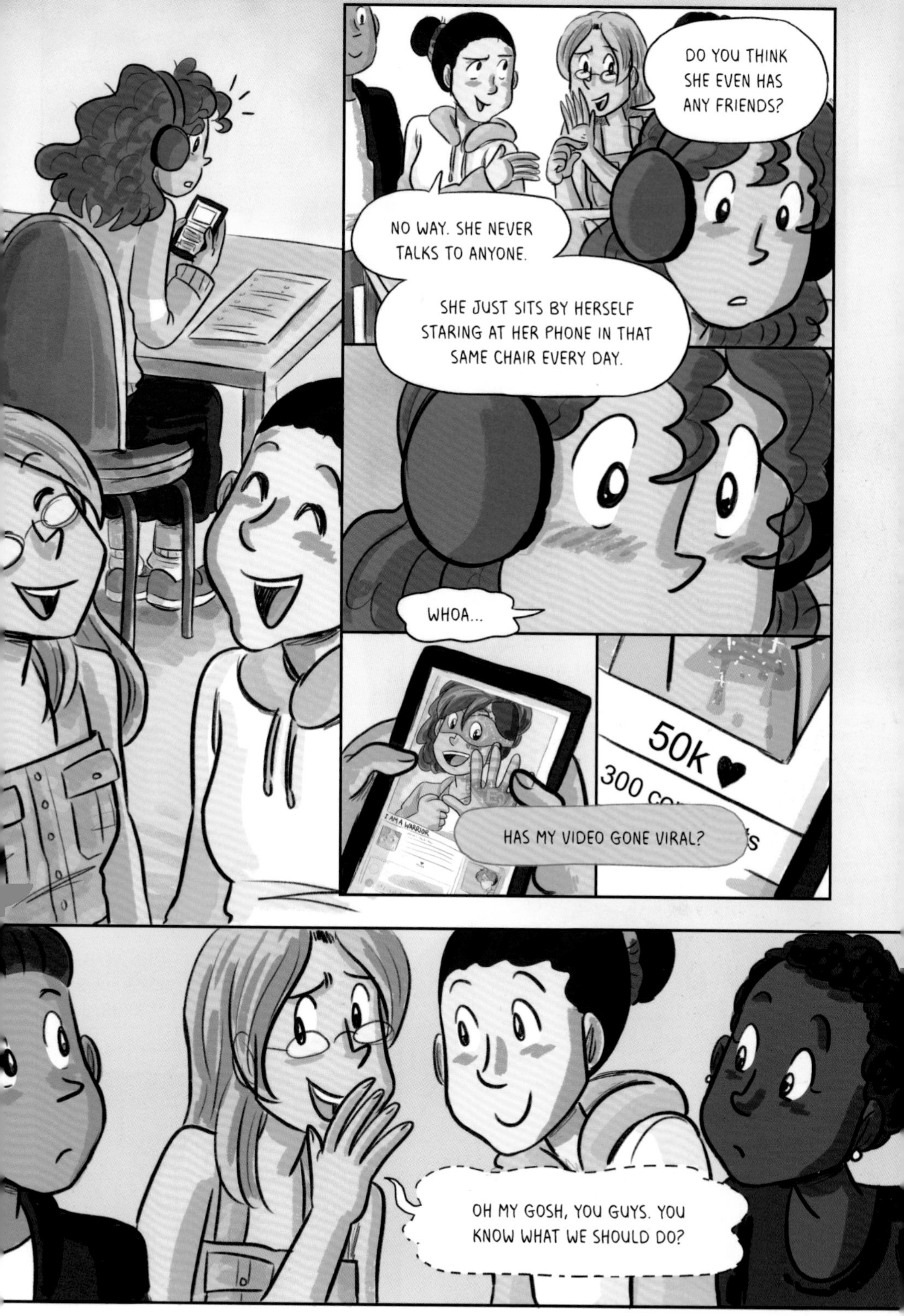
DO YOU THINK SHE EVEN HAS ANY FRIENDS?
NO WAY. SHE NEVER TALKS TO ANYONE.
SHE JUST SITS BY HERSELF STARING AT HER PHONE IN THAT SAME CHAIR EVERY DAY.
WHOA...
I AM A WARRIOR
50k ♥
HAS MY VIDEO GONE VIRAL?
OH MY GOSH, YOU GUYS. YOU KNOW WHAT WE SHOULD DO?

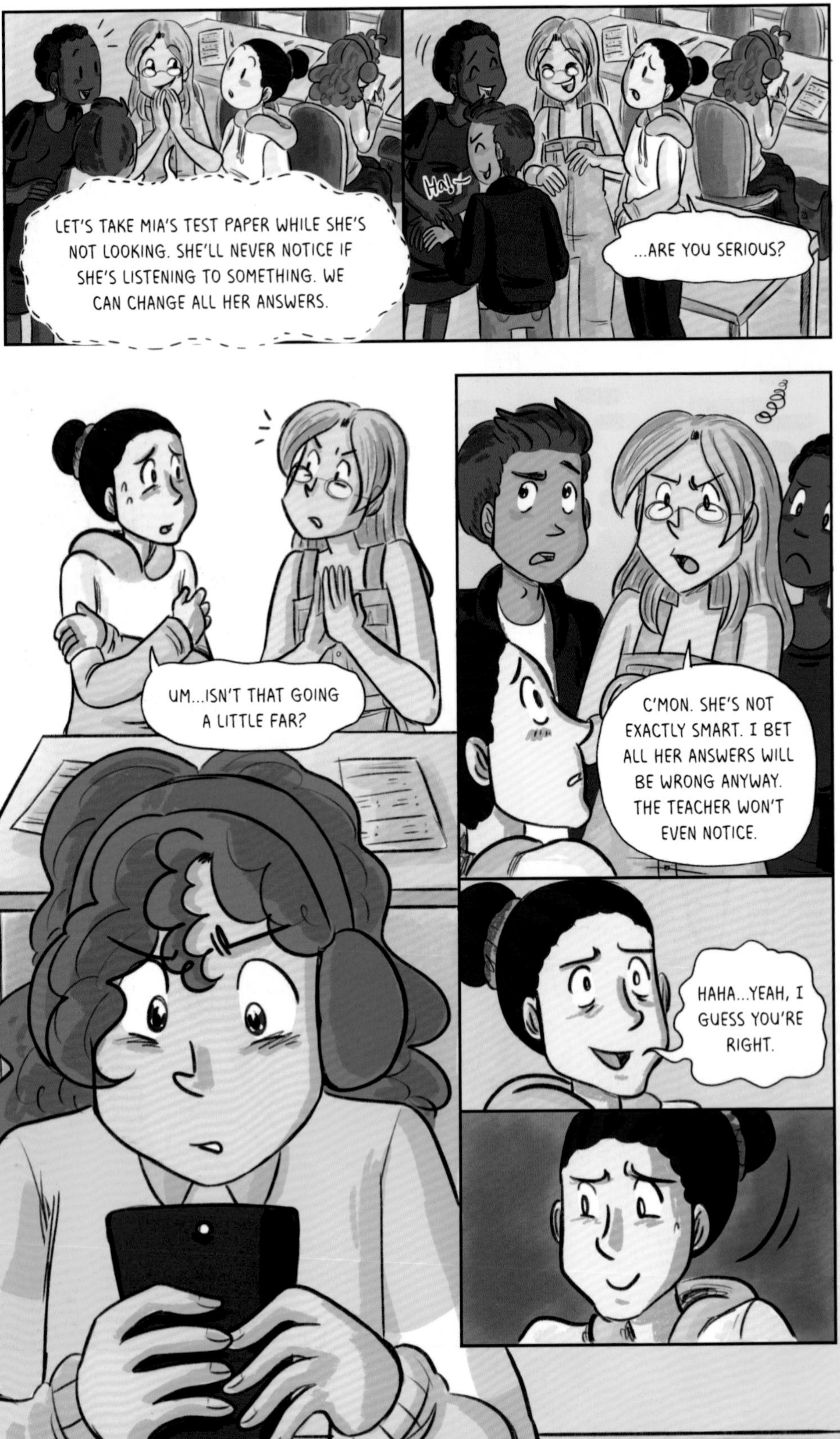

LET'S TAKE MIA'S TEST PAPER WHILE SHE'S NOT LOOKING. SHE'LL NEVER NOTICE IF SHE'S LISTENING TO SOMETHING. WE CAN CHANGE ALL HER ANSWERS.
Ha!
...ARE YOU SERIOUS?
UM...ISN'T THAT GOING A LITTLE FAR?
C'MON. SHE'S NOT EXACTLY SMART. I BET ALL HER ANSWERS WILL BE WRONG ANYWAY. THE TEACHER WON'T EVEN NOTICE.
HAHA...YEAH, I GUESS YOU'RE RIGHT.

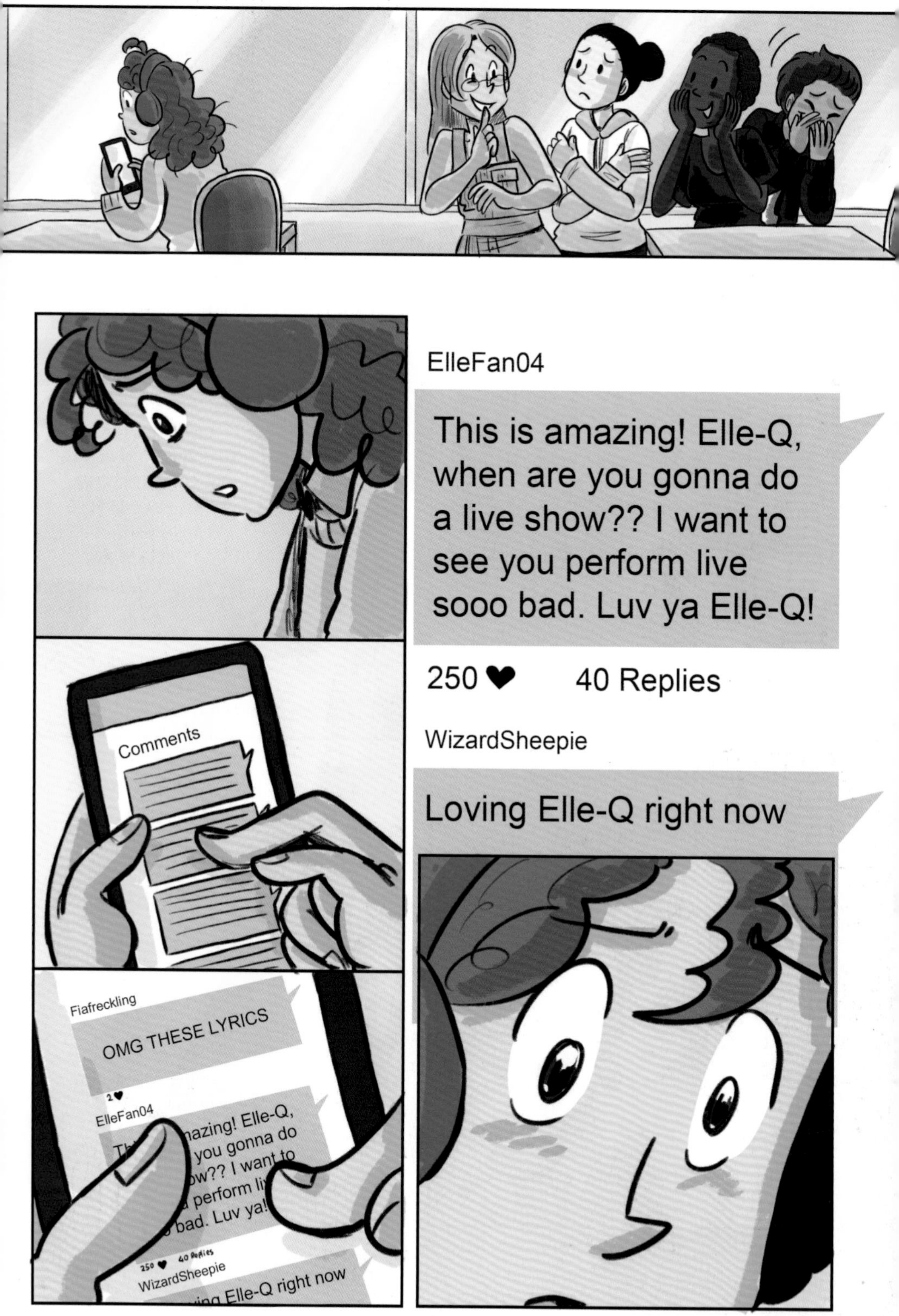
EllefFan04
This is amazing! Elle-Q, when are you gonna do a live show?? I want to see you perform live sooo bad. Luv ya Elle-Q!
250 ❤ 40 Replies
WizardSheepie
Loving Elle-Q right now
Comments
Fiafreckling
OMG THESE LYRICS
ElleFan04
WizardSheepie

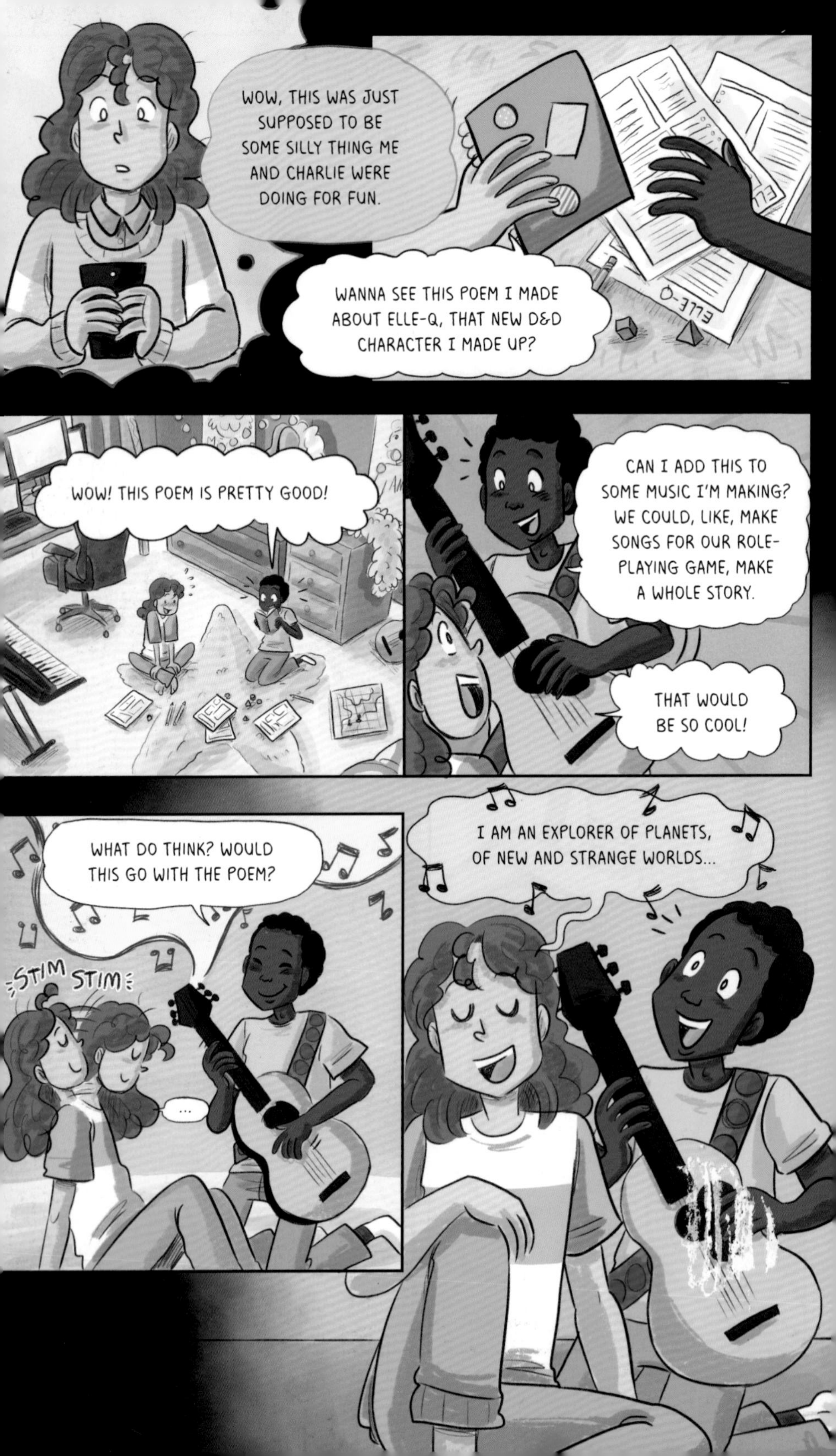

WOW, THIS WAS JUST SUPPOSED TO BE SOME SILLY THING ME AND CHARLIE WERE DOING FOR FUN.
WANNA SEE THIS POEM I MADE ABOUT ELLE-Q, THAT NEW D&D CHARACTER I MADE UP?
ELLE-Q
WOW! THIS POEM IS PRETTY GOOD!
CAN I ADD THIS TO SOME MUSIC I'M MAKING? WE COULD, LIKE, MAKE SONGS FOR OUR ROLE-PLAYING GAME, MAKE A WHOLE STORY.
THAT WOULD BE SO COOL!
WHAT DO THINK? WOULD THIS GO WITH THE POEM?
STIM STIM
...
I AM AN EXPLORER OF PLANETS, OF NEW AND STRANGE WORLDS...

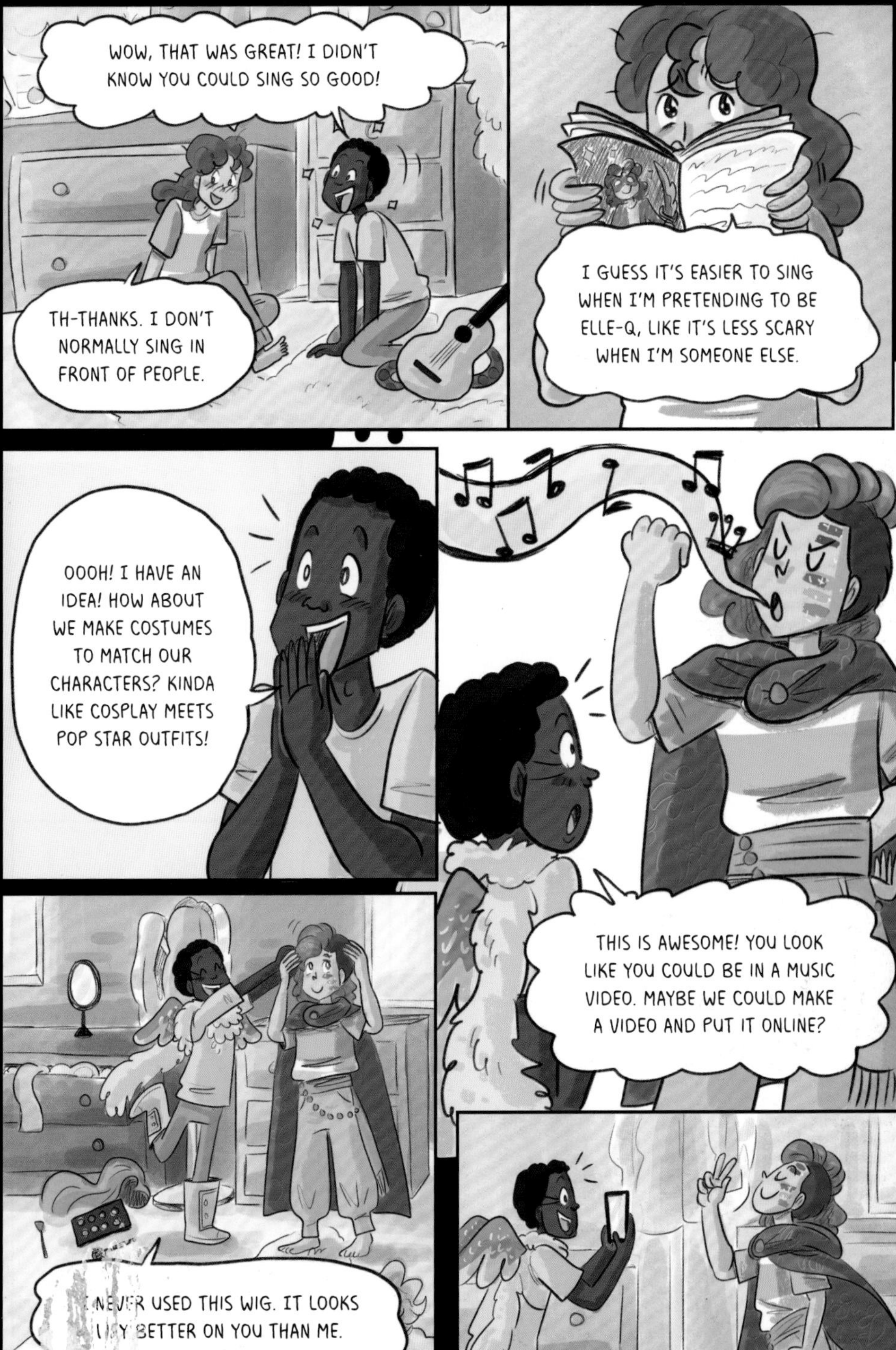
WOW, THAT WAS GREAT! I DIDN'T KNOW YOU COULD SING SO GOOD!
TH-THANKS. I DON'T NORMALLY SING IN FRONT OF PEOPLE.
I GUESS IT'S EASIER TO SING WHEN I'M PRETENDING TO BE ELLE-Q, LIKE IT'S LESS SCARY WHEN I'M SOMEONE ELSE.
OOOH! I HAVE AN IDEA! HOW ABOUT WE MAKE COSTUMES TO MATCH OUR CHARACTERS? KINDA LIKE COSPLAY MEETS POP STAR OUTFITS!
NEVER USED THIS WIG. IT LOOKS
BETTER ON YOU THAN ME.
THIS IS AWESOME! YOU LOOK LIKE YOU COULD BE IN A MUSIC VIDEO. MAYBE WE COULD MAKE A VIDEO AND PUT IT ONLINE?

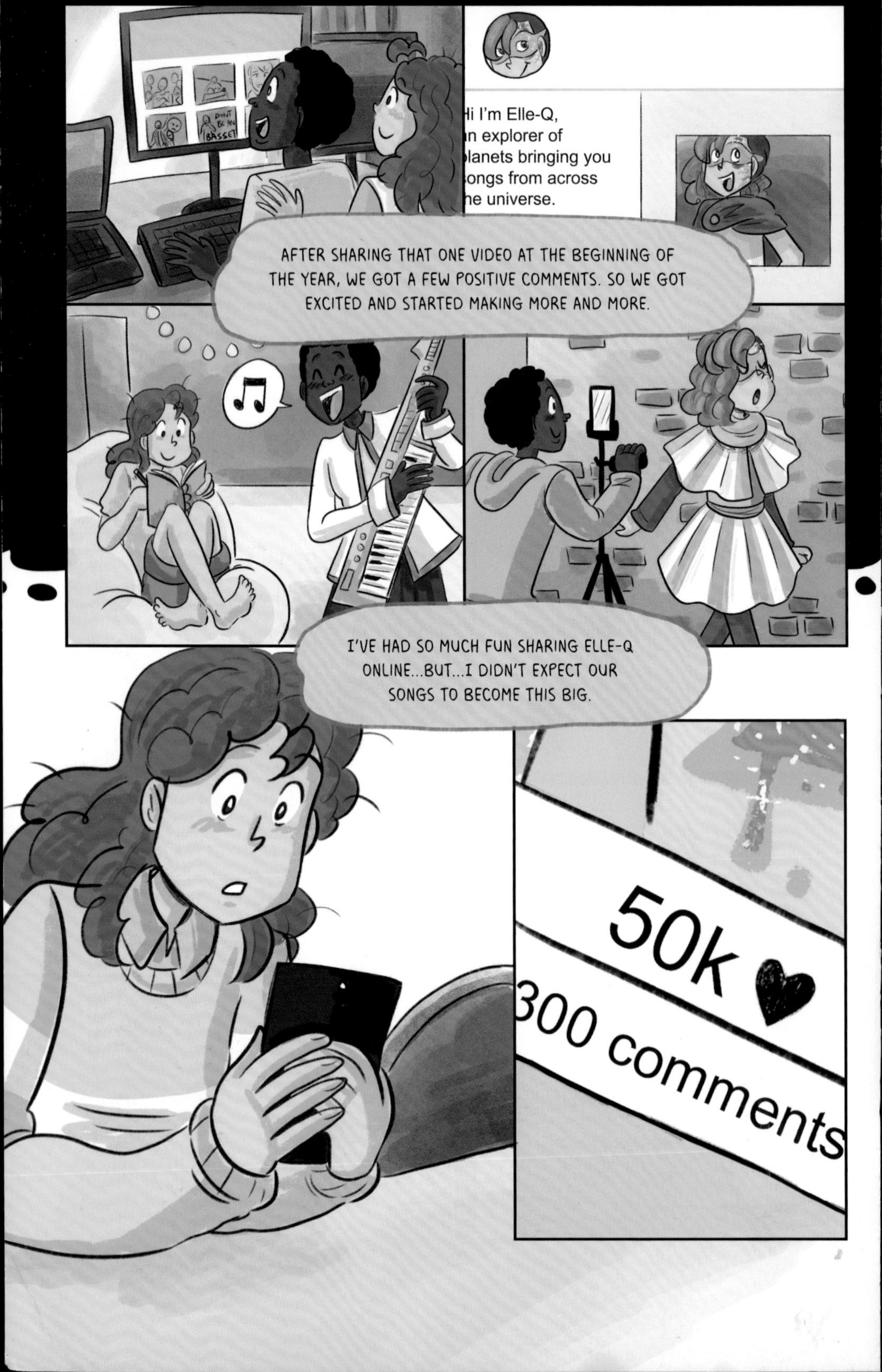

Hi I'm Elle-Q,
n explorer of
lanets bringing you
ongs from across
he universe.
AFTER SHARING THAT ONE VIDEO AT THE BEGINNING OF THE YEAR, WE GOT A FEW POSITIVE COMMENTS. SO WE GOT EXCITED AND STARTED MAKING MORE AND MORE.
I'VE HAD SO MUCH FUN SHARING ELLE-Q ONLINE...BUT...I DIDN'T EXPECT OUR SONGS TO BECOME THIS BIG.
50k
300 comments

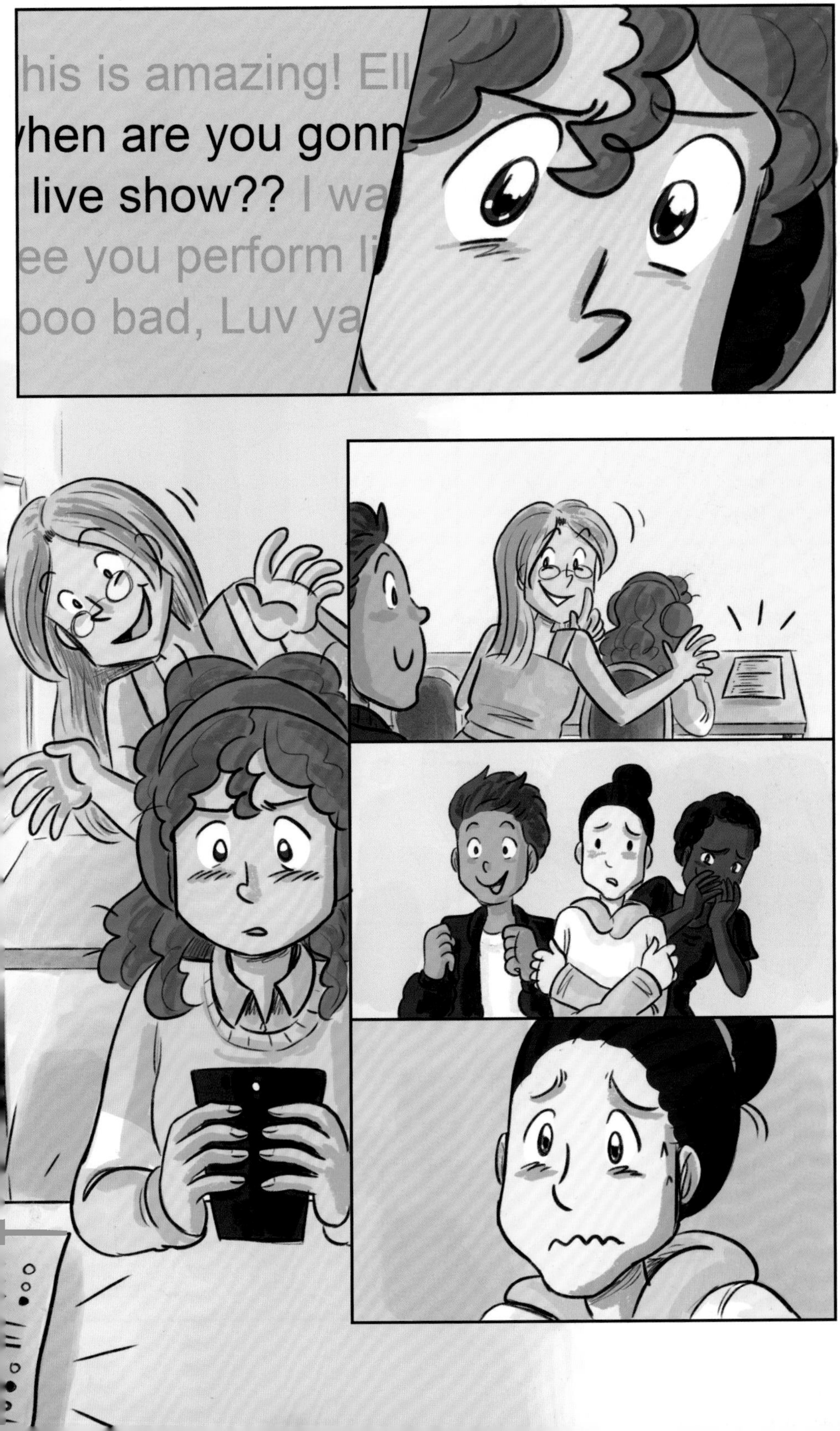
his is amazing! Ell
hen are you gonn
live show?? I wa
ee you perform li
ooo bad, Luv ya

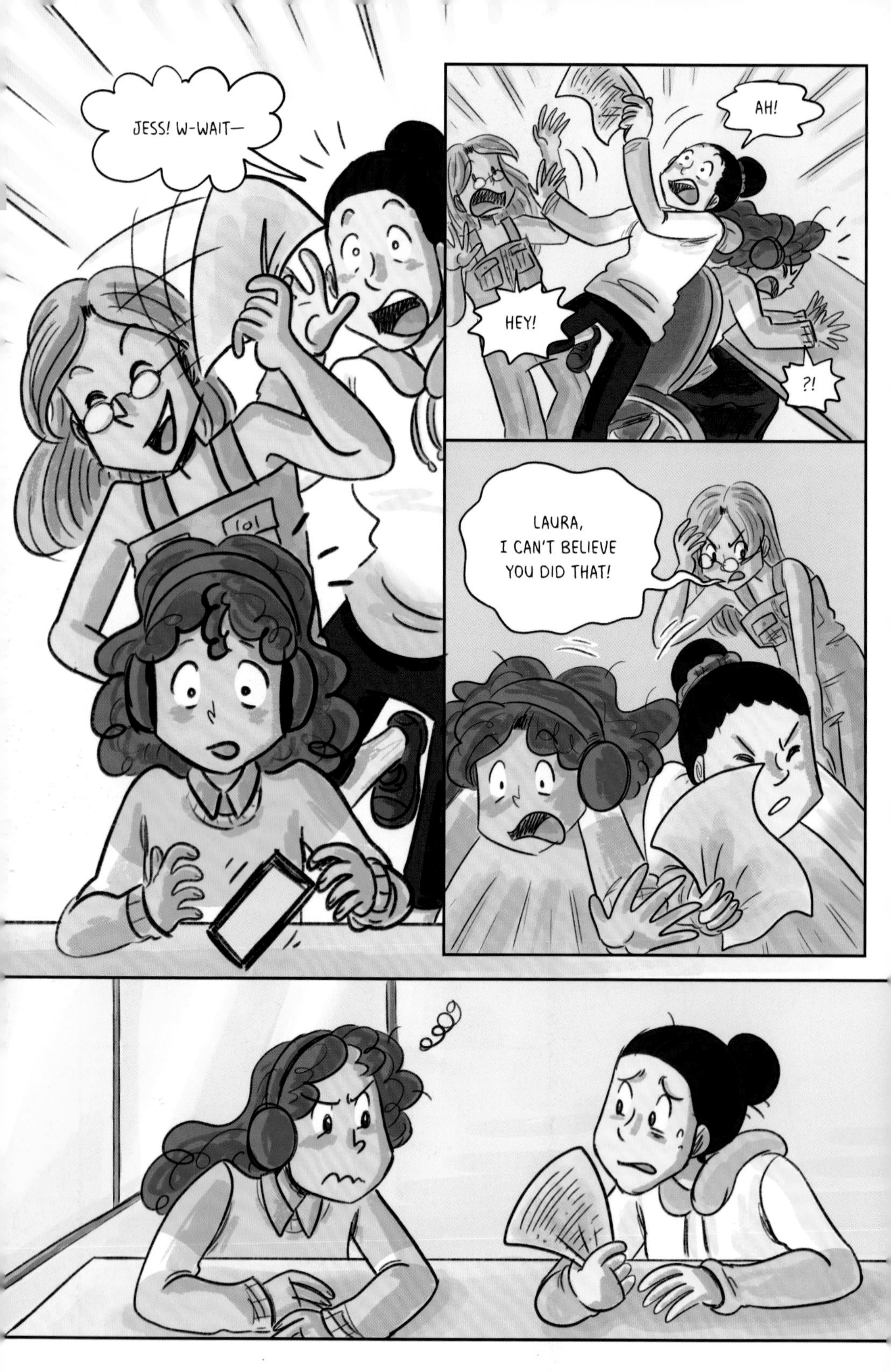
JESS! W-WAIT—
AH!
HEY!
?!
LAURA, I CAN'T BELIEVE YOU DID THAT!

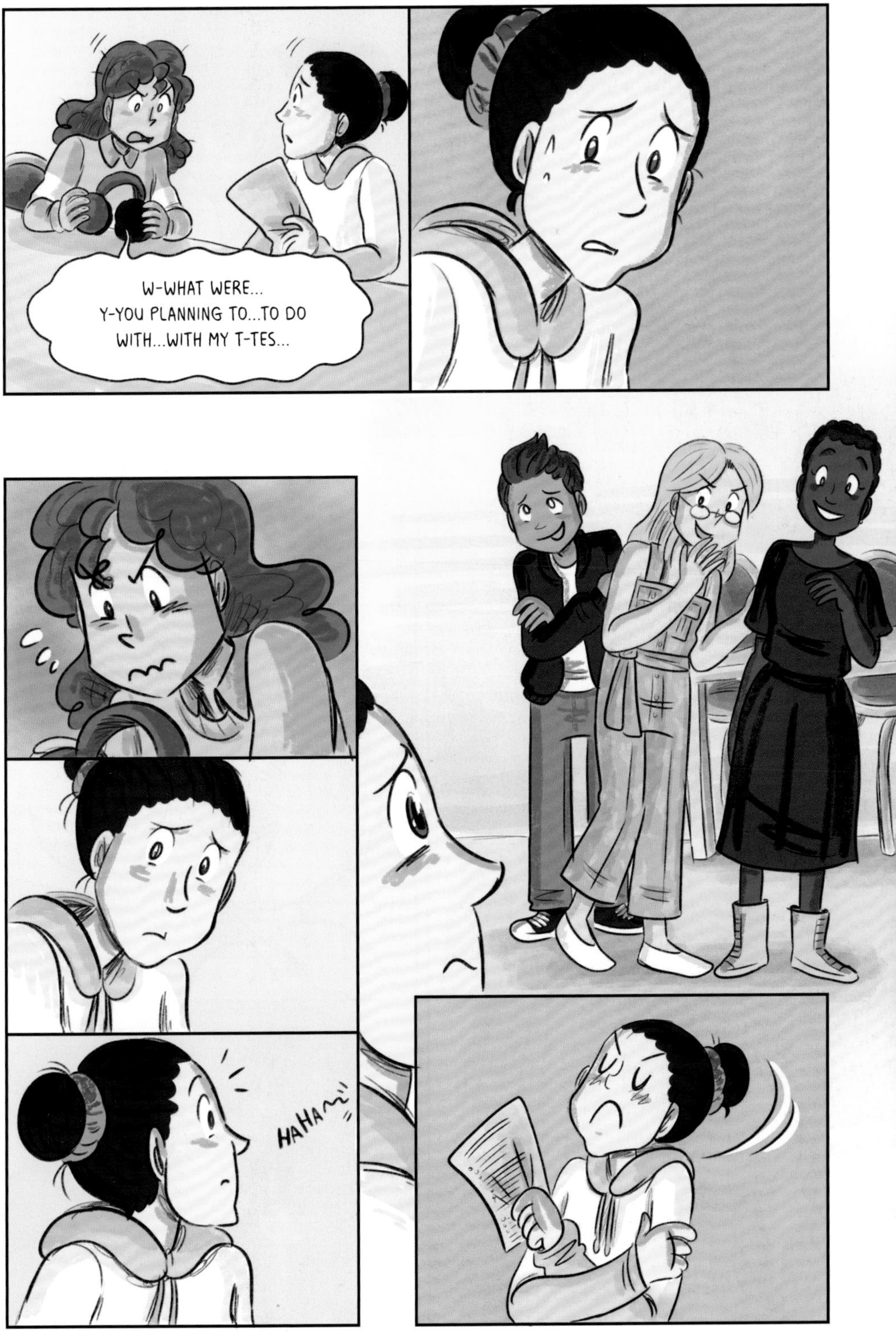
W-WHAT WERE...
Y-YOU PLANNING TO...TO DO
WITH...WITH MY T-TES...
HAHA

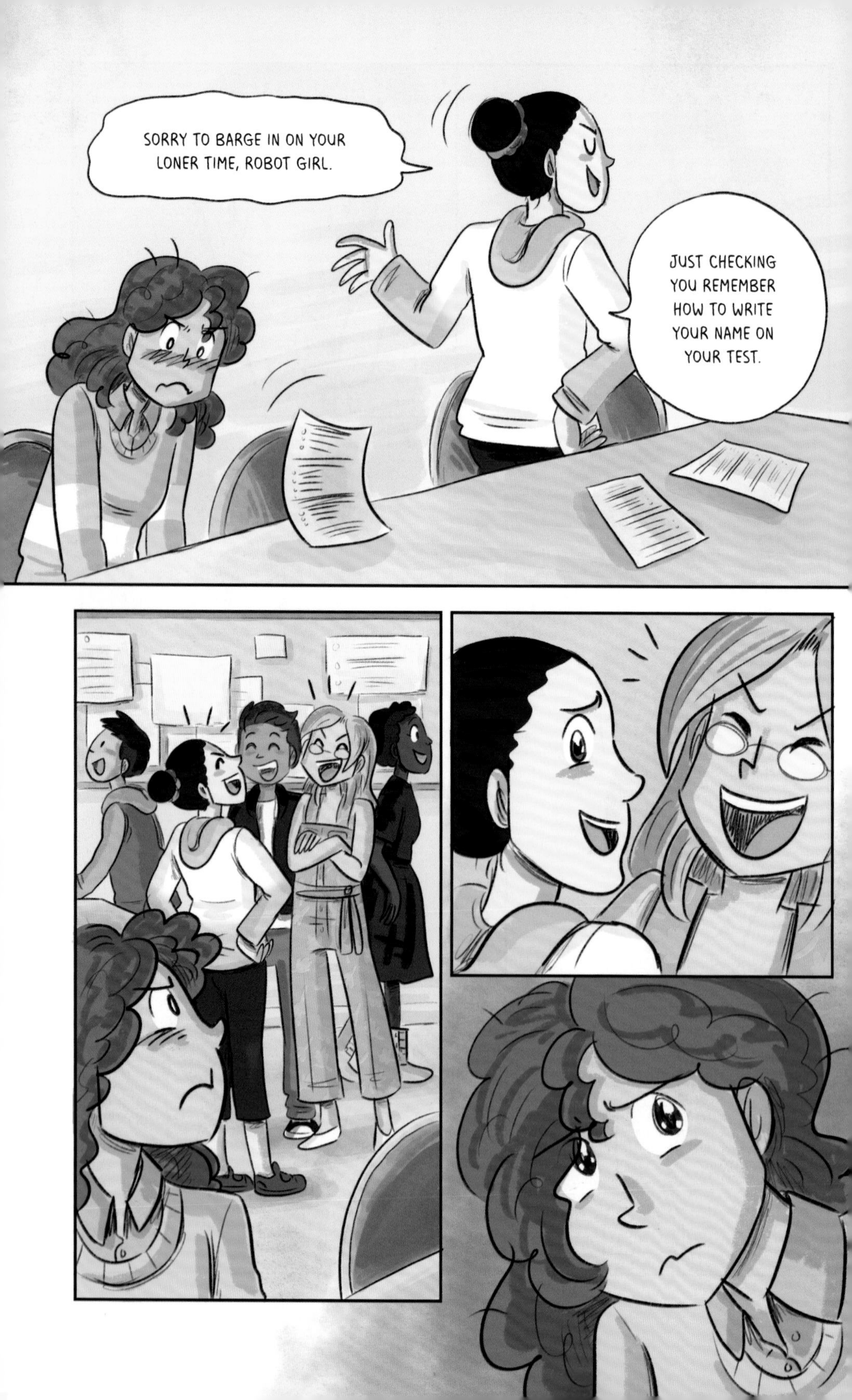
SORRY TO BARGE IN ON YOUR LONER TIME, ROBOT GIRL.
JUST CHECKING YOU REMEMBER HOW TO WRITE YOUR NAME ON YOUR TEST.

CHAPTER TWO

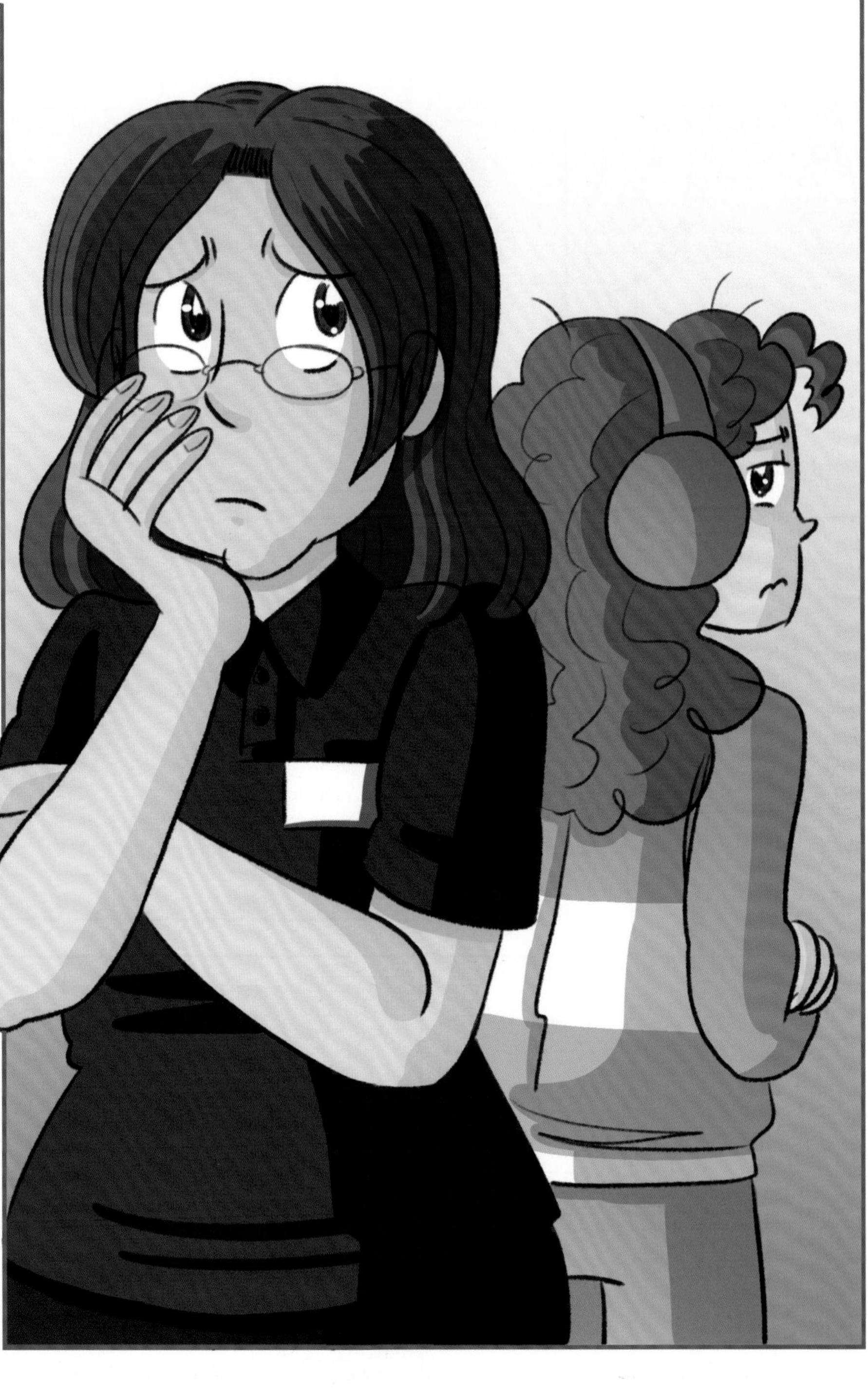

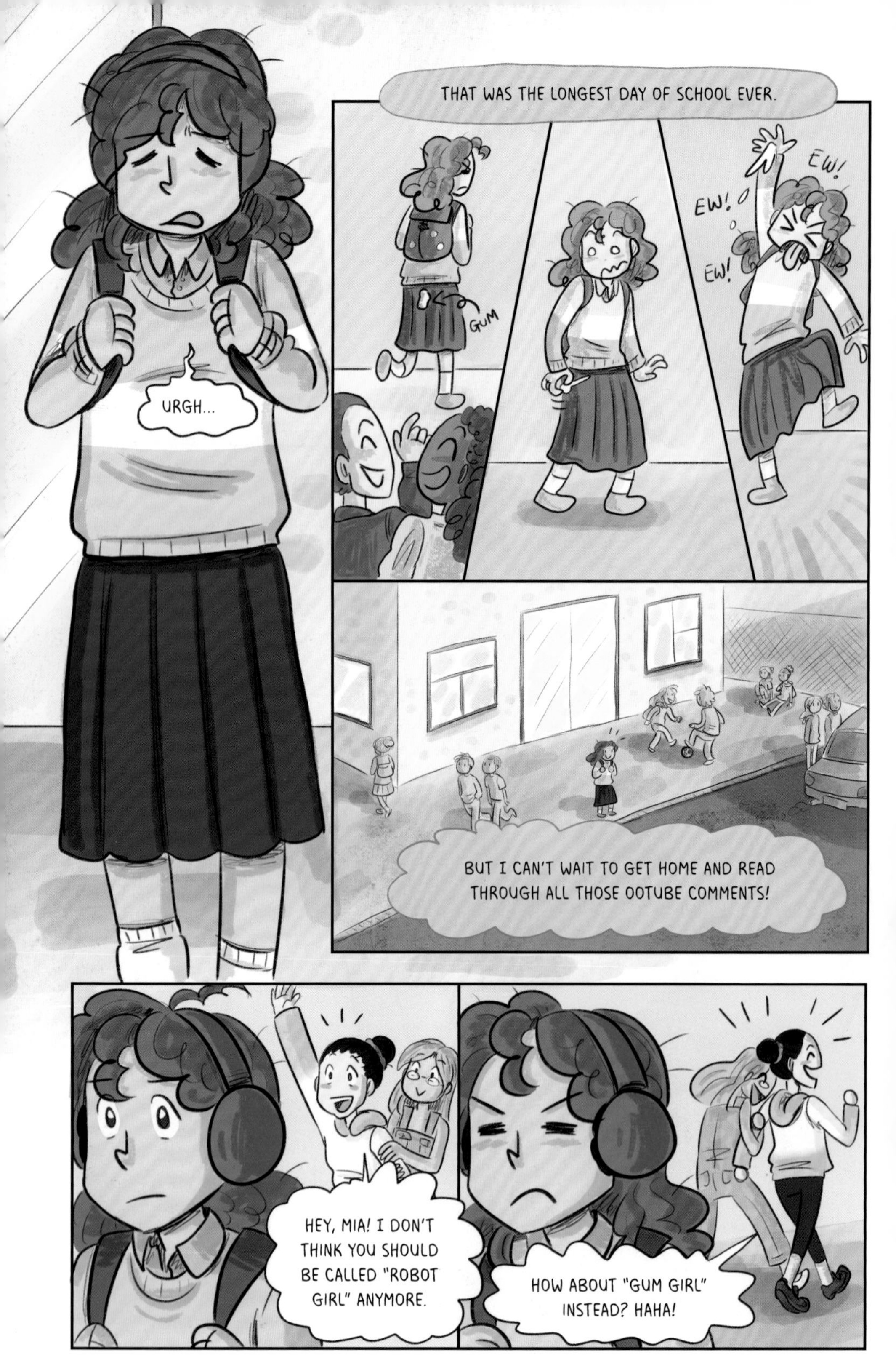
URGH...
THAT WAS THE LONGEST DAY OF SCHOOL EVER.
GUM
EW!
EW!
EW!
BUT I CAN'T WAIT TO GET HOME AND READ THROUGH ALL THOSE OOTUBE COMMENTS!
HEY, MIA! I DON'T THINK YOU SHOULD BE CALLED "ROBOT GIRL" ANYMORE.
HOW ABOUT "GUM GIRL" INSTEAD? HAHA!

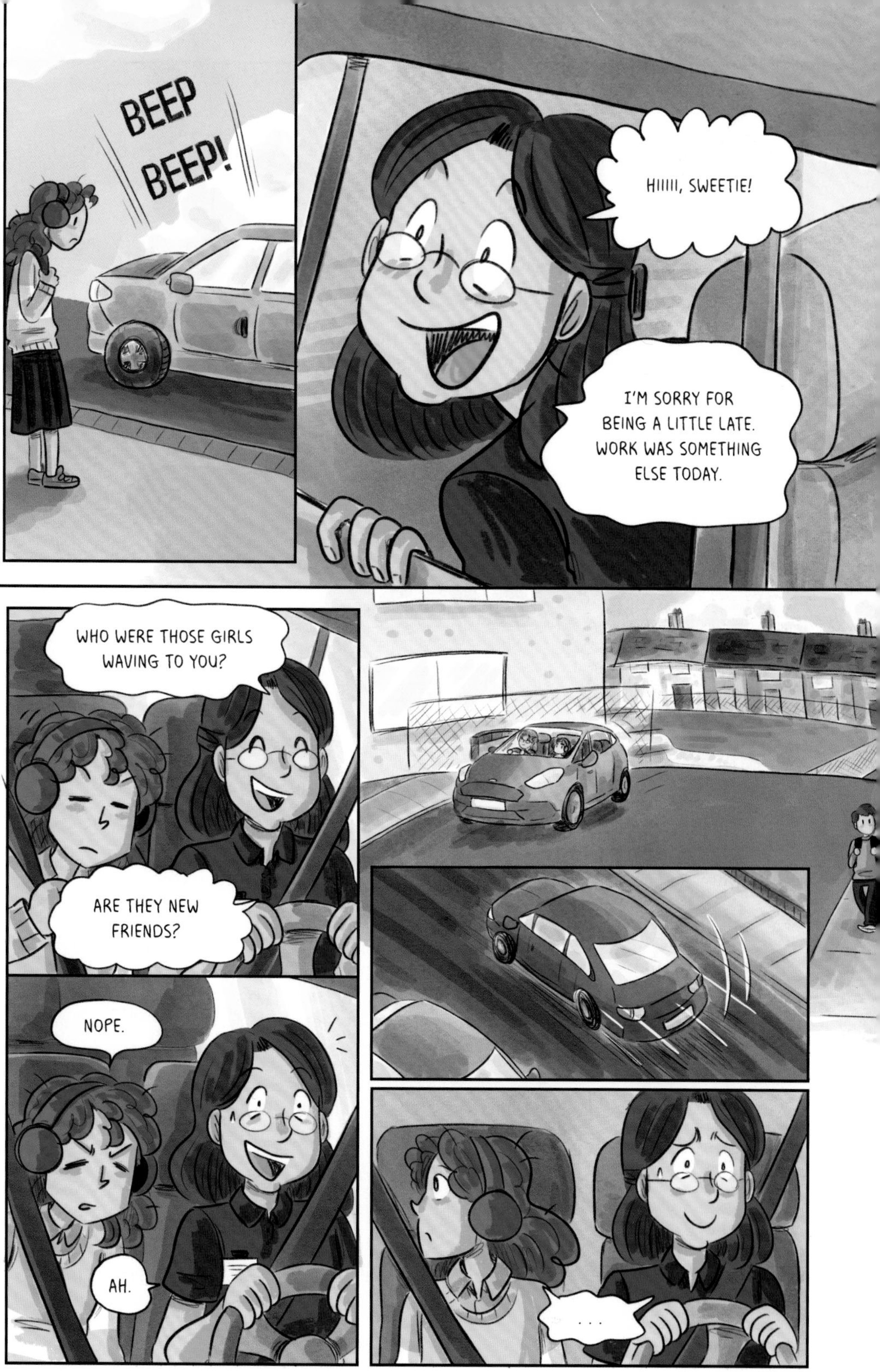
BEEP BEEP!
HIIIII, SWEETIE!
I'M SORRY FOR BEING A LITTLE LATE. WORK WAS SOMETHING ELSE TODAY.
WHO WERE THOSE GIRLS WAVING TO YOU?
ARE THEY NEW FRIENDS?
NOPE.
AH.
. . .

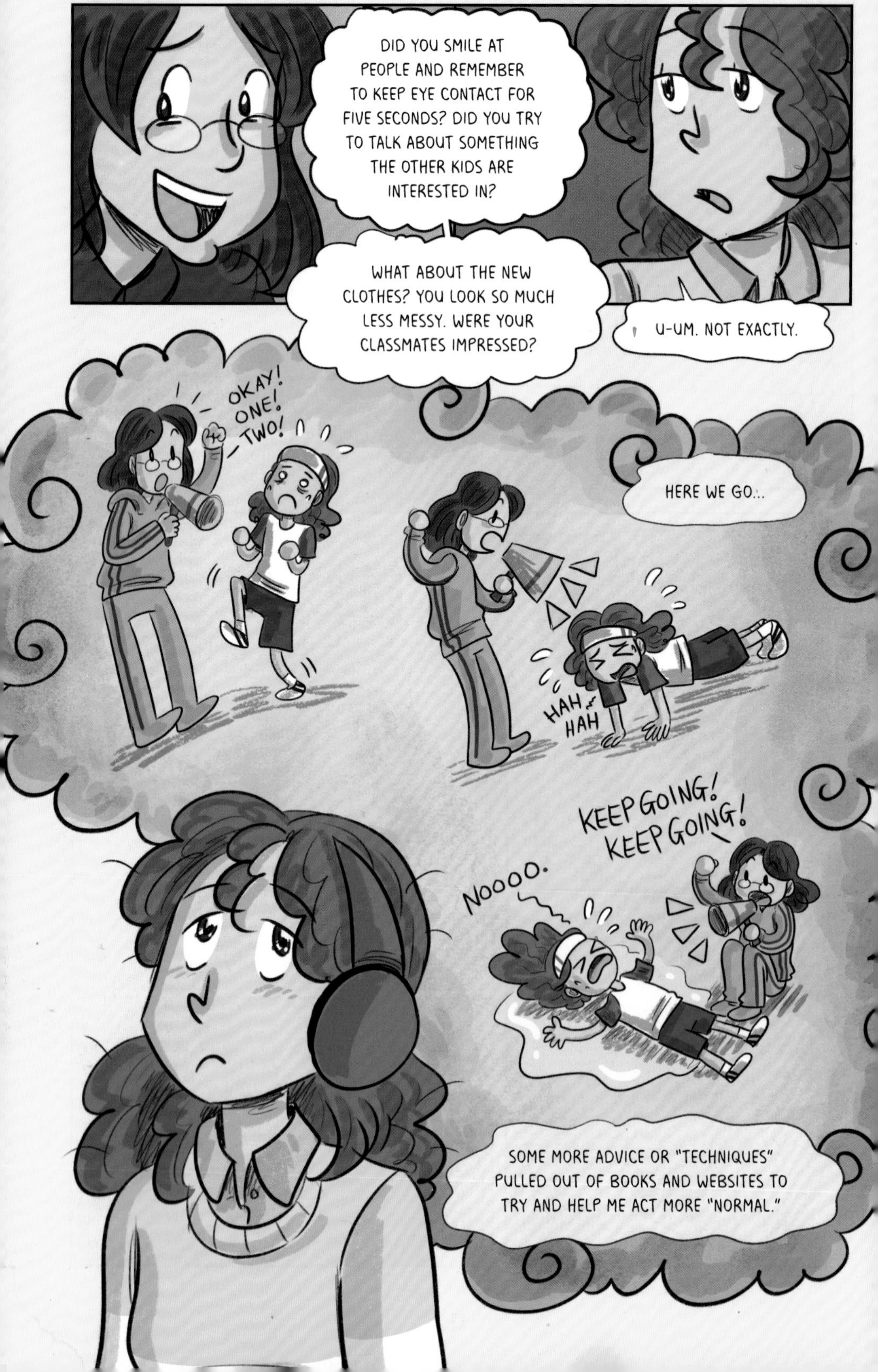
DID YOU SMILE AT PEOPLE AND REMEMBER TO KEEP EYE CONTACT FOR FIVE SECONDS? DID YOU TRY TO TALK ABOUT SOMETHING THE OTHER KIDS ARE INTERESTED IN?
WHAT ABOUT THE NEW CLOTHES? YOU LOOK SO MUCH LESS MESSY. WERE YOUR CLASSMATES IMPRESSED?
U-UM. NOT EXACTLY.
OKAY! ONE! TWO!
HERE WE GO...
HAH HAH
KEEP GOING! KEEP GOING!
NOOOO.
SOME MORE ADVICE OR "TECHNIQUES" PULLED OUT OF BOOKS AND WEBSITES TO TRY AND HELP ME ACT MORE "NORMAL."

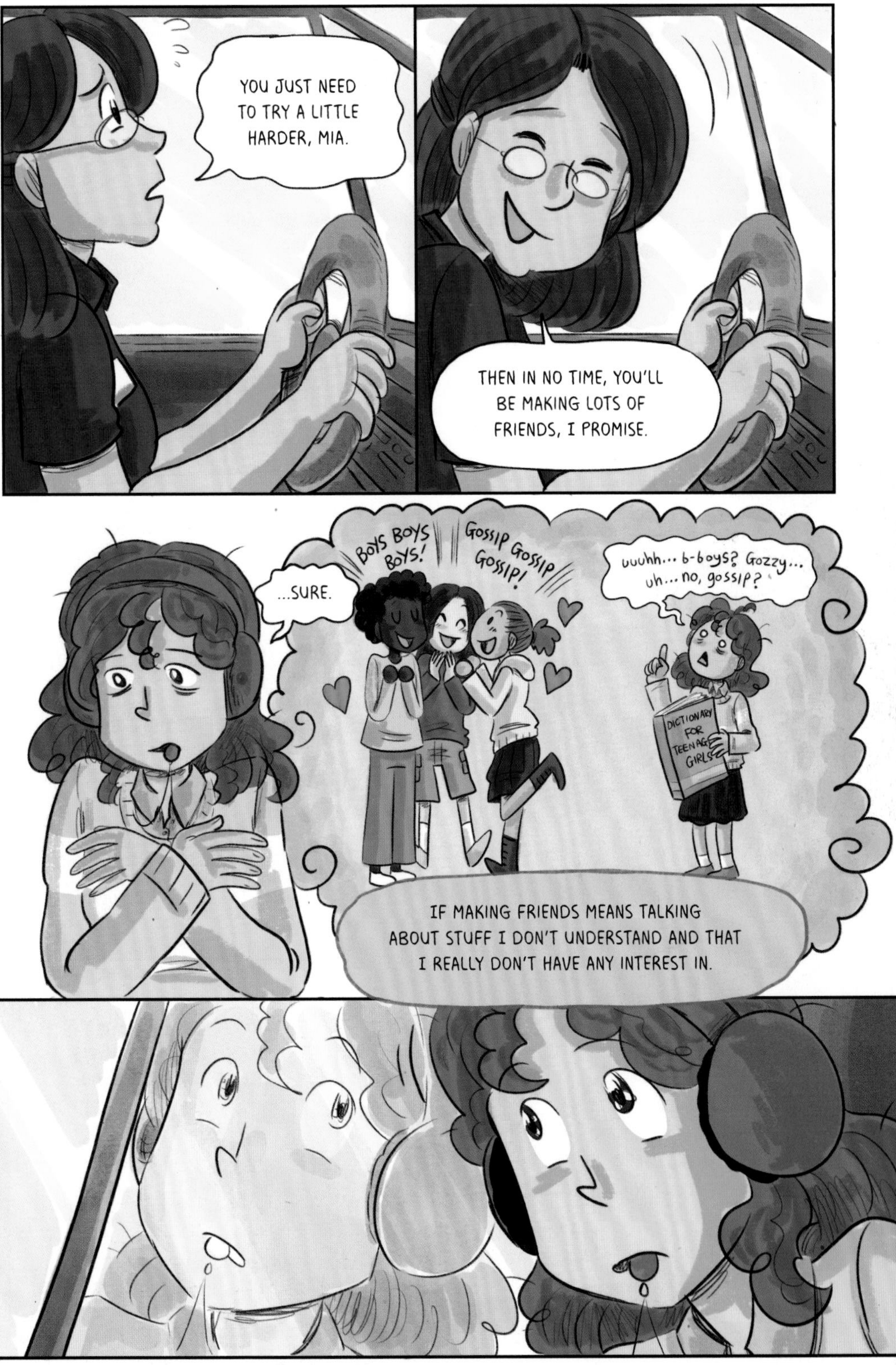
YOU JUST NEED TO TRY A LITTLE HARDER, MIA.
THEN IN NO TIME, YOU'LL BE MAKING LOTS OF FRIENDS, I PROMISE.
...SURE.
BOYS BOYS BOYS!
GOSSIP GOSSIP GOSSIP!
uuuhh... b-boys? Gozzy... uh... no, gossip?
DICTIONARY FOR TEENAGE GIRLS
IF MAKING FRIENDS MEANS TALKING ABOUT STUFF I DON'T UNDERSTAND AND THAT I REALLY DON'T HAVE ANY INTEREST IN.

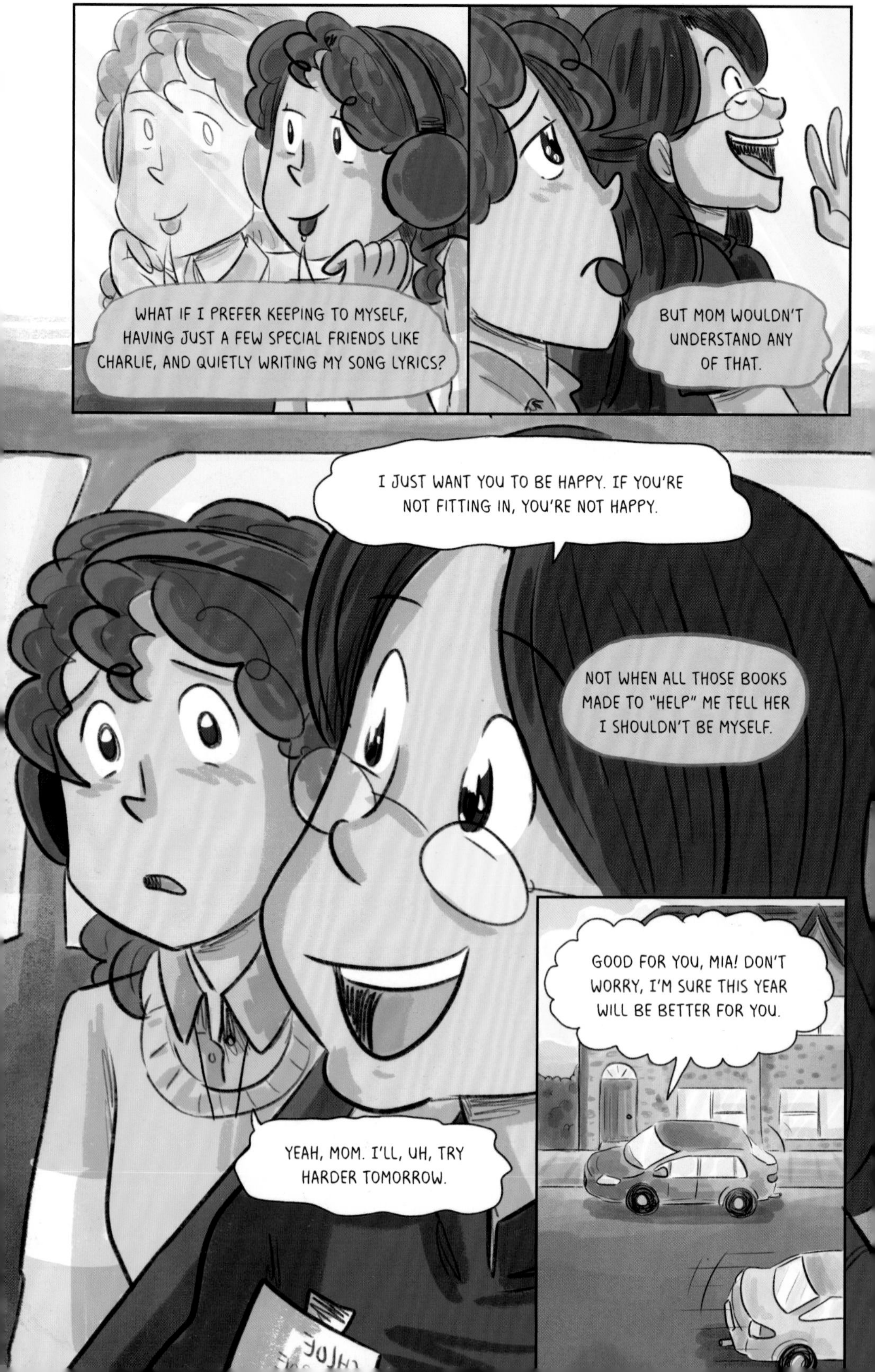
WHAT IF I PREFER KEEPING TO MYSELF, HAVING JUST A FEW SPECIAL FRIENDS LIKE CHARLIE, AND QUIETLY WRITING MY SONG LYRICS?
BUT MOM WOULDN'T UNDERSTAND ANY OF THAT.
I JUST WANT YOU TO BE HAPPY. IF YOU'RE NOT FITTING IN, YOU'RE NOT HAPPY.
NOT WHEN ALL THOSE BOOKS MADE TO "HELP" ME TELL HER I SHOULDN'T BE MYSELF.
YEAH, MOM. I'LL, UH, TRY HARDER TOMORROW.
GOOD FOR YOU, MIA! DON'T WORRY, I'M SURE THIS YEAR WILL BE BETTER FOR YOU.

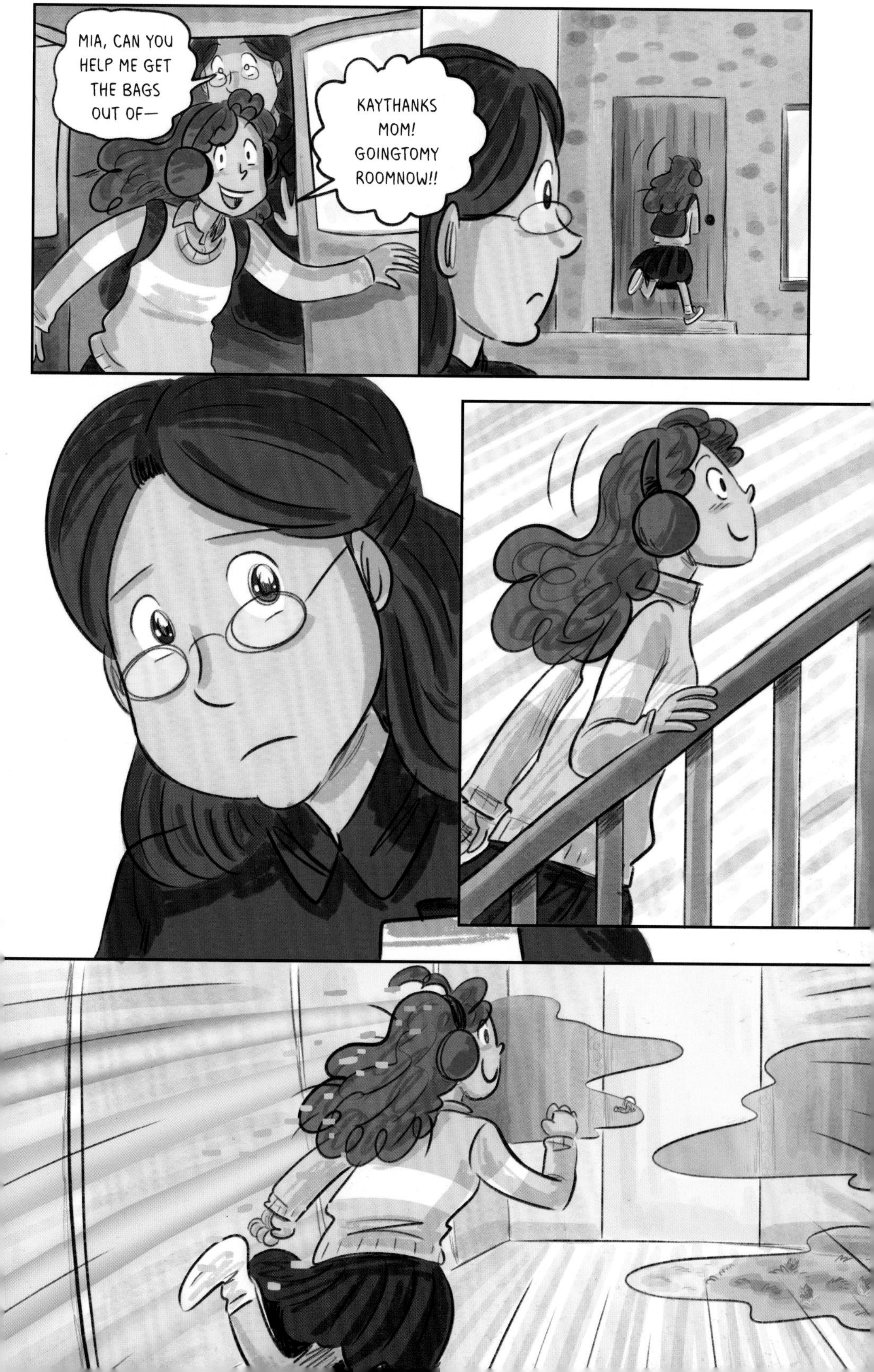
MIA, CAN YOU HELP ME GET THE BAGS OUT OF—
KAYTHANKS MOM! GOINGTOMY ROOMNOW!!

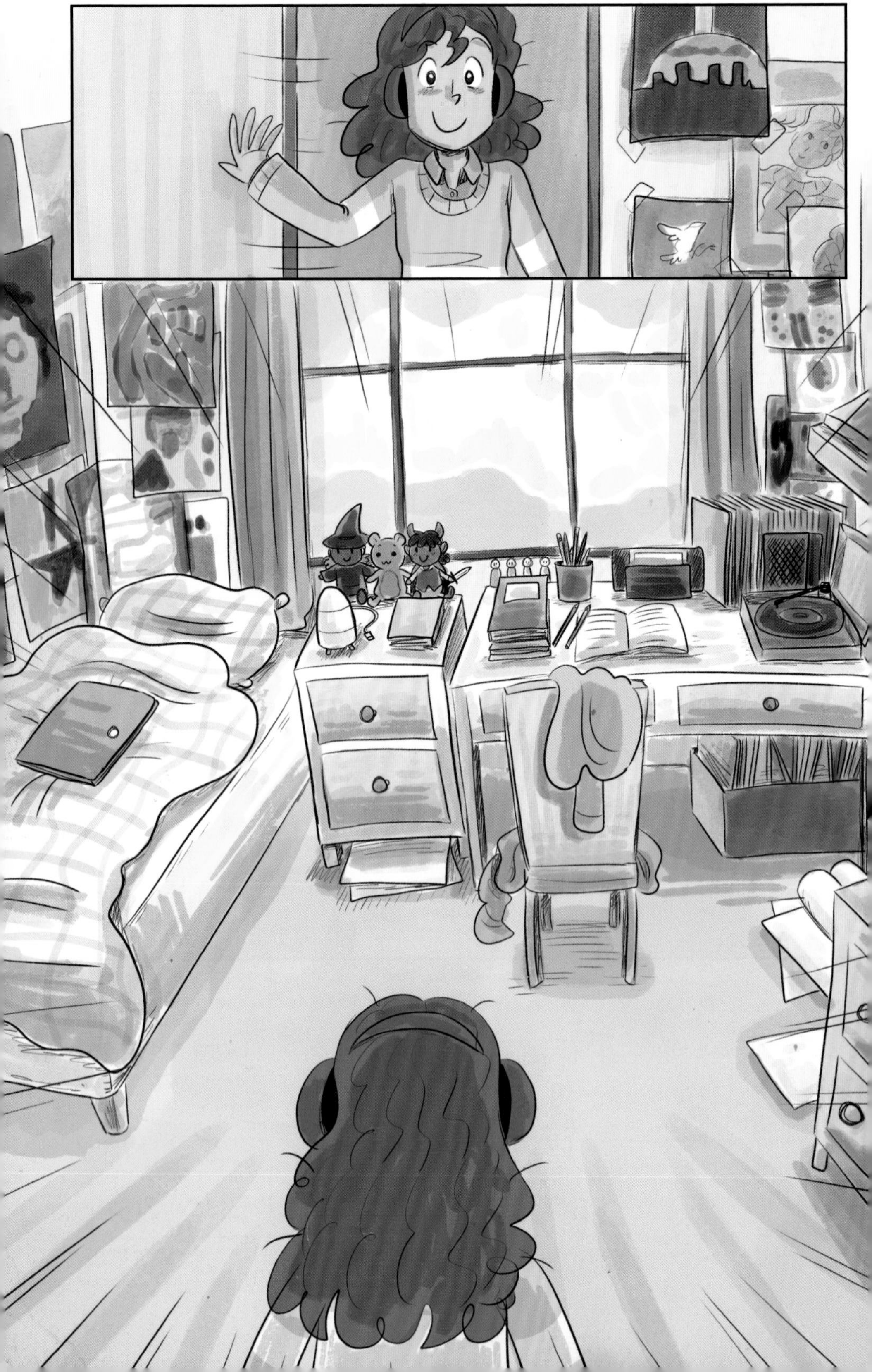

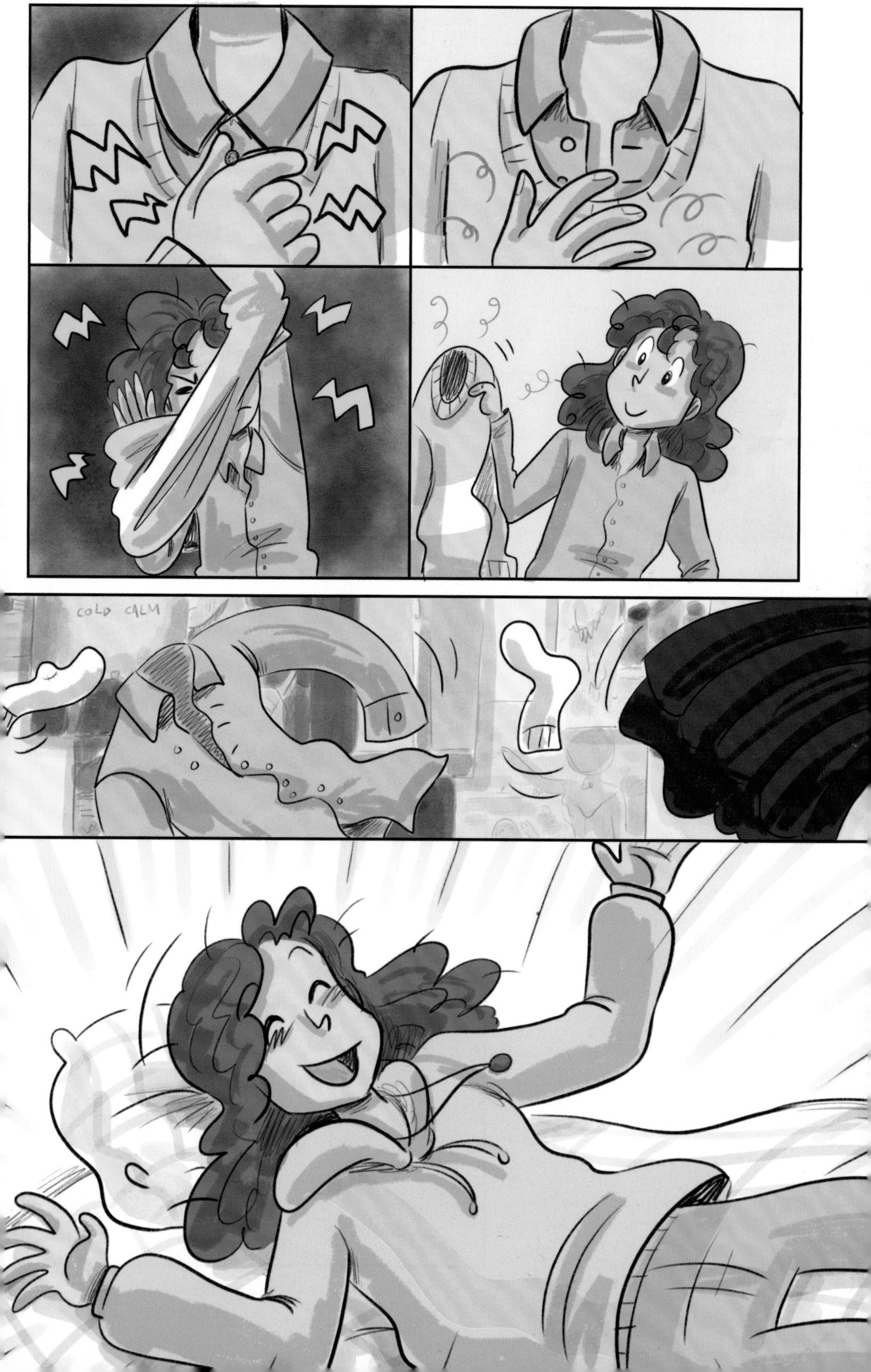
COLD CALM

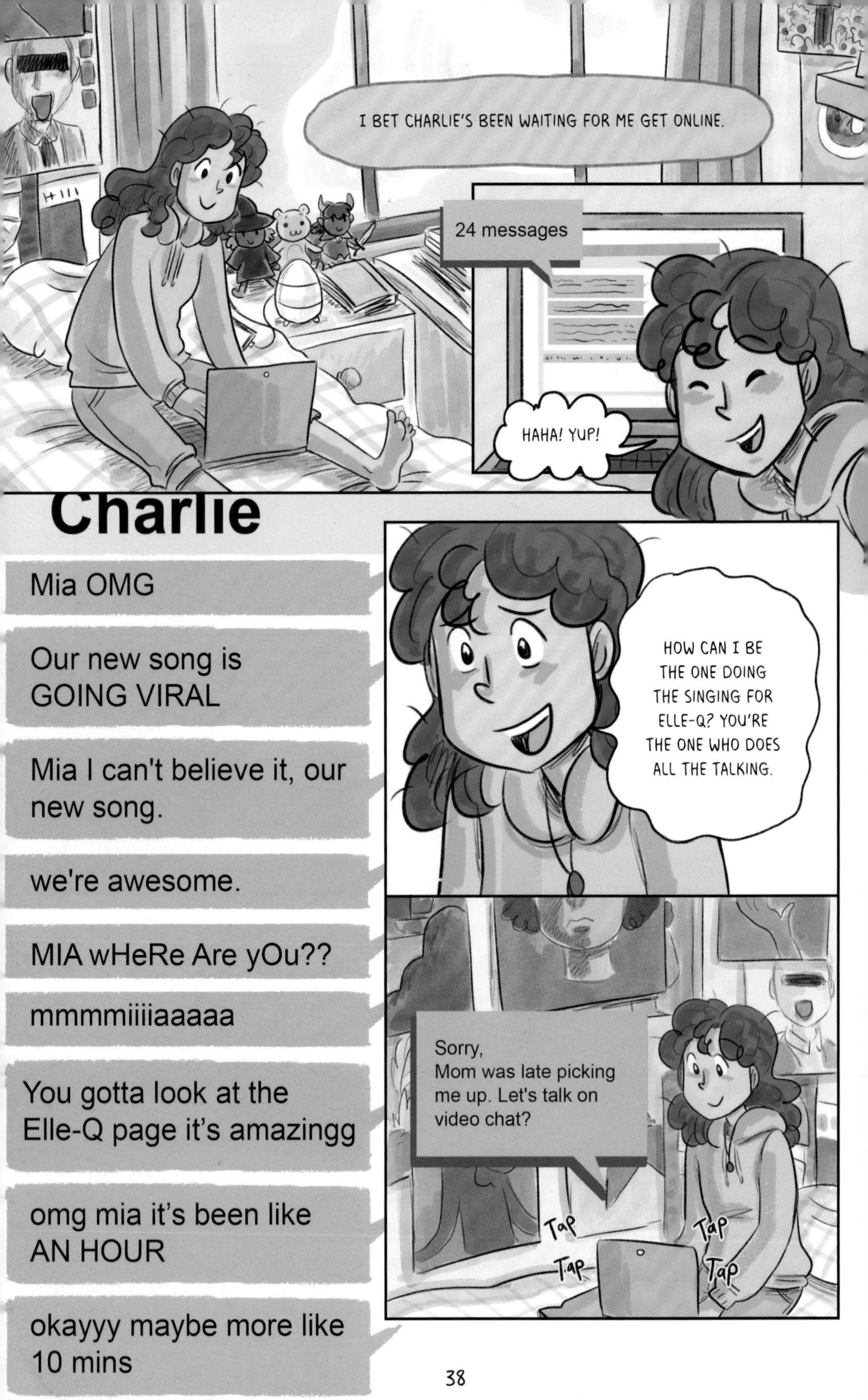

I BET CHARLIE'S BEEN WAITING FOR ME GET ONLINE.
24 messages
HAHA! YUP!
Charlie
Mia OMG
Our new song is GOING VIRAL
Mia I can't believe it, our new song.
we're awesome.
MIA wHeRe Are yOu??
mmmmiiiiaaaaa
You gotta look at the Elle-Q page it's amazingg
omg mia it's been like AN HOUR
okayyy maybe more like 10 mins
HOW CAN I BE THE ONE DOING THE SINGING FOR ELLE-Q? YOU'RE THE ONE WHO DOES ALL THE TALKING.
Sorry, Mom was late picking me up. Let's talk on video chat?
Tap
Tap
Tap
Tap

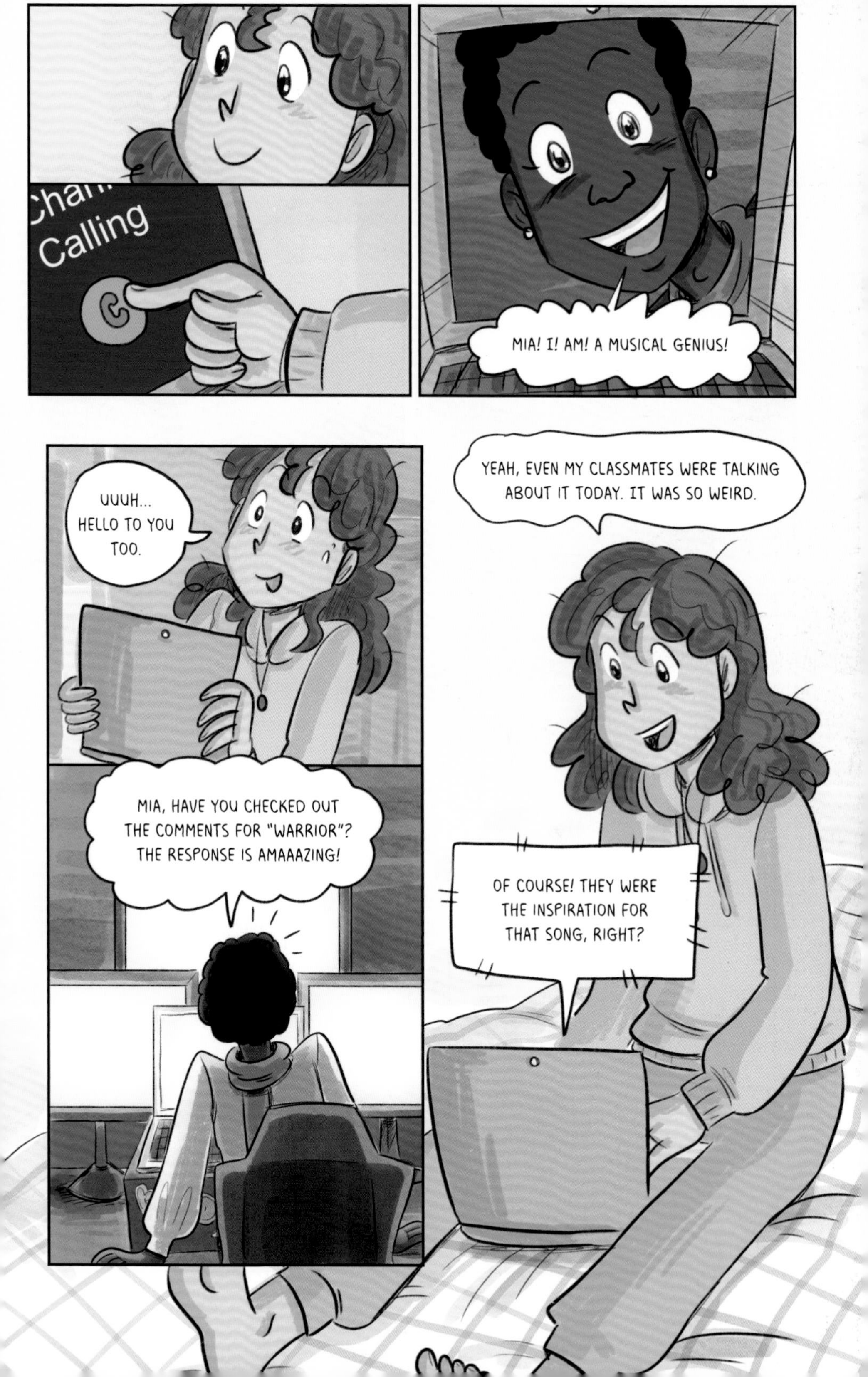
Calling
MIA! I! AM! A MUSICAL GENIUS!
UUUH...
HELLO TO YOU
TOO.
YEAH, EVEN MY CLASSMATES WERE TALKING
ABOUT IT TODAY. IT WAS SO WEIRD.
MIA, HAVE YOU CHECKED OUT
THE COMMENTS FOR "WARRIOR"?
THE RESPONSE IS AMAAAZING!
OF COURSE! THEY WERE
THE INSPIRATION FOR
THAT SONG, RIGHT?

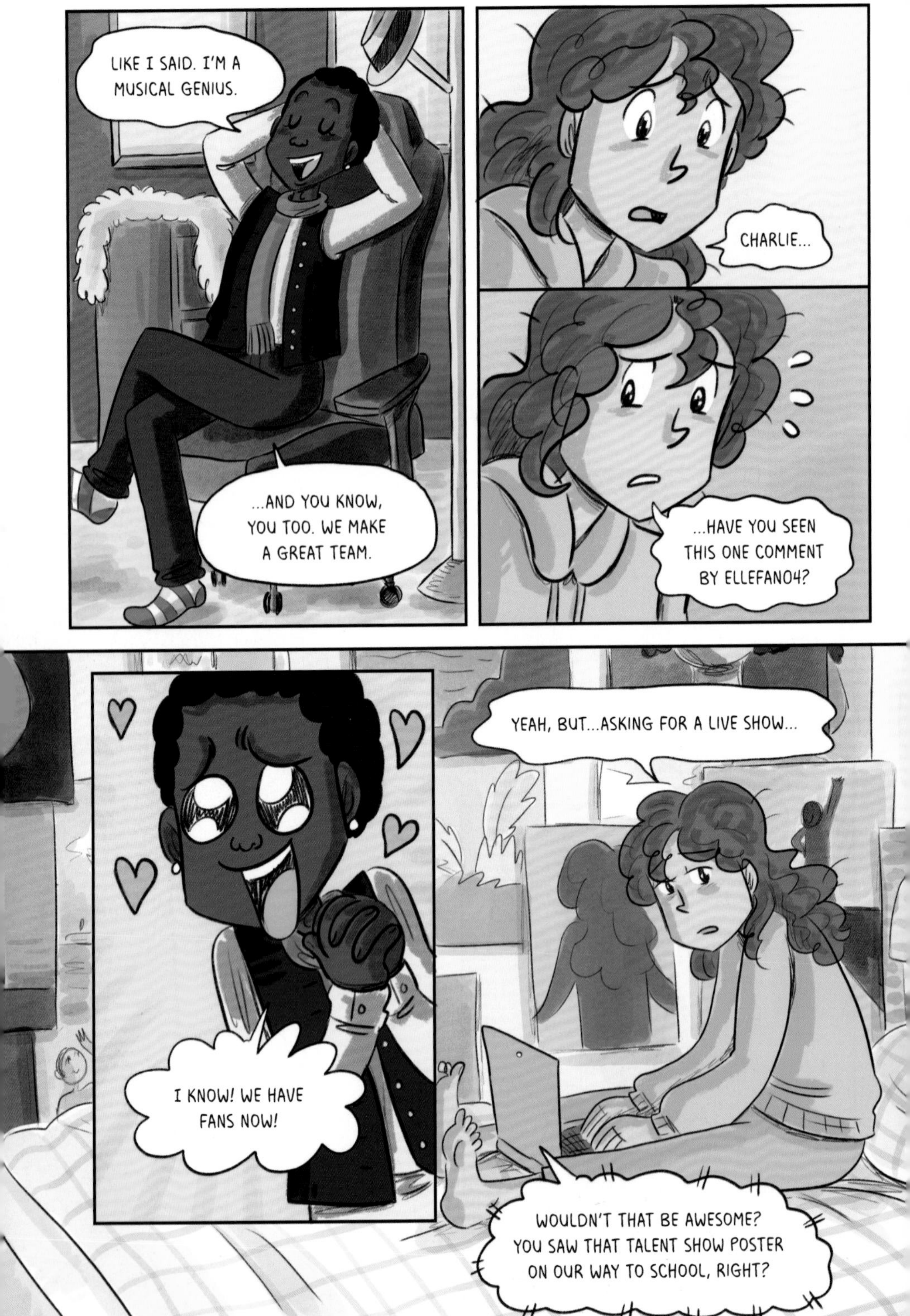
LIKE I SAID. I'M A MUSICAL GENIUS.
...AND YOU KNOW, YOU TOO. WE MAKE A GREAT TEAM.
CHARLIE...
...HAVE YOU SEEN THIS ONE COMMENT BY ELLEFAN04?
I KNOW! WE HAVE FANS NOW!
YEAH, BUT...ASKING FOR A LIVE SHOW...
WOULDN'T THAT BE AWESOME? YOU SAW THAT TALENT SHOW POSTER ON OUR WAY TO SCHOOL, RIGHT?

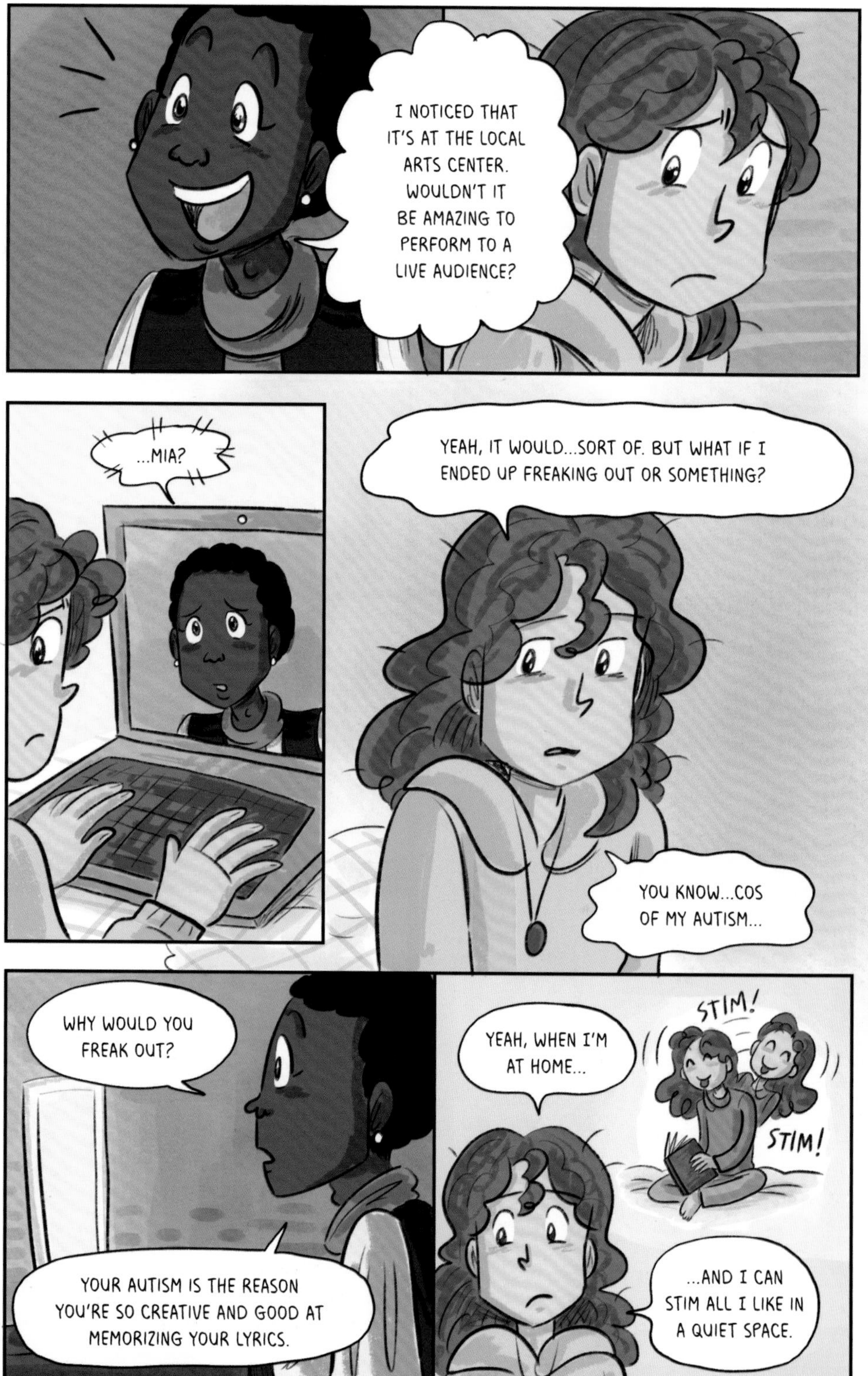
I NOTICED THAT IT'S AT THE LOCAL ARTS CENTER. WOULDN'T IT BE AMAZING TO PERFORM TO A LIVE AUDIENCE?
...MIA?
YEAH, IT WOULD...SORT OF. BUT WHAT IF I ENDED UP FREAKING OUT OR SOMETHING?
YOU KNOW...COS OF MY AUTISM...
WHY WOULD YOU FREAK OUT?
YOUR AUTISM IS THE REASON YOU'RE SO CREATIVE AND GOOD AT MEMORIZING YOUR LYRICS.
YEAH, WHEN I'M AT HOME...
STIM!
STIM!
...AND I CAN STIM ALL I LIKE IN A QUIET SPACE.

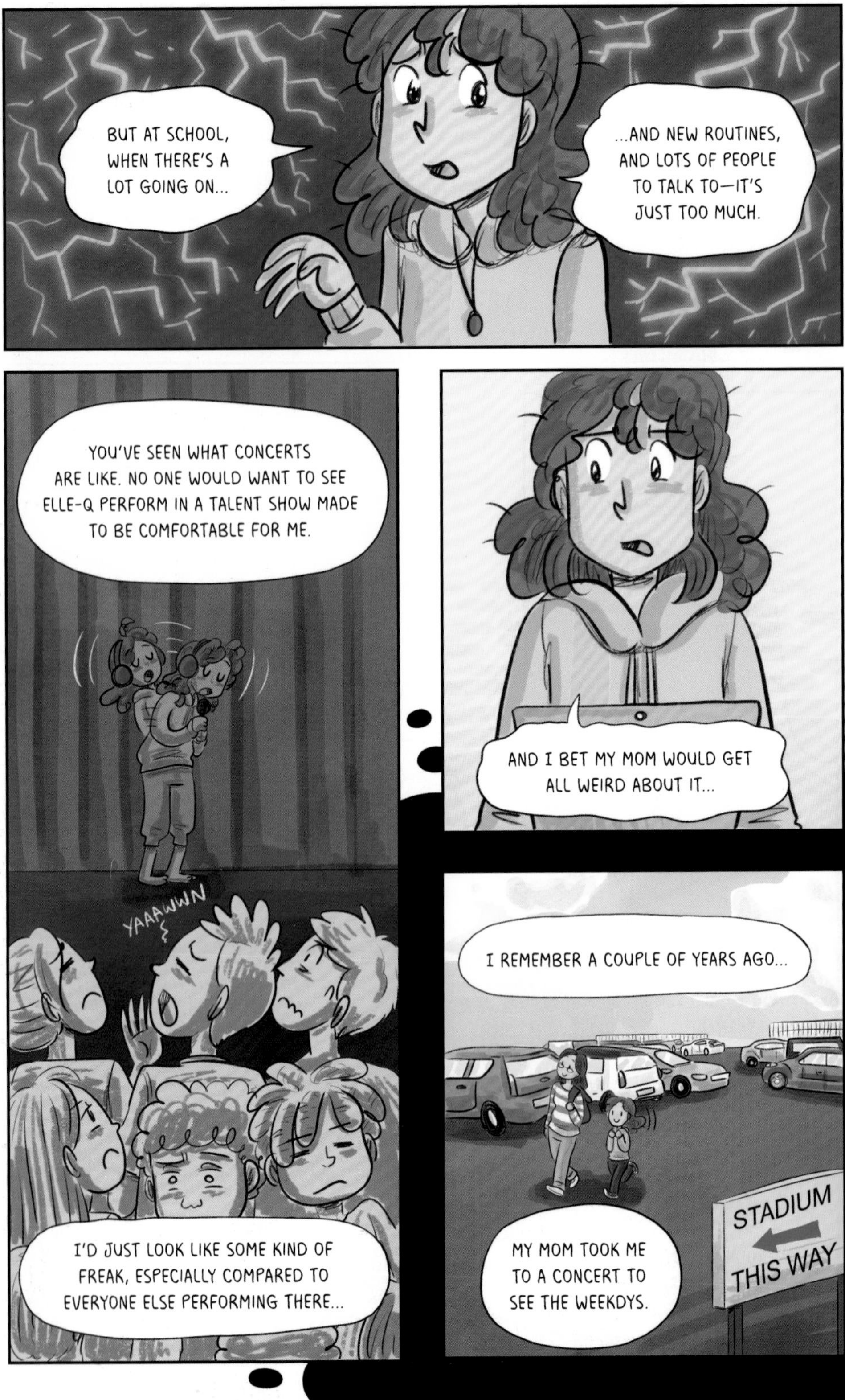
BUT AT SCHOOL, WHEN THERE'S A LOT GOING ON...
...AND NEW ROUTINES, AND LOTS OF PEOPLE TO TALK TO—IT'S JUST TOO MUCH.
YOU'VE SEEN WHAT CONCERTS ARE LIKE. NO ONE WOULD WANT TO SEE ELLE-Q PERFORM IN A TALENT SHOW MADE TO BE COMFORTABLE FOR ME.
YAAAWWN
I'D JUST LOOK LIKE SOME KIND OF FREAK, ESPECIALLY COMPARED TO EVERYONE ELSE PERFORMING THERE...
AND I BET MY MOM WOULD GET ALL WEIRD ABOUT IT...
I REMEMBER A COUPLE OF YEARS AGO...
MY MOM TOOK ME TO A CONCERT TO SEE THE WEEKDYS.
STADIUM
THIS WAY

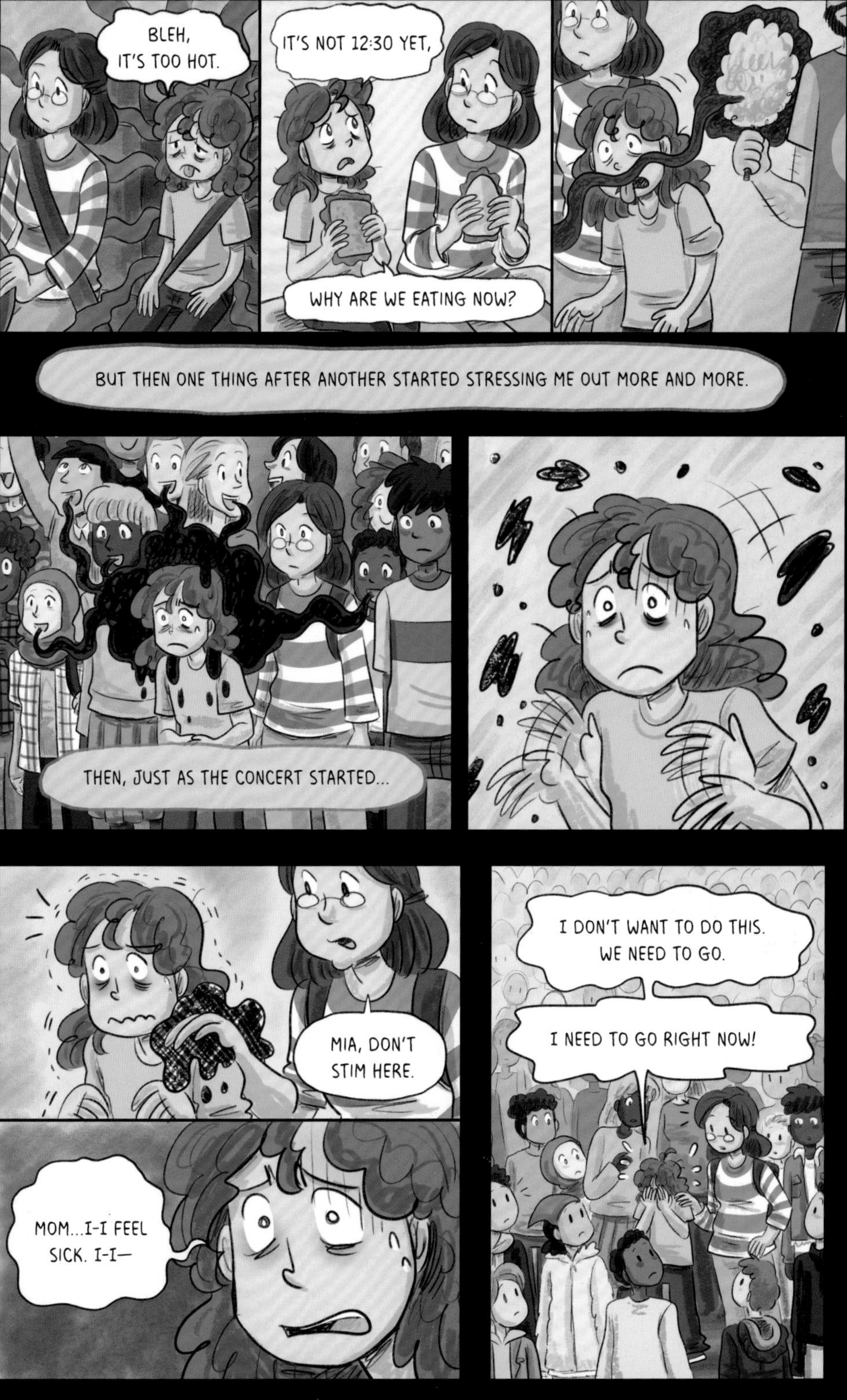

BLEH, IT'S TOO HOT.
IT'S NOT 12:30 YET,
WHY ARE WE EATING NOW?
BUT THEN ONE THING AFTER ANOTHER STARTED STRESSING ME OUT MORE AND MORE.
THEN, JUST AS THE CONCERT STARTED...
MIA, DON'T STIM HERE.
MOM...I-I FEEL SICK. I-I—
I DON'T WANT TO DO THIS. WE NEED TO GO.
I NEED TO GO RIGHT NOW!

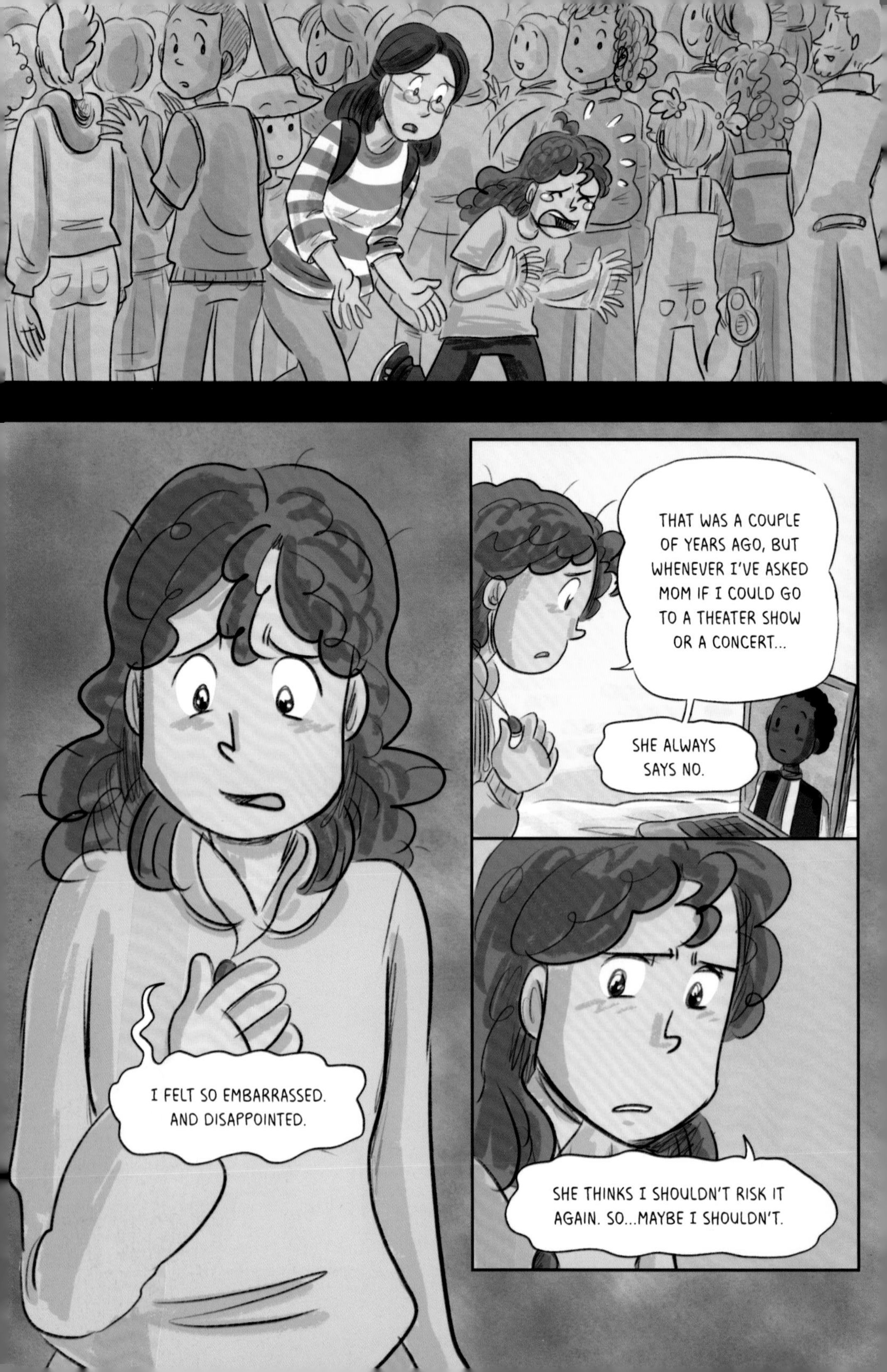
I FELT SO EMBARRASSED. AND DISAPPOINTED.
THAT WAS A COUPLE OF YEARS AGO, BUT WHENEVER I'VE ASKED MOM IF I COULD GO TO A THEATER SHOW OR A CONCERT...
SHE ALWAYS SAYS NO.
SHE THINKS I SHOULDN'T RISK IT AGAIN. SO...MAYBE I SHOULDN'T.

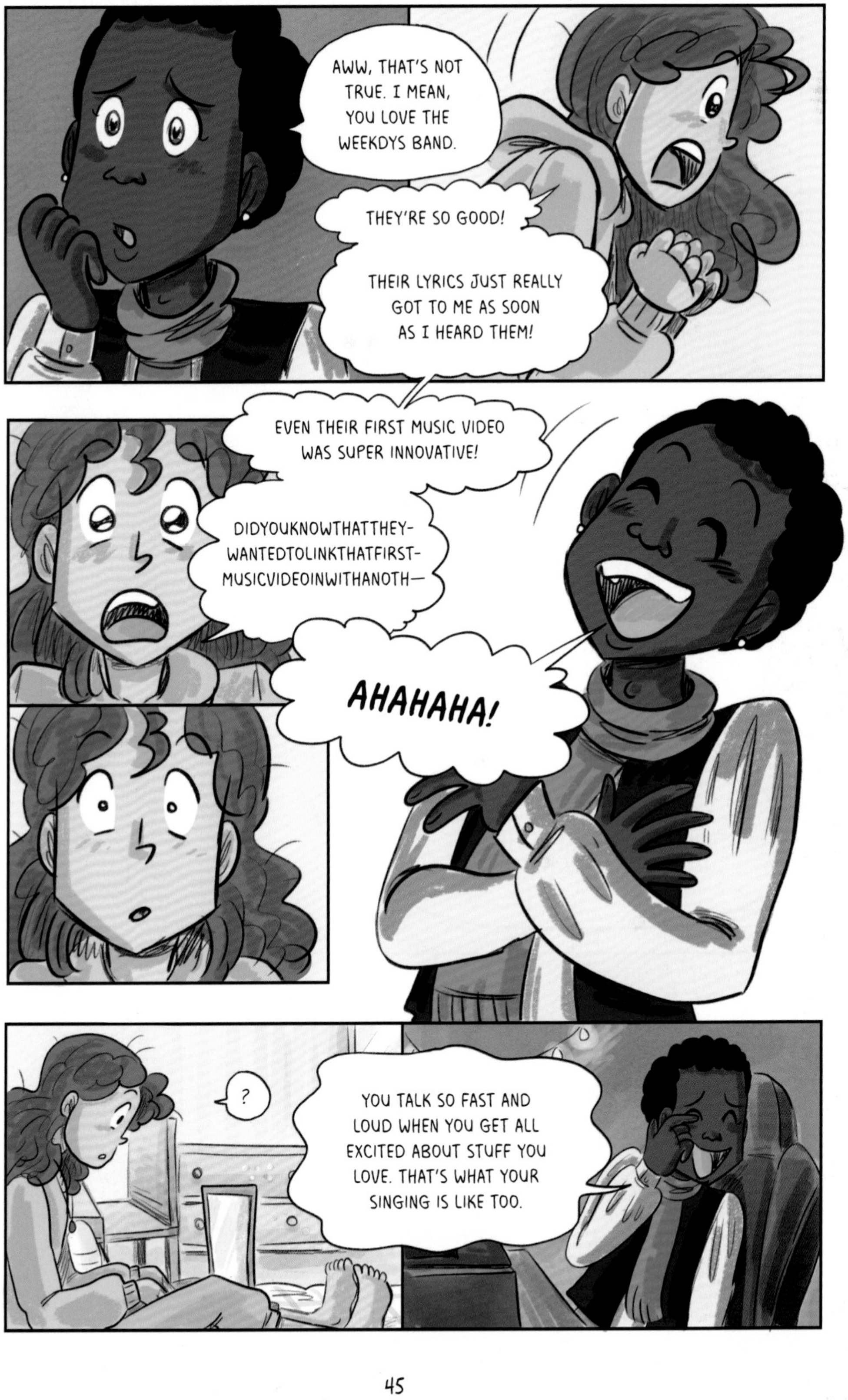
AWW, THAT'S NOT TRUE. I MEAN, YOU LOVE THE WEEKDYS BAND.
THEY'RE SO GOOD!
THEIR LYRICS JUST REALLY GOT TO ME AS SOON AS I HEARD THEM!
EVEN THEIR FIRST MUSIC VIDEO WAS SUPER INNOVATIVE!
DIDYOUKNOWTHATTHEY-WANTEDTOLINKTHATFIRST-MUSICVIDEOINWITHANOTH—
AHAHAHA!
?
YOU TALK SO FAST AND LOUD WHEN YOU GET ALL EXCITED ABOUT STUFF YOU LOVE. THAT'S WHAT YOUR SINGING IS LIKE TOO.

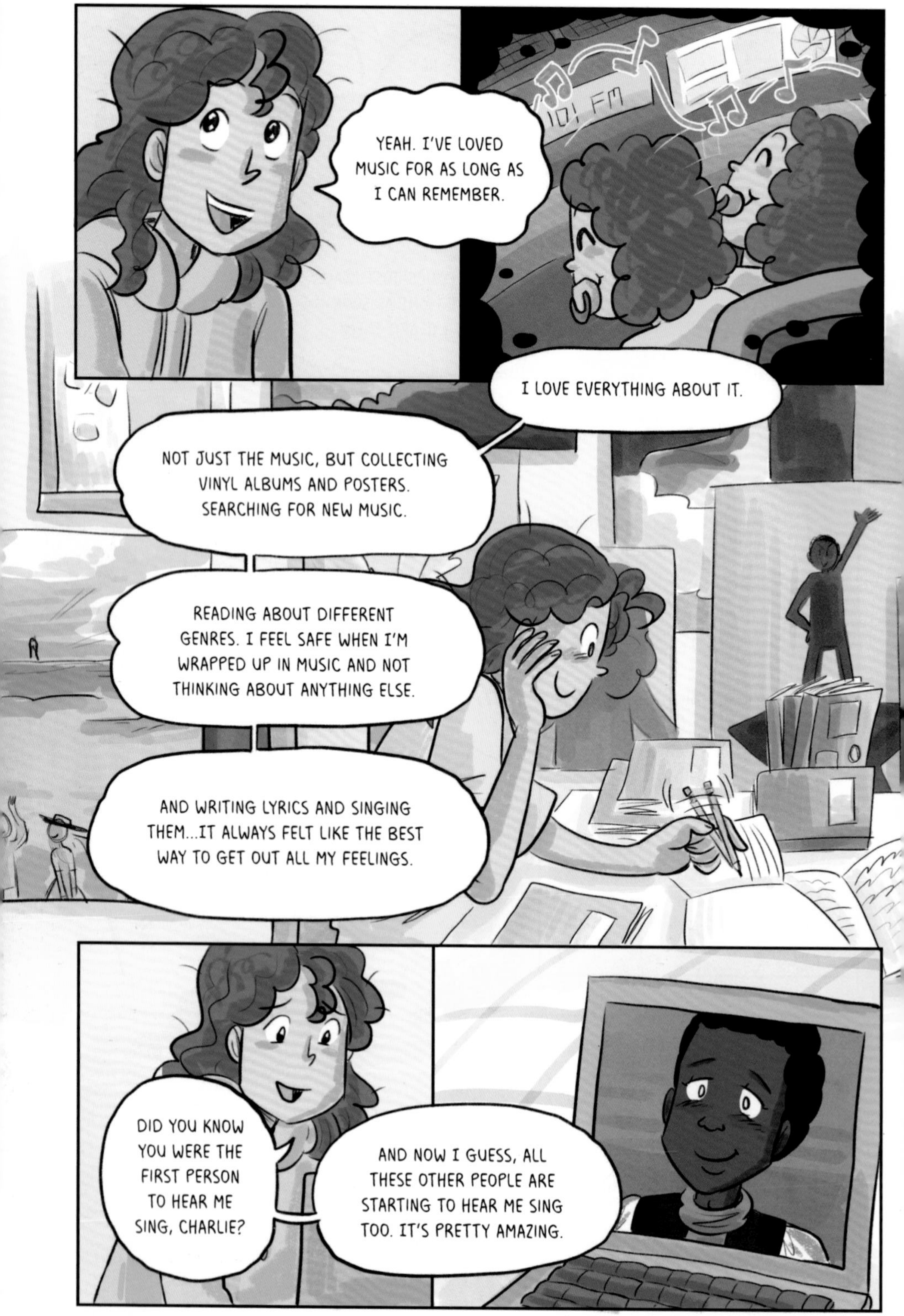
YEAH. I'VE LOVED MUSIC FOR AS LONG AS I CAN REMEMBER.
101 FM
I LOVE EVERYTHING ABOUT IT.
NOT JUST THE MUSIC, BUT COLLECTING VINYL ALBUMS AND POSTERS. SEARCHING FOR NEW MUSIC.
READING ABOUT DIFFERENT GENRES. I FEEL SAFE WHEN I'M WRAPPED UP IN MUSIC AND NOT THINKING ABOUT ANYTHING ELSE.
AND WRITING LYRICS AND SINGING THEM...IT ALWAYS FELT LIKE THE BEST WAY TO GET OUT ALL MY FEELINGS.
DID YOU KNOW YOU WERE THE FIRST PERSON TO HEAR ME SING, CHARLIE?
AND NOW I GUESS, ALL THESE OTHER PEOPLE ARE STARTING TO HEAR ME SING TOO. IT'S PRETTY AMAZING.

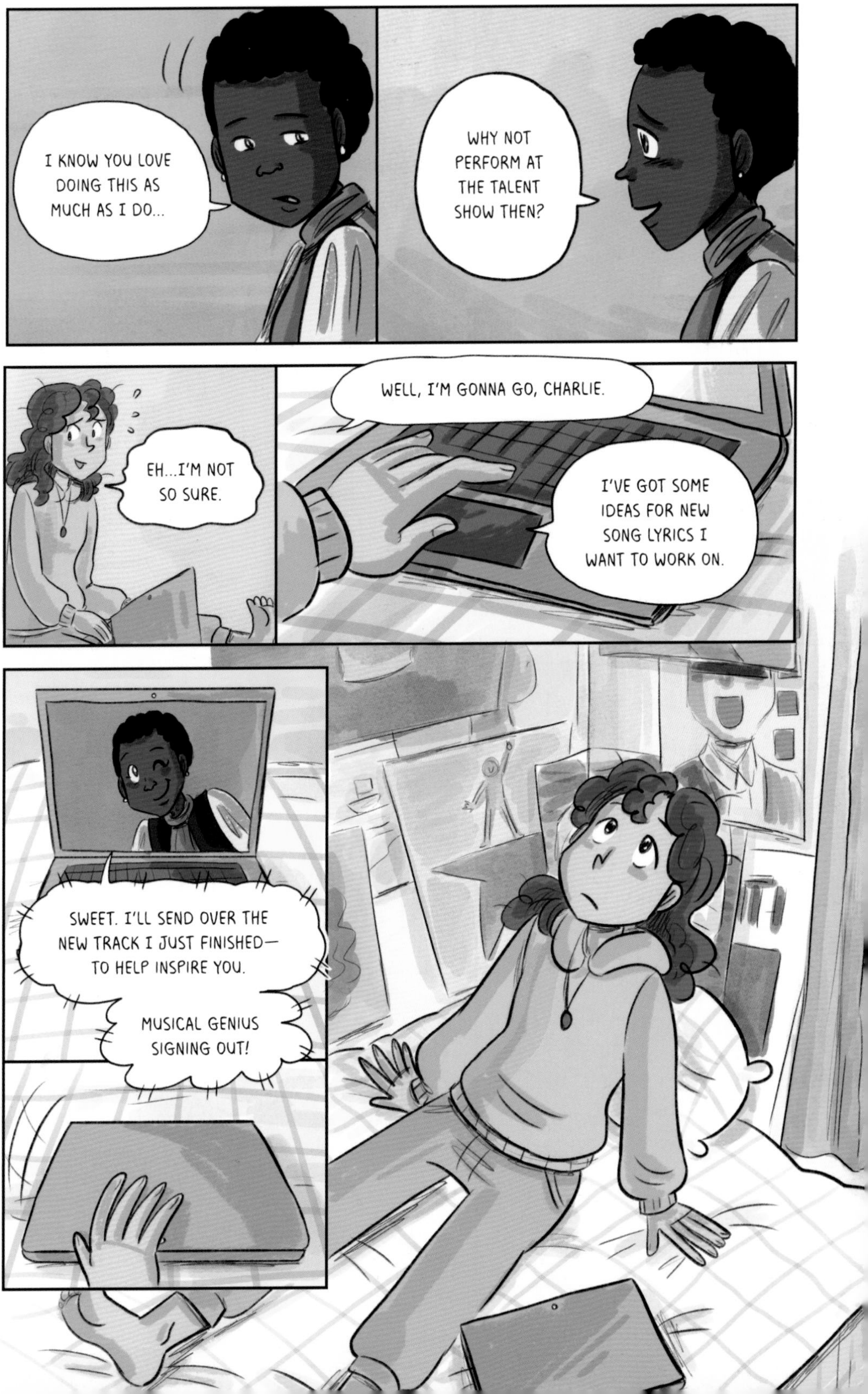
I KNOW YOU LOVE DOING THIS AS MUCH AS I DO...
WHY NOT PERFORM AT THE TALENT SHOW THEN?
EH...I'M NOT SO SURE.
WELL, I'M GONNA GO, CHARLIE.
I'VE GOT SOME IDEAS FOR NEW SONG LYRICS I WANT TO WORK ON.
SWEET. I'LL SEND OVER THE NEW TRACK I JUST FINISHED—TO HELP INSPIRE YOU.
MUSICAL GENIUS SIGNING OUT!

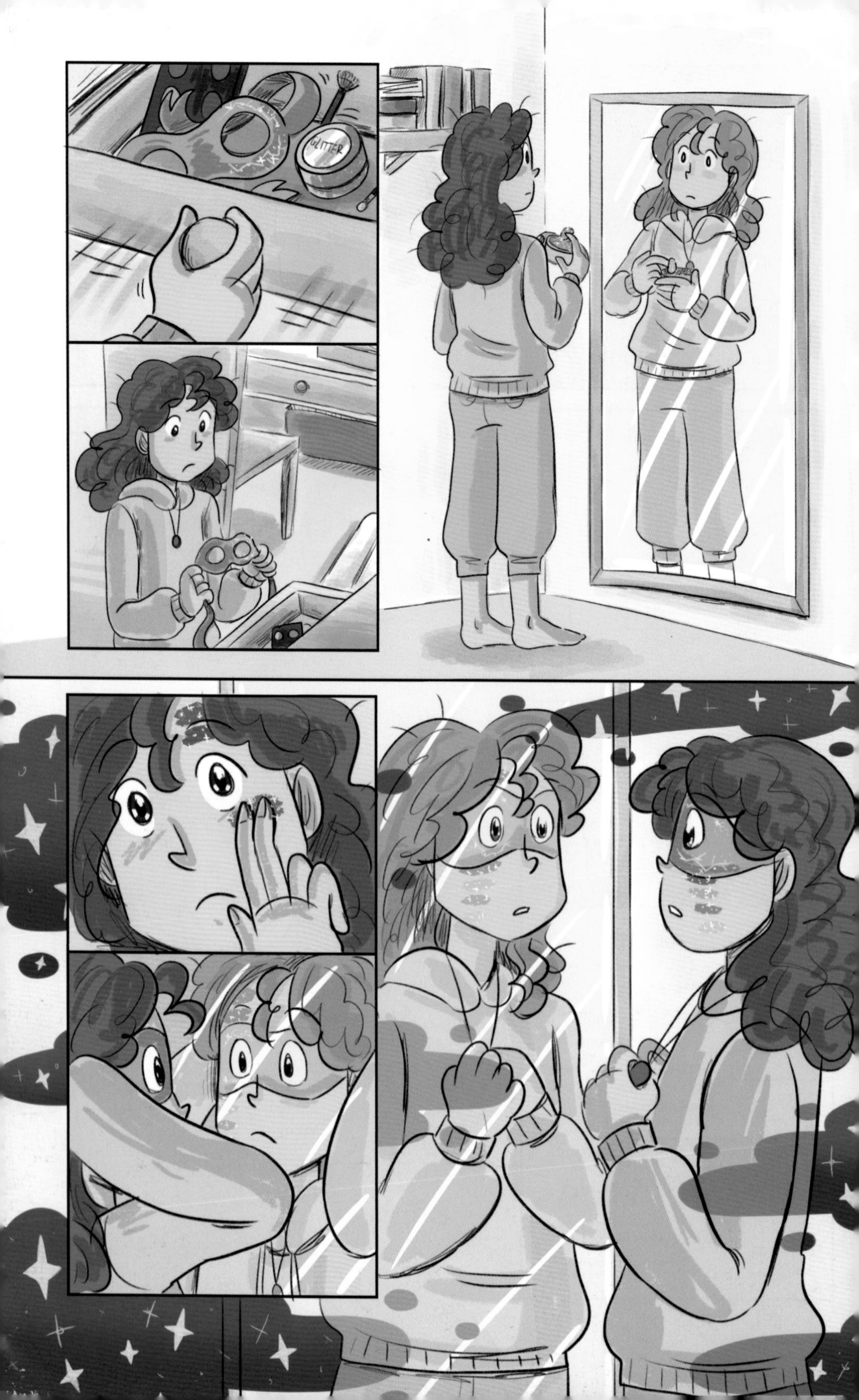
GLITTER

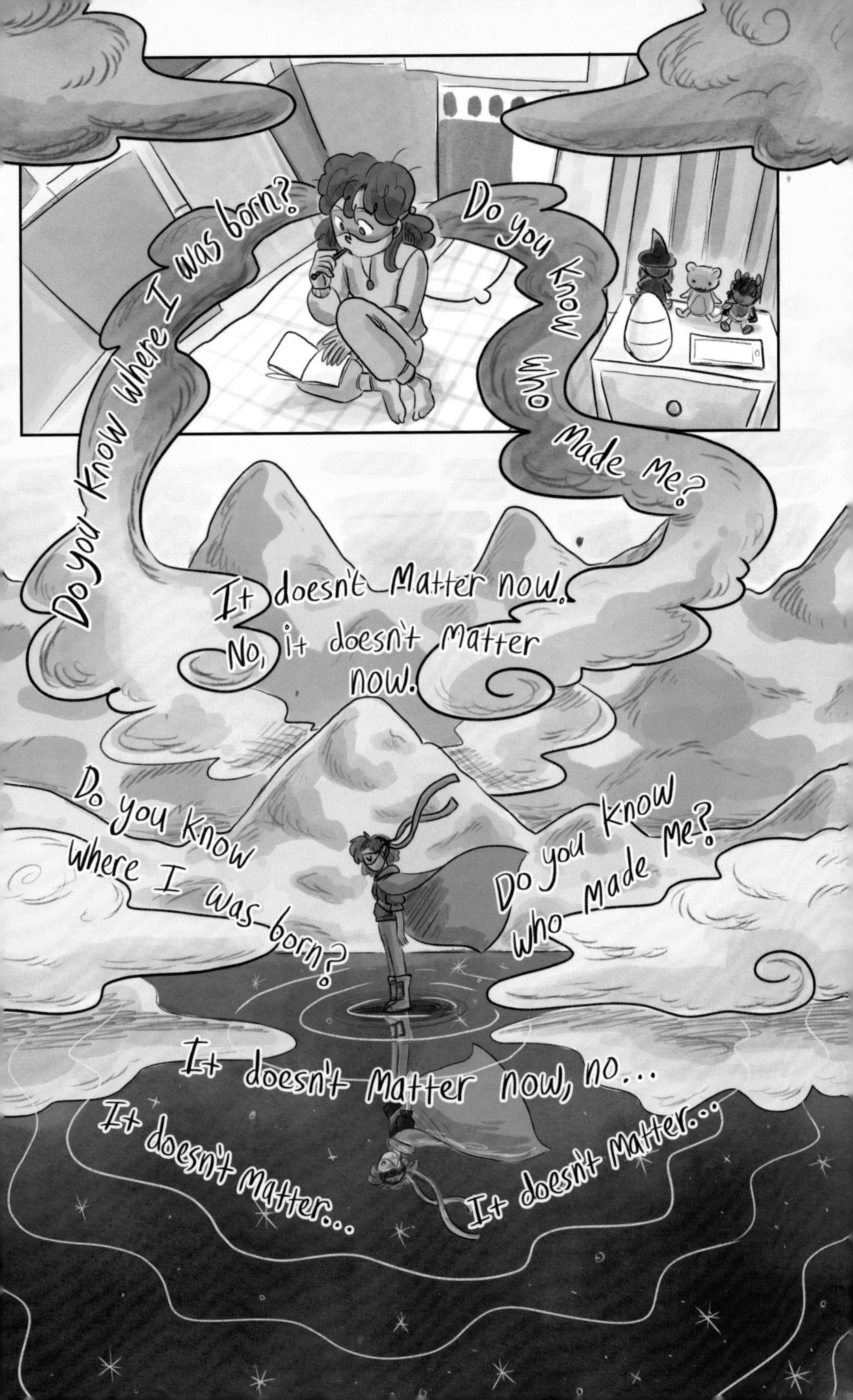

Do you know where I was born?
Do you know who made me?
It doesn't matter now.
No, it doesn't matter now.
Do you know where I was born?
Do you know who made me?
It doesn't matter now, no...
It doesn't matter...
It doesn't matter...

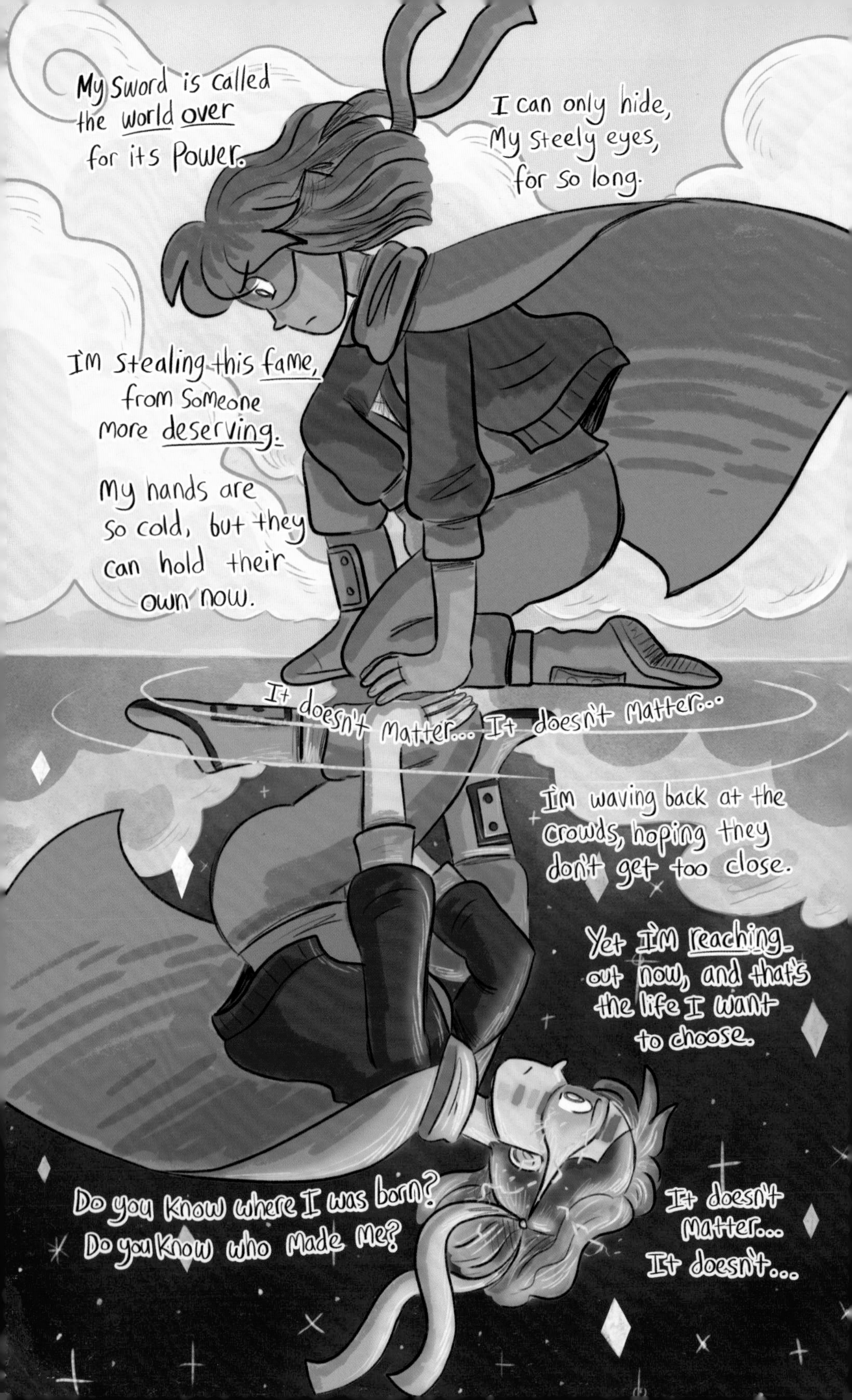
My sword is called the world over for its power.
I can only hide, my steely eyes, for so long.
I'm stealing this fame, from someone more deserving.
My hands are so cold, but they can hold their own now.
It doesn't matter... It doesn't matter...
I'm waving back at the crowds, hoping they don't get too close.
Yet I'm reaching out now, and that's the life I want to choose.
Do you know where I was born? Do you know who made me?
It doesn't matter... It doesn't...

CHAPTER THREE

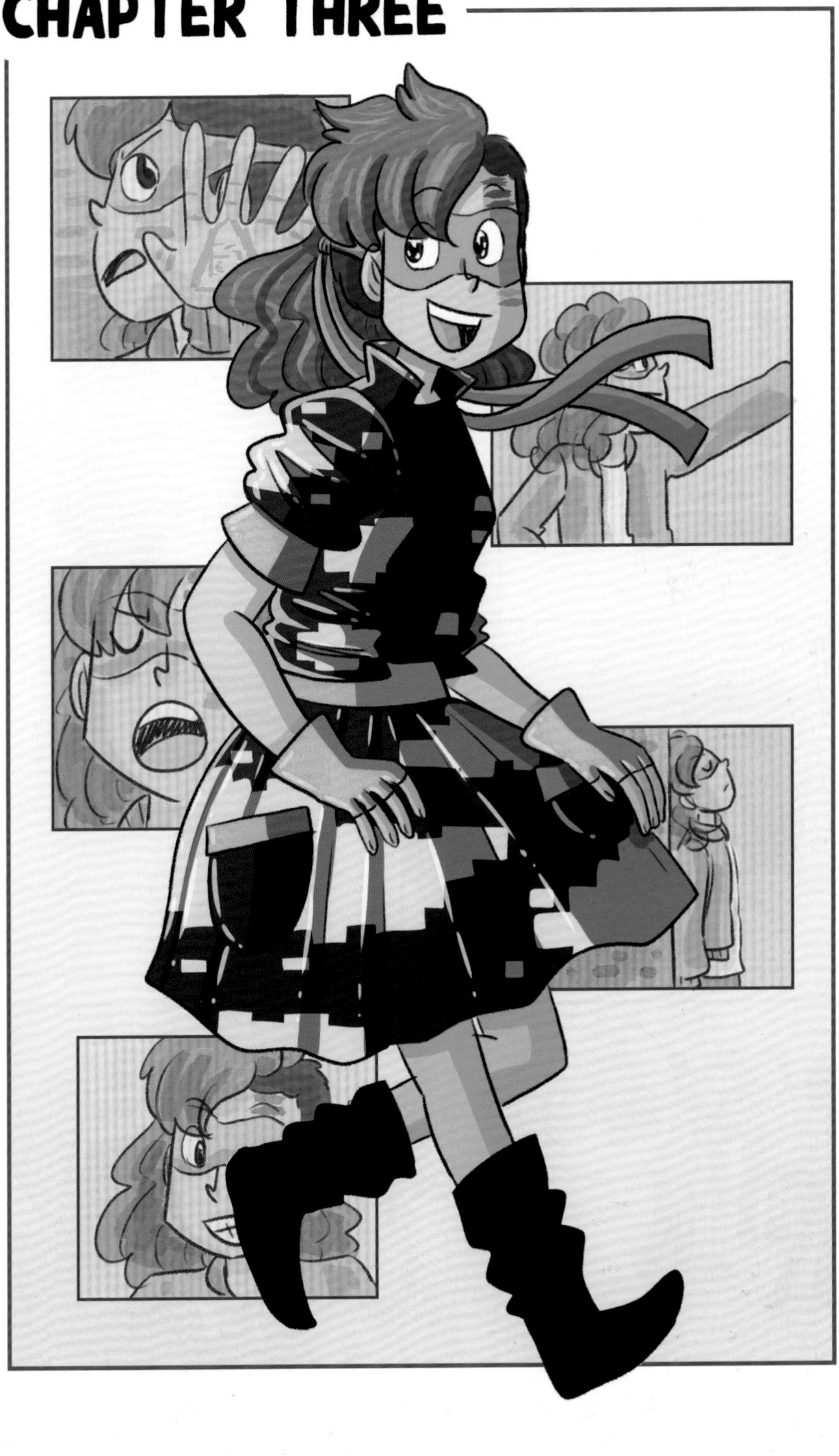

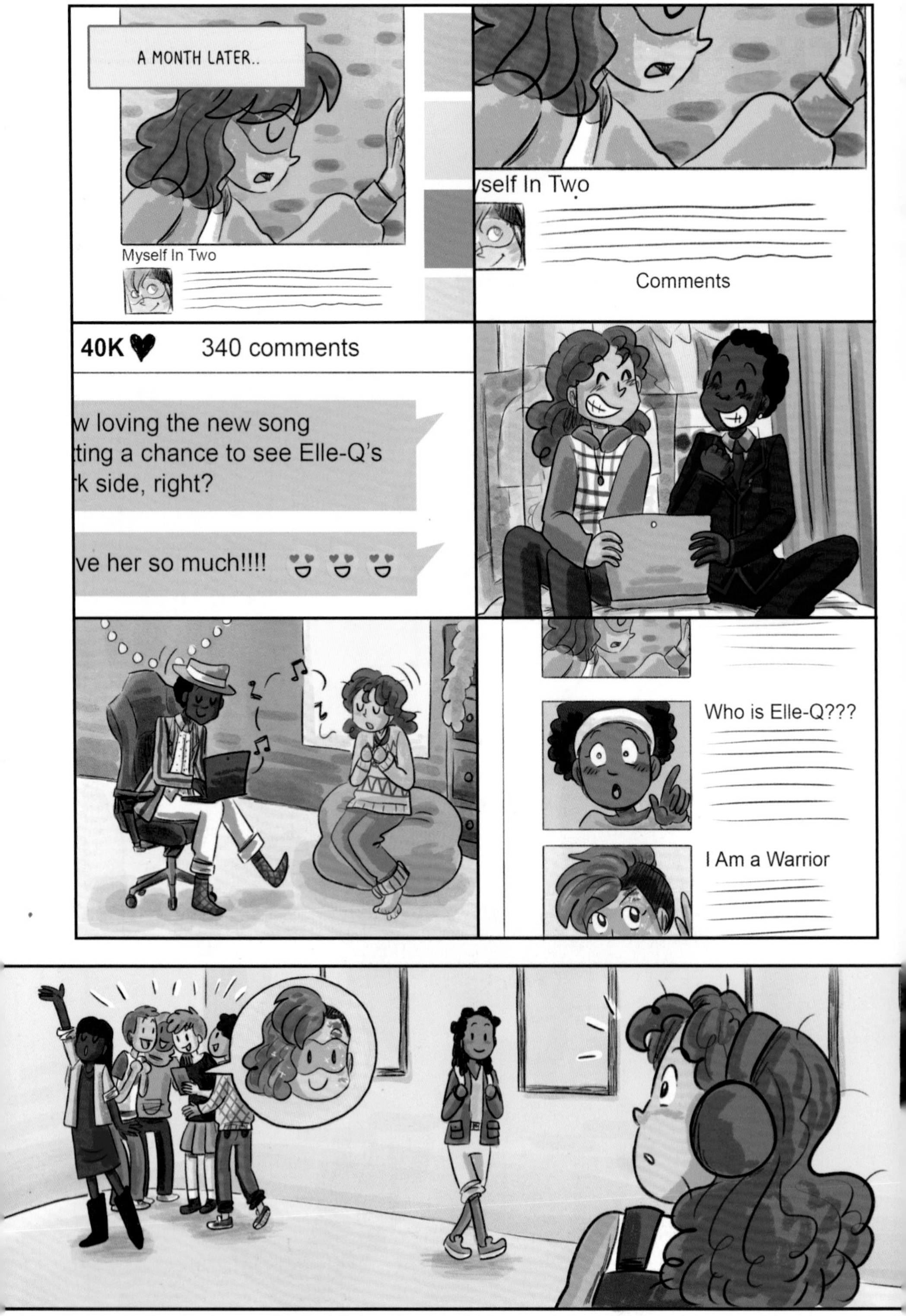
A MONTH LATER..
Myself In Two
yself In Two
Comments
40K
340 comments
w loving the new song
tting a chance to see Elle-Q's
rk side, right?
ve her so much!!!!
Who is Elle-Q???
I Am a Warrior

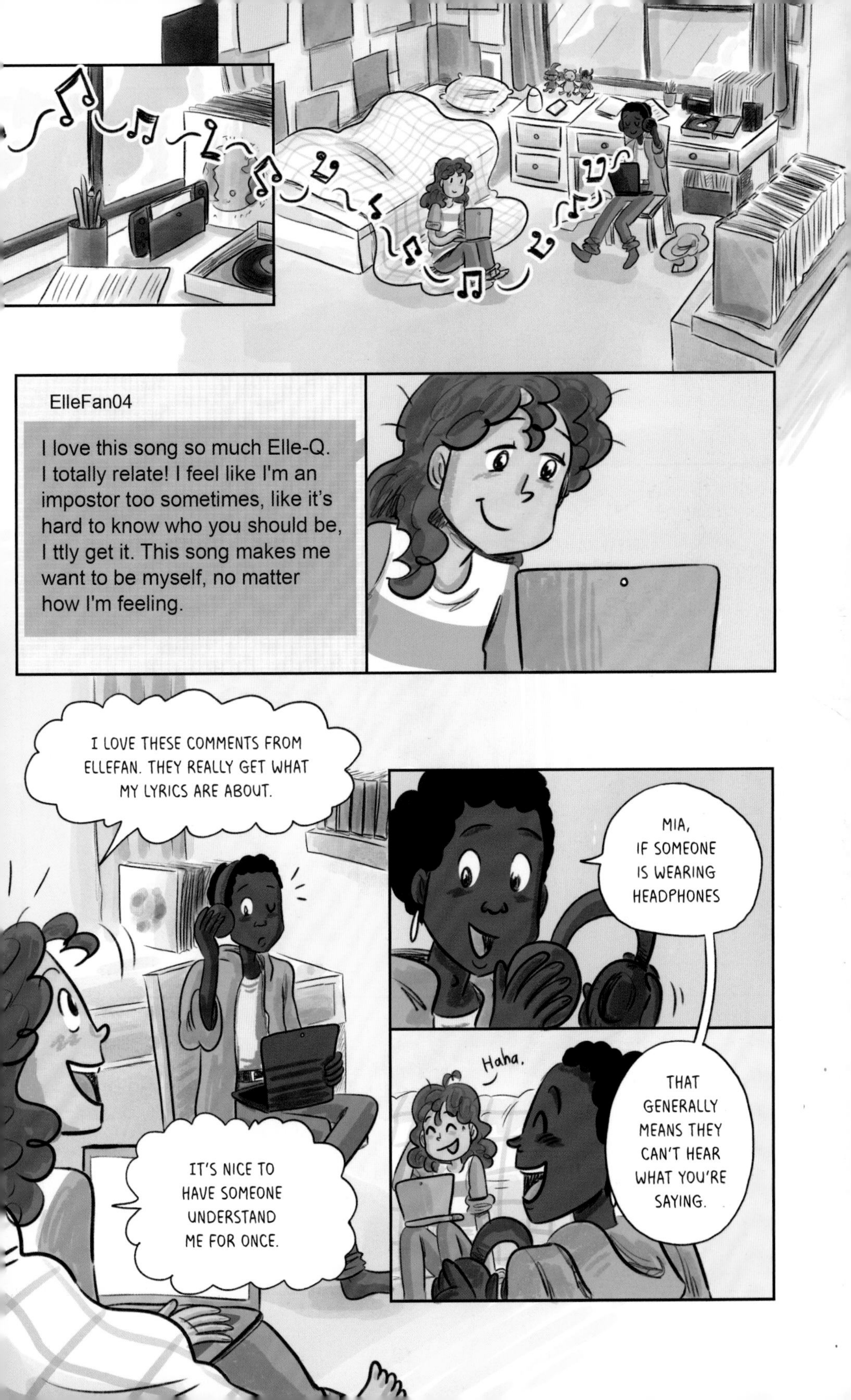

ElleFan04
I love this song so much Elle-Q. I totally relate! I feel like I'm an impostor too sometimes, like it's hard to know who you should be, I ttly get it. This song makes me want to be myself, no matter how I'm feeling.
I LOVE THESE COMMENTS FROM ELLEFAN. THEY REALLY GET WHAT MY LYRICS ARE ABOUT.
IT'S NICE TO HAVE SOMEONE UNDERSTAND ME FOR ONCE.
MIA, IF SOMEONE IS WEARING HEADPHONES
Haha.
THAT GENERALLY MEANS THEY CAN'T HEAR WHAT YOU'RE SAYING.

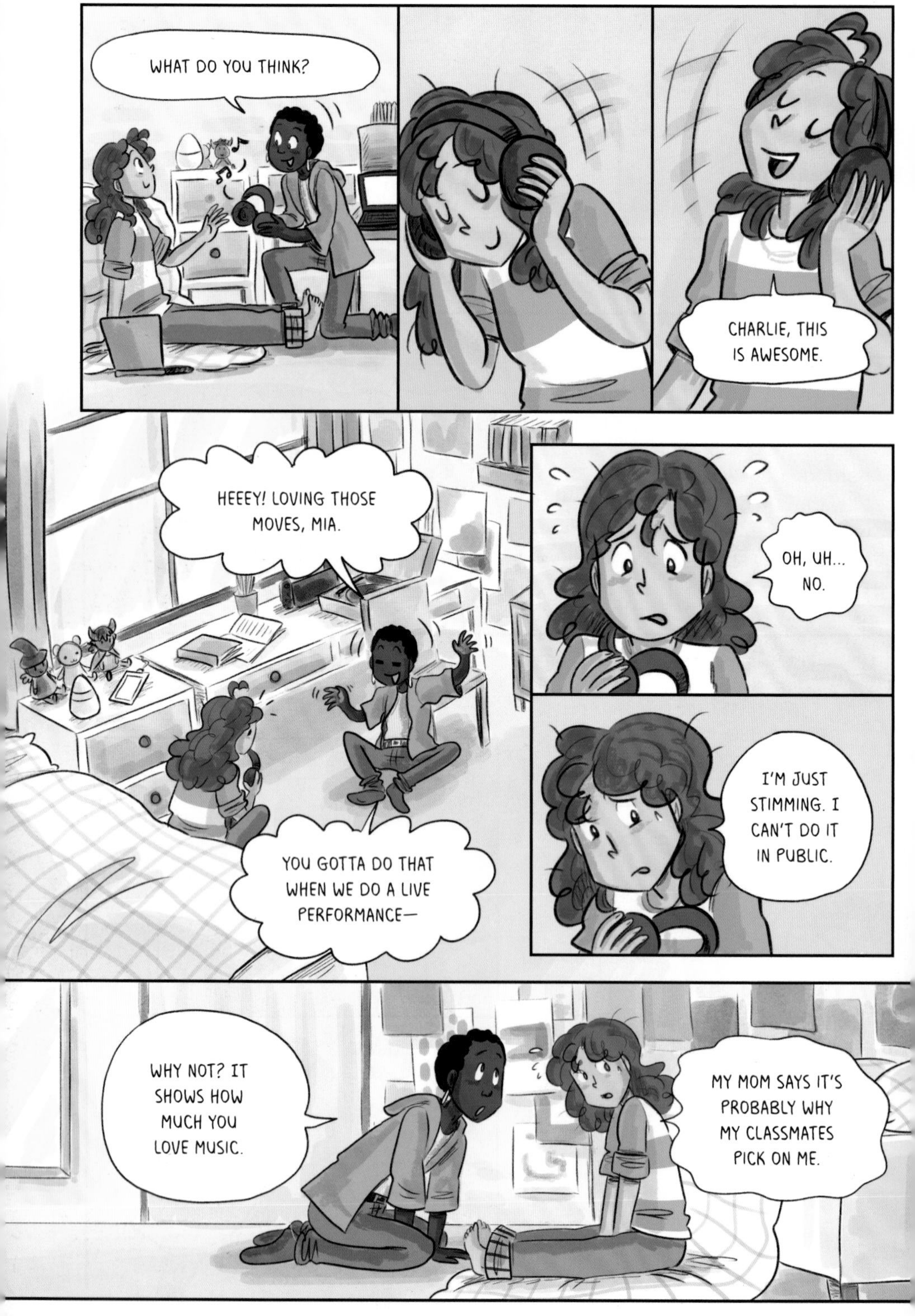
WHAT DO YOU THINK?
CHARLIE, THIS IS AWESOME.
HEEEY! LOVING THOSE MOVES, MIA.
YOU GOTTA DO THAT WHEN WE DO A LIVE PERFORMANCE—
OH, UH... NO.
I'M JUST STIMMING. I CAN'T DO IT IN PUBLIC.
WHY NOT? IT SHOWS HOW MUCH YOU LOVE MUSIC.
MY MOM SAYS IT'S PROBABLY WHY MY CLASSMATES PICK ON ME.

BESIDES, WE'RE NOT EVEN DOING A LIVE PERFORMANCE.

I DUNNO...I JUST THOUGHT, SINCE OUR MUSIC IS DOING SO WELL...AND WITH THAT TALENT SHOW COMING UP...IT WOULD BE THIS GREAT OPPORTUNITY FOR US BOTH.

WOULDN'T IT BE COOL TO CONNECT WITH MORE PEOPLE LIKE ELLEFANO4?

I totally relate! I feel like I'm an impostor too sometimes, like it's hard to know who you should be. I ttly get it. This song makes me want to be myself, no matter how I'm feeling.

I KNOW IT MAKES YOU NERVOUS, BUT THERE'S A DEADLINE FOR ENTERING THE TALENT SHOW. CAN'T WE AT LEAST TALK ABOUT THE IDEA OF—

MIAAA! IT'S TIME TO GET GOING. I HAVE ERRANDS TO RUN!

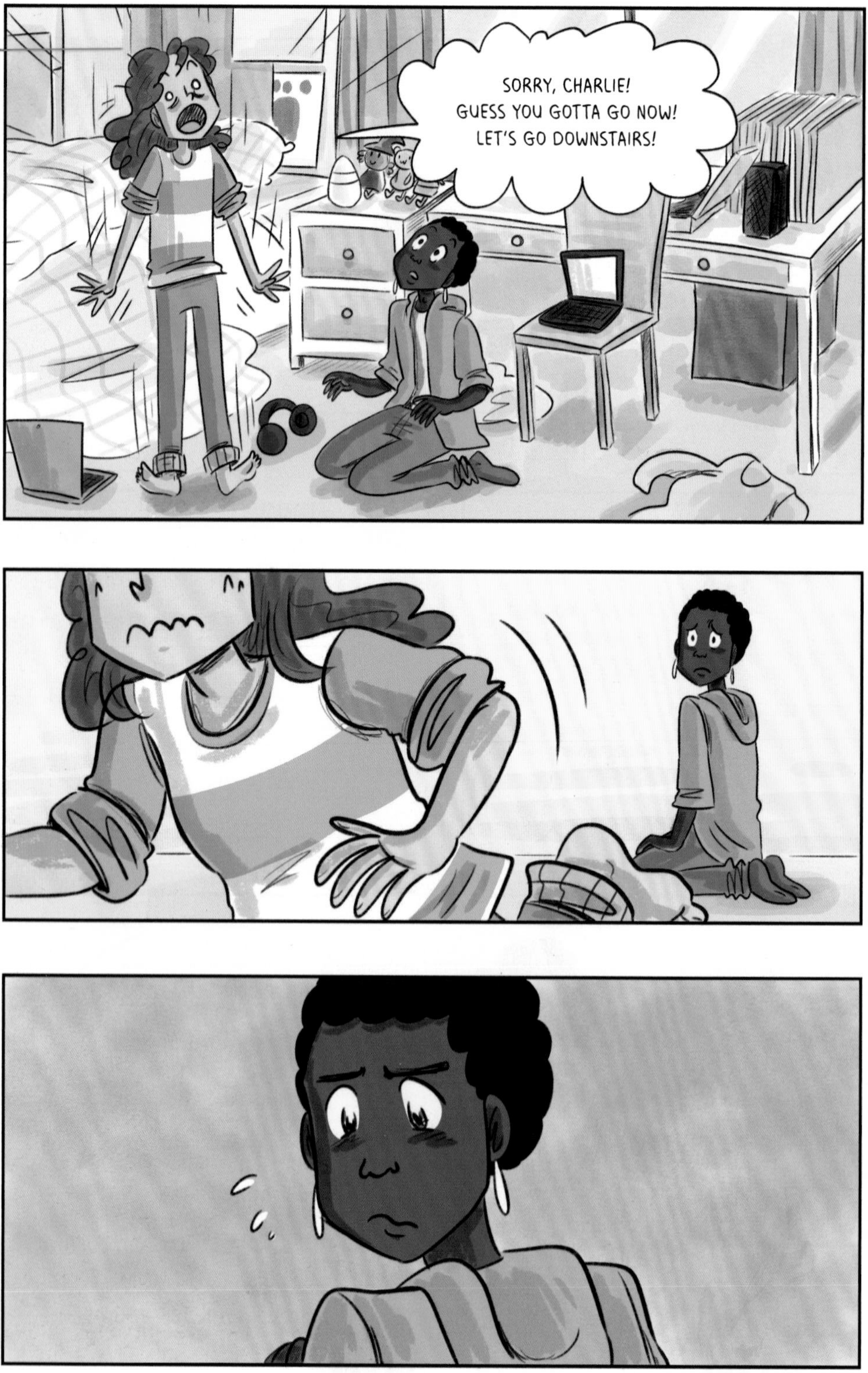
SORRY, CHARLIE!
GUESS YOU GOTTA GO NOW!
LET'S GO DOWNSTAIRS!

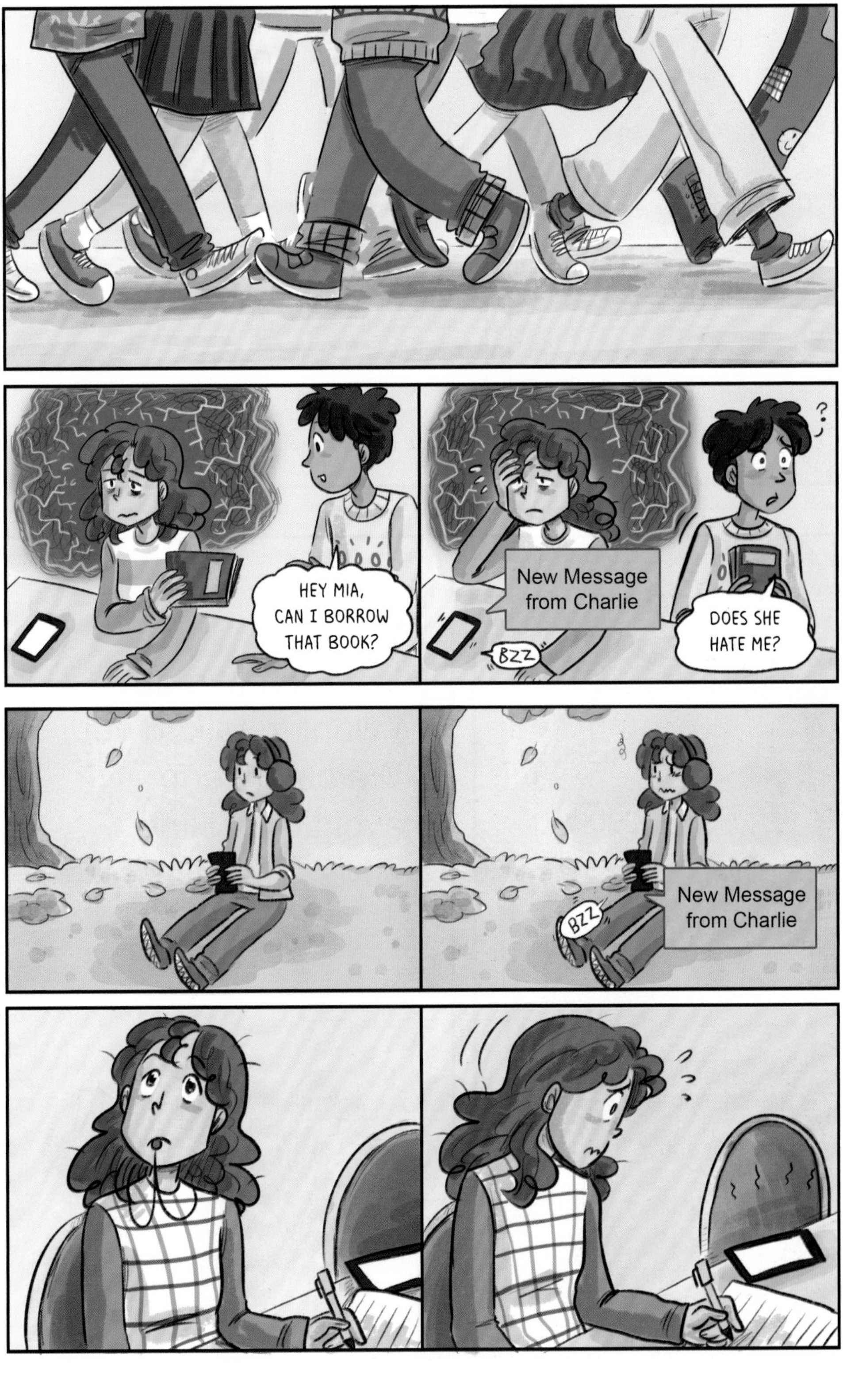
HEY MIA,
CAN I BORROW
THAT BOOK?
New Message
from Charlie
BZZ
DOES SHE
HATE ME?
BZZ
New Message
from Charlie

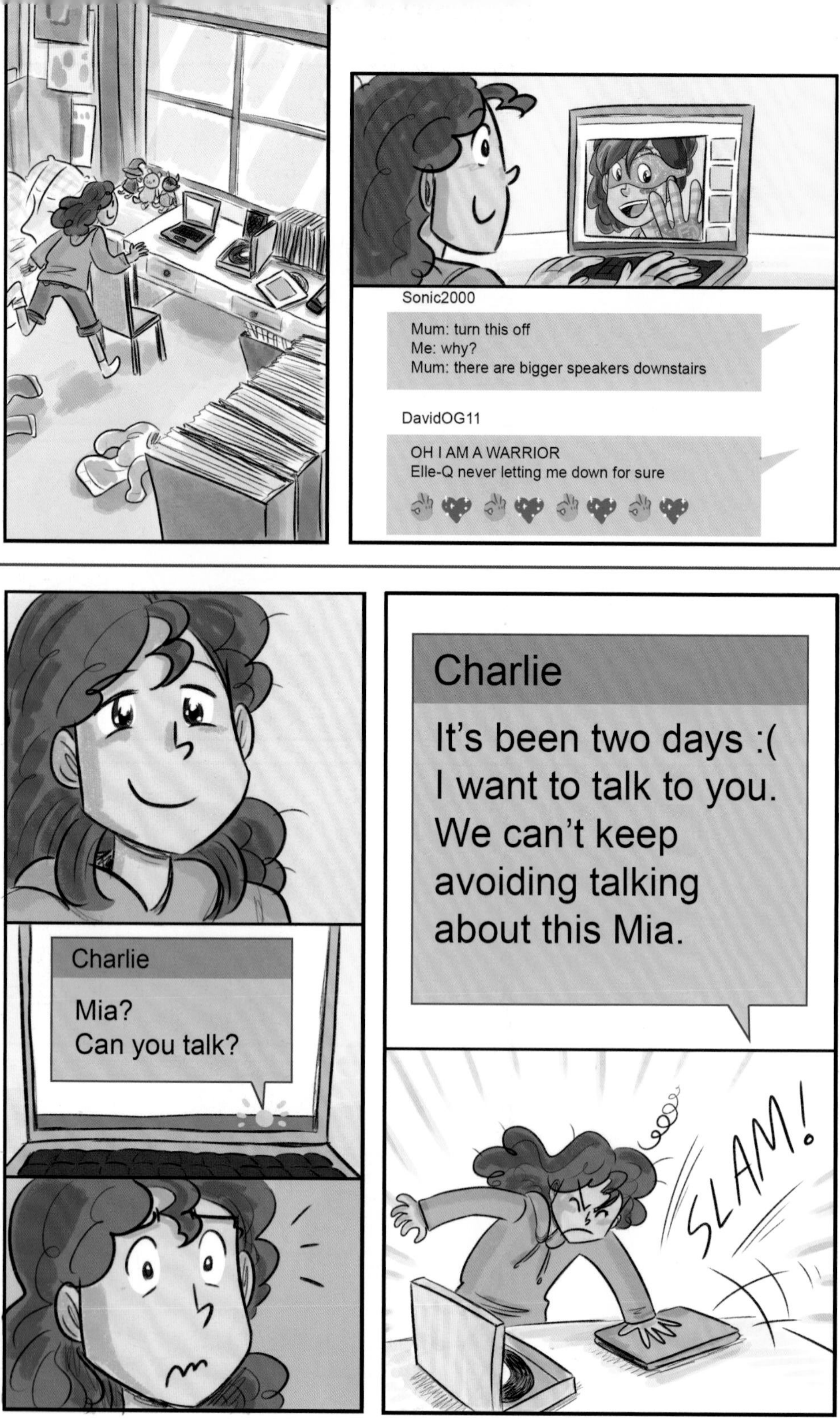
Sonic2000
Mum: turn this off
Me: why?
Mum: there are bigger speakers downstairs
DavidOG11
OH I AM A WARRIOR
Elle-Q never letting me down for sure
Charlie
Mia?
Can you talk?
Charlie
It's been two days :(
I want to talk to you.
We can't keep avoiding talking about this Mia.
SLAM!

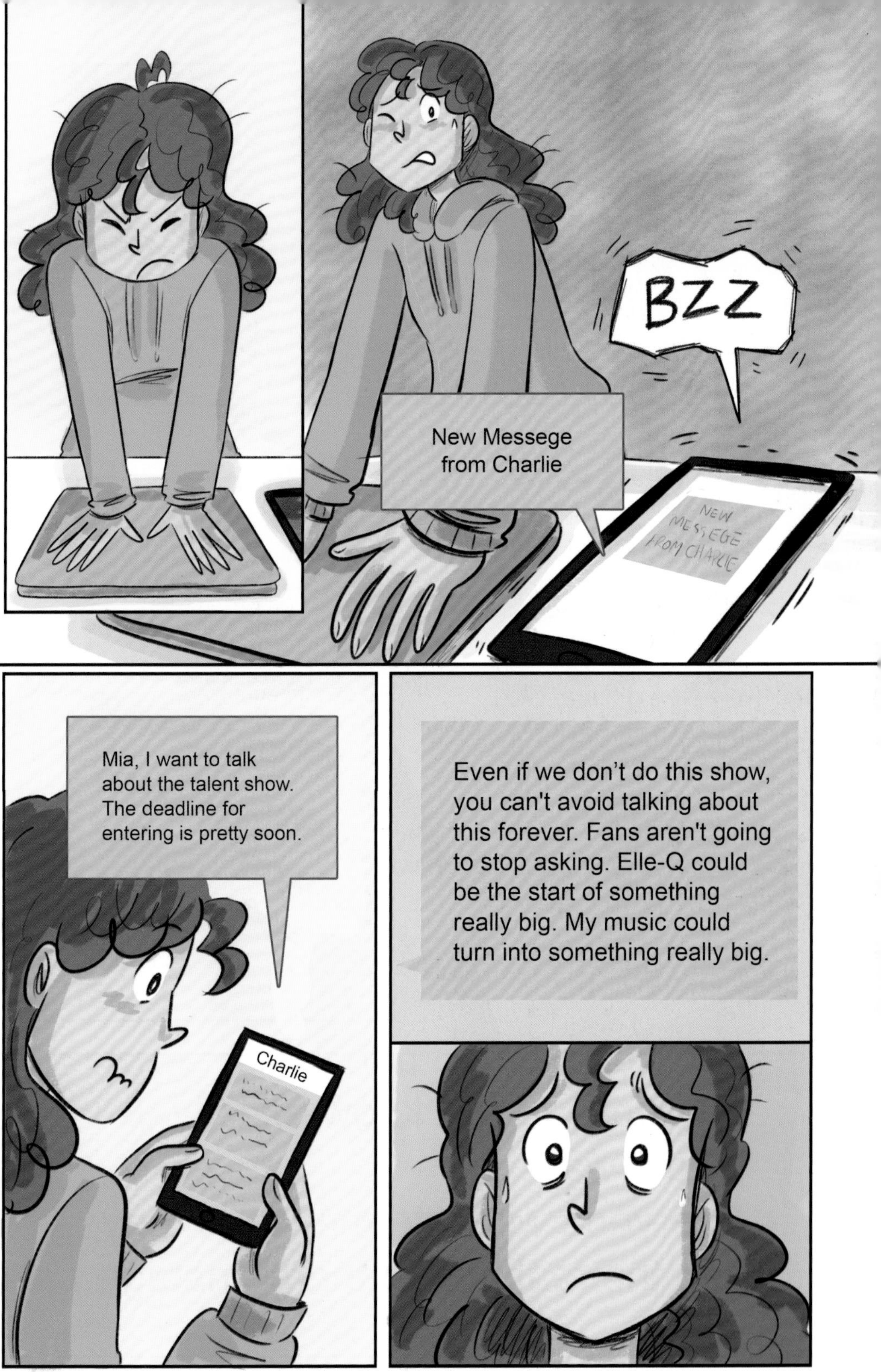
BZZ
New Messege from Charlie
NEW MESSEGE FROM CHARLIE
Mia, I want to talk about the talent show. The deadline for entering is pretty soon.
Charlie
Even if we don't do this show, you can't avoid talking about this forever. Fans aren't going to stop asking. Elle-Q could be the start of something really big. My music could turn into something really big.

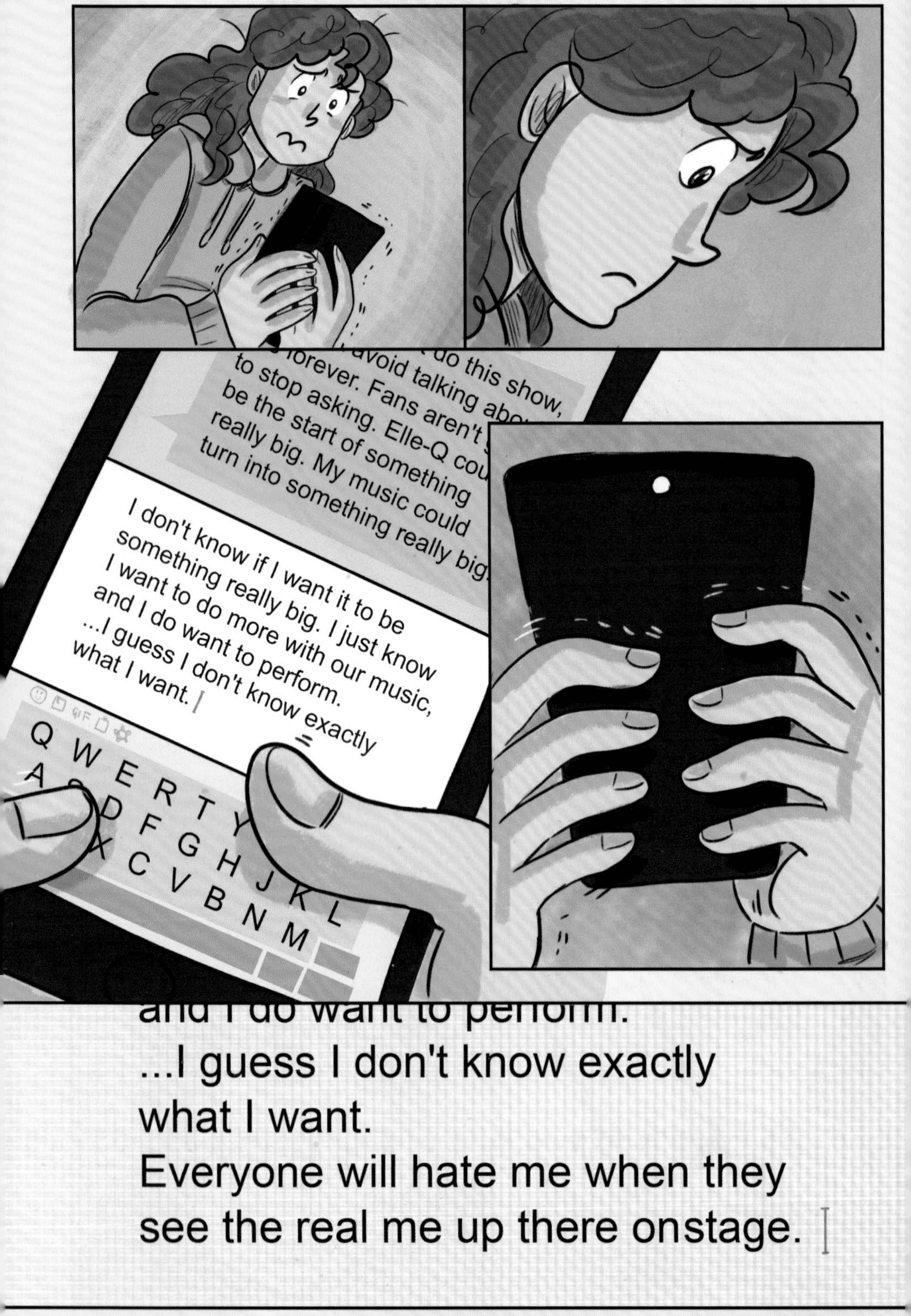
do this show,
avoid talking abo
forever. Fans aren't
to stop asking. Elle-Q cou
be the start of something
really big. My music could
turn into something really big.
I don't know if I want it to be something really big. I just know I want to do more with our music, and I do want to perform. ...I guess I don't know exactly what I want.
QWERTY
ADFGHJKL
XCVBNM
and I do want to perform.
...I guess I don't know exactly what I want.
Everyone will hate me when they see the real me up there onstage.

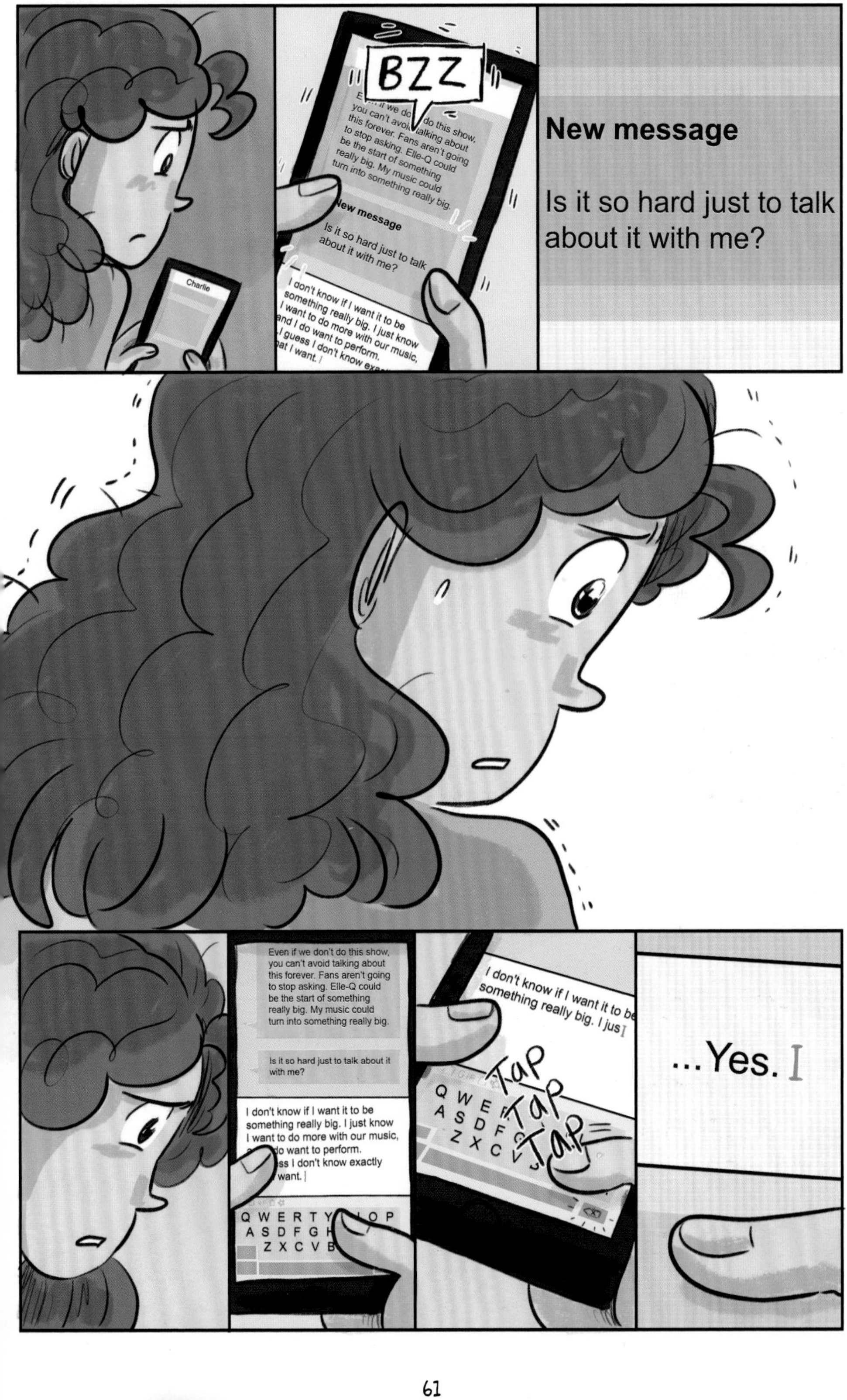
Charlie
BZZ
New message
Is it so hard just to talk about it with me?
New message
Is it so hard just to talk about it with me?
Even if we don't do this show, you can't avoid talking about this forever. Fans aren't going to stop asking. Elle-Q could be the start of something really big. My music could turn into something really big.
Is it so hard just to talk about it with me?
I don't know if I want it to be something really big. I just know I want to do more with our music,
I don't know if I want it to be something really big. I jus
TAP
TAP
TAP
...Yes.

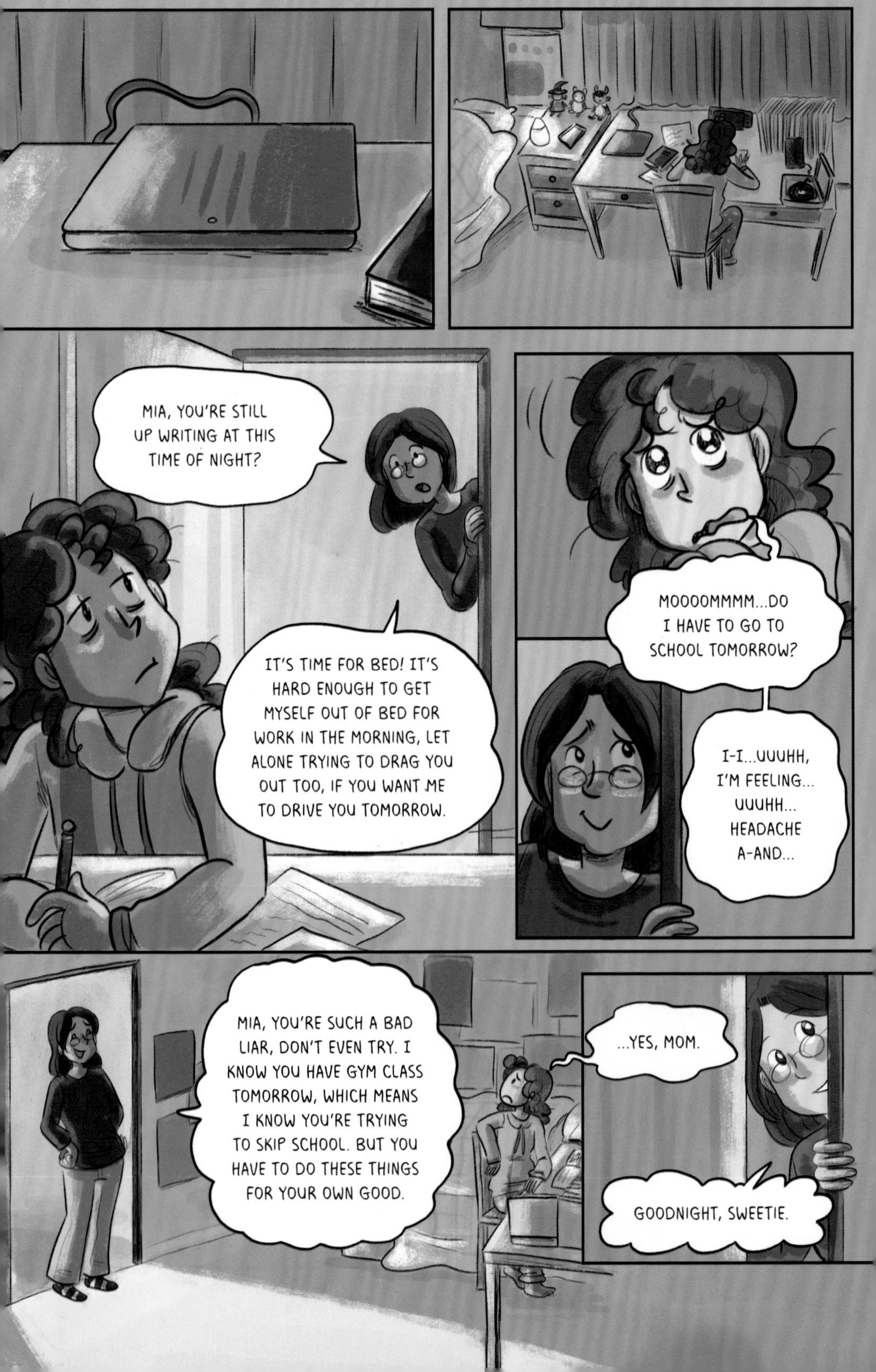
MIA, YOU'RE STILL UP WRITING AT THIS TIME OF NIGHT?
IT'S TIME FOR BED! IT'S HARD ENOUGH TO GET MYSELF OUT OF BED FOR WORK IN THE MORNING, LET ALONE TRYING TO DRAG YOU OUT TOO, IF YOU WANT ME TO DRIVE YOU TOMORROW.
MOOOOMMMM...DO I HAVE TO GO TO SCHOOL TOMORROW?
I-I...UUUHH, I'M FEELING... UUUHH... HEADACHE A-AND...
MIA, YOU'RE SUCH A BAD LIAR, DON'T EVEN TRY. I KNOW YOU HAVE GYM CLASS TOMORROW, WHICH MEANS I KNOW YOU'RE TRYING TO SKIP SCHOOL. BUT YOU HAVE TO DO THESE THINGS FOR YOUR OWN GOOD.
...YES, MOM.
GOODNIGHT, SWEETIE.

CHAPTER FOUR

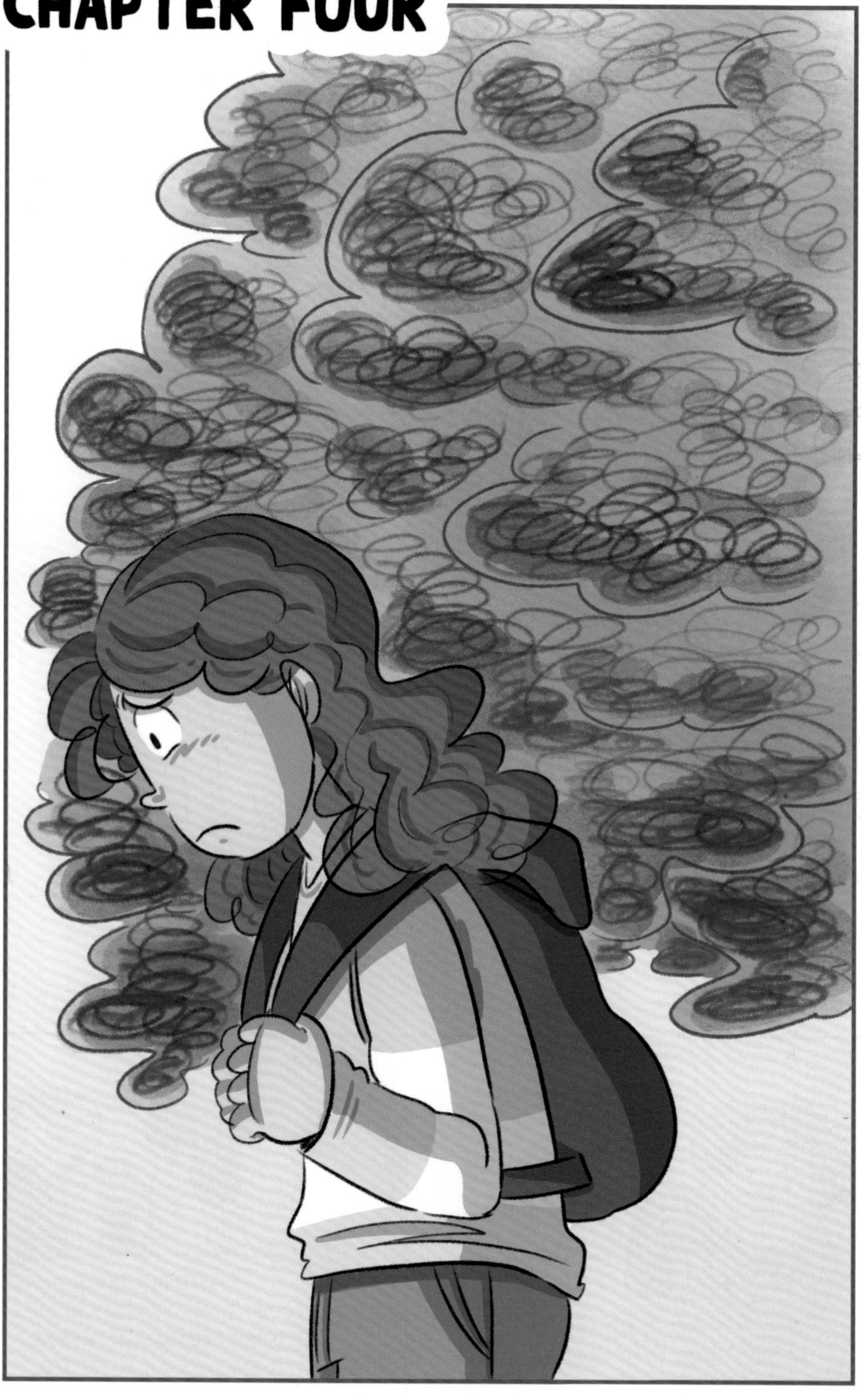

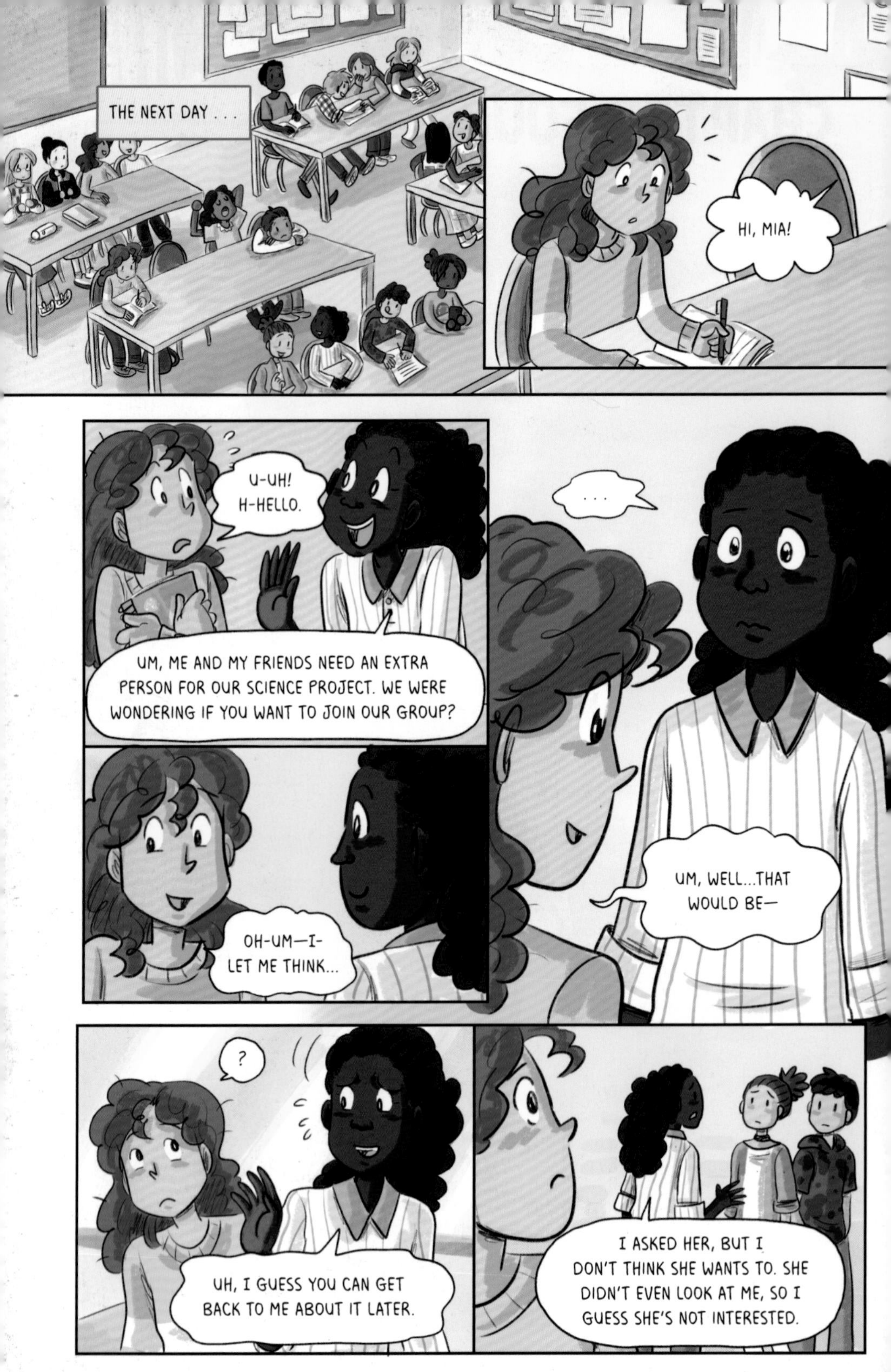
THE NEXT DAY . . .
HI, MIA!
U-UH!
H-HELLO.
UM, ME AND MY FRIENDS NEED AN EXTRA PERSON FOR OUR SCIENCE PROJECT. WE WERE WONDERING IF YOU WANT TO JOIN OUR GROUP?
. . .
OH-UM—I-
LET ME THINK...
UM, WELL...THAT WOULD BE—
?
UH, I GUESS YOU CAN GET BACK TO ME ABOUT IT LATER.
I ASKED HER, BUT I DON'T THINK SHE WANTS TO. SHE DIDN'T EVEN LOOK AT ME, SO I GUESS SHE'S NOT INTERESTED.

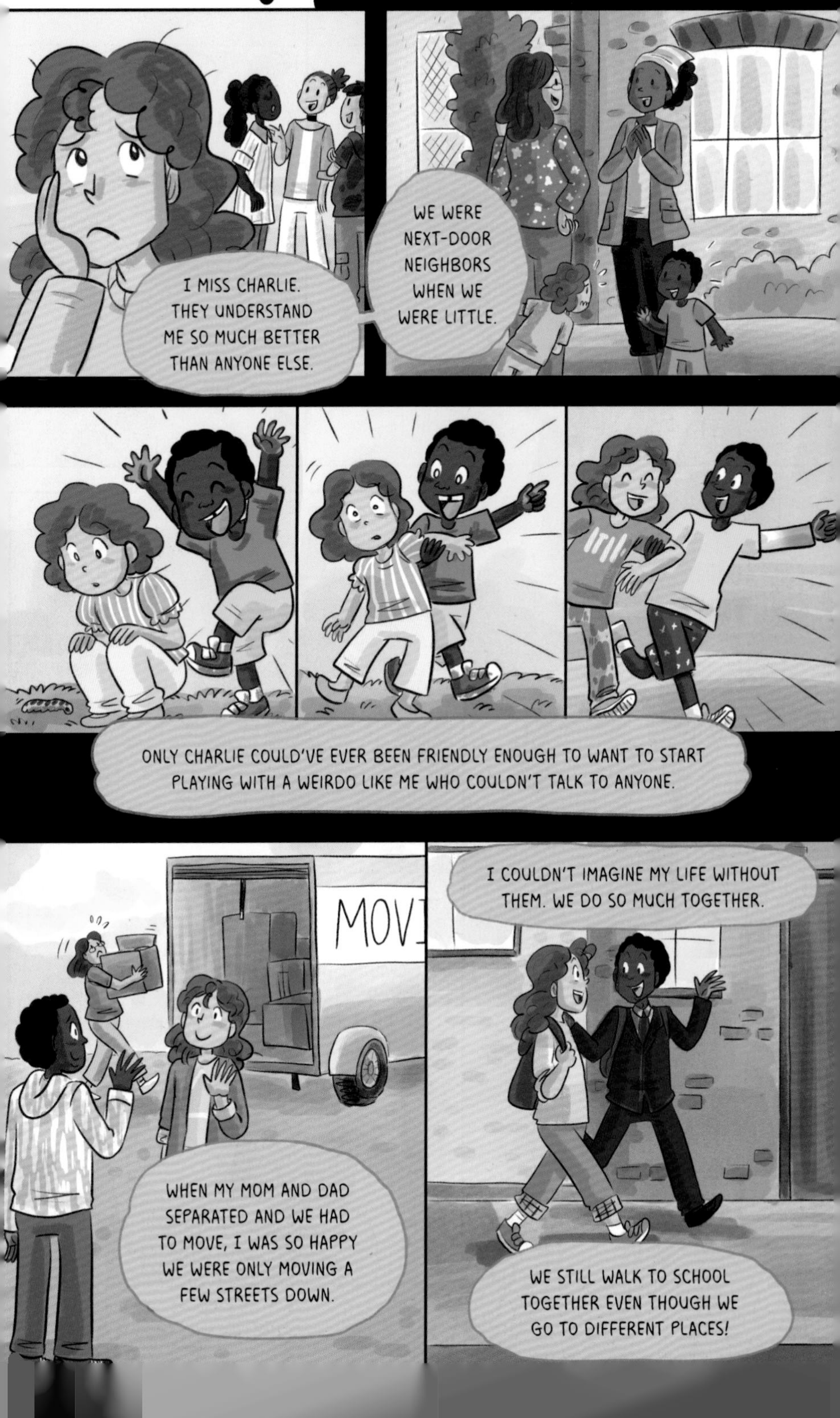
I MISS CHARLIE. THEY UNDERSTAND ME SO MUCH BETTER THAN ANYONE ELSE.
WE WERE NEXT-DOOR NEIGHBORS WHEN WE WERE LITTLE.
ONLY CHARLIE COULD'VE EVER BEEN FRIENDLY ENOUGH TO WANT TO START PLAYING WITH A WEIRDO LIKE ME WHO COULDN'T TALK TO ANYONE.
MOVI
WHEN MY MOM AND DAD SEPARATED AND WE HAD TO MOVE, I WAS SO HAPPY WE WERE ONLY MOVING A FEW STREETS DOWN.
I COULDN'T IMAGINE MY LIFE WITHOUT THEM. WE DO SO MUCH TOGETHER.
WE STILL WALK TO SCHOOL TOGETHER EVEN THOUGH WE GO TO DIFFERENT PLACES!

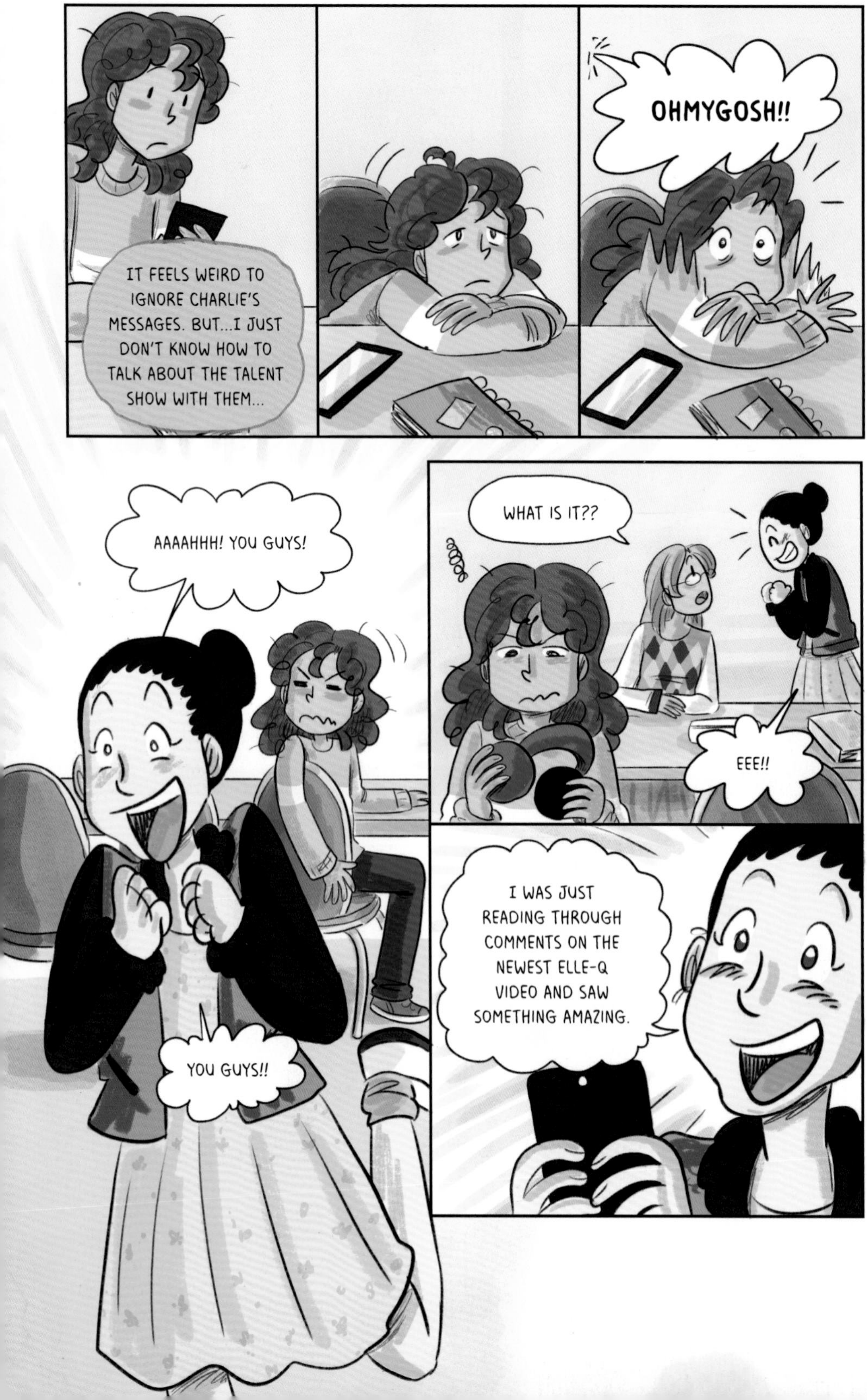
IT FEELS WEIRD TO IGNORE CHARLIE'S MESSAGES. BUT...I JUST DON'T KNOW HOW TO TALK ABOUT THE TALENT SHOW WITH THEM...
OHMYGOSH!!
AAAAHHH! YOU GUYS!
YOU GUYS!!
WHAT IS IT??
EEE!!
I WAS JUST READING THROUGH COMMENTS ON THE NEWEST ELLE-Q VIDEO AND SAW SOMETHING AMAZING.

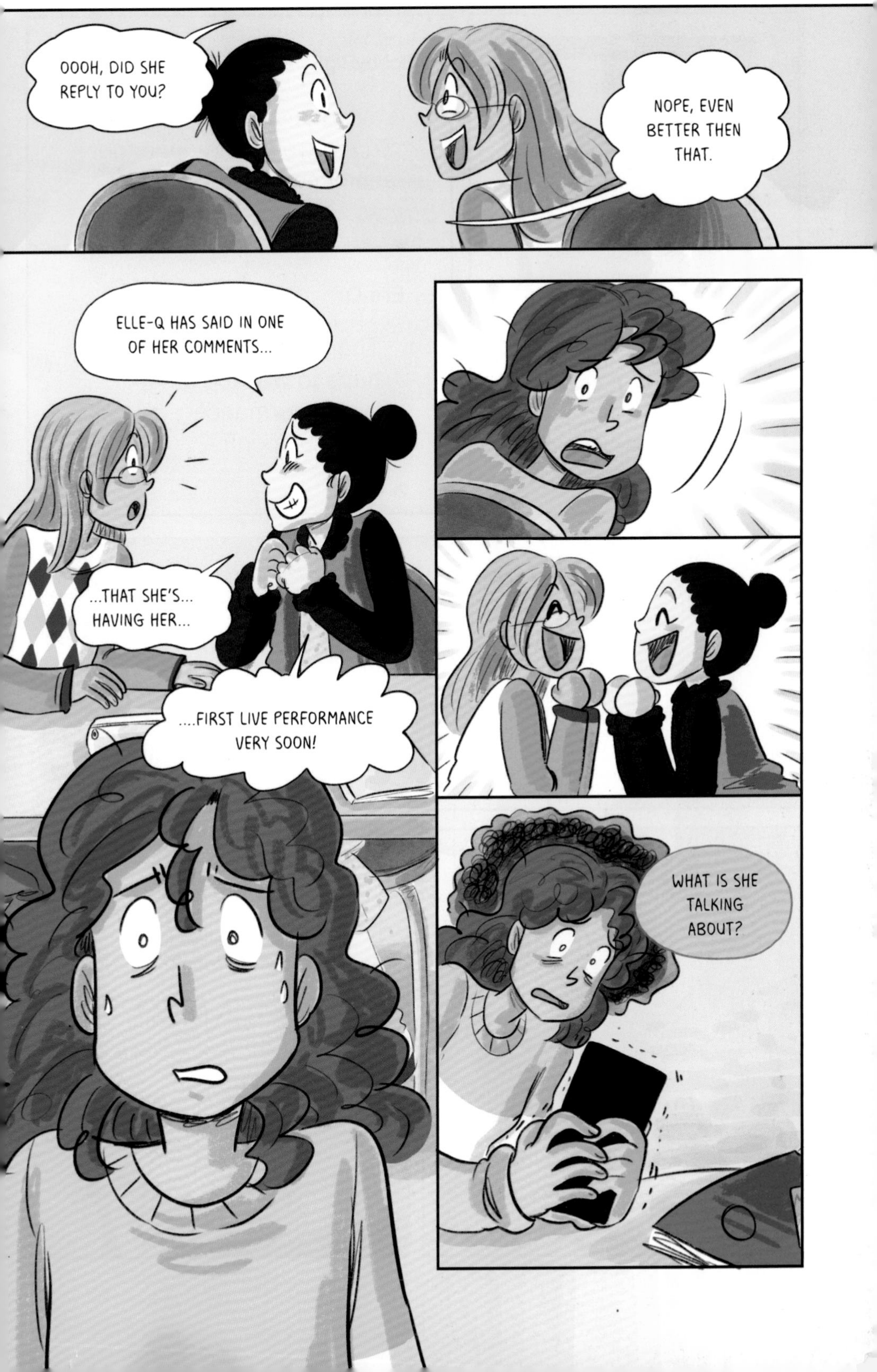
OOOH, DID SHE REPLY TO YOU?
NOPE, EVEN BETTER THEN THAT.
ELLE-Q HAS SAID IN ONE OF HER COMMENTS...
...THAT SHE'S... HAVING HER...
....FIRST LIVE PERFORMANCE VERY SOON!
WHAT IS SHE TALKING ABOUT?

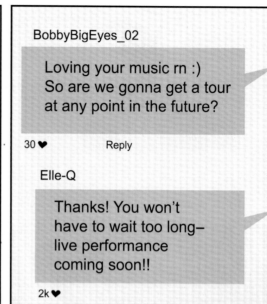

Changes

BobbyBigEyes_02

Loving your music rn :)
So are we gonna get a tour
at any point in the future?

30 ❤   Reply

Elle-Q

Thanks! You won't
have to wait too long–
live performance
coming soon!!

2k ❤

Tap
Tap
Tap

Charlie, why is there a
comment from ME on our
video saying a live show is
coming soon???

Q W E R T Y U
A S D F G H
Z X C V B N M

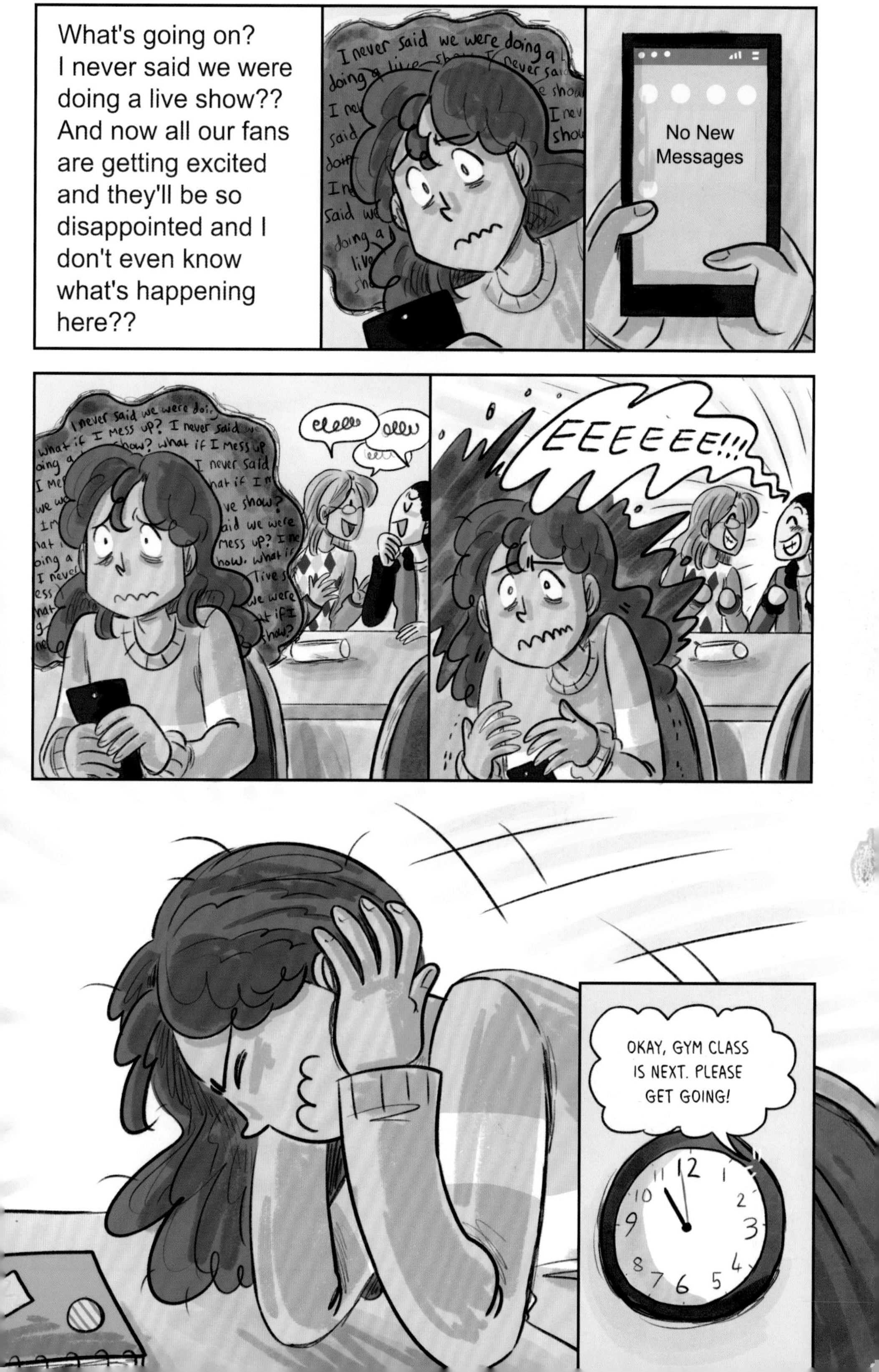
What's going on? I never said we were doing a live show?? And now all our fans are getting excited and they'll be so disappointed and I don't even know what's happening here??
No New Messages
EEEEEE!!!
OKAY, GYM CLASS IS NEXT. PLEASE GET GOING!

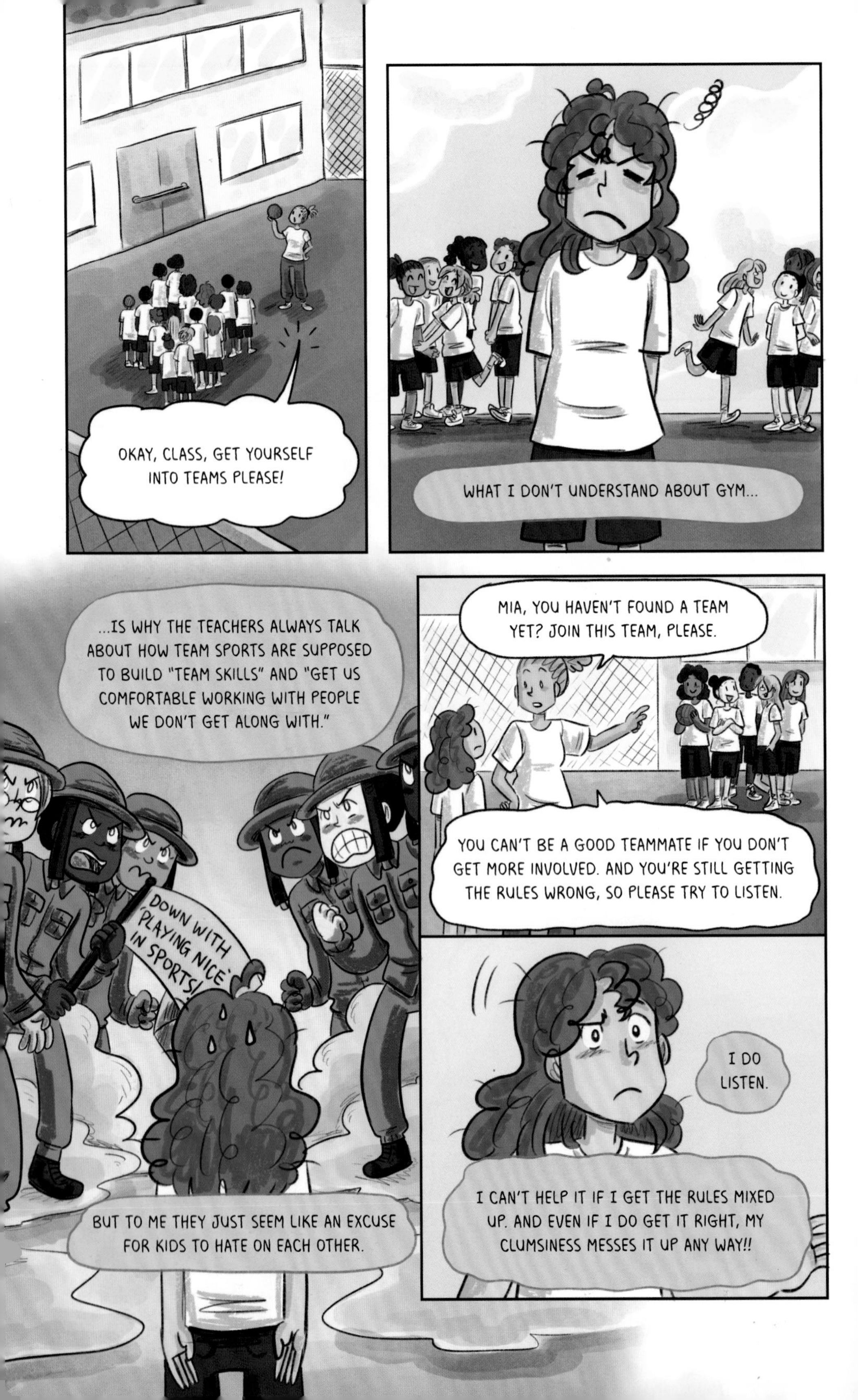
OKAY, CLASS, GET YOURSELF INTO TEAMS PLEASE!
WHAT I DON'T UNDERSTAND ABOUT GYM...
...IS WHY THE TEACHERS ALWAYS TALK ABOUT HOW TEAM SPORTS ARE SUPPOSED TO BUILD "TEAM SKILLS" AND "GET US COMFORTABLE WORKING WITH PEOPLE WE DON'T GET ALONG WITH."
DOWN WITH 'PLAYING NICE' IN SPORTS!
BUT TO ME THEY JUST SEEM LIKE AN EXCUSE FOR KIDS TO HATE ON EACH OTHER.
MIA, YOU HAVEN'T FOUND A TEAM YET? JOIN THIS TEAM, PLEASE.
YOU CAN'T BE A GOOD TEAMMATE IF YOU DON'T GET MORE INVOLVED. AND YOU'RE STILL GETTING THE RULES WRONG, SO PLEASE TRY TO LISTEN.
I DO LISTEN.
I CAN'T HELP IT IF I GET THE RULES MIXED UP. AND EVEN IF I DO GET IT RIGHT, MY CLUMSINESS MESSES IT UP ANY WAY!!

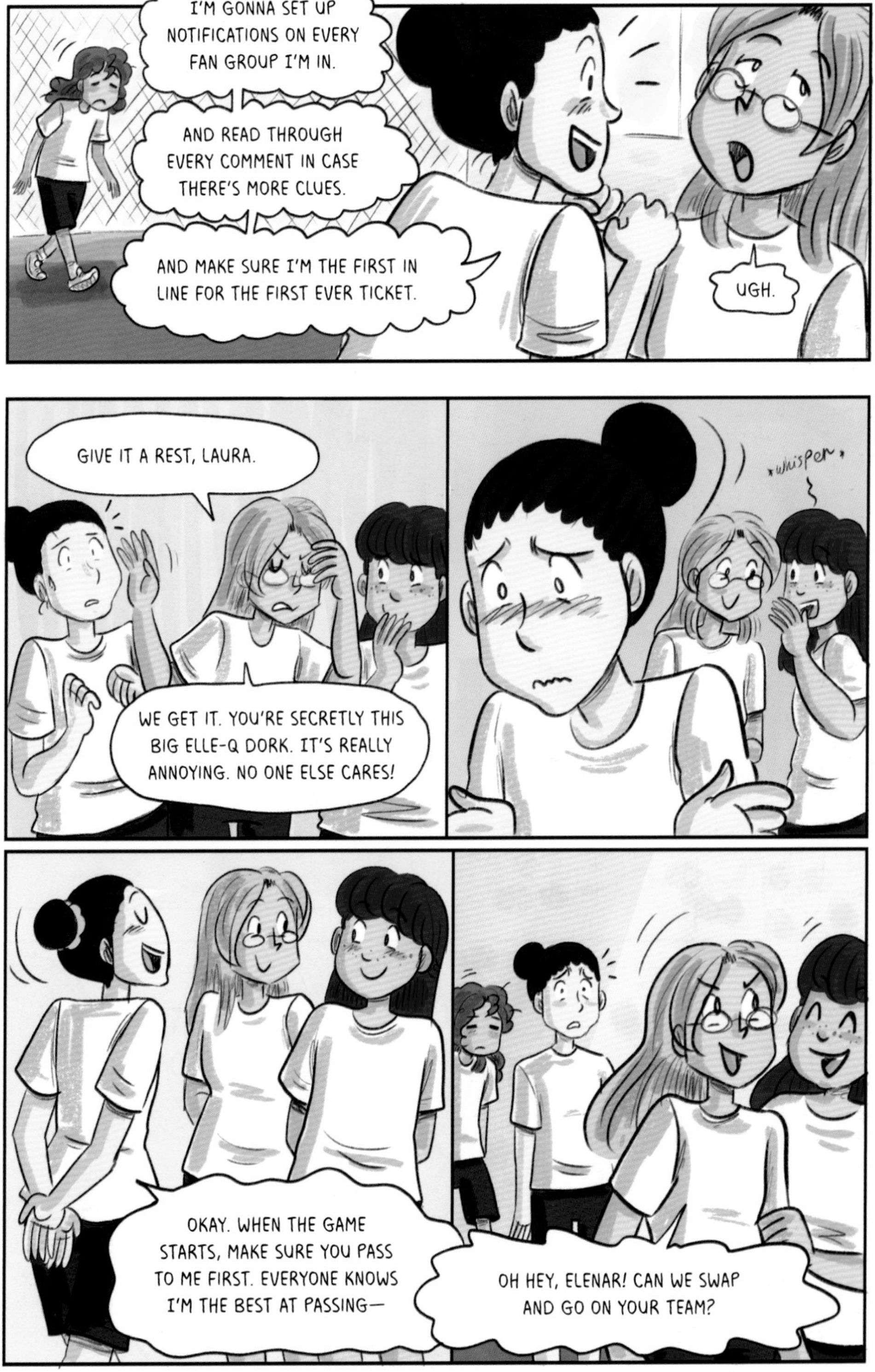
I'M GONNA SET UP NOTIFICATIONS ON EVERY FAN GROUP I'M IN.
AND READ THROUGH EVERY COMMENT IN CASE THERE'S MORE CLUES.
AND MAKE SURE I'M THE FIRST IN LINE FOR THE FIRST EVER TICKET.
UGH.
GIVE IT A REST, LAURA.
WE GET IT. YOU'RE SECRETLY THIS BIG ELLE-Q DORK. IT'S REALLY ANNOYING. NO ONE ELSE CARES!
whisper
OKAY. WHEN THE GAME STARTS, MAKE SURE YOU PASS TO ME FIRST. EVERYONE KNOWS I'M THE BEST AT PASSING—
OH HEY, ELENAR! CAN WE SWAP AND GO ON YOUR TEAM?

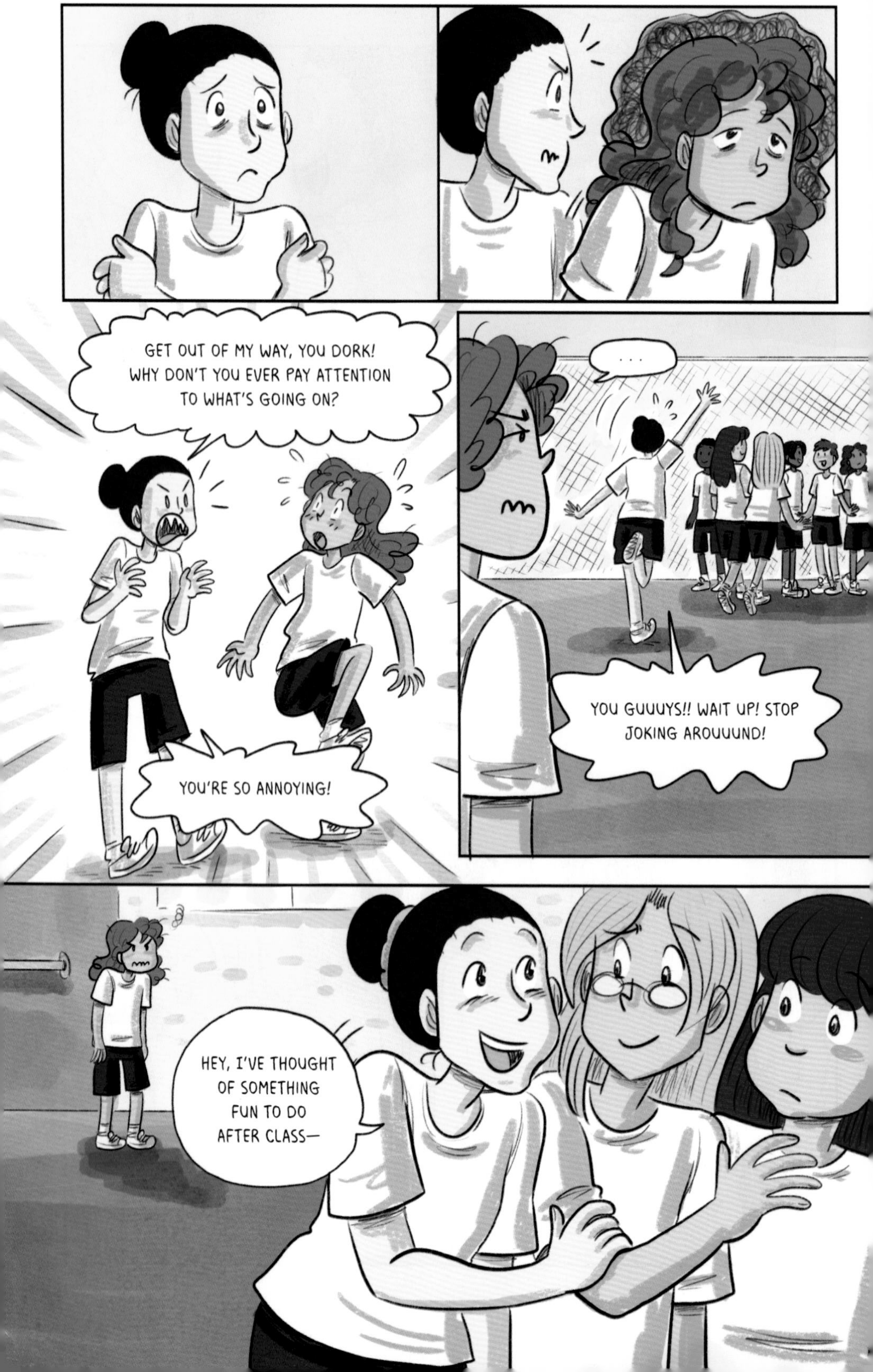
GET OUT OF MY WAY, YOU DORK! WHY DON'T YOU EVER PAY ATTENTION TO WHAT'S GOING ON?
YOU'RE SO ANNOYING!
. . .
YOU GUUUYS!! WAIT UP! STOP JOKING AROUUUND!
HEY, I'VE THOUGHT OF SOMETHING FUN TO DO AFTER CLASS—

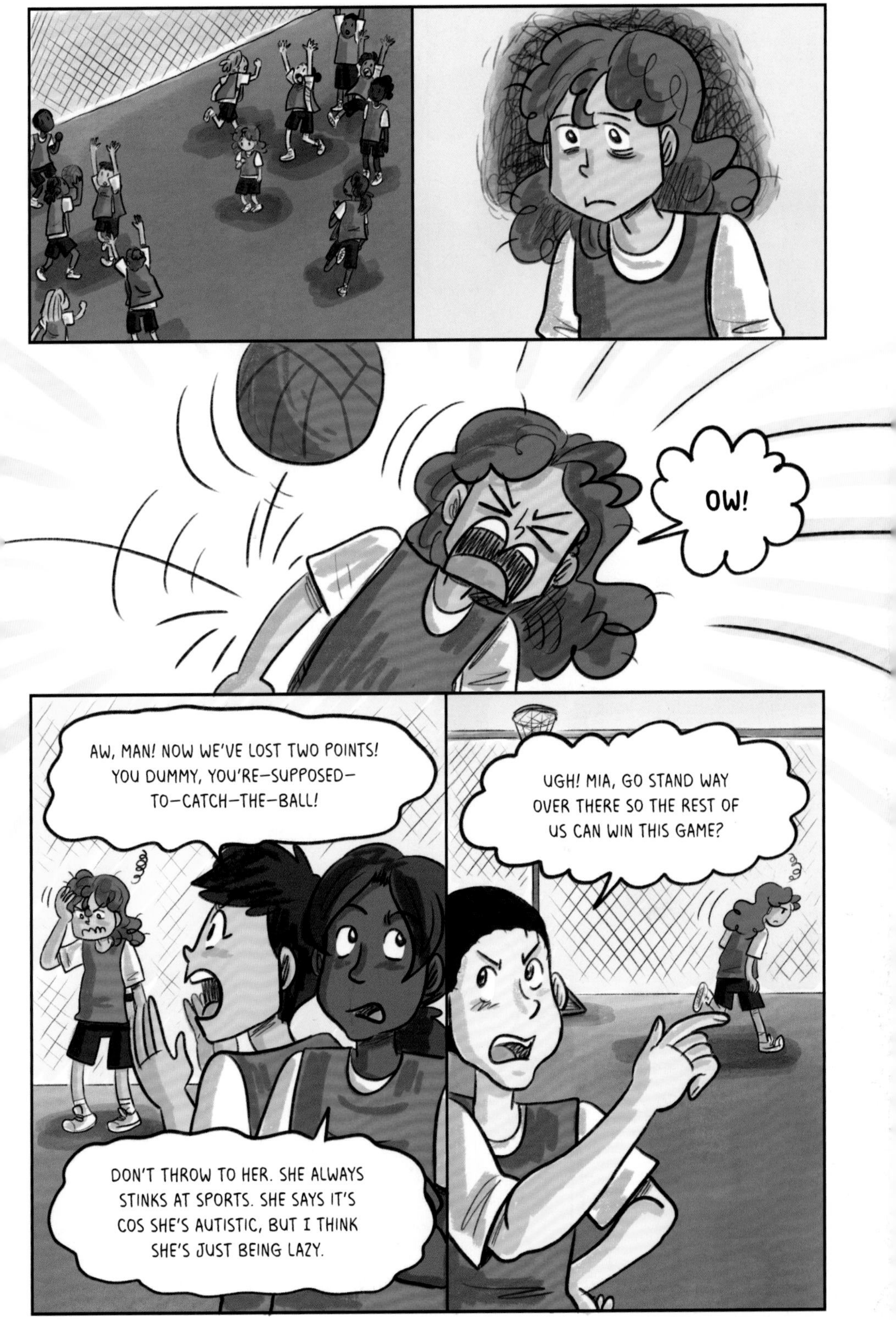
OW!
AW, MAN! NOW WE'VE LOST TWO POINTS! YOU DUMMY, YOU'RE—SUPPOSED—TO—CATCH—THE—BALL!
DON'T THROW TO HER. SHE ALWAYS STINKS AT SPORTS. SHE SAYS IT'S COS SHE'S AUTISTIC, BUT I THINK SHE'S JUST BEING LAZY.
UGH! MIA, GO STAND WAY OVER THERE SO THE REST OF US CAN WIN THIS GAME?

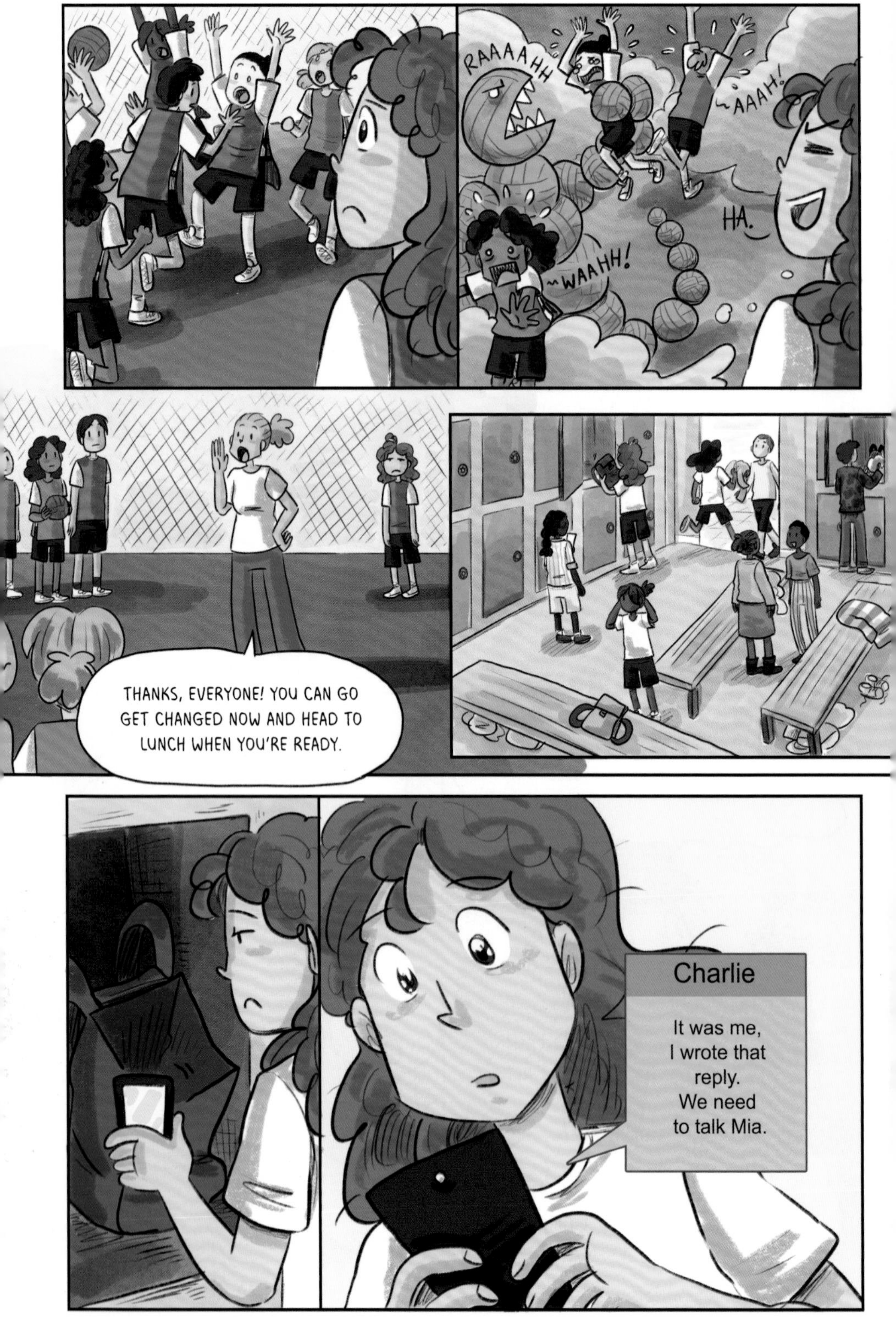
RAAAAAHH
~AAAH!
HA.
~WAAHH!
THANKS, EVERYONE! YOU CAN GO GET CHANGED NOW AND HEAD TO LUNCH WHEN YOU'RE READY.
Charlie
It was me, I wrote that reply. We need to talk Mia.

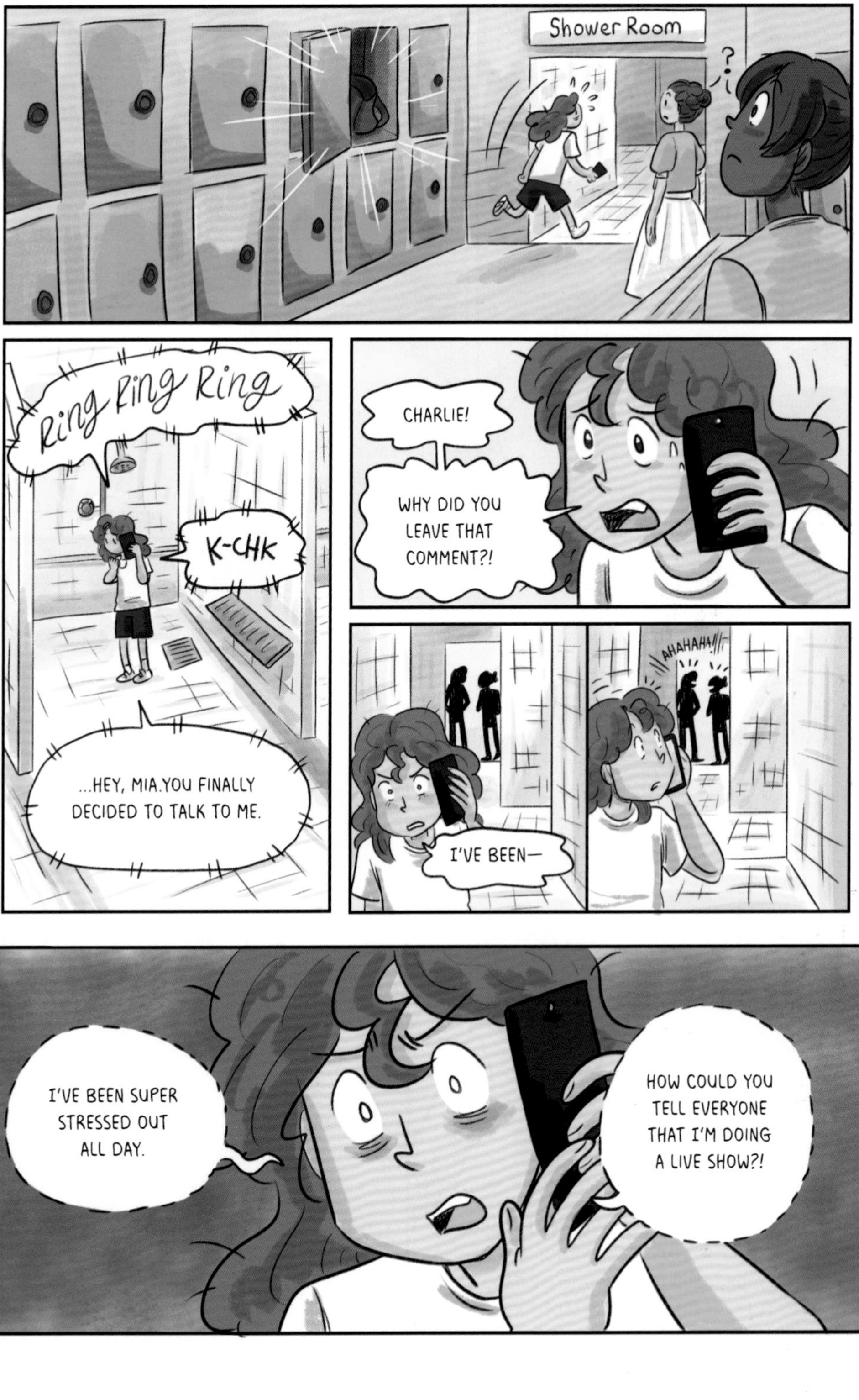
Shower Room
?
Ring Ring Ring
K-CHK
...HEY, MIA.YOU FINALLY DECIDED TO TALK TO ME.
CHARLIE!
WHY DID YOU LEAVE THAT COMMENT?!
I'VE BEEN—
AHAHAHA!!
I'VE BEEN SUPER STRESSED OUT ALL DAY.
HOW COULD YOU TELL EVERYONE THAT I'M DOING A LIVE SHOW?!

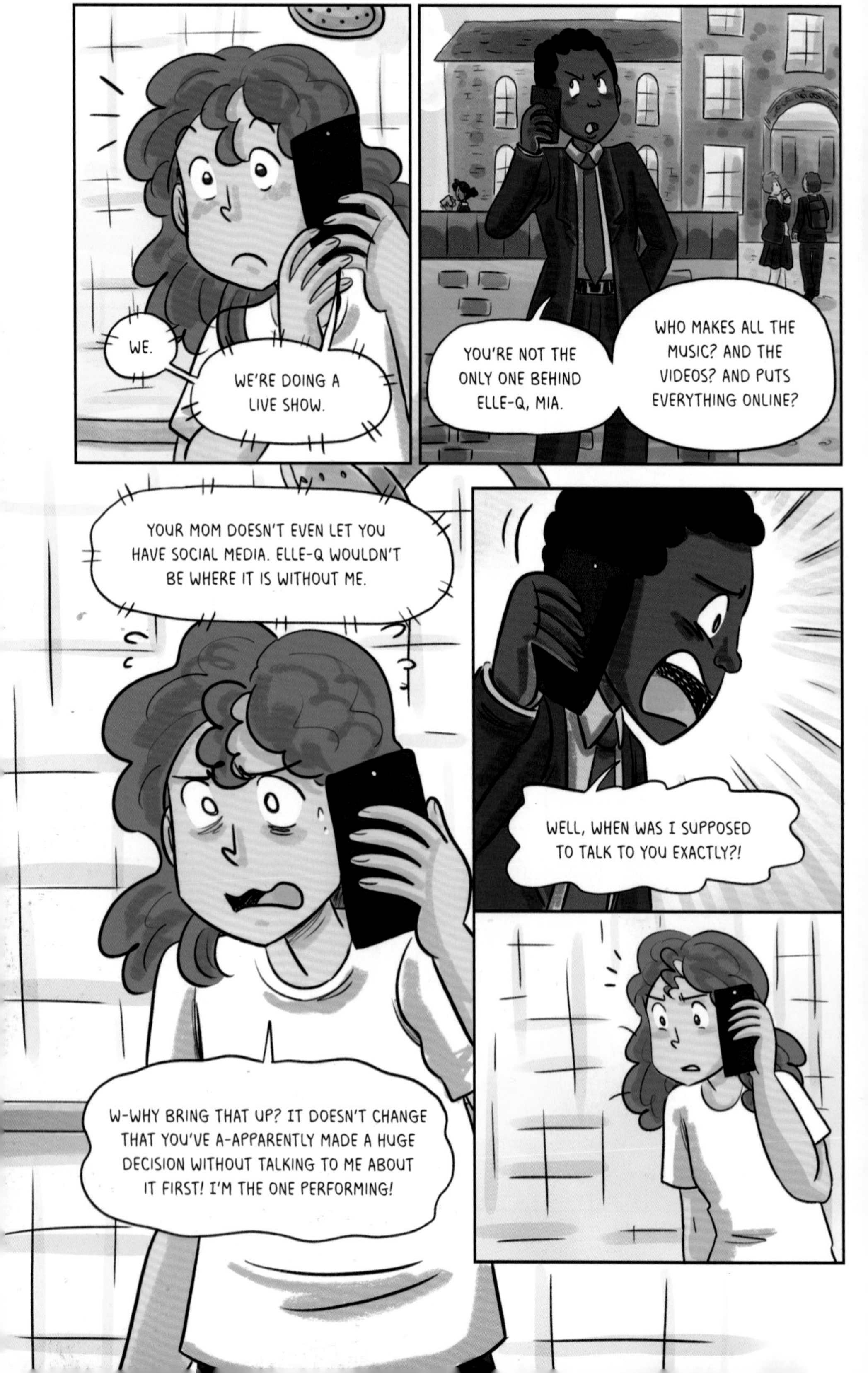
WE.
WE'RE DOING A LIVE SHOW.
YOU'RE NOT THE ONLY ONE BEHIND ELLE-Q, MIA.
WHO MAKES ALL THE MUSIC? AND THE VIDEOS? AND PUTS EVERYTHING ONLINE?
YOUR MOM DOESN'T EVEN LET YOU HAVE SOCIAL MEDIA. ELLE-Q WOULDN'T BE WHERE IT IS WITHOUT ME.
W-WHY BRING THAT UP? IT DOESN'T CHANGE THAT YOU'VE A-APPARENTLY MADE A HUGE DECISION WITHOUT TALKING TO ME ABOUT IT FIRST! I'M THE ONE PERFORMING!
WELL, WHEN WAS I SUPPOSED TO TALK TO YOU EXACTLY?!

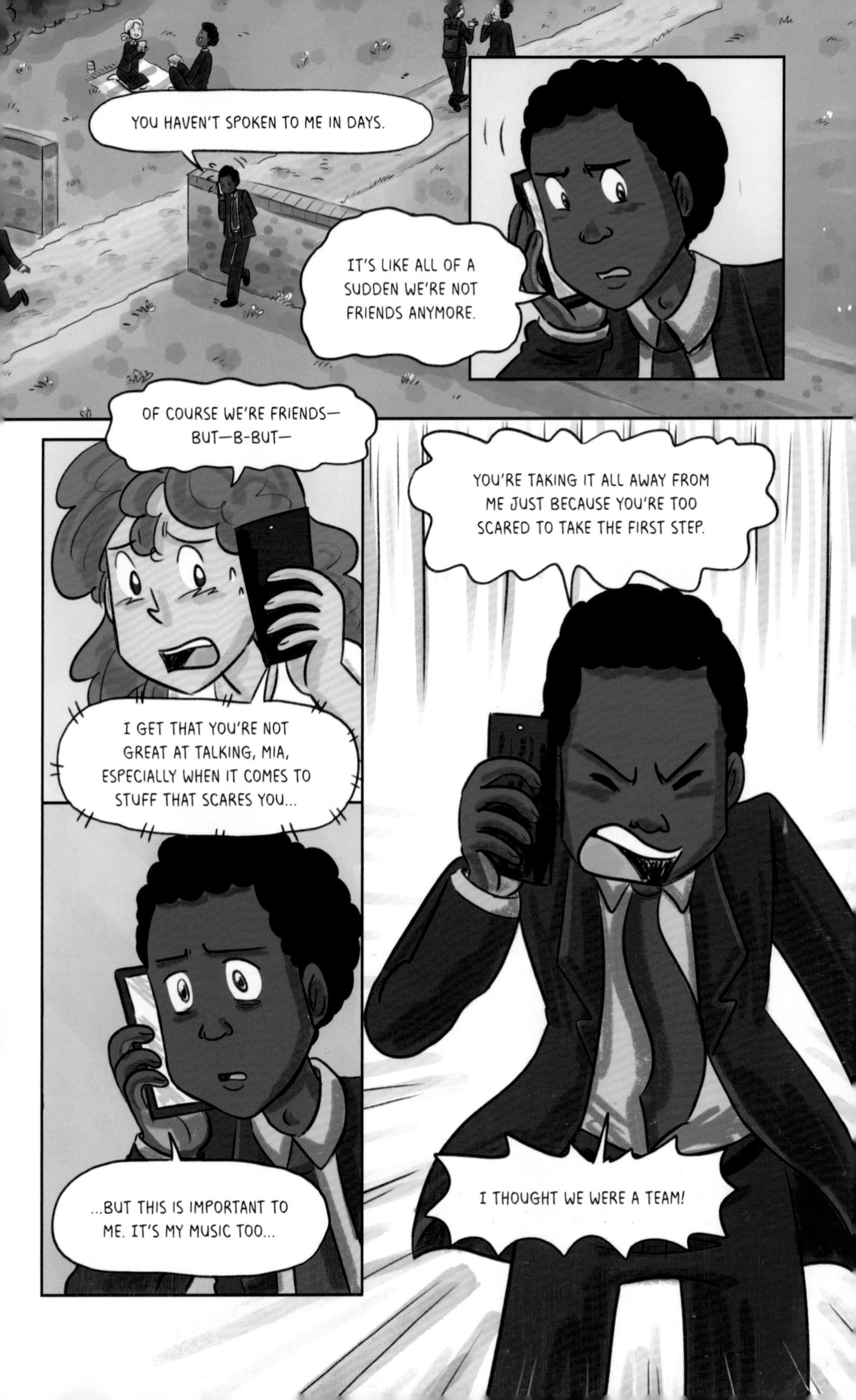
YOU HAVEN'T SPOKEN TO ME IN DAYS.
IT'S LIKE ALL OF A SUDDEN WE'RE NOT FRIENDS ANYMORE.
OF COURSE WE'RE FRIENDS—BUT—B-BUT—
YOU'RE TAKING IT ALL AWAY FROM ME JUST BECAUSE YOU'RE TOO SCARED TO TAKE THE FIRST STEP.
I GET THAT YOU'RE NOT GREAT AT TALKING, MIA, ESPECIALLY WHEN IT COMES TO STUFF THAT SCARES YOU...
...BUT THIS IS IMPORTANT TO ME. IT'S MY MUSIC TOO...
I THOUGHT WE WERE A TEAM!

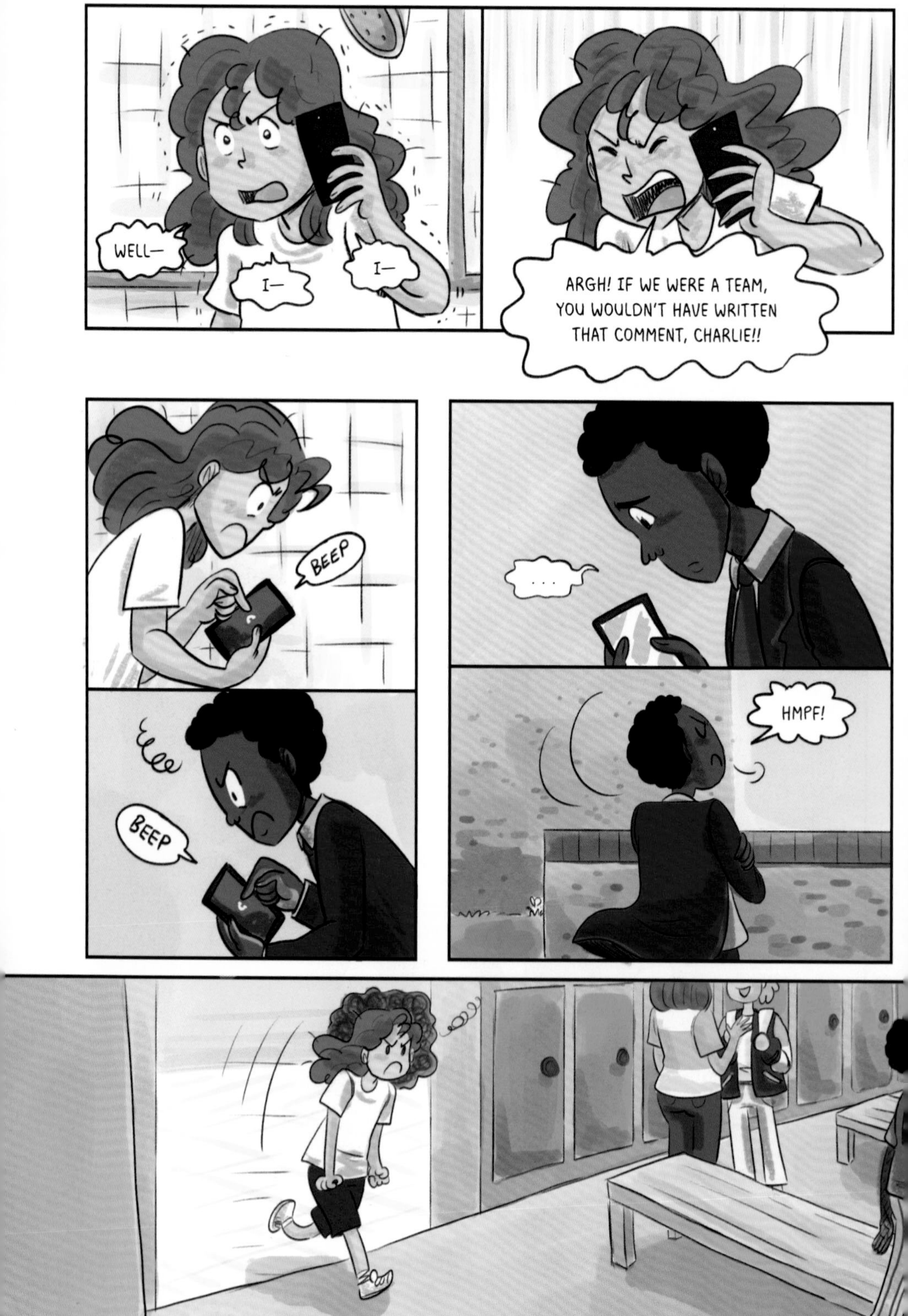
WELL—
I—
I—
ARGH! IF WE WERE A TEAM, YOU WOULDN'T HAVE WRITTEN THAT COMMENT, CHARLIE!!
BEEP
. . .
BEEP
HMPF!

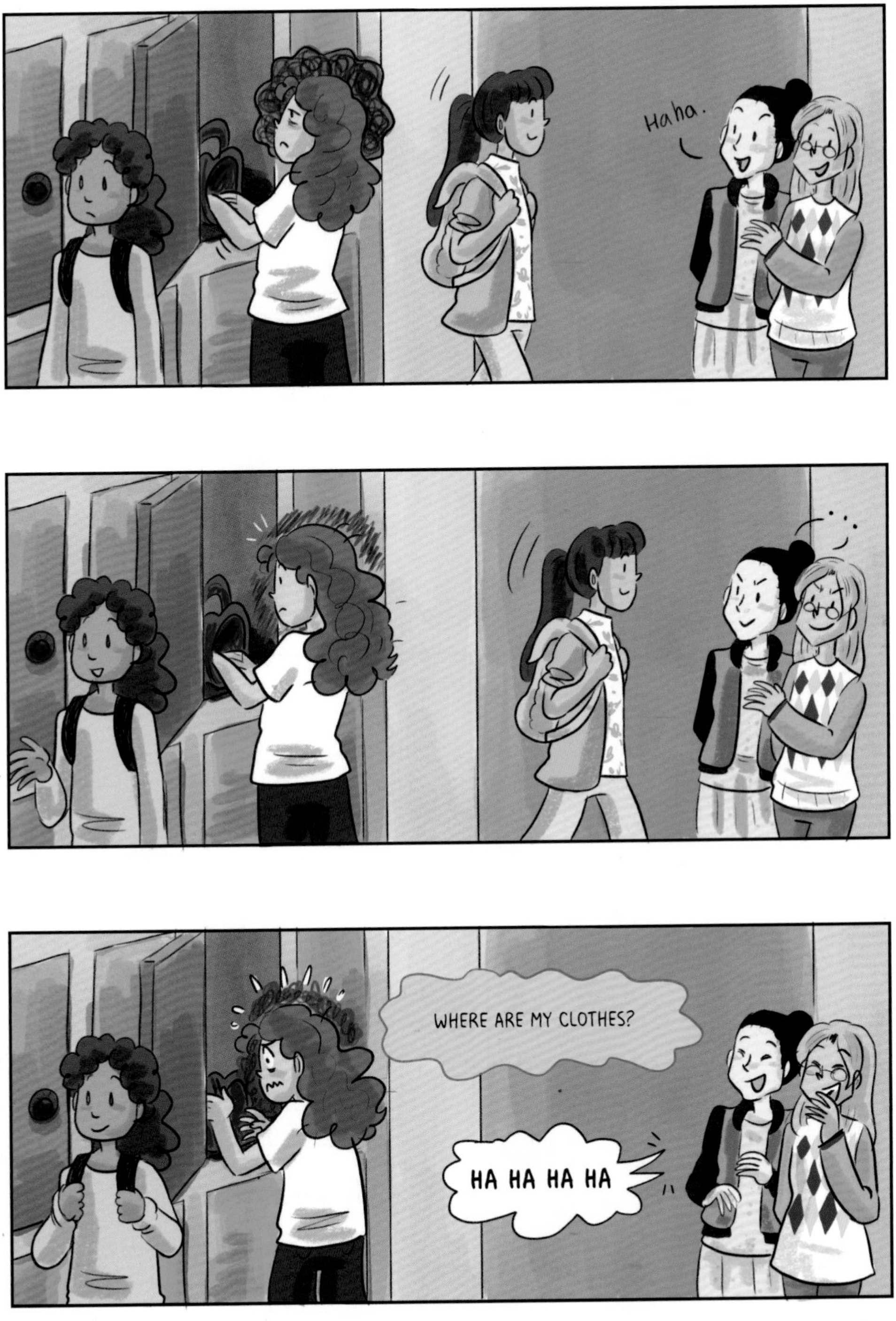
Haha.
WHERE ARE MY CLOTHES?
HA HA HA HA

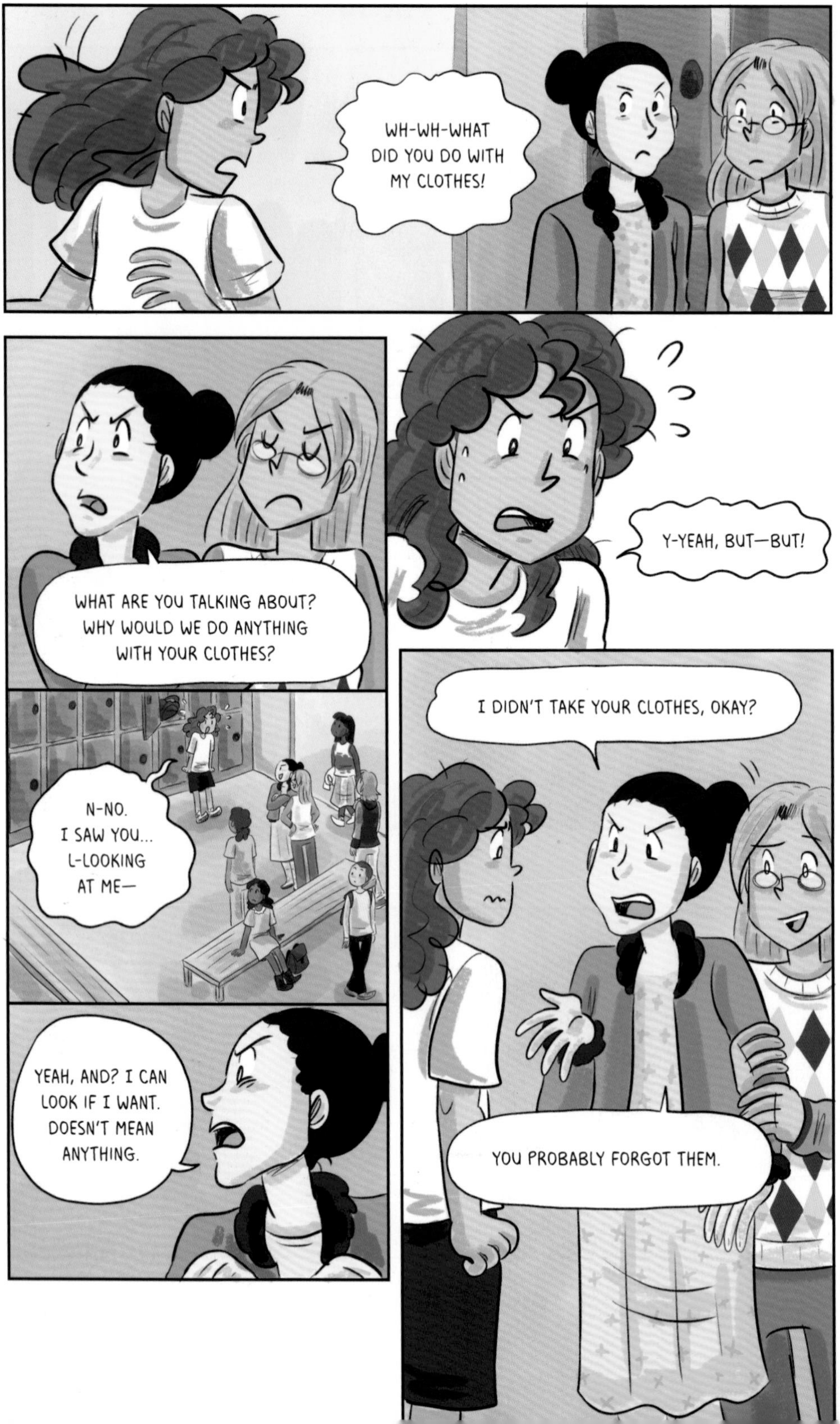
WH-WH-WHAT DID YOU DO WITH MY CLOTHES!
WHAT ARE YOU TALKING ABOUT? WHY WOULD WE DO ANYTHING WITH YOUR CLOTHES?
Y-YEAH, BUT—BUT!
N-NO. I SAW YOU... L-LOOKING AT ME—
YEAH, AND? I CAN LOOK IF I WANT. DOESN'T MEAN ANYTHING.
I DIDN'T TAKE YOUR CLOTHES, OKAY?
YOU PROBABLY FORGOT THEM.

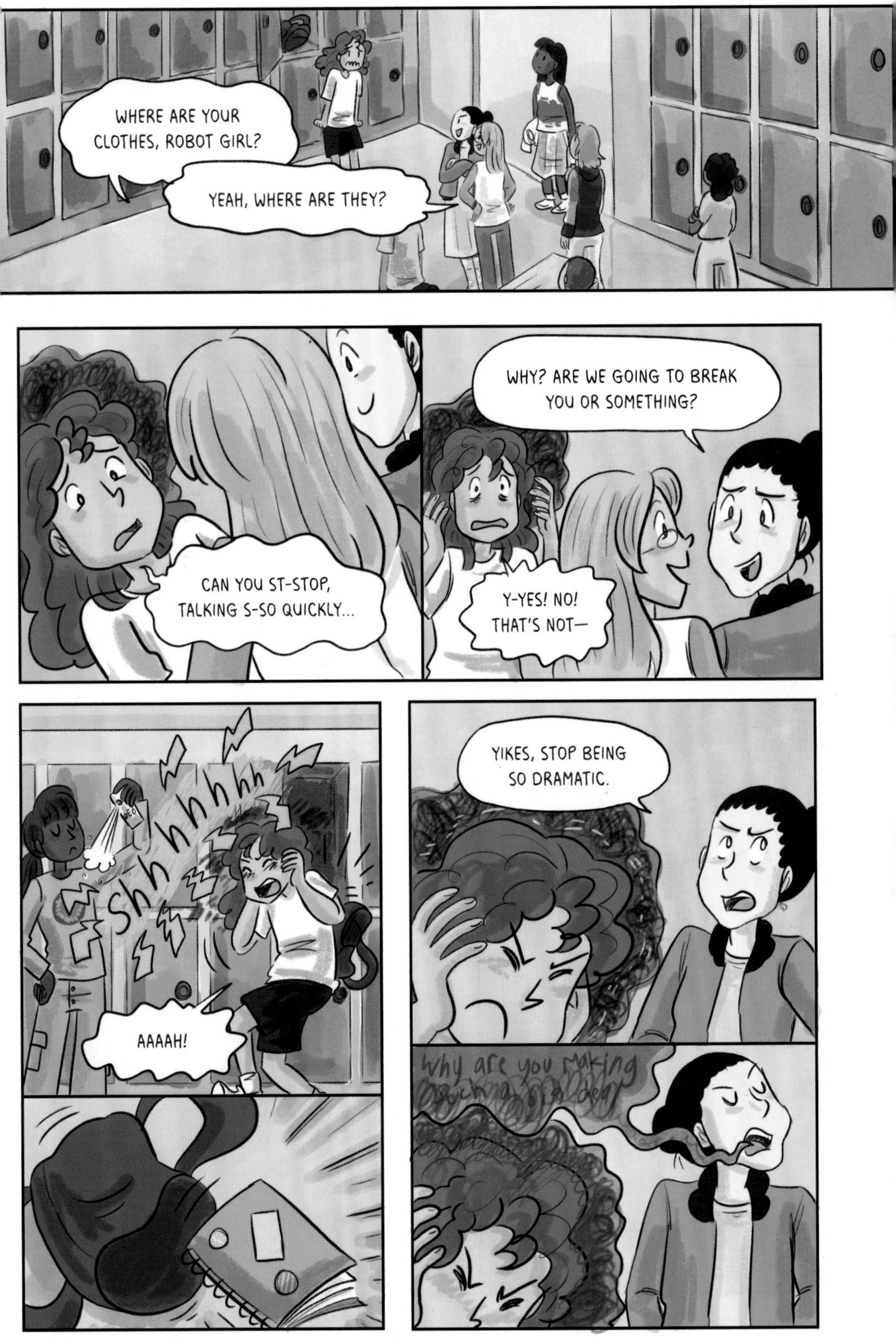
WHERE ARE YOUR CLOTHES, ROBOT GIRL?
YEAH, WHERE ARE THEY?
CAN YOU ST-STOP, TALKING S-SO QUICKLY...
WHY? ARE WE GOING TO BREAK YOU OR SOMETHING?
Y-YES! NO! THAT'S NOT—
DEO
Shhhhhhhhh
AAAAH!
YIKES, STOP BEING SO DRAMATIC.
why are you making

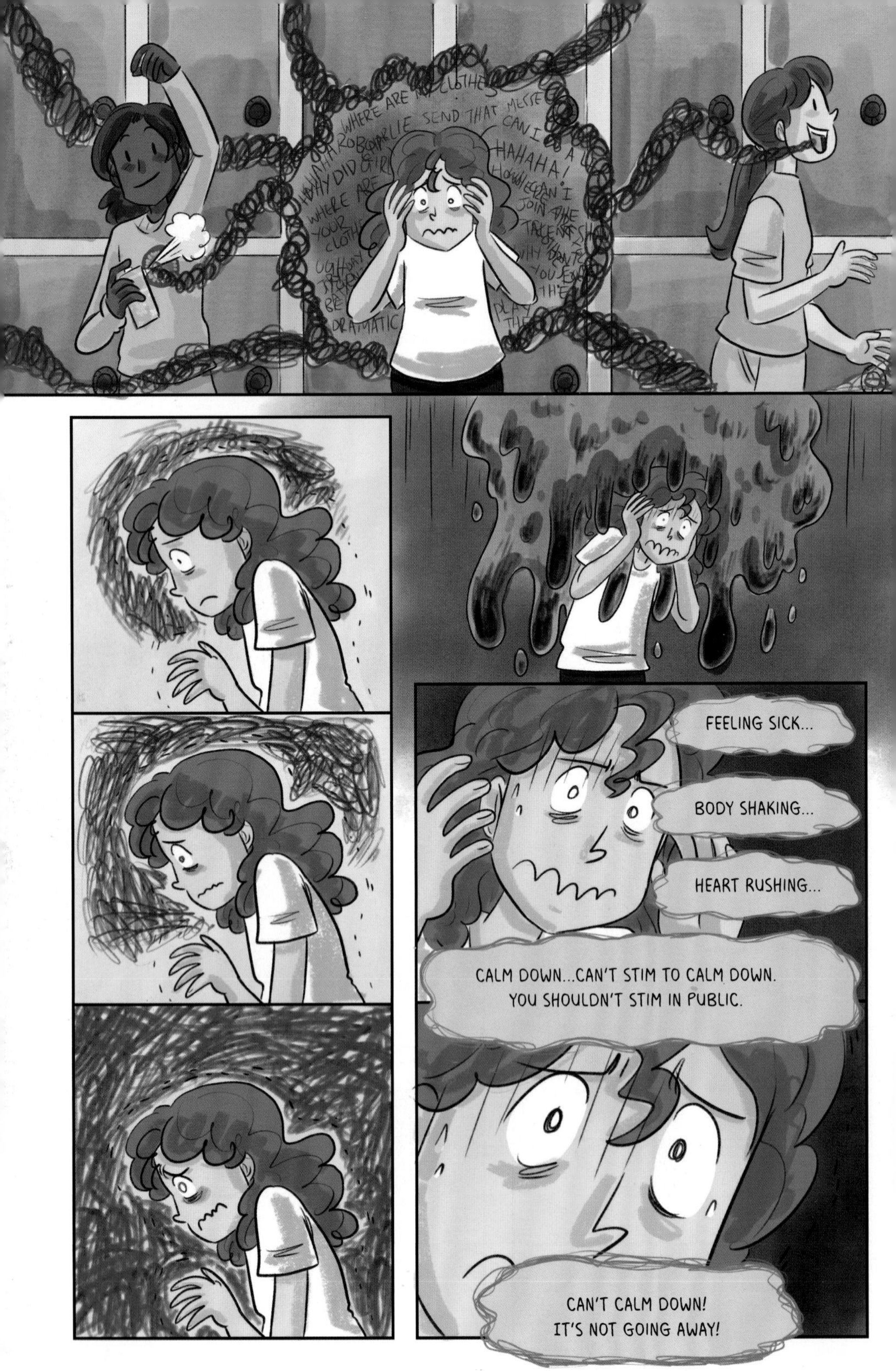
FEELING SICK...
BODY SHAKING...
HEART RUSHING...
CALM DOWN...CAN'T STIM TO CALM DOWN. YOU SHOULDN'T STIM IN PUBLIC.
CAN'T CALM DOWN! IT'S NOT GOING AWAY!

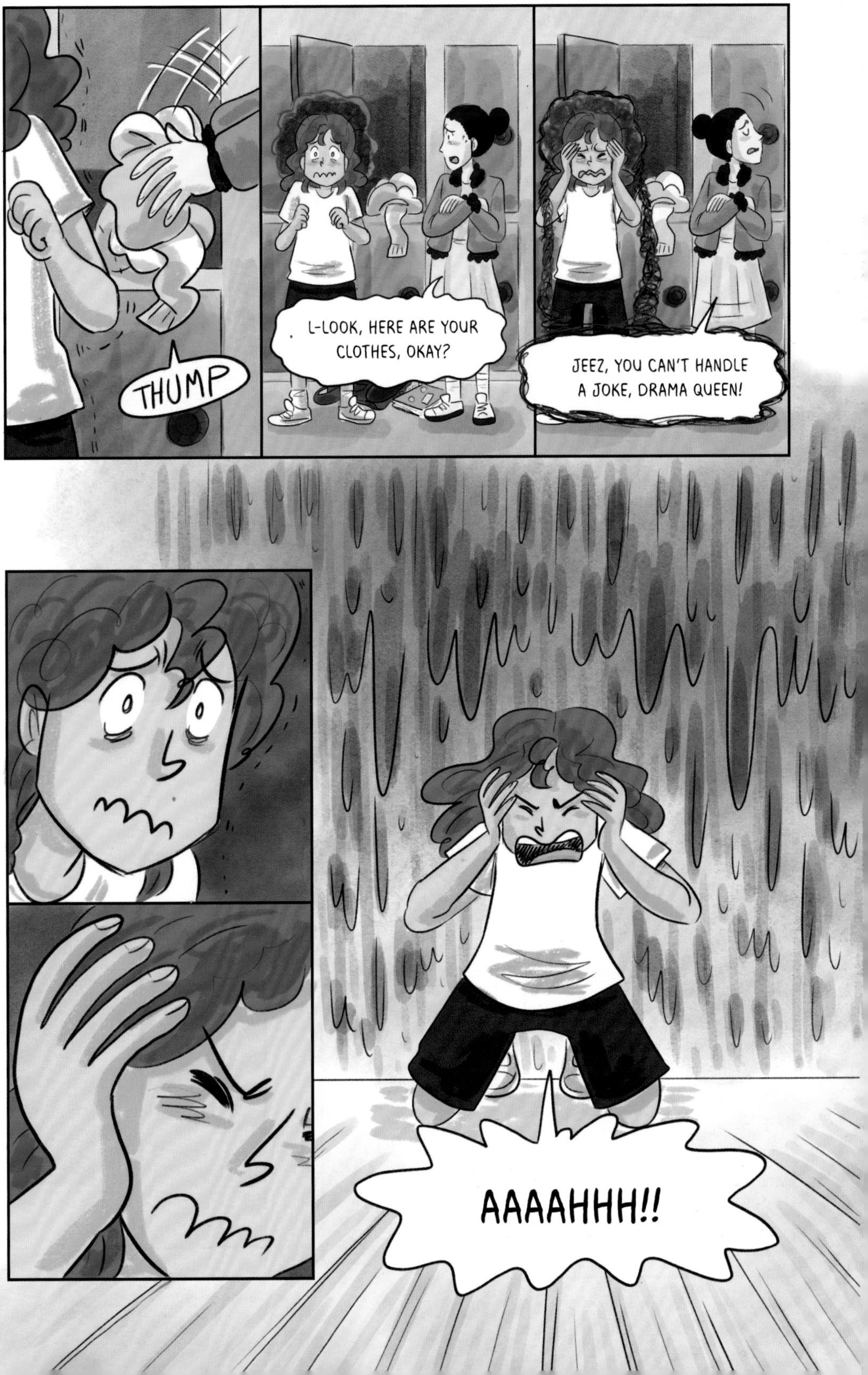
THUMP
L-LOOK, HERE ARE YOUR CLOTHES, OKAY?
JEEZ, YOU CAN'T HANDLE A JOKE, DRAMA QUEEN!
AAAAHHH!!

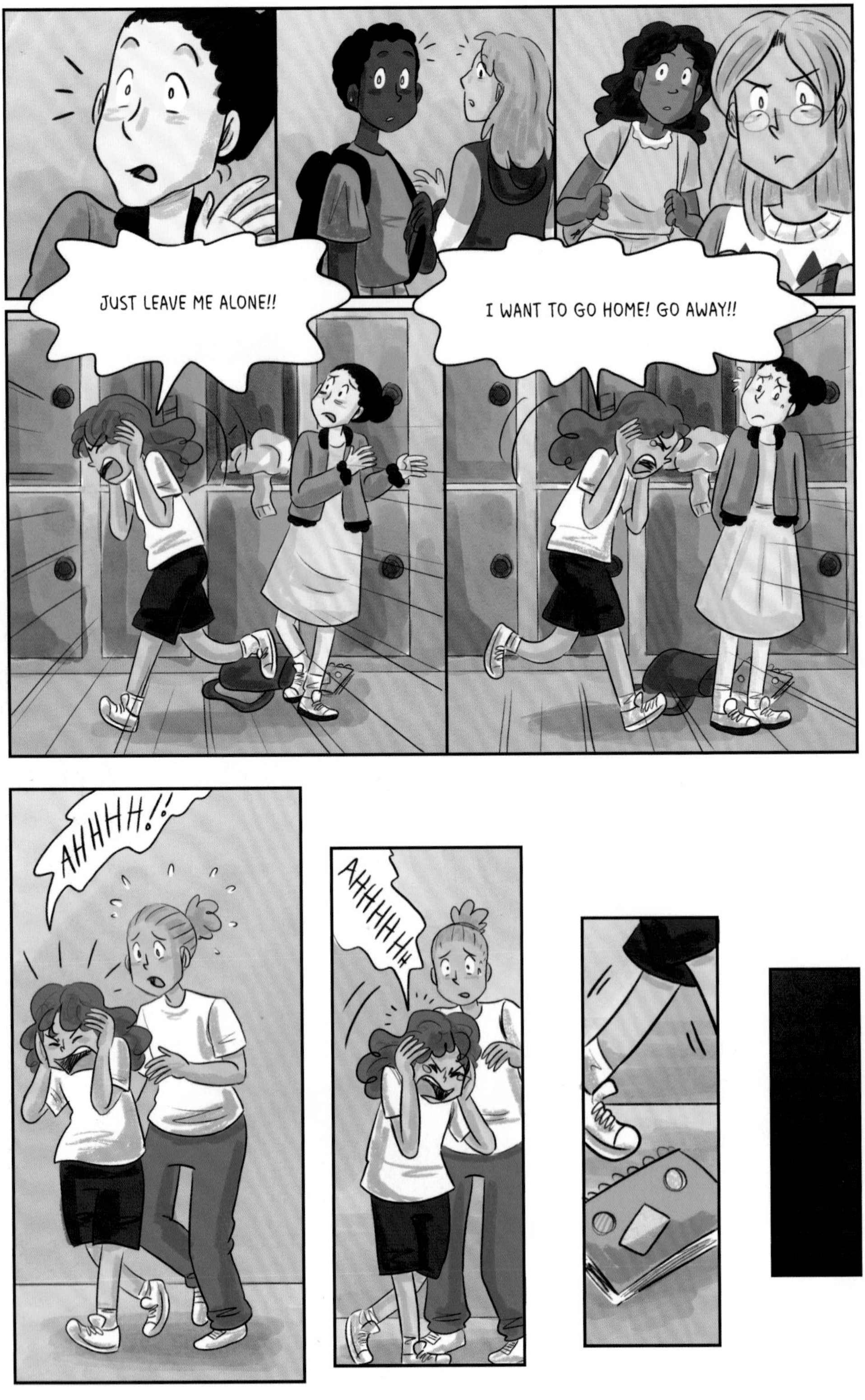
JUST LEAVE ME ALONE!!
I WANT TO GO HOME! GO AWAY!!
AHHHH!!
AHHHHH

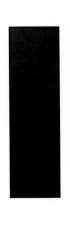

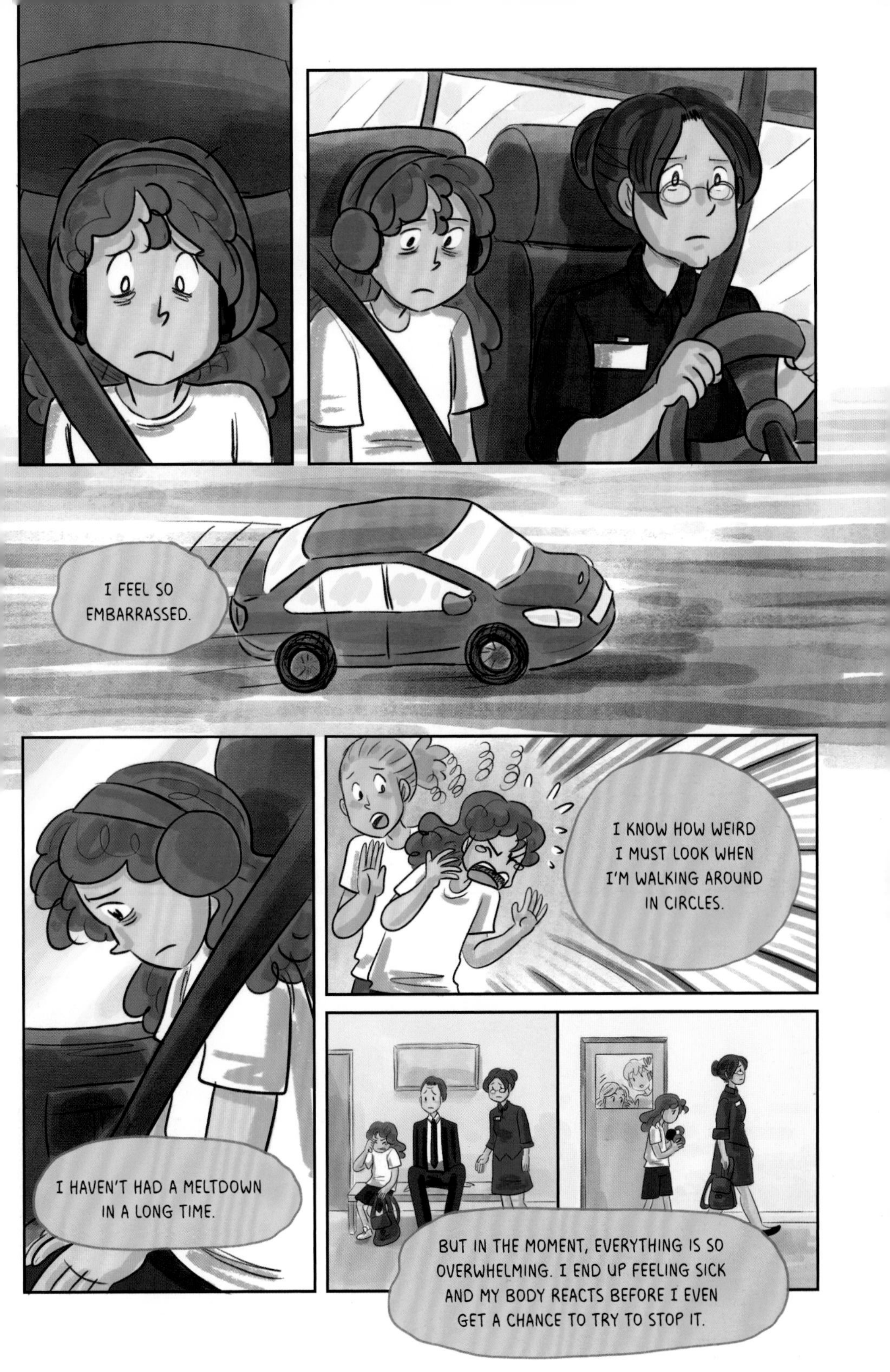
I FEEL SO EMBARRASSED.
I HAVEN'T HAD A MELTDOWN IN A LONG TIME.
I KNOW HOW WEIRD I MUST LOOK WHEN I'M WALKING AROUND IN CIRCLES.
BUT IN THE MOMENT, EVERYTHING IS SO OVERWHELMING. I END UP FEELING SICK AND MY BODY REACTS BEFORE I EVEN GET A CHANCE TO TRY TO STOP IT.

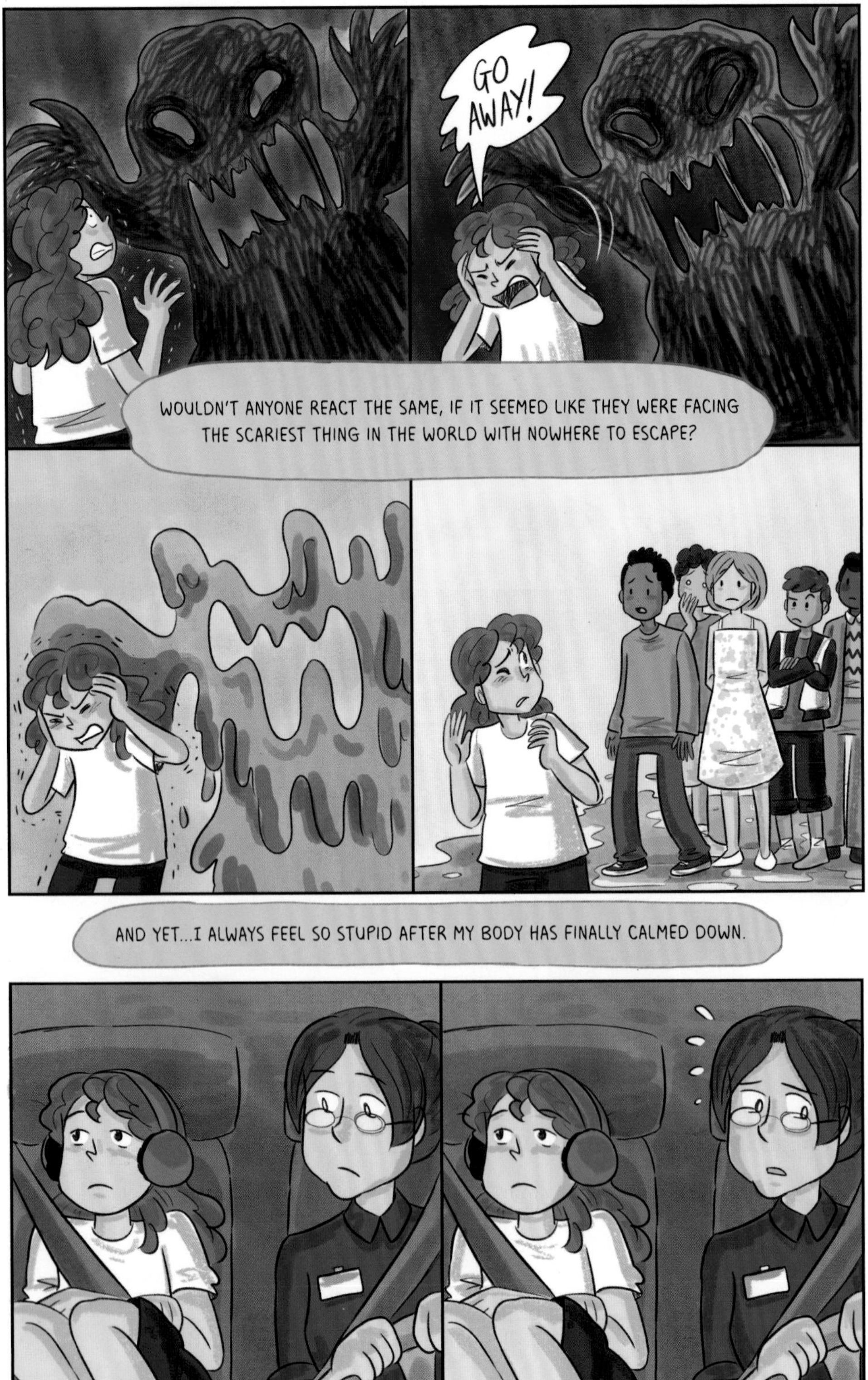
GO AWAY!
WOULDN'T ANYONE REACT THE SAME, IF IT SEEMED LIKE THEY WERE FACING THE SCARIEST THING IN THE WORLD WITH NOWHERE TO ESCAPE?
AND YET...I ALWAYS FEEL SO STUPID AFTER MY BODY HAS FINALLY CALMED DOWN.

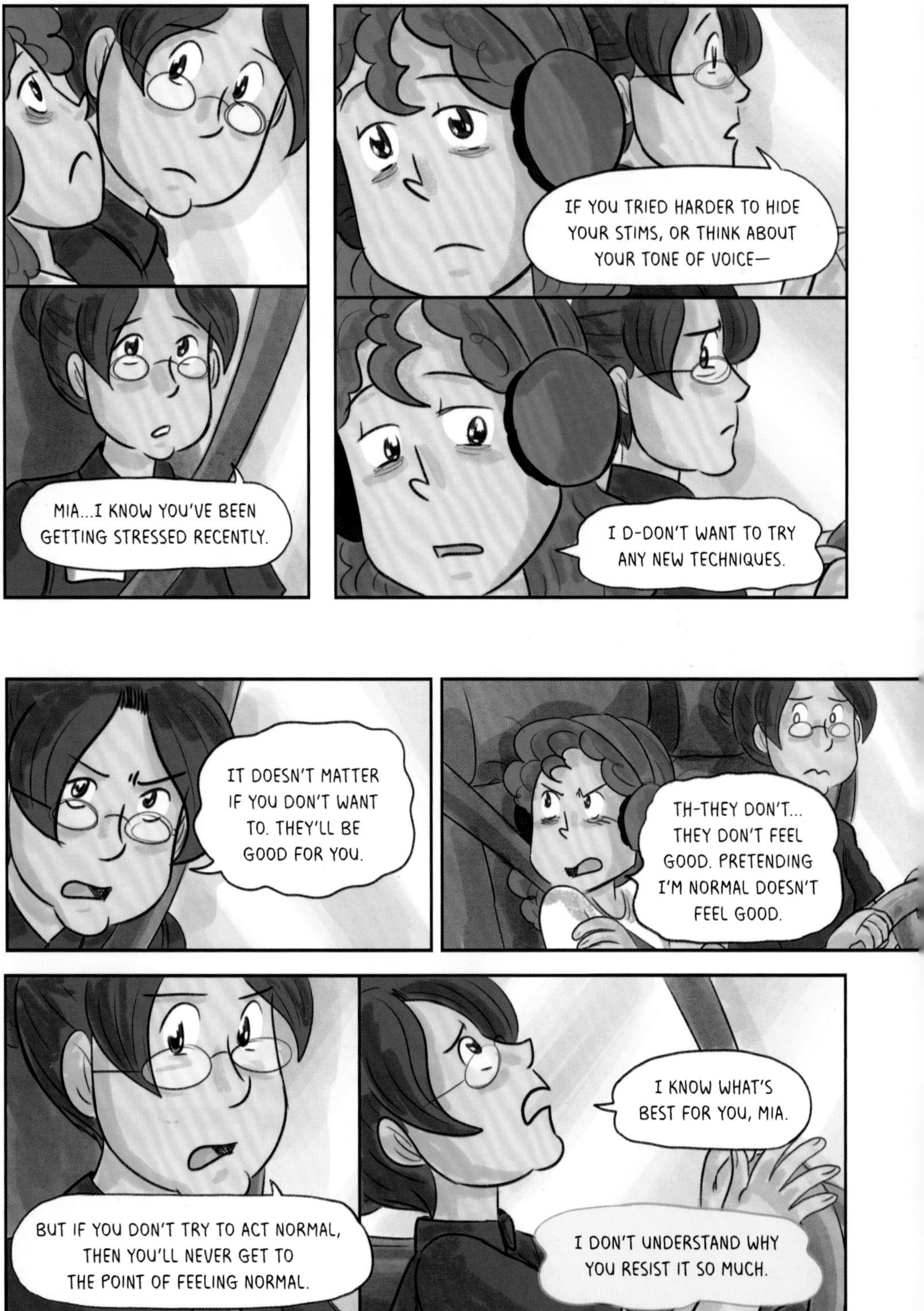
IF YOU TRIED HARDER TO HIDE YOUR STIMS, OR THINK ABOUT YOUR TONE OF VOICE—
MIA...I KNOW YOU'VE BEEN GETTING STRESSED RECENTLY.
I D-DON'T WANT TO TRY ANY NEW TECHNIQUES.
IT DOESN'T MATTER IF YOU DON'T WANT TO. THEY'LL BE GOOD FOR YOU.
TH-THEY DON'T... THEY DON'T FEEL GOOD. PRETENDING I'M NORMAL DOESN'T FEEL GOOD.
BUT IF YOU DON'T TRY TO ACT NORMAL, THEN YOU'LL NEVER GET TO THE POINT OF FEELING NORMAL.
I KNOW WHAT'S BEST FOR YOU, MIA.
I DON'T UNDERSTAND WHY YOU RESIST IT SO MUCH.

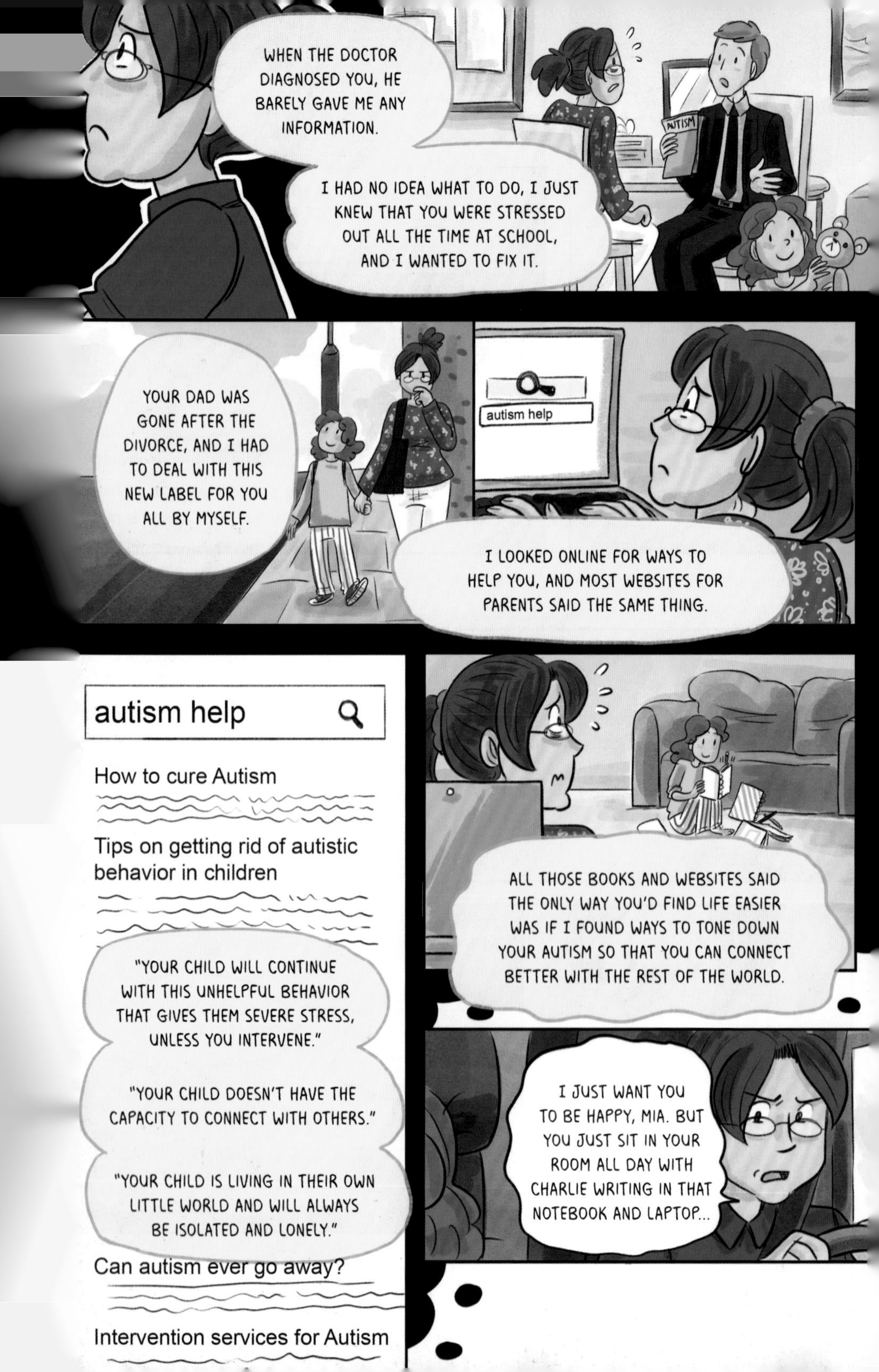
WHEN THE DOCTOR DIAGNOSED YOU, HE BARELY GAVE ME ANY INFORMATION.
I HAD NO IDEA WHAT TO DO, I JUST KNEW THAT YOU WERE STRESSED OUT ALL THE TIME AT SCHOOL, AND I WANTED TO FIX IT.
AUTISM
YOUR DAD WAS GONE AFTER THE DIVORCE, AND I HAD TO DEAL WITH THIS NEW LABEL FOR YOU ALL BY MYSELF.
autism help
I LOOKED ONLINE FOR WAYS TO HELP YOU, AND MOST WEBSITES FOR PARENTS SAID THE SAME THING.
autism help
How to cure Autism
Tips on getting rid of autistic behavior in children
"YOUR CHILD WILL CONTINUE WITH THIS UNHELPFUL BEHAVIOR THAT GIVES THEM SEVERE STRESS, UNLESS YOU INTERVENE."
"YOUR CHILD DOESN'T HAVE THE CAPACITY TO CONNECT WITH OTHERS."
"YOUR CHILD IS LIVING IN THEIR OWN LITTLE WORLD AND WILL ALWAYS BE ISOLATED AND LONELY."
Can autism ever go away?
Intervention services for Autism
ALL THOSE BOOKS AND WEBSITES SAID THE ONLY WAY YOU'D FIND LIFE EASIER WAS IF I FOUND WAYS TO TONE DOWN YOUR AUTISM SO THAT YOU CAN CONNECT BETTER WITH THE REST OF THE WORLD.
I JUST WANT YOU TO BE HAPPY, MIA. BUT YOU JUST SIT IN YOUR ROOM ALL DAY WITH CHARLIE WRITING IN THAT NOTEBOOK AND LAPTOP...

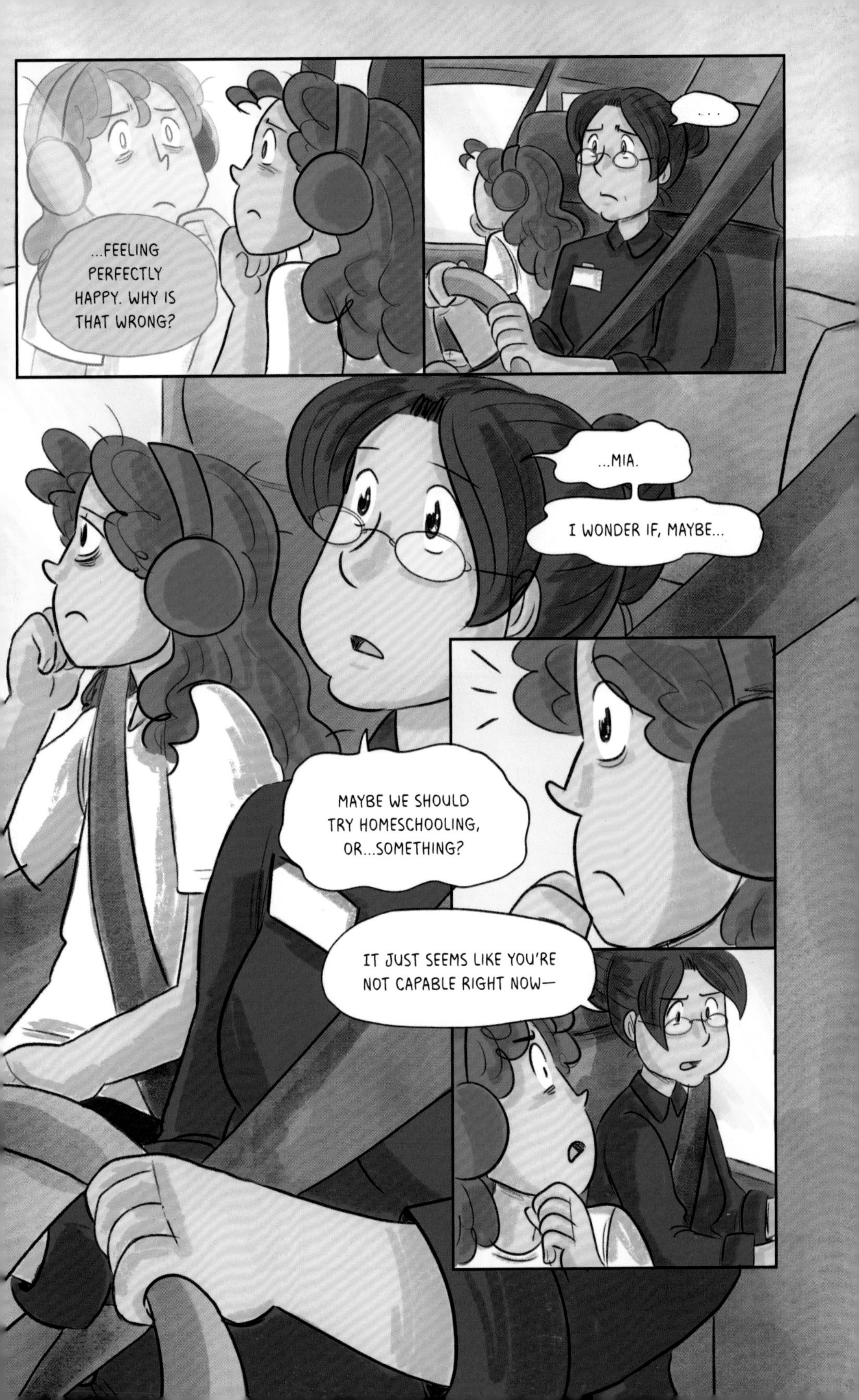
...FEELING PERFECTLY HAPPY. WHY IS THAT WRONG?
...
...MIA.
I WONDER IF, MAYBE...
MAYBE WE SHOULD TRY HOMESCHOOLING, OR...SOMETHING?
IT JUST SEEMS LIKE YOU'RE NOT CAPABLE RIGHT NOW—

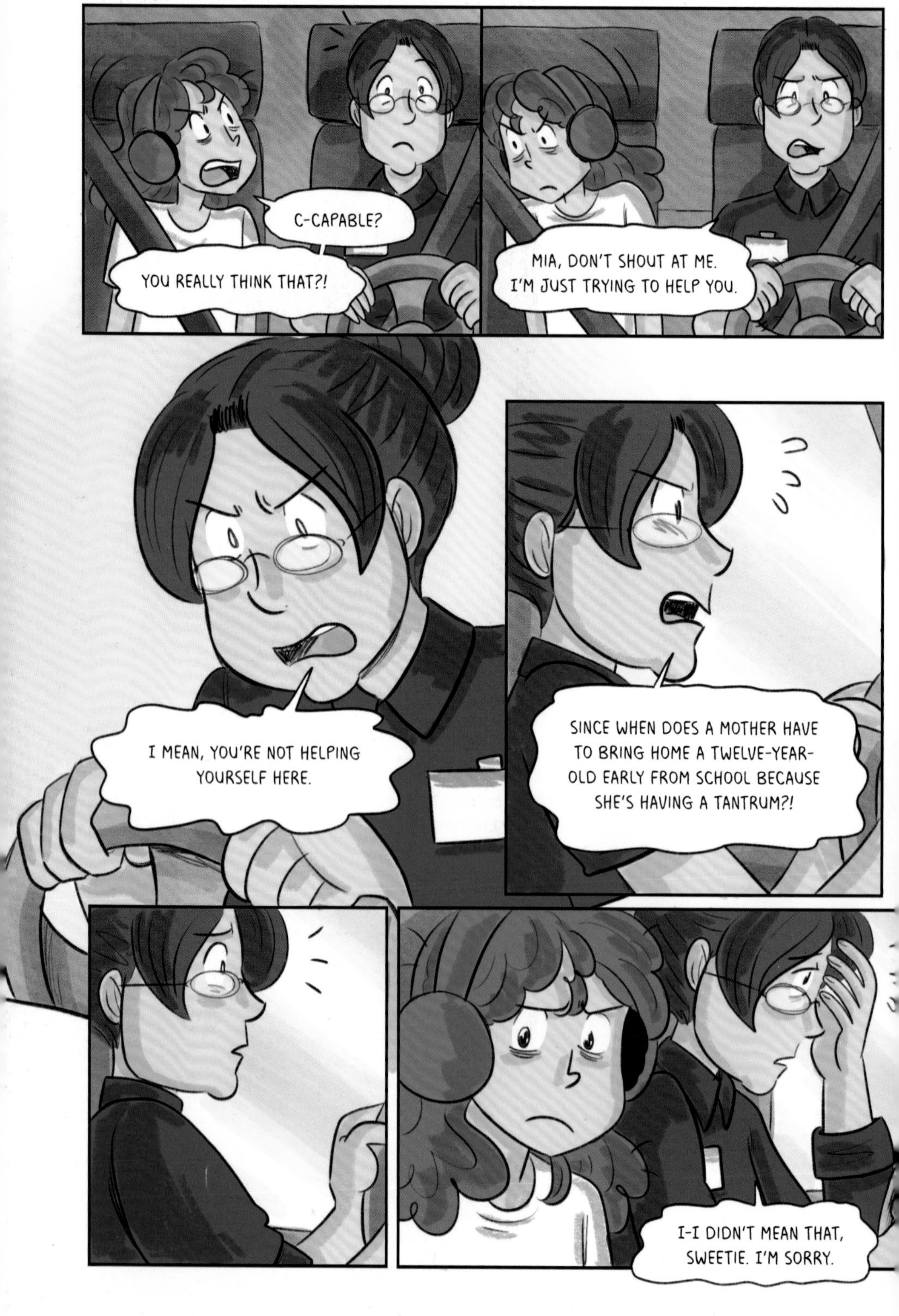
C-CAPABLE?
YOU REALLY THINK THAT?!
MIA, DON'T SHOUT AT ME. I'M JUST TRYING TO HELP YOU.
I MEAN, YOU'RE NOT HELPING YOURSELF HERE.
SINCE WHEN DOES A MOTHER HAVE TO BRING HOME A TWELVE-YEAR-OLD EARLY FROM SCHOOL BECAUSE SHE'S HAVING A TANTRUM?!
I-I DIDN'T MEAN THAT, SWEETIE. I'M SORRY.

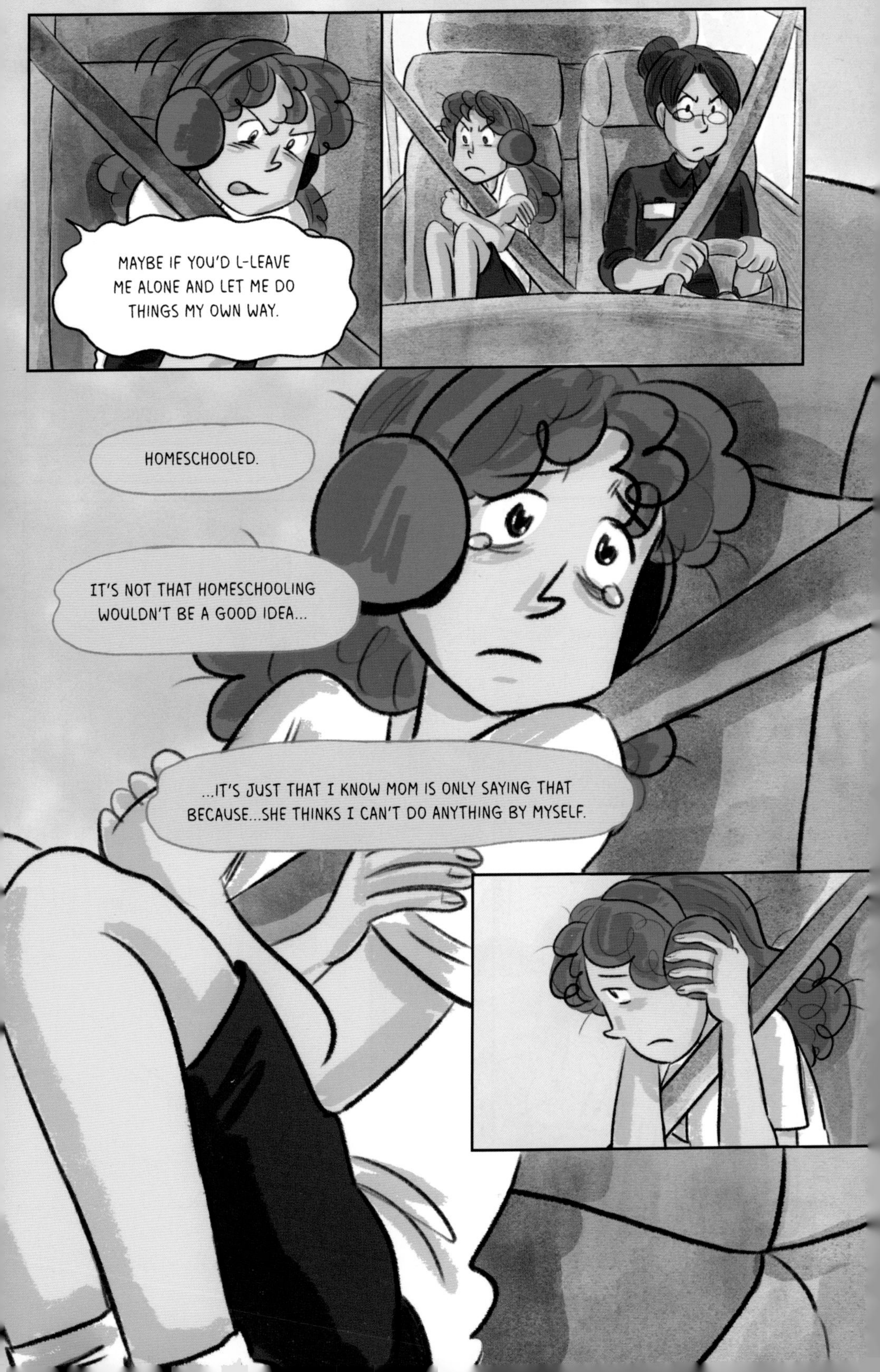
MAYBE IF YOU'D L-LEAVE ME ALONE AND LET ME DO THINGS MY OWN WAY.
HOMESCHOOLED.
IT'S NOT THAT HOMESCHOOLING WOULDN'T BE A GOOD IDEA...
...IT'S JUST THAT I KNOW MOM IS ONLY SAYING THAT BECAUSE...SHE THINKS I CAN'T DO ANYTHING BY MYSELF.

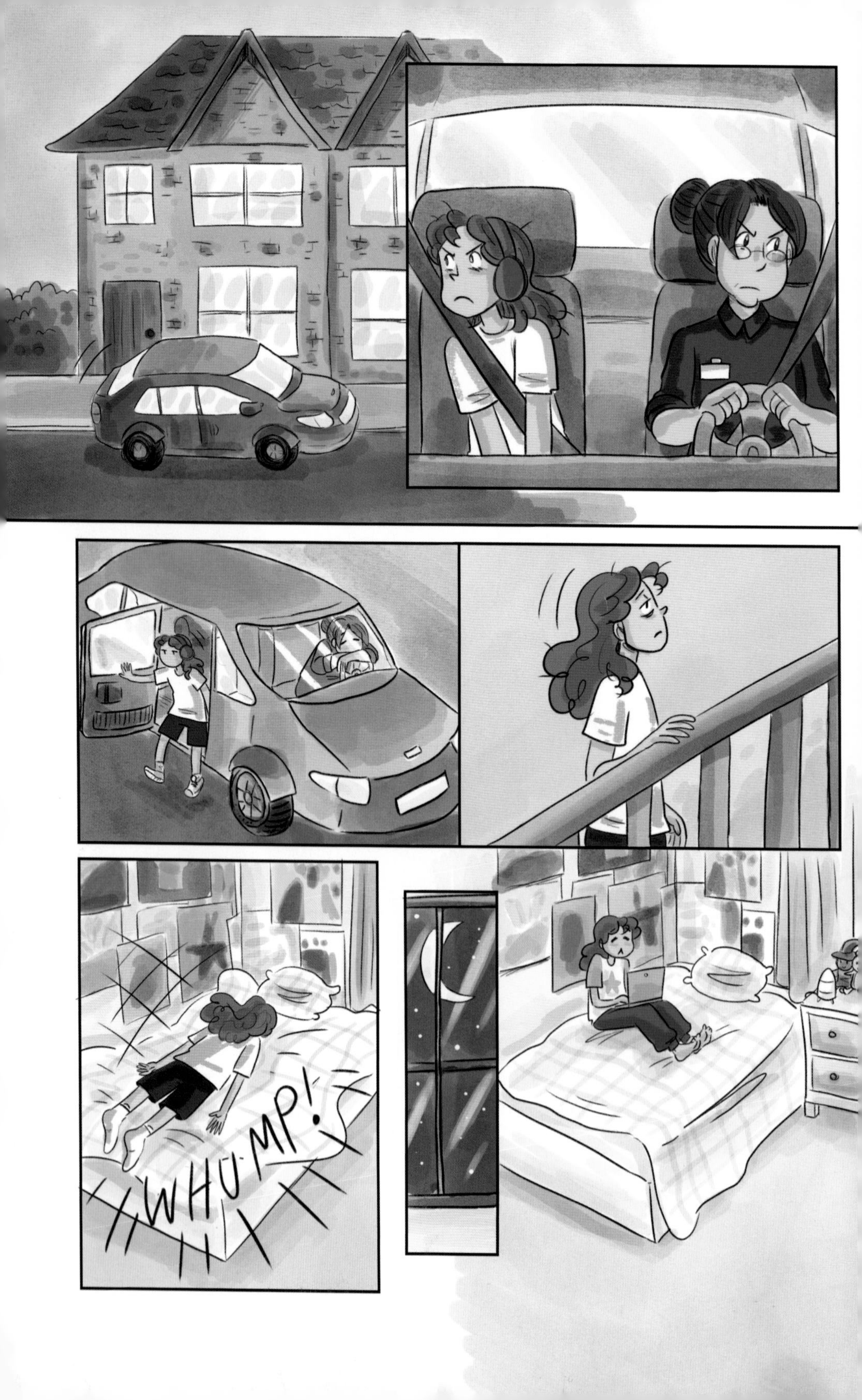
WHUMP!

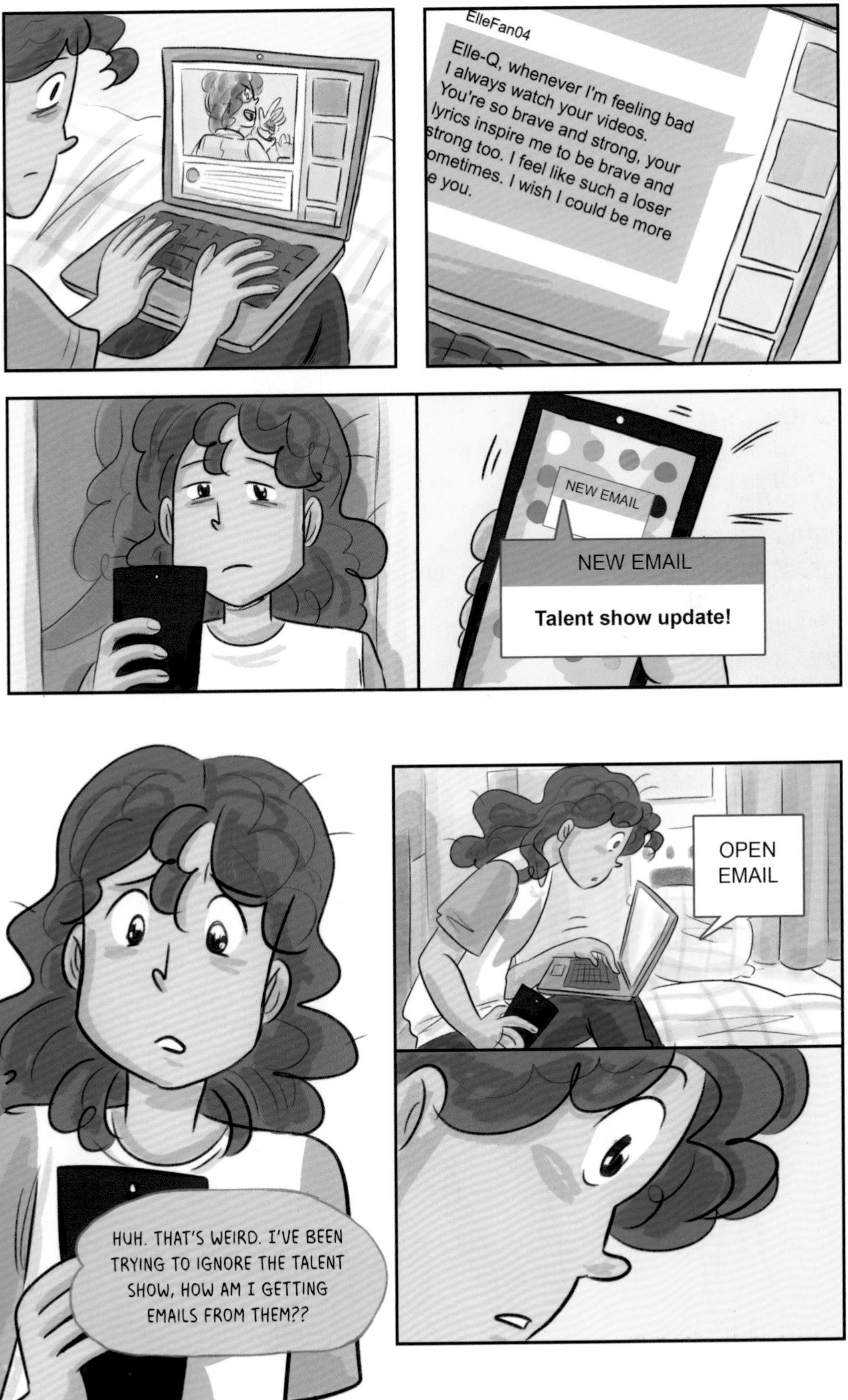
ElleFan04
Elle-Q, whenever I'm feeling bad
I always watch your videos.
You're so brave and strong, your
lyrics inspire me to be brave and
strong too. I feel like such a loser
ometimes. I wish I could be more
e you.
NEW EMAIL
NEW EMAIL
Talent show update!
HUH. THAT'S WEIRD. I'VE BEEN TRYING TO IGNORE THE TALENT SHOW, HOW AM I GETTING EMAILS FROM THEM??
OPEN EMAIL

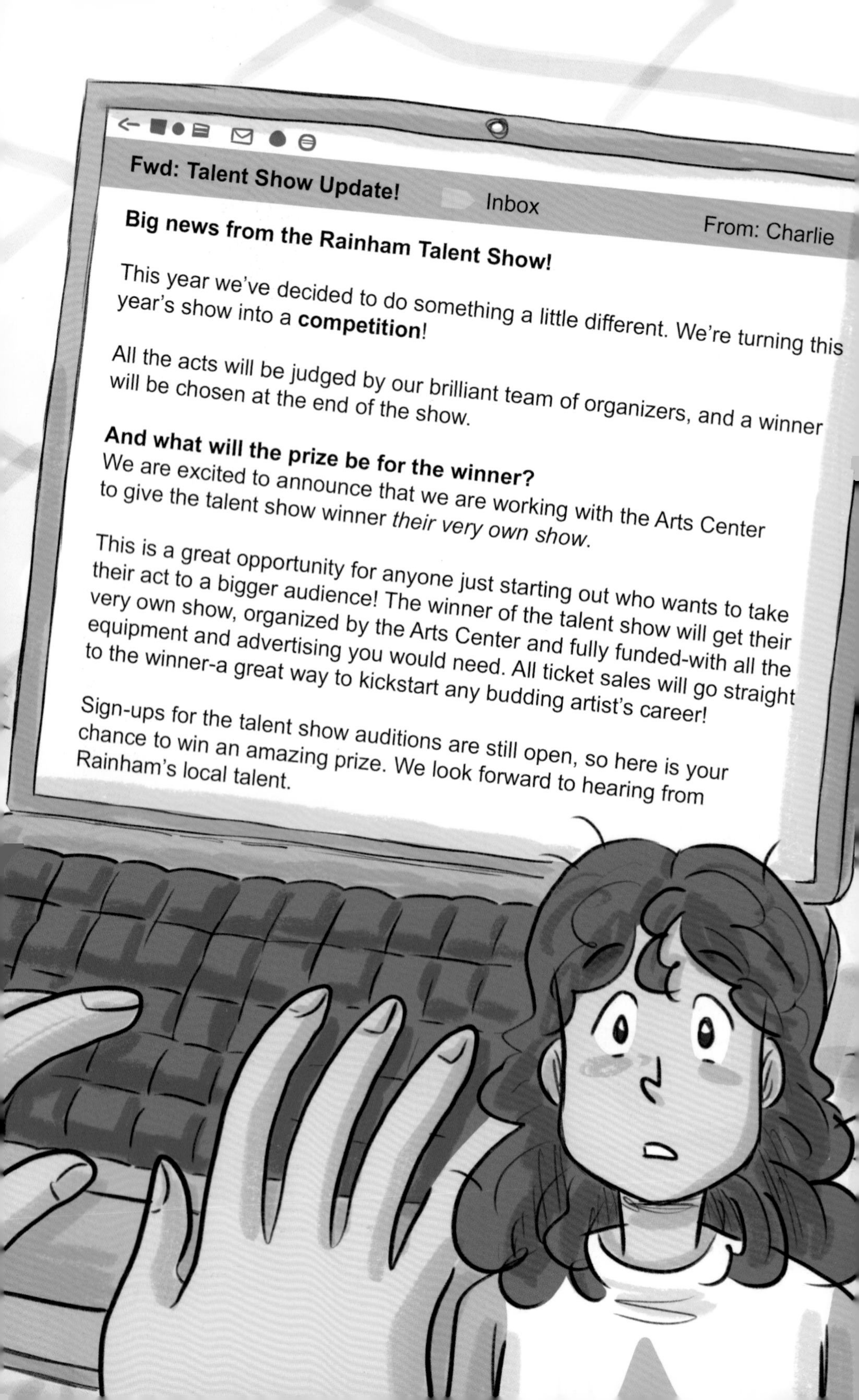
Fwd: Talent Show Update!
Inbox
From: Charlie
Big news from the Rainham Talent Show!
This year we've decided to do something a little different. We're turning this year's show into a competition!
All the acts will be judged by our brilliant team of organizers, and a winner will be chosen at the end of the show.
And what will the prize be for the winner?
We are excited to announce that we are working with the Arts Center to give the talent show winner their very own show.
This is a great opportunity for anyone just starting out who wants to take their act to a bigger audience! The winner of the talent show will get their very own show, organized by the Arts Center and fully funded-with all the equipment and advertising you would need. All ticket sales will go straight to the winner-a great way to kickstart any budding artist's career!
Sign-ups for the talent show auditions are still open, so here is your chance to win an amazing prize. We look forward to hearing from Rainham's local talent.

CHAPTER FIVE

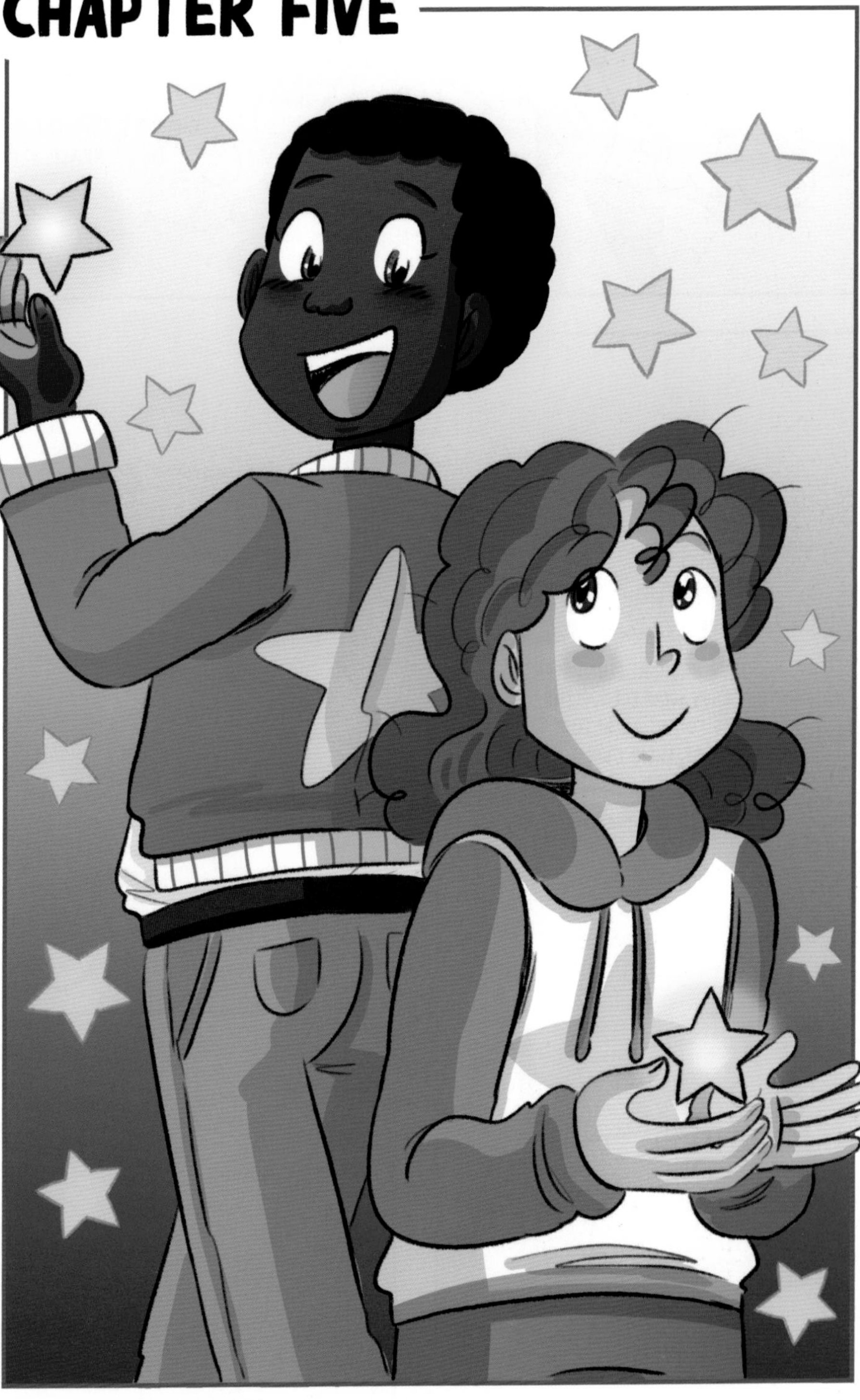

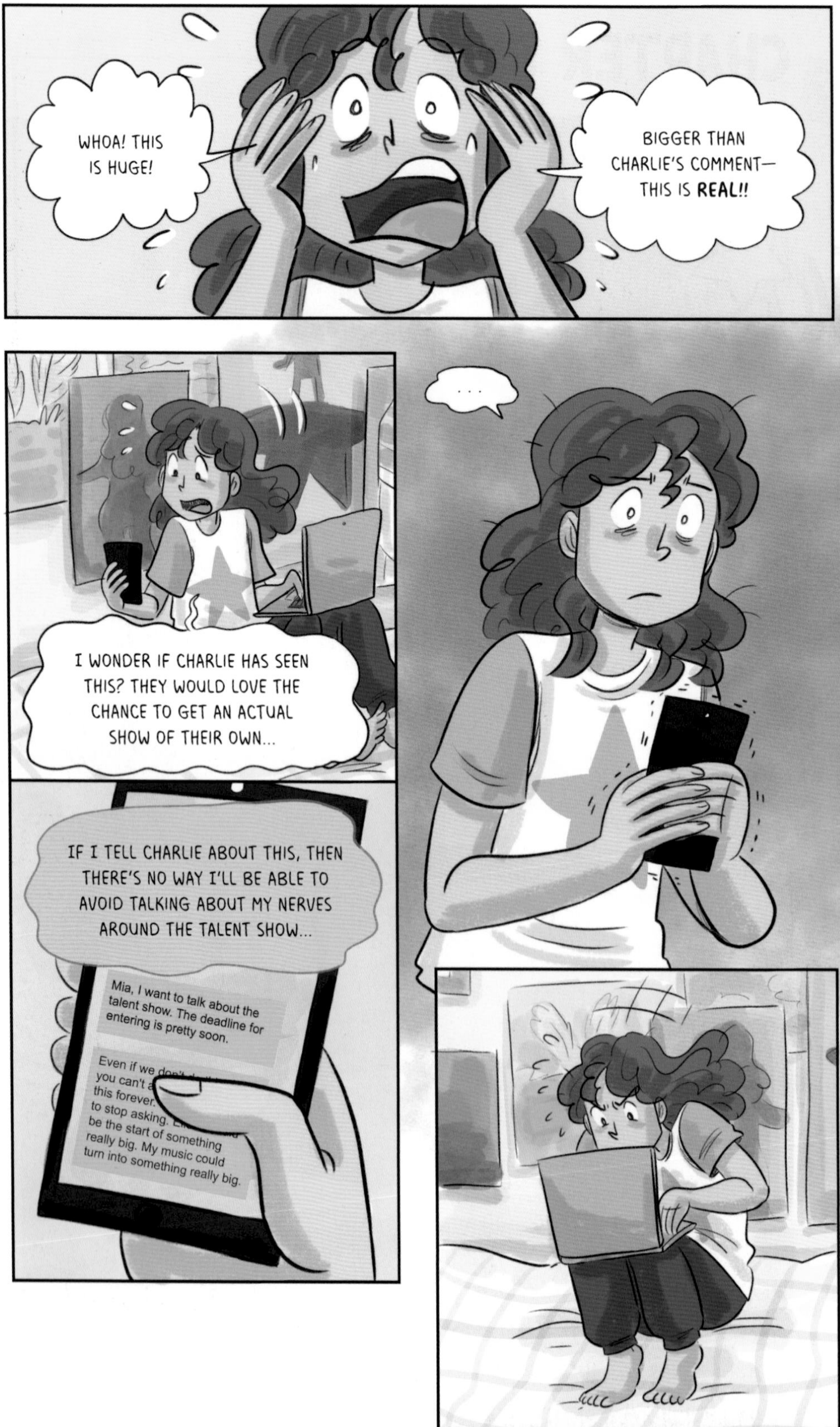
WHOA! THIS IS HUGE!
BIGGER THAN CHARLIE'S COMMENT—THIS IS **REAL!!**
I WONDER IF CHARLIE HAS SEEN THIS? THEY WOULD LOVE THE CHANCE TO GET AN ACTUAL SHOW OF THEIR OWN...
...
IF I TELL CHARLIE ABOUT THIS, THEN THERE'S NO WAY I'LL BE ABLE TO AVOID TALKING ABOUT MY NERVES AROUND THE TALENT SHOW...
Mia, I want to talk about the talent show. The deadline for entering is pretty soon.
Even if we
you can't
this forever.
to stop asking.
be the start of something
really big. My music could
turn into something really big.

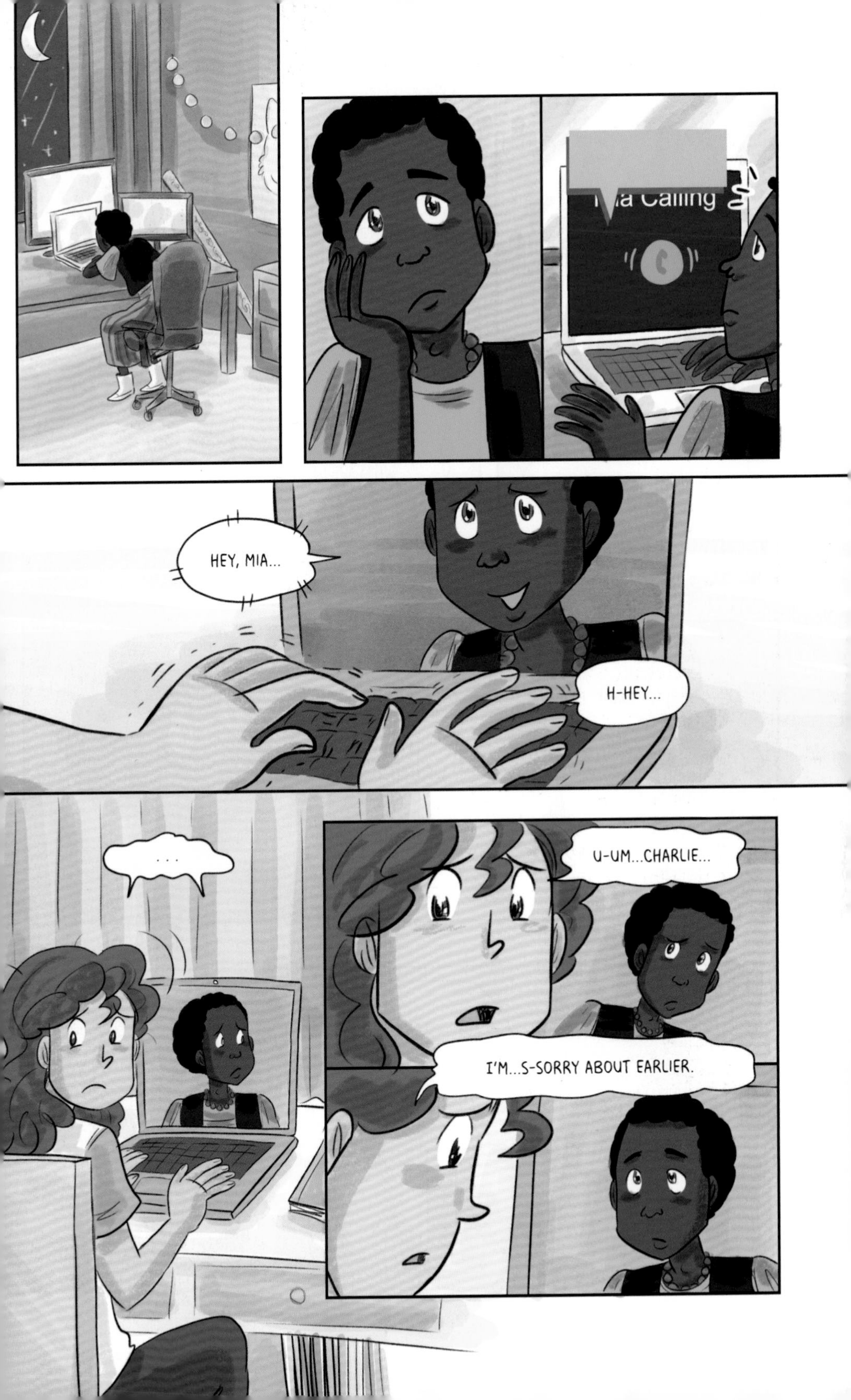
Calling
HEY, MIA...
H-HEY...
. . .
U-UM...CHARLIE...
I'M...S-SORRY ABOUT EARLIER.

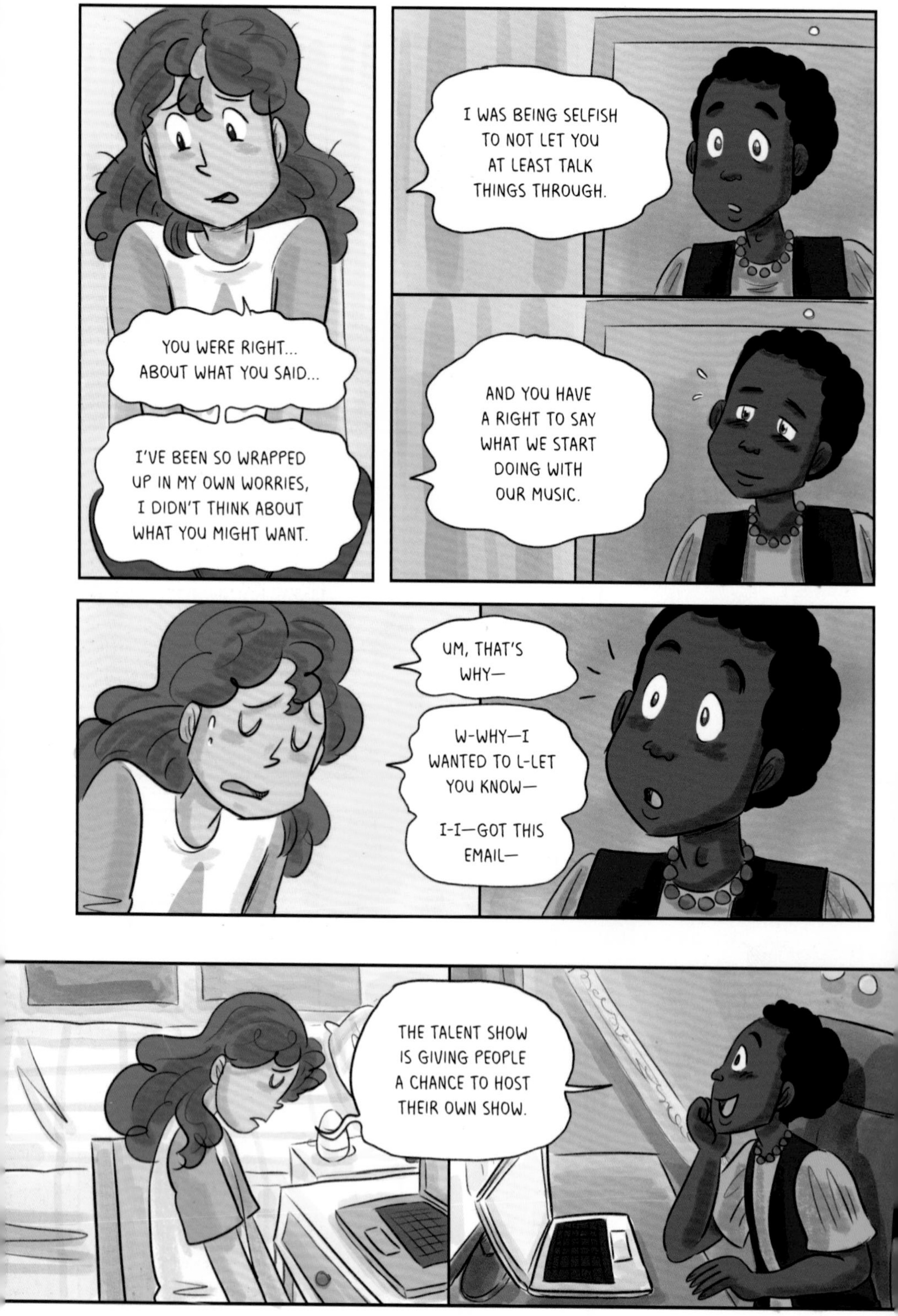
YOU WERE RIGHT... ABOUT WHAT YOU SAID...
I'VE BEEN SO WRAPPED UP IN MY OWN WORRIES, I DIDN'T THINK ABOUT WHAT YOU MIGHT WANT.
I WAS BEING SELFISH TO NOT LET YOU AT LEAST TALK THINGS THROUGH.
AND YOU HAVE A RIGHT TO SAY WHAT WE START DOING WITH OUR MUSIC.
UM, THAT'S WHY—
W-WHY—I WANTED TO L-LET YOU KNOW—
I-I—GOT THIS EMAIL—
THE TALENT SHOW IS GIVING PEOPLE A CHANCE TO HOST THEIR OWN SHOW.

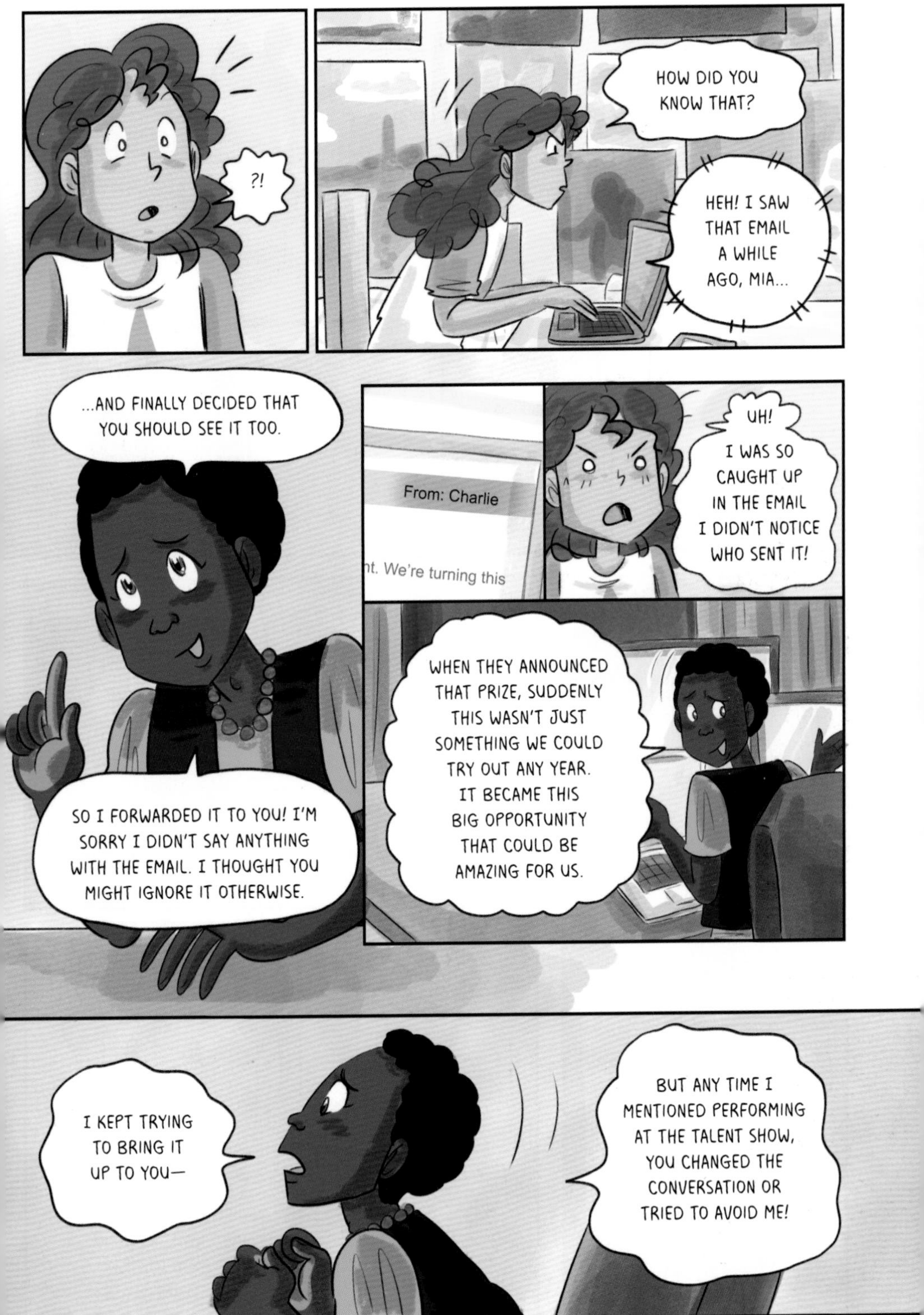
?!
HOW DID YOU KNOW THAT?
HEH! I SAW THAT EMAIL A WHILE AGO, MIA...
...AND FINALLY DECIDED THAT YOU SHOULD SEE IT TOO.
From: Charlie
nt. We're turning this
UH! I WAS SO CAUGHT UP IN THE EMAIL I DIDN'T NOTICE WHO SENT IT!
SO I FORWARDED IT TO YOU! I'M SORRY I DIDN'T SAY ANYTHING WITH THE EMAIL. I THOUGHT YOU MIGHT IGNORE IT OTHERWISE.
WHEN THEY ANNOUNCED THAT PRIZE, SUDDENLY THIS WASN'T JUST SOMETHING WE COULD TRY OUT ANY YEAR. IT BECAME THIS BIG OPPORTUNITY THAT COULD BE AMAZING FOR US.
I KEPT TRYING TO BRING IT UP TO YOU—
BUT ANY TIME I MENTIONED PERFORMING AT THE TALENT SHOW, YOU CHANGED THE CONVERSATION OR TRIED TO AVOID ME!

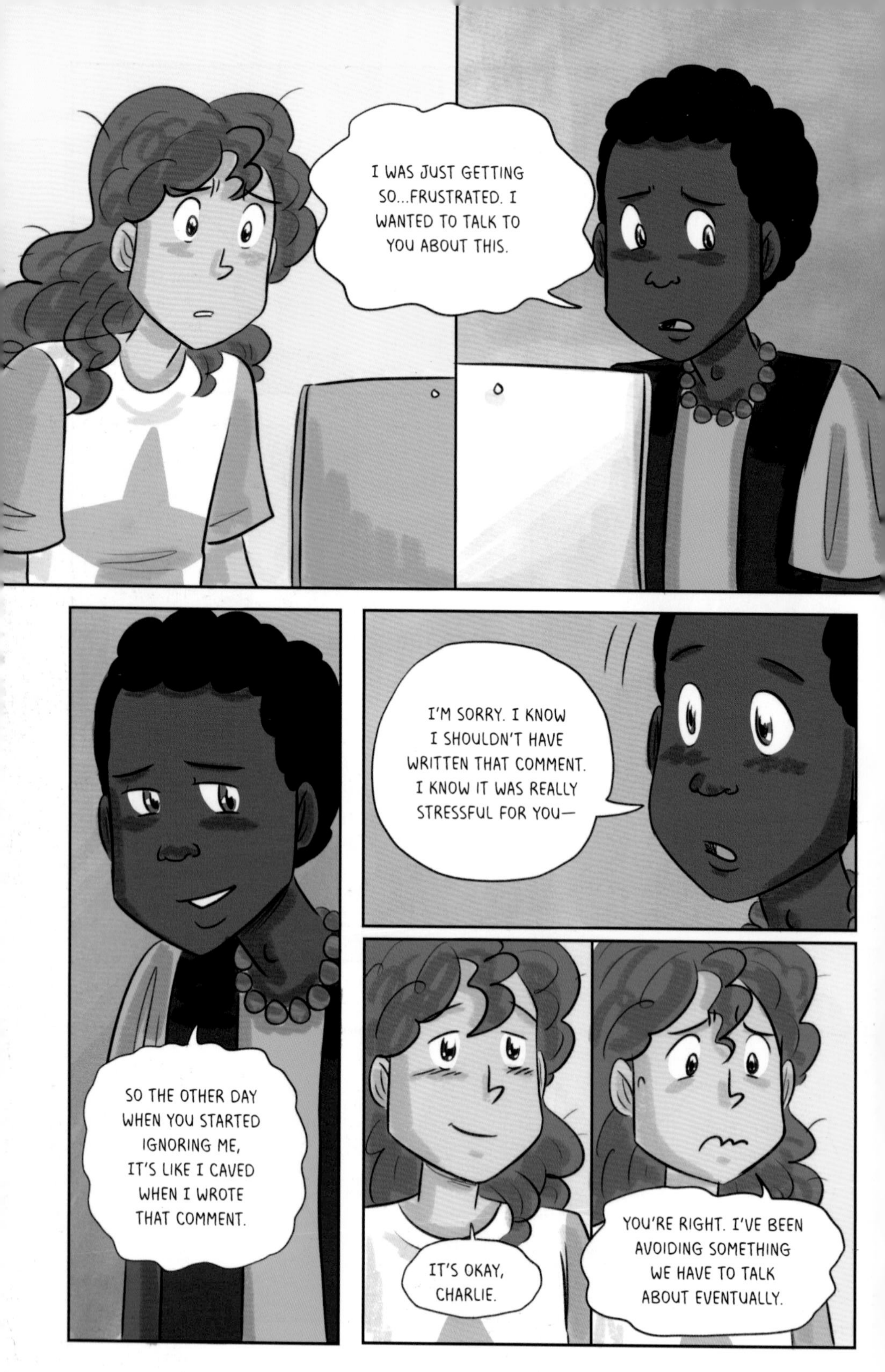
I WAS JUST GETTING SO...FRUSTRATED. I WANTED TO TALK TO YOU ABOUT THIS.
SO THE OTHER DAY WHEN YOU STARTED IGNORING ME, IT'S LIKE I CAVED WHEN I WROTE THAT COMMENT.
I'M SORRY. I KNOW I SHOULDN'T HAVE WRITTEN THAT COMMENT. I KNOW IT WAS REALLY STRESSFUL FOR YOU—
IT'S OKAY, CHARLIE.
YOU'RE RIGHT. I'VE BEEN AVOIDING SOMETHING WE HAVE TO TALK ABOUT EVENTUALLY.

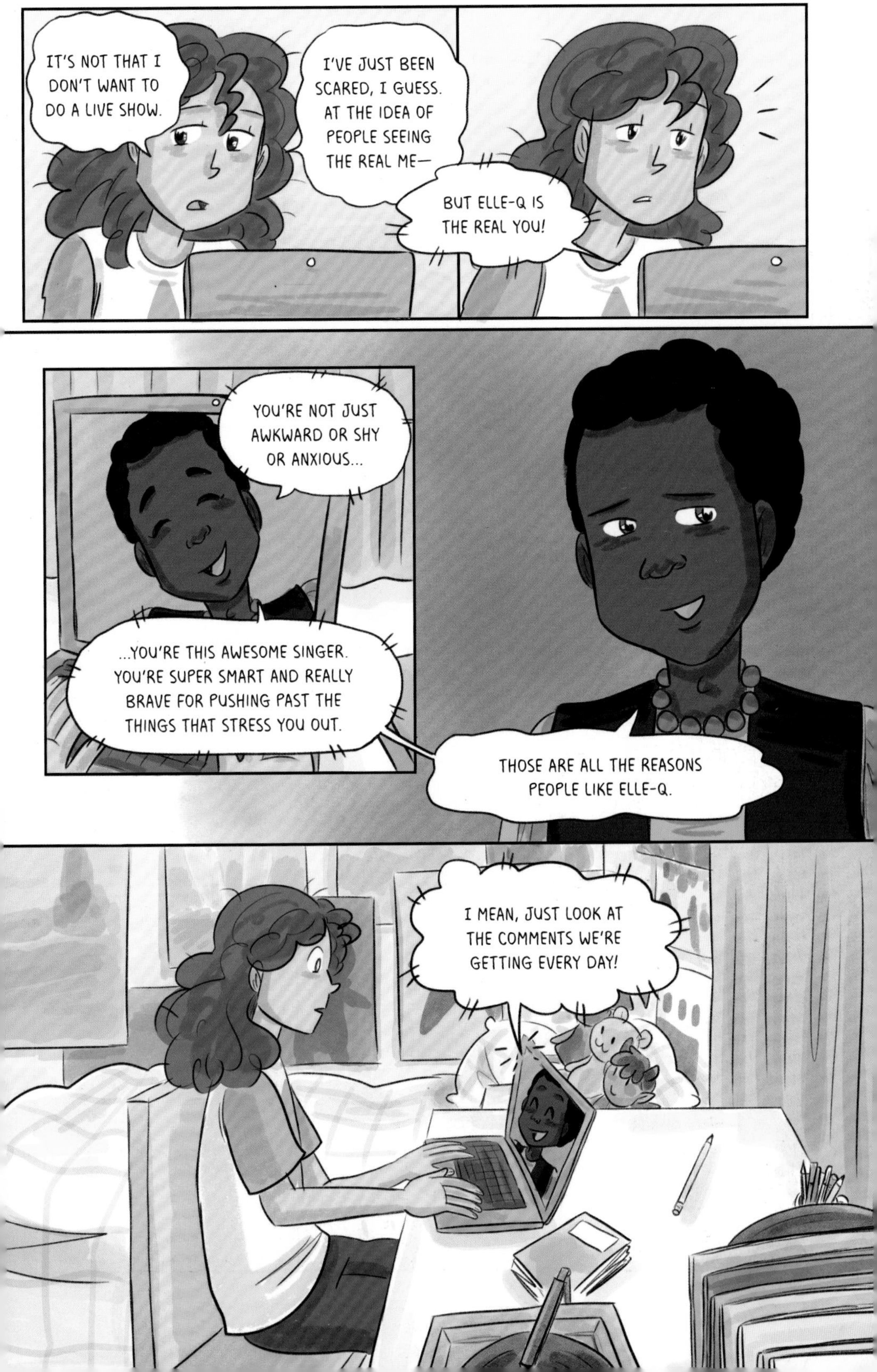
IT'S NOT THAT I DON'T WANT TO DO A LIVE SHOW.
I'VE JUST BEEN SCARED, I GUESS. AT THE IDEA OF PEOPLE SEEING THE REAL ME—
BUT ELLE-Q IS THE REAL YOU!
YOU'RE NOT JUST AWKWARD OR SHY OR ANXIOUS...
...YOU'RE THIS AWESOME SINGER. YOU'RE SUPER SMART AND REALLY BRAVE FOR PUSHING PAST THE THINGS THAT STRESS YOU OUT.
THOSE ARE ALL THE REASONS PEOPLE LIKE ELLE-Q.
I MEAN, JUST LOOK AT THE COMMENTS WE'RE GETTING EVERY DAY!

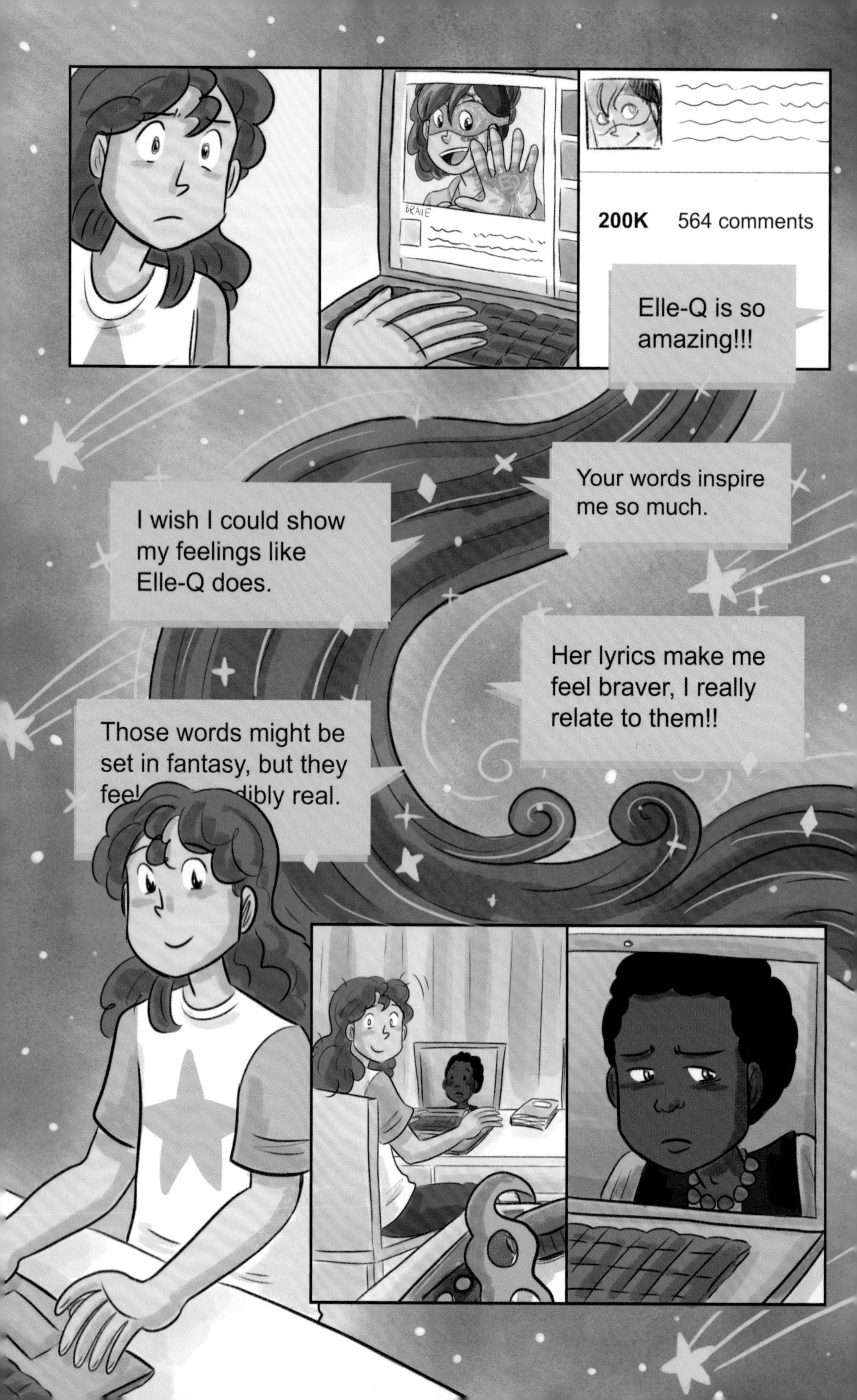
BRAVE
200K
564 comments
Elle-Q is so amazing!!!
Your words inspire me so much.
I wish I could show my feelings like Elle-Q does.
Her lyrics make me feel braver, I really relate to them!!
Those words might be set in fantasy, but they
fee
dibly real.

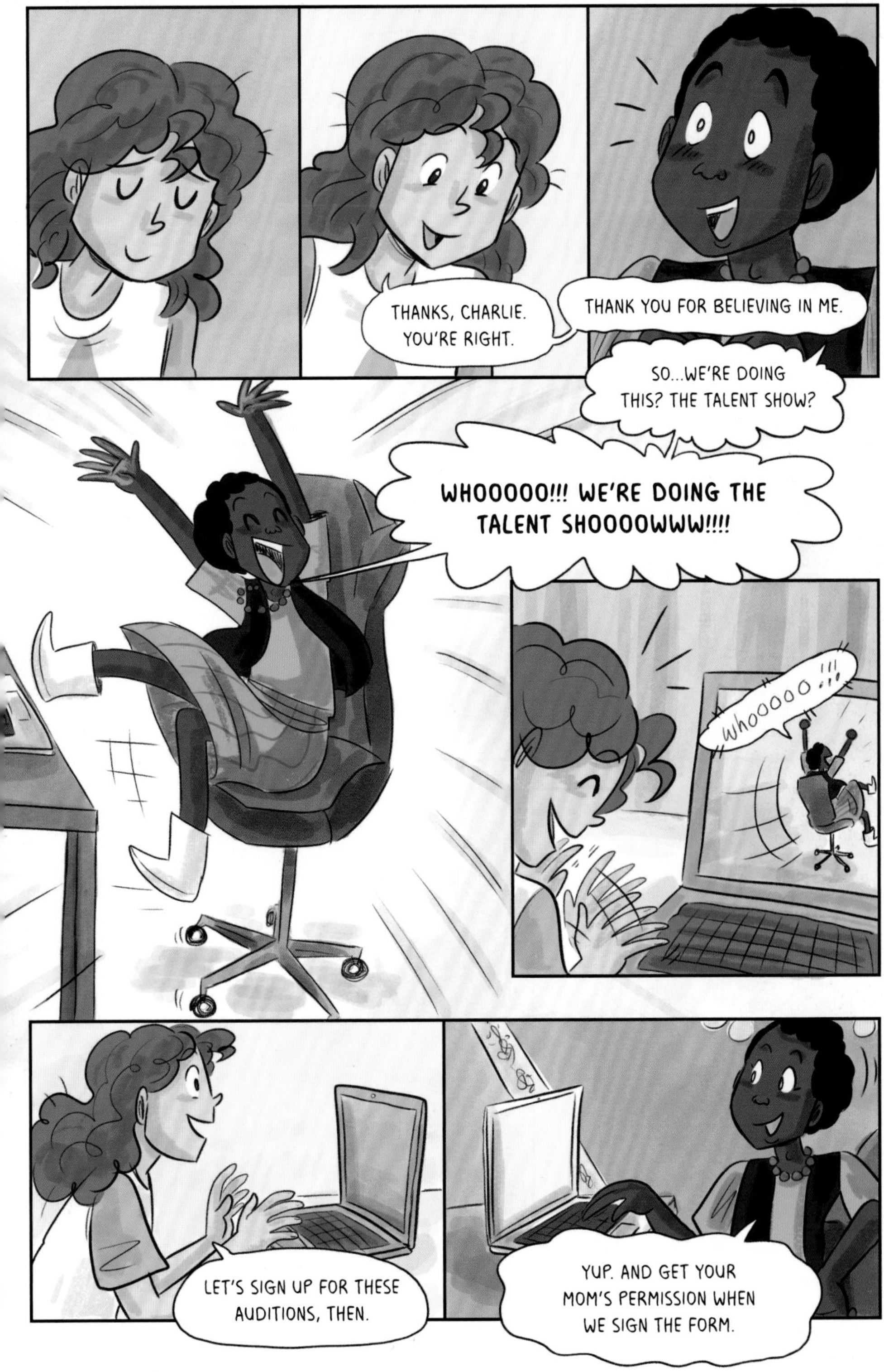
THANKS, CHARLIE. YOU'RE RIGHT.
THANK YOU FOR BELIEVING IN ME.
SO...WE'RE DOING THIS? THE TALENT SHOW?
WHOOOOO!!! WE'RE DOING THE TALENT SHOOOOWWW!!!!
WHOOOOO!!!
LET'S SIGN UP FOR THESE AUDITIONS, THEN.
YUP. AND GET YOUR MOM'S PERMISSION WHEN WE SIGN THE FORM.

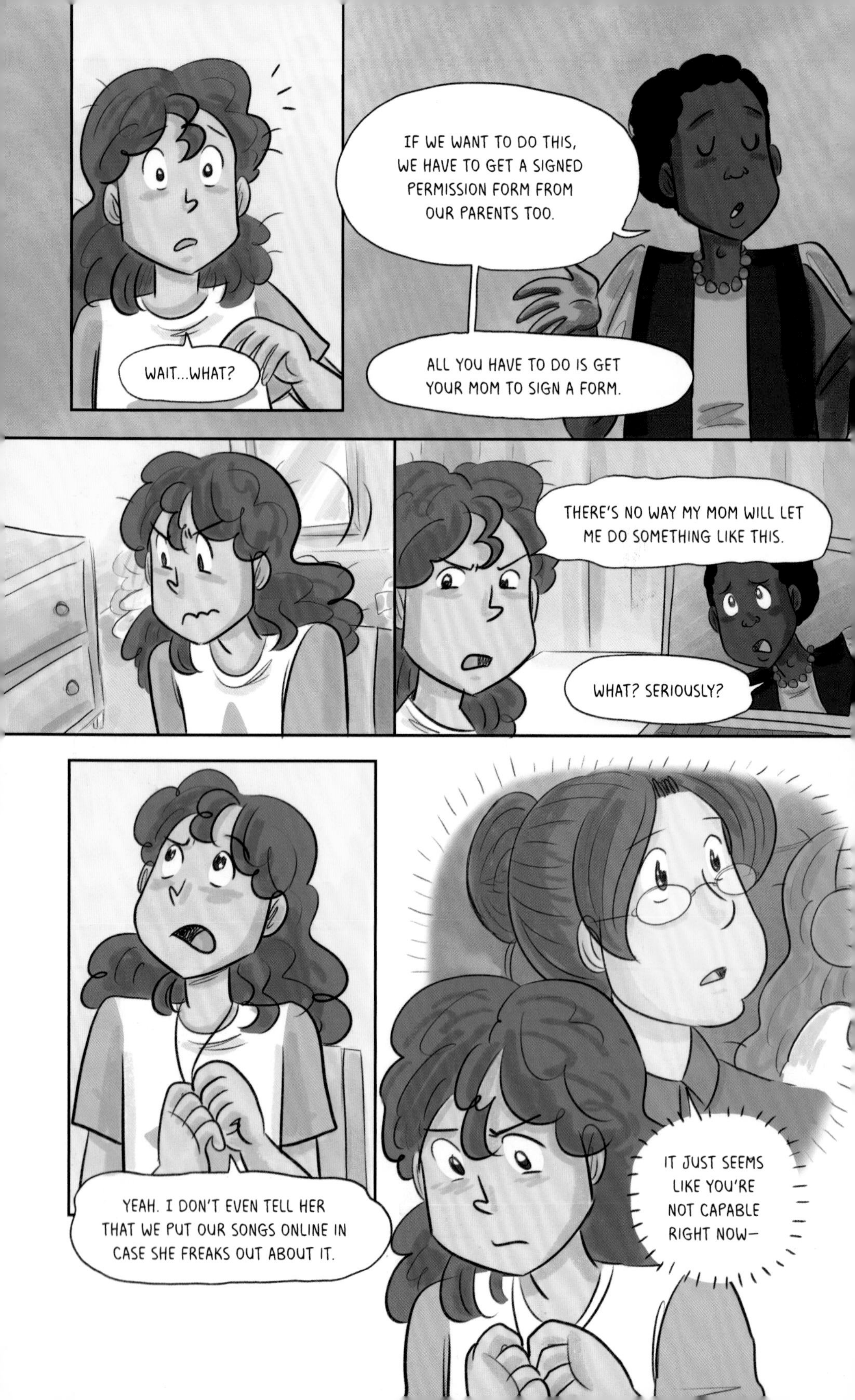
IF WE WANT TO DO THIS, WE HAVE TO GET A SIGNED PERMISSION FORM FROM OUR PARENTS TOO.
WAIT...WHAT?
ALL YOU HAVE TO DO IS GET YOUR MOM TO SIGN A FORM.
THERE'S NO WAY MY MOM WILL LET ME DO SOMETHING LIKE THIS.
WHAT? SERIOUSLY?
YEAH. I DON'T EVEN TELL HER THAT WE PUT OUR SONGS ONLINE IN CASE SHE FREAKS OUT ABOUT IT.
IT JUST SEEMS LIKE YOU'RE NOT CAPABLE RIGHT NOW—

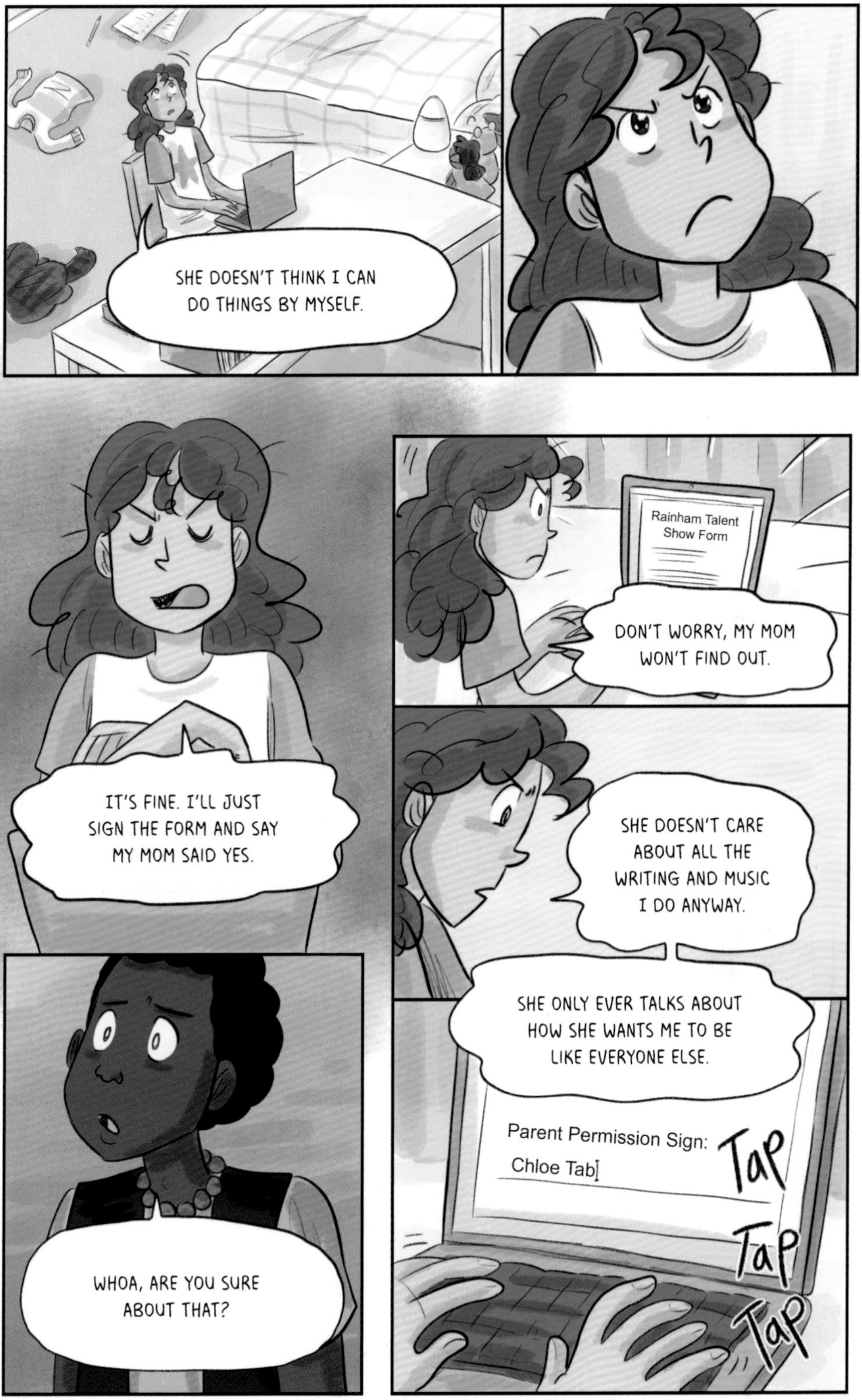
SHE DOESN'T THINK I CAN DO THINGS BY MYSELF.
IT'S FINE. I'LL JUST SIGN THE FORM AND SAY MY MOM SAID YES.
Rainham Talent Show Form
DON'T WORRY, MY MOM WON'T FIND OUT.
SHE DOESN'T CARE ABOUT ALL THE WRITING AND MUSIC I DO ANYWAY.
SHE ONLY EVER TALKS ABOUT HOW SHE WANTS ME TO BE LIKE EVERYONE ELSE.
Parent Permission Sign:
Chloe Tab
Tap
Tap
Tap
WHOA, ARE YOU SURE ABOUT THAT?

ainham Tale

Show Form

nning the below you hereby give permis
ur child, if under 18, to participate in
uns and main performance of the Rainh
ent show. Please sign your name and s

Name: Mia Tabolt   Age: 12

Are you performing by yourself or
If participating in a group, name of

Parent Permission Sign:

Chloe Tabolt

Email Sent!

HEY, MAYBE WE COULD DEBUT A NEW SONG AT THE TALENT SHOW. WHAT DO YOU THINK?

OH COOL! DO YOU KNOW WHAT SONG YOU WANNA DO?

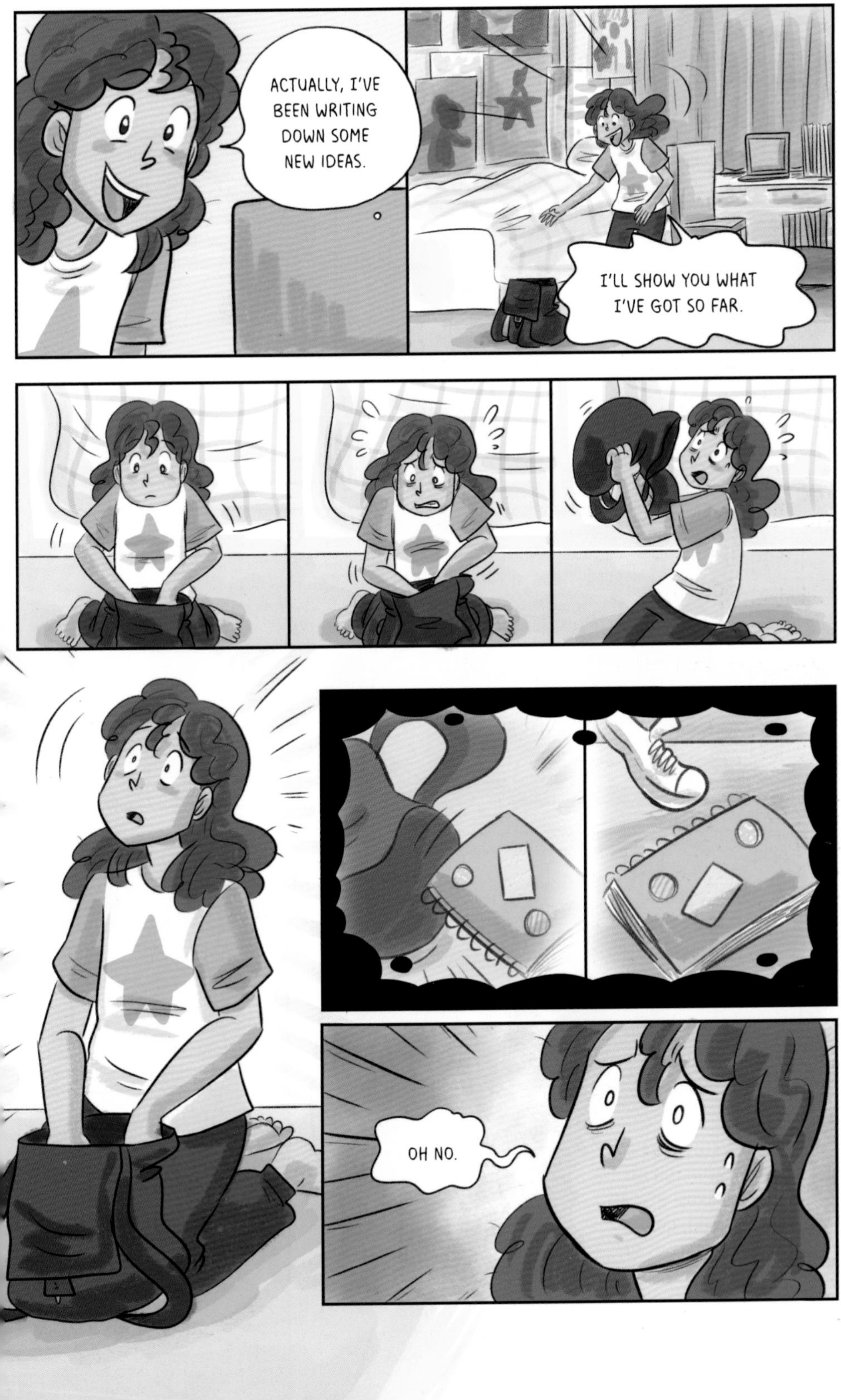
ACTUALLY, I'VE BEEN WRITING DOWN SOME NEW IDEAS.
I'LL SHOW YOU WHAT I'VE GOT SO FAR.
OH NO.

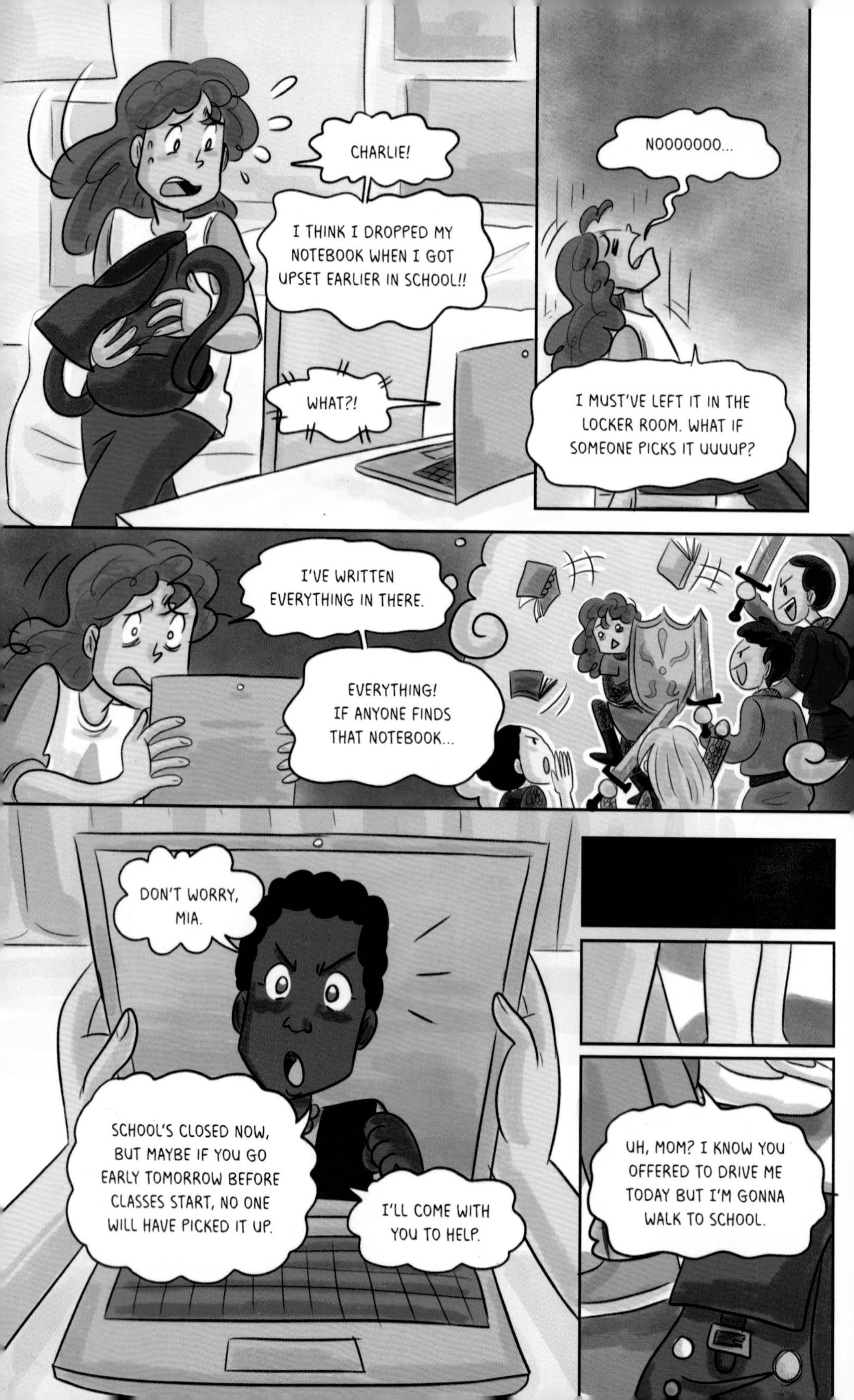
CHARLIE!
I THINK I DROPPED MY NOTEBOOK WHEN I GOT UPSET EARLIER IN SCHOOL!!
WHAT?!
NOOOOOOO...
I MUST'VE LEFT IT IN THE LOCKER ROOM. WHAT IF SOMEONE PICKS IT UUUUP?
I'VE WRITTEN EVERYTHING IN THERE.
EVERYTHING! IF ANYONE FINDS THAT NOTEBOOK...
DON'T WORRY, MIA.
SCHOOL'S CLOSED NOW, BUT MAYBE IF YOU GO EARLY TOMORROW BEFORE CLASSES START, NO ONE WILL HAVE PICKED IT UP.
I'LL COME WITH YOU TO HELP.
UH, MOM? I KNOW YOU OFFERED TO DRIVE ME TODAY BUT I'M GONNA WALK TO SCHOOL.

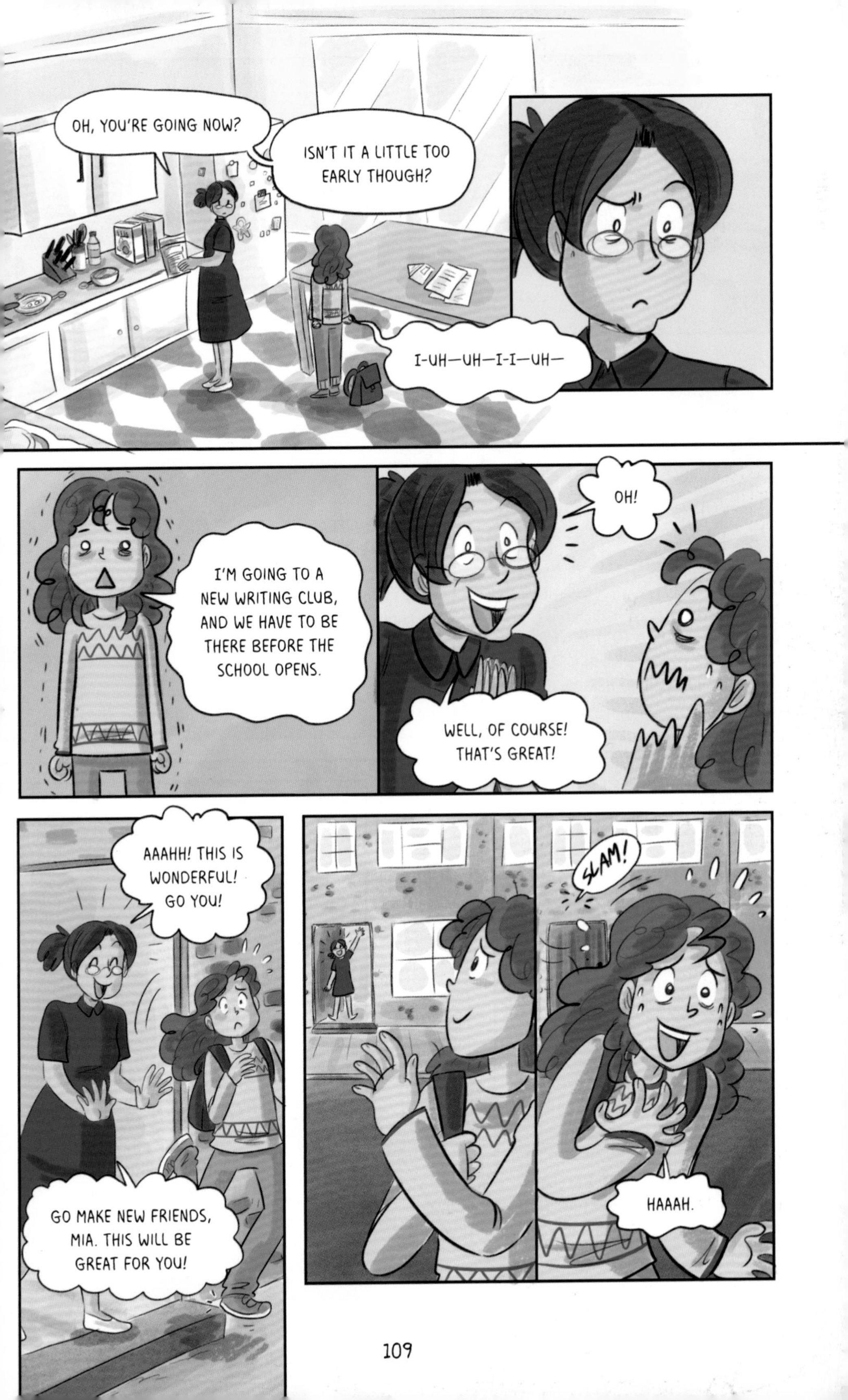
OH, YOU'RE GOING NOW?
ISN'T IT A LITTLE TOO EARLY THOUGH?
I-UH—UH—I-I—UH—
I'M GOING TO A NEW WRITING CLUB, AND WE HAVE TO BE THERE BEFORE THE SCHOOL OPENS.
OH!
WELL, OF COURSE! THAT'S GREAT!
AAAHH! THIS IS WONDERFUL! GO YOU!
GO MAKE NEW FRIENDS, MIA. THIS WILL BE GREAT FOR YOU!
SLAM!
HAAAH.

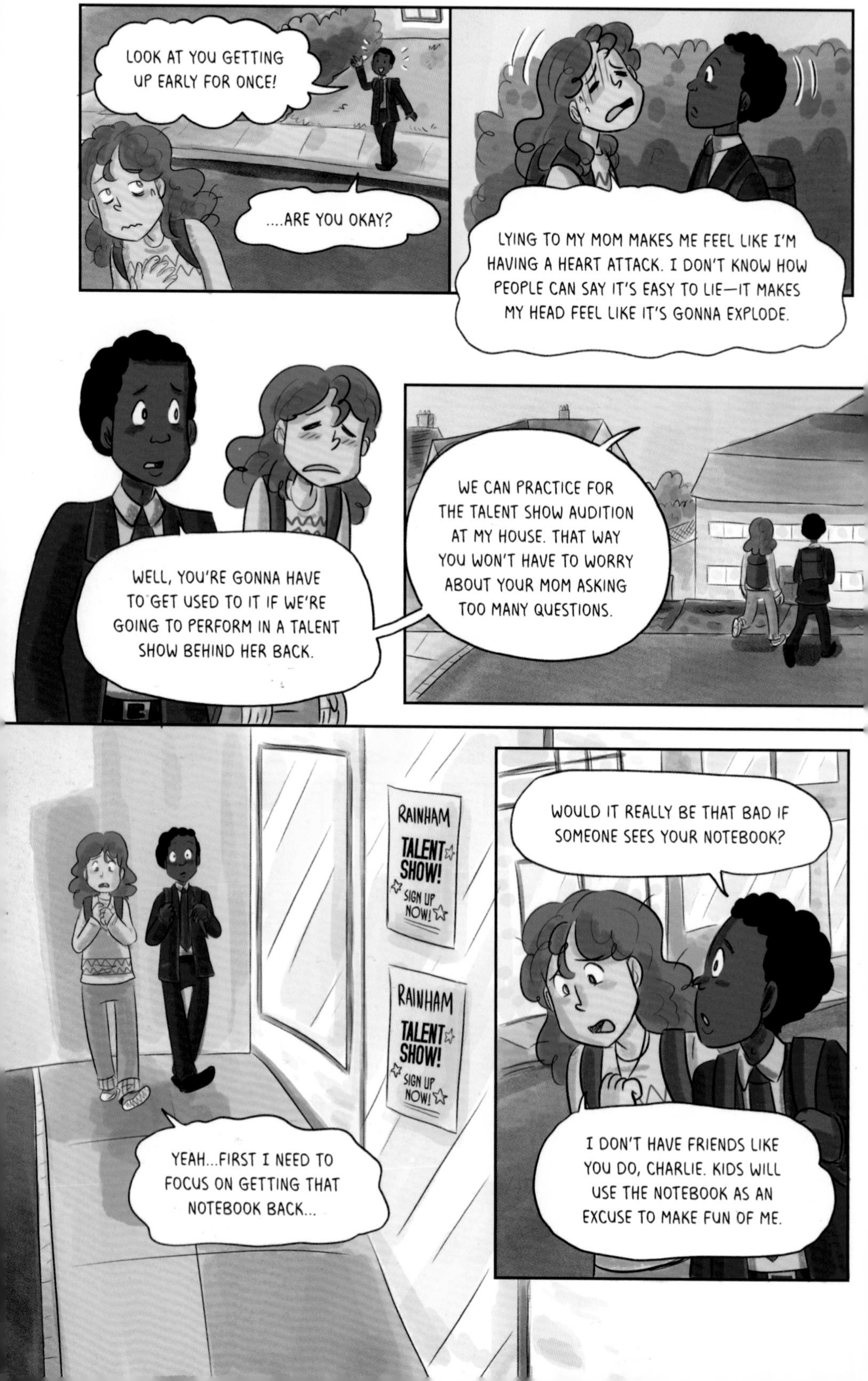
LOOK AT YOU GETTING UP EARLY FOR ONCE!
....ARE YOU OKAY?
LYING TO MY MOM MAKES ME FEEL LIKE I'M HAVING A HEART ATTACK. I DON'T KNOW HOW PEOPLE CAN SAY IT'S EASY TO LIE—IT MAKES MY HEAD FEEL LIKE IT'S GONNA EXPLODE.
WELL, YOU'RE GONNA HAVE TO GET USED TO IT IF WE'RE GOING TO PERFORM IN A TALENT SHOW BEHIND HER BACK.
WE CAN PRACTICE FOR THE TALENT SHOW AUDITION AT MY HOUSE. THAT WAY YOU WON'T HAVE TO WORRY ABOUT YOUR MOM ASKING TOO MANY QUESTIONS.
RAINHAM TALENT SHOW! SIGN UP NOW!
RAINHAM TALENT SHOW! SIGN UP NOW!
YEAH...FIRST I NEED TO FOCUS ON GETTING THAT NOTEBOOK BACK...
WOULD IT REALLY BE THAT BAD IF SOMEONE SEES YOUR NOTEBOOK?
I DON'T HAVE FRIENDS LIKE YOU DO, CHARLIE. KIDS WILL USE THE NOTEBOOK AS AN EXCUSE TO MAKE FUN OF ME.

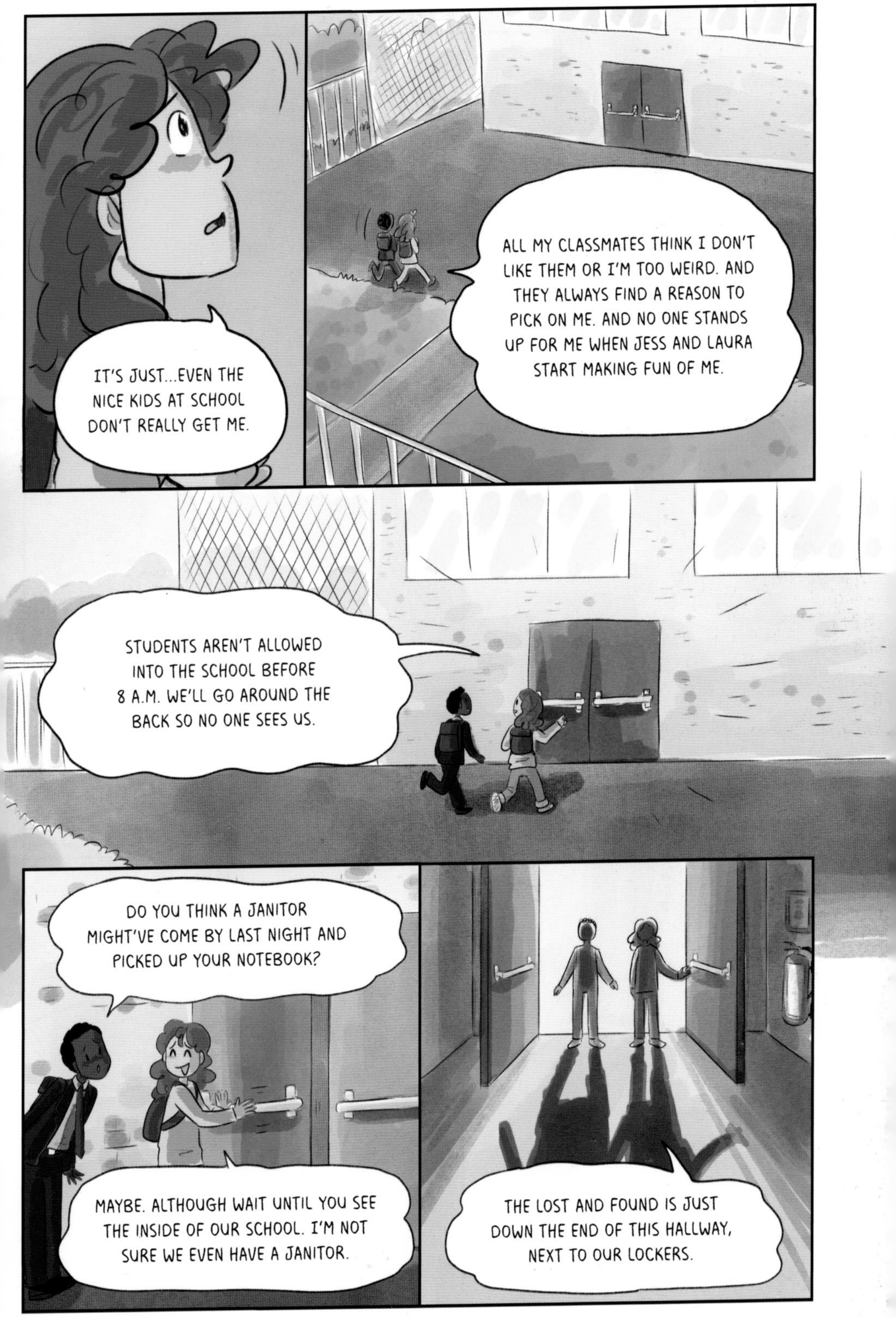
IT'S JUST...EVEN THE NICE KIDS AT SCHOOL DON'T REALLY GET ME.
ALL MY CLASSMATES THINK I DON'T LIKE THEM OR I'M TOO WEIRD. AND THEY ALWAYS FIND A REASON TO PICK ON ME. AND NO ONE STANDS UP FOR ME WHEN JESS AND LAURA START MAKING FUN OF ME.
STUDENTS AREN'T ALLOWED INTO THE SCHOOL BEFORE 8 A.M. WE'LL GO AROUND THE BACK SO NO ONE SEES US.
DO YOU THINK A JANITOR MIGHT'VE COME BY LAST NIGHT AND PICKED UP YOUR NOTEBOOK?
MAYBE. ALTHOUGH WAIT UNTIL YOU SEE THE INSIDE OF OUR SCHOOL. I'M NOT SURE WE EVEN HAVE A JANITOR.
THE LOST AND FOUND IS JUST DOWN THE END OF THIS HALLWAY, NEXT TO OUR LOCKERS.

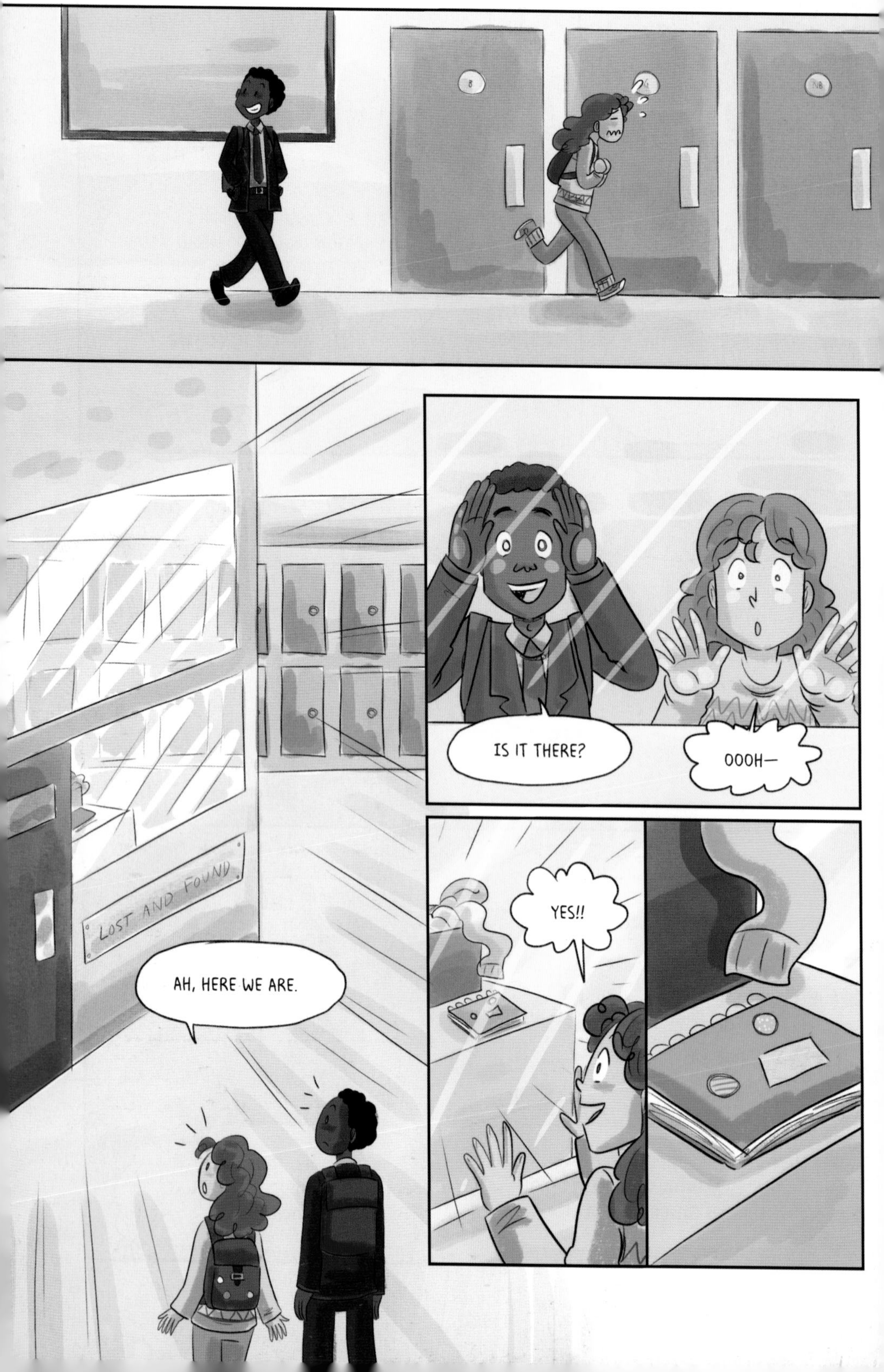
LOST AND FOUND
AH, HERE WE ARE.
IS IT THERE?
OOOH—
YES!!

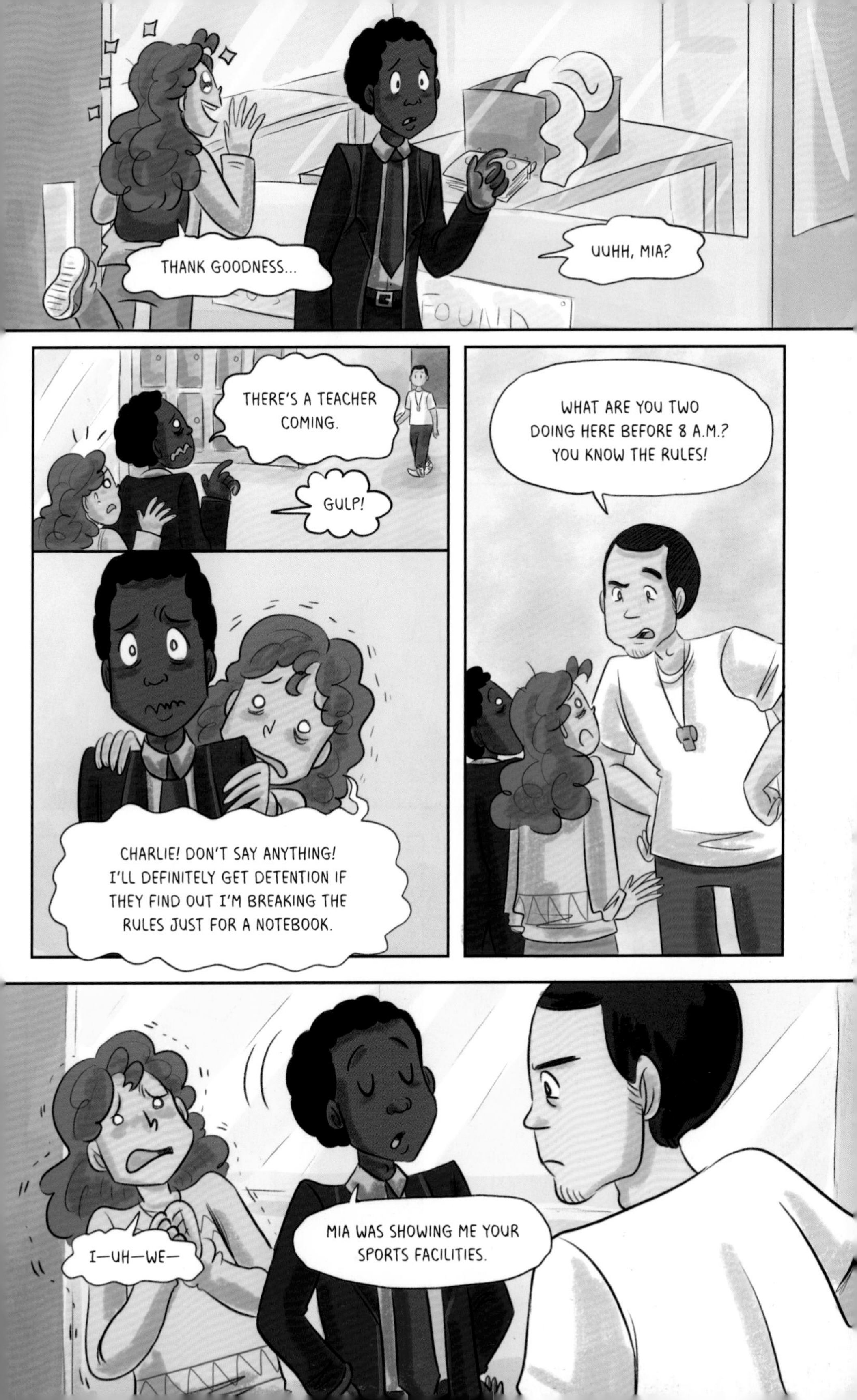
THANK GOODNESS...
UUHH, MIA?
THERE'S A TEACHER COMING.
GULP!
CHARLIE! DON'T SAY ANYTHING! I'LL DEFINITELY GET DETENTION IF THEY FIND OUT I'M BREAKING THE RULES JUST FOR A NOTEBOOK.
WHAT ARE YOU TWO DOING HERE BEFORE 8 A.M.? YOU KNOW THE RULES!
I—UH—WE—
MIA WAS SHOWING ME YOUR SPORTS FACILITIES.

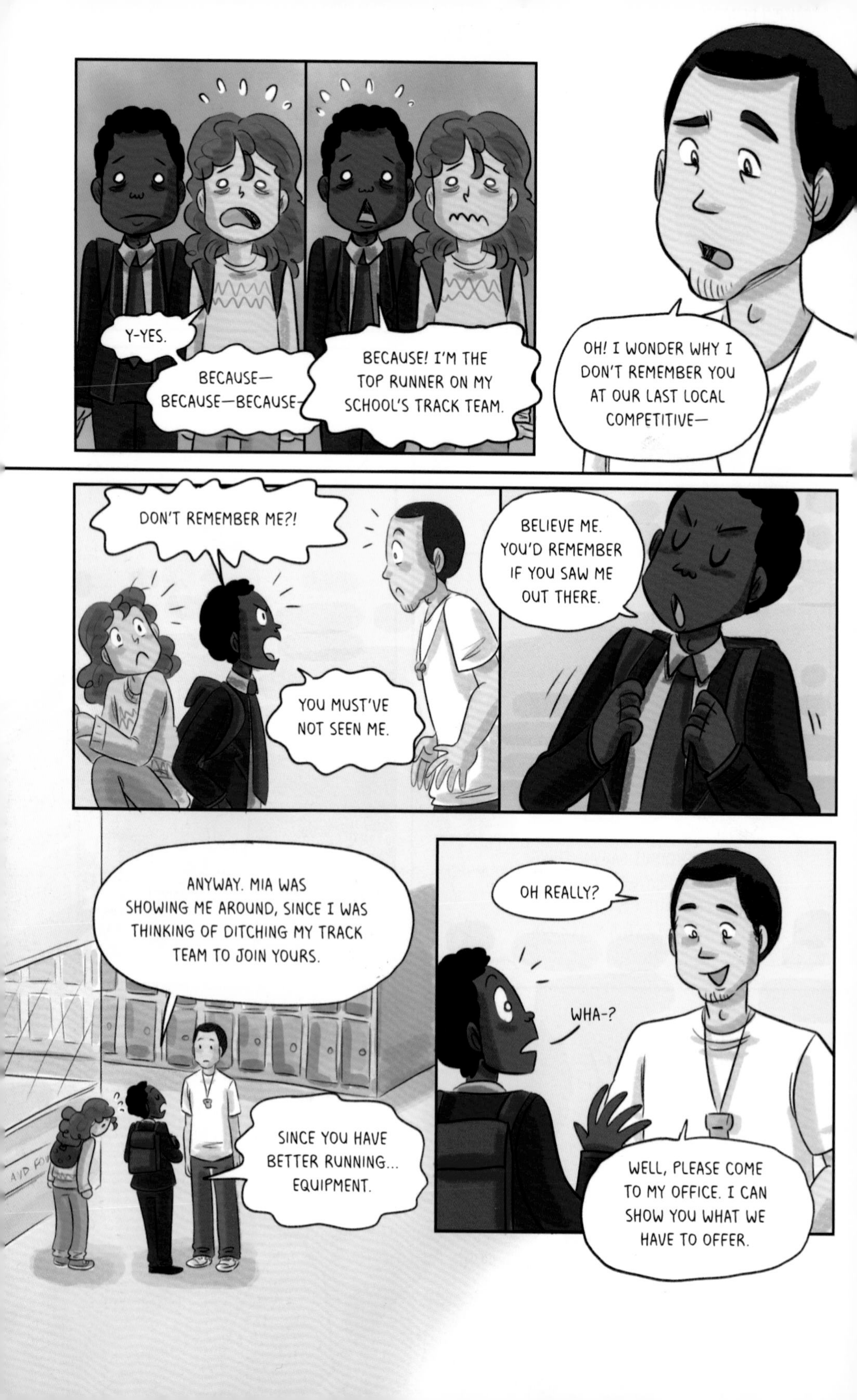
Y-YES.
BECAUSE—
BECAUSE—BECAUSE—
BECAUSE! I'M THE TOP RUNNER ON MY SCHOOL'S TRACK TEAM.
OH! I WONDER WHY I DON'T REMEMBER YOU AT OUR LAST LOCAL COMPETITIVE—
DON'T REMEMBER ME?!
YOU MUST'VE NOT SEEN ME.
BELIEVE ME. YOU'D REMEMBER IF YOU SAW ME OUT THERE.
ANYWAY. MIA WAS SHOWING ME AROUND, SINCE I WAS THINKING OF DITCHING MY TRACK TEAM TO JOIN YOURS.
SINCE YOU HAVE BETTER RUNNING... EQUIPMENT.
OH REALLY?
WHA-?
WELL, PLEASE COME TO MY OFFICE. I CAN SHOW YOU WHAT WE HAVE TO OFFER.

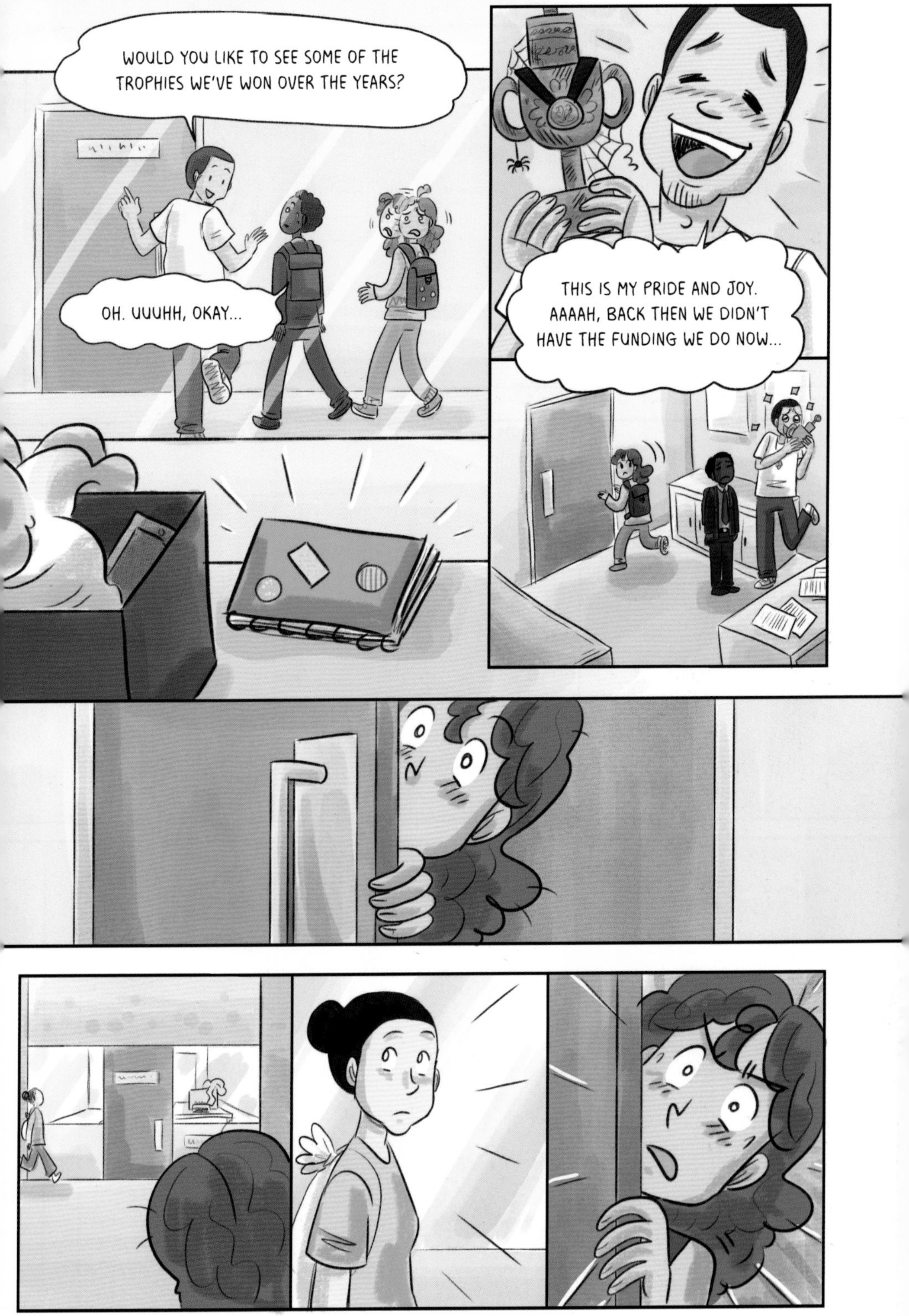
WOULD YOU LIKE TO SEE SOME OF THE TROPHIES WE'VE WON OVER THE YEARS?
OH. UUUHH, OKAY...
THIS IS MY PRIDE AND JOY. AAAAH, BACK THEN WE DIDN'T HAVE THE FUNDING WE DO NOW...

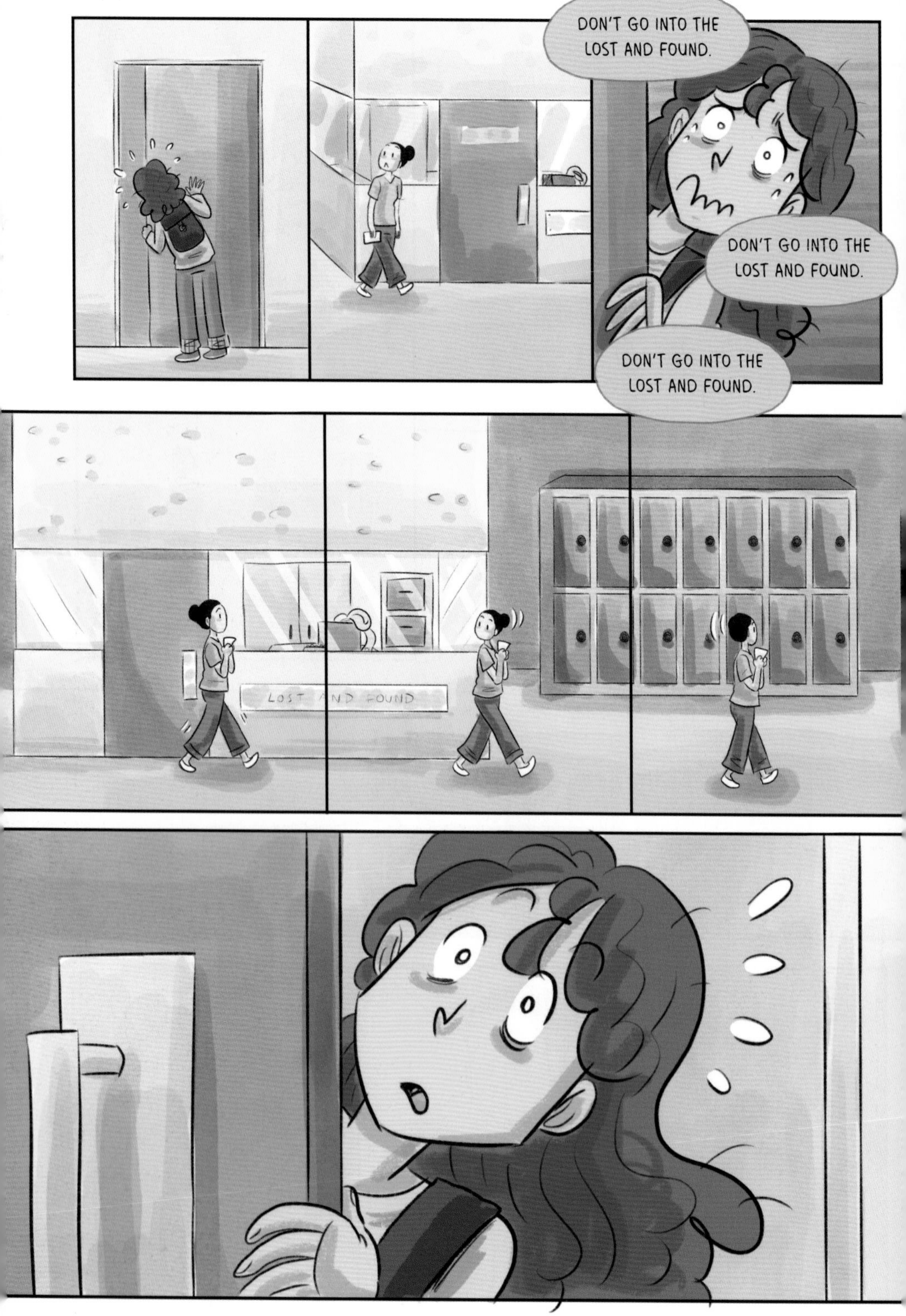
DON'T GO INTO THE LOST AND FOUND.
DON'T GO INTO THE LOST AND FOUND.
DON'T GO INTO THE LOST AND FOUND.
LOST AND FOUND

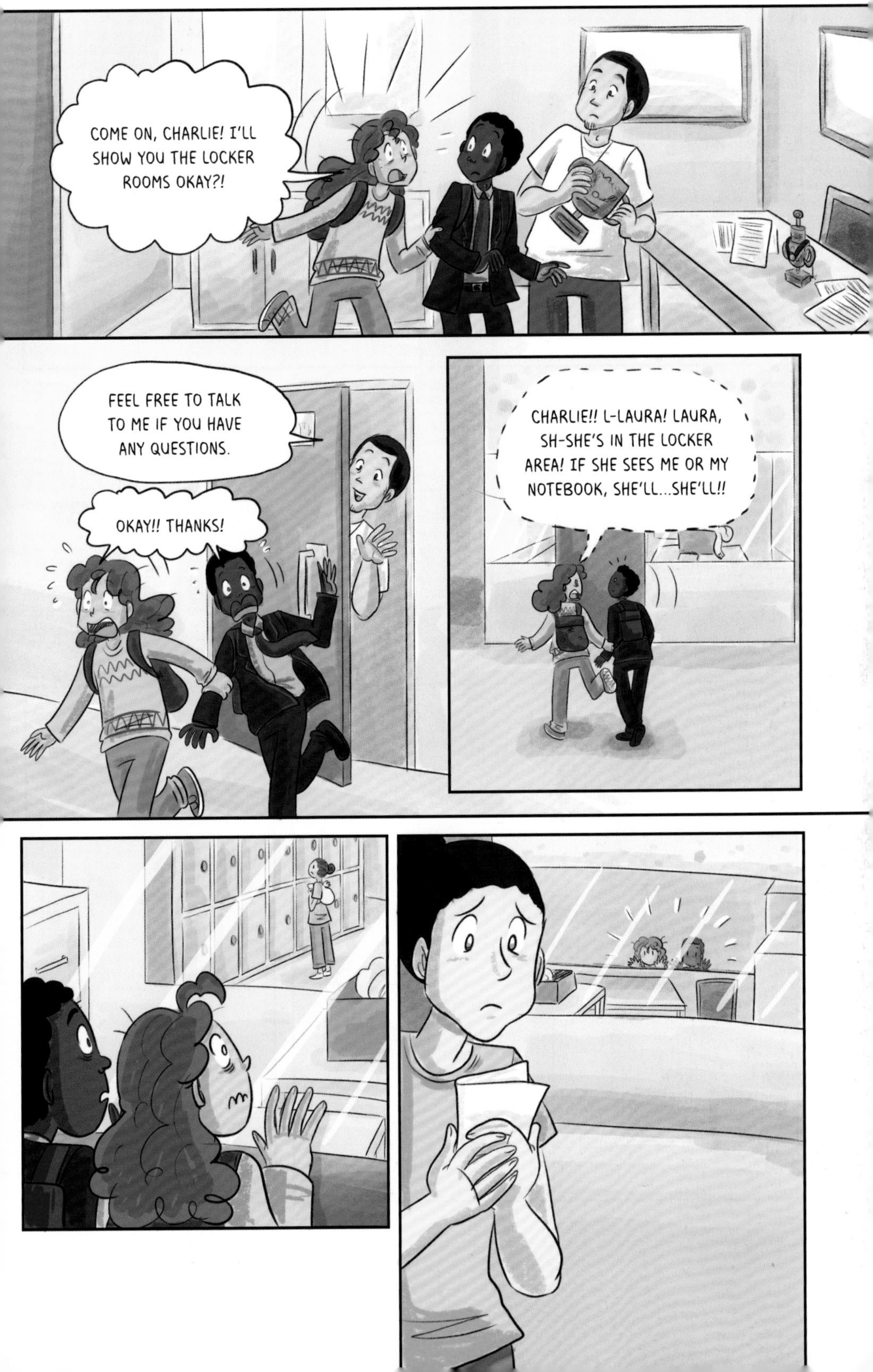
COME ON, CHARLIE! I'LL SHOW YOU THE LOCKER ROOMS OKAY?!
FEEL FREE TO TALK TO ME IF YOU HAVE ANY QUESTIONS.
OKAY!! THANKS!
CHARLIE!! L-LAURA! LAURA, SH-SHE'S IN THE LOCKER AREA! IF SHE SEES ME OR MY NOTEBOOK, SHE'LL...SHE'LL!!

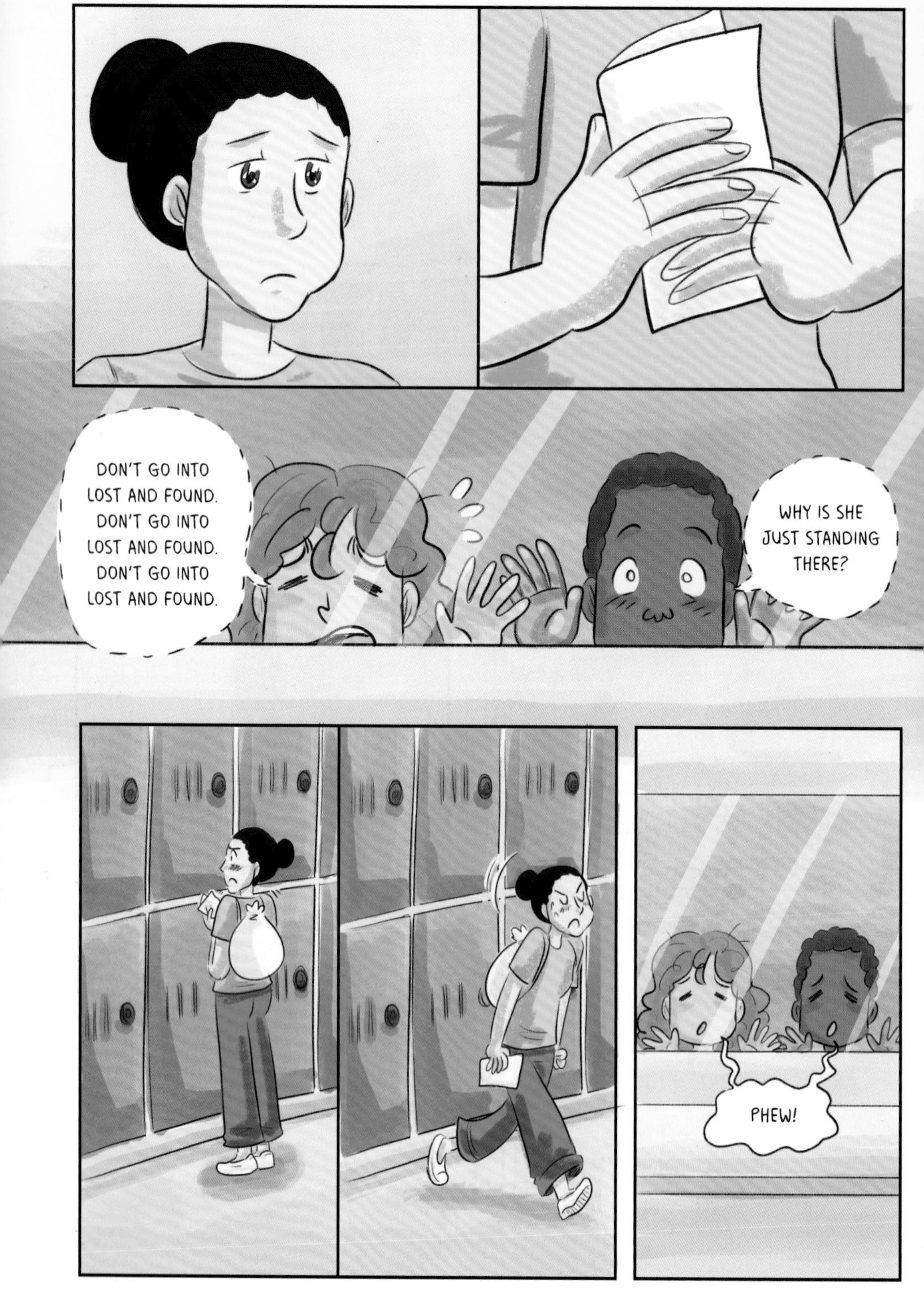
DON'T GO INTO LOST AND FOUND. DON'T GO INTO LOST AND FOUND. DON'T GO INTO LOST AND FOUND.
WHY IS SHE JUST STANDING THERE?
PHEW!

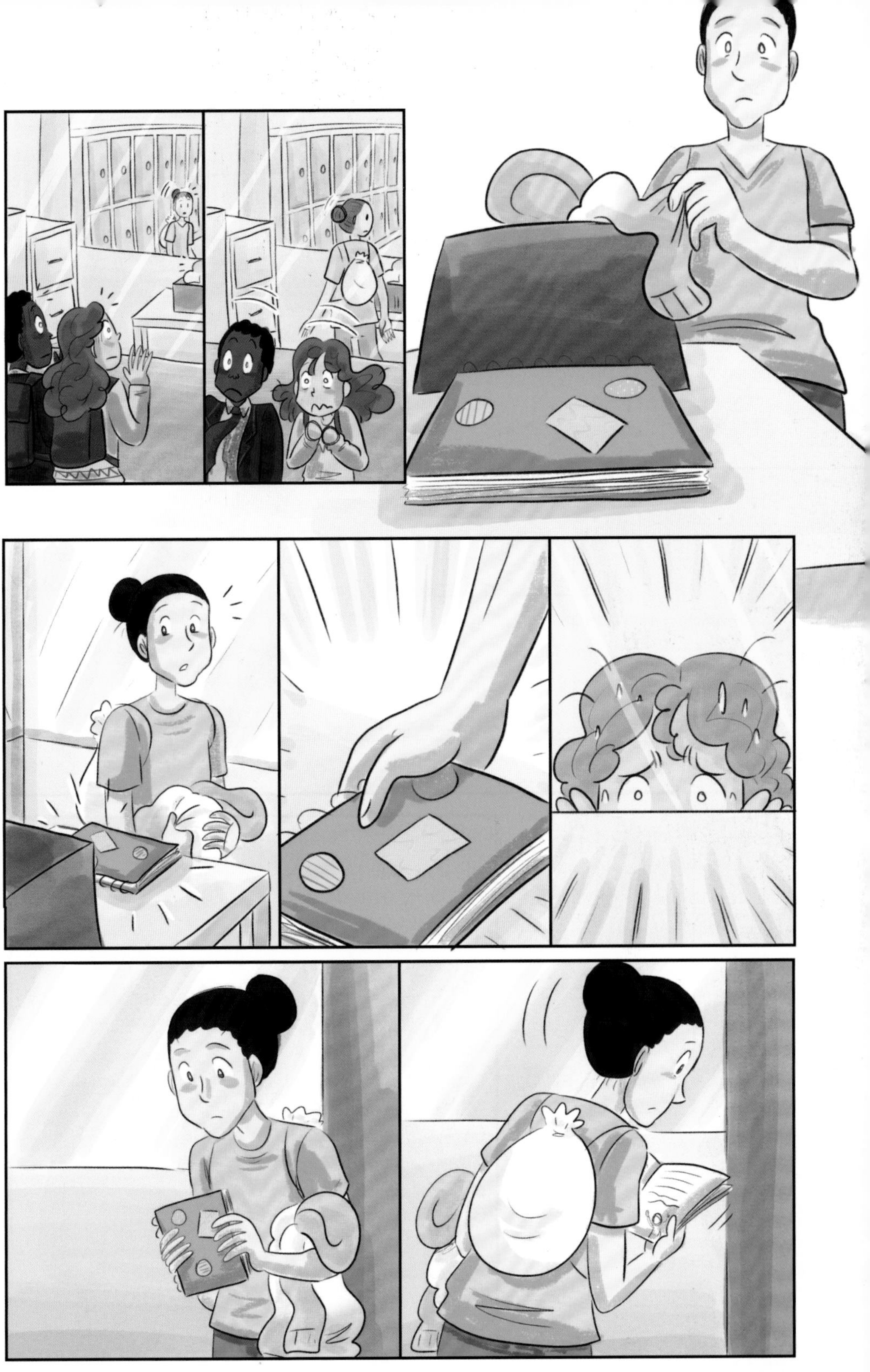

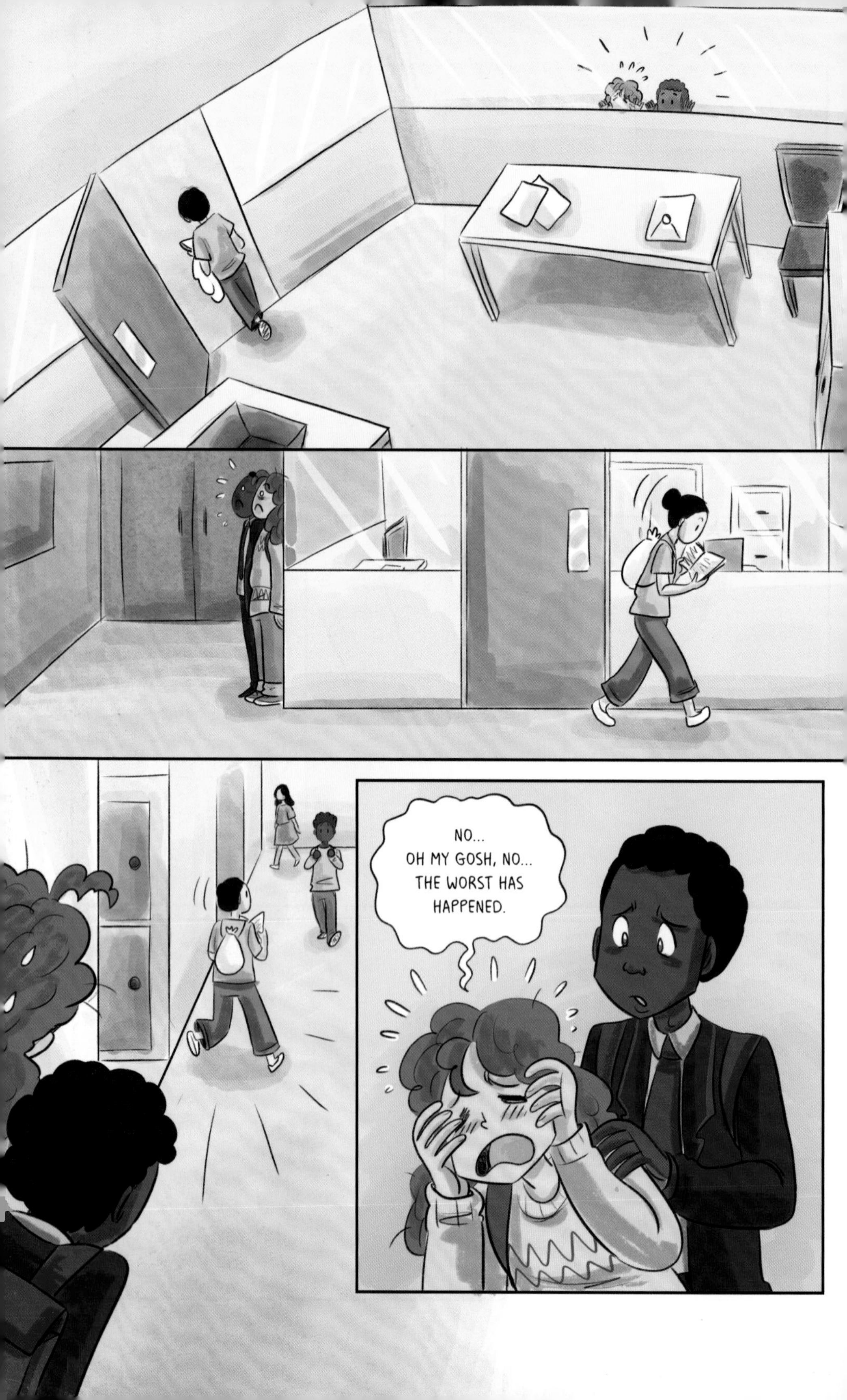
NO...
OH MY GOSH, NO...
THE WORST HAS
HAPPENED.

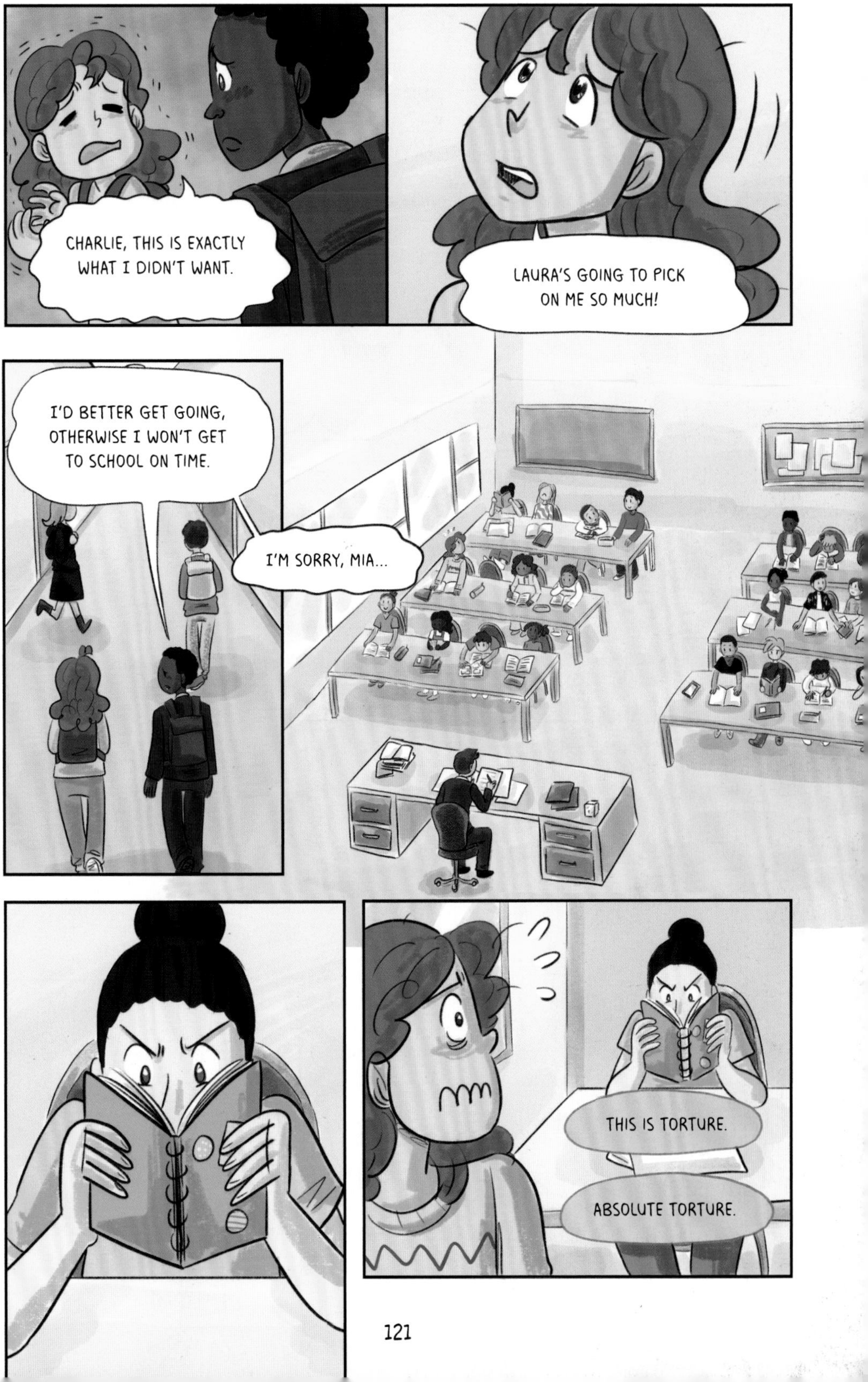
CHARLIE, THIS IS EXACTLY WHAT I DIDN'T WANT.
LAURA'S GOING TO PICK ON ME SO MUCH!
I'D BETTER GET GOING, OTHERWISE I WON'T GET TO SCHOOL ON TIME.
I'M SORRY, MIA...
THIS IS TORTURE.
ABSOLUTE TORTURE.

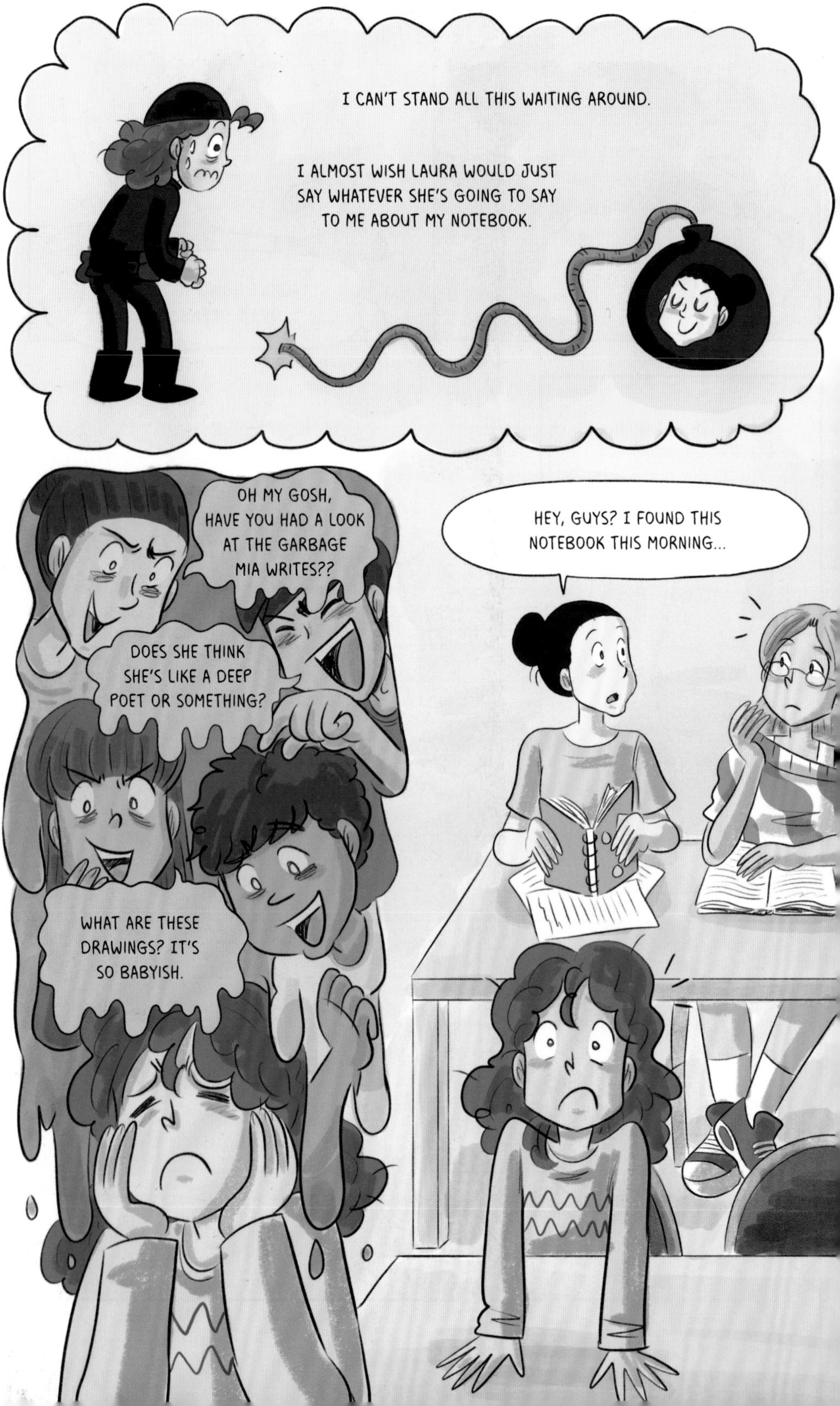
I CAN'T STAND ALL THIS WAITING AROUND.
I ALMOST WISH LAURA WOULD JUST SAY WHATEVER SHE'S GOING TO SAY TO ME ABOUT MY NOTEBOOK.
OH MY GOSH, HAVE YOU HAD A LOOK AT THE GARBAGE MIA WRITES??
DOES SHE THINK SHE'S LIKE A DEEP POET OR SOMETHING?
WHAT ARE THESE DRAWINGS? IT'S SO BABYISH.
HEY, GUYS? I FOUND THIS NOTEBOOK THIS MORNING...

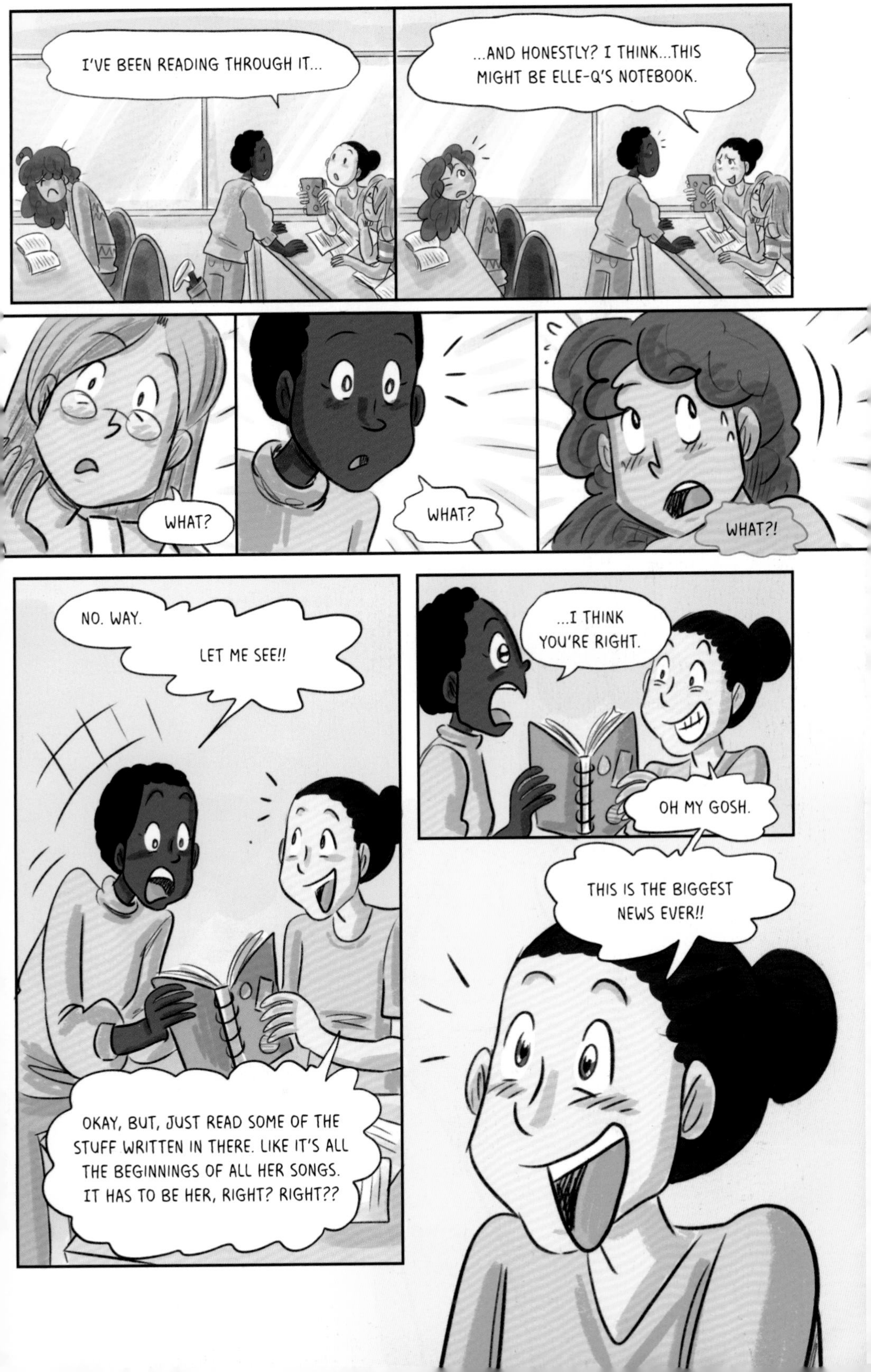
I'VE BEEN READING THROUGH IT...
...AND HONESTLY? I THINK...THIS MIGHT BE ELLE-Q'S NOTEBOOK.
WHAT?
WHAT?
WHAT?!
NO. WAY.
LET ME SEE!!
OKAY, BUT, JUST READ SOME OF THE STUFF WRITTEN IN THERE. LIKE IT'S ALL THE BEGINNINGS OF ALL HER SONGS. IT HAS TO BE HER, RIGHT? RIGHT??
...I THINK YOU'RE RIGHT.
OH MY GOSH.
THIS IS THE BIGGEST NEWS EVER!!

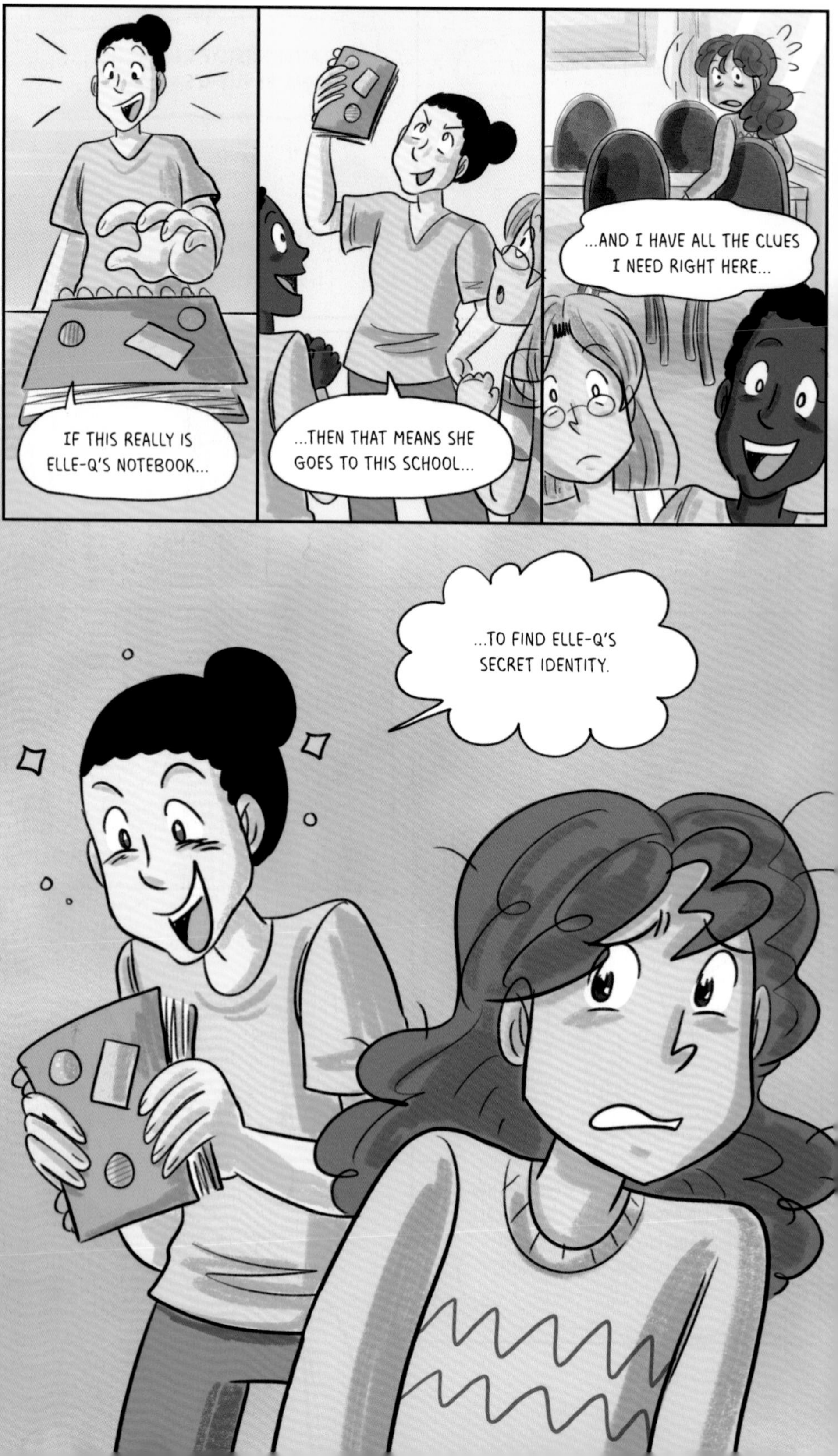
IF THIS REALLY IS ELLE-Q'S NOTEBOOK...
...THEN THAT MEANS SHE GOES TO THIS SCHOOL...
...AND I HAVE ALL THE CLUES I NEED RIGHT HERE...
...TO FIND ELLE-Q'S SECRET IDENTITY.

CHAPTER SIX

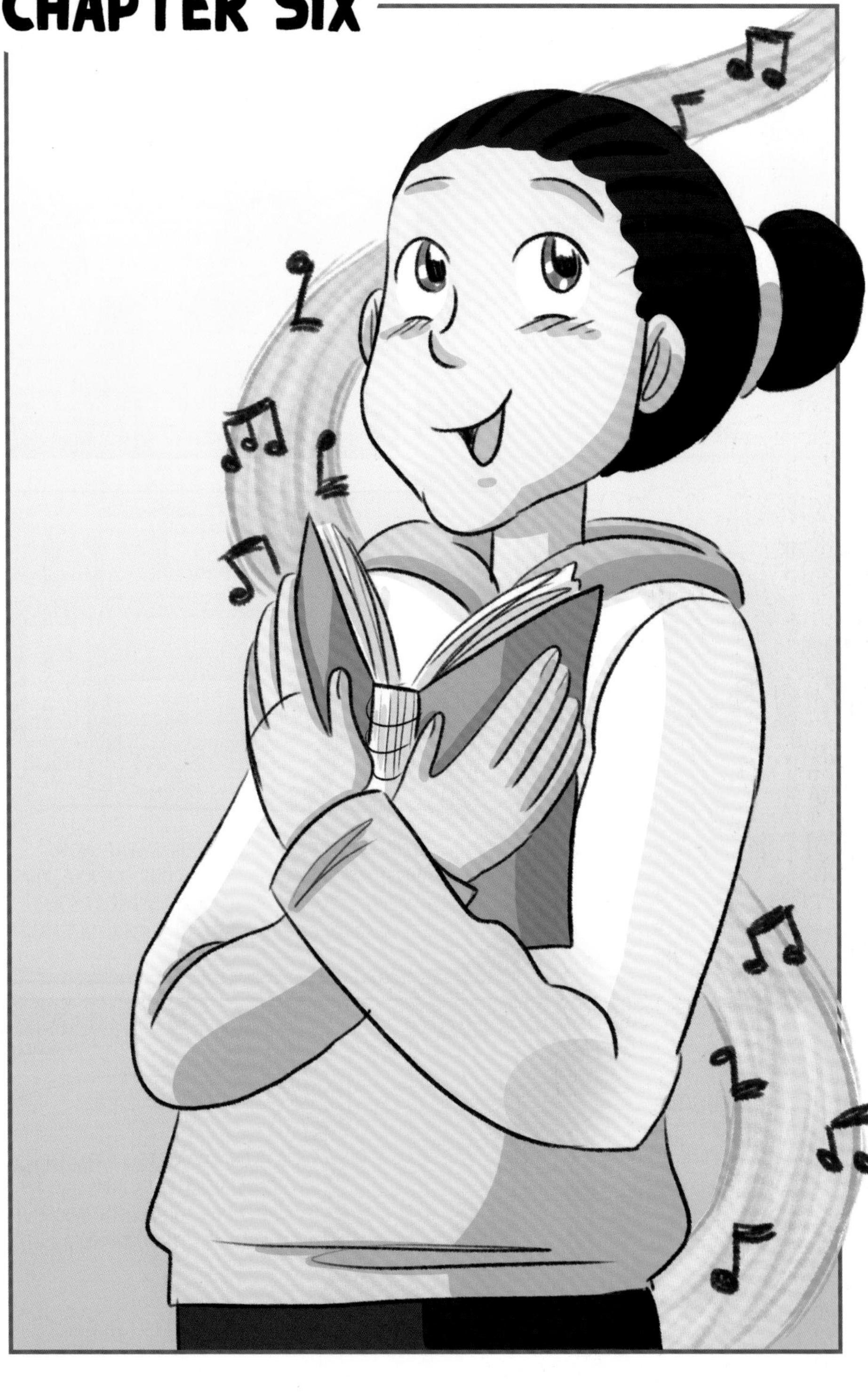

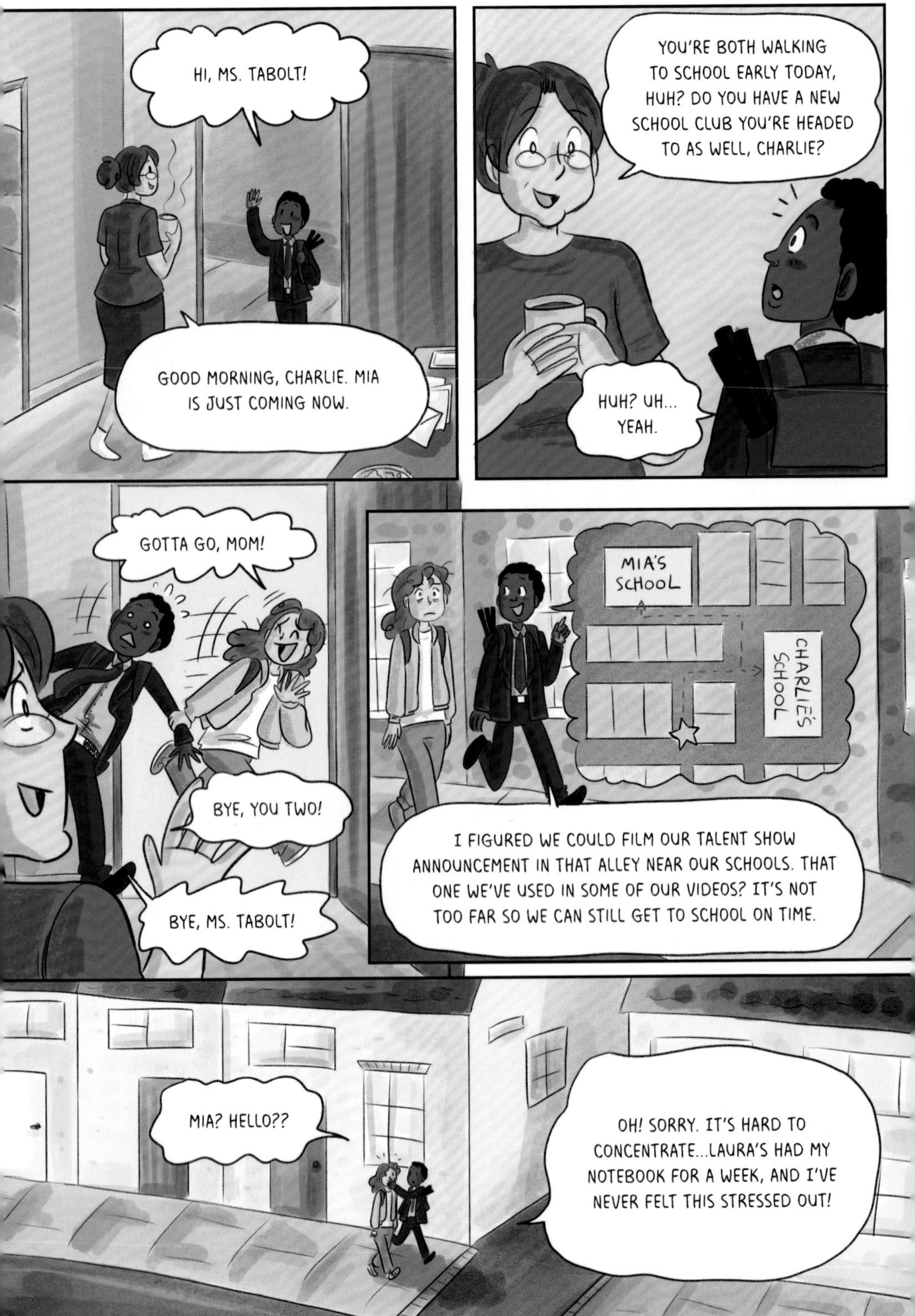
HI, MS. TABOLT!
GOOD MORNING, CHARLIE. MIA IS JUST COMING NOW.
YOU'RE BOTH WALKING TO SCHOOL EARLY TODAY, HUH? DO YOU HAVE A NEW SCHOOL CLUB YOU'RE HEADED TO AS WELL, CHARLIE?
HUH? UH... YEAH.
GOTTA GO, MOM!
BYE, YOU TWO!
BYE, MS. TABOLT!
MIA'S SCHOOL
CHARLIE'S SCHOOL
I FIGURED WE COULD FILM OUR TALENT SHOW ANNOUNCEMENT IN THAT ALLEY NEAR OUR SCHOOLS. THAT ONE WE'VE USED IN SOME OF OUR VIDEOS? IT'S NOT TOO FAR SO WE CAN STILL GET TO SCHOOL ON TIME.
MIA? HELLO??
OH! SORRY. IT'S HARD TO CONCENTRATE...LAURA'S HAD MY NOTEBOOK FOR A WEEK, AND I'VE NEVER FELT THIS STRESSED OUT!

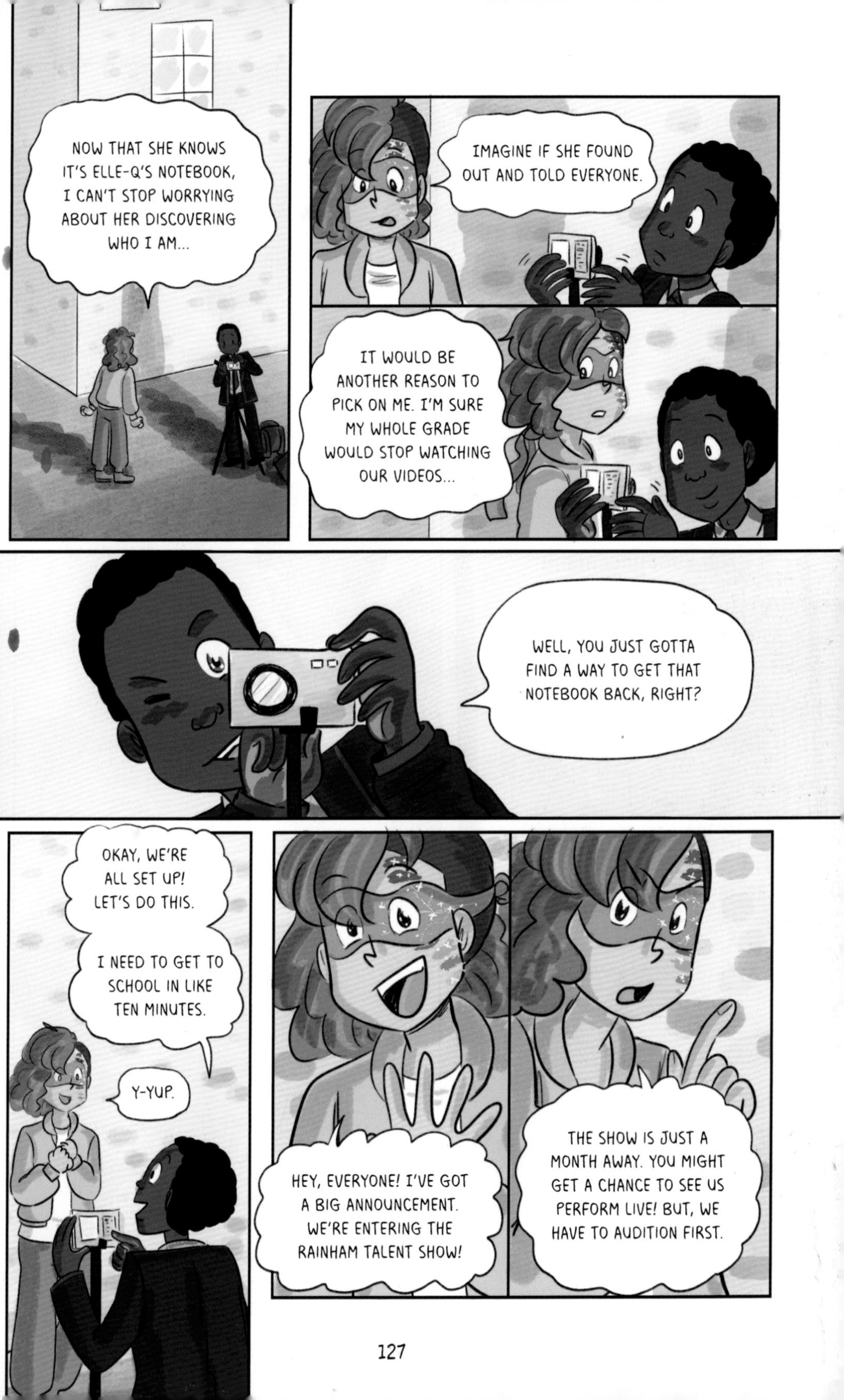
NOW THAT SHE KNOWS IT'S ELLE-Q'S NOTEBOOK, I CAN'T STOP WORRYING ABOUT HER DISCOVERING WHO I AM...
IMAGINE IF SHE FOUND OUT AND TOLD EVERYONE.
IT WOULD BE ANOTHER REASON TO PICK ON ME. I'M SURE MY WHOLE GRADE WOULD STOP WATCHING OUR VIDEOS...
WELL, YOU JUST GOTTA FIND A WAY TO GET THAT NOTEBOOK BACK, RIGHT?
OKAY, WE'RE ALL SET UP! LET'S DO THIS.
I NEED TO GET TO SCHOOL IN LIKE TEN MINUTES.
Y-YUP.
HEY, EVERYONE! I'VE GOT A BIG ANNOUNCEMENT. WE'RE ENTERING THE RAINHAM TALENT SHOW!
THE SHOW IS JUST A MONTH AWAY. YOU MIGHT GET A CHANCE TO SEE US PERFORM LIVE! BUT, WE HAVE TO AUDITION FIRST.

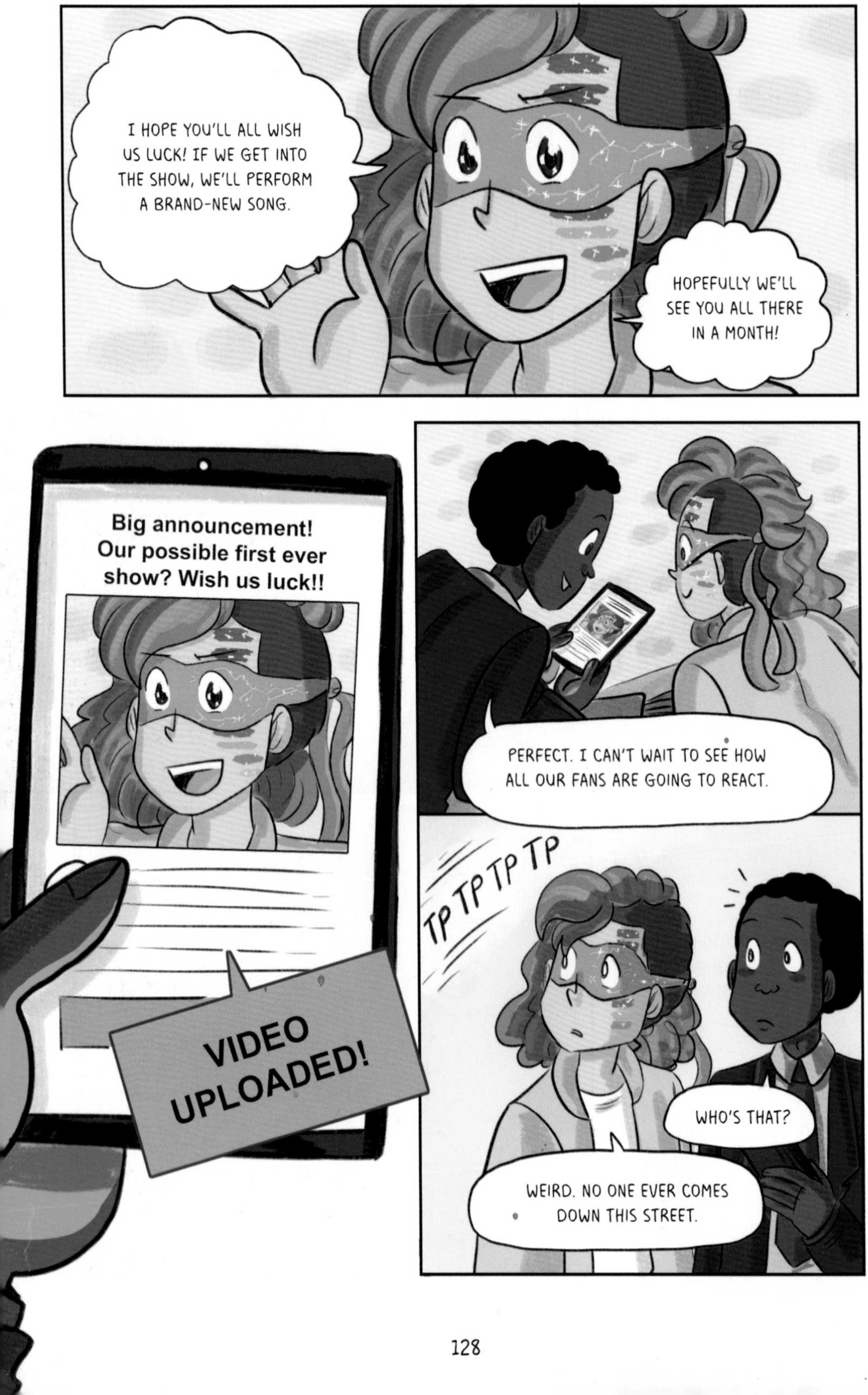

I HOPE YOU'LL ALL WISH US LUCK! IF WE GET INTO THE SHOW, WE'LL PERFORM A BRAND-NEW SONG.
HOPEFULLY WE'LL SEE YOU ALL THERE IN A MONTH!
Big announcement! Our possible first ever show? Wish us luck!!
VIDEO UPLOADED!
PERFECT. I CAN'T WAIT TO SEE HOW ALL OUR FANS ARE GOING TO REACT.
TP TP TP TP
WHO'S THAT?
WEIRD. NO ONE EVER COMES DOWN THIS STREET.

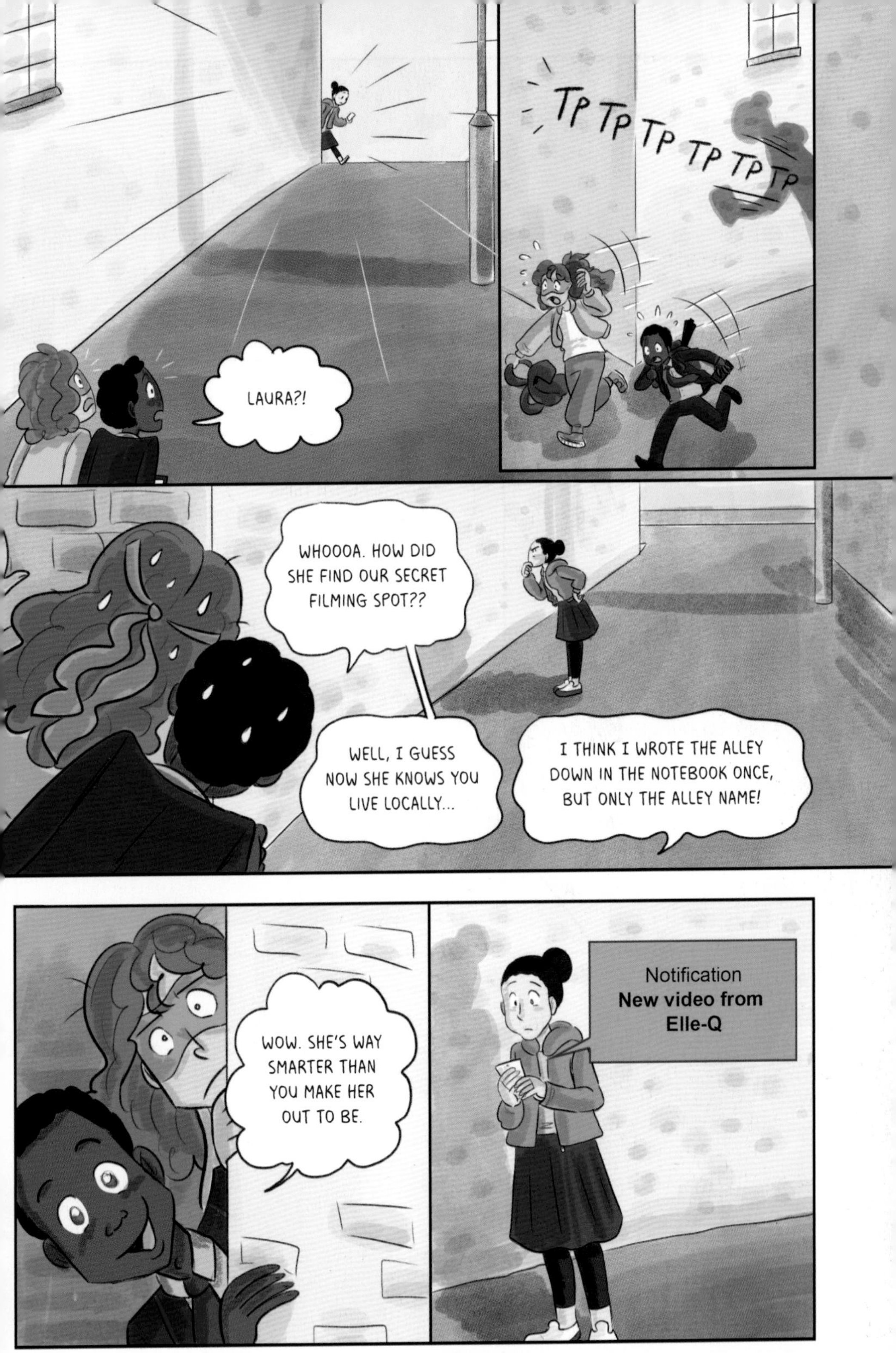
LAURA?!
TP TP TP TP TP TP
WHOOOA. HOW DID SHE FIND OUR SECRET FILMING SPOT??
WELL, I GUESS NOW SHE KNOWS YOU LIVE LOCALLY...
I THINK I WROTE THE ALLEY DOWN IN THE NOTEBOOK ONCE, BUT ONLY THE ALLEY NAME!
WOW. SHE'S WAY SMARTER THAN YOU MAKE HER OUT TO BE.
Notification
New video from Elle-Q

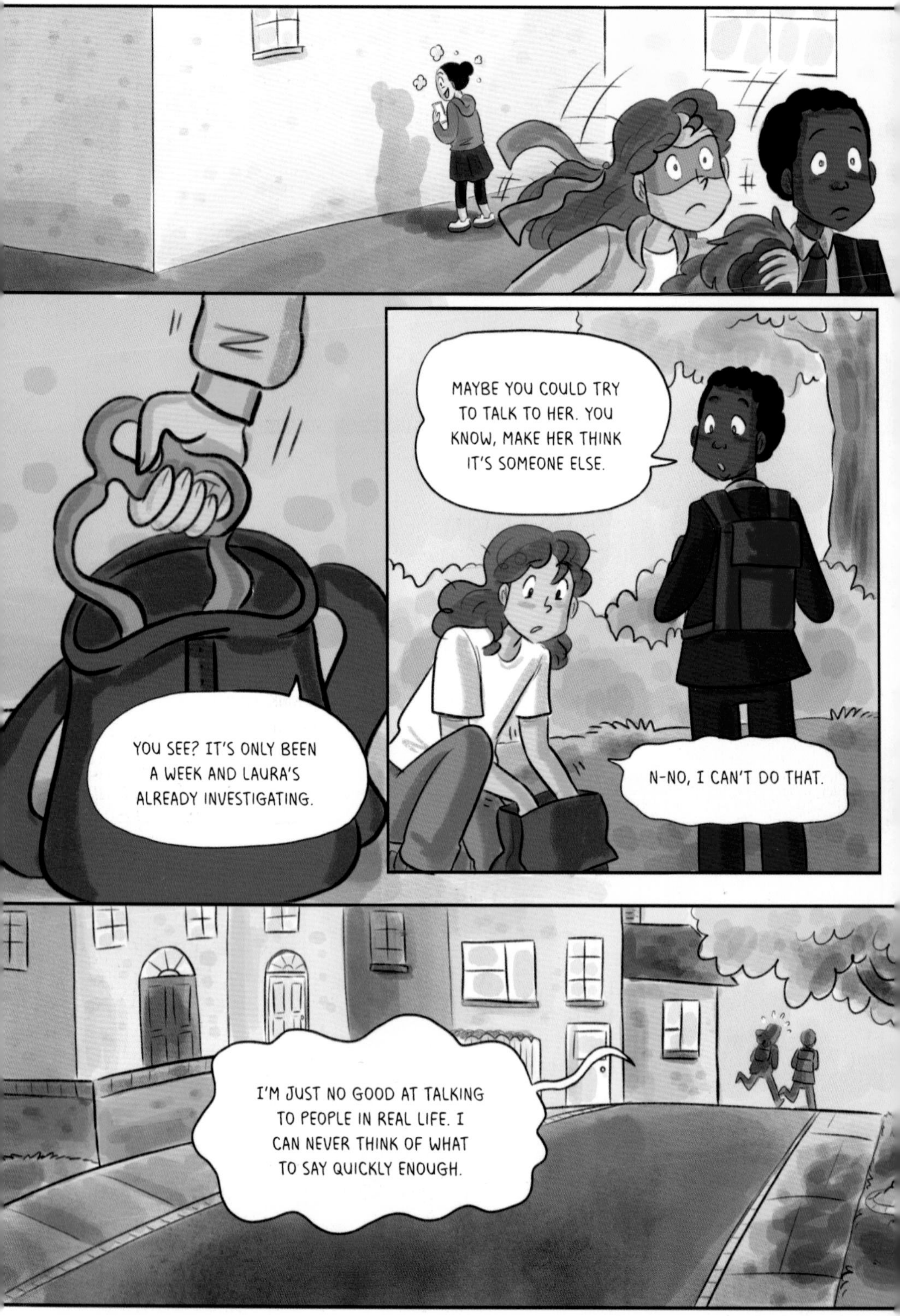
YOU SEE? IT'S ONLY BEEN A WEEK AND LAURA'S ALREADY INVESTIGATING.
MAYBE YOU COULD TRY TO TALK TO HER. YOU KNOW, MAKE HER THINK IT'S SOMEONE ELSE.
N-NO, I CAN'T DO THAT.
I'M JUST NO GOOD AT TALKING TO PEOPLE IN REAL LIFE. I CAN NEVER THINK OF WHAT TO SAY QUICKLY ENOUGH.

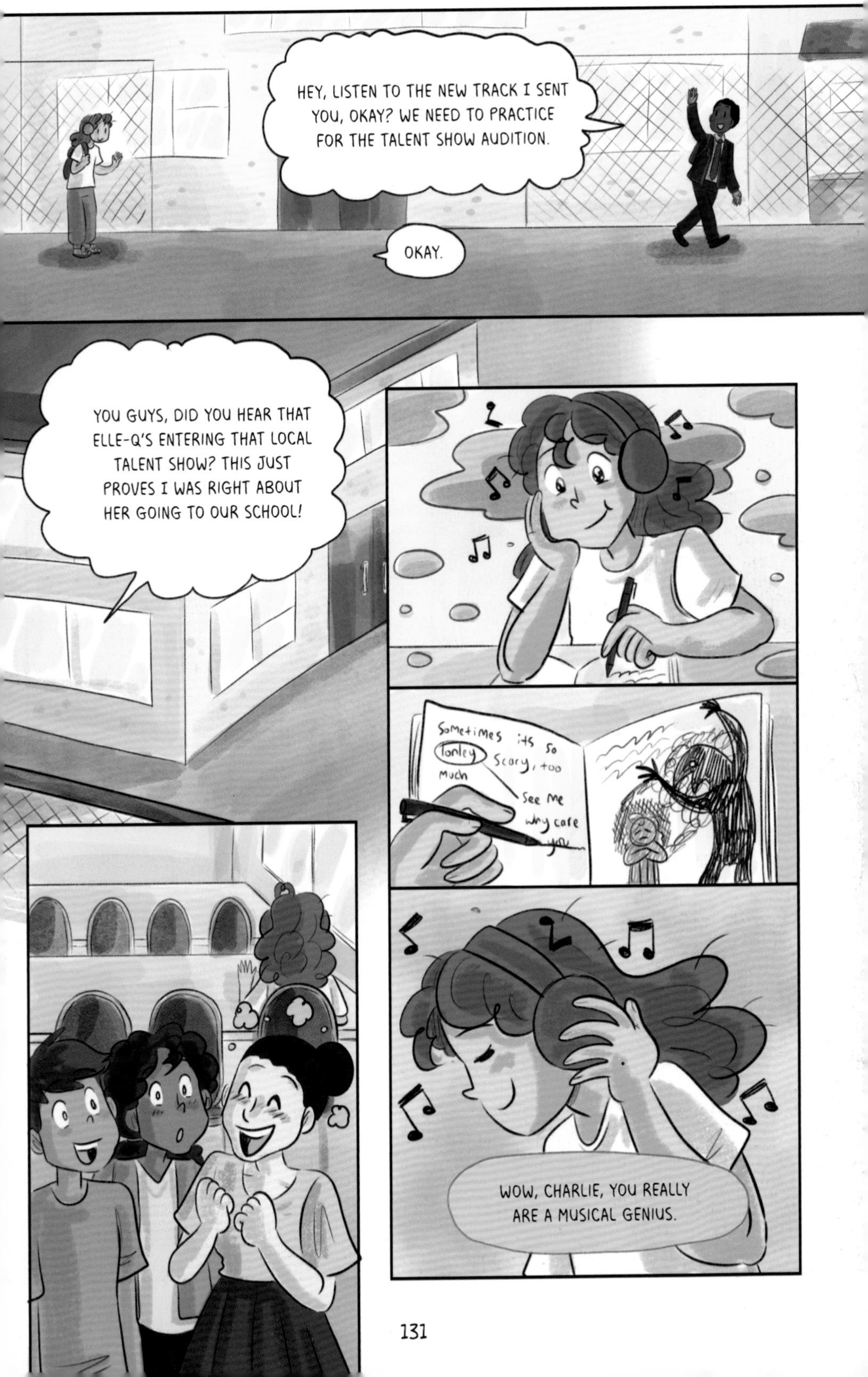
HEY, LISTEN TO THE NEW TRACK I SENT YOU, OKAY? WE NEED TO PRACTICE FOR THE TALENT SHOW AUDITION.
OKAY.
YOU GUYS, DID YOU HEAR THAT ELLE-Q'S ENTERING THAT LOCAL TALENT SHOW? THIS JUST PROVES I WAS RIGHT ABOUT HER GOING TO OUR SCHOOL!
Sometimes its so
Tonley Scary, too
Much
See me
why care
WOW, CHARLIE, YOU REALLY ARE A MUSICAL GENIUS.

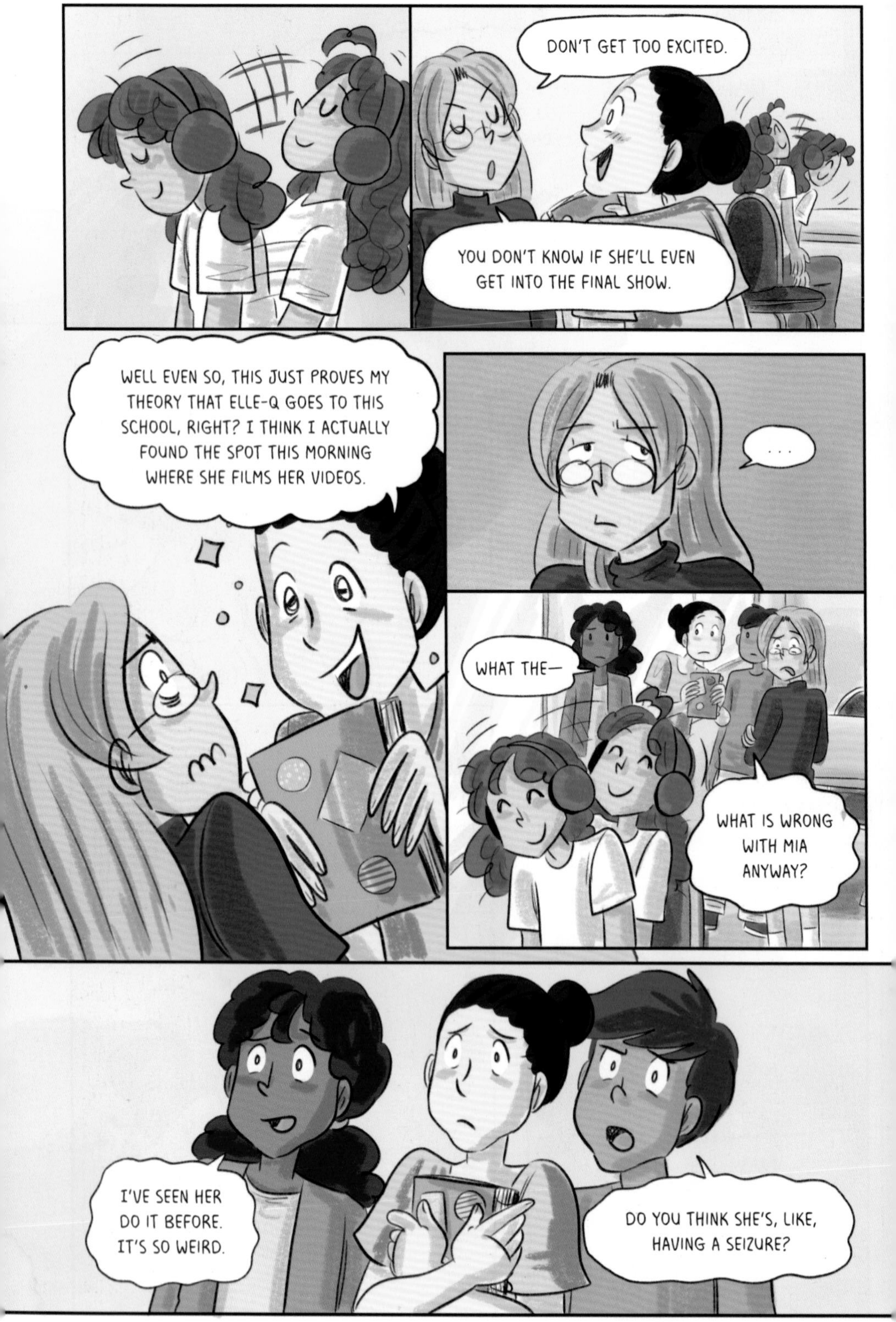
DON'T GET TOO EXCITED.
YOU DON'T KNOW IF SHE'LL EVEN GET INTO THE FINAL SHOW.
WELL EVEN SO, THIS JUST PROVES MY THEORY THAT ELLE-Q GOES TO THIS SCHOOL, RIGHT? I THINK I ACTUALLY FOUND THE SPOT THIS MORNING WHERE SHE FILMS HER VIDEOS.
. . .
WHAT THE—
WHAT IS WRONG WITH MIA ANYWAY?
I'VE SEEN HER DO IT BEFORE. IT'S SO WEIRD.
DO YOU THINK SHE'S, LIKE, HAVING A SEIZURE?

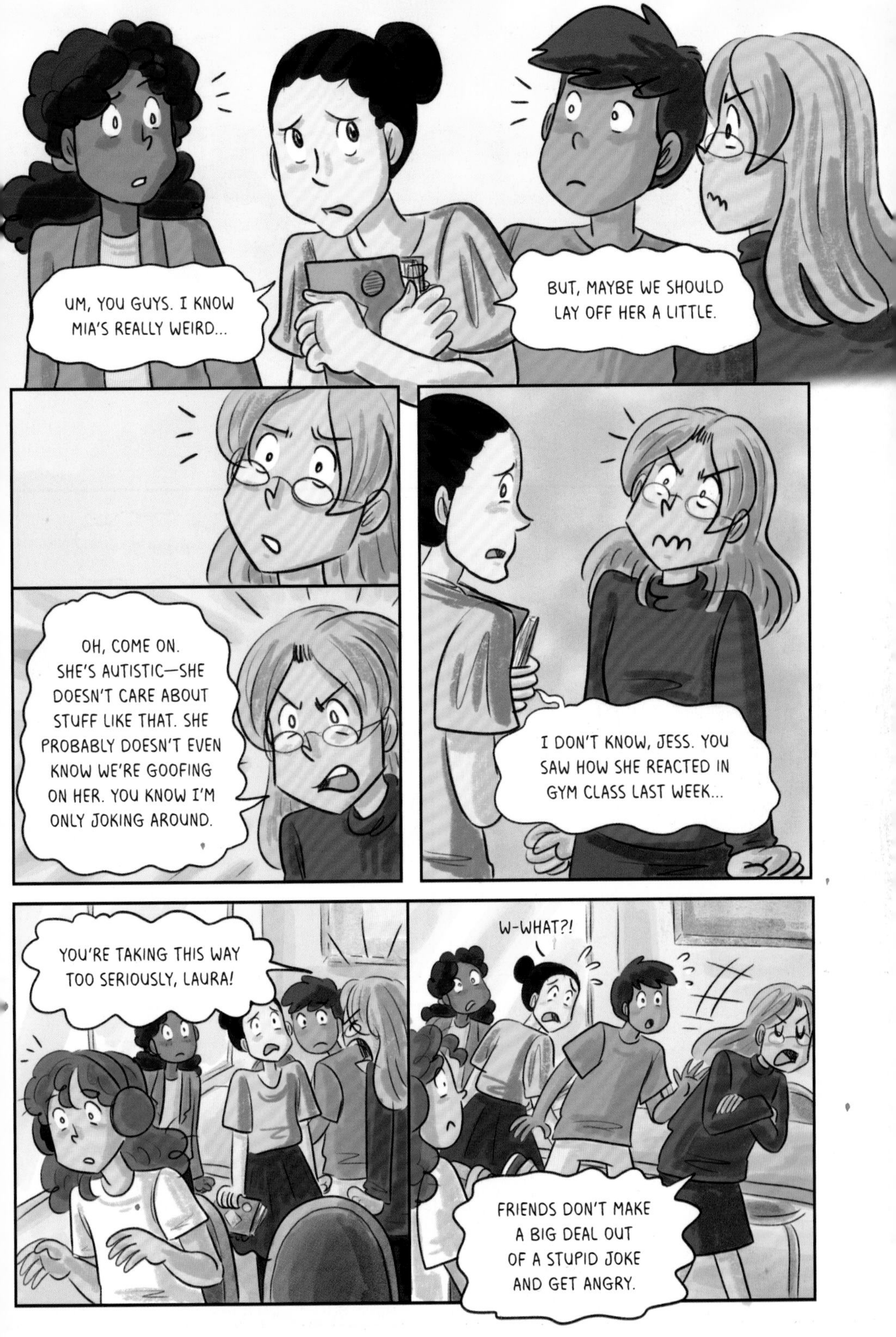
UM, YOU GUYS. I KNOW MIA'S REALLY WEIRD...
BUT, MAYBE WE SHOULD LAY OFF HER A LITTLE.
OH, COME ON. SHE'S AUTISTIC—SHE DOESN'T CARE ABOUT STUFF LIKE THAT. SHE PROBABLY DOESN'T EVEN KNOW WE'RE GOOFING ON HER. YOU KNOW I'M ONLY JOKING AROUND.
I DON'T KNOW, JESS. YOU SAW HOW SHE REACTED IN GYM CLASS LAST WEEK...
YOU'RE TAKING THIS WAY TOO SERIOUSLY, LAURA!
W-WHAT?!
FRIENDS DON'T MAKE A BIG DEAL OUT OF A STUPID JOKE AND GET ANGRY.

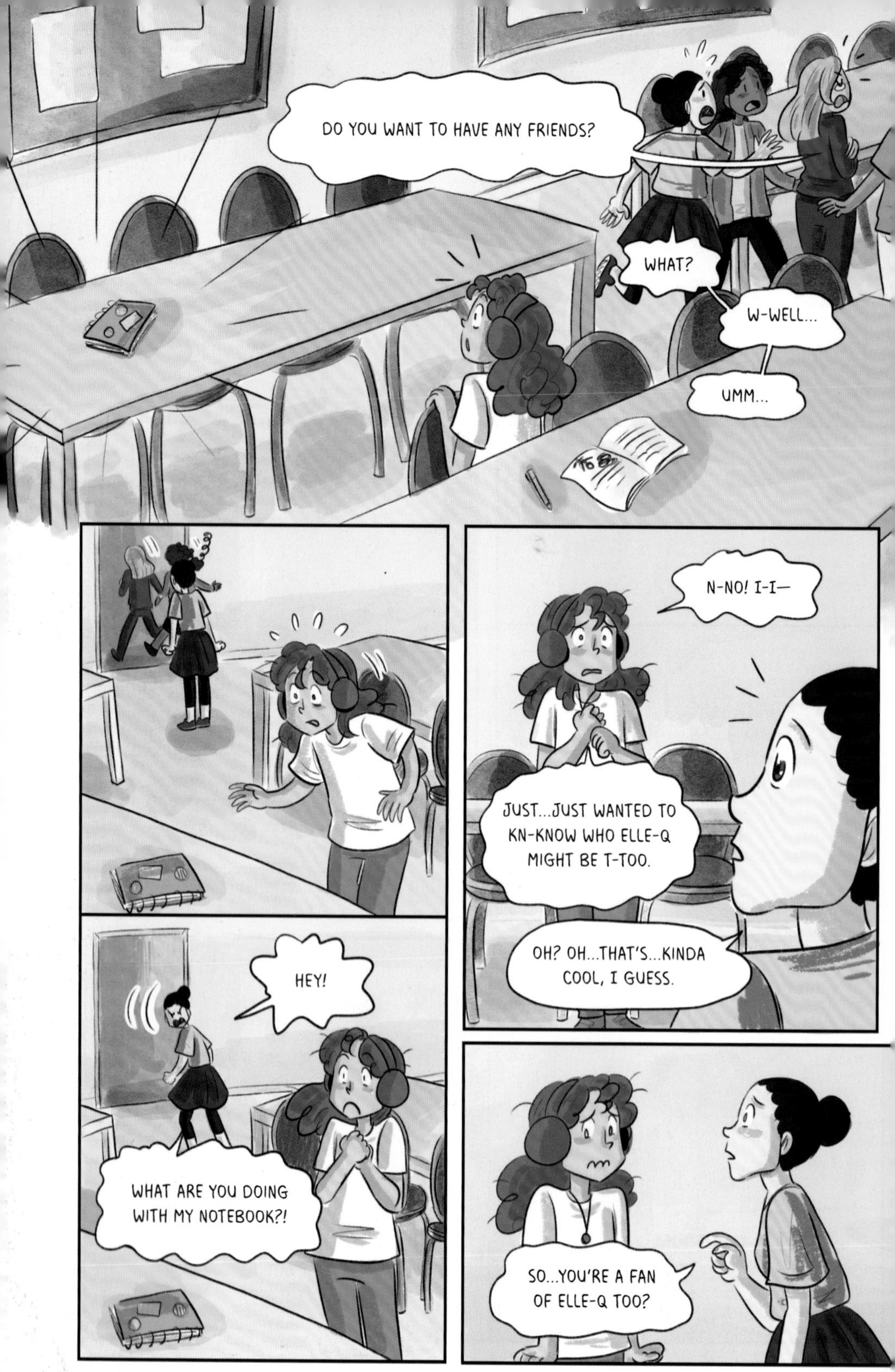

DO YOU WANT TO HAVE ANY FRIENDS?
WHAT?
W-WELL...
UMM...
N-NO! I-I—
JUST...JUST WANTED TO KN-KNOW WHO ELLE-Q MIGHT BE T-TOO.
OH? OH...THAT'S...KINDA COOL, I GUESS.
HEY!
WHAT ARE YOU DOING WITH MY NOTEBOOK?!
SO...YOU'RE A FAN OF ELLE-Q TOO?

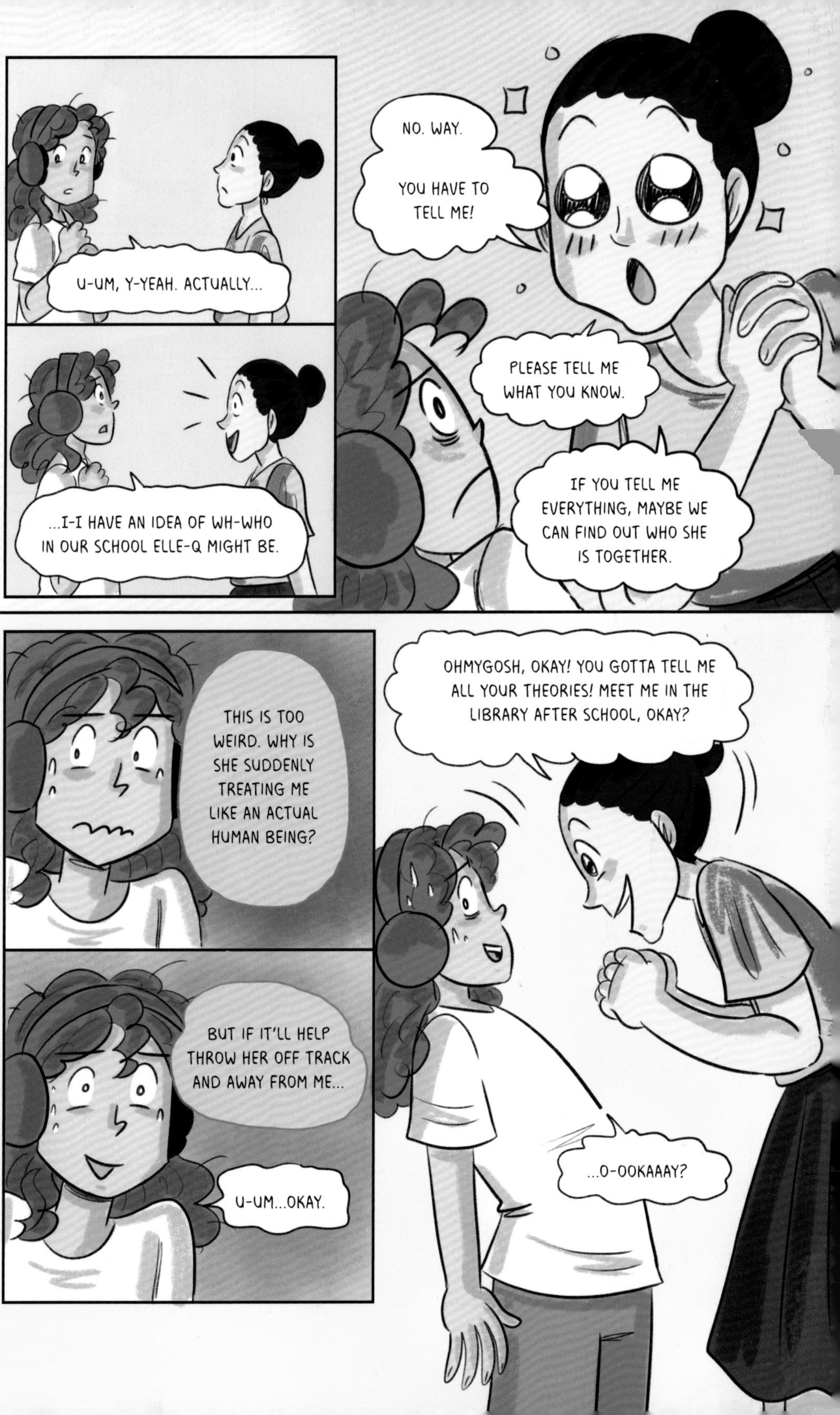
U-UM, Y-YEAH. ACTUALLY...
...I-I HAVE AN IDEA OF WH-WHO IN OUR SCHOOL ELLE-Q MIGHT BE.
NO. WAY.
YOU HAVE TO TELL ME!
PLEASE TELL ME WHAT YOU KNOW.
IF YOU TELL ME EVERYTHING, MAYBE WE CAN FIND OUT WHO SHE IS TOGETHER.
THIS IS TOO WEIRD. WHY IS SHE SUDDENLY TREATING ME LIKE AN ACTUAL HUMAN BEING?
BUT IF IT'LL HELP THROW HER OFF TRACK AND AWAY FROM ME...
U-UM...OKAY.
OHMYGOSH, OKAY! YOU GOTTA TELL ME ALL YOUR THEORIES! MEET ME IN THE LIBRARY AFTER SCHOOL, OKAY?
...O-OOKAAAY?

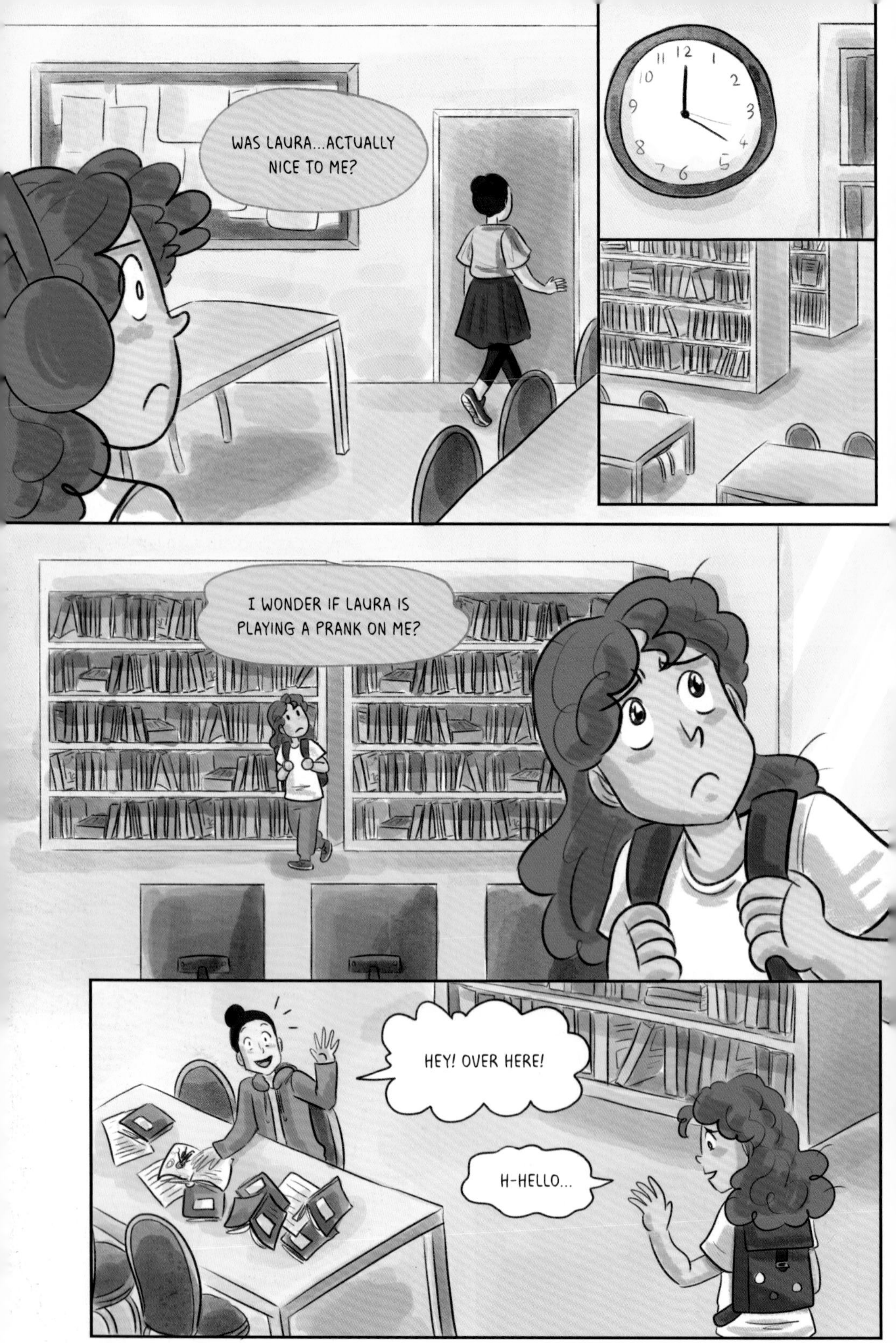
WAS LAURA...ACTUALLY NICE TO ME?
I WONDER IF LAURA IS PLAYING A PRANK ON ME?
HEY! OVER HERE!
H-HELLO...

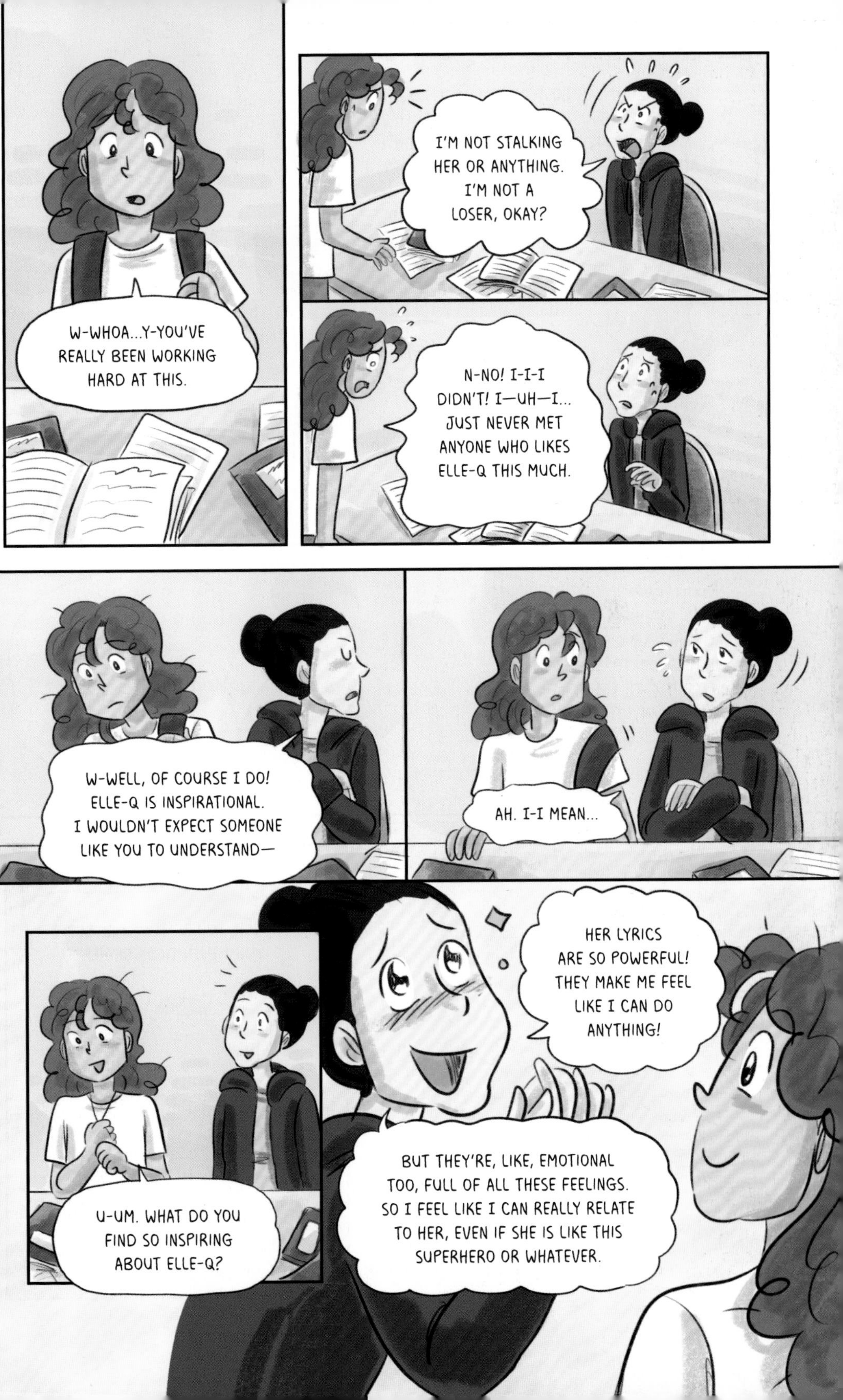
W-WHOA...Y-YOU'VE REALLY BEEN WORKING HARD AT THIS.
I'M NOT STALKING HER OR ANYTHING. I'M NOT A LOSER, OKAY?
N-NO! I-I-I DIDN'T! I—UH—I... JUST NEVER MET ANYONE WHO LIKES ELLE-Q THIS MUCH.
W-WELL, OF COURSE I DO! ELLE-Q IS INSPIRATIONAL. I WOULDN'T EXPECT SOMEONE LIKE YOU TO UNDERSTAND—
AH. I-I MEAN...
U-UM. WHAT DO YOU FIND SO INSPIRING ABOUT ELLE-Q?
HER LYRICS ARE SO POWERFUL! THEY MAKE ME FEEL LIKE I CAN DO ANYTHING!
BUT THEY'RE, LIKE, EMOTIONAL TOO, FULL OF ALL THESE FEELINGS. SO I FEEL LIKE I CAN REALLY RELATE TO HER, EVEN IF SHE IS LIKE THIS SUPERHERO OR WHATEVER.

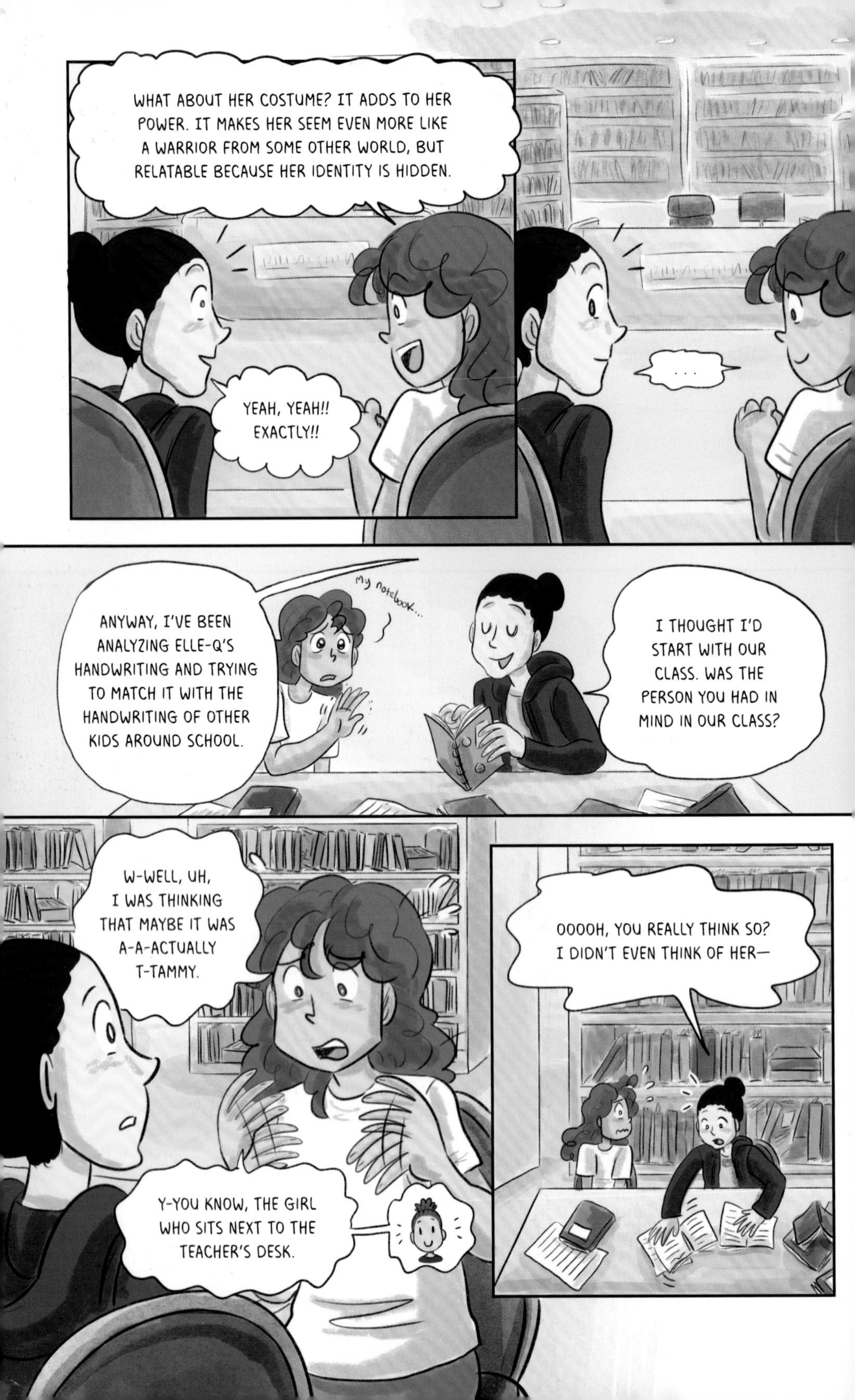
WHAT ABOUT HER COSTUME? IT ADDS TO HER POWER. IT MAKES HER SEEM EVEN MORE LIKE A WARRIOR FROM SOME OTHER WORLD, BUT RELATABLE BECAUSE HER IDENTITY IS HIDDEN.
YEAH, YEAH!! EXACTLY!!
. . .
ANYWAY, I'VE BEEN ANALYZING ELLE-Q'S HANDWRITING AND TRYING TO MATCH IT WITH THE HANDWRITING OF OTHER KIDS AROUND SCHOOL.
My notebook...
I THOUGHT I'D START WITH OUR CLASS. WAS THE PERSON YOU HAD IN MIND IN OUR CLASS?
W-WELL, UH, I WAS THINKING THAT MAYBE IT WAS A-A-ACTUALLY T-TAMMY.
Y-YOU KNOW, THE GIRL WHO SITS NEXT TO THE TEACHER'S DESK.
OOOOH, YOU REALLY THINK SO? I DIDN'T EVEN THINK OF HER—

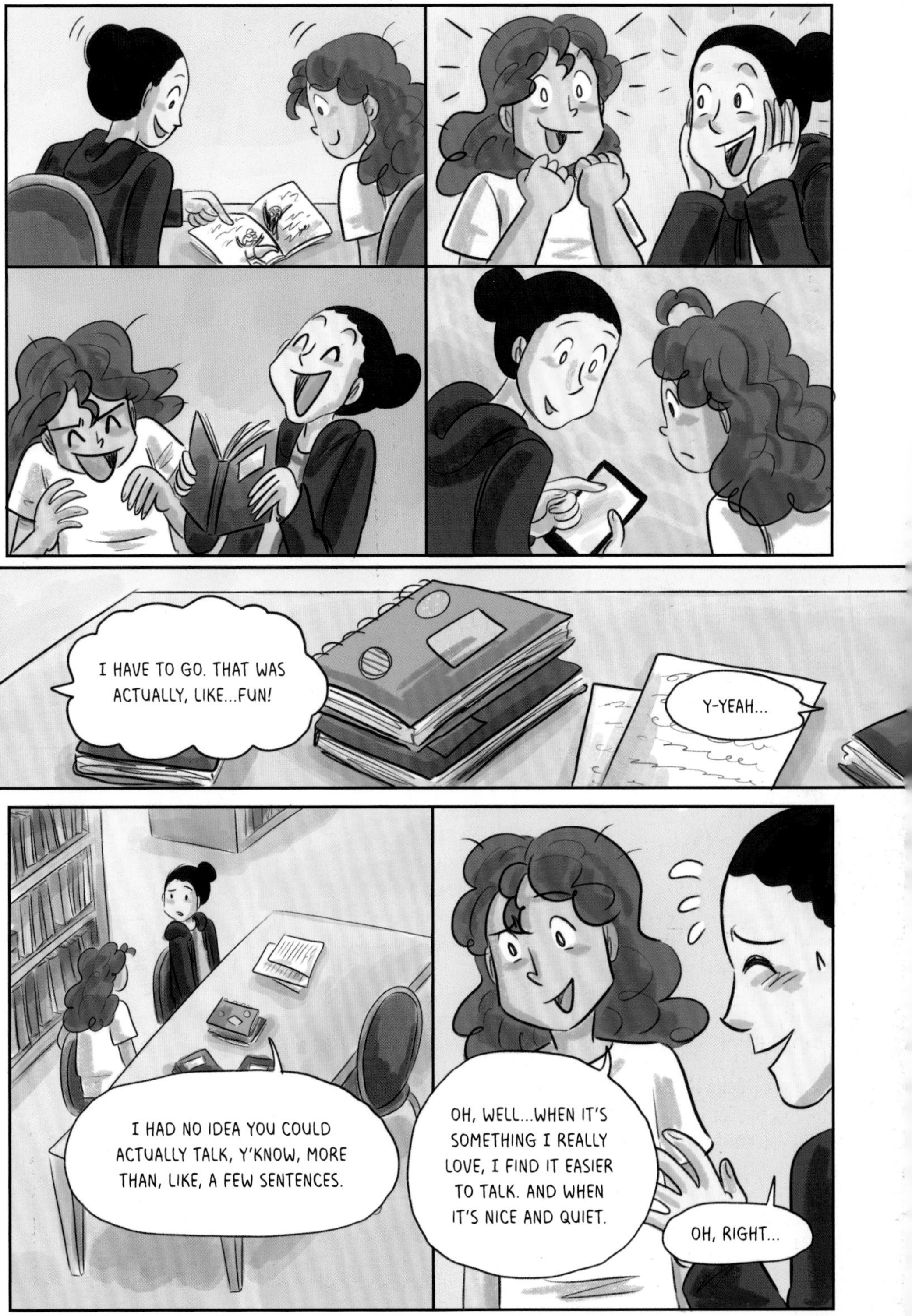
I HAVE TO GO. THAT WAS ACTUALLY, LIKE...FUN!
Y-YEAH...
I HAD NO IDEA YOU COULD ACTUALLY TALK, Y'KNOW, MORE THAN, LIKE, A FEW SENTENCES.
OH, WELL...WHEN IT'S SOMETHING I REALLY LOVE, I FIND IT EASIER TO TALK. AND WHEN IT'S NICE AND QUIET.
OH, RIGHT...

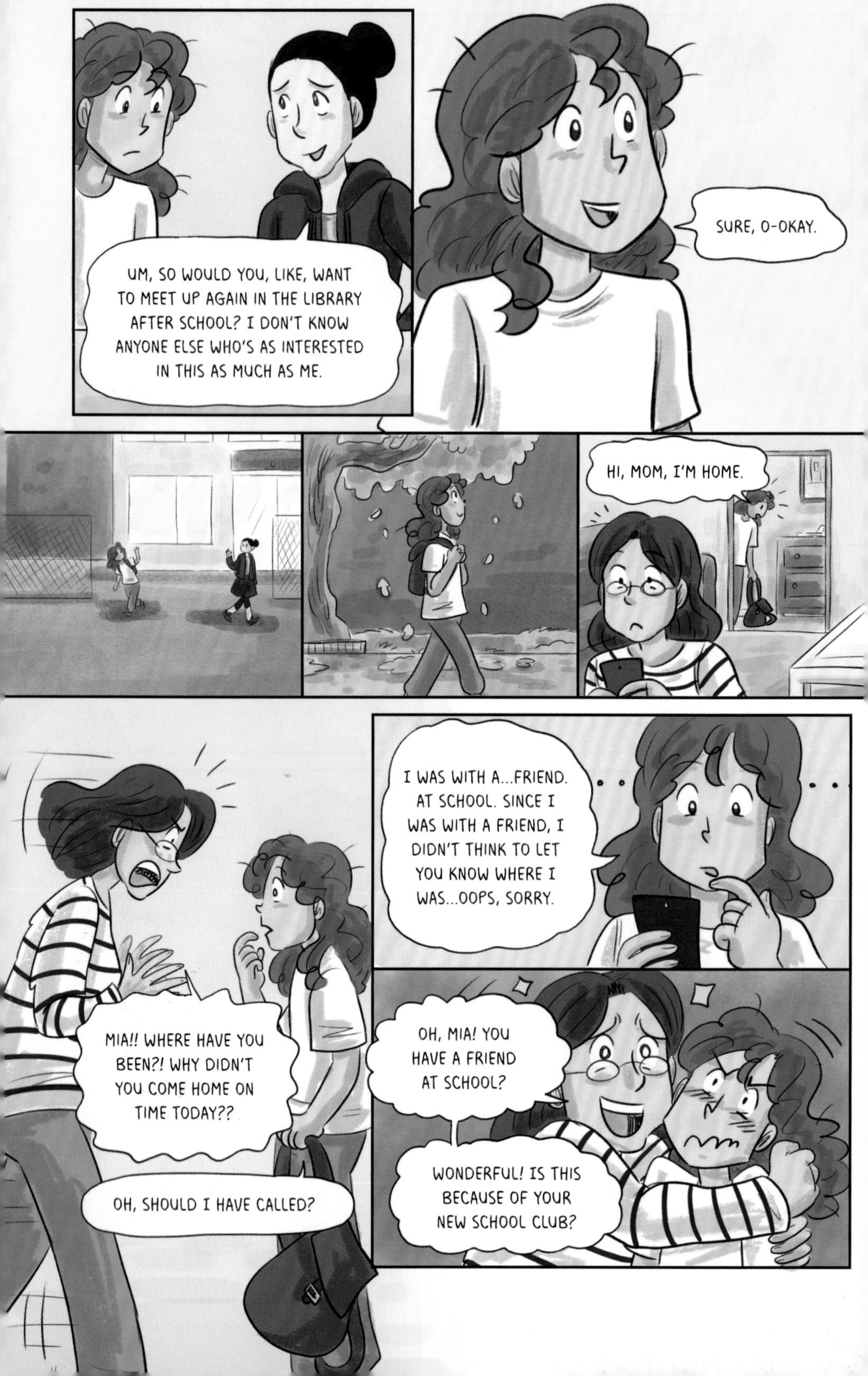
UM, SO WOULD YOU, LIKE, WANT TO MEET UP AGAIN IN THE LIBRARY AFTER SCHOOL? I DON'T KNOW ANYONE ELSE WHO'S AS INTERESTED IN THIS AS MUCH AS ME.
SURE, O-OKAY.
HI, MOM, I'M HOME.
MIA!! WHERE HAVE YOU BEEN?! WHY DIDN'T YOU COME HOME ON TIME TODAY??
OH, SHOULD I HAVE CALLED?
I WAS WITH A...FRIEND. AT SCHOOL. SINCE I WAS WITH A FRIEND, I DIDN'T THINK TO LET YOU KNOW WHERE I WAS...OOPS, SORRY.
OH, MIA! YOU HAVE A FRIEND AT SCHOOL?
WONDERFUL! IS THIS BECAUSE OF YOUR NEW SCHOOL CLUB?

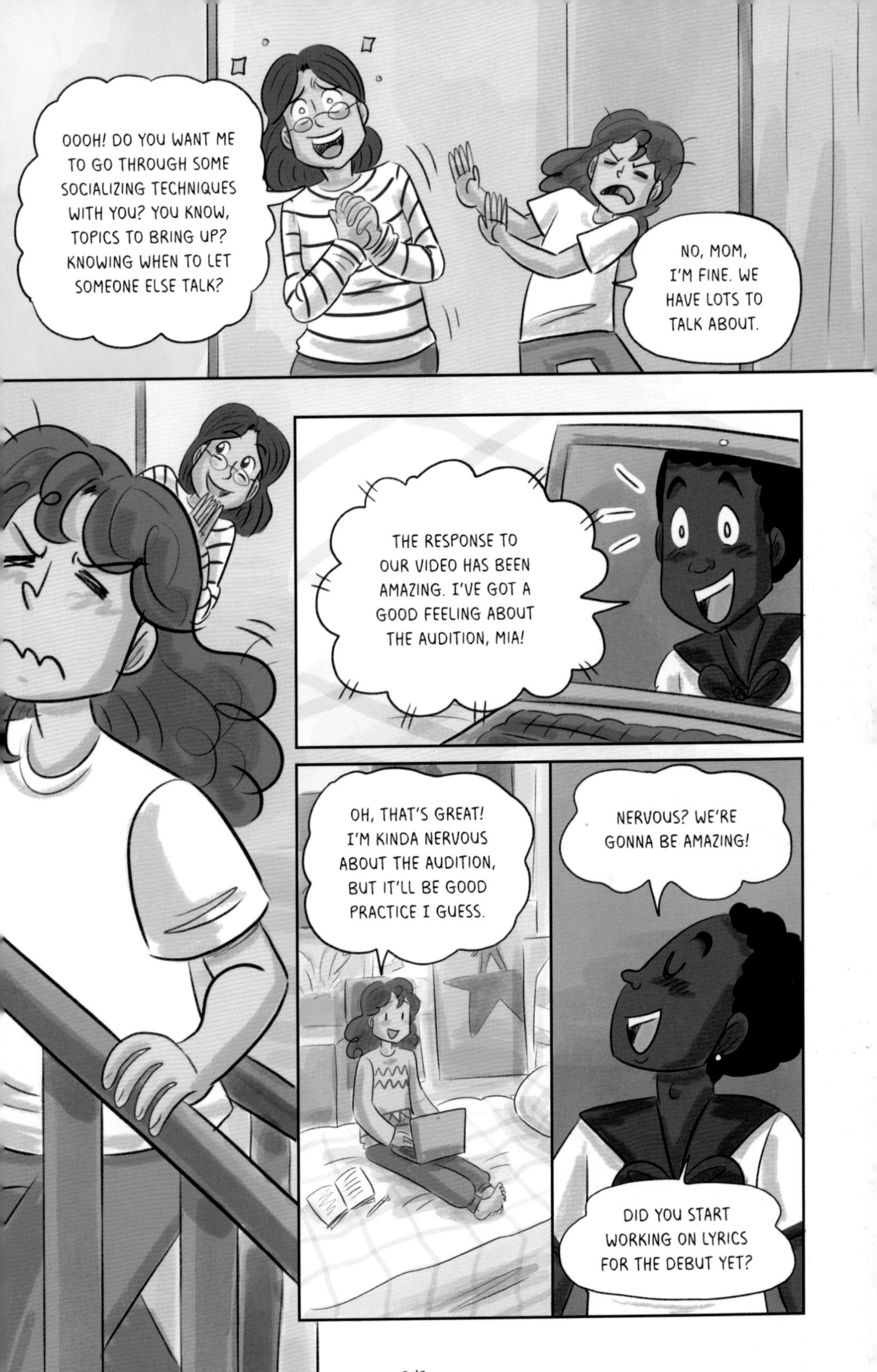
OOOH! DO YOU WANT ME TO GO THROUGH SOME SOCIALIZING TECHNIQUES WITH YOU? YOU KNOW, TOPICS TO BRING UP? KNOWING WHEN TO LET SOMEONE ELSE TALK?
NO, MOM, I'M FINE. WE HAVE LOTS TO TALK ABOUT.
THE RESPONSE TO OUR VIDEO HAS BEEN AMAZING. I'VE GOT A GOOD FEELING ABOUT THE AUDITION, MIA!
OH, THAT'S GREAT! I'M KINDA NERVOUS ABOUT THE AUDITION, BUT IT'LL BE GOOD PRACTICE I GUESS.
NERVOUS? WE'RE GONNA BE AMAZING!
DID YOU START WORKING ON LYRICS FOR THE DEBUT YET?

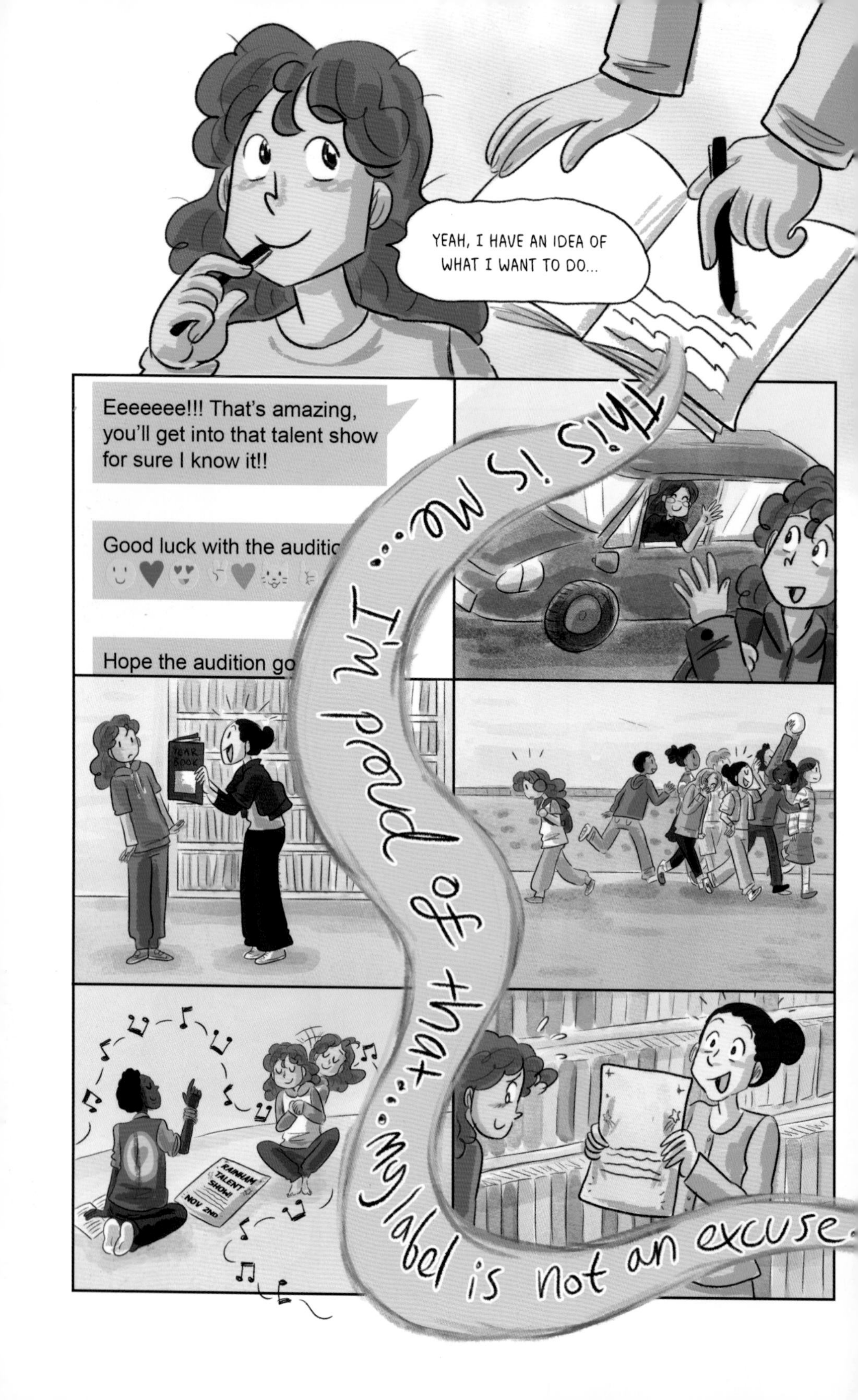
YEAH, I HAVE AN IDEA OF WHAT I WANT TO DO...
Eeeeeee!!! That's amazing, you'll get into that talent show for sure I know it!!
Good luck with the auditio
Hope the audition go
This is me... I'm proud of that... My label is not an excuse.
YEAR BOOK
RAINHAM TALENT SHOW!
NOV 2ND

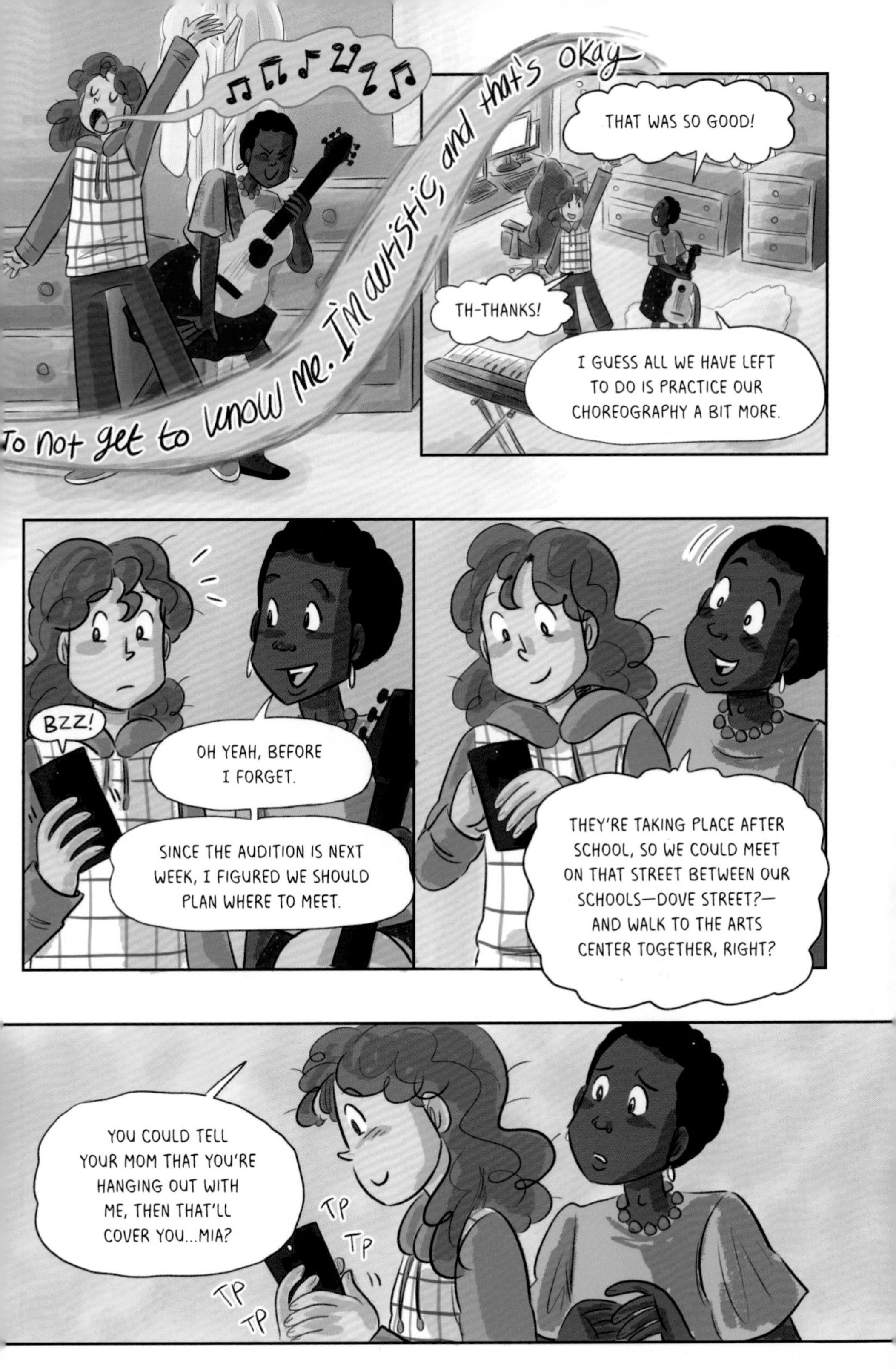
To not get to know me. I'm autistic, and that's okay
THAT WAS SO GOOD!
TH-THANKS!
I GUESS ALL WE HAVE LEFT TO DO IS PRACTICE OUR CHOREOGRAPHY A BIT MORE.
BZZ!
OH YEAH, BEFORE I FORGET.
SINCE THE AUDITION IS NEXT WEEK, I FIGURED WE SHOULD PLAN WHERE TO MEET.
THEY'RE TAKING PLACE AFTER SCHOOL, SO WE COULD MEET ON THAT STREET BETWEEN OUR SCHOOLS—DOVE STREET?—AND WALK TO THE ARTS CENTER TOGETHER, RIGHT?
YOU COULD TELL YOUR MOM THAT YOU'RE HANGING OUT WITH ME, THEN THAT'LL COVER YOU...MIA?
TP
TP
TP
TP

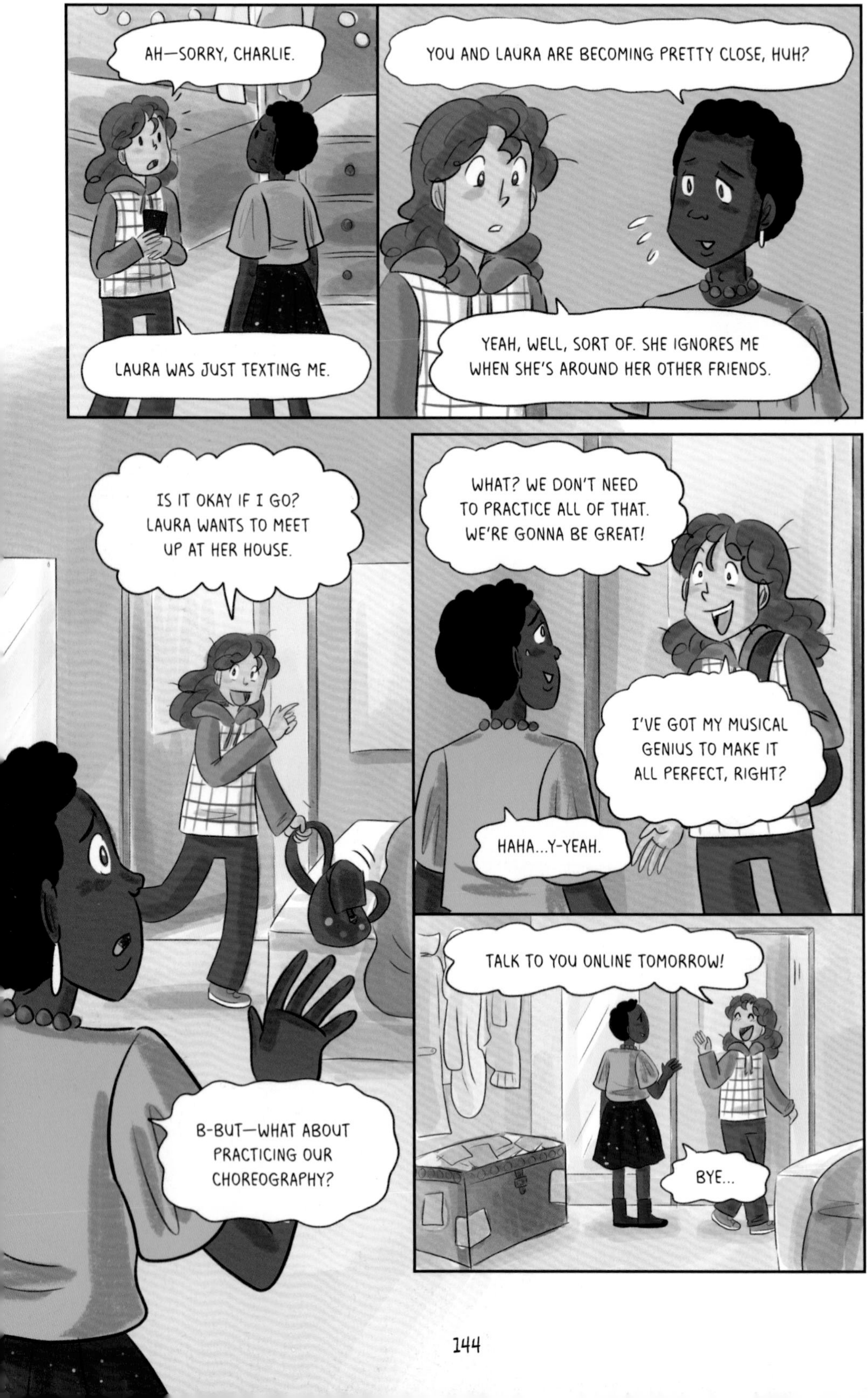
AH—SORRY, CHARLIE.
LAURA WAS JUST TEXTING ME.
YOU AND LAURA ARE BECOMING PRETTY CLOSE, HUH?
YEAH, WELL, SORT OF. SHE IGNORES ME WHEN SHE'S AROUND HER OTHER FRIENDS.
IS IT OKAY IF I GO? LAURA WANTS TO MEET UP AT HER HOUSE.
B-BUT—WHAT ABOUT PRACTICING OUR CHOREOGRAPHY?
WHAT? WE DON'T NEED TO PRACTICE ALL OF THAT. WE'RE GONNA BE GREAT!
I'VE GOT MY MUSICAL GENIUS TO MAKE IT ALL PERFECT, RIGHT?
HAHA...Y-YEAH.
TALK TO YOU ONLINE TOMORROW!
BYE...

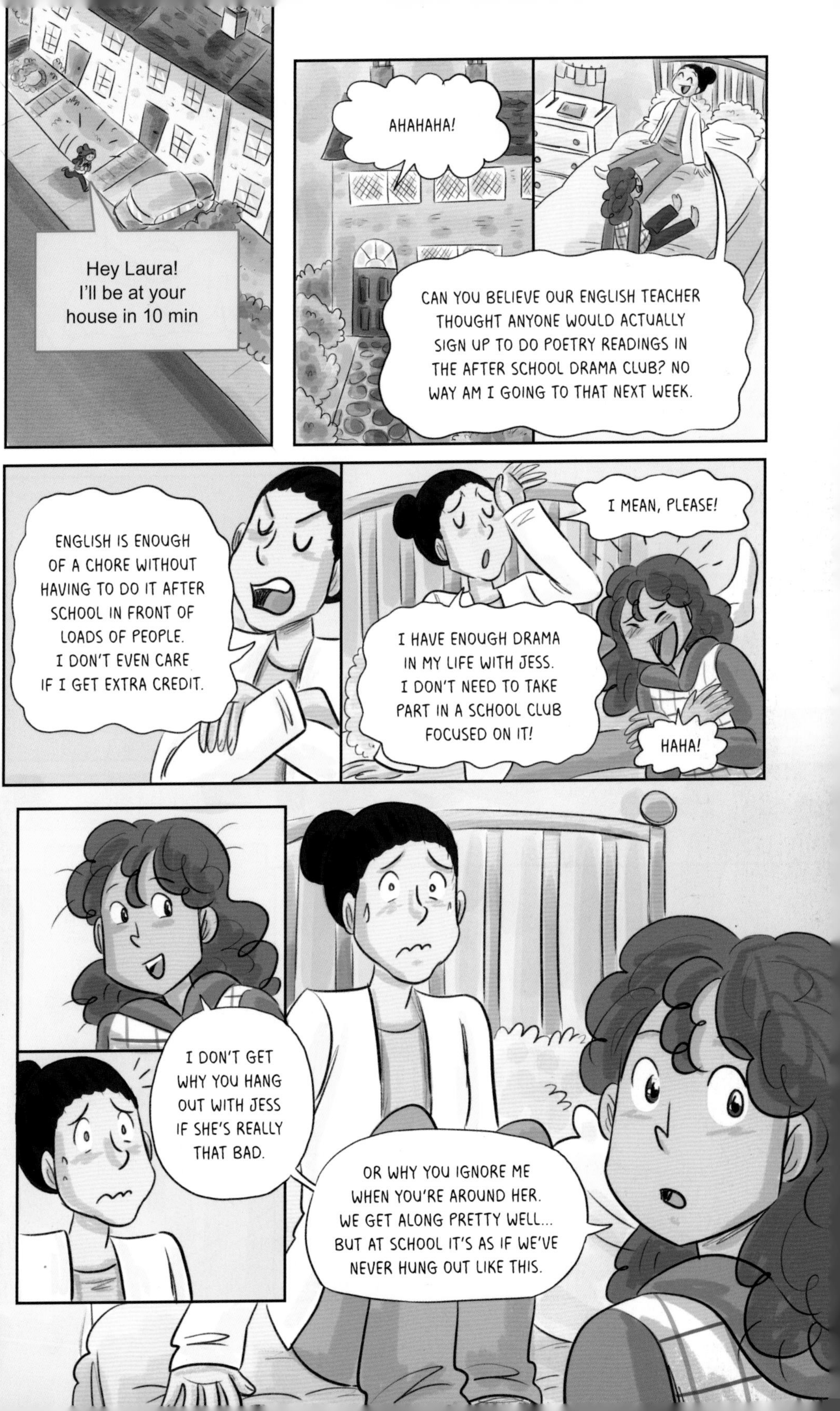
Hey Laura!
I'll be at your house in 10 min
AHAHAHA!
CAN YOU BELIEVE OUR ENGLISH TEACHER THOUGHT ANYONE WOULD ACTUALLY SIGN UP TO DO POETRY READINGS IN THE AFTER SCHOOL DRAMA CLUB? NO WAY AM I GOING TO THAT NEXT WEEK.
ENGLISH IS ENOUGH OF A CHORE WITHOUT HAVING TO DO IT AFTER SCHOOL IN FRONT OF LOADS OF PEOPLE. I DON'T EVEN CARE IF I GET EXTRA CREDIT.
I MEAN, PLEASE!
I HAVE ENOUGH DRAMA IN MY LIFE WITH JESS. I DON'T NEED TO TAKE PART IN A SCHOOL CLUB FOCUSED ON IT!
HAHA!
I DON'T GET WHY YOU HANG OUT WITH JESS IF SHE'S REALLY THAT BAD.
OR WHY YOU IGNORE ME WHEN YOU'RE AROUND HER. WE GET ALONG PRETTY WELL... BUT AT SCHOOL IT'S AS IF WE'VE NEVER HUNG OUT LIKE THIS.

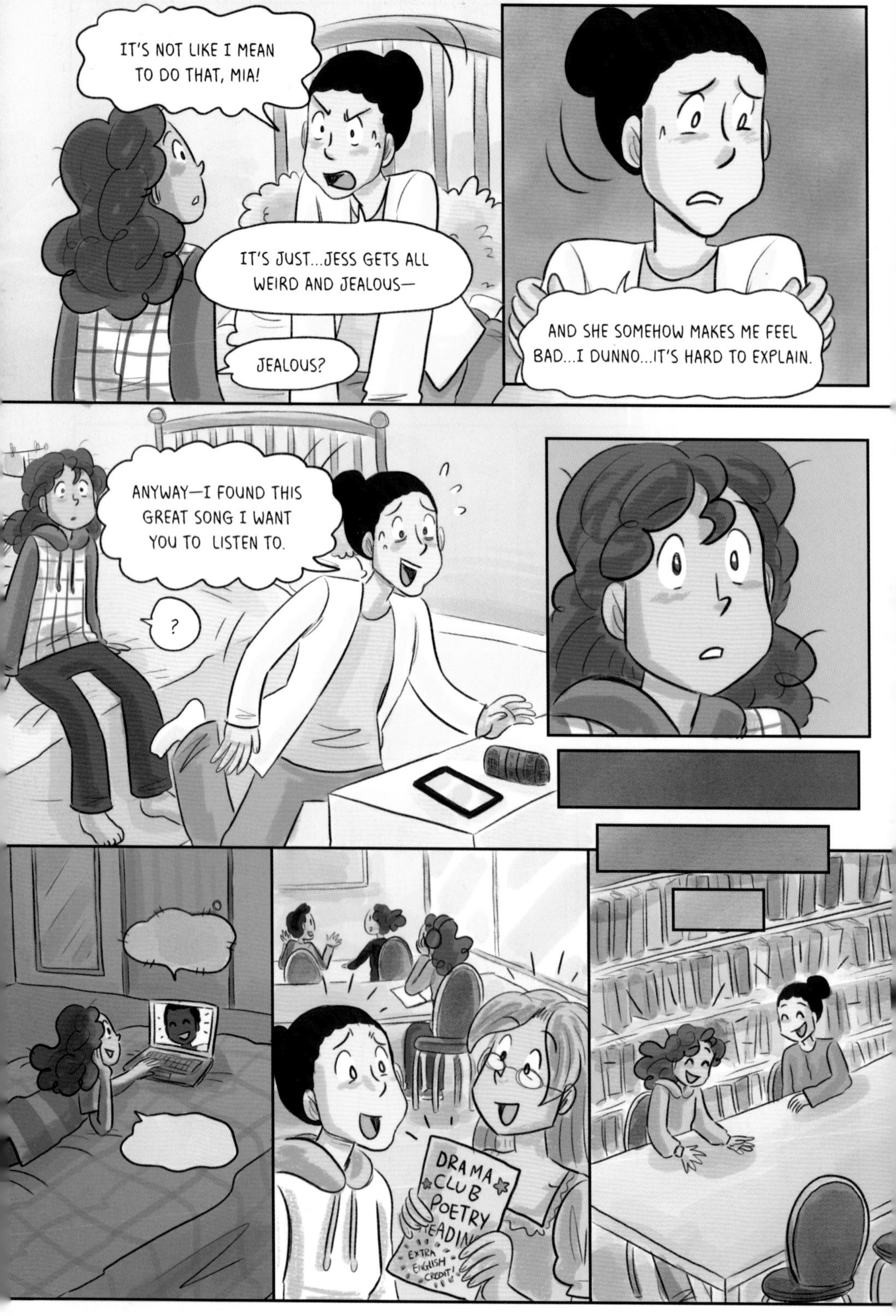
IT'S NOT LIKE I MEAN TO DO THAT, MIA!
IT'S JUST...JESS GETS ALL WEIRD AND JEALOUS—
JEALOUS?
AND SHE SOMEHOW MAKES ME FEEL BAD...I DUNNO...IT'S HARD TO EXPLAIN.
ANYWAY—I FOUND THIS GREAT SONG I WANT YOU TO LISTEN TO.
?
DRAMA CLUB POETRY READING
EXTRA ENGLISH CREDIT!

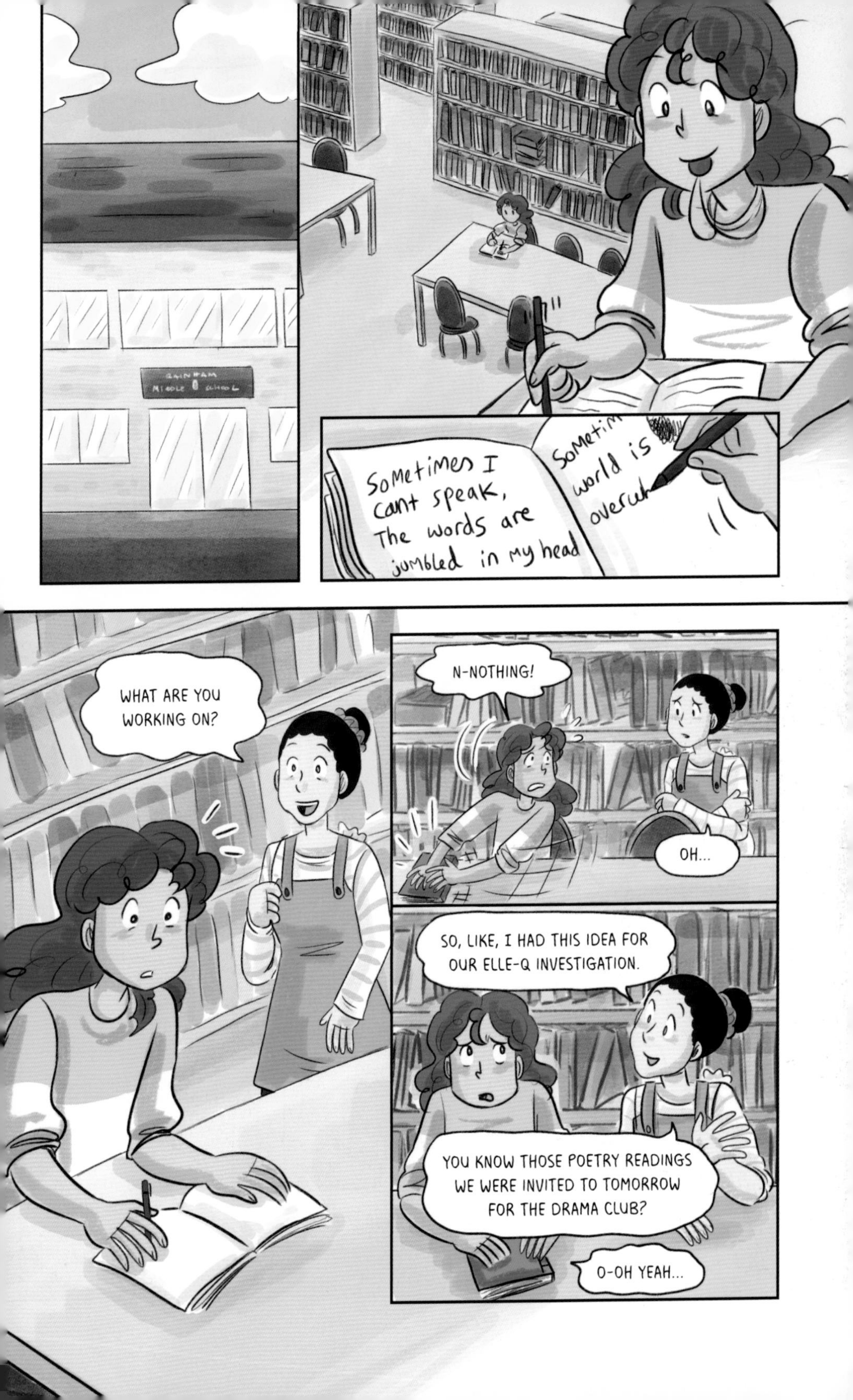

Sometimes I cant speak, The words are jumbled in my head
Sometim
world is
WHAT ARE YOU WORKING ON?
N-NOTHING!
OH...
SO, LIKE, I HAD THIS IDEA FOR OUR ELLE-Q INVESTIGATION.
YOU KNOW THOSE POETRY READINGS WE WERE INVITED TO TOMORROW FOR THE DRAMA CLUB?
O-OH YEAH...

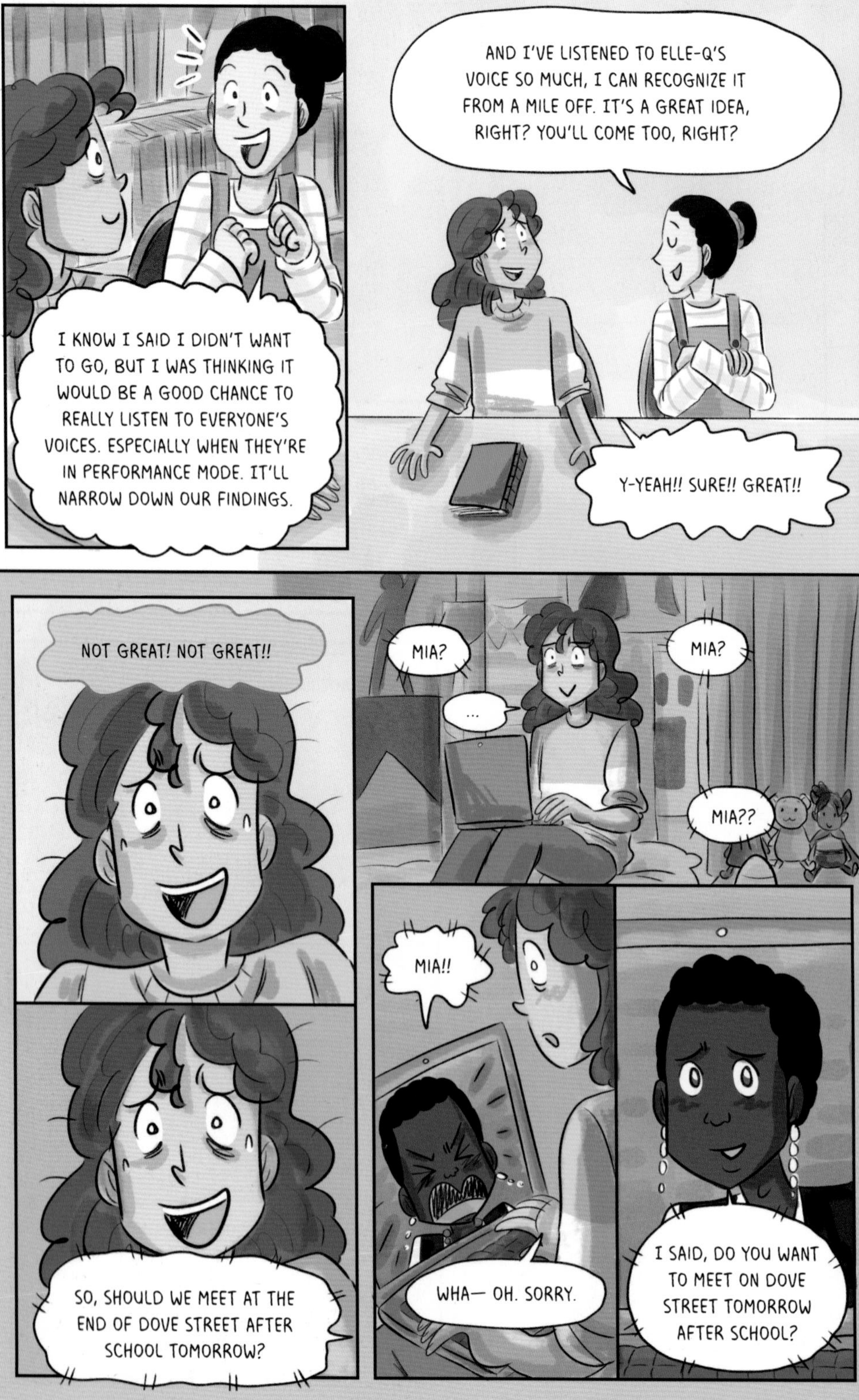
I KNOW I SAID I DIDN'T WANT TO GO, BUT I WAS THINKING IT WOULD BE A GOOD CHANCE TO REALLY LISTEN TO EVERYONE'S VOICES. ESPECIALLY WHEN THEY'RE IN PERFORMANCE MODE. IT'LL NARROW DOWN OUR FINDINGS.
AND I'VE LISTENED TO ELLE-Q'S VOICE SO MUCH, I CAN RECOGNIZE IT FROM A MILE OFF. IT'S A GREAT IDEA, RIGHT? YOU'LL COME TOO, RIGHT?
Y-YEAH!! SURE!! GREAT!!
NOT GREAT! NOT GREAT!!
SO, SHOULD WE MEET AT THE END OF DOVE STREET AFTER SCHOOL TOMORROW?
MIA?
MIA?
...
MIA??
MIA!!
WHA— OH. SORRY.
I SAID, DO YOU WANT TO MEET ON DOVE STREET TOMORROW AFTER SCHOOL?

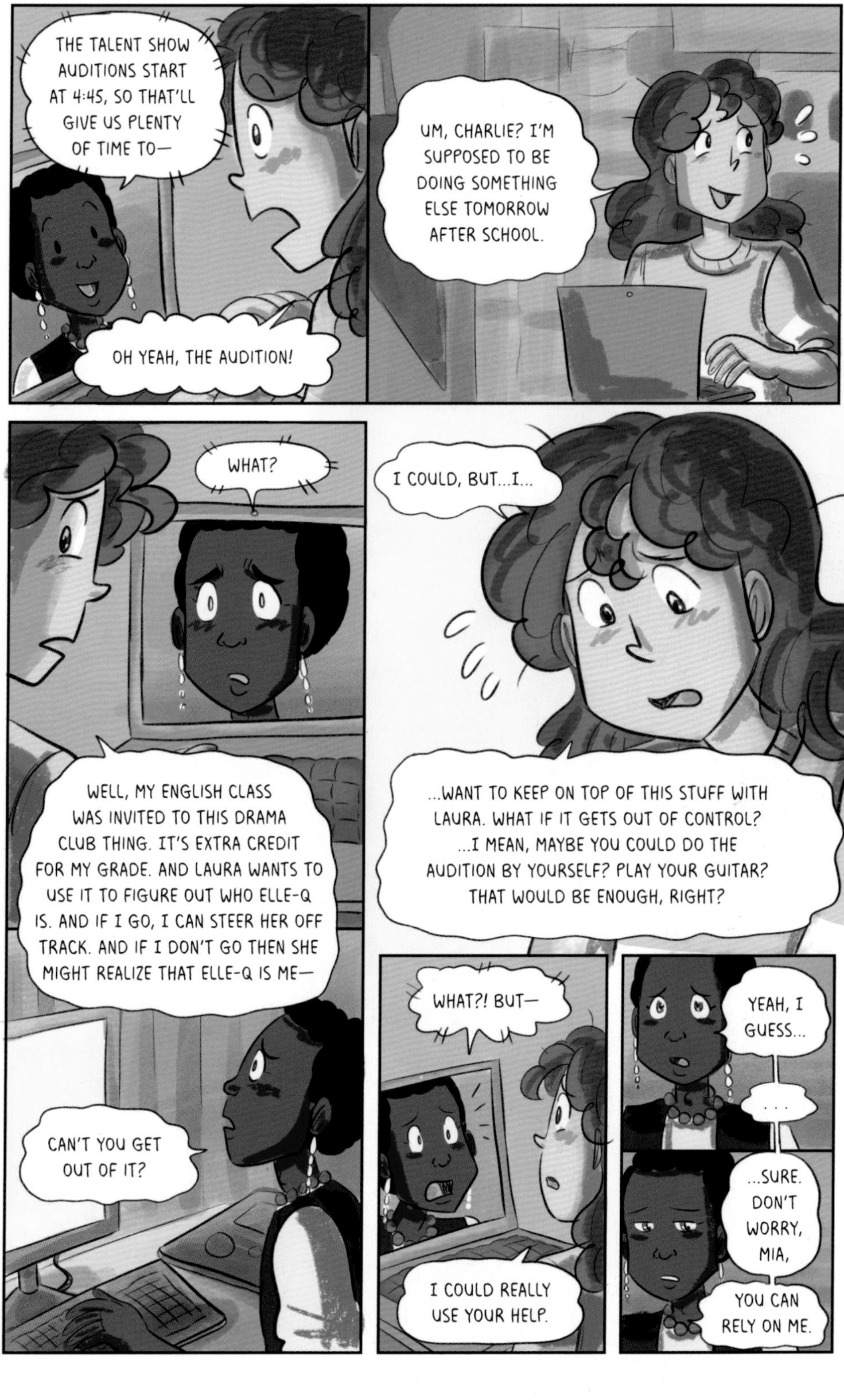
THE TALENT SHOW AUDITIONS START AT 4:45, SO THAT'LL GIVE US PLENTY OF TIME TO—
OH YEAH, THE AUDITION!
UM, CHARLIE? I'M SUPPOSED TO BE DOING SOMETHING ELSE TOMORROW AFTER SCHOOL.
WHAT?
WELL, MY ENGLISH CLASS WAS INVITED TO THIS DRAMA CLUB THING. IT'S EXTRA CREDIT FOR MY GRADE. AND LAURA WANTS TO USE IT TO FIGURE OUT WHO ELLE-Q IS. AND IF I GO, I CAN STEER HER OFF TRACK. AND IF I DON'T GO THEN SHE MIGHT REALIZE THAT ELLE-Q IS ME—
CAN'T YOU GET OUT OF IT?
I COULD, BUT...I...
...WANT TO KEEP ON TOP OF THIS STUFF WITH LAURA. WHAT IF IT GETS OUT OF CONTROL? ...I MEAN, MAYBE YOU COULD DO THE AUDITION BY YOURSELF? PLAY YOUR GUITAR? THAT WOULD BE ENOUGH, RIGHT?
WHAT?! BUT—
I COULD REALLY USE YOUR HELP.
YEAH, I GUESS...
. . .
...SURE. DON'T WORRY, MIA,
YOU CAN RELY ON ME.

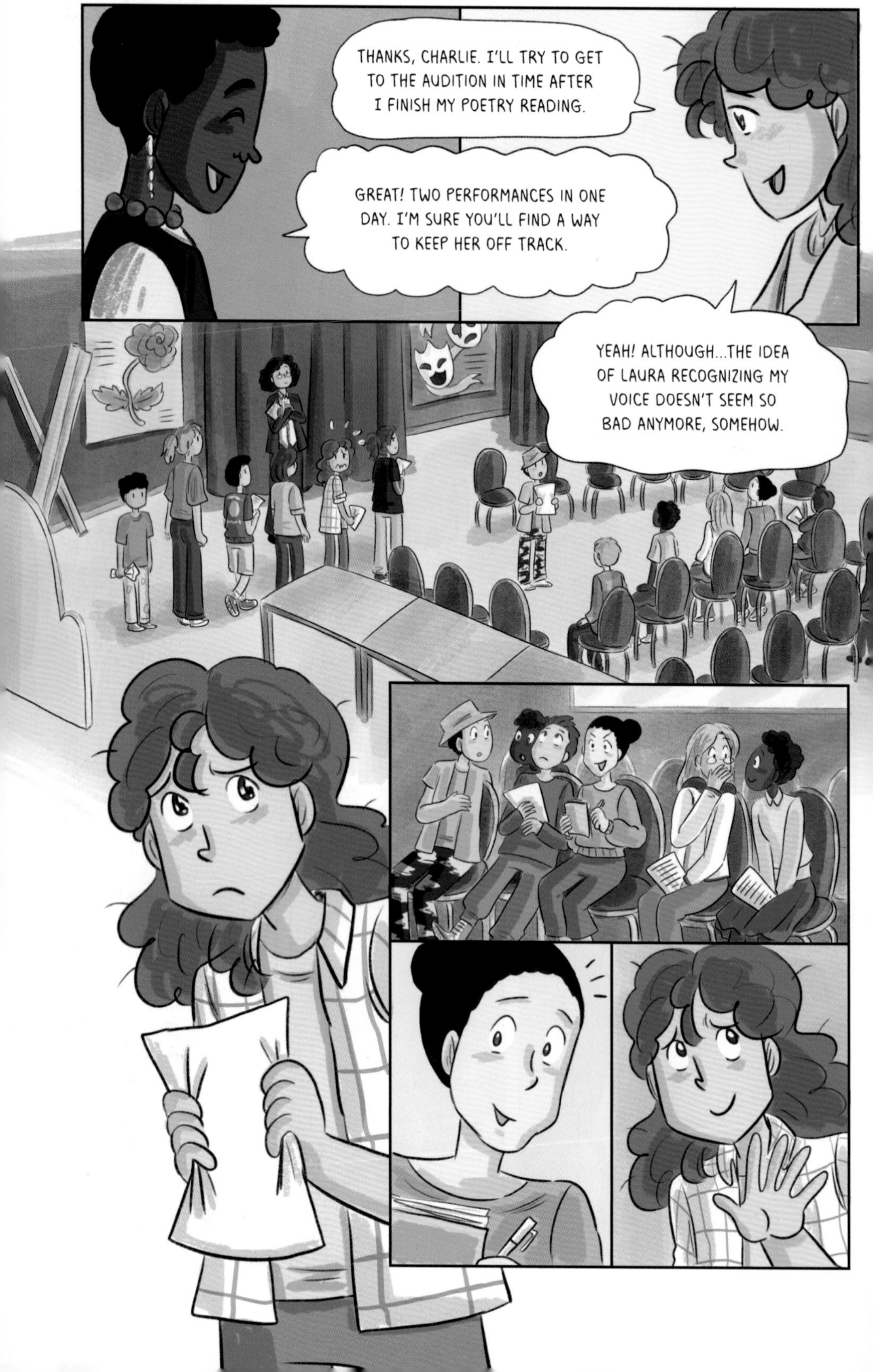
THANKS, CHARLIE. I'LL TRY TO GET TO THE AUDITION IN TIME AFTER I FINISH MY POETRY READING.
GREAT! TWO PERFORMANCES IN ONE DAY. I'M SURE YOU'LL FIND A WAY TO KEEP HER OFF TRACK.
YEAH! ALTHOUGH...THE IDEA OF LAURA RECOGNIZING MY VOICE DOESN'T SEEM SO BAD ANYMORE, SOMEHOW.

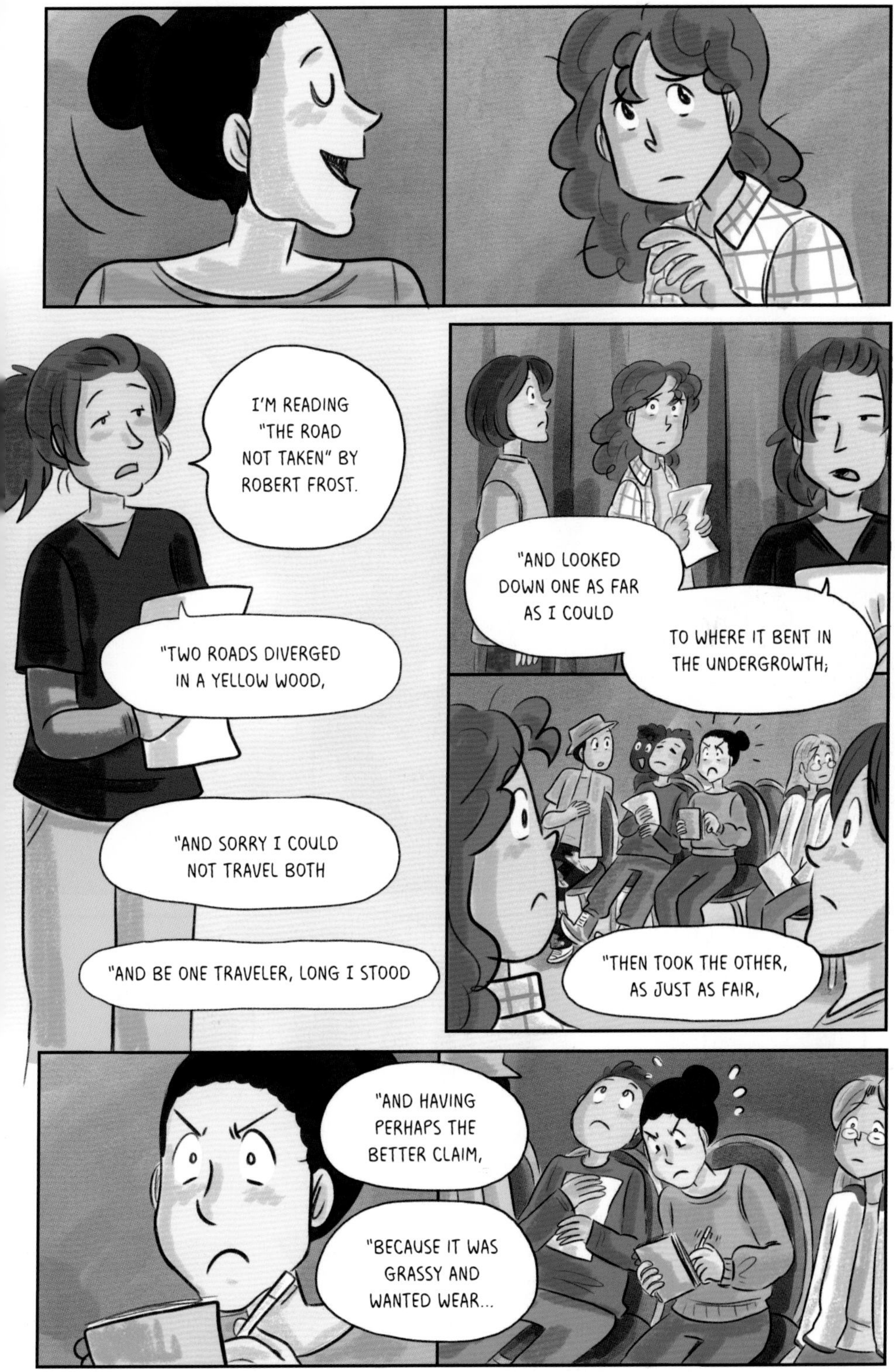
I'M READING "THE ROAD NOT TAKEN" BY ROBERT FROST.
"TWO ROADS DIVERGED IN A YELLOW WOOD,
"AND SORRY I COULD NOT TRAVEL BOTH
"AND BE ONE TRAVELER, LONG I STOOD
"AND LOOKED DOWN ONE AS FAR AS I COULD
TO WHERE IT BENT IN THE UNDERGROWTH;
"THEN TOOK THE OTHER, AS JUST AS FAIR,
"AND HAVING PERHAPS THE BETTER CLAIM,
"BECAUSE IT WAS GRASSY AND WANTED WEAR...

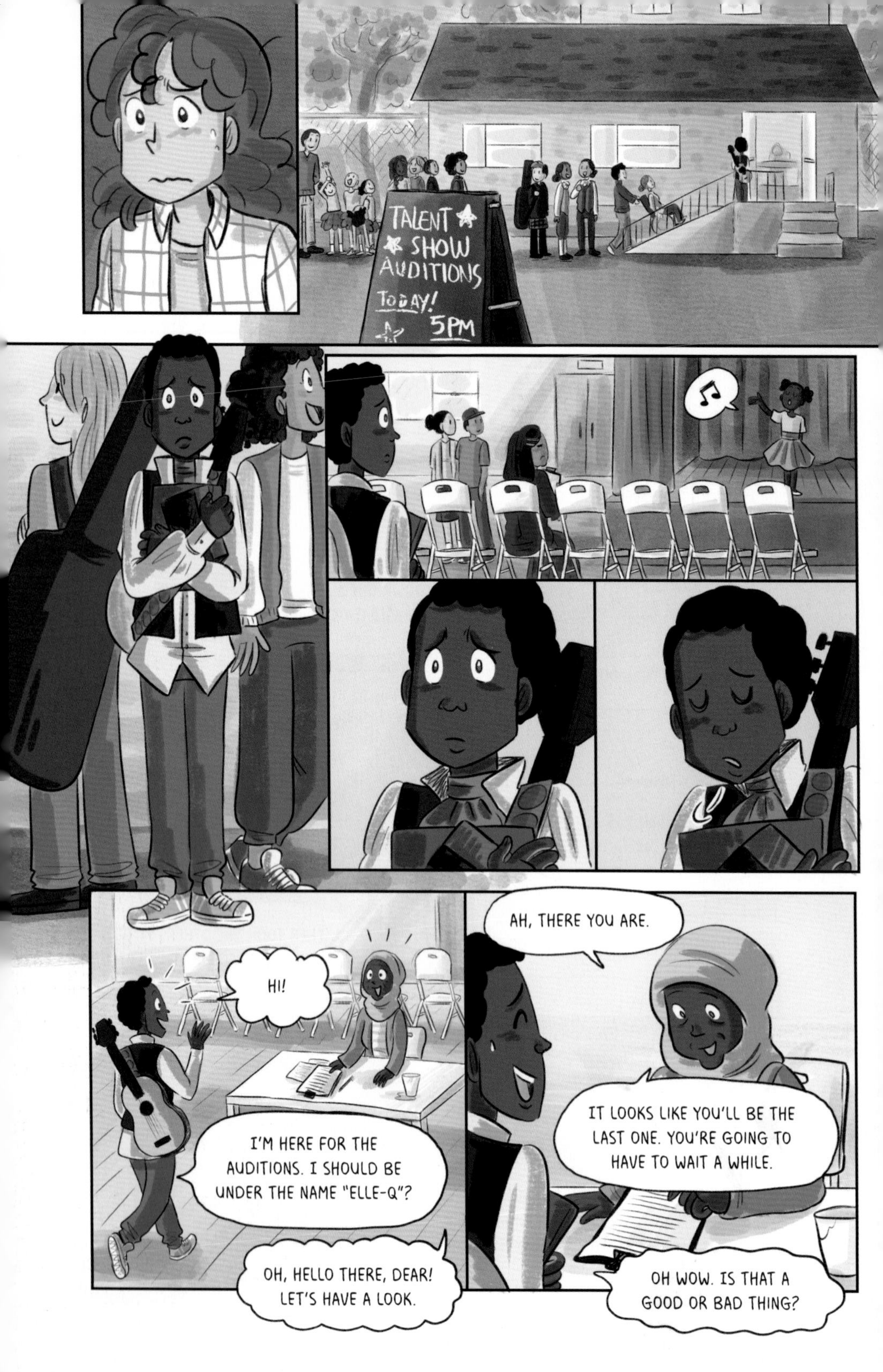
TALENT SHOW AUDITIONS TODAY! 5PM
HI!
I'M HERE FOR THE AUDITIONS. I SHOULD BE UNDER THE NAME "ELLE-Q"?
OH, HELLO THERE, DEAR! LET'S HAVE A LOOK.
AH, THERE YOU ARE.
IT LOOKS LIKE YOU'LL BE THE LAST ONE. YOU'RE GOING TO HAVE TO WAIT A WHILE.
OH WOW. IS THAT A GOOD OR BAD THING?

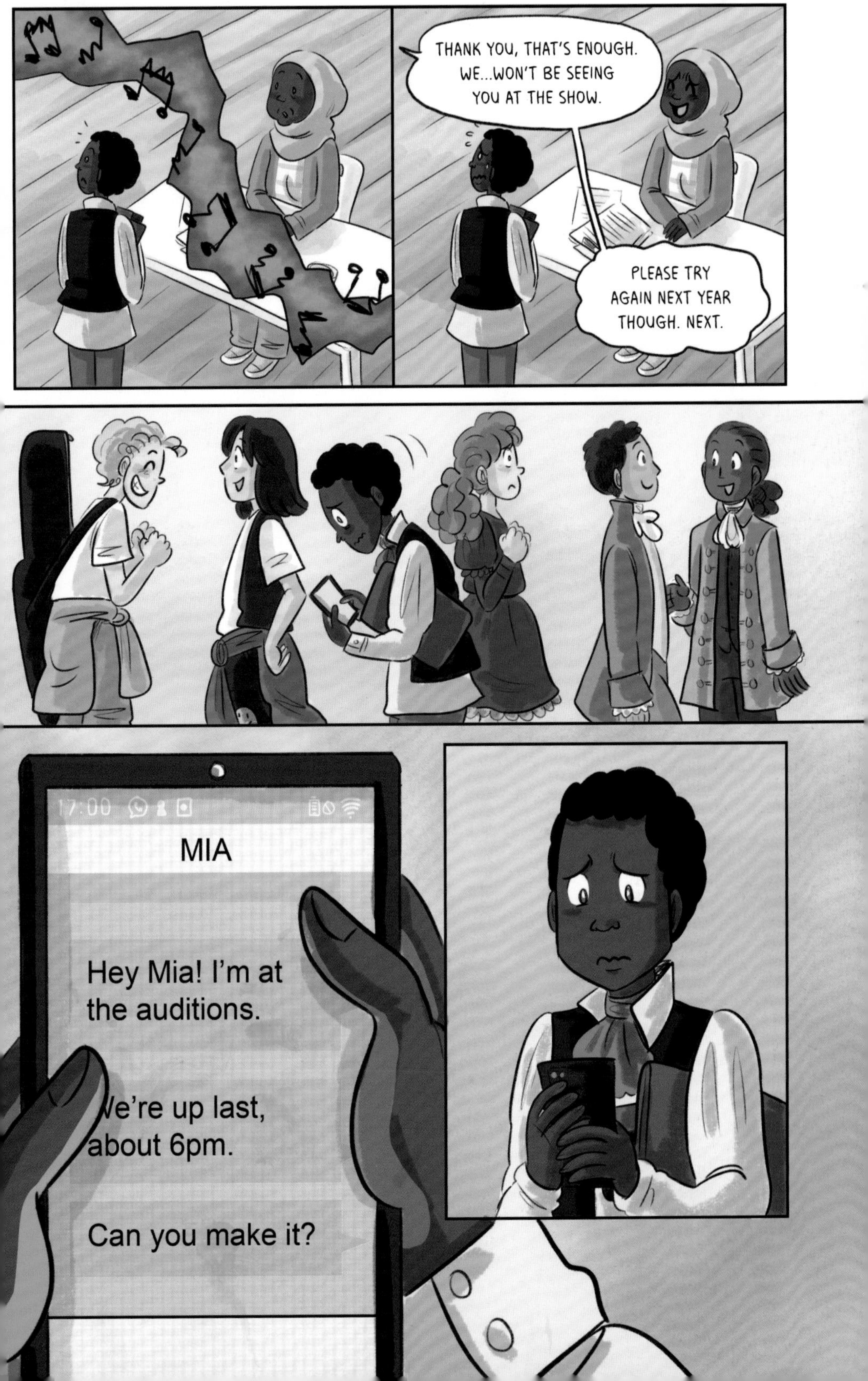
THANK YOU, THAT'S ENOUGH. WE...WON'T BE SEEING YOU AT THE SHOW.
PLEASE TRY AGAIN NEXT YEAR THOUGH. NEXT.
17:00
MIA
Hey Mia! I'm at the auditions.
We're up last, about 6pm.
Can you make it?

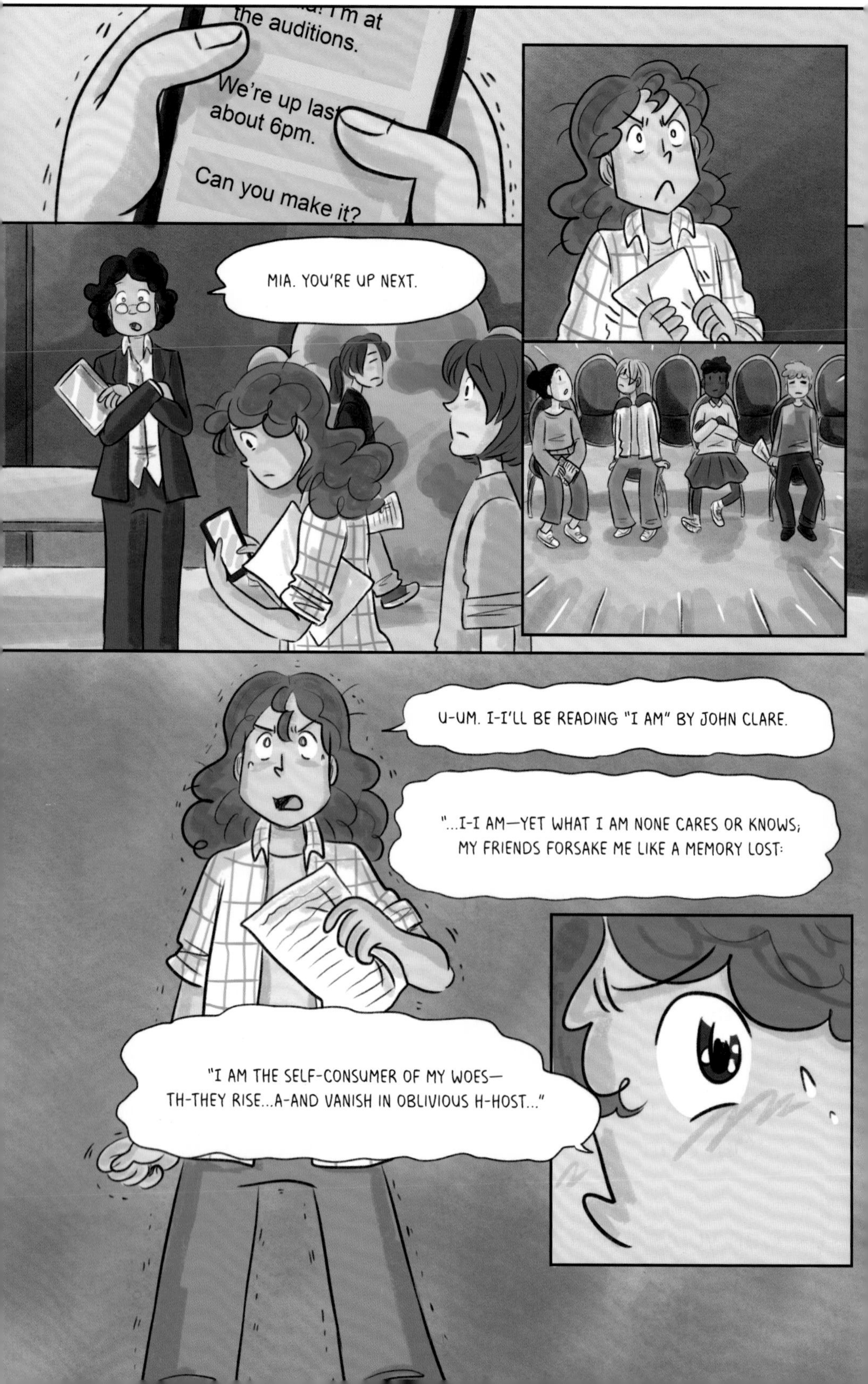
I'm at
the auditions.
We're up las
about 6pm.
Can you make it?
MIA. YOU'RE UP NEXT.
U-UM. I-I'LL BE READING "I AM" BY JOHN CLARE.
"...I-I AM—YET WHAT I AM NONE CARES OR KNOWS;
MY FRIENDS FORSAKE ME LIKE A MEMORY LOST:
"I AM THE SELF-CONSUMER OF MY WOES—
TH-THEY RISE...A-AND VANISH IN OBLIVIOUS H-HOST..."

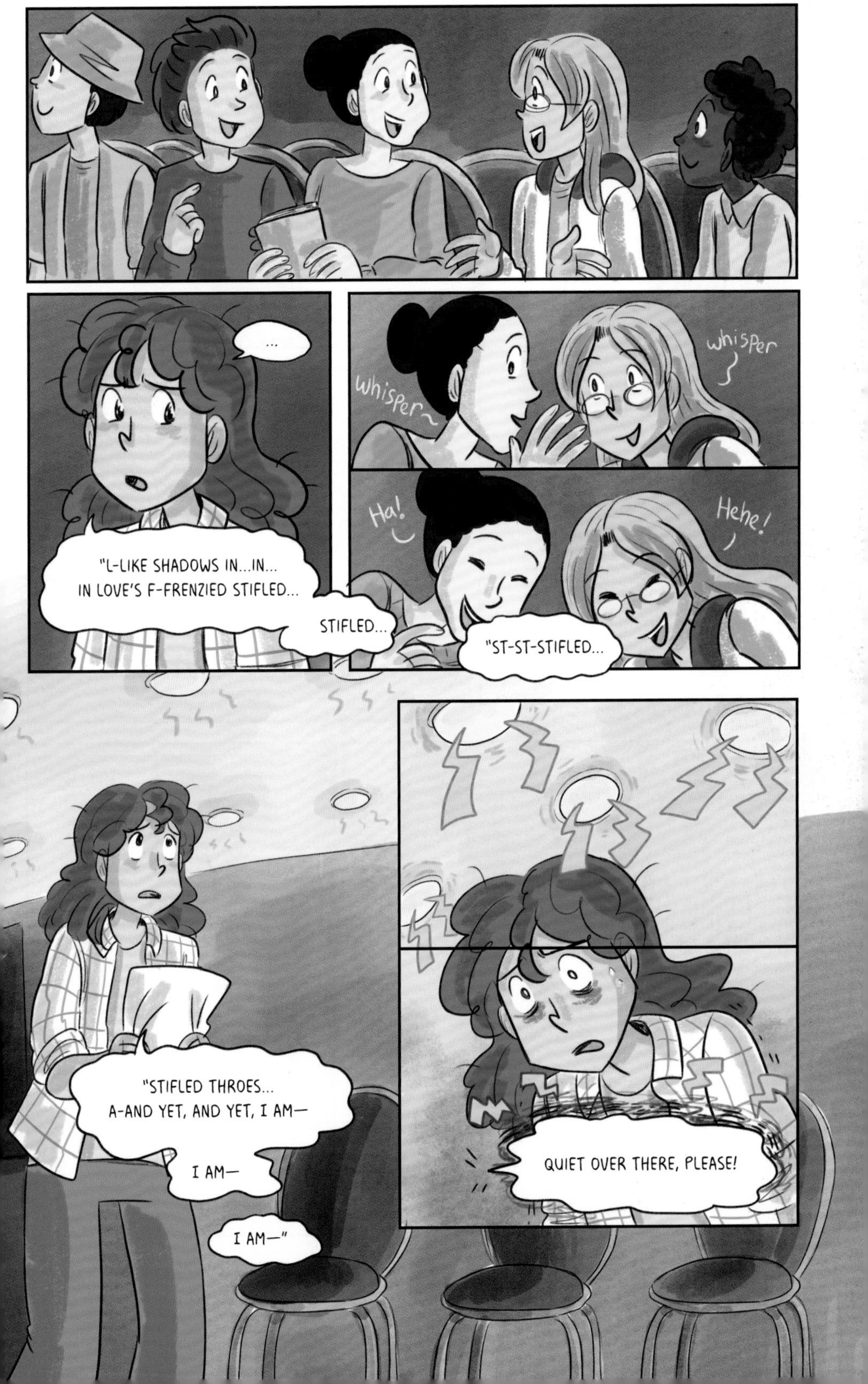
...
whisper~
whisper
"L-LIKE SHADOWS IN...IN... IN LOVE'S F-FRENZIED STIFLED...
STIFLED...
Ha!
Hehe!
"ST-ST-STIFLED...
"STIFLED THROES... A-AND YET, AND YET, I AM—
I AM—
I AM—"
QUIET OVER THERE, PLEASE!

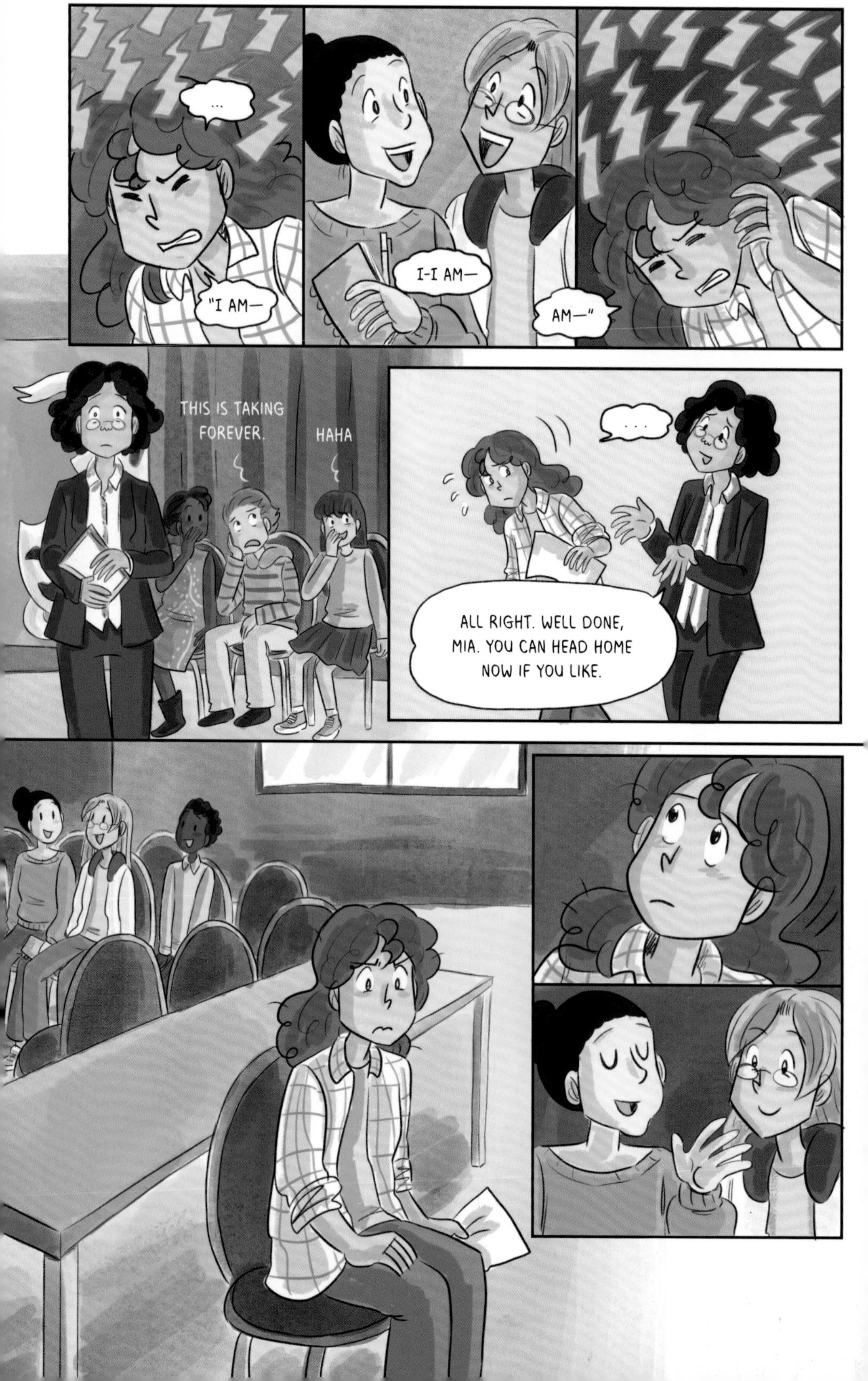
...
"I AM—
I-I AM—
AM—"
THIS IS TAKING FOREVER.
HAHA
. . .
ALL RIGHT. WELL DONE, MIA. YOU CAN HEAD HOME NOW IF YOU LIKE.

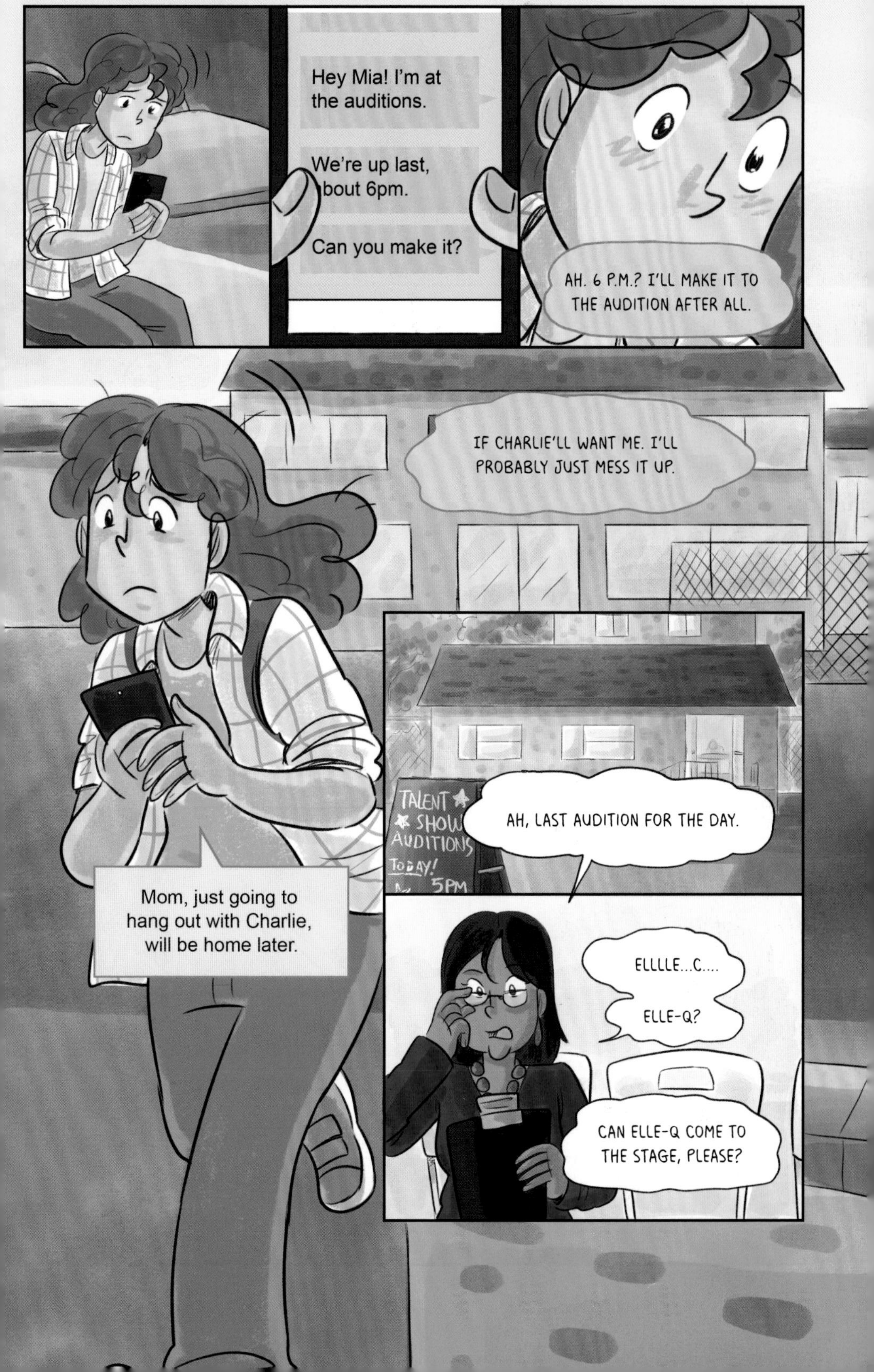
Hey Mia! I'm at the auditions.
We're up last, 'bout 6pm.
Can you make it?
AH. 6 P.M.? I'LL MAKE IT TO THE AUDITION AFTER ALL.
IF CHARLIE'LL WANT ME. I'LL PROBABLY JUST MESS IT UP.
Mom, just going to hang out with Charlie, will be home later.
TALENT SHOW AUDITIONS TODAY! 5PM
AH, LAST AUDITION FOR THE DAY.
ELLLLE...C....
ELLE-Q?
CAN ELLE-Q COME TO THE STAGE, PLEASE?

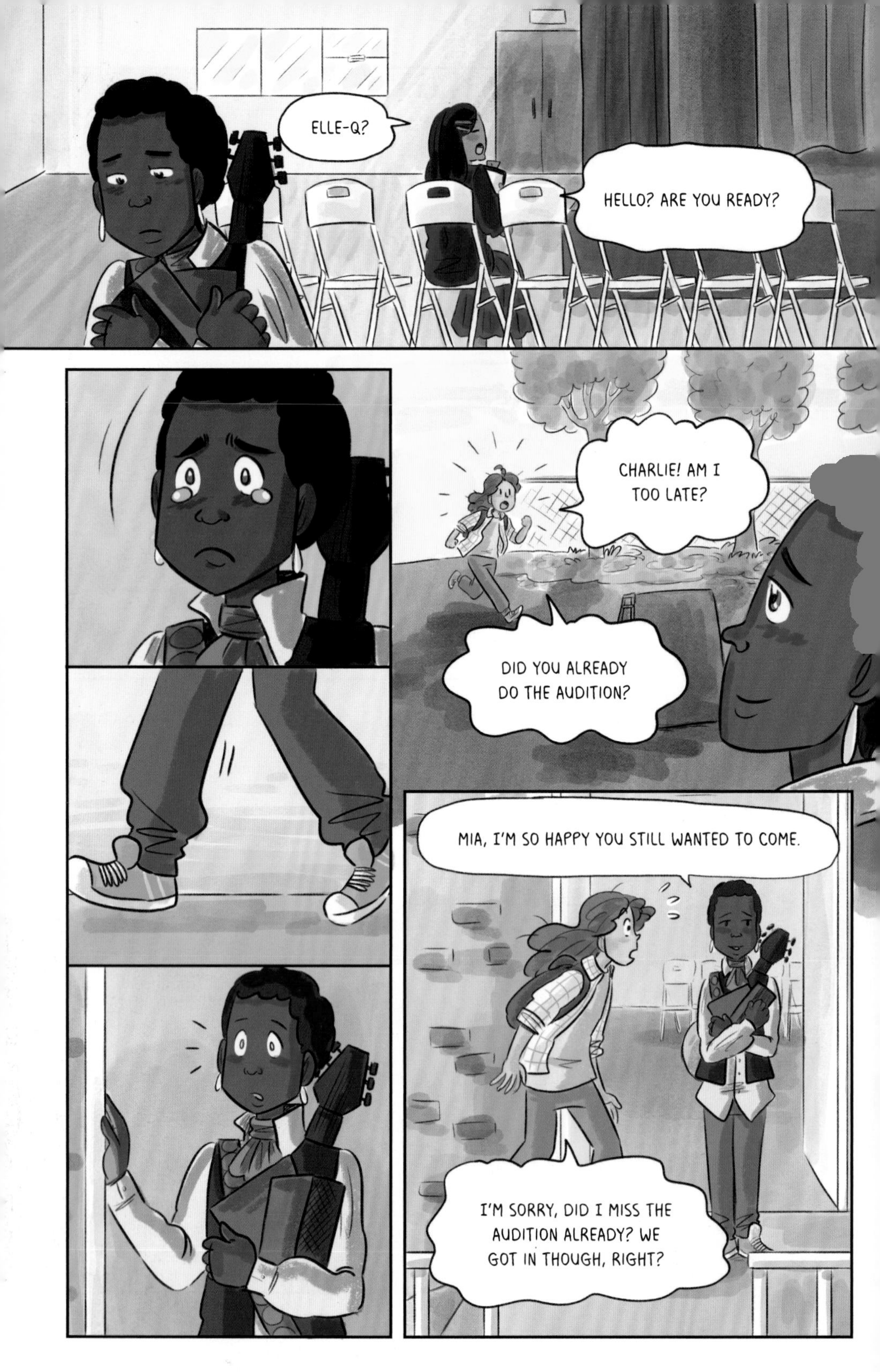
ELLE-Q?
HELLO? ARE YOU READY?
CHARLIE! AM I TOO LATE?
DID YOU ALREADY DO THE AUDITION?
MIA, I'M SO HAPPY YOU STILL WANTED TO COME.
I'M SORRY, DID I MISS THE AUDITION ALREADY? WE GOT IN THOUGH, RIGHT?

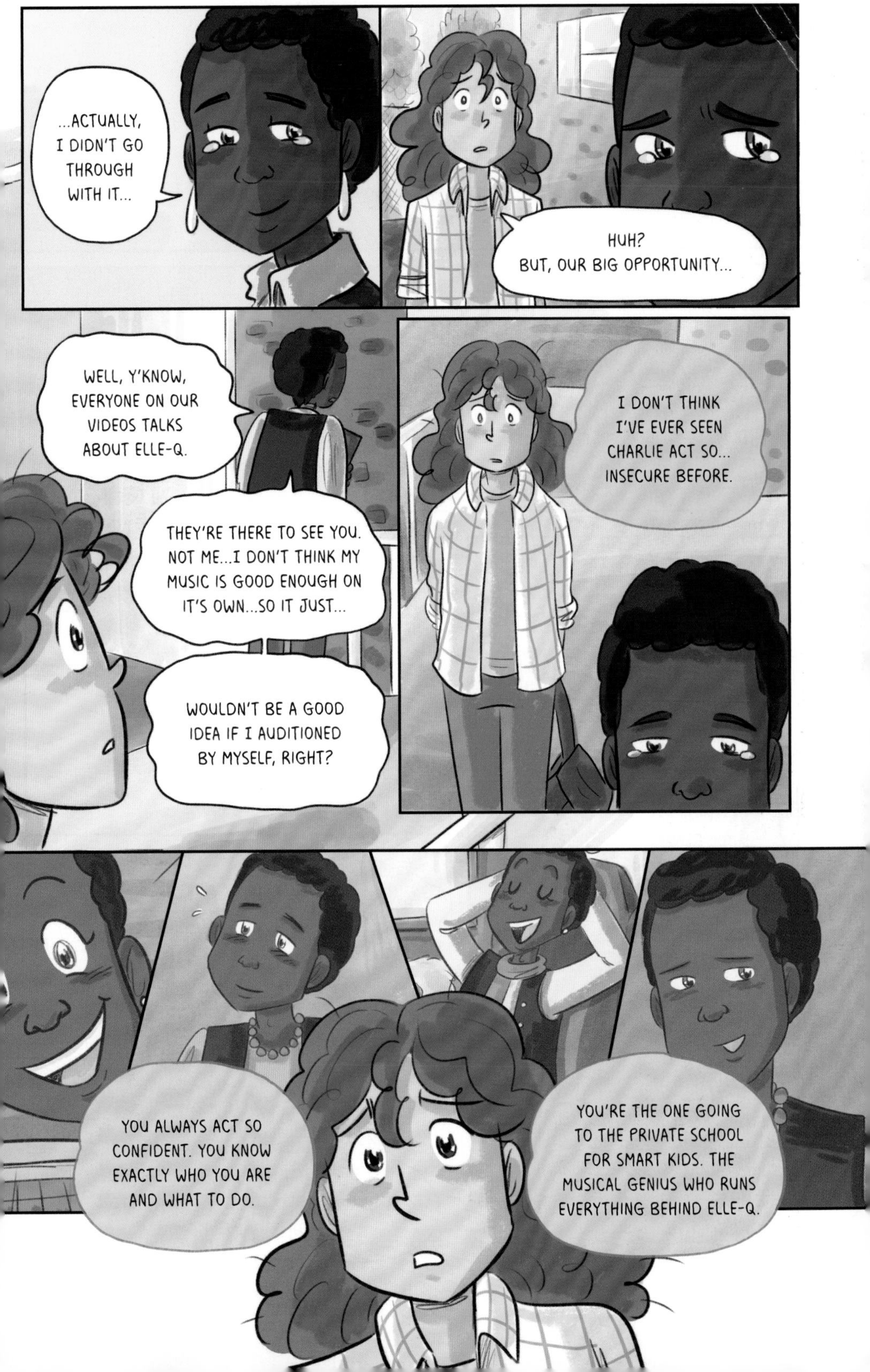
...ACTUALLY, I DIDN'T GO THROUGH WITH IT...
HUH? BUT, OUR BIG OPPORTUNITY...
WELL, Y'KNOW, EVERYONE ON OUR VIDEOS TALKS ABOUT ELLE-Q.
THEY'RE THERE TO SEE YOU. NOT ME...I DON'T THINK MY MUSIC IS GOOD ENOUGH ON IT'S OWN...SO IT JUST...
WOULDN'T BE A GOOD IDEA IF I AUDITIONED BY MYSELF, RIGHT?
I DON'T THINK I'VE EVER SEEN CHARLIE ACT SO... INSECURE BEFORE.
YOU ALWAYS ACT SO CONFIDENT. YOU KNOW EXACTLY WHO YOU ARE AND WHAT TO DO.
YOU'RE THE ONE GOING TO THE PRIVATE SCHOOL FOR SMART KIDS. THE MUSICAL GENIUS WHO RUNS EVERYTHING BEHIND ELLE-Q.

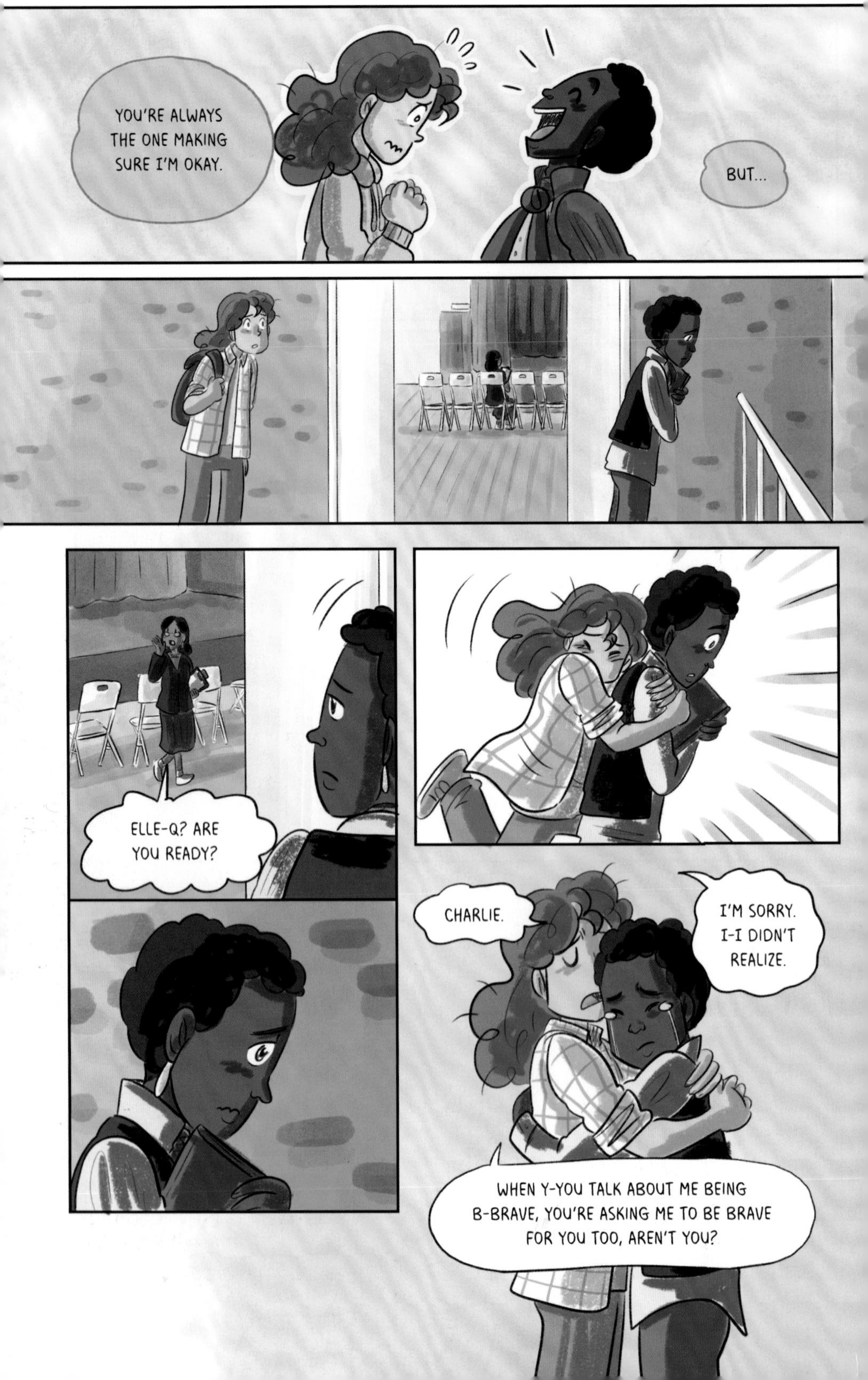
YOU'RE ALWAYS THE ONE MAKING SURE I'M OKAY.
BUT...
ELLE-Q? ARE YOU READY?
CHARLIE.
I'M SORRY. I-I DIDN'T REALIZE.
WHEN Y-YOU TALK ABOUT ME BEING B-BRAVE, YOU'RE ASKING ME TO BE BRAVE FOR YOU TOO, AREN'T YOU?

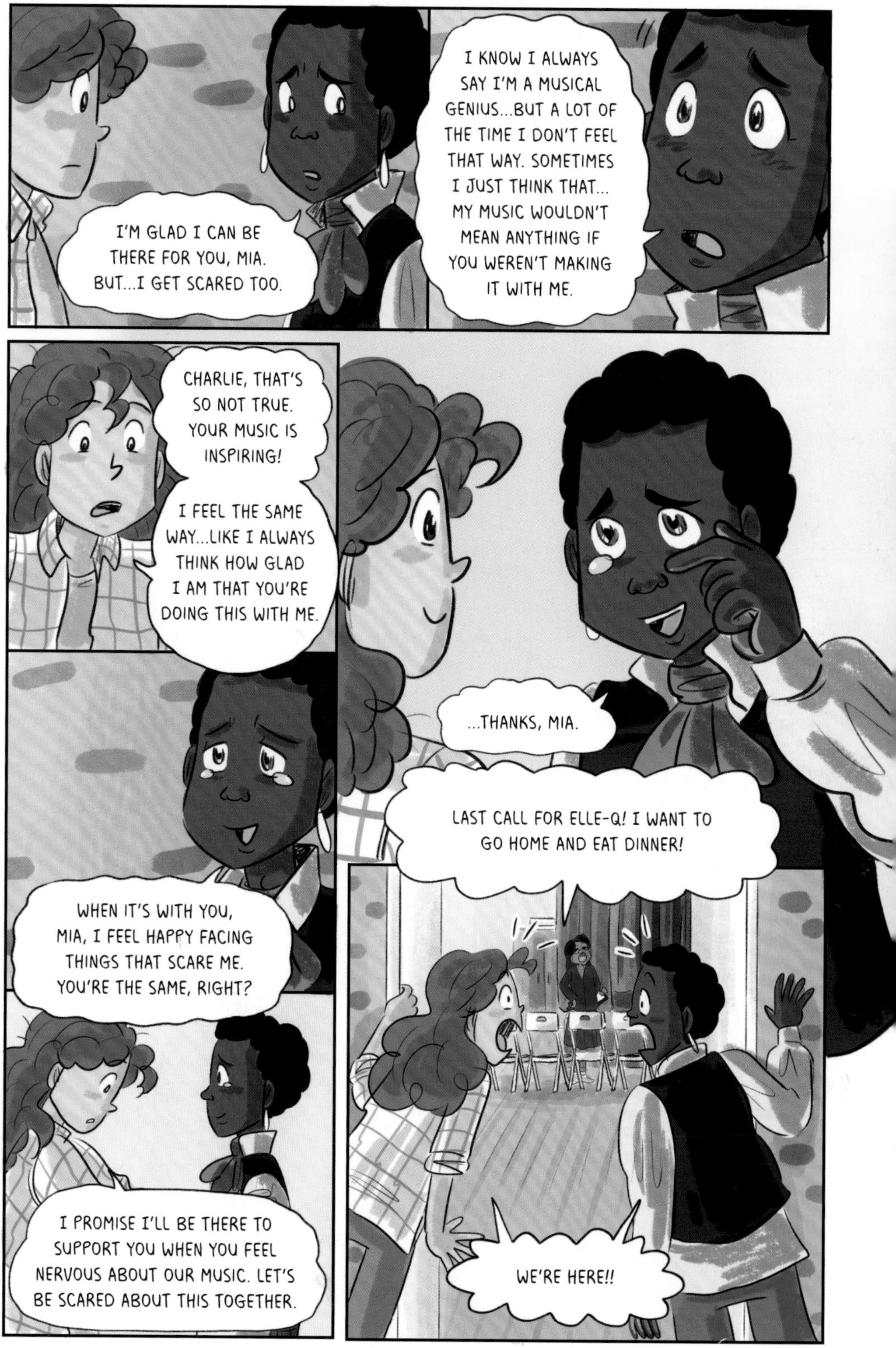
I'M GLAD I CAN BE THERE FOR YOU, MIA. BUT...I GET SCARED TOO.
I KNOW I ALWAYS SAY I'M A MUSICAL GENIUS...BUT A LOT OF THE TIME I DON'T FEEL THAT WAY. SOMETIMES I JUST THINK THAT... MY MUSIC WOULDN'T MEAN ANYTHING IF YOU WEREN'T MAKING IT WITH ME.
CHARLIE, THAT'S SO NOT TRUE. YOUR MUSIC IS INSPIRING!
I FEEL THE SAME WAY...LIKE I ALWAYS THINK HOW GLAD I AM THAT YOU'RE DOING THIS WITH ME.
WHEN IT'S WITH YOU, MIA, I FEEL HAPPY FACING THINGS THAT SCARE ME. YOU'RE THE SAME, RIGHT?
I PROMISE I'LL BE THERE TO SUPPORT YOU WHEN YOU FEEL NERVOUS ABOUT OUR MUSIC. LET'S BE SCARED ABOUT THIS TOGETHER.
...THANKS, MIA.
LAST CALL FOR ELLE-Q! I WANT TO GO HOME AND EAT DINNER!
WE'RE HERE!!

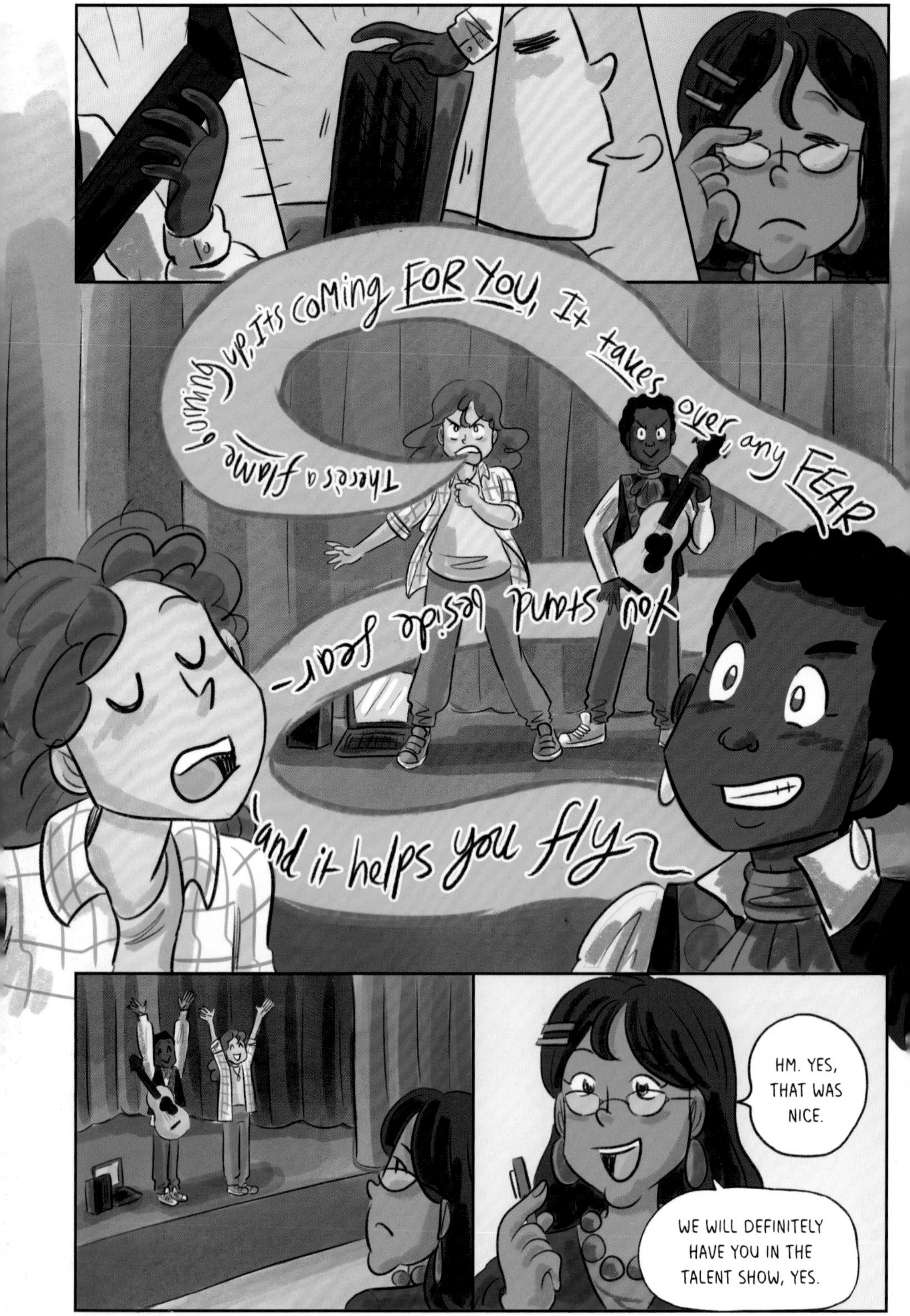
There's a flame burning up, it's coming FOR YOU, It takes over, any FEAR
You stand beside fear–
and it helps you fly~
HM. YES, THAT WAS NICE.
WE WILL DEFINITELY HAVE YOU IN THE TALENT SHOW, YES.

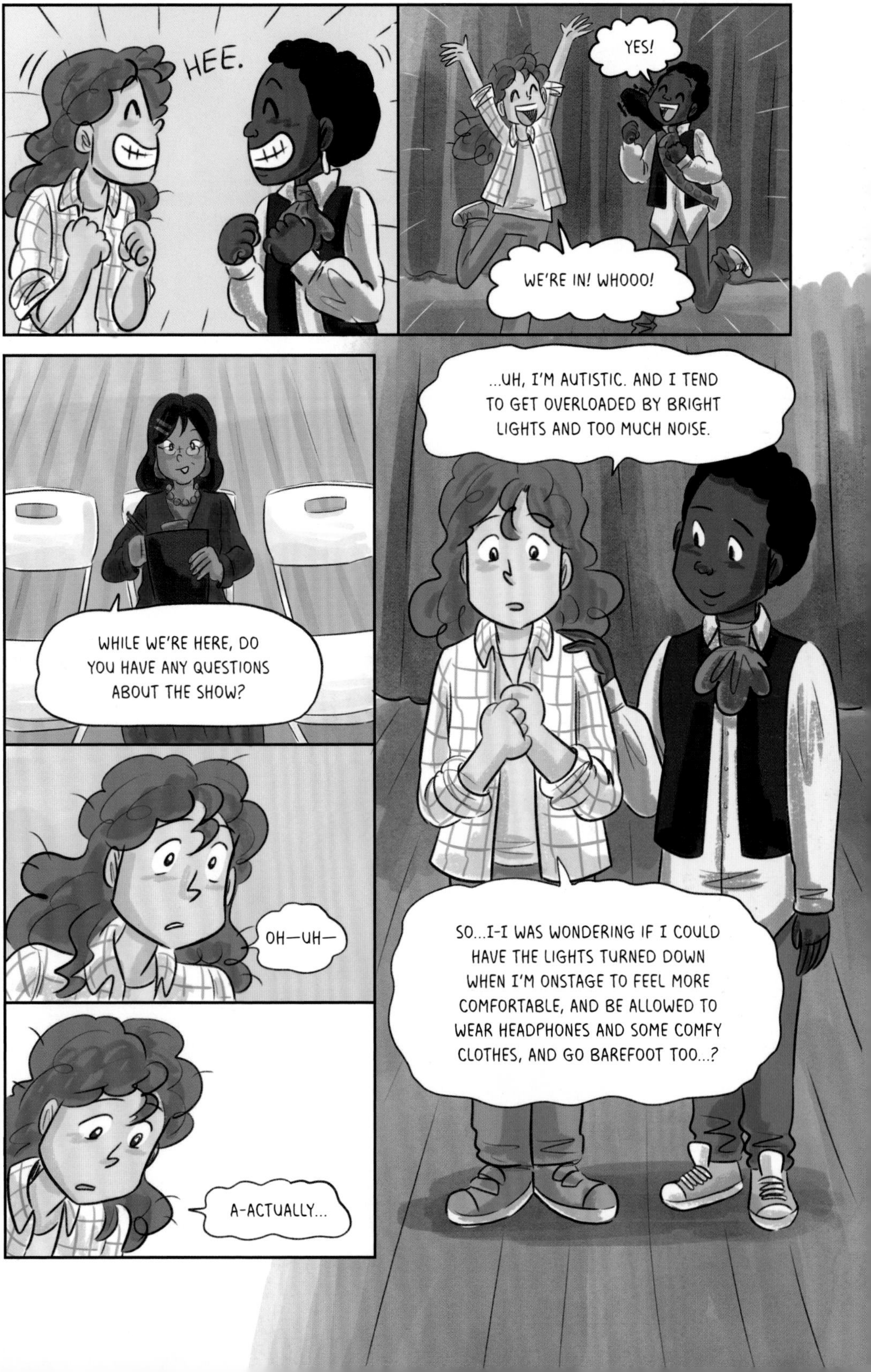
HEE.
YES!
WE'RE IN! WHOOO!
WHILE WE'RE HERE, DO YOU HAVE ANY QUESTIONS ABOUT THE SHOW?
OH—UH—
A-ACTUALLY...
...UH, I'M AUTISTIC. AND I TEND TO GET OVERLOADED BY BRIGHT LIGHTS AND TOO MUCH NOISE.
SO...I-I WAS WONDERING IF I COULD HAVE THE LIGHTS TURNED DOWN WHEN I'M ONSTAGE TO FEEL MORE COMFORTABLE, AND BE ALLOWED TO WEAR HEADPHONES AND SOME COMFY CLOTHES, AND GO BAREFOOT TOO...?

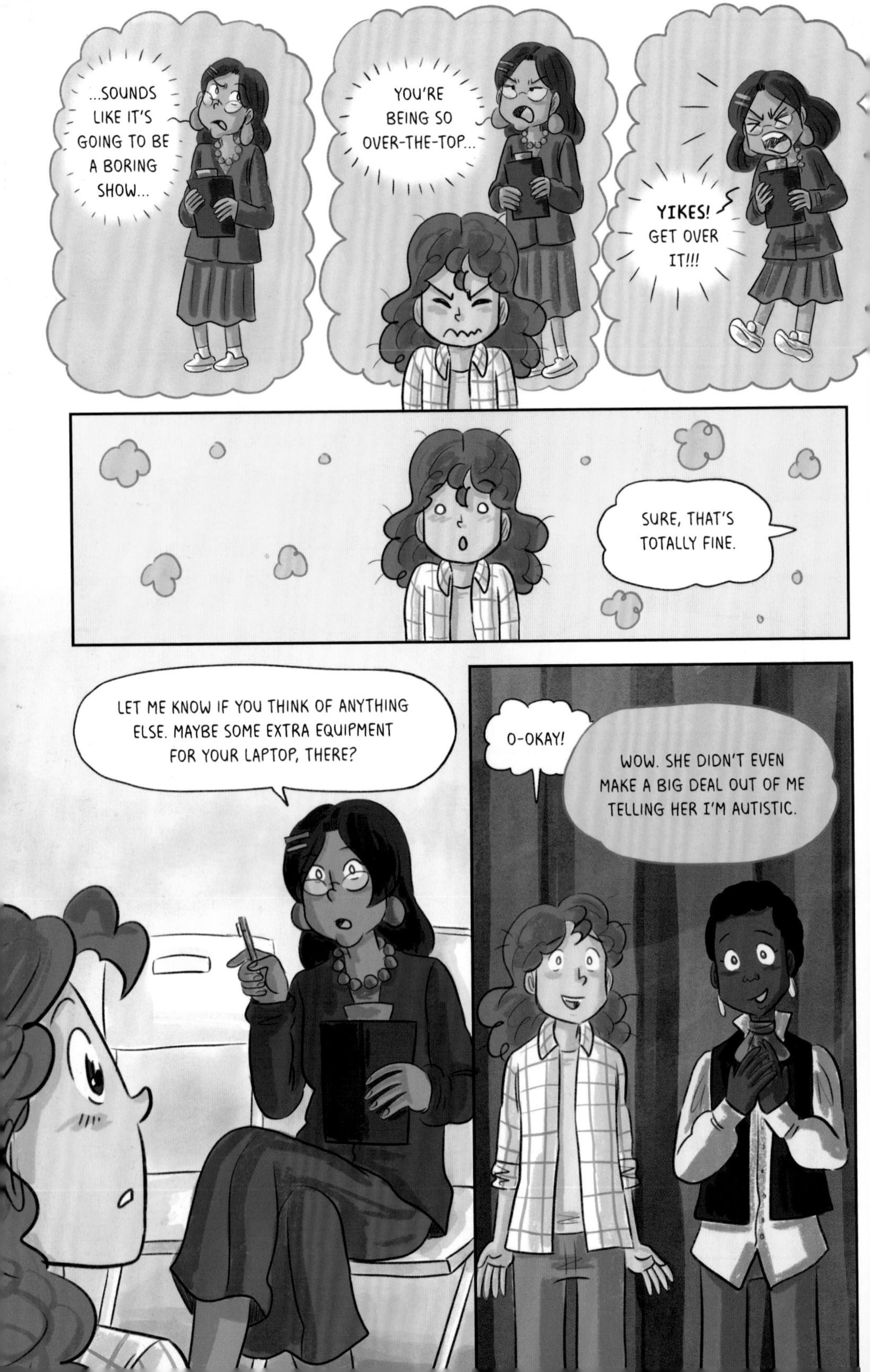
...SOUNDS LIKE IT'S GOING TO BE A BORING SHOW...
YOU'RE BEING SO OVER-THE-TOP...
YIKES! GET OVER IT!!!
SURE, THAT'S TOTALLY FINE.
LET ME KNOW IF YOU THINK OF ANYTHING ELSE. MAYBE SOME EXTRA EQUIPMENT FOR YOUR LAPTOP, THERE?
O-OKAY!
WOW. SHE DIDN'T EVEN MAKE A BIG DEAL OUT OF ME TELLING HER I'M AUTISTIC.

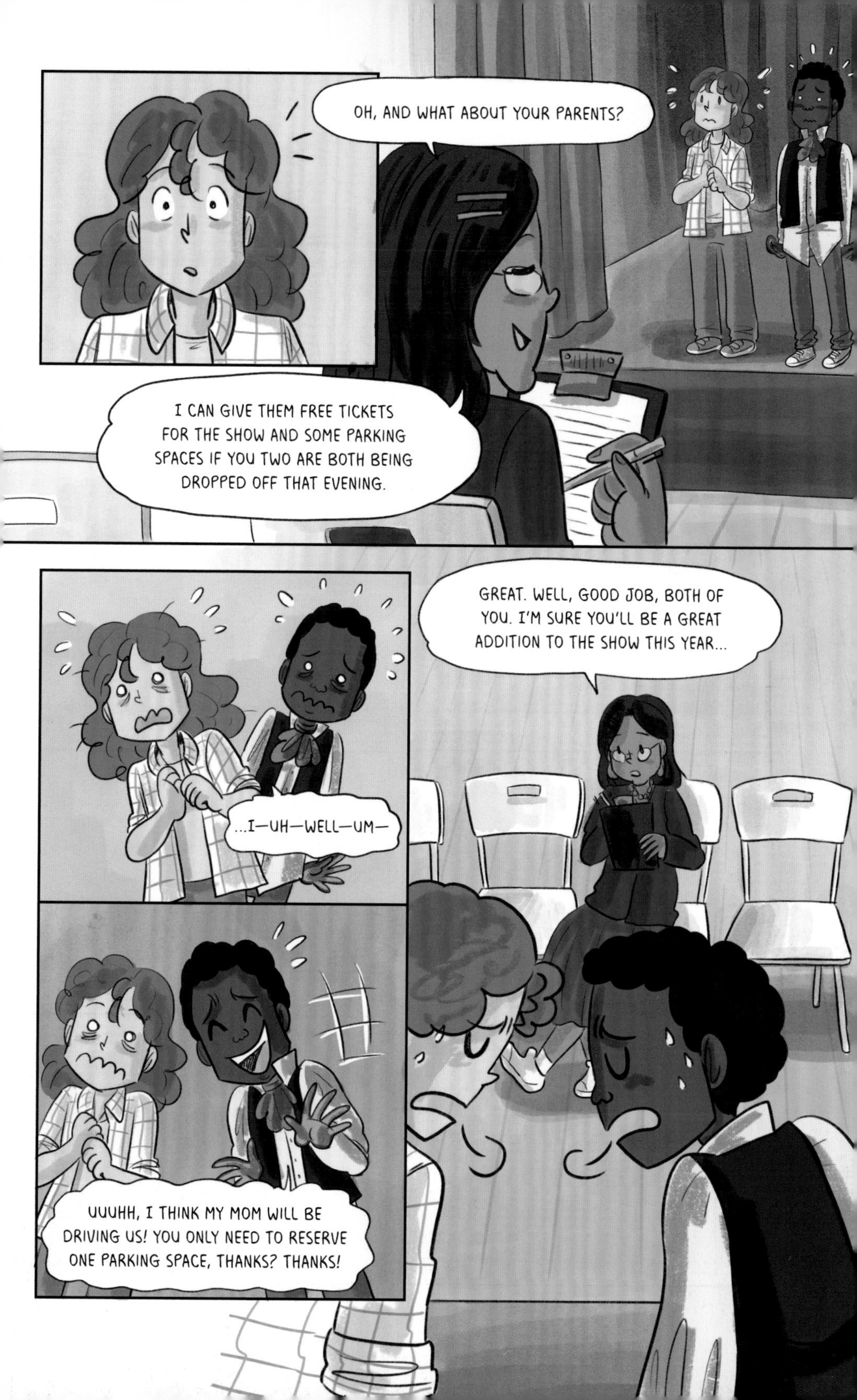
OH, AND WHAT ABOUT YOUR PARENTS?
I CAN GIVE THEM FREE TICKETS FOR THE SHOW AND SOME PARKING SPACES IF YOU TWO ARE BOTH BEING DROPPED OFF THAT EVENING.
GREAT. WELL, GOOD JOB, BOTH OF YOU. I'M SURE YOU'LL BE A GREAT ADDITION TO THE SHOW THIS YEAR...
...I—UH—WELL—UM—
UUUHH, I THINK MY MOM WILL BE DRIVING US! YOU ONLY NEED TO RESERVE ONE PARKING SPACE, THANKS? THANKS!

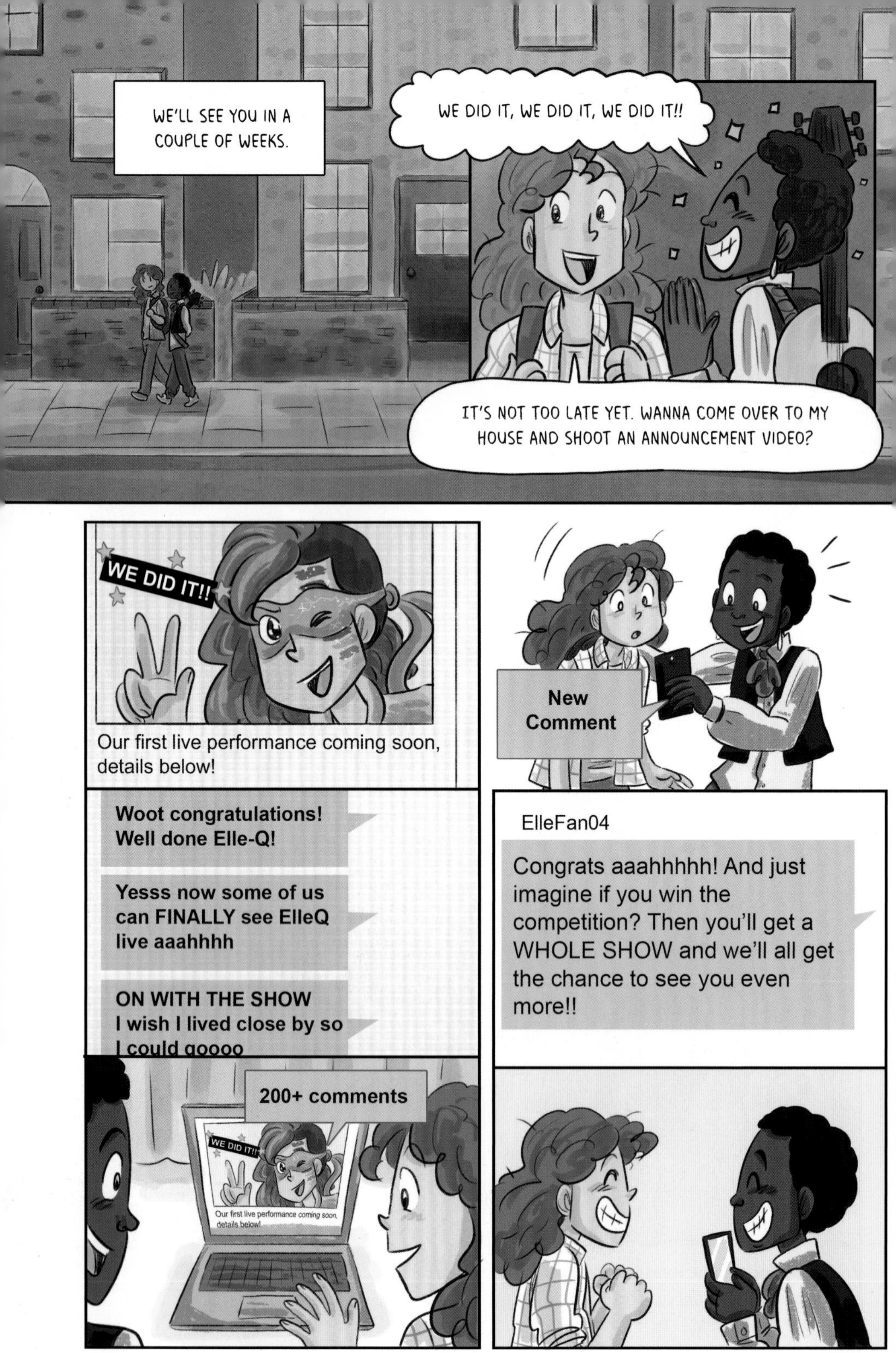
WE'LL SEE YOU IN A COUPLE OF WEEKS.
WE DID IT, WE DID IT, WE DID IT!!
IT'S NOT TOO LATE YET. WANNA COME OVER TO MY HOUSE AND SHOOT AN ANNOUNCEMENT VIDEO?
WE DID IT!!
Our first live performance coming soon, details below!
New Comment
Woot congratulations! Well done Elle-Q!
Yesss now some of us can FINALLY see ElleQ live aaahhhh
ON WITH THE SHOW I wish I lived close by so I could goooo
ElleFan04
Congrats aaahhhhh! And just imagine if you win the competition? Then you'll get a WHOLE SHOW and we'll all get the chance to see you even more!!
200+ comments
WE DID IT!!
Our first live performance coming soon, details below!

CHAPTER SEVEN

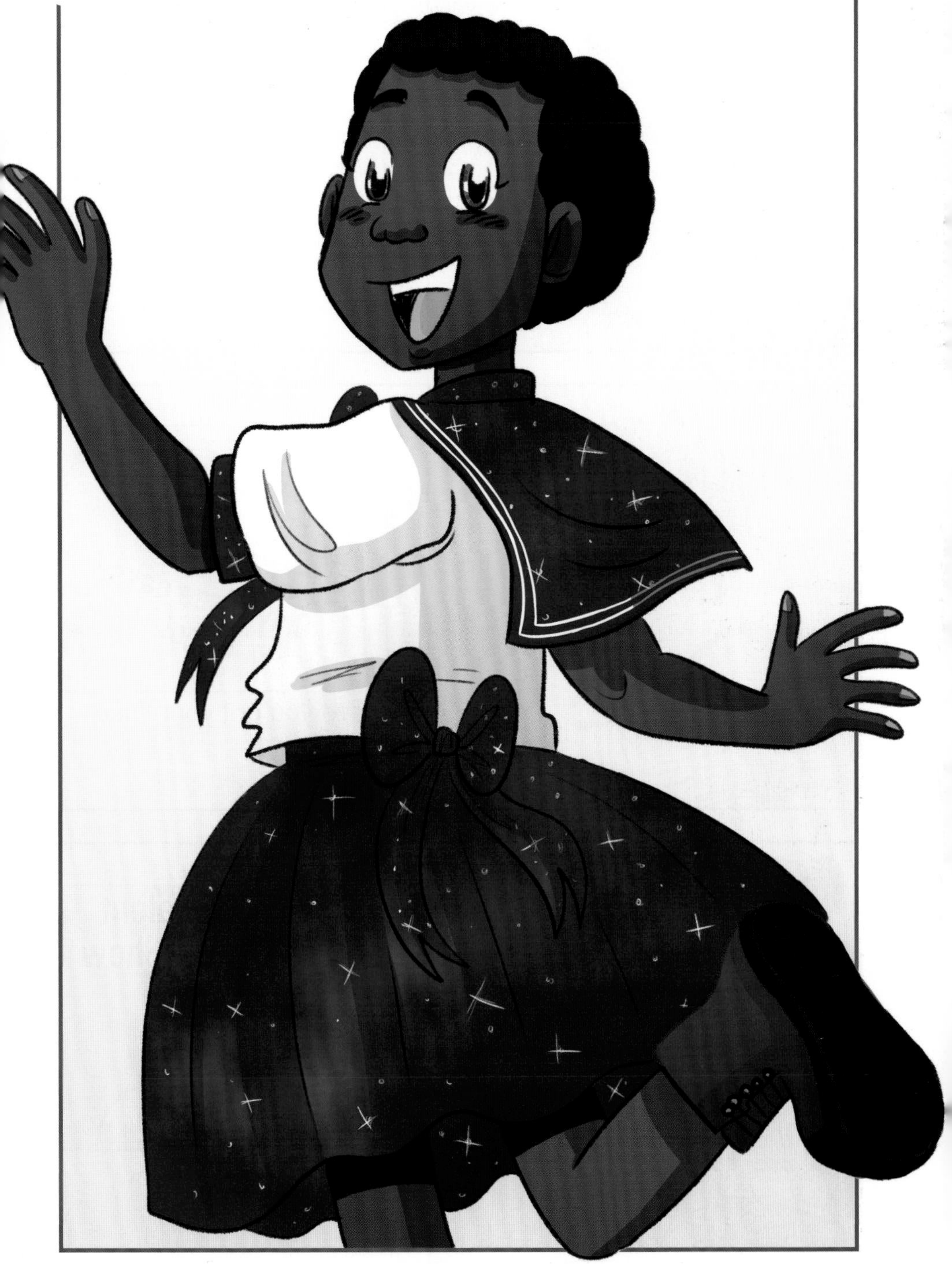

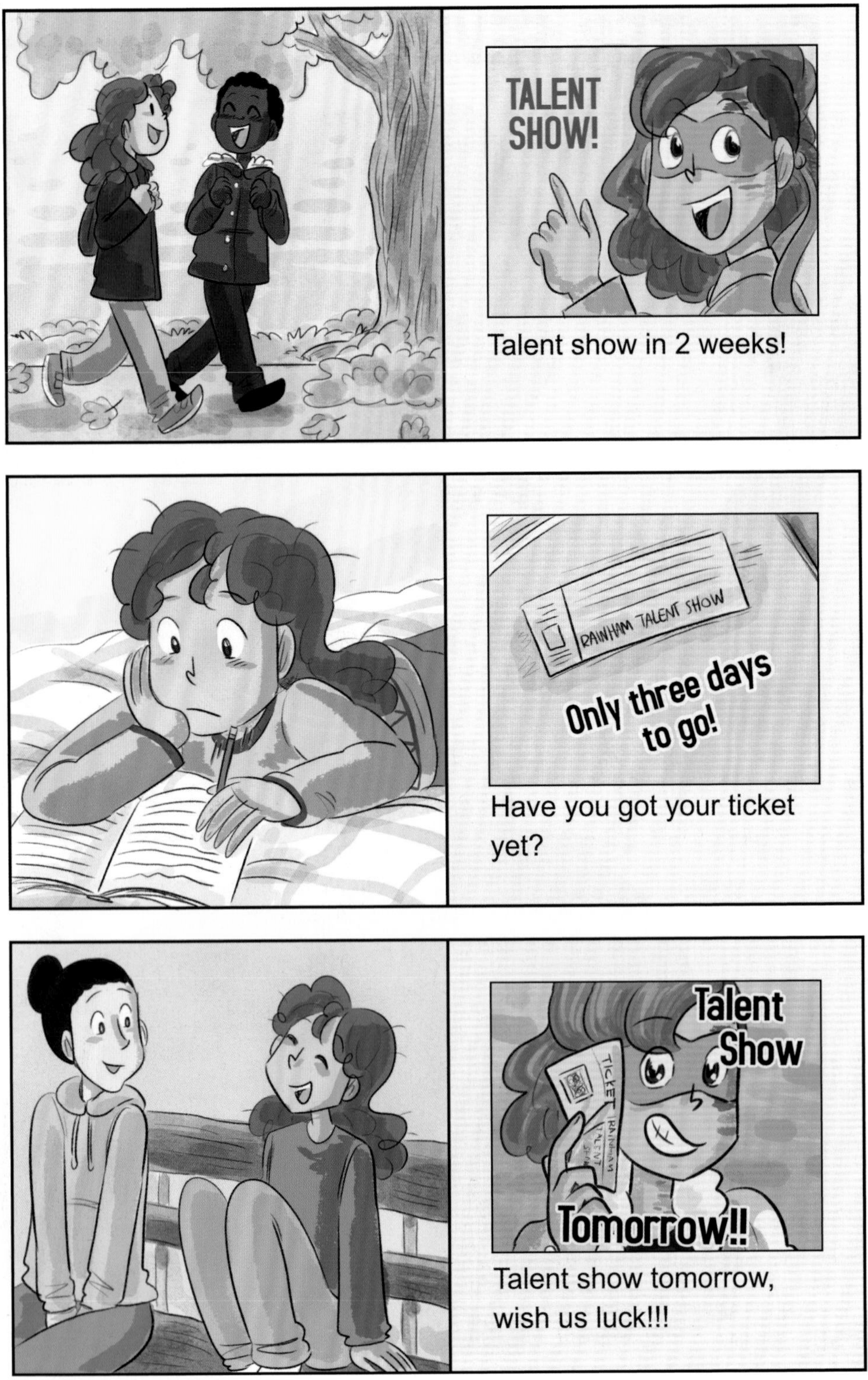
TALENT SHOW!
Talent show in 2 weeks!
RAINHAM TALENT SHOW
Only three days to go!
Have you got your ticket yet?
TICKET
Talent Show
Tomorrow!!
Talent show tomorrow, wish us luck!!!

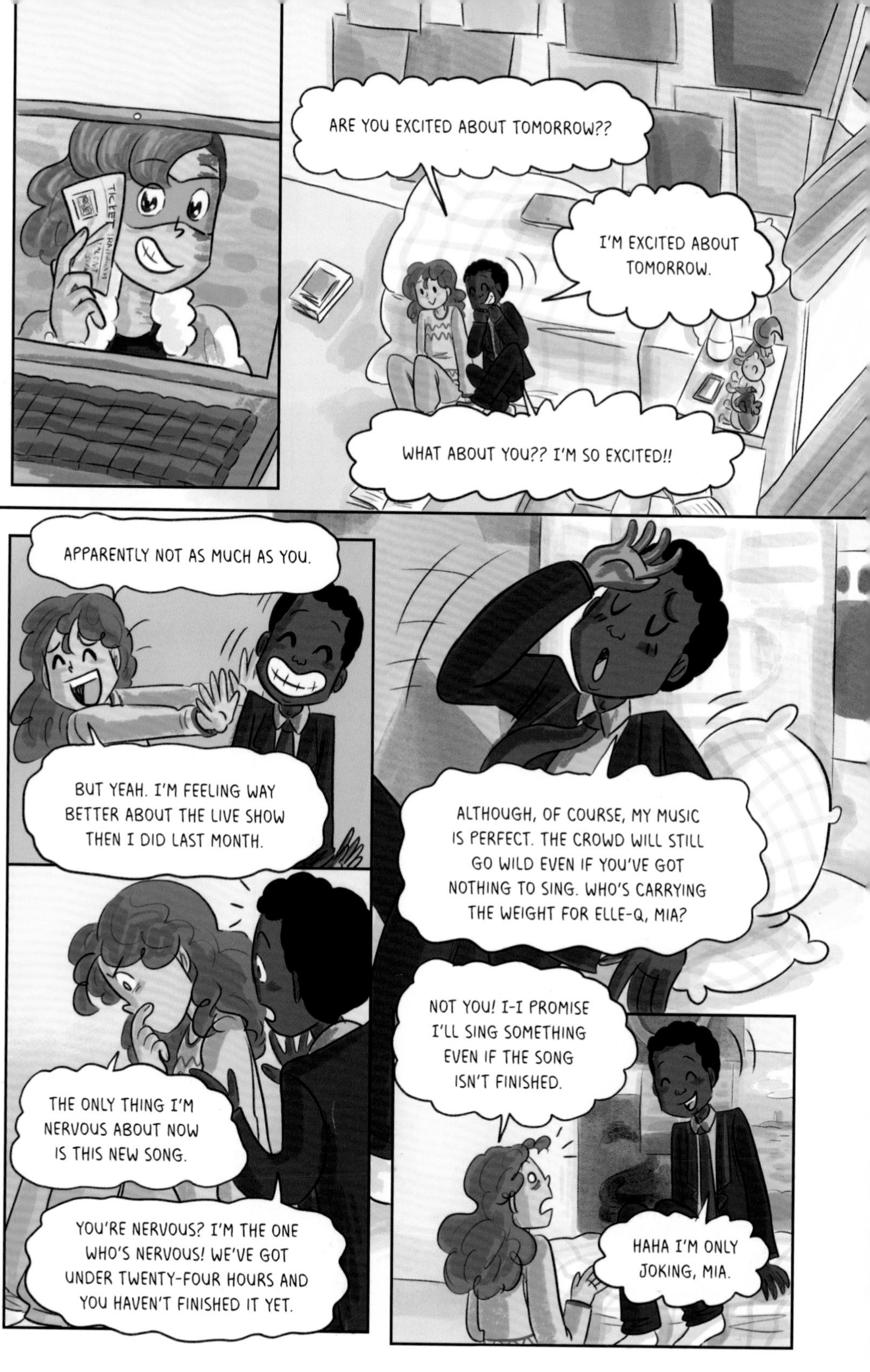
ARE YOU EXCITED ABOUT TOMORROW??
I'M EXCITED ABOUT TOMORROW.
WHAT ABOUT YOU?? I'M SO EXCITED!!
APPARENTLY NOT AS MUCH AS YOU.
BUT YEAH. I'M FEELING WAY BETTER ABOUT THE LIVE SHOW THEN I DID LAST MONTH.
THE ONLY THING I'M NERVOUS ABOUT NOW IS THIS NEW SONG.
YOU'RE NERVOUS? I'M THE ONE WHO'S NERVOUS! WE'VE GOT UNDER TWENTY-FOUR HOURS AND YOU HAVEN'T FINISHED IT YET.
ALTHOUGH, OF COURSE, MY MUSIC IS PERFECT. THE CROWD WILL STILL GO WILD EVEN IF YOU'VE GOT NOTHING TO SING. WHO'S CARRYING THE WEIGHT FOR ELLE-Q, MIA?
NOT YOU! I-I PROMISE I'LL SING SOMETHING EVEN IF THE SONG ISN'T FINISHED.
HAHA I'M ONLY JOKING, MIA.

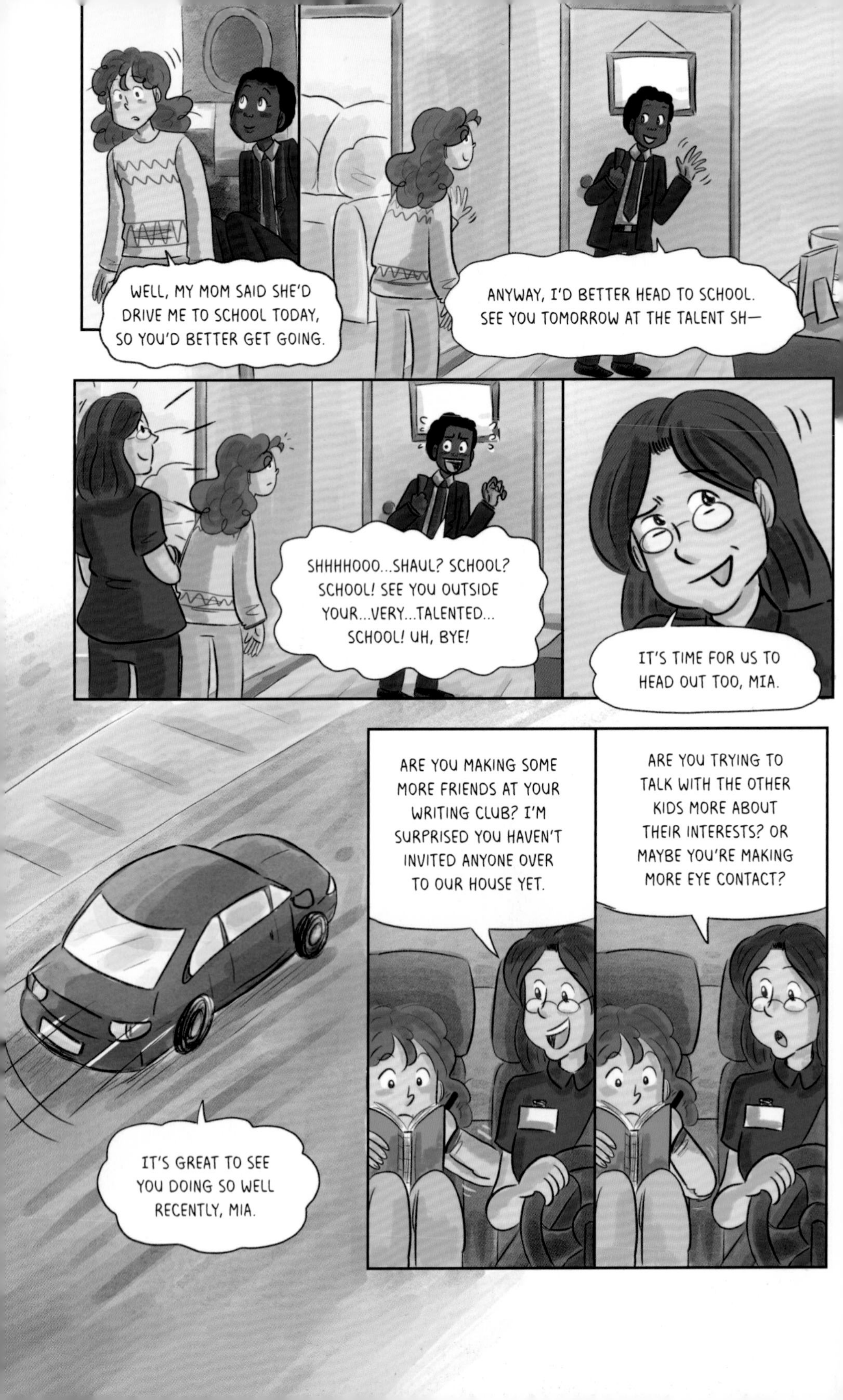
WELL, MY MOM SAID SHE'D DRIVE ME TO SCHOOL TODAY, SO YOU'D BETTER GET GOING.
ANYWAY, I'D BETTER HEAD TO SCHOOL. SEE YOU TOMORROW AT THE TALENT SH—
SHHHHOOO...SHAUL? SCHOOL? SCHOOL! SEE YOU OUTSIDE YOUR...VERY...TALENTED... SCHOOL! UH, BYE!
IT'S TIME FOR US TO HEAD OUT TOO, MIA.
IT'S GREAT TO SEE YOU DOING SO WELL RECENTLY, MIA.
ARE YOU MAKING SOME MORE FRIENDS AT YOUR WRITING CLUB? I'M SURPRISED YOU HAVEN'T INVITED ANYONE OVER TO OUR HOUSE YET.
ARE YOU TRYING TO TALK WITH THE OTHER KIDS MORE ABOUT THEIR INTERESTS? OR MAYBE YOU'RE MAKING MORE EYE CONTACT?

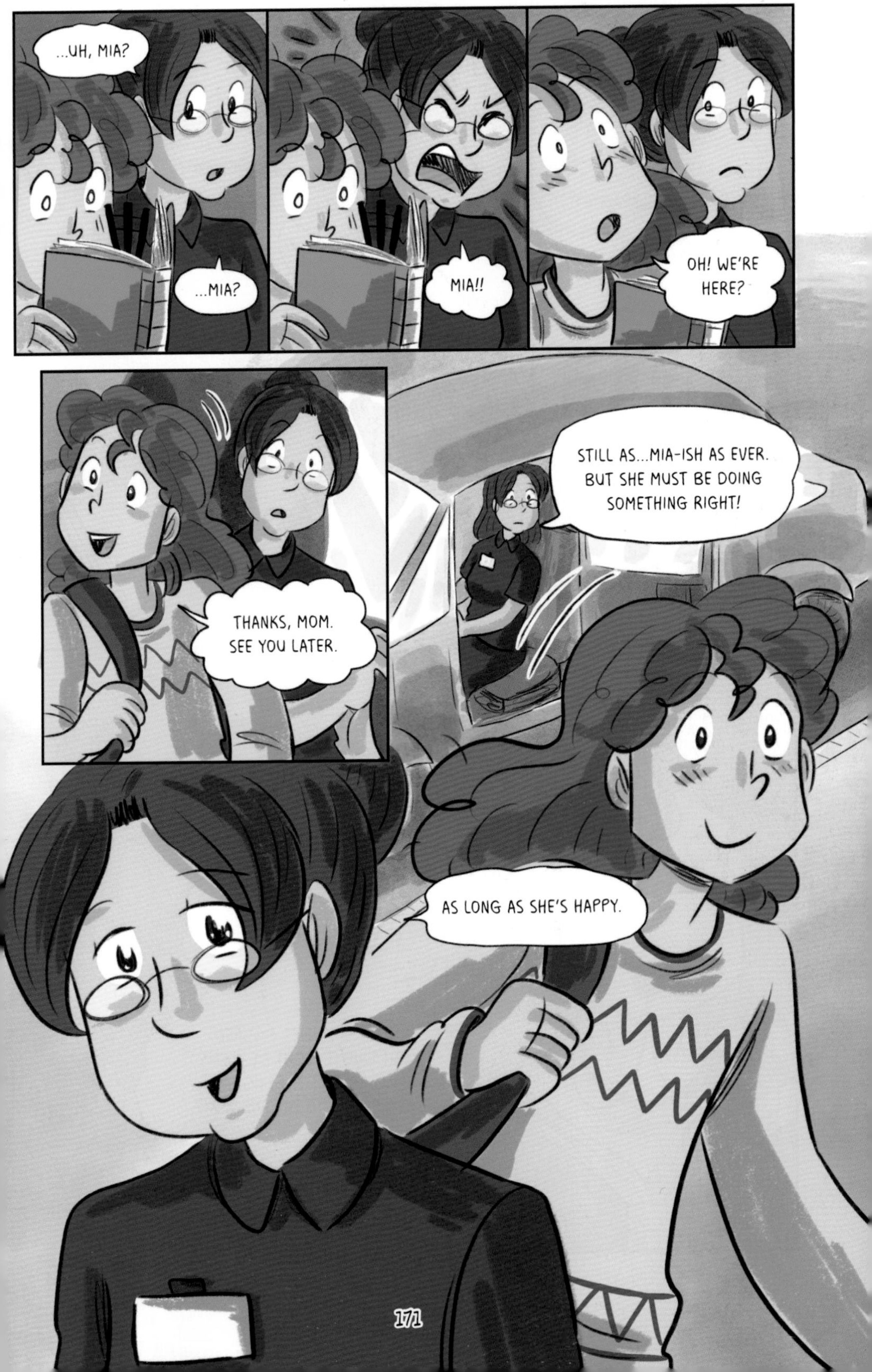
...UH, MIA?
...MIA?
MIA!!
OH! WE'RE HERE?
THANKS, MOM. SEE YOU LATER.
STILL AS...MIA-ISH AS EVER. BUT SHE MUST BE DOING SOMETHING RIGHT!
AS LONG AS SHE'S HAPPY.

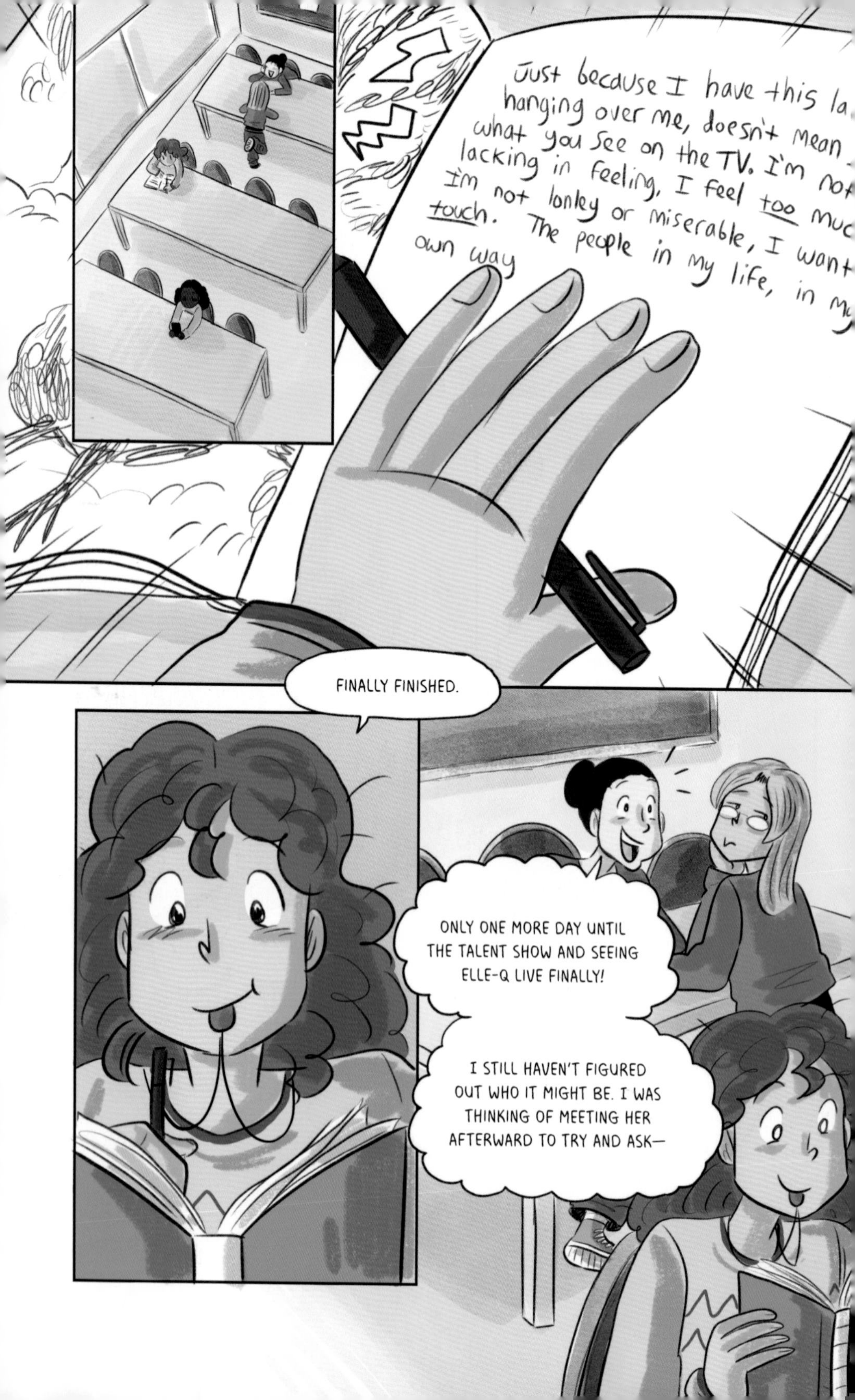
Just because I have this la
hanging over me, doesn't mean
what you See on the TV. I'm not
lacking in feeling, I feel too muc
I'm not lonley or miserable, I want
touch. The people in my life, in my
own way
FINALLY FINISHED.
ONLY ONE MORE DAY UNTIL THE TALENT SHOW AND SEEING ELLE-Q LIVE FINALLY!
I STILL HAVEN'T FIGURED OUT WHO IT MIGHT BE. I WAS THINKING OF MEETING HER AFTERWARD TO TRY AND ASK—

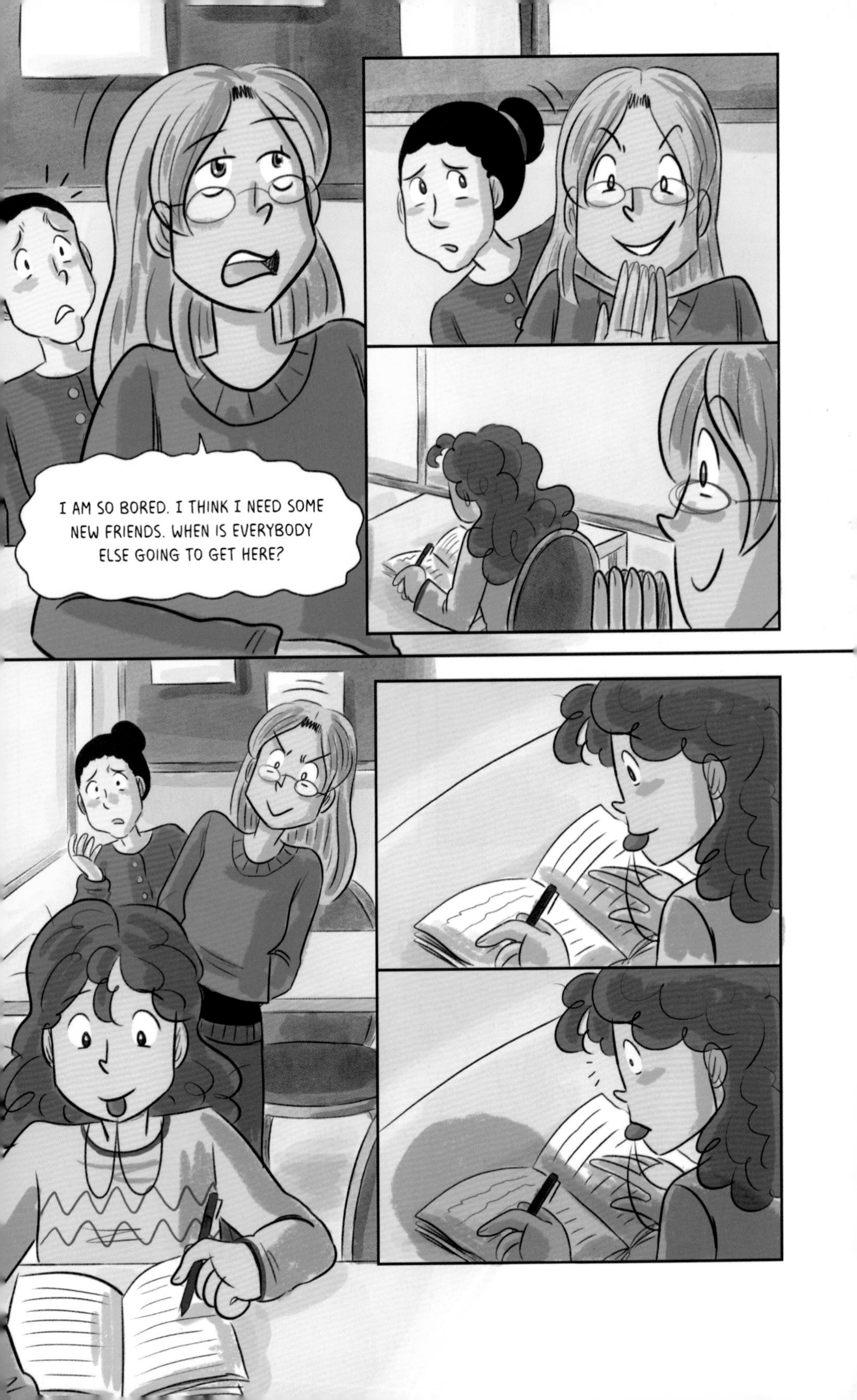
I AM SO BORED. I THINK I NEED SOME NEW FRIENDS. WHEN IS EVERYBODY ELSE GOING TO GET HERE?

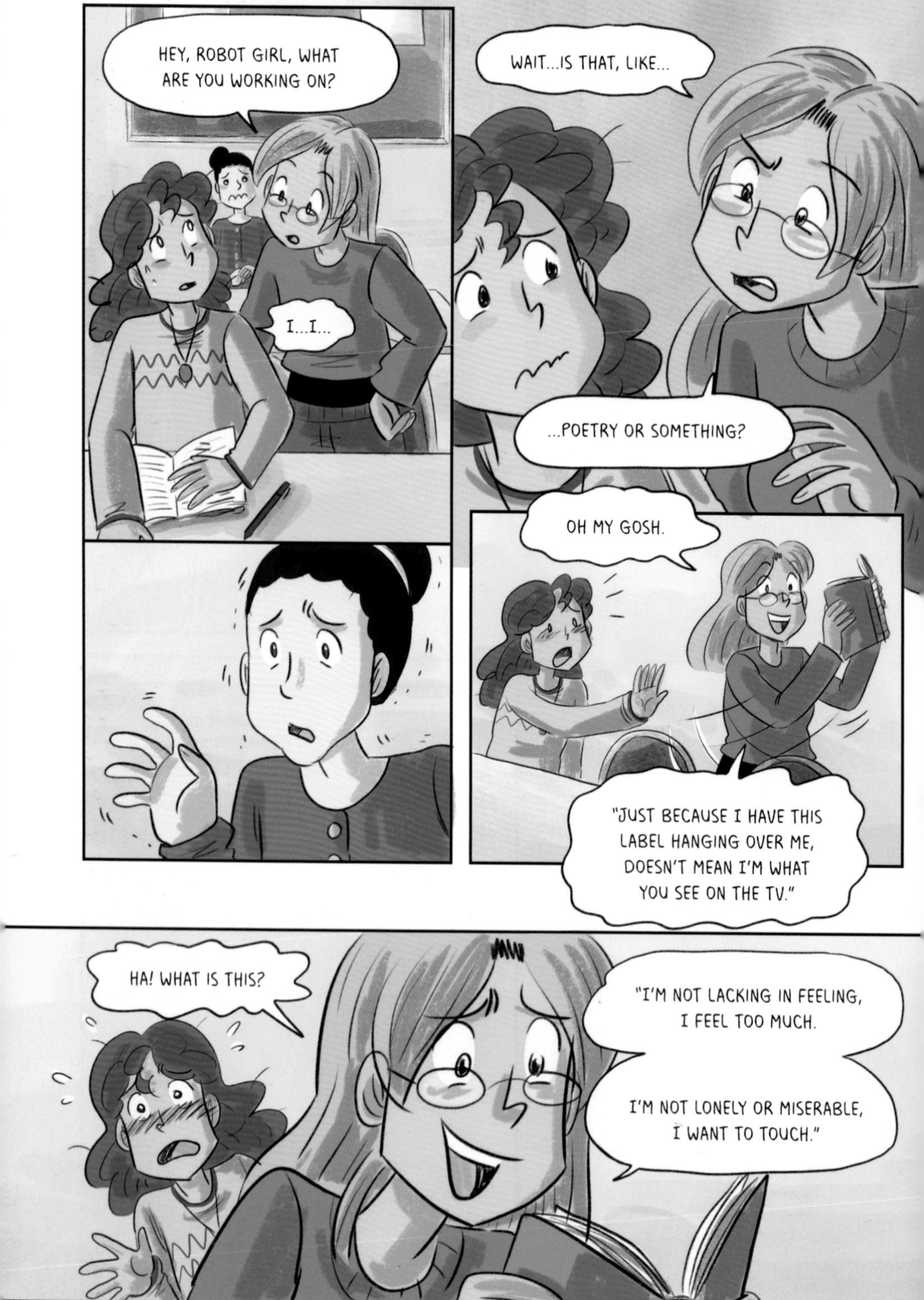
HEY, ROBOT GIRL, WHAT ARE YOU WORKING ON?
I...I...
WAIT...IS THAT, LIKE...
...POETRY OR SOMETHING?
OH MY GOSH.
"JUST BECAUSE I HAVE THIS LABEL HANGING OVER ME, DOESN'T MEAN I'M WHAT YOU SEE ON THE TV."
HA! WHAT IS THIS?
"I'M NOT LACKING IN FEELING, I FEEL TOO MUCH.
I'M NOT LONELY OR MISERABLE, I WANT TO TOUCH."

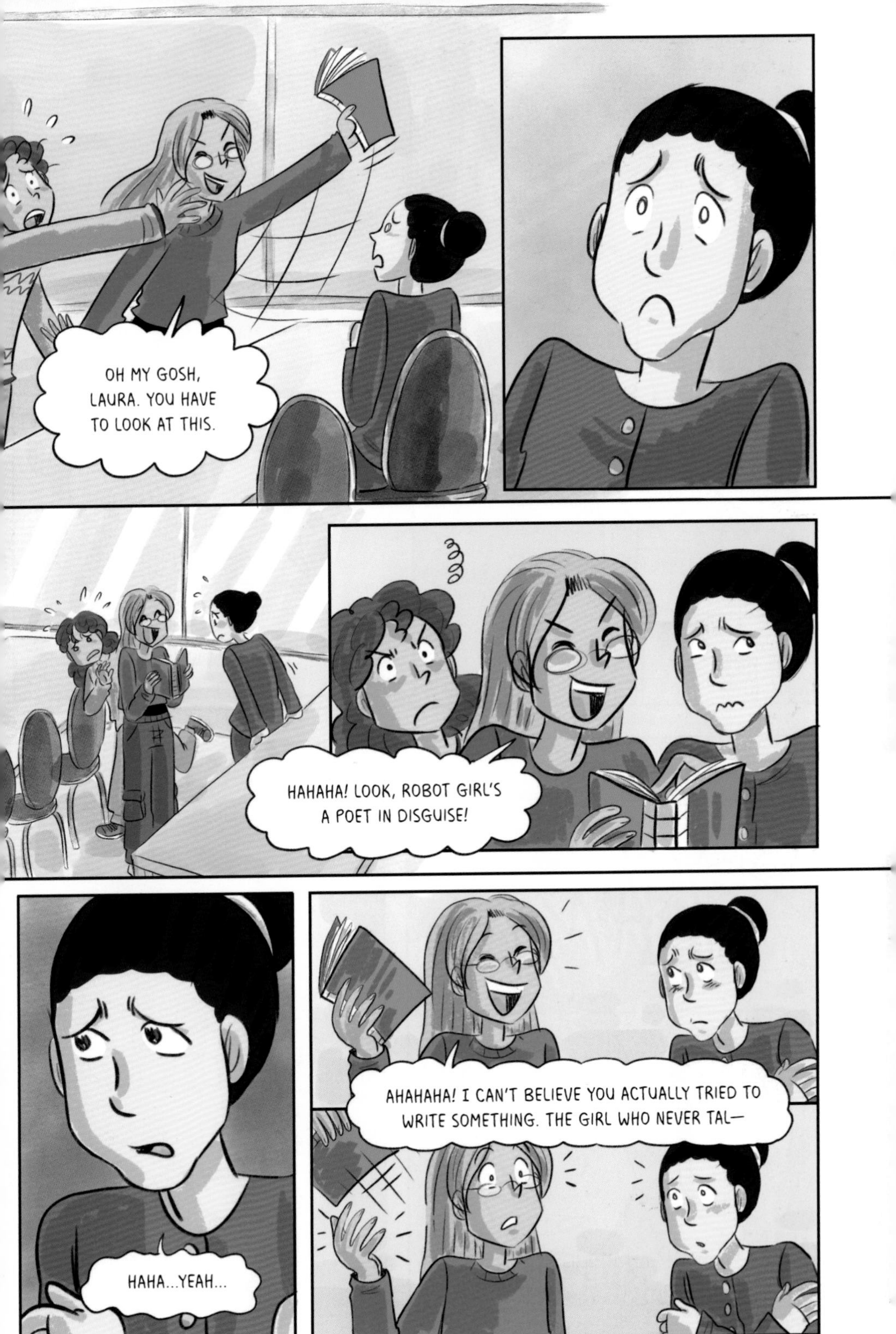
OH MY GOSH, LAURA. YOU HAVE TO LOOK AT THIS.
HAHAHA! LOOK, ROBOT GIRL'S A POET IN DISGUISE!
HAHA...YEAH...
AHAHAHA! I CAN'T BELIEVE YOU ACTUALLY TRIED TO WRITE SOMETHING. THE GIRL WHO NEVER TAL—

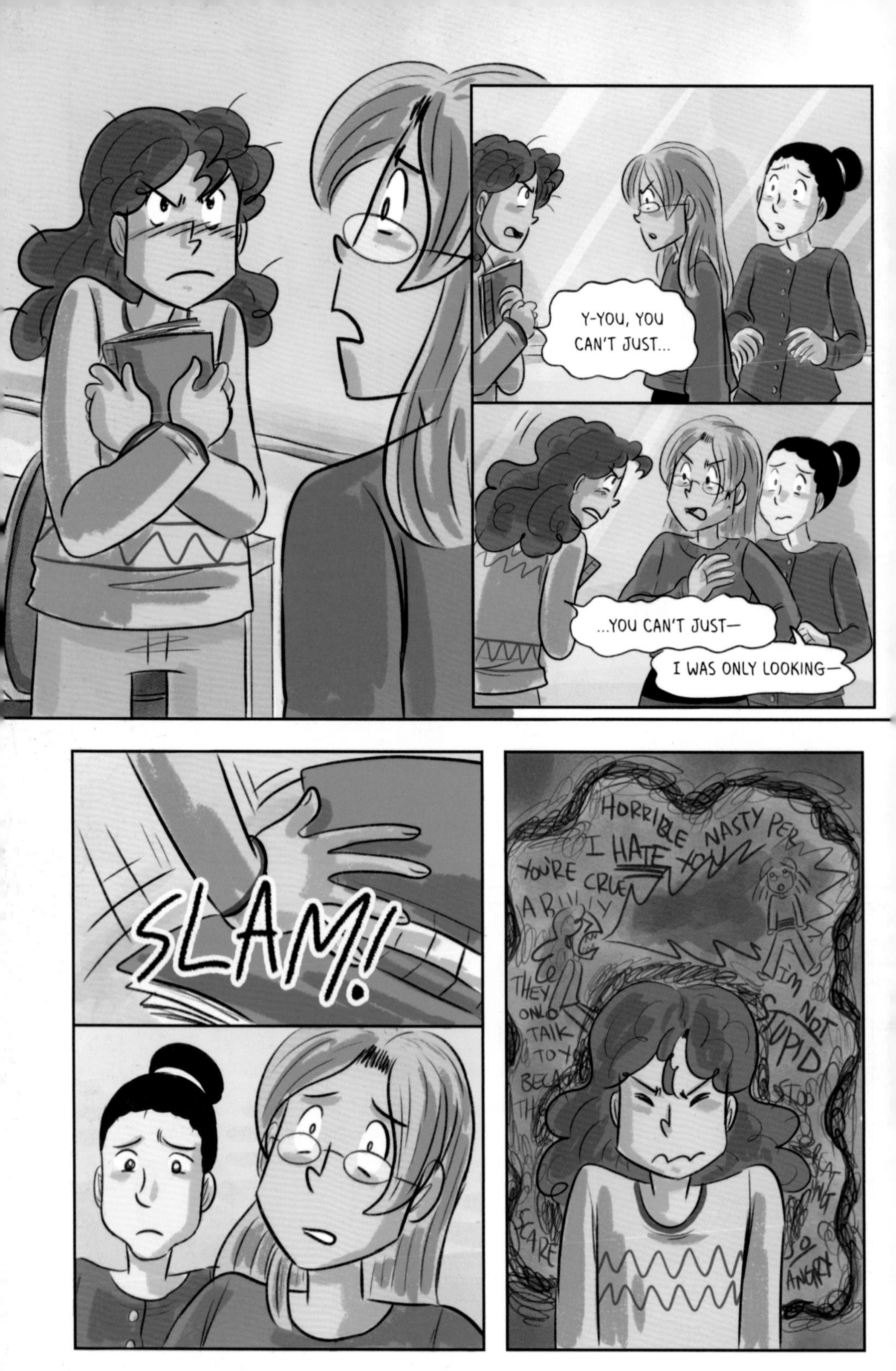
Y-YOU, YOU CAN'T JUST...
...YOU CAN'T JUST—
I WAS ONLY LOOKING—
SLAM!
HORRIBLE NASTY
I HATE
YOU'RE
I'M NOT STUPID
SCARE
ANGRY

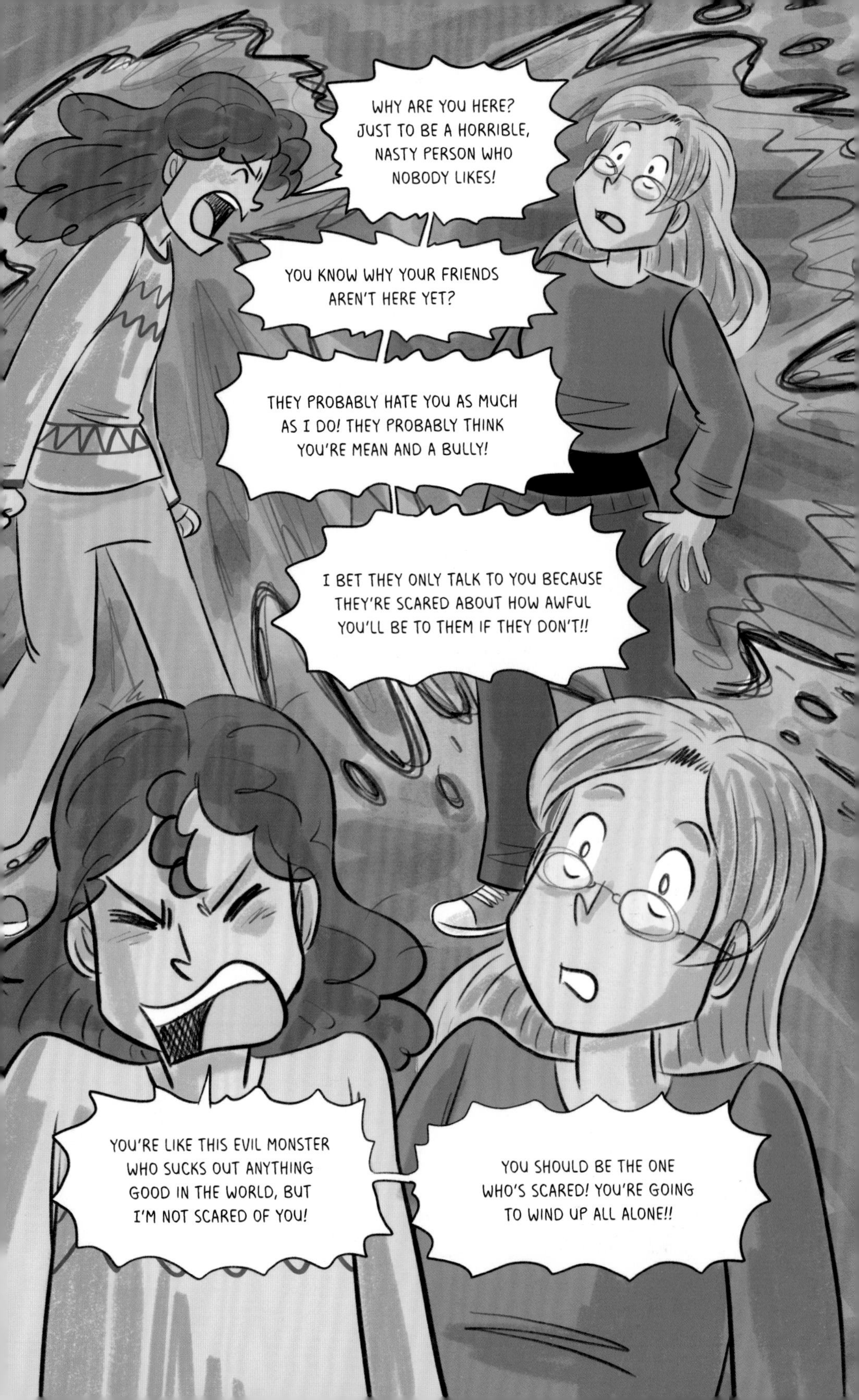
WHY ARE YOU HERE? JUST TO BE A HORRIBLE, NASTY PERSON WHO NOBODY LIKES!
YOU KNOW WHY YOUR FRIENDS AREN'T HERE YET?
THEY PROBABLY HATE YOU AS MUCH AS I DO! THEY PROBABLY THINK YOU'RE MEAN AND A BULLY!
I BET THEY ONLY TALK TO YOU BECAUSE THEY'RE SCARED ABOUT HOW AWFUL YOU'LL BE TO THEM IF THEY DON'T!!
YOU'RE LIKE THIS EVIL MONSTER WHO SUCKS OUT ANYTHING GOOD IN THE WORLD, BUT I'M NOT SCARED OF YOU!
YOU SHOULD BE THE ONE WHO'S SCARED! YOU'RE GOING TO WIND UP ALL ALONE!!

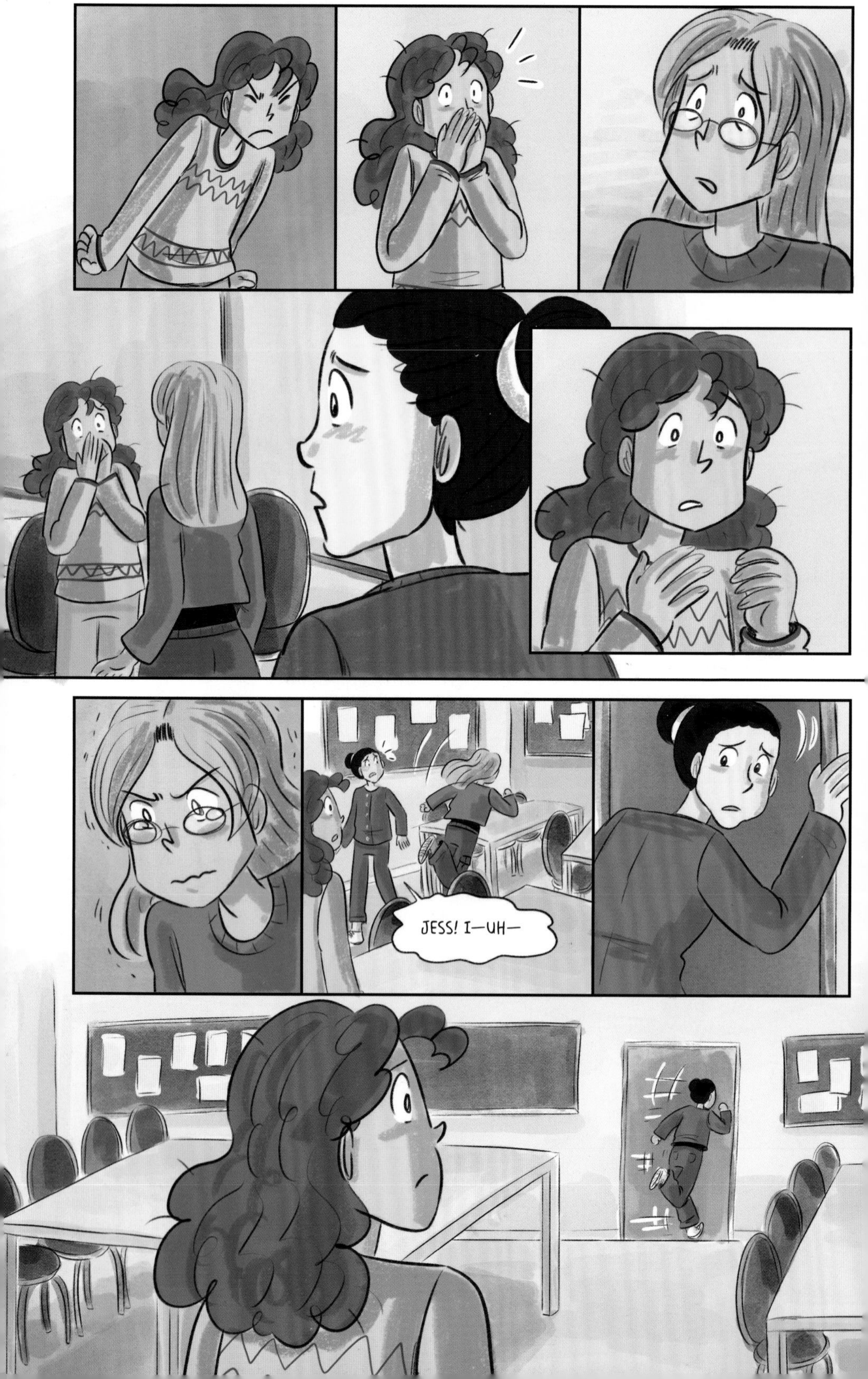
JESS! I—UH—

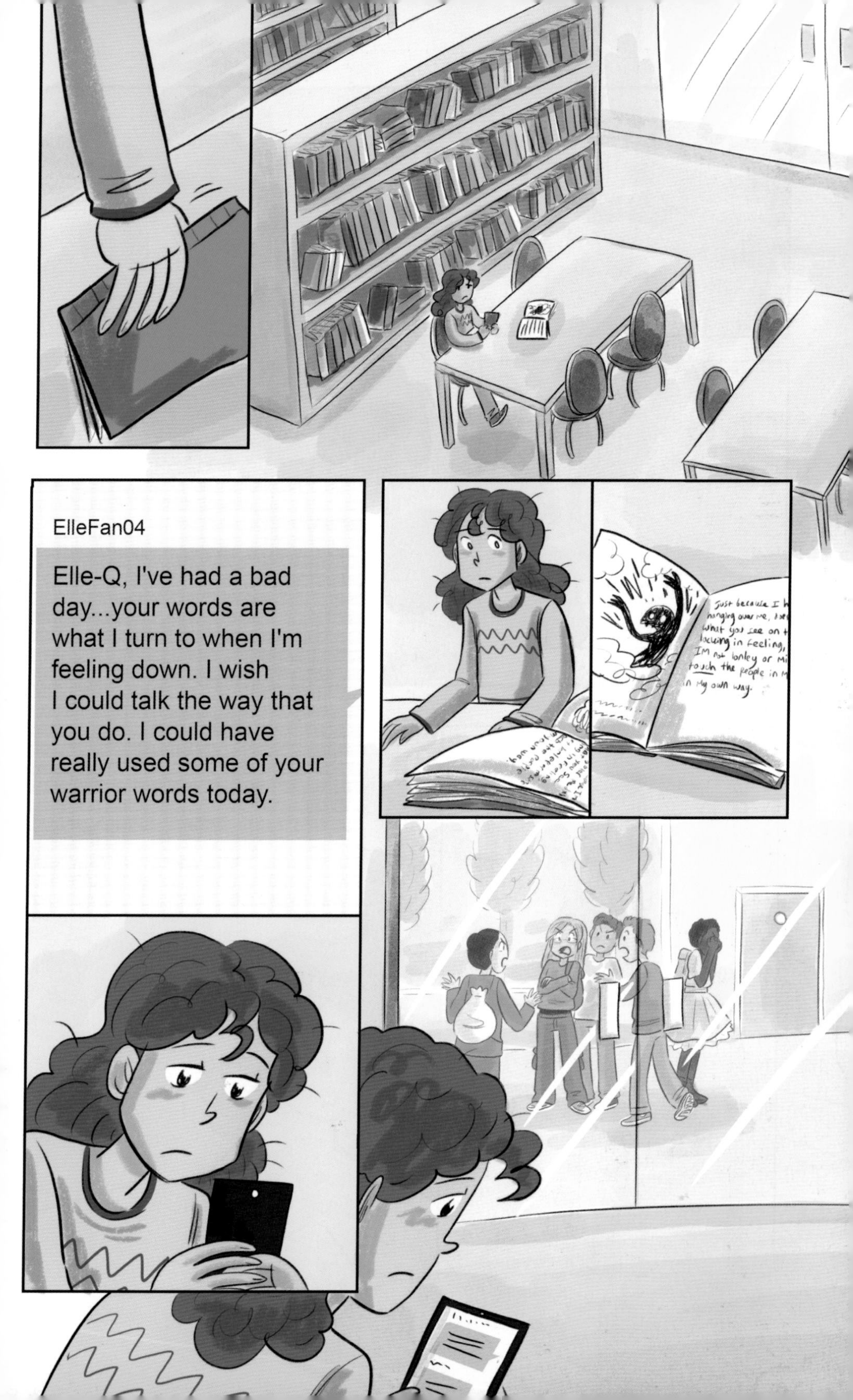
ElleFan04
Elle-Q, I've had a bad day...your words are what I turn to when I'm feeling down. I wish I could talk the way that you do. I could have really used some of your warrior words today.

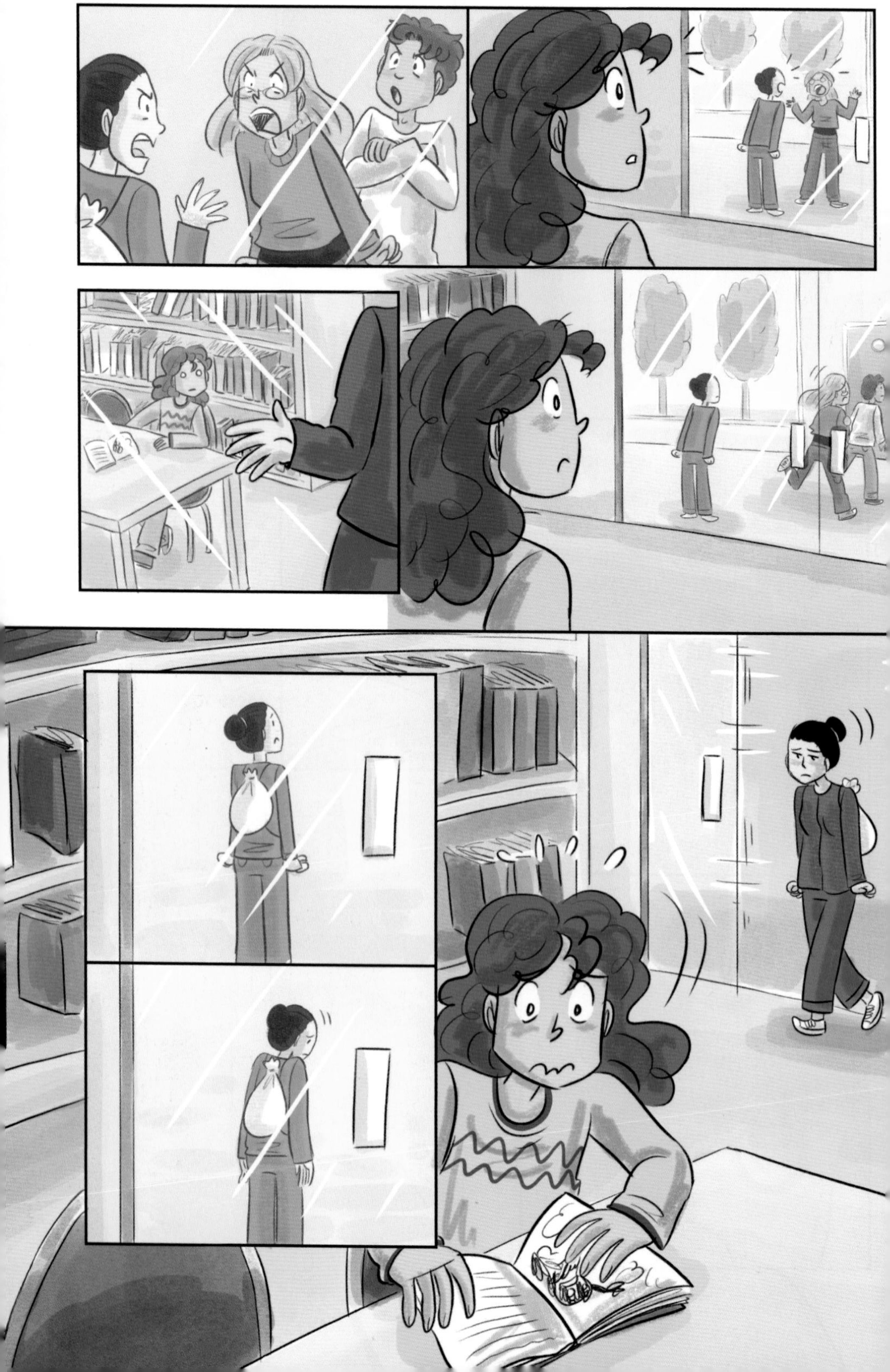

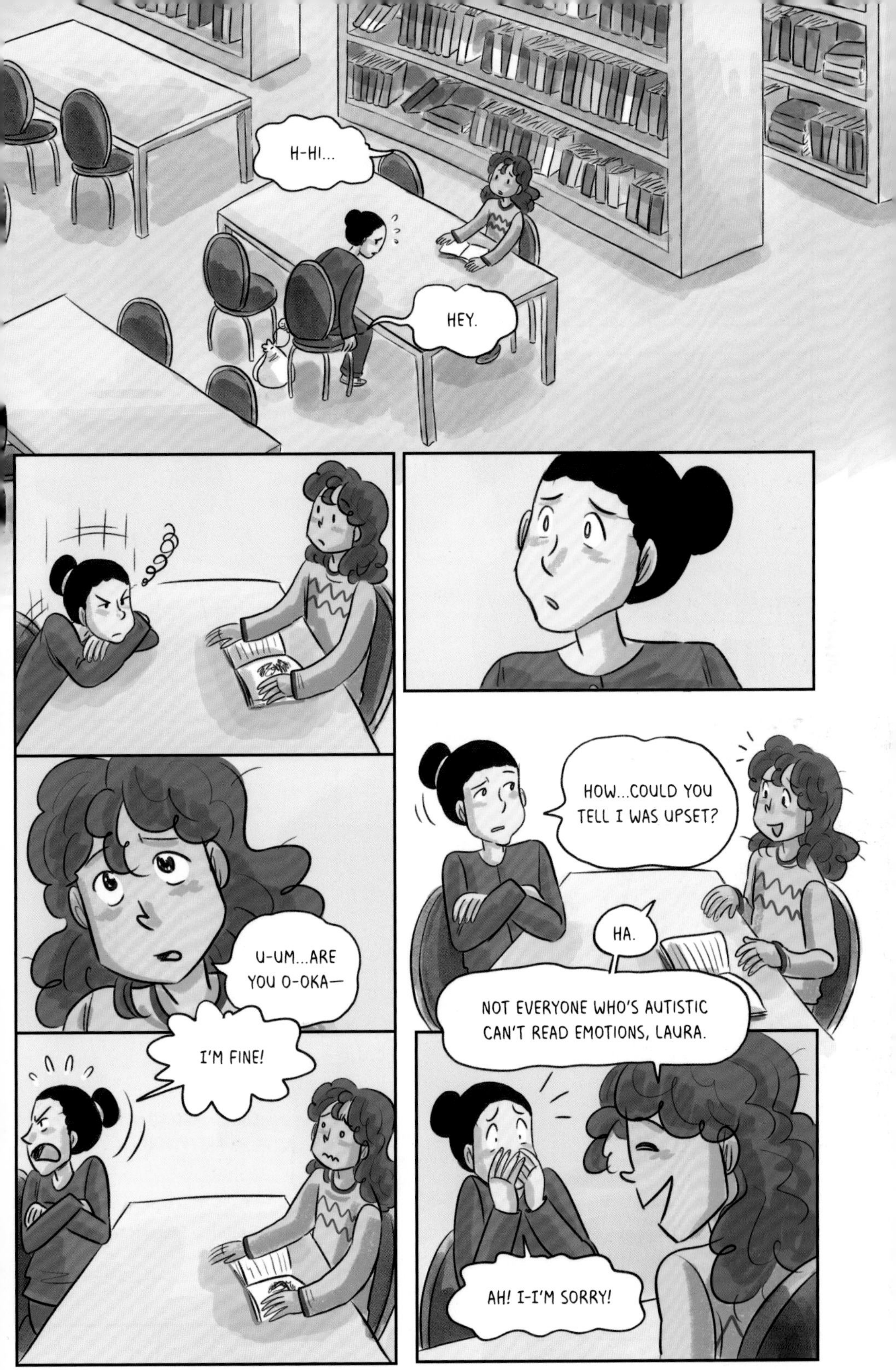
H-HI...
HEY.
U-UM...ARE YOU O-OKA—
I'M FINE!
HOW...COULD YOU TELL I WAS UPSET?
HA.
NOT EVERYONE WHO'S AUTISTIC CAN'T READ EMOTIONS, LAURA.
AH! I-I'M SORRY!

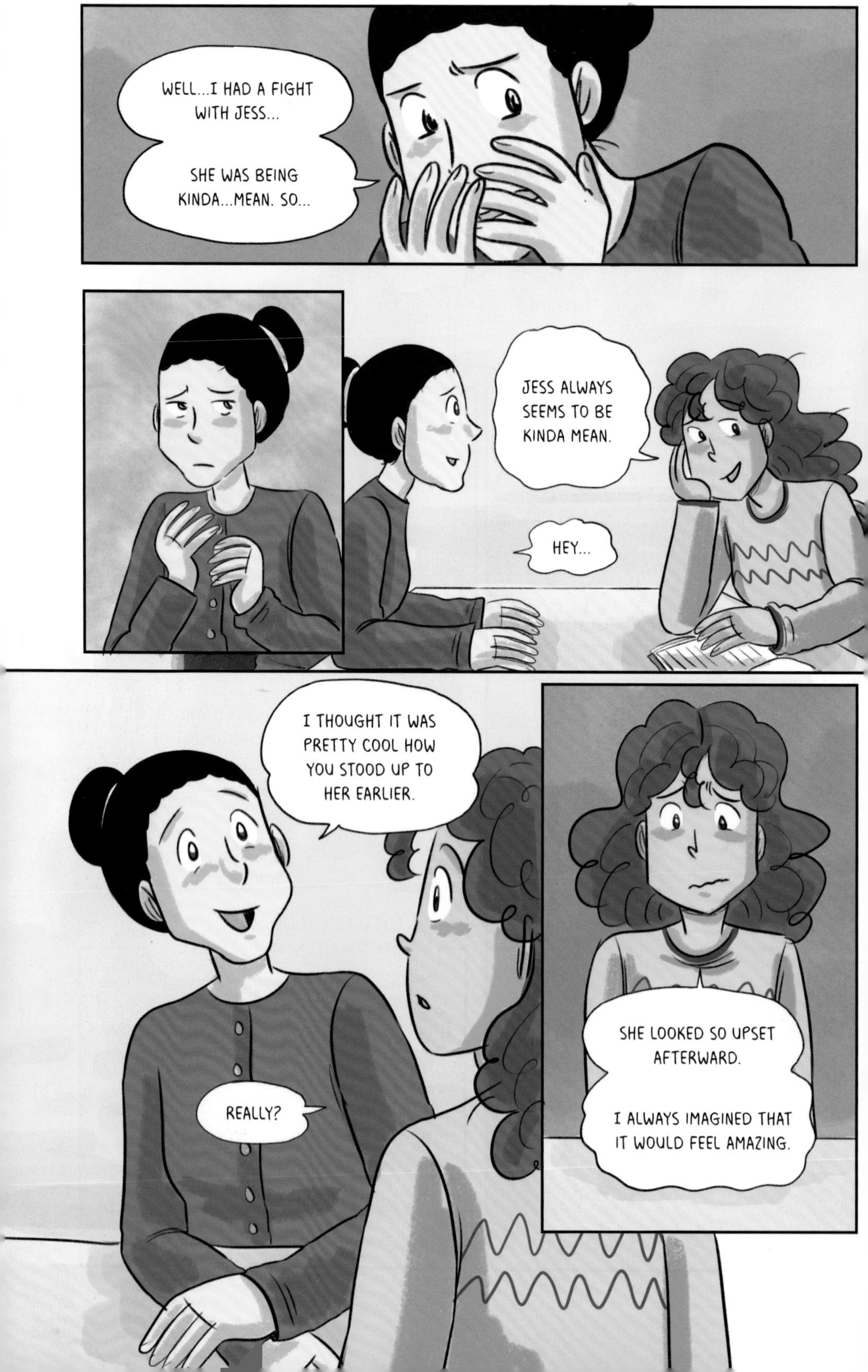
WELL...I HAD A FIGHT WITH JESS...
SHE WAS BEING KINDA...MEAN. SO...
JESS ALWAYS SEEMS TO BE KINDA MEAN.
HEY...
I THOUGHT IT WAS PRETTY COOL HOW YOU STOOD UP TO HER EARLIER.
REALLY?
SHE LOOKED SO UPSET AFTERWARD.
I ALWAYS IMAGINED THAT IT WOULD FEEL AMAZING.

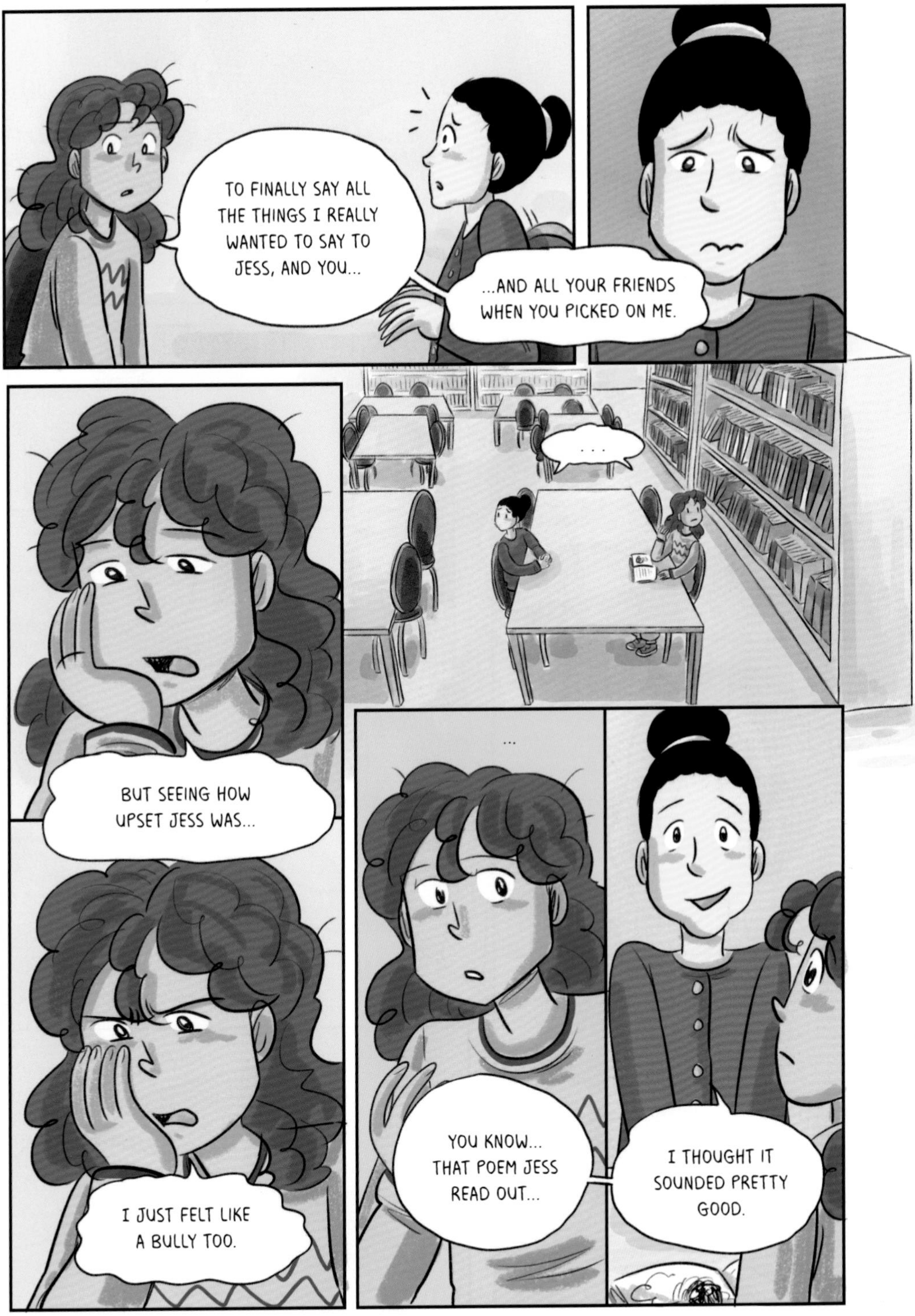
TO FINALLY SAY ALL THE THINGS I REALLY WANTED TO SAY TO JESS, AND YOU...
...AND ALL YOUR FRIENDS WHEN YOU PICKED ON ME.
. . .
BUT SEEING HOW UPSET JESS WAS...
I JUST FELT LIKE A BULLY TOO.
...
YOU KNOW... THAT POEM JESS READ OUT...
I THOUGHT IT SOUNDED PRETTY GOOD.

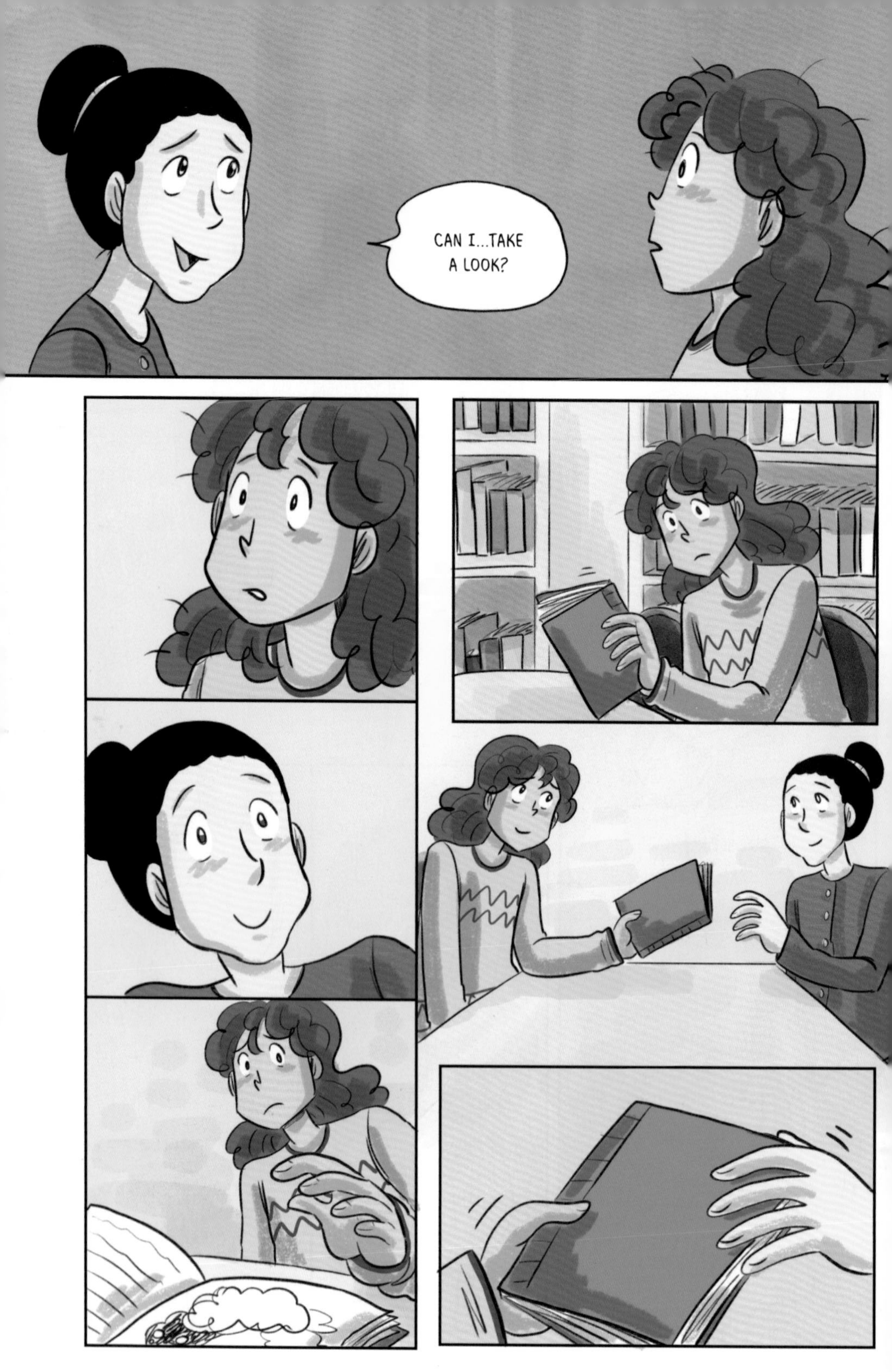
CAN I...TAKE A LOOK?

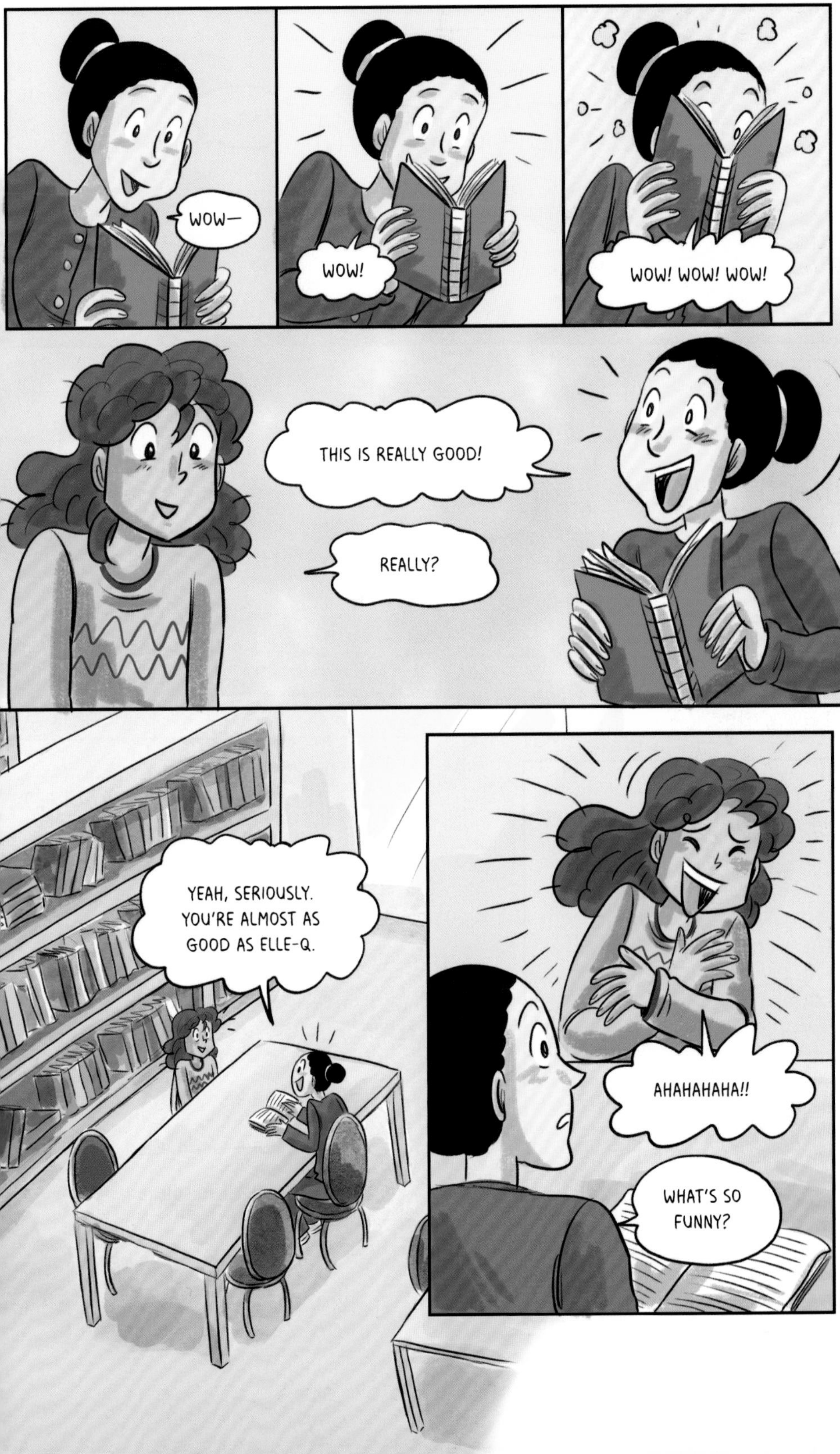
WOW—
WOW!
WOW! WOW! WOW!
THIS IS REALLY GOOD!
REALLY?
YEAH, SERIOUSLY. YOU'RE ALMOST AS GOOD AS ELLE-Q.
AHAHAHAHA!!
WHAT'S SO FUNNY?

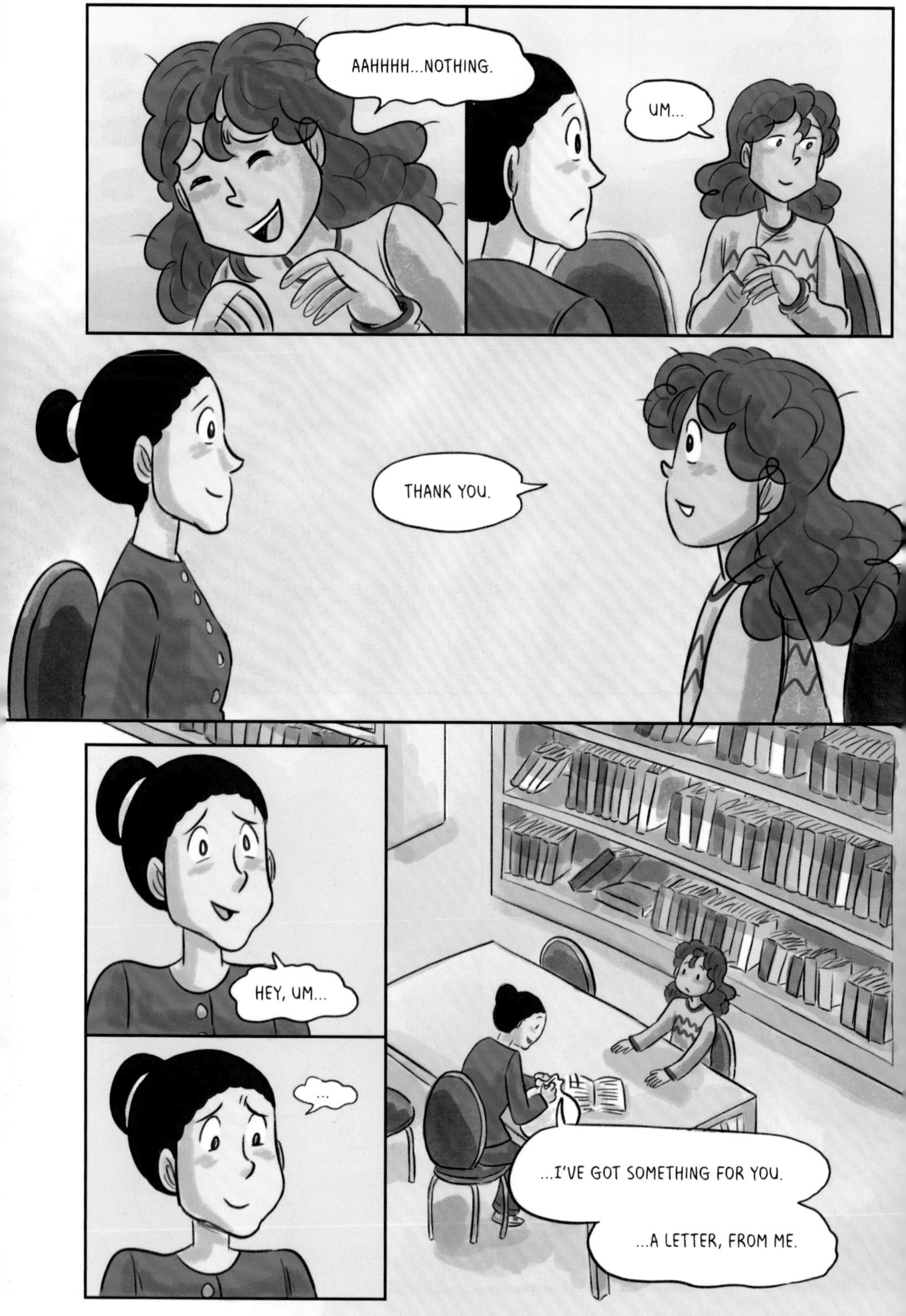
AAHHHH...NOTHING.
UM...
THANK YOU.
HEY, UM...
...
...I'VE GOT SOMETHING FOR YOU.
...A LETTER, FROM ME.

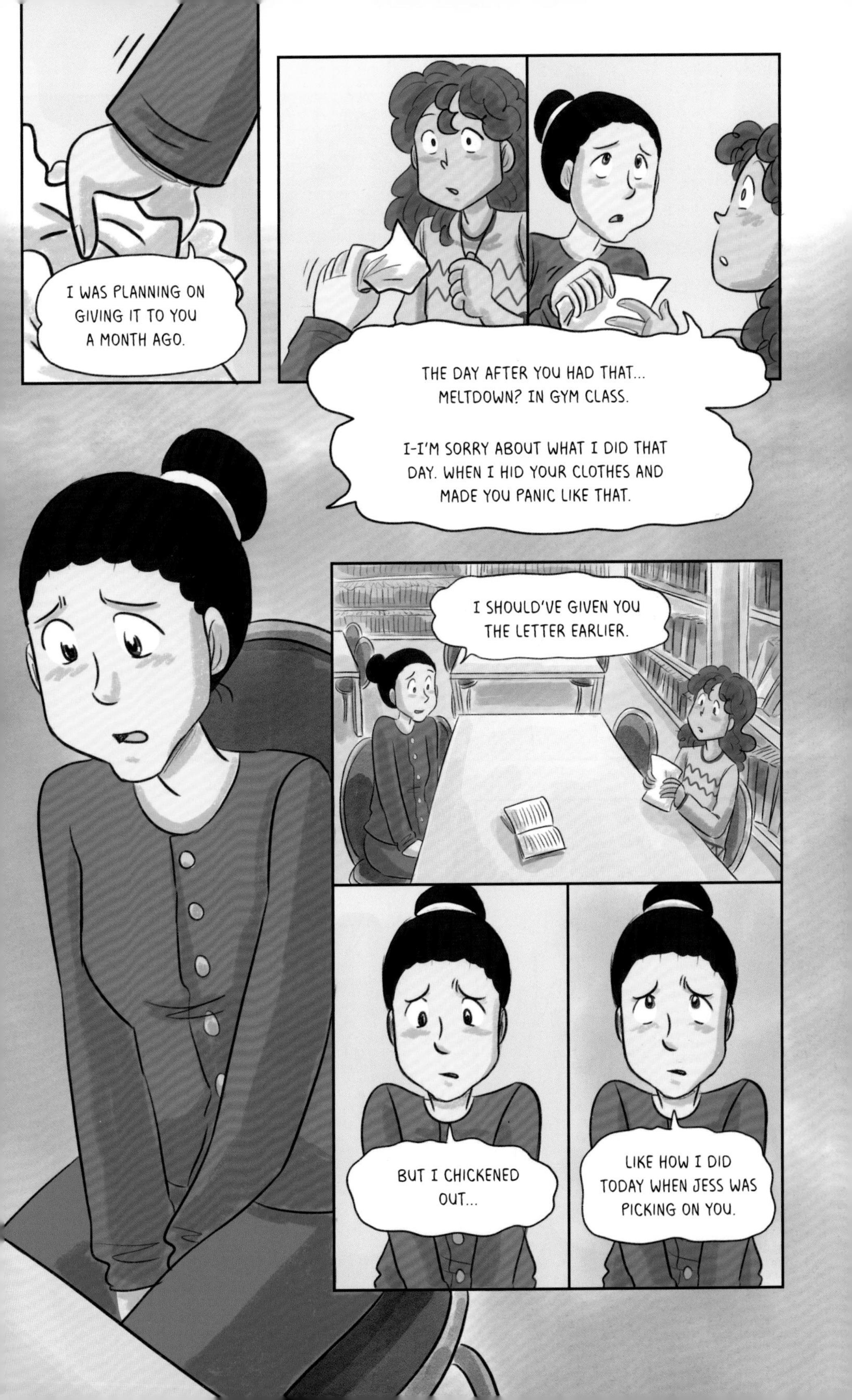
I WAS PLANNING ON GIVING IT TO YOU A MONTH AGO.
THE DAY AFTER YOU HAD THAT... MELTDOWN? IN GYM CLASS.
I-I'M SORRY ABOUT WHAT I DID THAT DAY. WHEN I HID YOUR CLOTHES AND MADE YOU PANIC LIKE THAT.
I SHOULD'VE GIVEN YOU THE LETTER EARLIER.
BUT I CHICKENED OUT...
LIKE HOW I DID TODAY WHEN JESS WAS PICKING ON YOU.

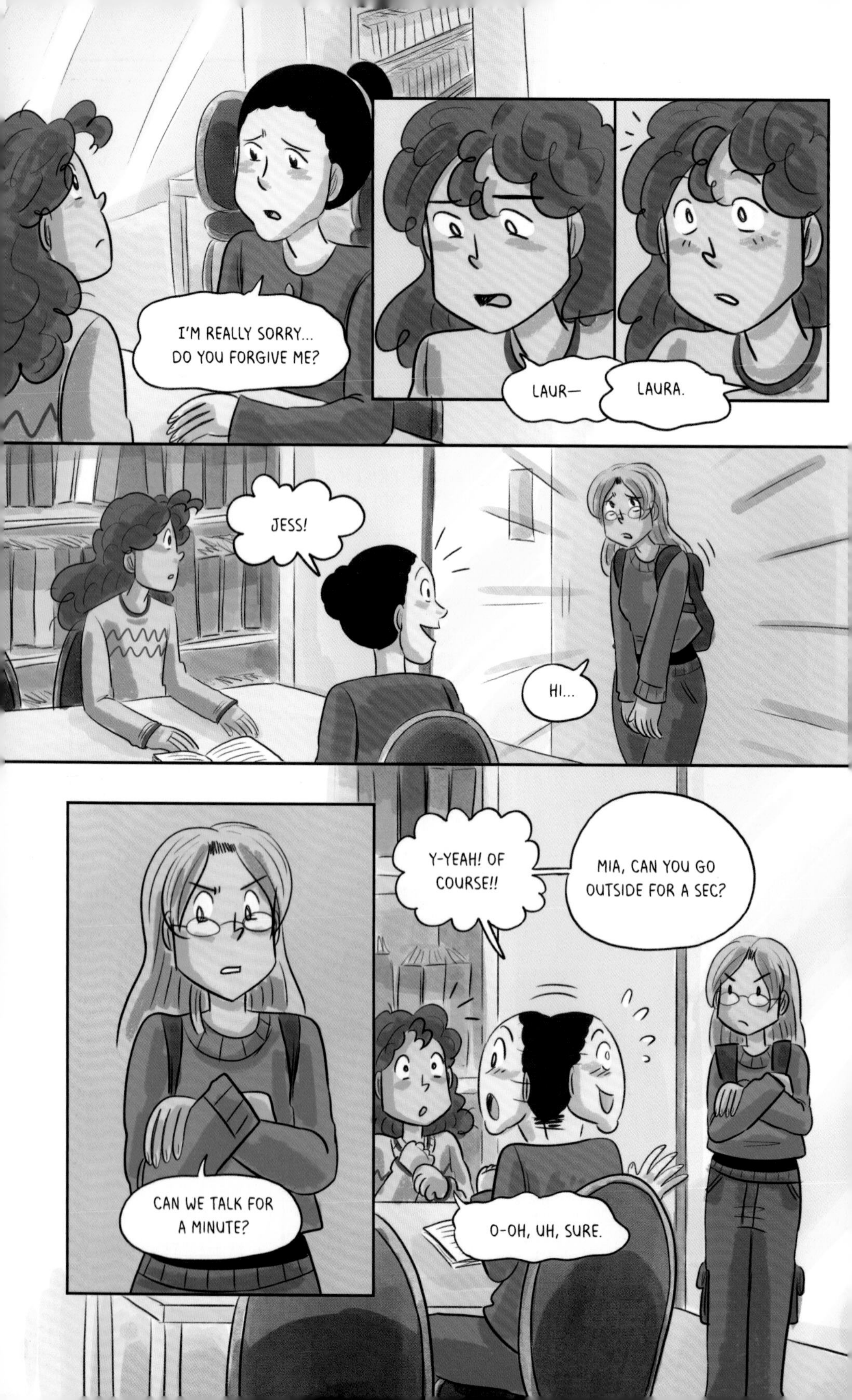
I'M REALLY SORRY... DO YOU FORGIVE ME?
LAUR—
LAURA.
JESS!
HI...
CAN WE TALK FOR A MINUTE?
Y-YEAH! OF COURSE!!
MIA, CAN YOU GO OUTSIDE FOR A SEC?
O-OH, UH, SURE.

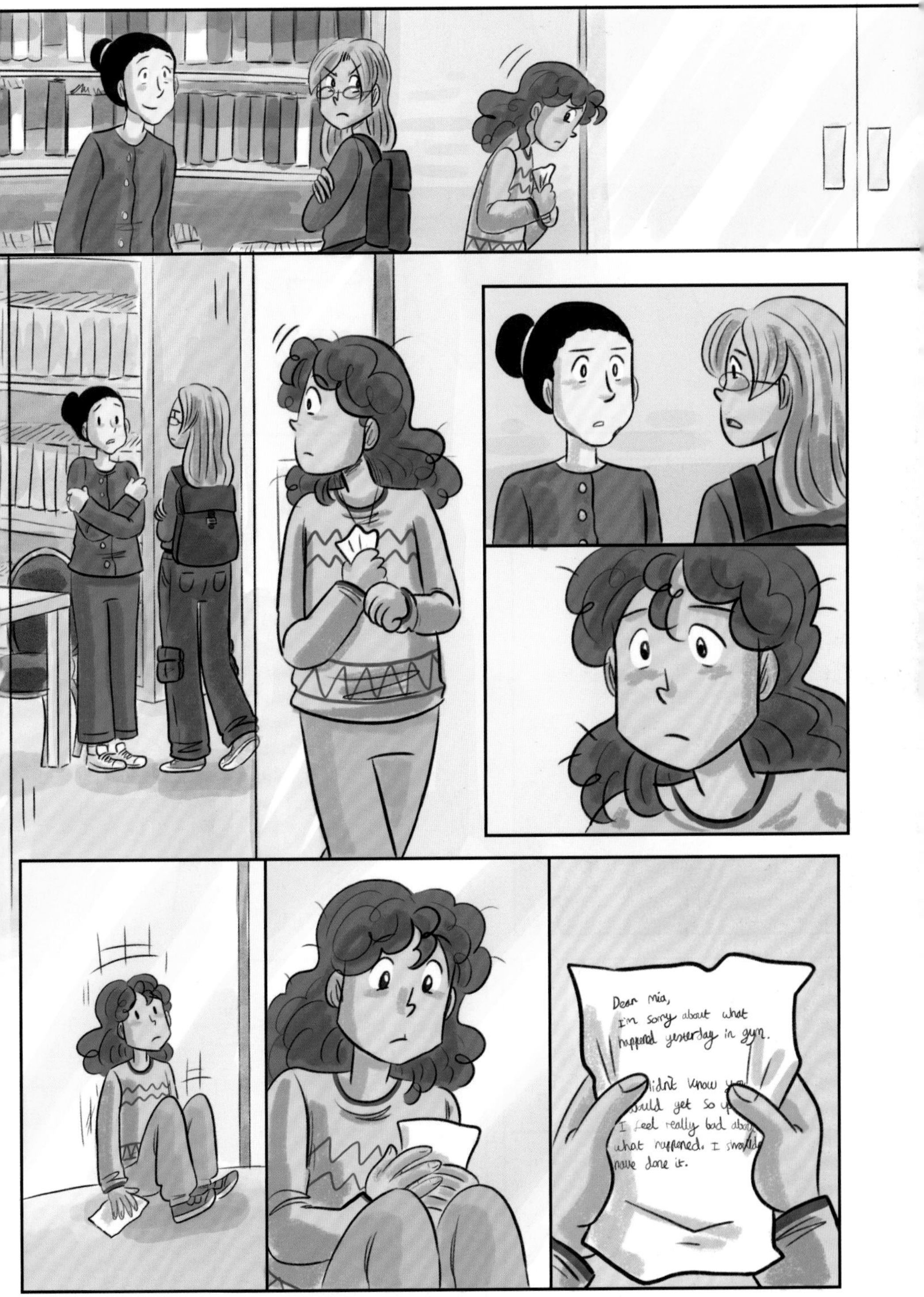
Dear mia,
I'm sorry about what
happened yesterday in gym.
idn't know
uld get so
I feel really bad
what happened. I
have done it.

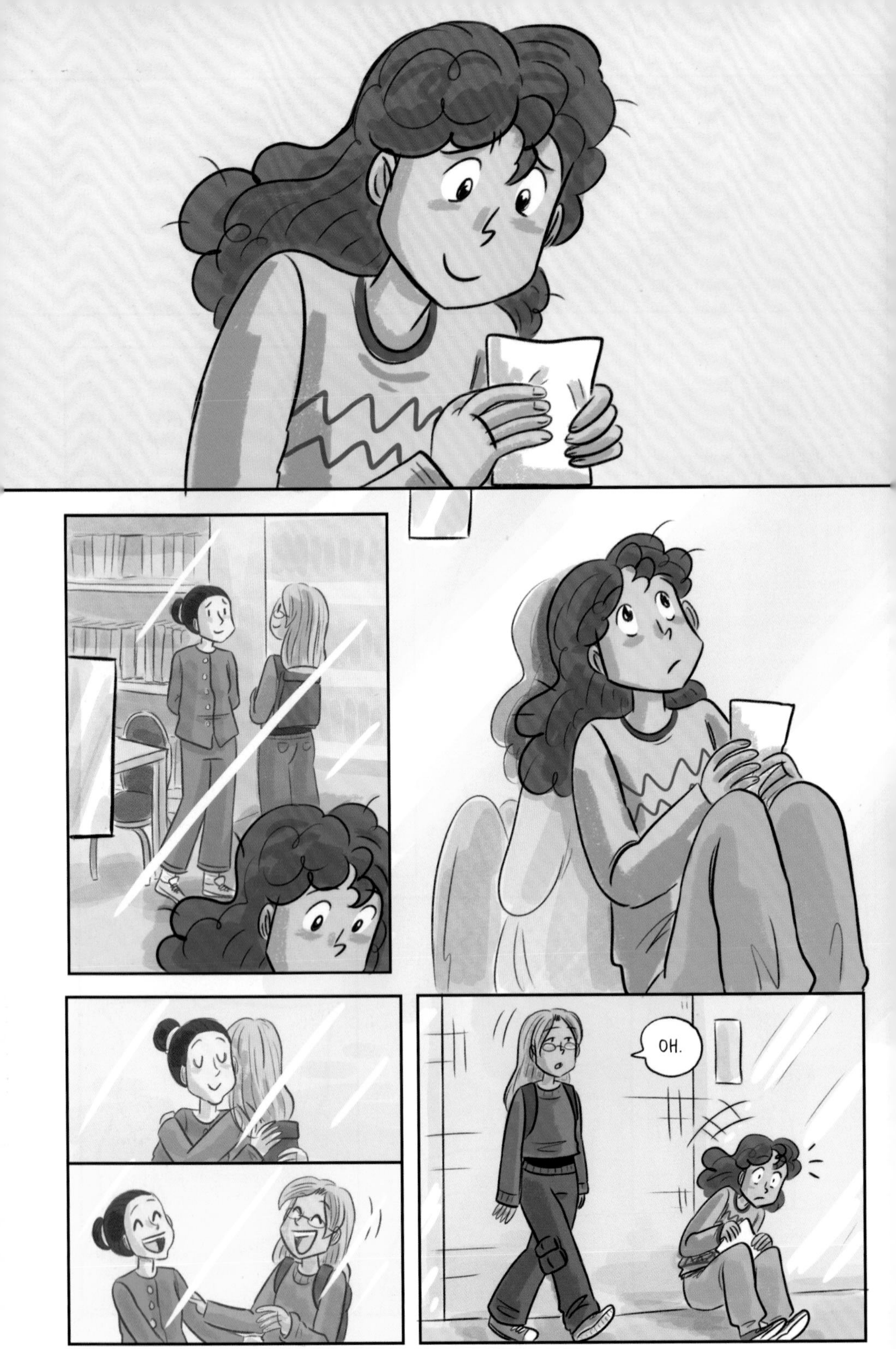
OH.

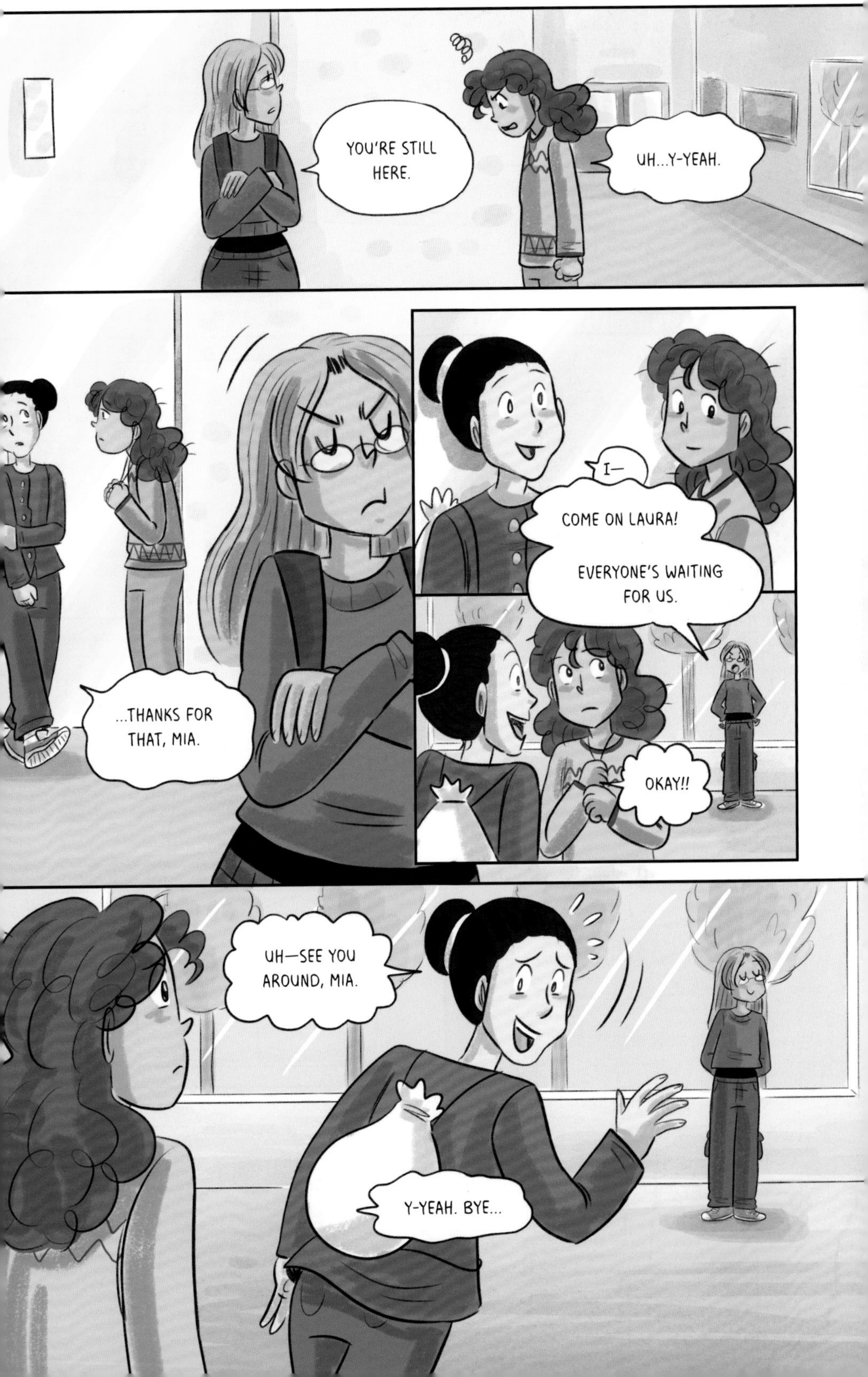
YOU'RE STILL HERE.
UH...Y-YEAH.
...THANKS FOR THAT, MIA.
I—
COME ON LAURA!
EVERYONE'S WAITING FOR US.
OKAY!!
UH—SEE YOU AROUND, MIA.
Y-YEAH. BYE...

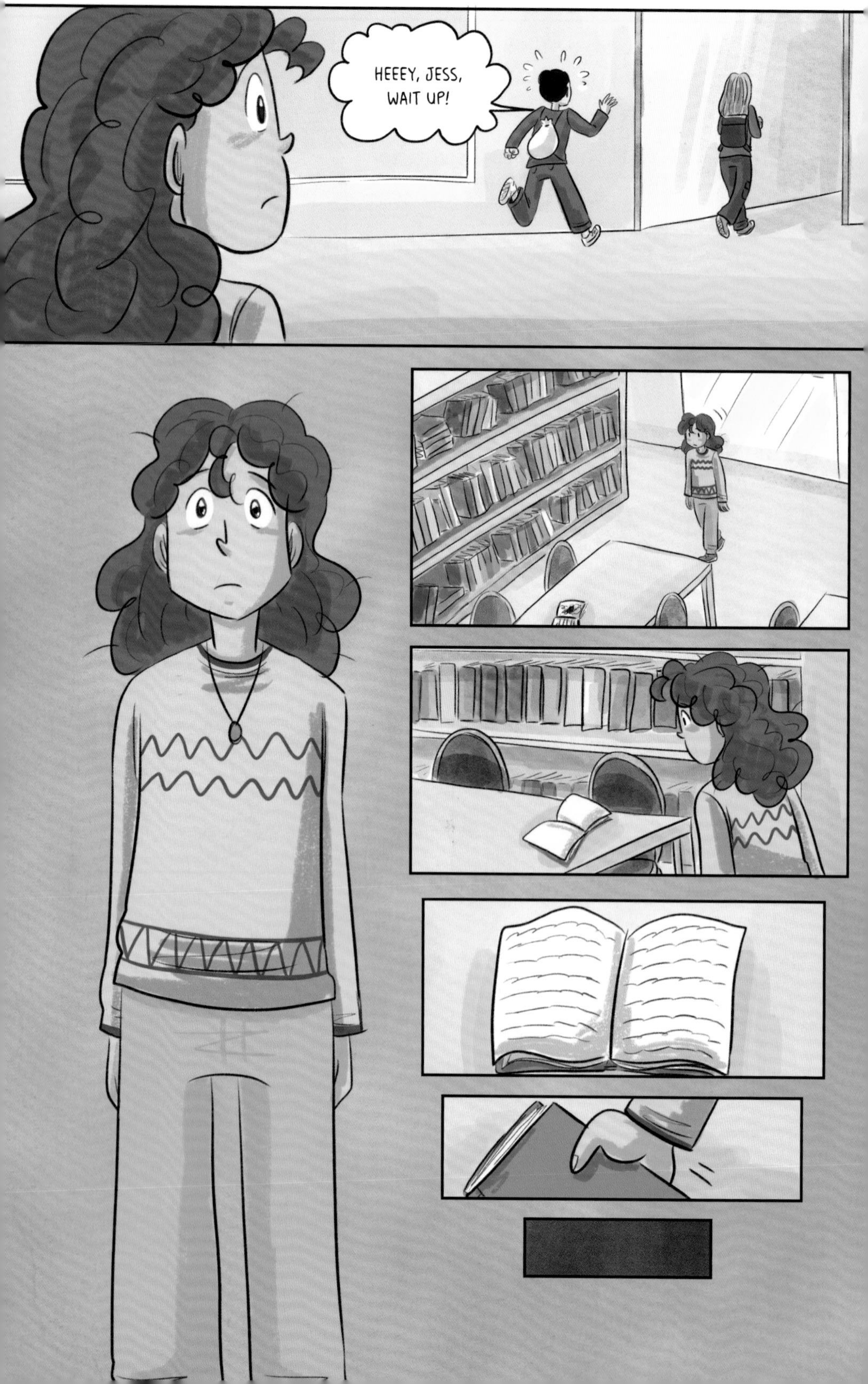
HEEEY, JESS, WAIT UP!

CHAPTER EIGHT

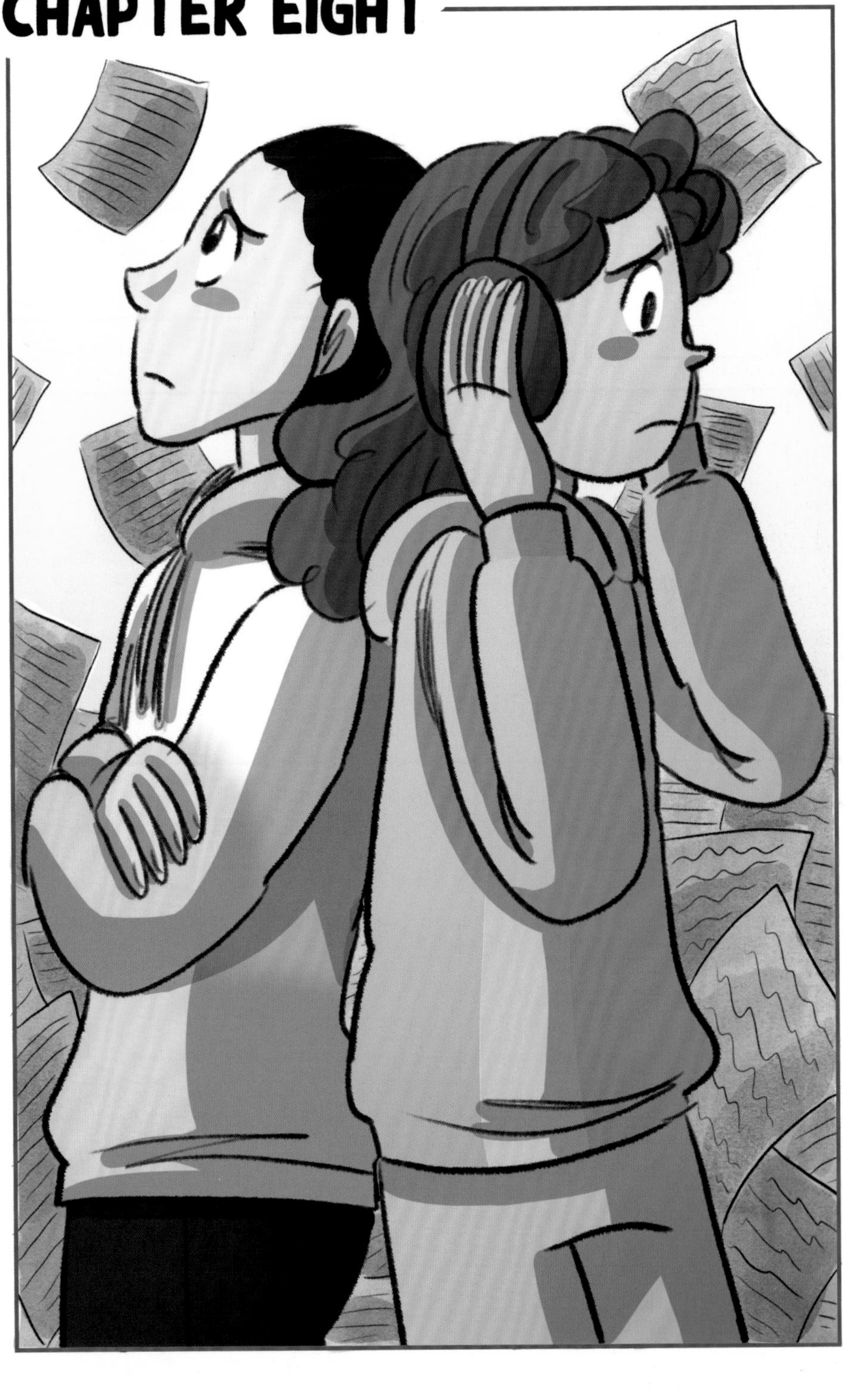

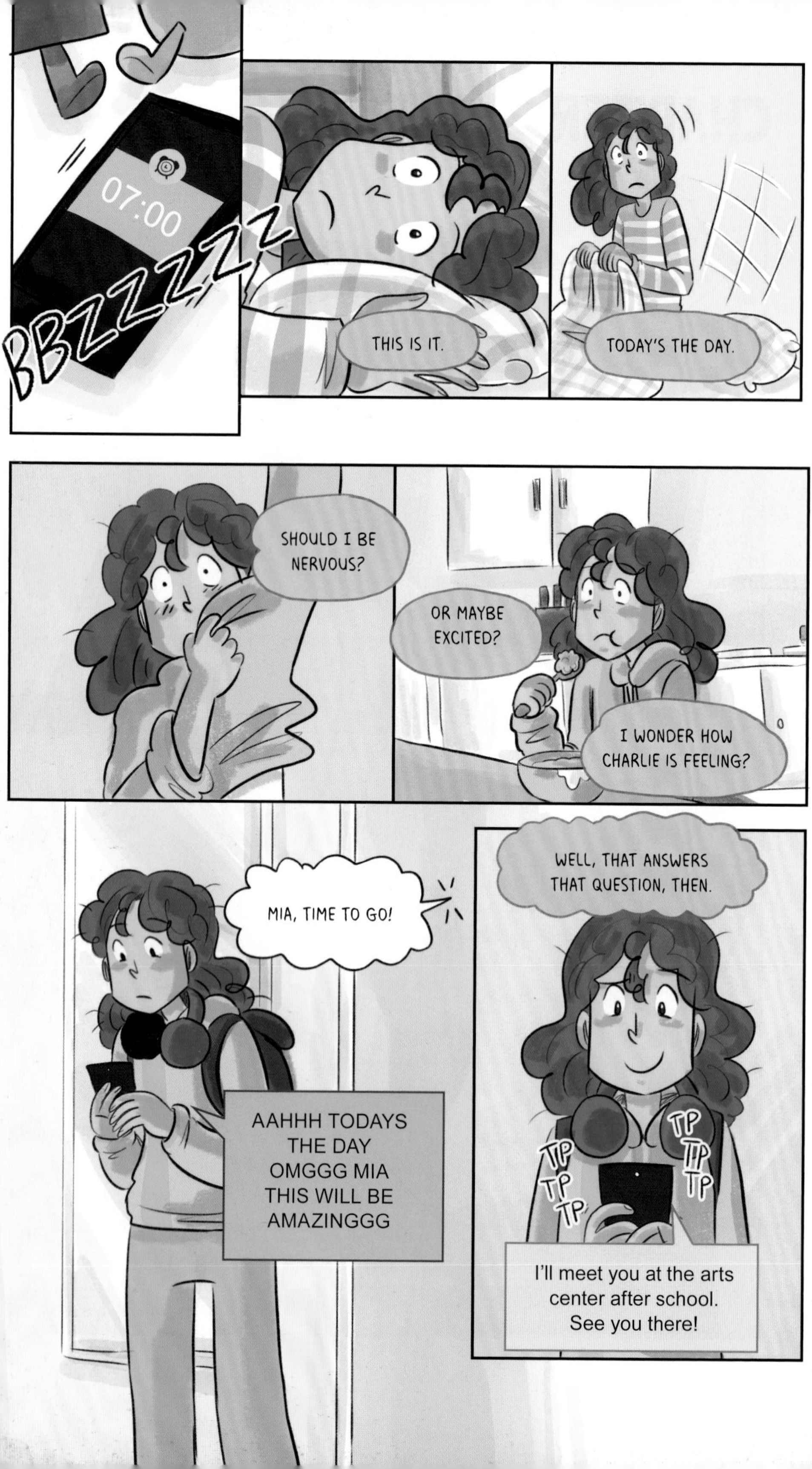
07:00
BBZZZZZZ
THIS IS IT.
TODAY'S THE DAY.
SHOULD I BE NERVOUS?
OR MAYBE EXCITED?
I WONDER HOW CHARLIE IS FEELING?
MIA, TIME TO GO!
AAHHH TODAYS THE DAY OMGGG MIA THIS WILL BE AMAZINGGG
WELL, THAT ANSWERS THAT QUESTION, THEN.
TP TP TP
TP TP TP
I'll meet you at the arts center after school. See you there!

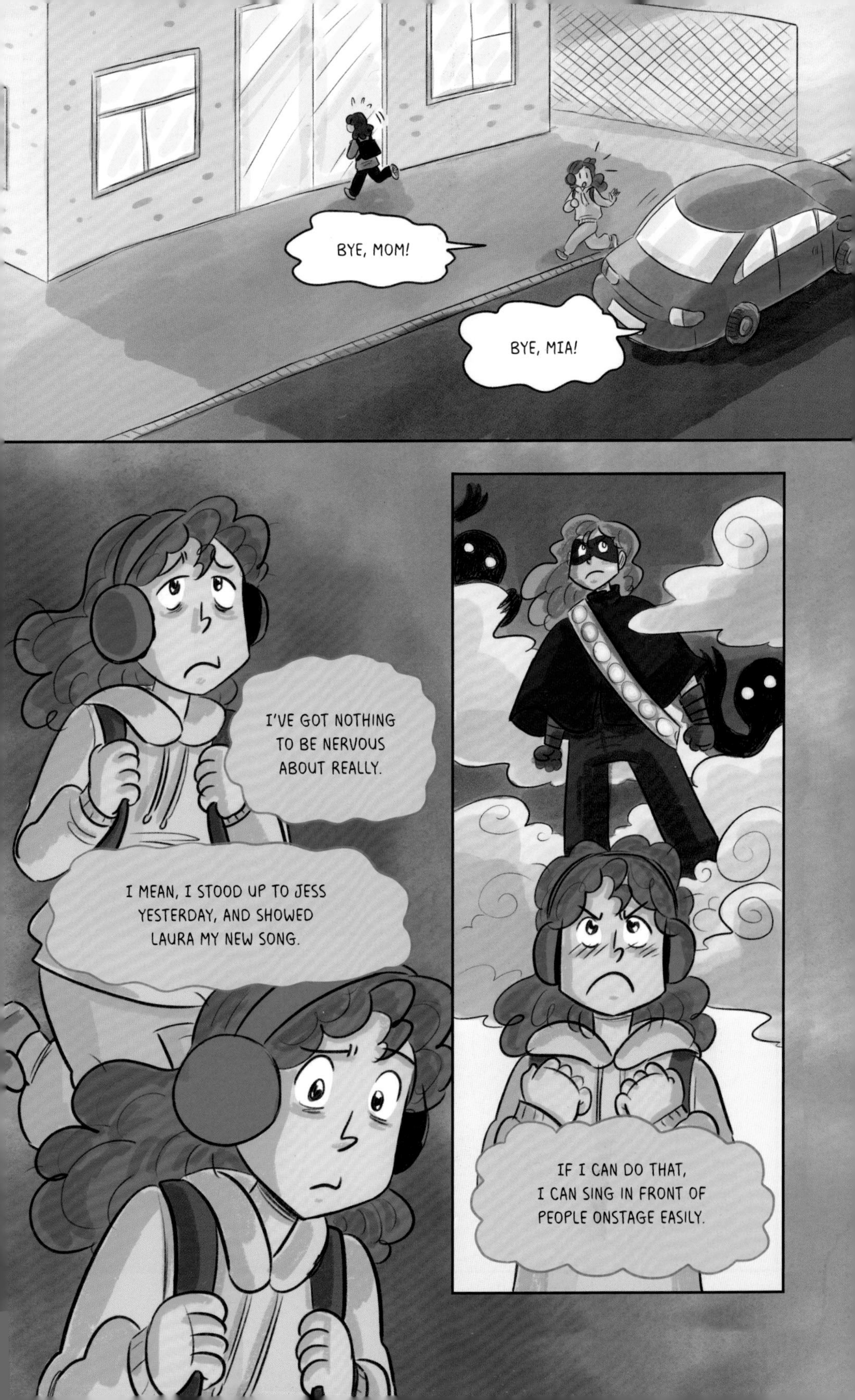
BYE, MOM!
BYE, MIA!
I'VE GOT NOTHING TO BE NERVOUS ABOUT REALLY.
I MEAN, I STOOD UP TO JESS YESTERDAY, AND SHOWED LAURA MY NEW SONG.
IF I CAN DO THAT, I CAN SING IN FRONT OF PEOPLE ONSTAGE EASILY.

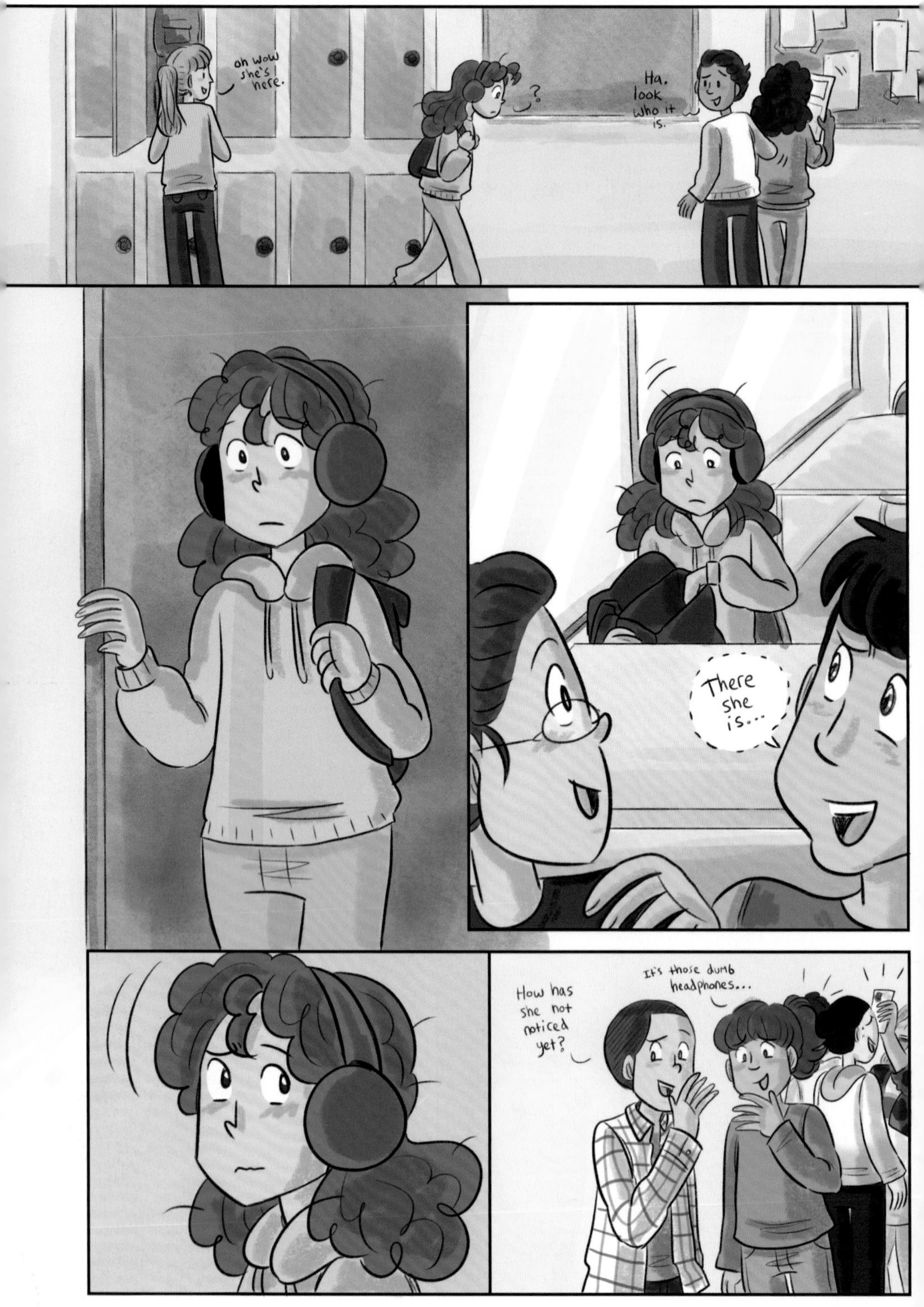
oh wow she's here.
?
Ha. look who it is.
There she is...
How has she not noticed yet?
It's those dumb headphones...

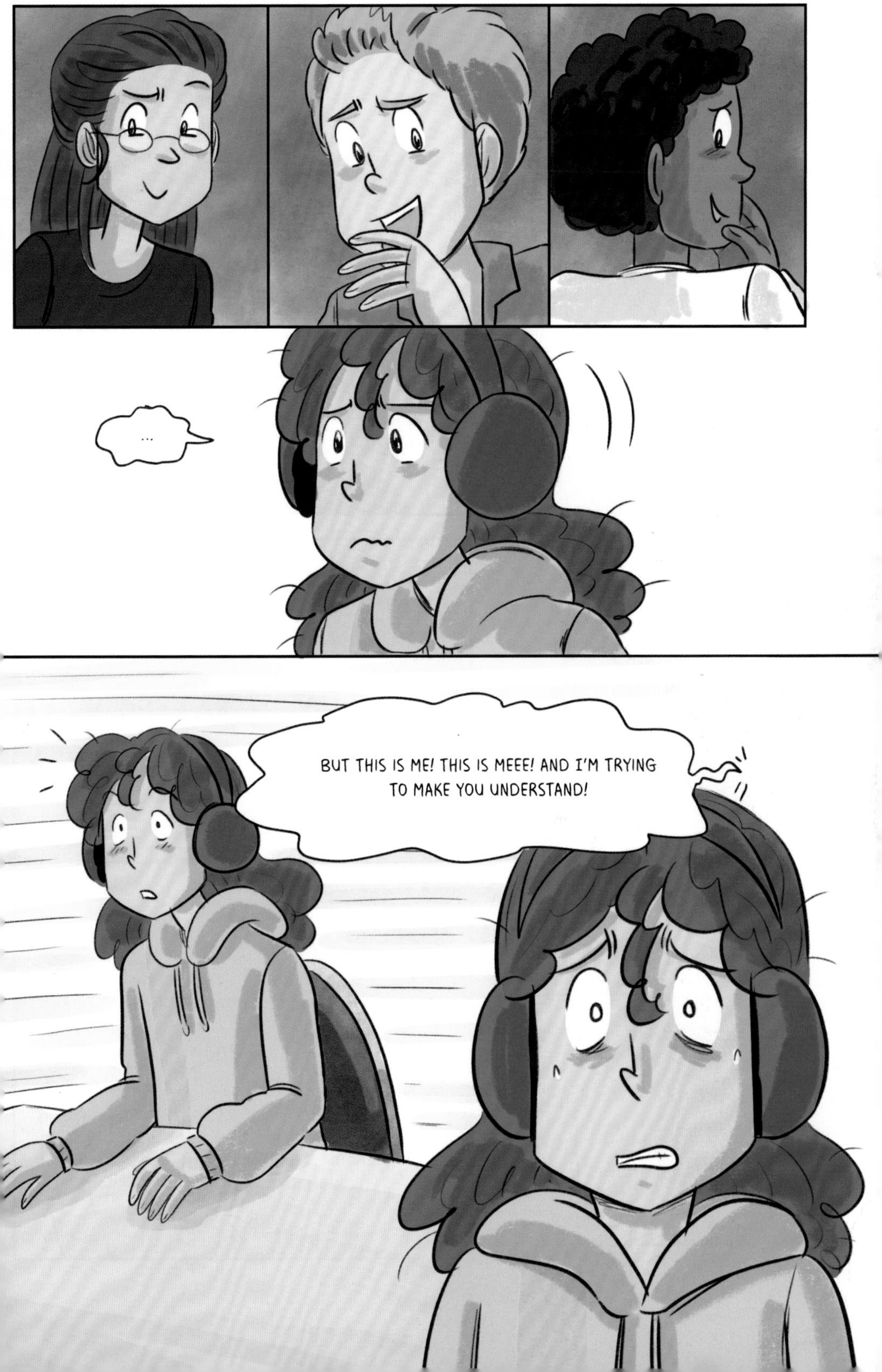
...
BUT THIS IS ME! THIS IS MEEE! AND I'M TRYING TO MAKE YOU UNDERSTAND!

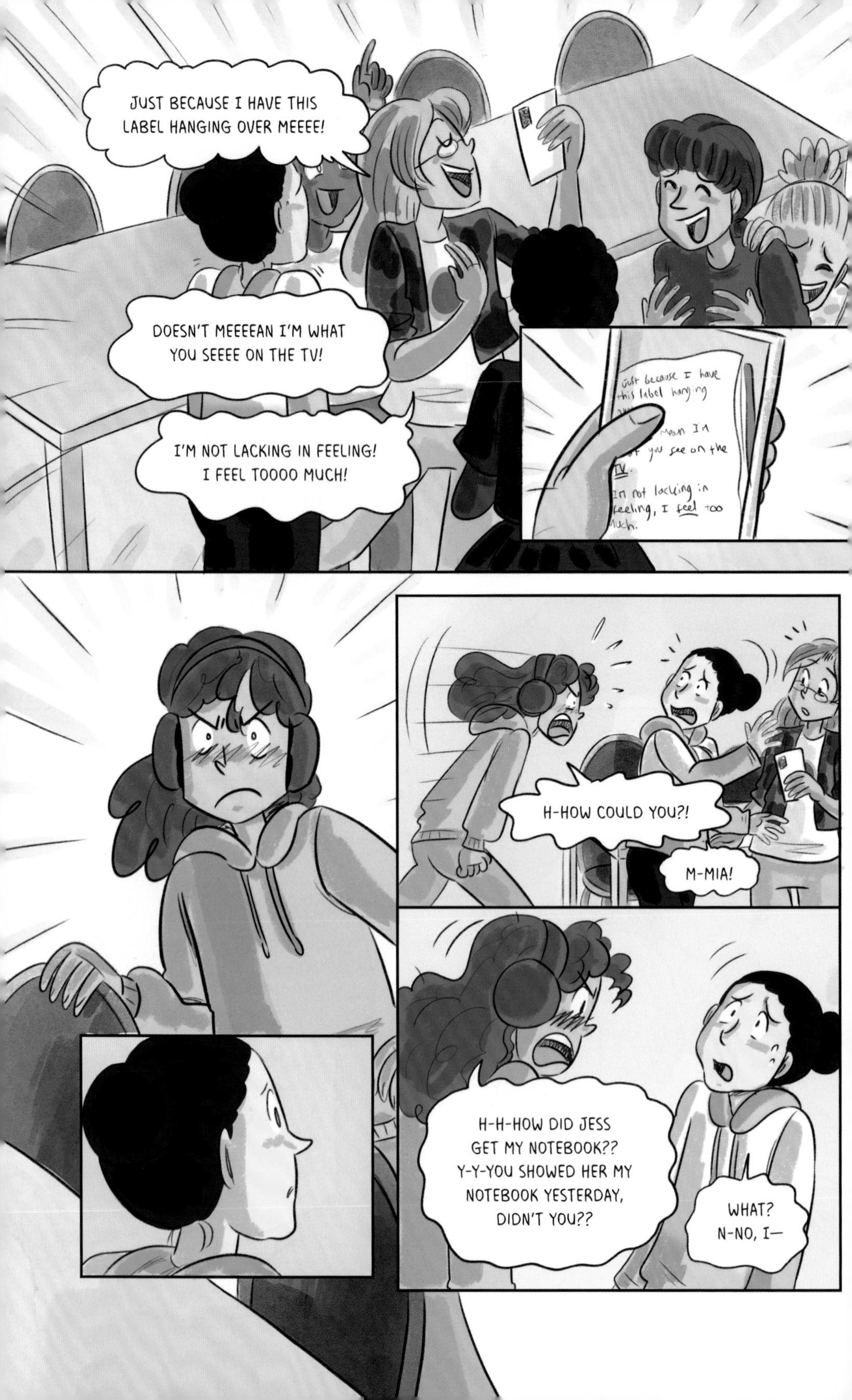

JUST BECAUSE I HAVE THIS LABEL HANGING OVER MEEEE!
DOESN'T MEEEEAN I'M WHAT YOU SEEEE ON THE TV!
I'M NOT LACKING IN FEELING! I FEEL TOOOO MUCH!
H-HOW COULD YOU?!
M-MIA!
H-H-HOW DID JESS GET MY NOTEBOOK?? Y-Y-YOU SHOWED HER MY NOTEBOOK YESTERDAY, DIDN'T YOU??
WHAT? N-NO, I—

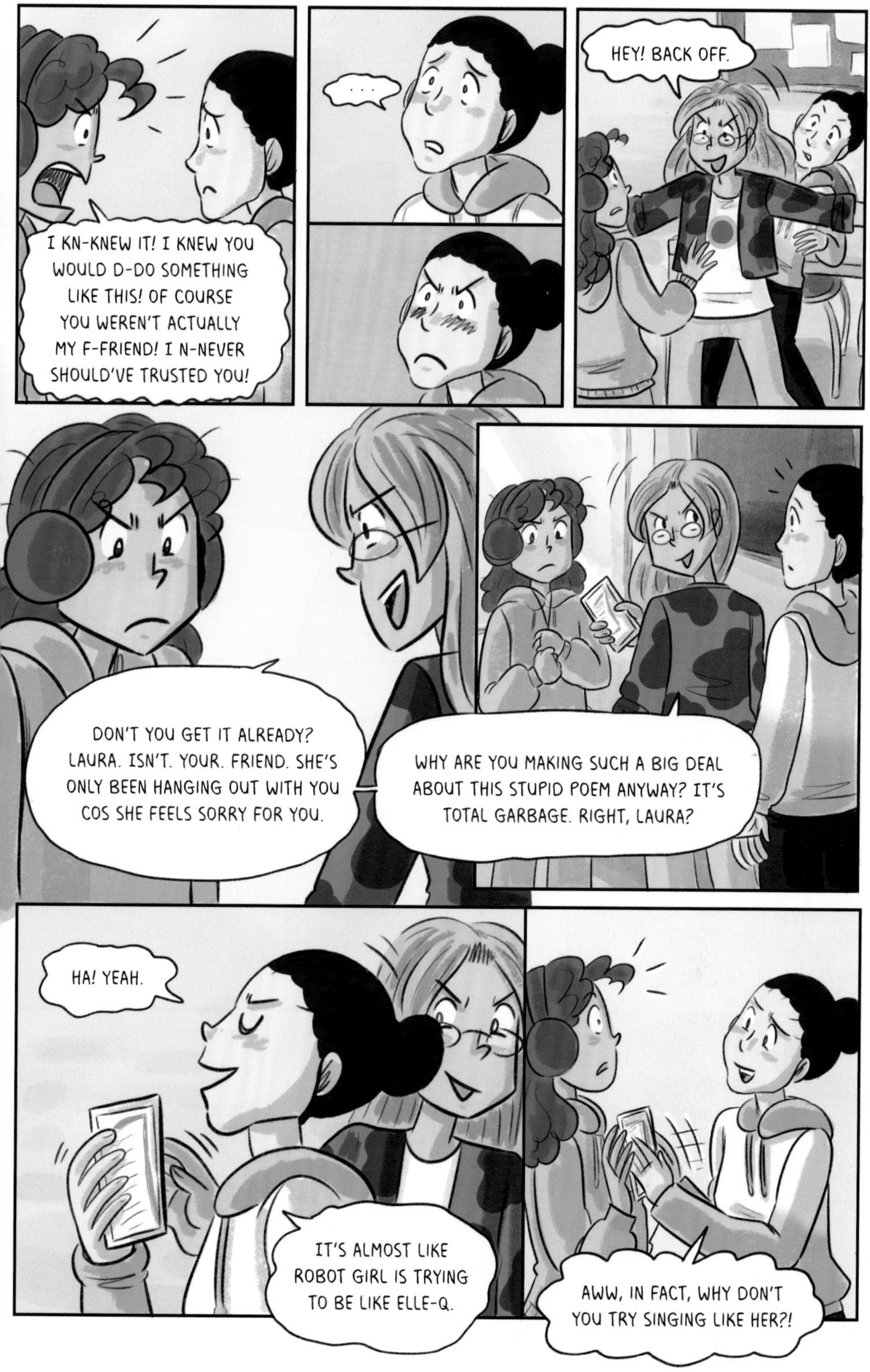

I KN-KNEW IT! I KNEW YOU WOULD D-DO SOMETHING LIKE THIS! OF COURSE YOU WEREN'T ACTUALLY MY F-FRIEND! I N-NEVER SHOULD'VE TRUSTED YOU!
. . . .
HEY! BACK OFF.
DON'T YOU GET IT ALREADY? LAURA. ISN'T. YOUR. FRIEND. SHE'S ONLY BEEN HANGING OUT WITH YOU COS SHE FEELS SORRY FOR YOU.
WHY ARE YOU MAKING SUCH A BIG DEAL ABOUT THIS STUPID POEM ANYWAY? IT'S TOTAL GARBAGE. RIGHT, LAURA?
HA! YEAH.
IT'S ALMOST LIKE ROBOT GIRL IS TRYING TO BE LIKE ELLE-Q.
AWW, IN FACT, WHY DON'T YOU TRY SINGING LIKE HER?!

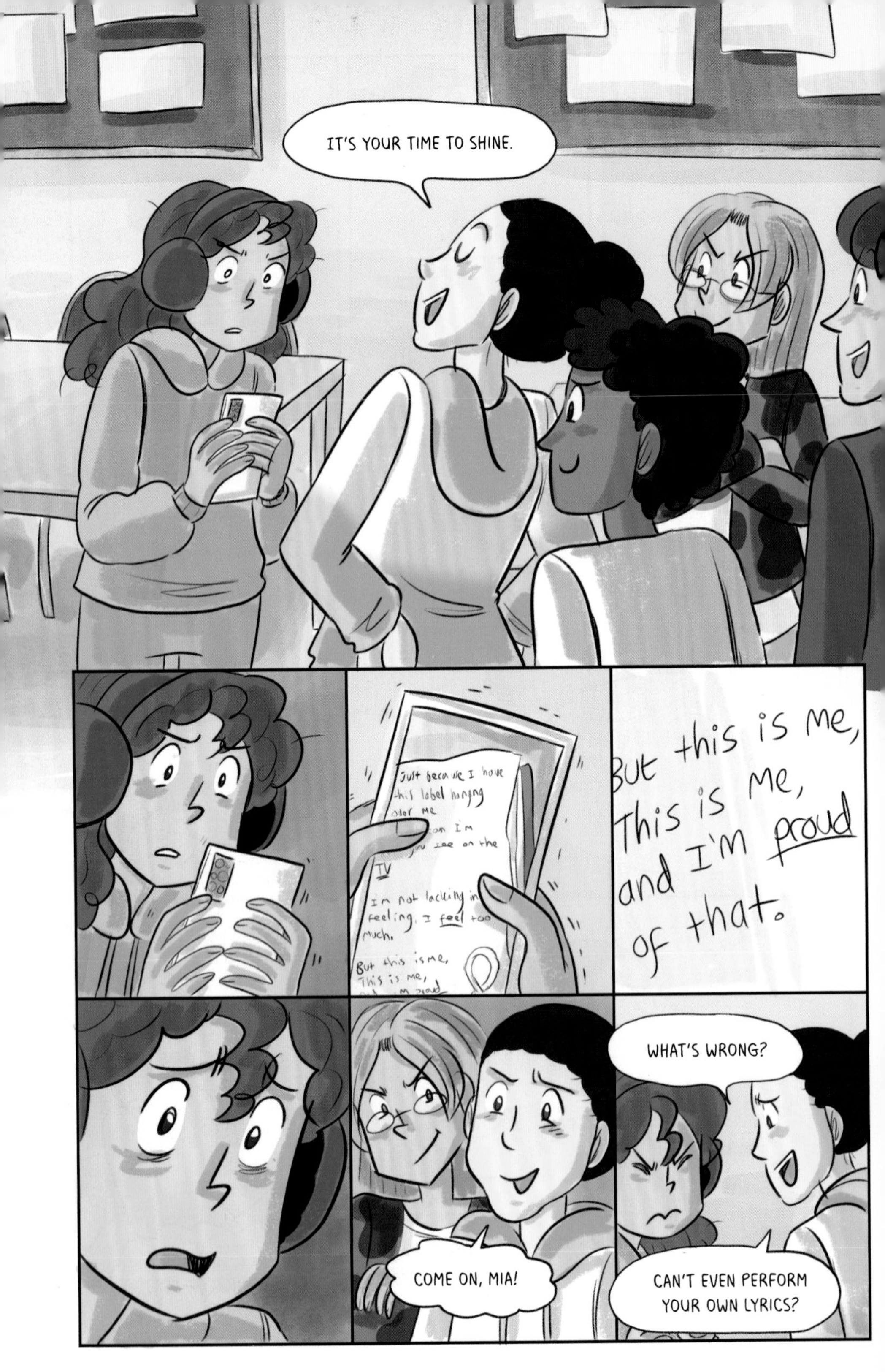
IT'S YOUR TIME TO SHINE.
Just because I have
this label hanging
over me
I'm not lacking in
feeling, I feel too
much.
But this is me,
This is me,
But this is me,
This is me,
and I'm proud
of that.
WHAT'S WRONG?
COME ON, MIA!
CAN'T EVEN PERFORM
YOUR OWN LYRICS?

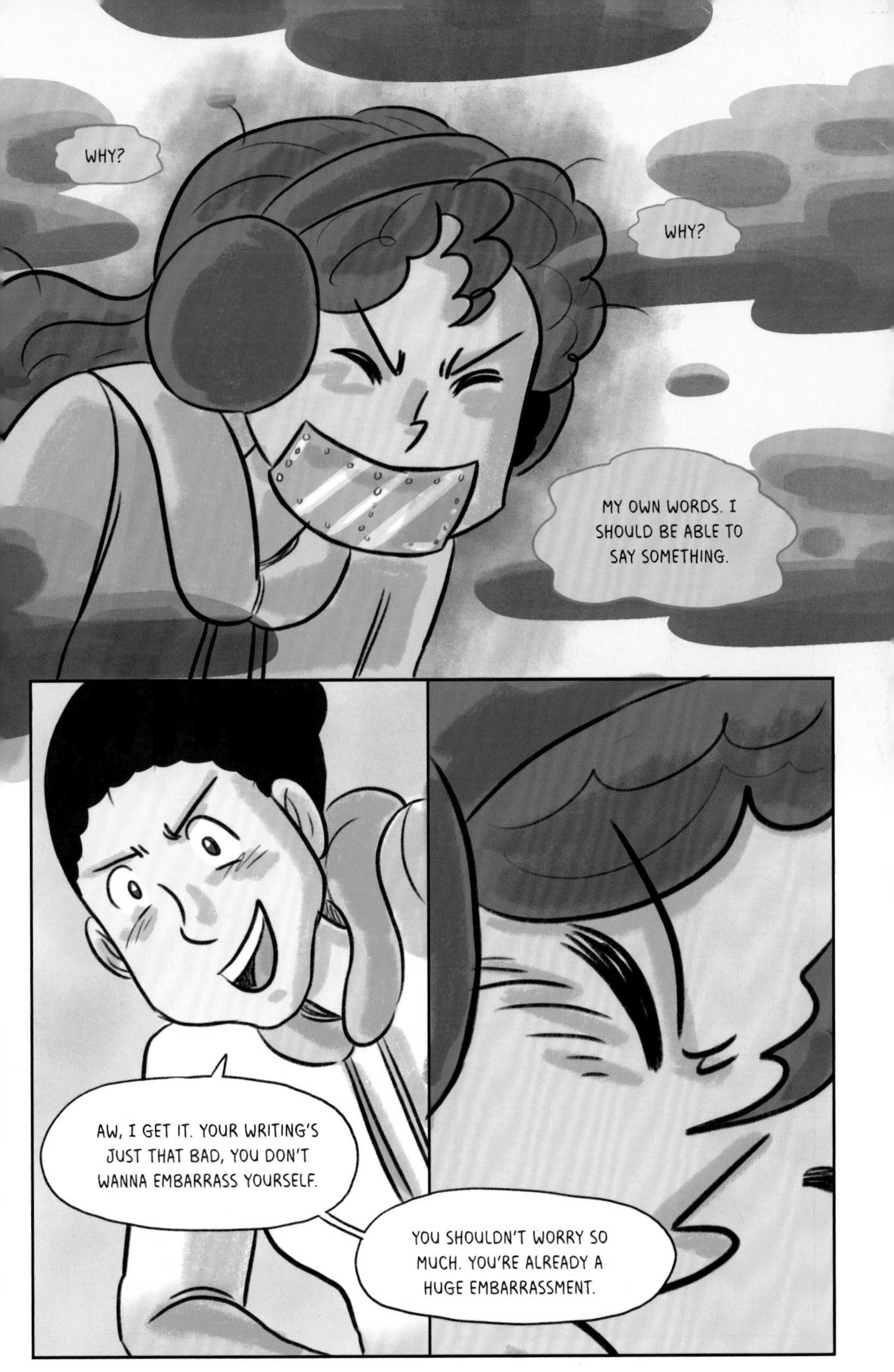
WHY?
WHY?
MY OWN WORDS. I SHOULD BE ABLE TO SAY SOMETHING.
AW, I GET IT. YOUR WRITING'S JUST THAT BAD, YOU DON'T WANNA EMBARRASS YOURSELF.
YOU SHOULDN'T WORRY SO MUCH. YOU'RE ALREADY A HUGE EMBARRASSMENT.

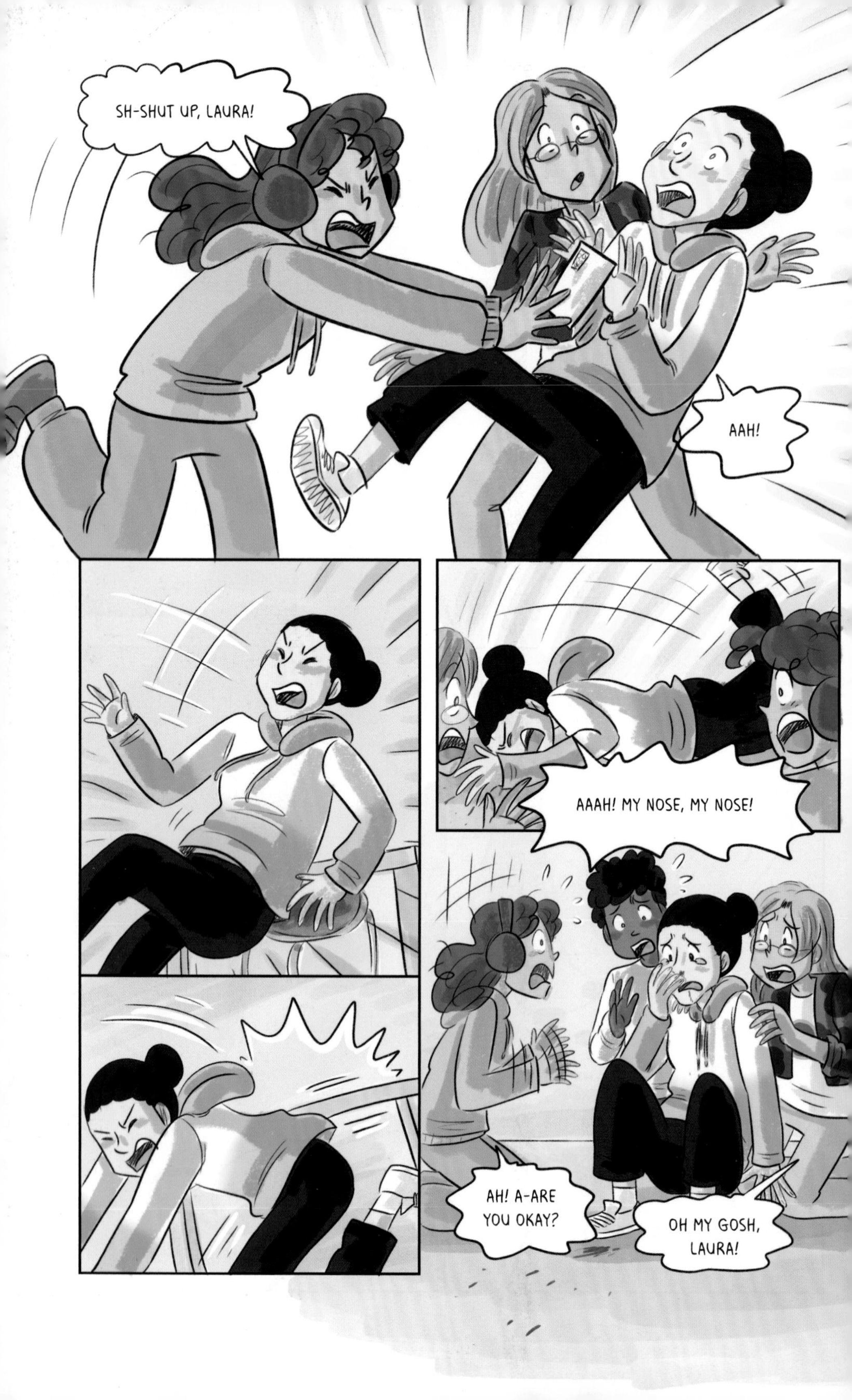
SH-SHUT UP, LAURA!
AAH!
AAAH! MY NOSE, MY NOSE!
AH! A-ARE YOU OKAY?
OH MY GOSH, LAURA!

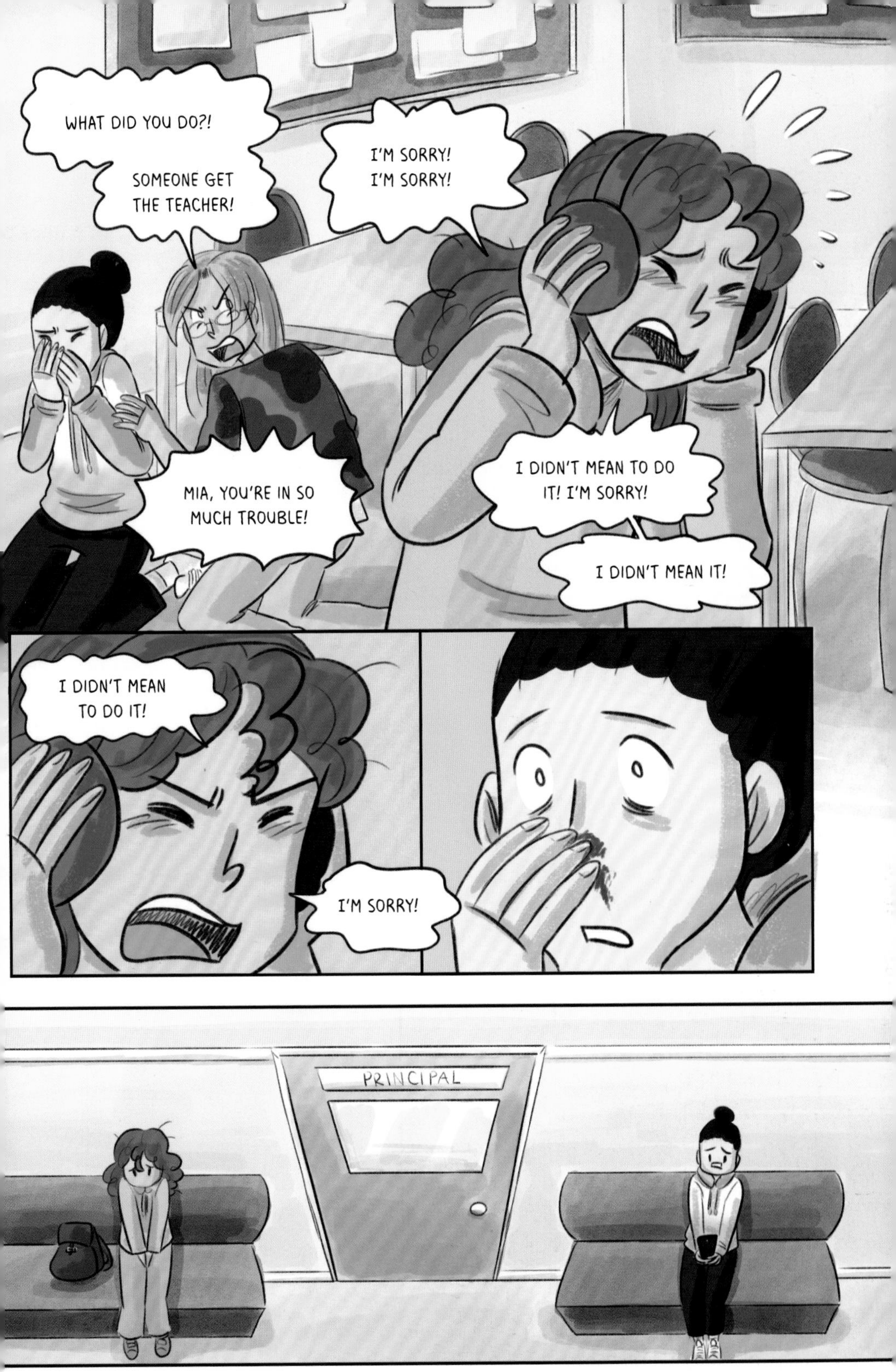
WHAT DID YOU DO?!
SOMEONE GET THE TEACHER!
I'M SORRY! I'M SORRY!
MIA, YOU'RE IN SO MUCH TROUBLE!
I DIDN'T MEAN TO DO IT! I'M SORRY!
I DIDN'T MEAN IT!
I DIDN'T MEAN TO DO IT!
I'M SORRY!
PRINCIPAL

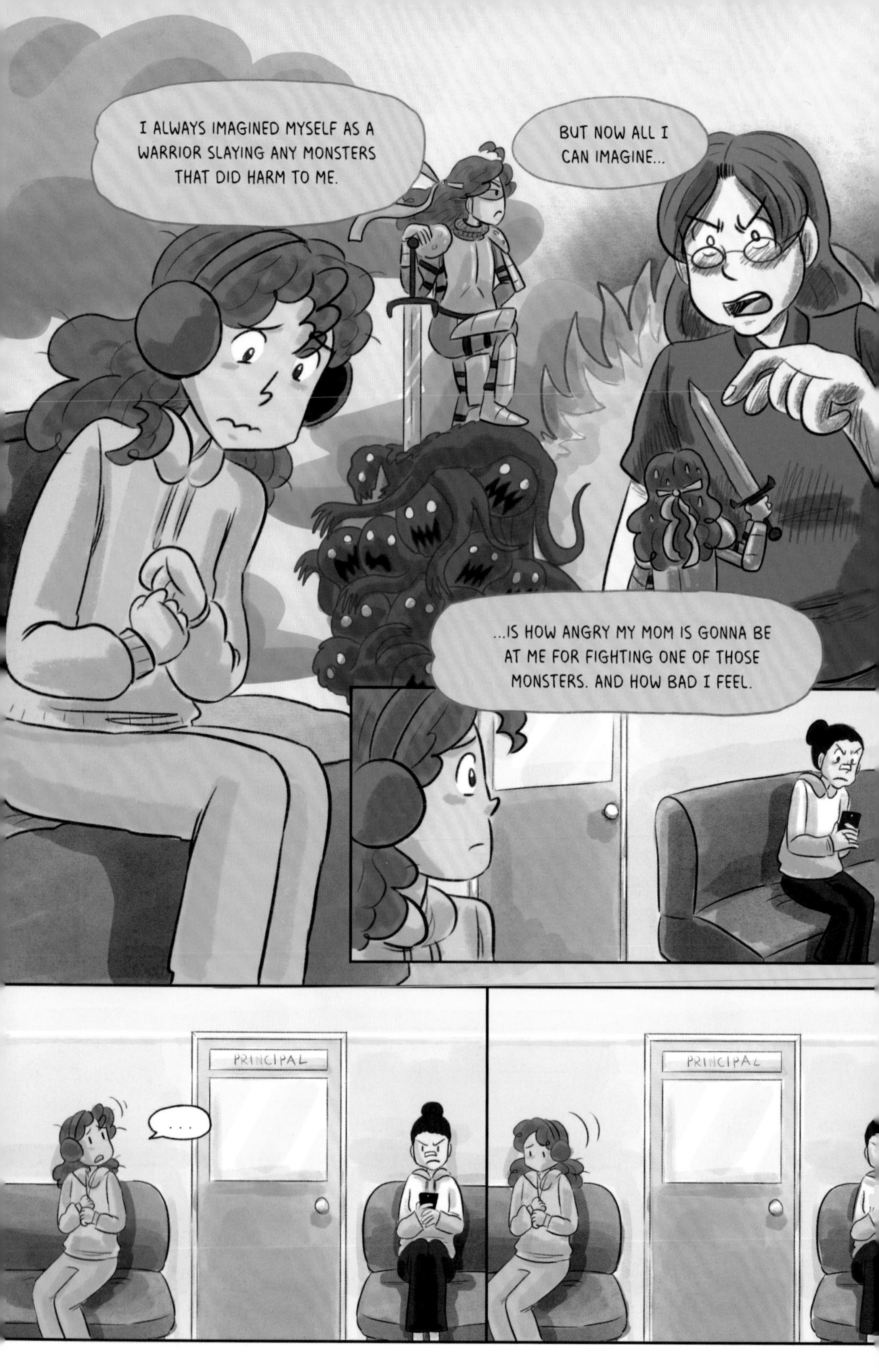
I ALWAYS IMAGINED MYSELF AS A WARRIOR SLAYING ANY MONSTERS THAT DID HARM TO ME.
BUT NOW ALL I CAN IMAGINE...
...IS HOW ANGRY MY MOM IS GONNA BE AT ME FOR FIGHTING ONE OF THOSE MONSTERS. AND HOW BAD I FEEL.
PRINCIPAL
...
PRINCIPAL

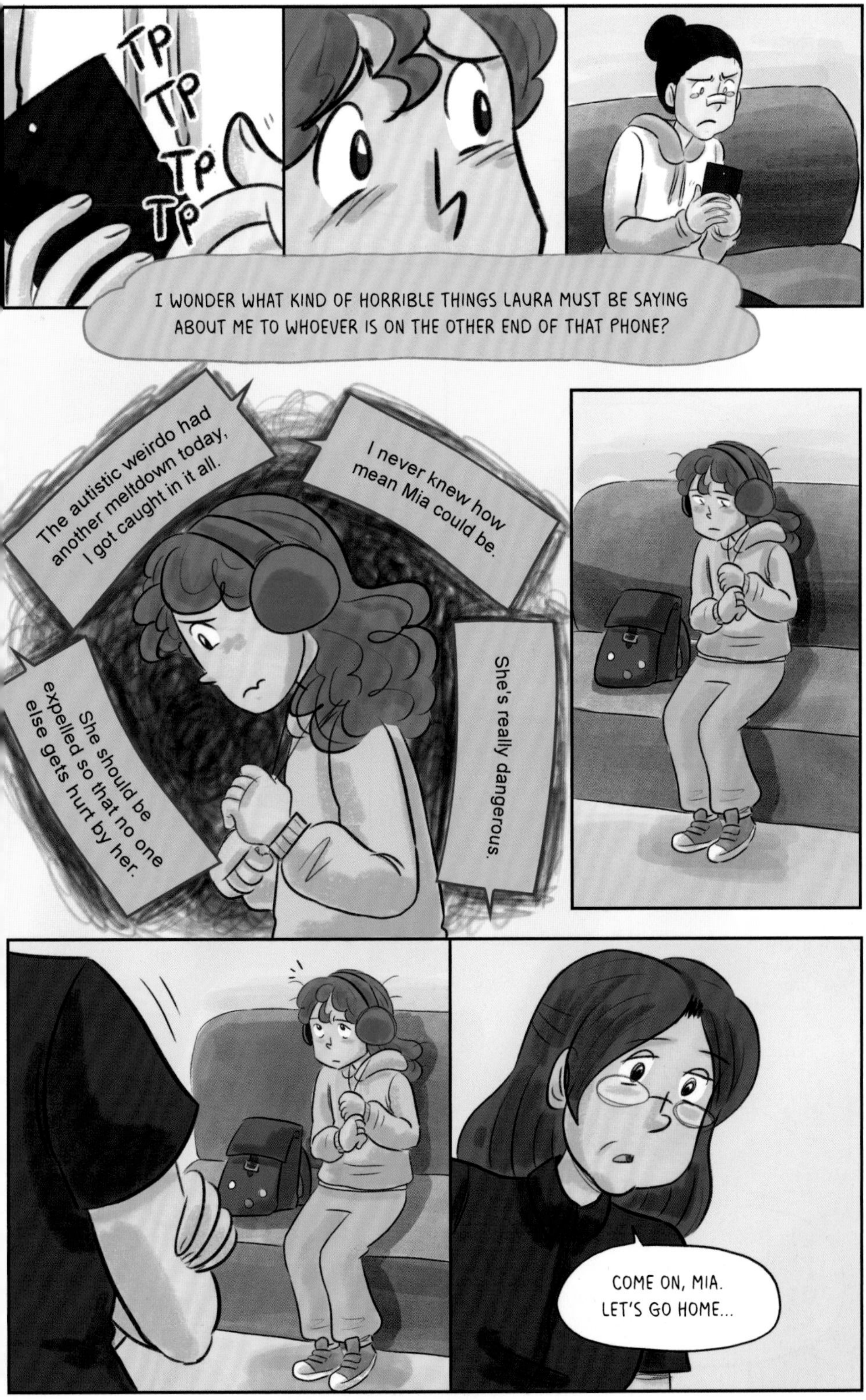
TP
TP
TP
TP
I WONDER WHAT KIND OF HORRIBLE THINGS LAURA MUST BE SAYING ABOUT ME TO WHOEVER IS ON THE OTHER END OF THAT PHONE?
The autistic weirdo had another meltdown today, I got caught in it all.
I never knew how mean Mia could be.
She should be expelled so that no one else gets hurt by her.
She's really dangerous.
COME ON, MIA. LET'S GO HOME...

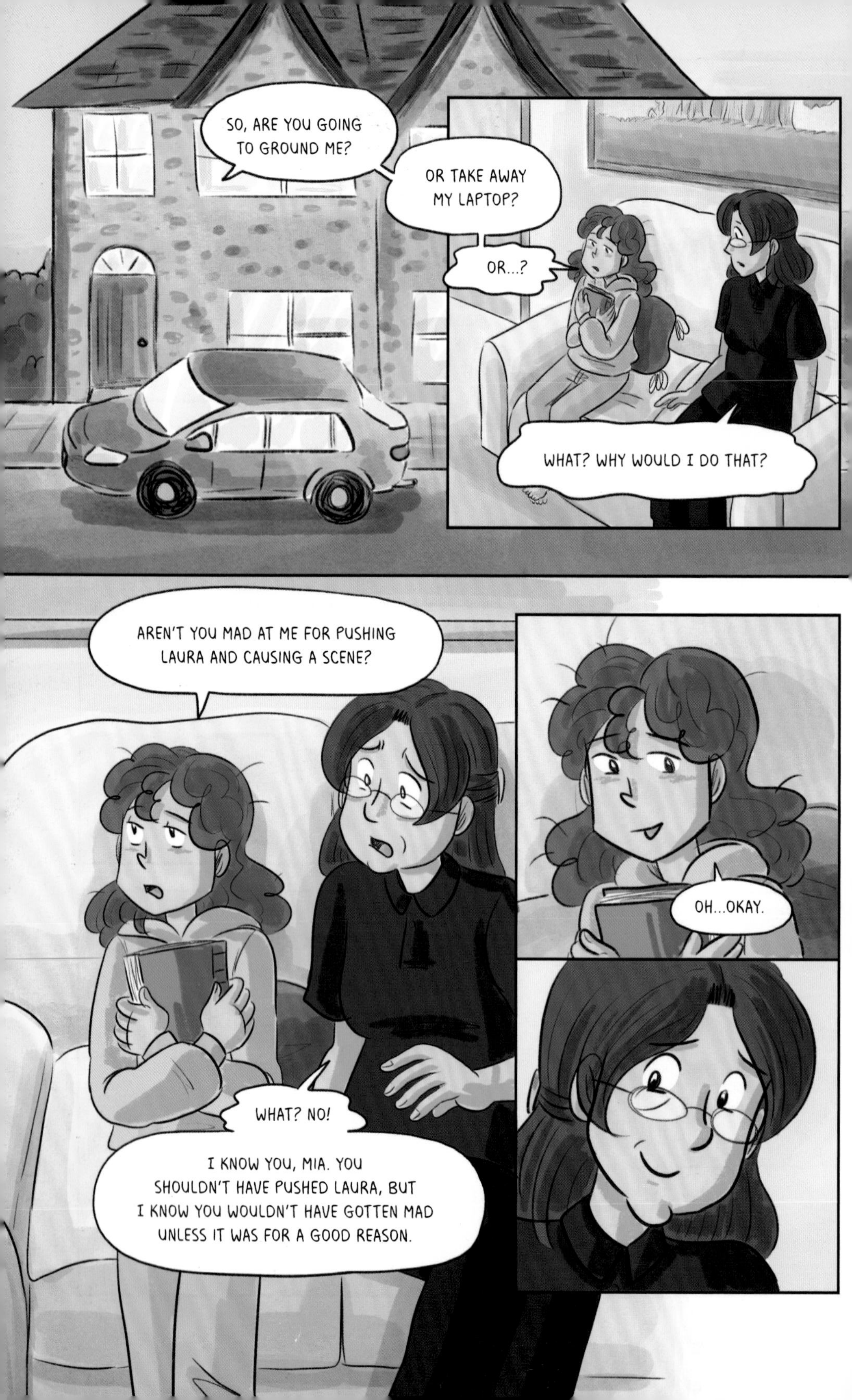
SO, ARE YOU GOING TO GROUND ME?
OR TAKE AWAY MY LAPTOP?
OR...?
WHAT? WHY WOULD I DO THAT?
AREN'T YOU MAD AT ME FOR PUSHING LAURA AND CAUSING A SCENE?
WHAT? NO!
I KNOW YOU, MIA. YOU SHOULDN'T HAVE PUSHED LAURA, BUT I KNOW YOU WOULDN'T HAVE GOTTEN MAD UNLESS IT WAS FOR A GOOD REASON.
OH...OKAY.

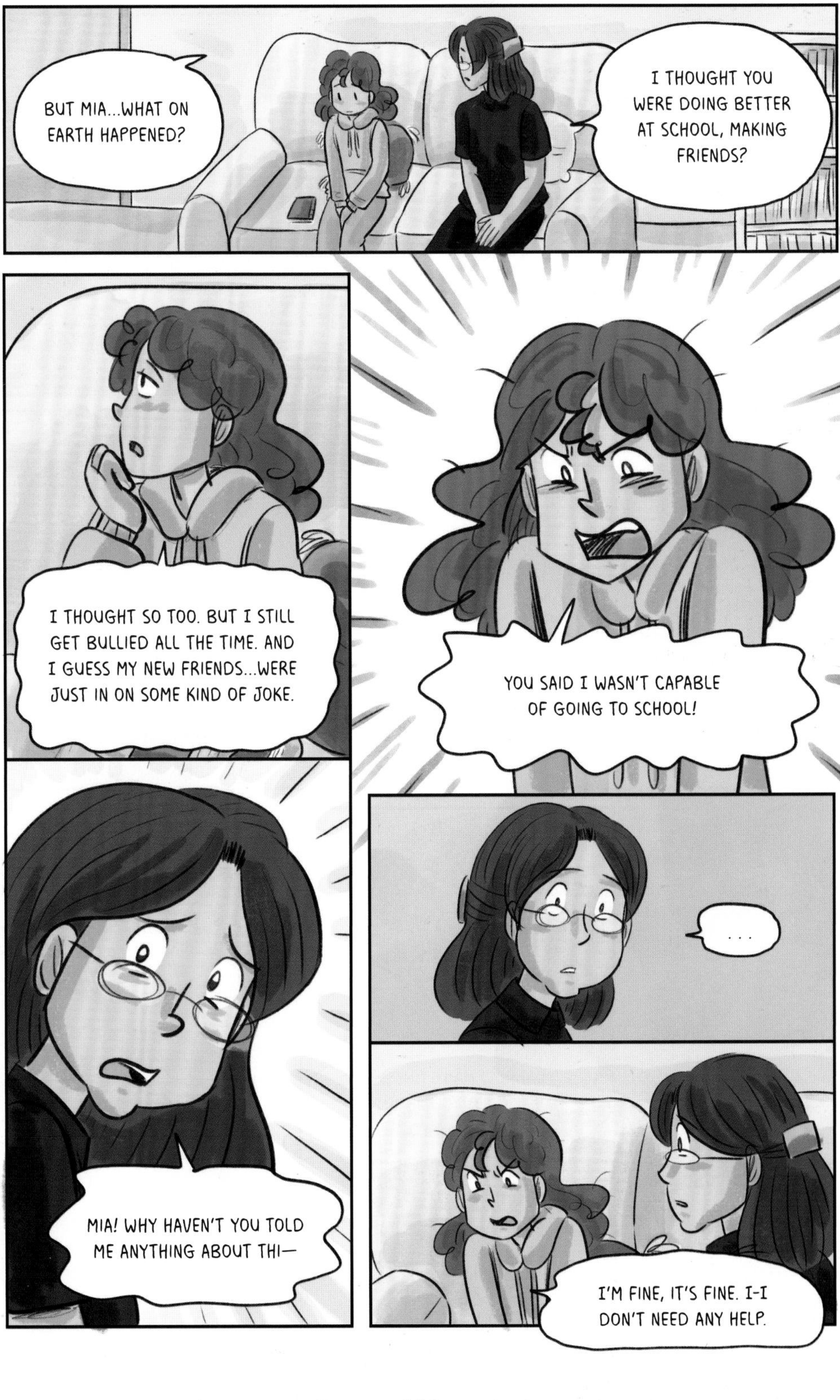

BUT MIA...WHAT ON EARTH HAPPENED?
I THOUGHT YOU WERE DOING BETTER AT SCHOOL, MAKING FRIENDS?
I THOUGHT SO TOO. BUT I STILL GET BULLIED ALL THE TIME. AND I GUESS MY NEW FRIENDS...WERE JUST IN ON SOME KIND OF JOKE.
YOU SAID I WASN'T CAPABLE OF GOING TO SCHOOL!
MIA! WHY HAVEN'T YOU TOLD ME ANYTHING ABOUT THI—
. . .
I'M FINE, IT'S FINE. I-I DON'T NEED ANY HELP.

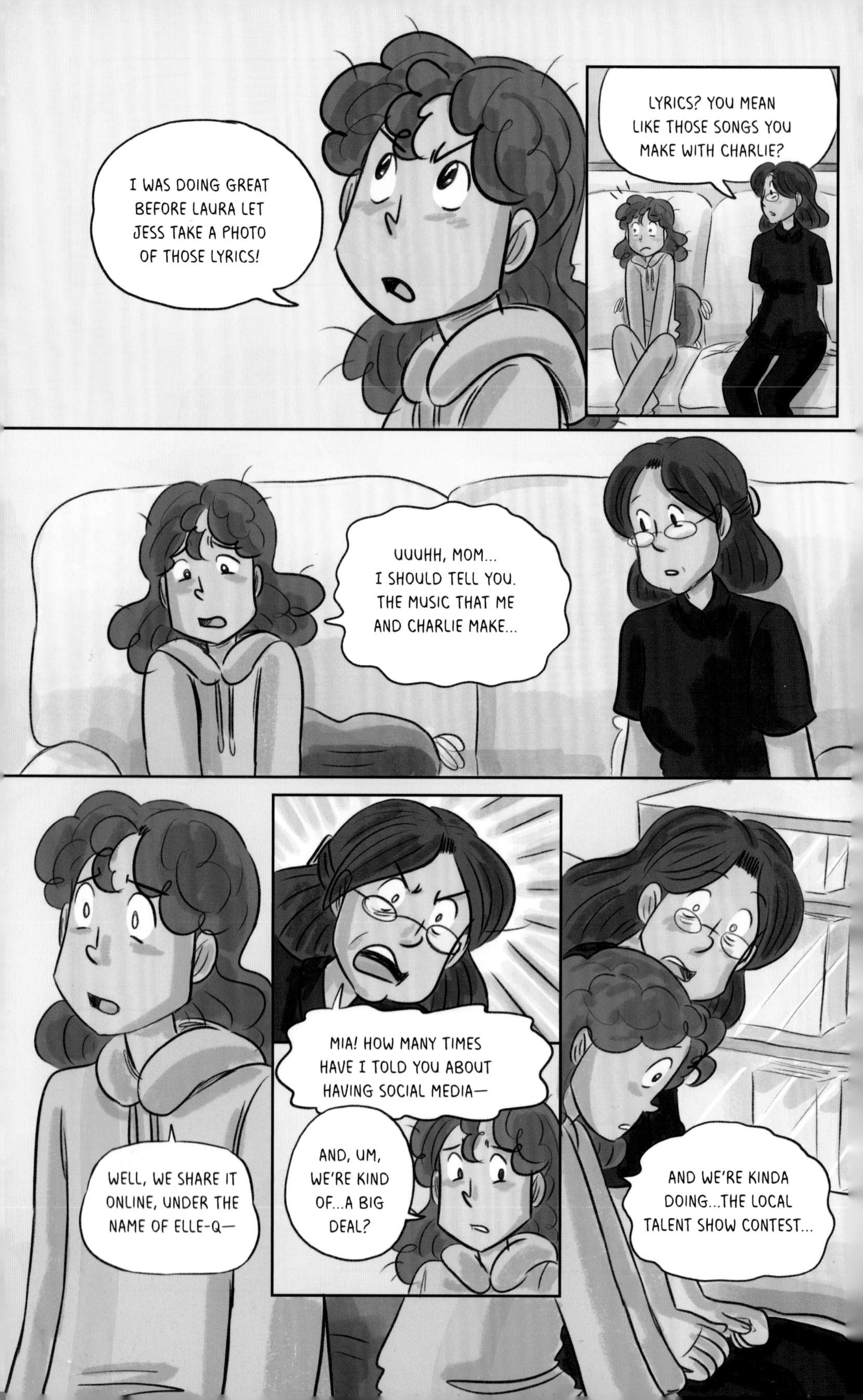
I WAS DOING GREAT BEFORE LAURA LET JESS TAKE A PHOTO OF THOSE LYRICS!
LYRICS? YOU MEAN LIKE THOSE SONGS YOU MAKE WITH CHARLIE?
UUUHH, MOM... I SHOULD TELL YOU. THE MUSIC THAT ME AND CHARLIE MAKE...
WELL, WE SHARE IT ONLINE, UNDER THE NAME OF ELLE-Q—
MIA! HOW MANY TIMES HAVE I TOLD YOU ABOUT HAVING SOCIAL MEDIA—
AND, UM, WE'RE KIND OF...A BIG DEAL?
AND WE'RE KINDA DOING...THE LOCAL TALENT SHOW CONTEST...

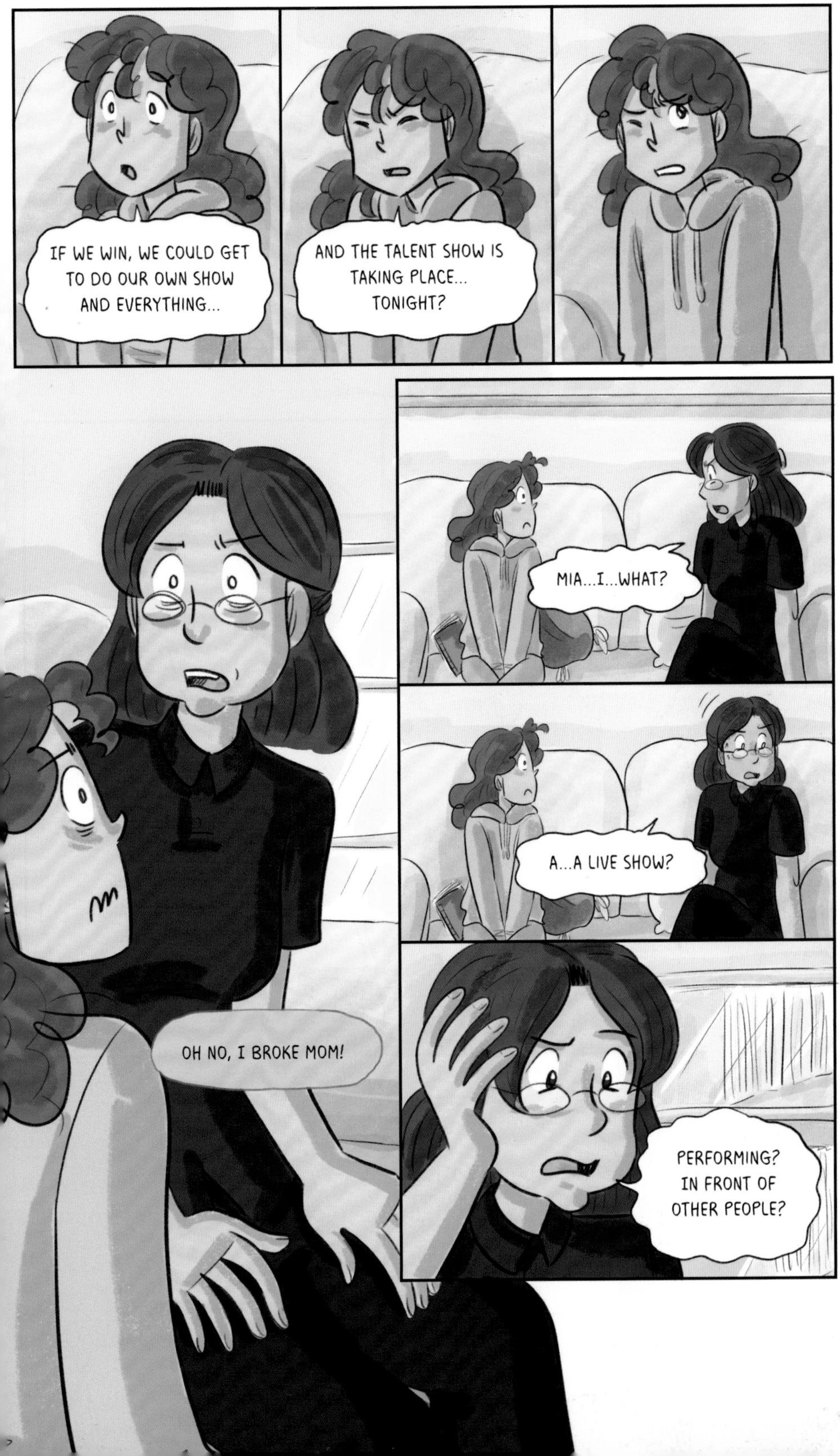
IF WE WIN, WE COULD GET TO DO OUR OWN SHOW AND EVERYTHING...
AND THE TALENT SHOW IS TAKING PLACE... TONIGHT?
MIA...I...WHAT?
A...A LIVE SHOW?
OH NO, I BROKE MOM!
PERFORMING? IN FRONT OF OTHER PEOPLE?

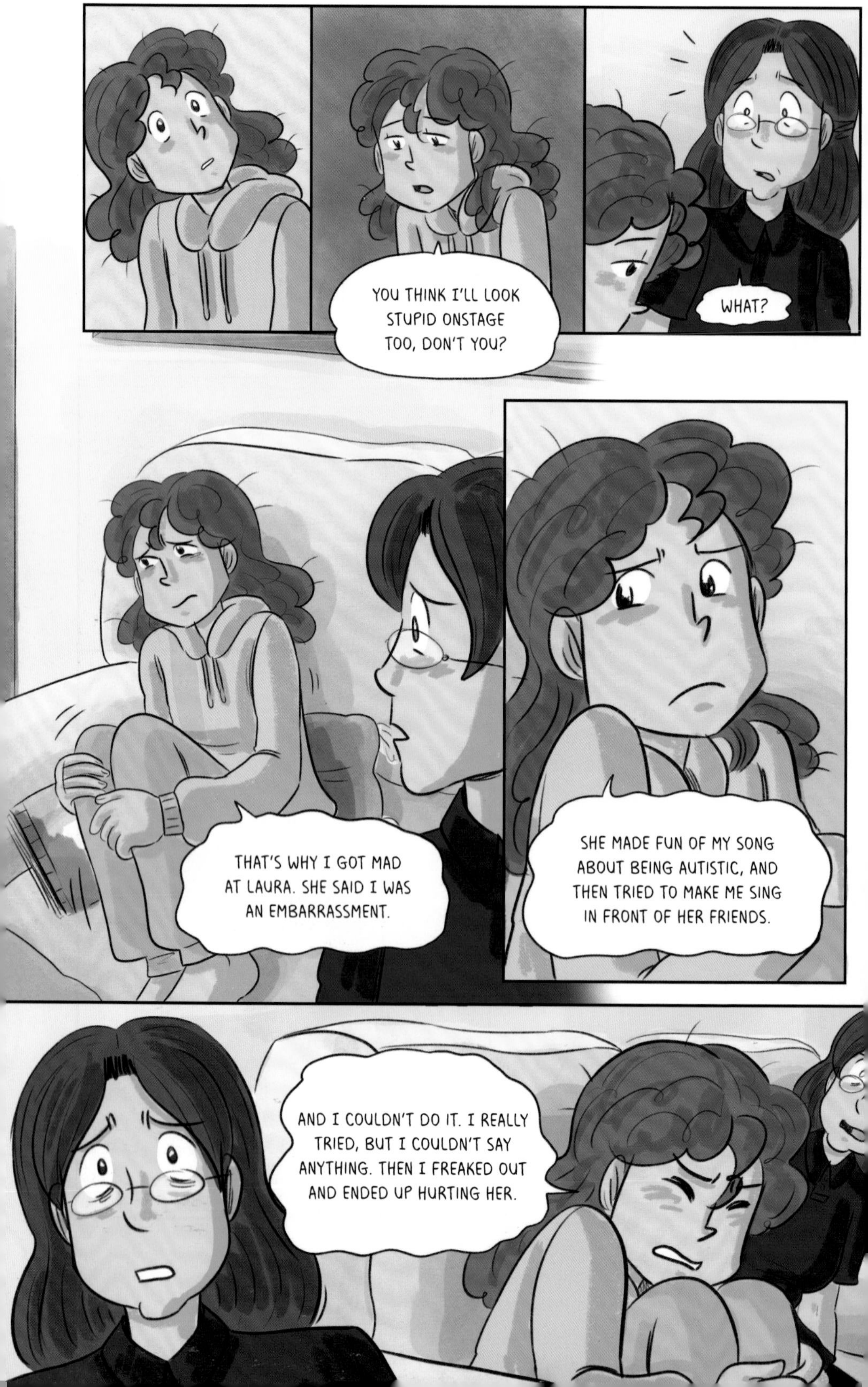
YOU THINK I'LL LOOK STUPID ONSTAGE TOO, DON'T YOU?
WHAT?
THAT'S WHY I GOT MAD AT LAURA. SHE SAID I WAS AN EMBARRASSMENT.
SHE MADE FUN OF MY SONG ABOUT BEING AUTISTIC, AND THEN TRIED TO MAKE ME SING IN FRONT OF HER FRIENDS.
AND I COULDN'T DO IT. I REALLY TRIED, BUT I COULDN'T SAY ANYTHING. THEN I FREAKED OUT AND ENDED UP HURTING HER.

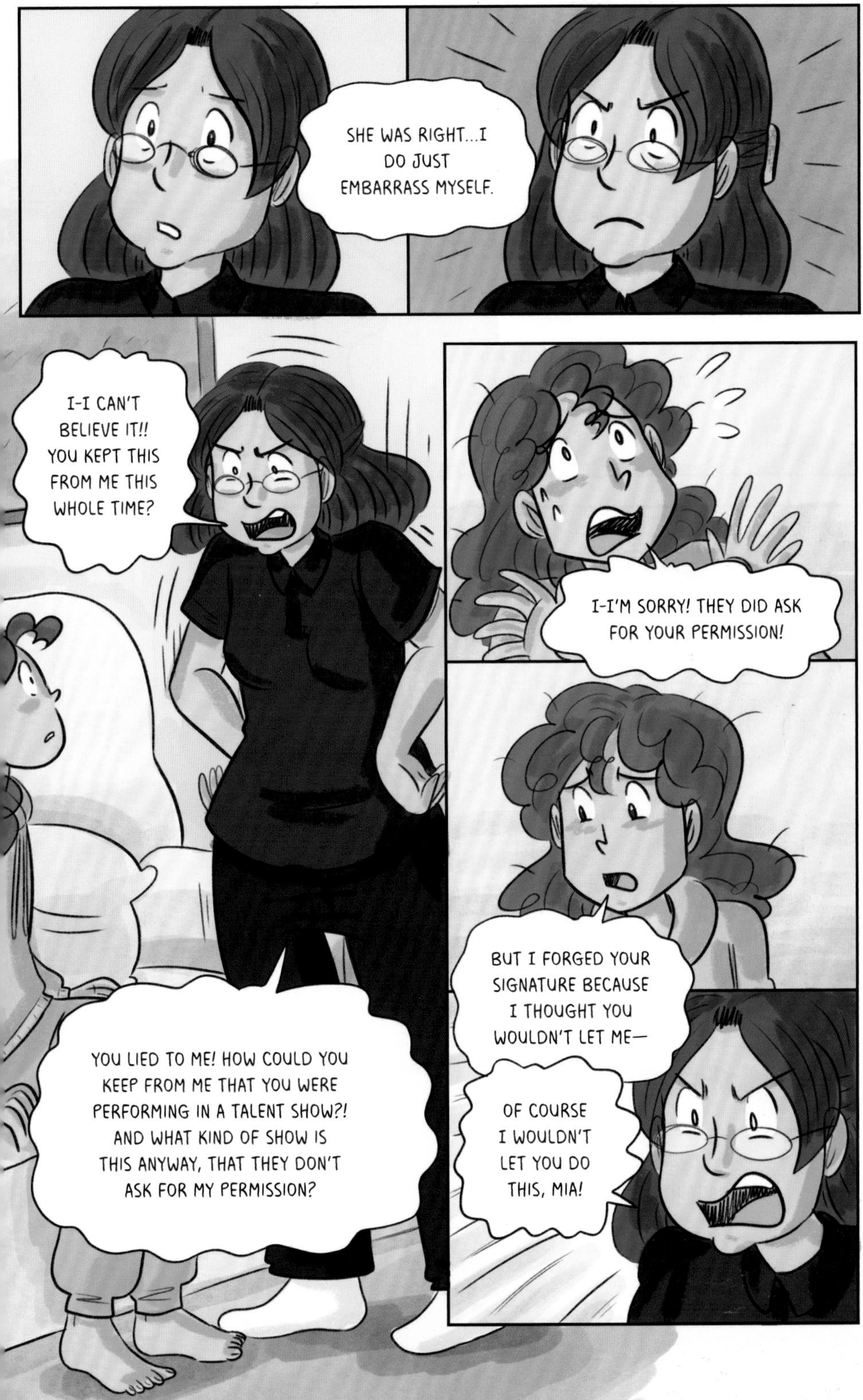
SHE WAS RIGHT...I DO JUST EMBARRASS MYSELF.
I-I CAN'T BELIEVE IT!! YOU KEPT THIS FROM ME THIS WHOLE TIME?
YOU LIED TO ME! HOW COULD YOU KEEP FROM ME THAT YOU WERE PERFORMING IN A TALENT SHOW?! AND WHAT KIND OF SHOW IS THIS ANYWAY, THAT THEY DON'T ASK FOR MY PERMISSION?
I-I'M SORRY! THEY DID ASK FOR YOUR PERMISSION!
BUT I FORGED YOUR SIGNATURE BECAUSE I THOUGHT YOU WOULDN'T LET ME—
OF COURSE I WOULDN'T LET YOU DO THIS, MIA!

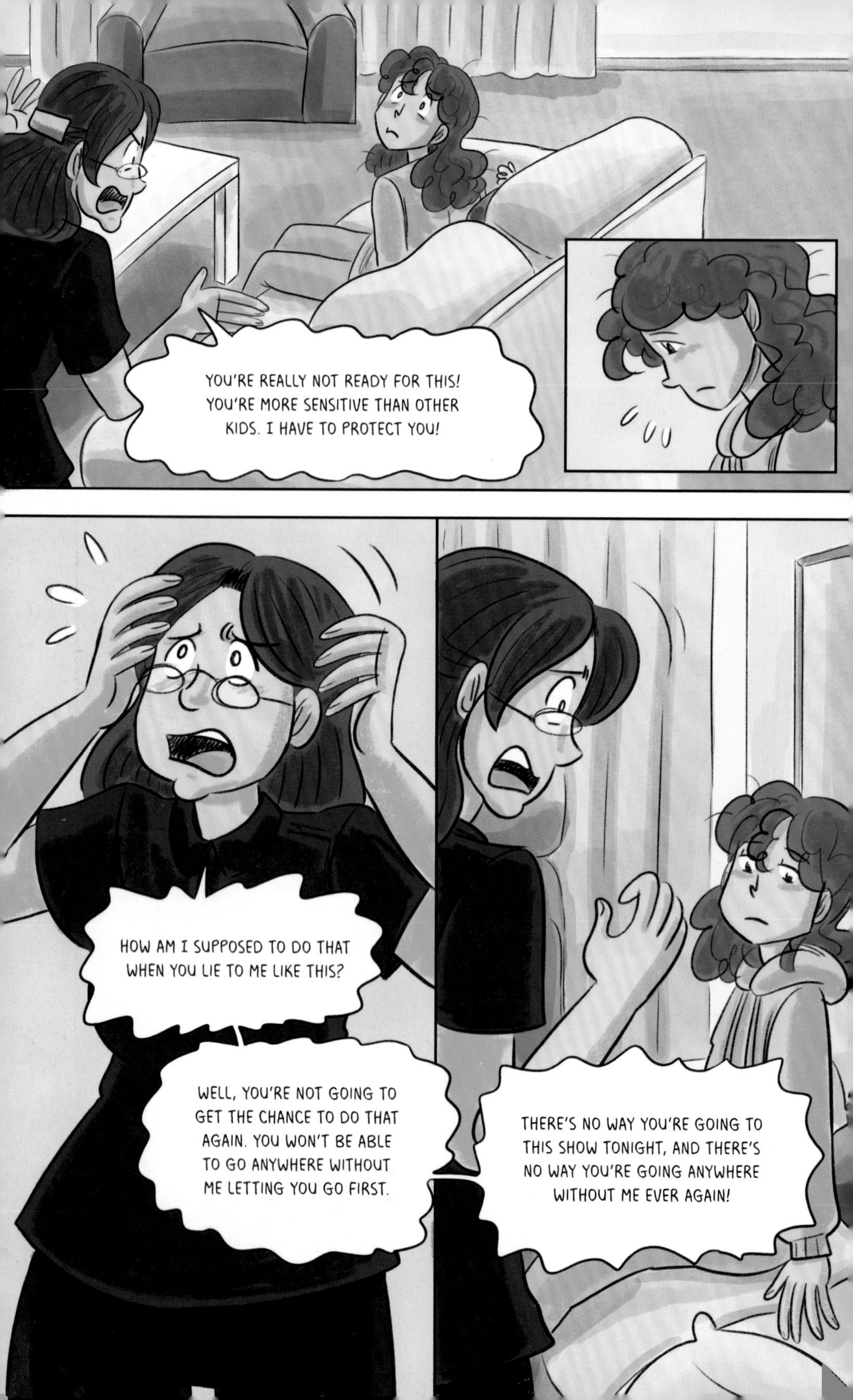
YOU'RE REALLY NOT READY FOR THIS! YOU'RE MORE SENSITIVE THAN OTHER KIDS. I HAVE TO PROTECT YOU!
HOW AM I SUPPOSED TO DO THAT WHEN YOU LIE TO ME LIKE THIS?
WELL, YOU'RE NOT GOING TO GET THE CHANCE TO DO THAT AGAIN. YOU WON'T BE ABLE TO GO ANYWHERE WITHOUT ME LETTING YOU GO FIRST.
THERE'S NO WAY YOU'RE GOING TO THIS SHOW TONIGHT, AND THERE'S NO WAY YOU'RE GOING ANYWHERE WITHOUT ME EVER AGAIN!

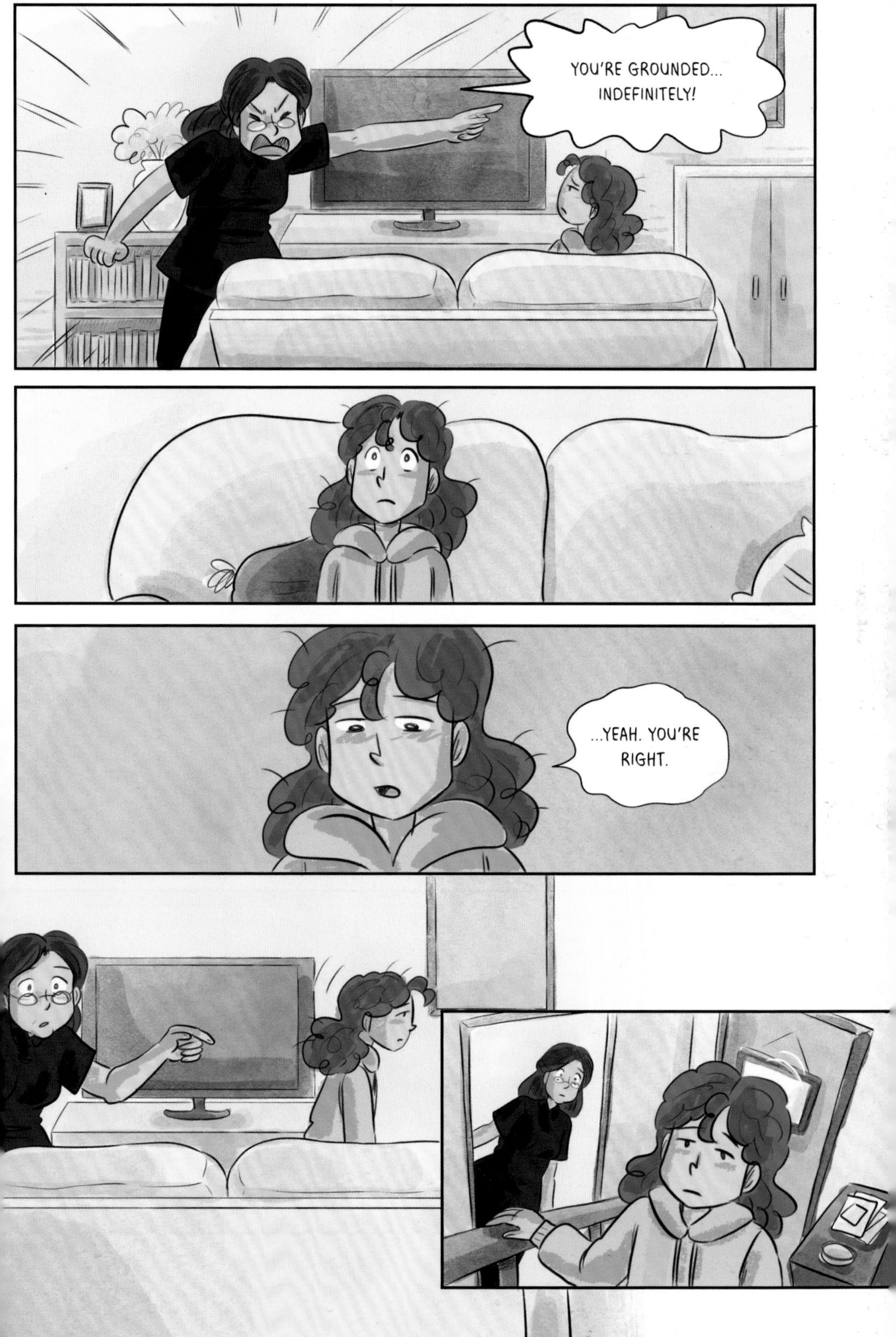
YOU'RE GROUNDED...
INDEFINITELY!
...YEAH. YOU'RE RIGHT.

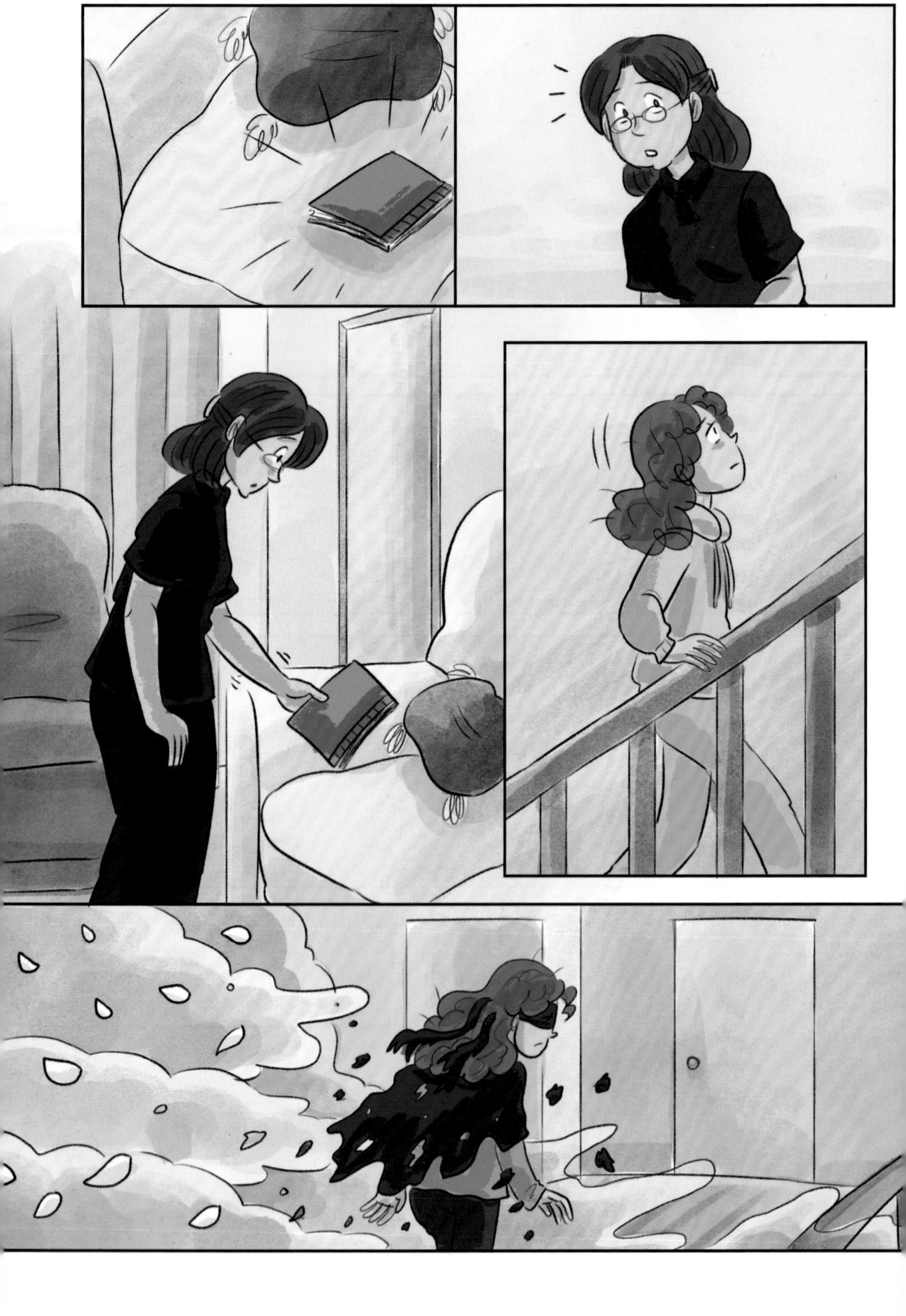

CHAPTER NINE

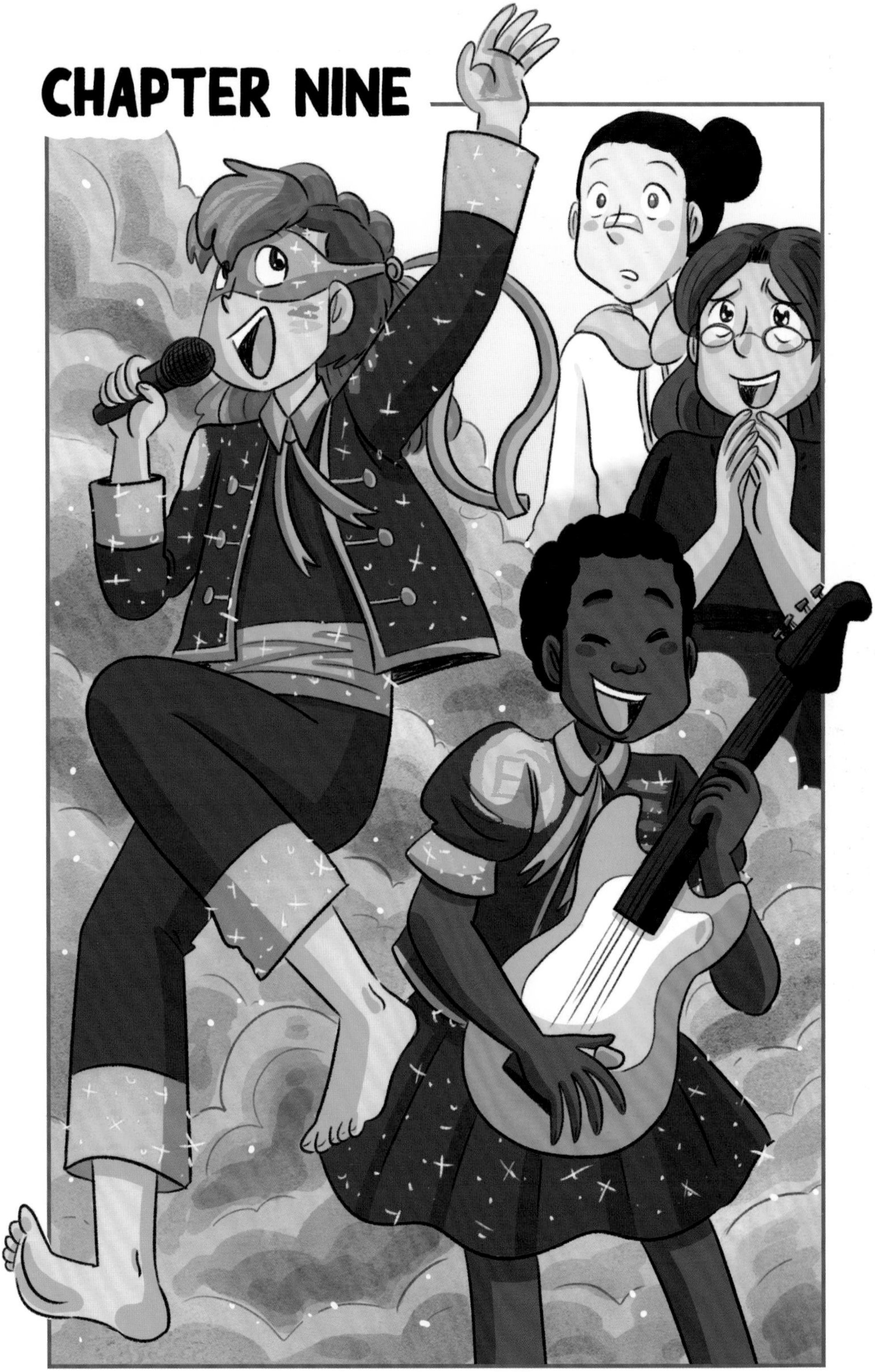

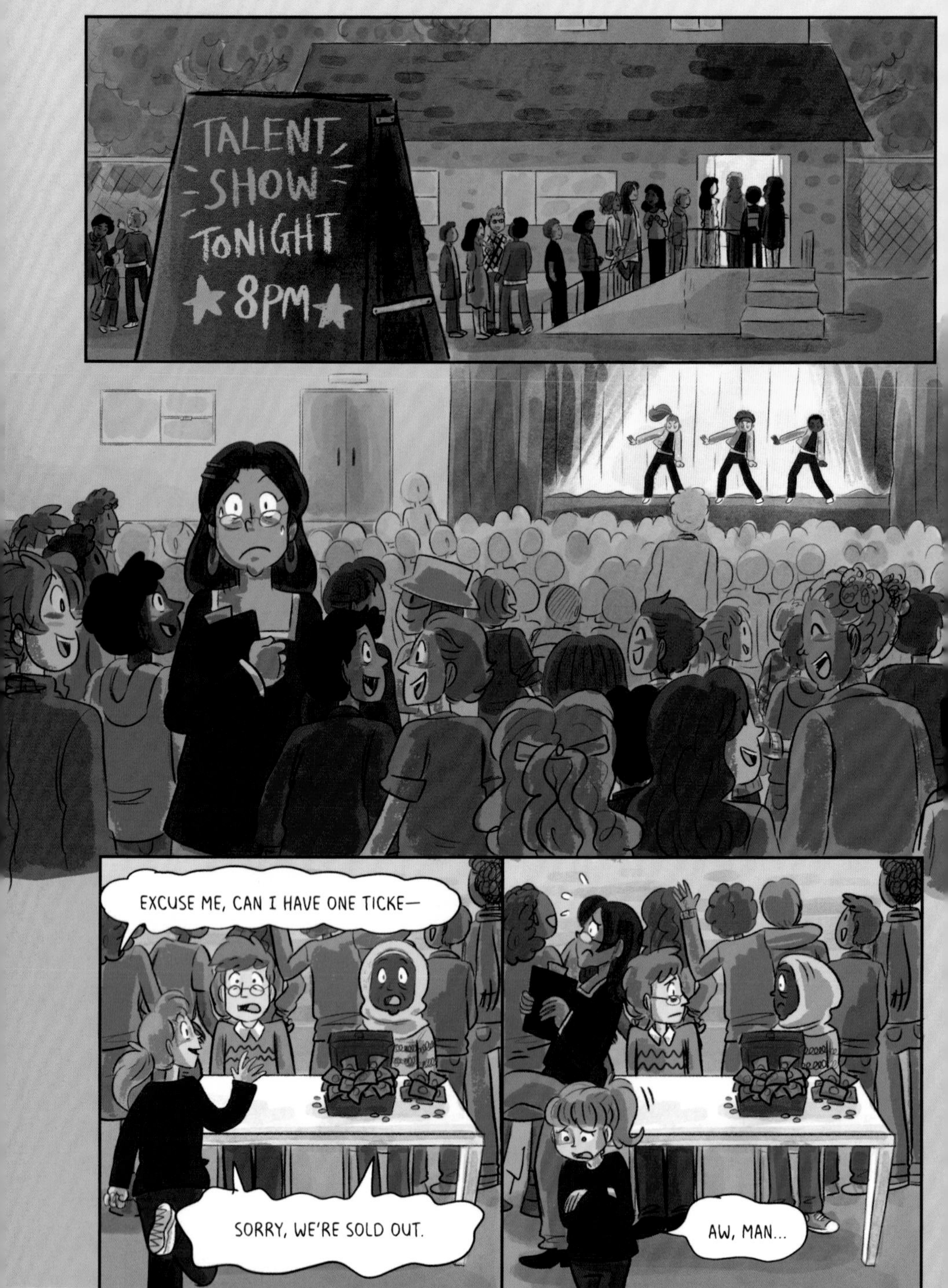
TALENT SHOW TONIGHT 8PM
EXCUSE ME, CAN I HAVE ONE TICKE—
SORRY, WE'RE SOLD OUT.
AW, MAN...

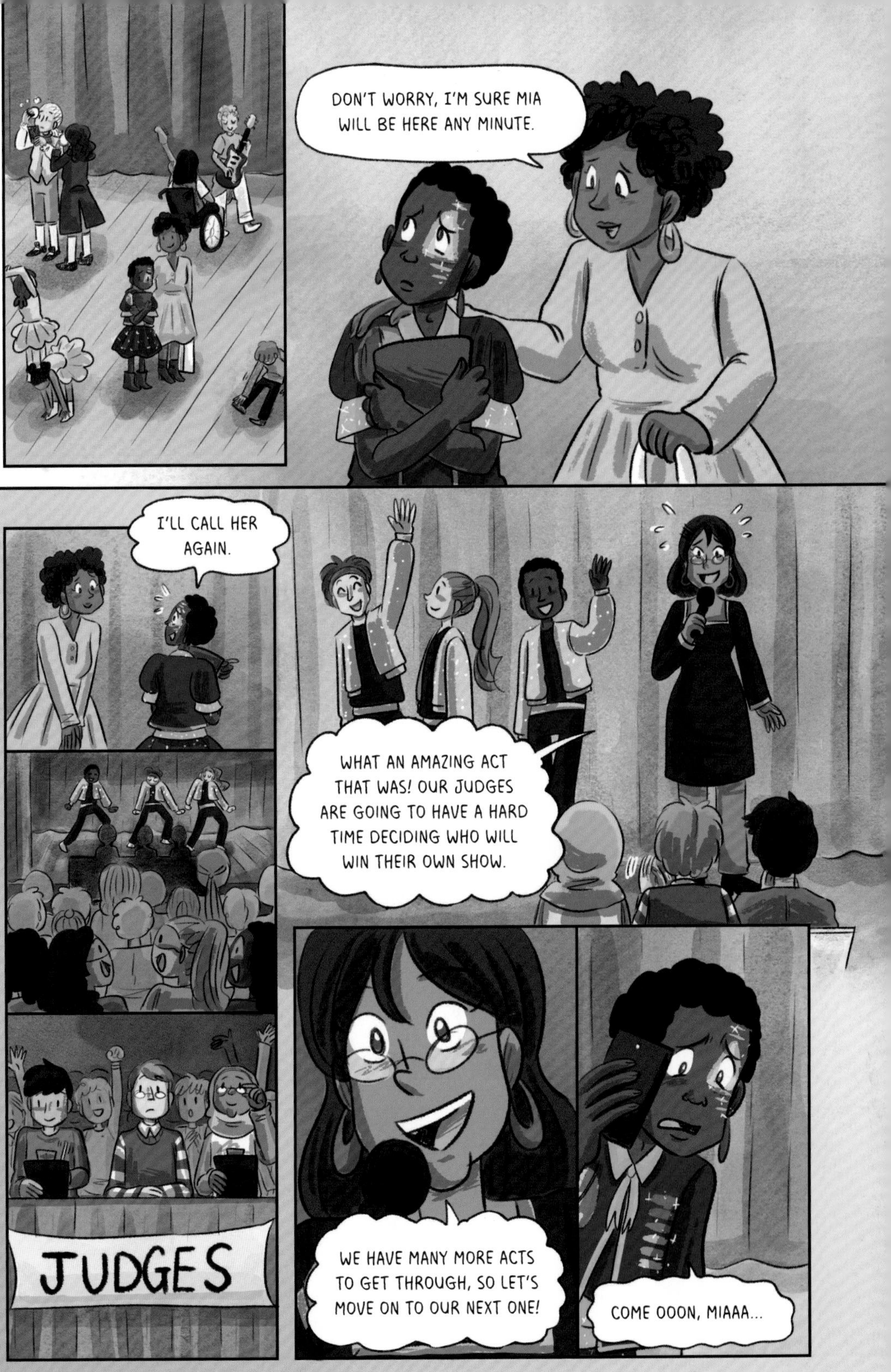
DON'T WORRY, I'M SURE MIA WILL BE HERE ANY MINUTE.
I'LL CALL HER AGAIN.
WHAT AN AMAZING ACT THAT WAS! OUR JUDGES ARE GOING TO HAVE A HARD TIME DECIDING WHO WILL WIN THEIR OWN SHOW.
JUDGES
WE HAVE MANY MORE ACTS TO GET THROUGH, SO LET'S MOVE ON TO OUR NEXT ONE!
COME OOON, MIAAA...

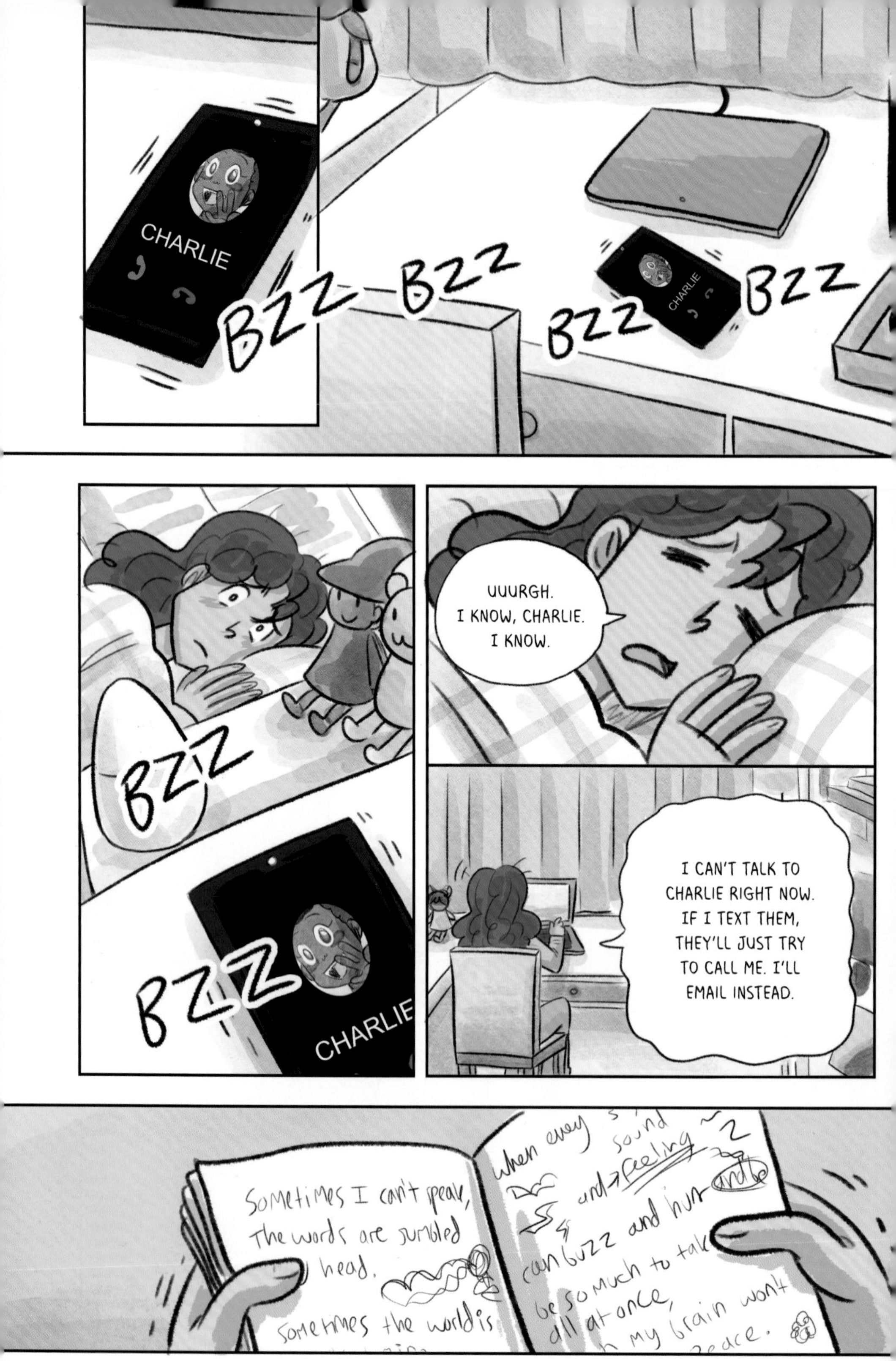
CHARLIE
BZZ BZZ
CHARLIE
BZZ BZZ
BZZ
BZZ
CHARLIE
UUURGH. I KNOW, CHARLIE. I KNOW.
I CAN'T TALK TO CHARLIE RIGHT NOW. IF I TEXT THEM, THEY'LL JUST TRY TO CALL ME. I'LL EMAIL INSTEAD.
Sometimes I can't speak,
The words are jumbled
head.
Sometimes the world is
when every
sound
and feeling
can buzz and hurt
be so much to take
all at once,
my brain won't
peace.

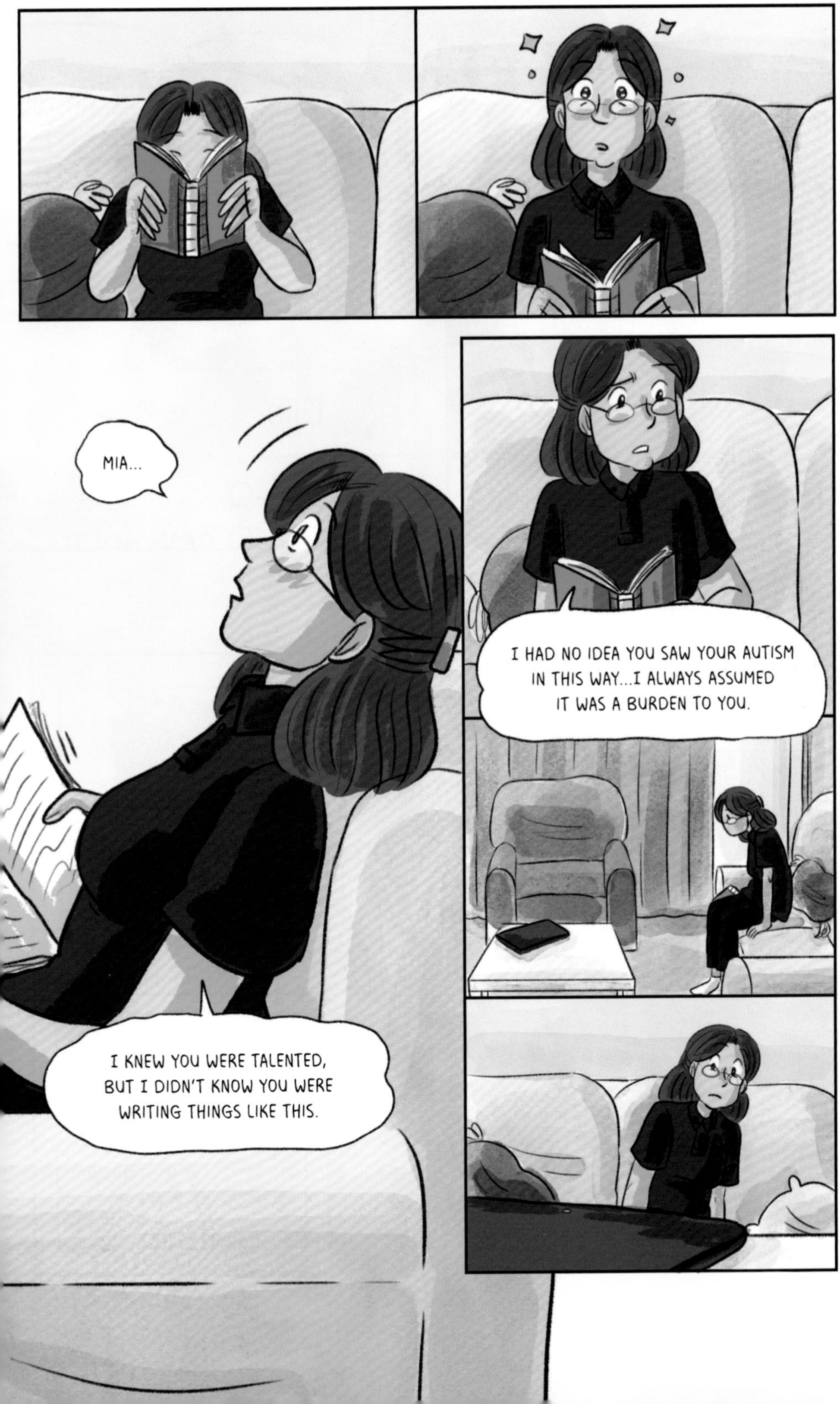
MIA...
I KNEW YOU WERE TALENTED, BUT I DIDN'T KNOW YOU WERE WRITING THINGS LIKE THIS.
I HAD NO IDEA YOU SAW YOUR AUTISM IN THIS WAY...I ALWAYS ASSUMED IT WAS A BURDEN TO YOU.

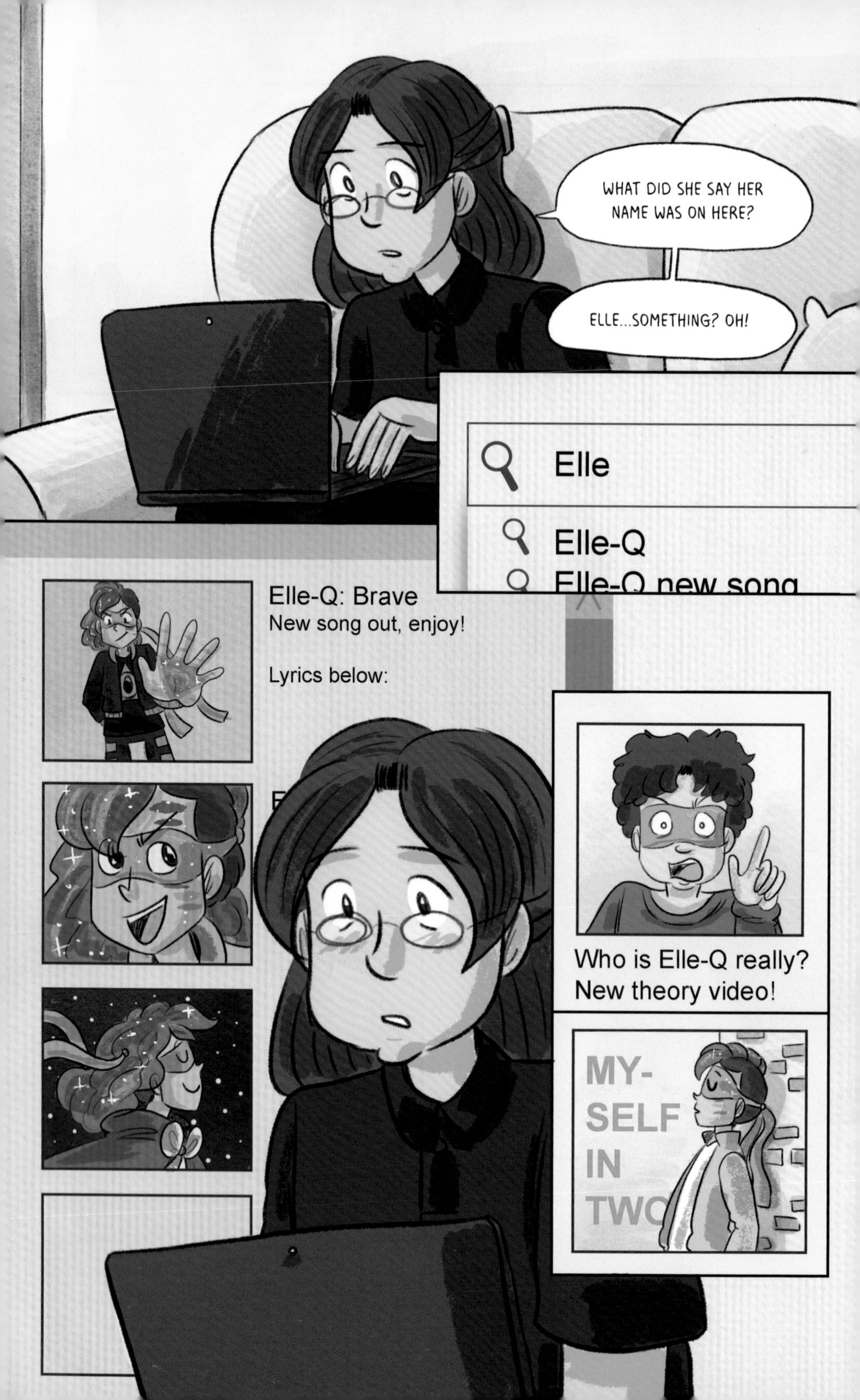
WHAT DID SHE SAY HER NAME WAS ON HERE?
ELLE...SOMETHING? OH!
Elle
Elle-Q
Elle-Q new song
Elle-Q: Brave
New song out, enjoy!
Lyrics below:
Who is Elle-Q really?
New theory video!
MY-
SELF
IN
TWO

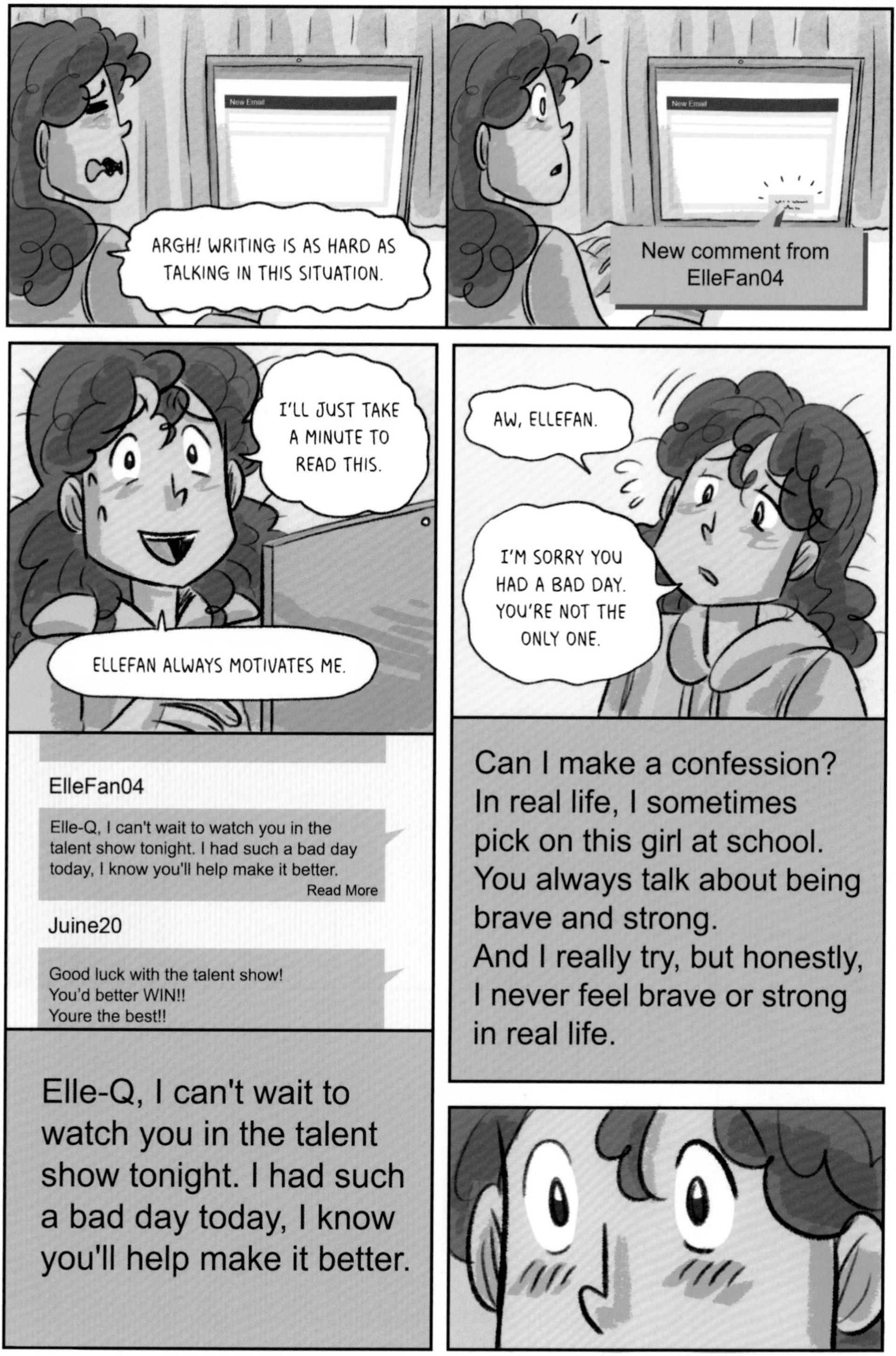

ARGH! WRITING IS AS HARD AS TALKING IN THIS SITUATION.
New comment from ElleFan04
I'LL JUST TAKE A MINUTE TO READ THIS.
ELLEFAN ALWAYS MOTIVATES ME.
AW, ELLEFAN.
I'M SORRY YOU HAD A BAD DAY. YOU'RE NOT THE ONLY ONE.
ElleFan04
Elle-Q, I can't wait to watch you in the talent show tonight. I had such a bad day today, I know you'll help make it better.
Read More
Juine20
Good luck with the talent show! You'd better WIN!! Youre the best!!
Can I make a confession? In real life, I sometimes pick on this girl at school. You always talk about being brave and strong. And I really try, but honestly, I never feel brave or strong in real life.
Elle-Q, I can't wait to watch you in the talent show tonight. I had such a bad day today, I know you'll help make it better.

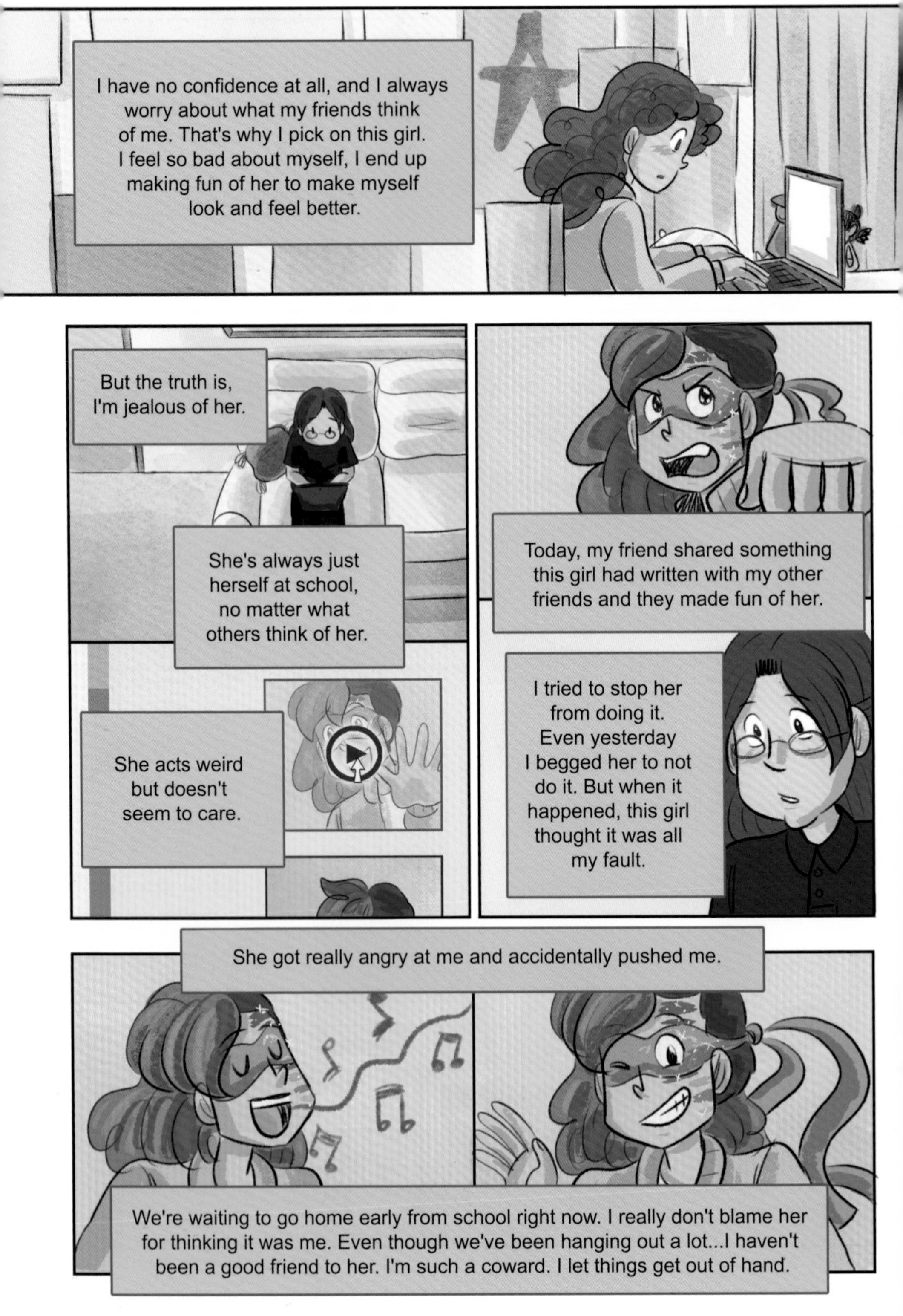
I have no confidence at all, and I always worry about what my friends think of me. That's why I pick on this girl. I feel so bad about myself, I end up making fun of her to make myself look and feel better.
But the truth is, I'm jealous of her.
She's always just herself at school, no matter what others think of her.
She acts weird but doesn't seem to care.
Today, my friend shared something this girl had written with my other friends and they made fun of her.
I tried to stop her from doing it. Even yesterday I begged her to not do it. But when it happened, this girl thought it was all my fault.
She got really angry at me and accidentally pushed me.
We're waiting to go home early from school right now. I really don't blame her for thinking it was me. Even though we've been hanging out a lot...I haven't been a good friend to her. I'm such a coward. I let things get out of hand.

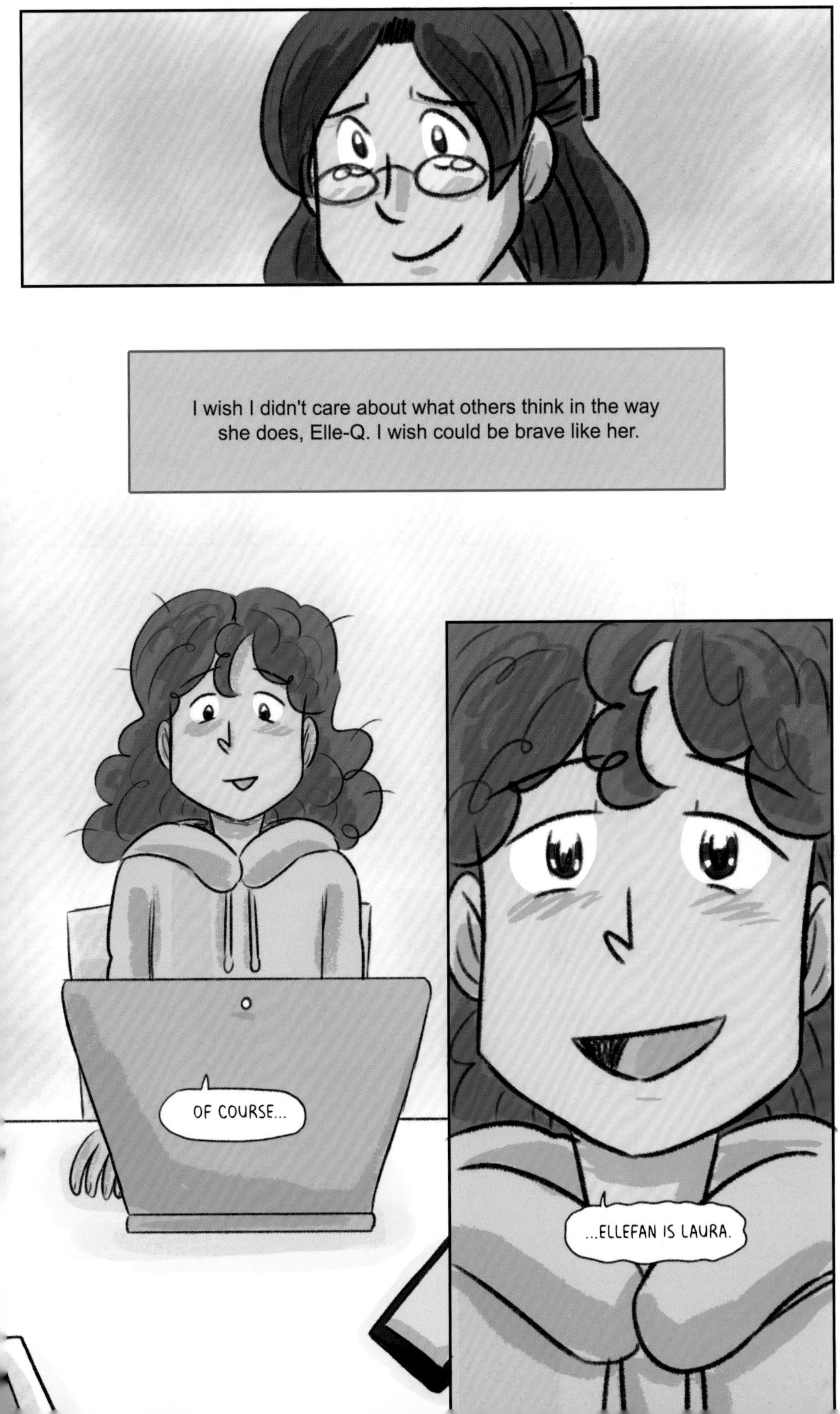
I wish I didn't care about what others think in the way she does, Elle-Q. I wish could be brave like her.
OF COURSE...
...ELLEFAN IS LAURA.

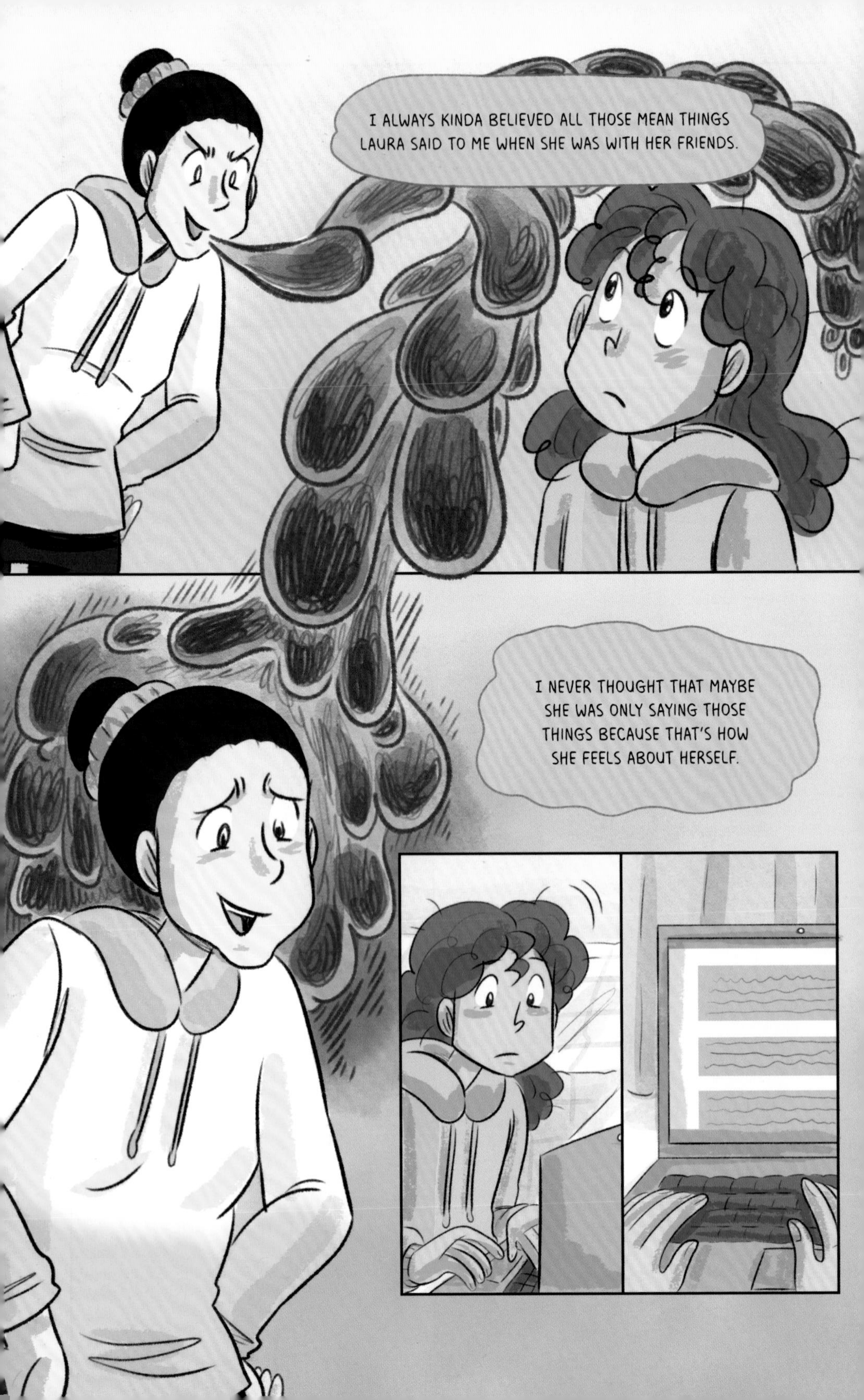
I ALWAYS KINDA BELIEVED ALL THOSE MEAN THINGS LAURA SAID TO ME WHEN SHE WAS WITH HER FRIENDS.
I NEVER THOUGHT THAT MAYBE SHE WAS ONLY SAYING THOSE THINGS BECAUSE THAT'S HOW SHE FEELS ABOUT HERSELF.

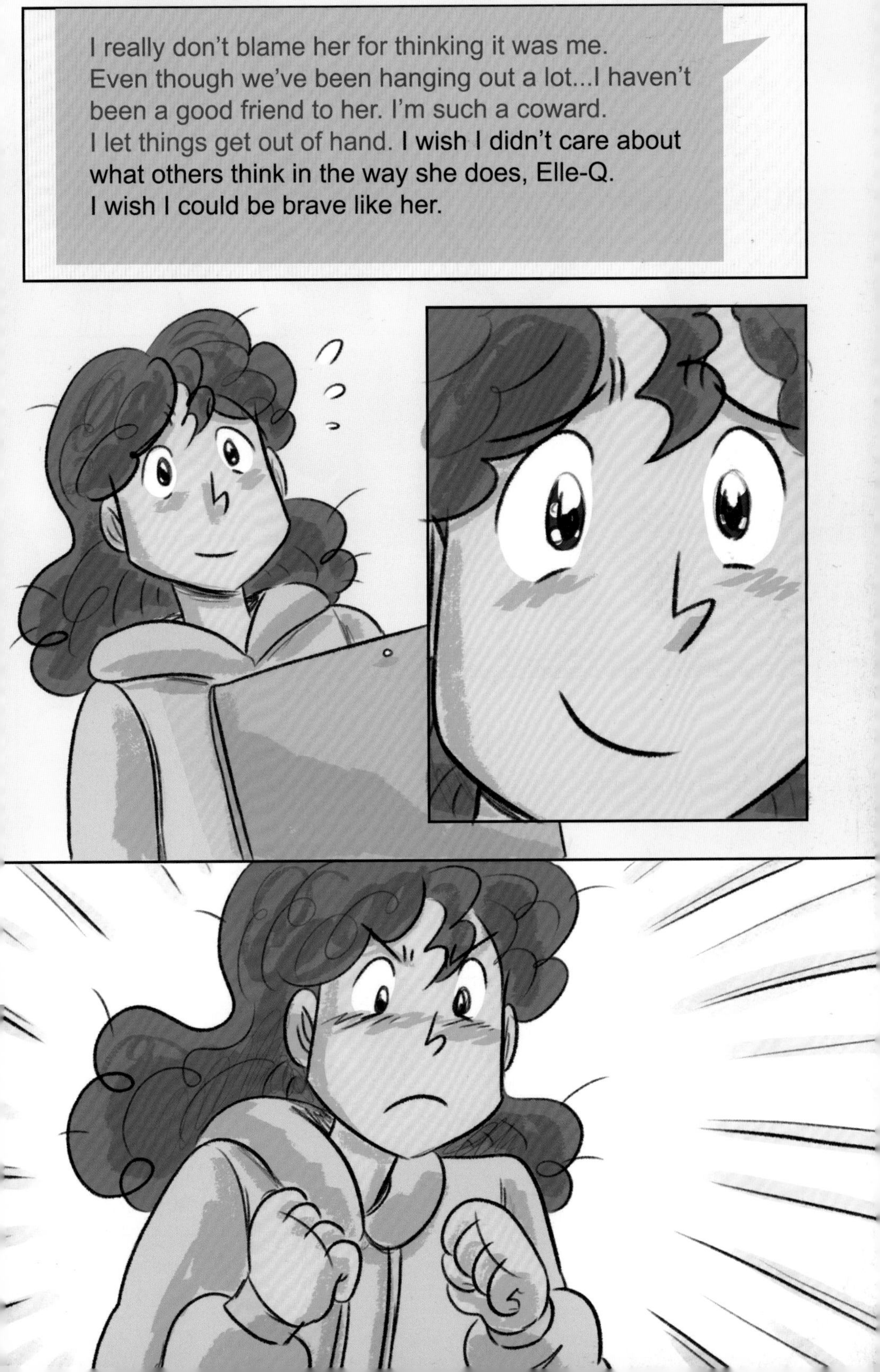
I really don't blame her for thinking it was me. Even though we've been hanging out a lot...I haven't been a good friend to her. I'm such a coward. I let things get out of hand. I wish I didn't care about what others think in the way she does, Elle-Q. I wish I could be brave like her.

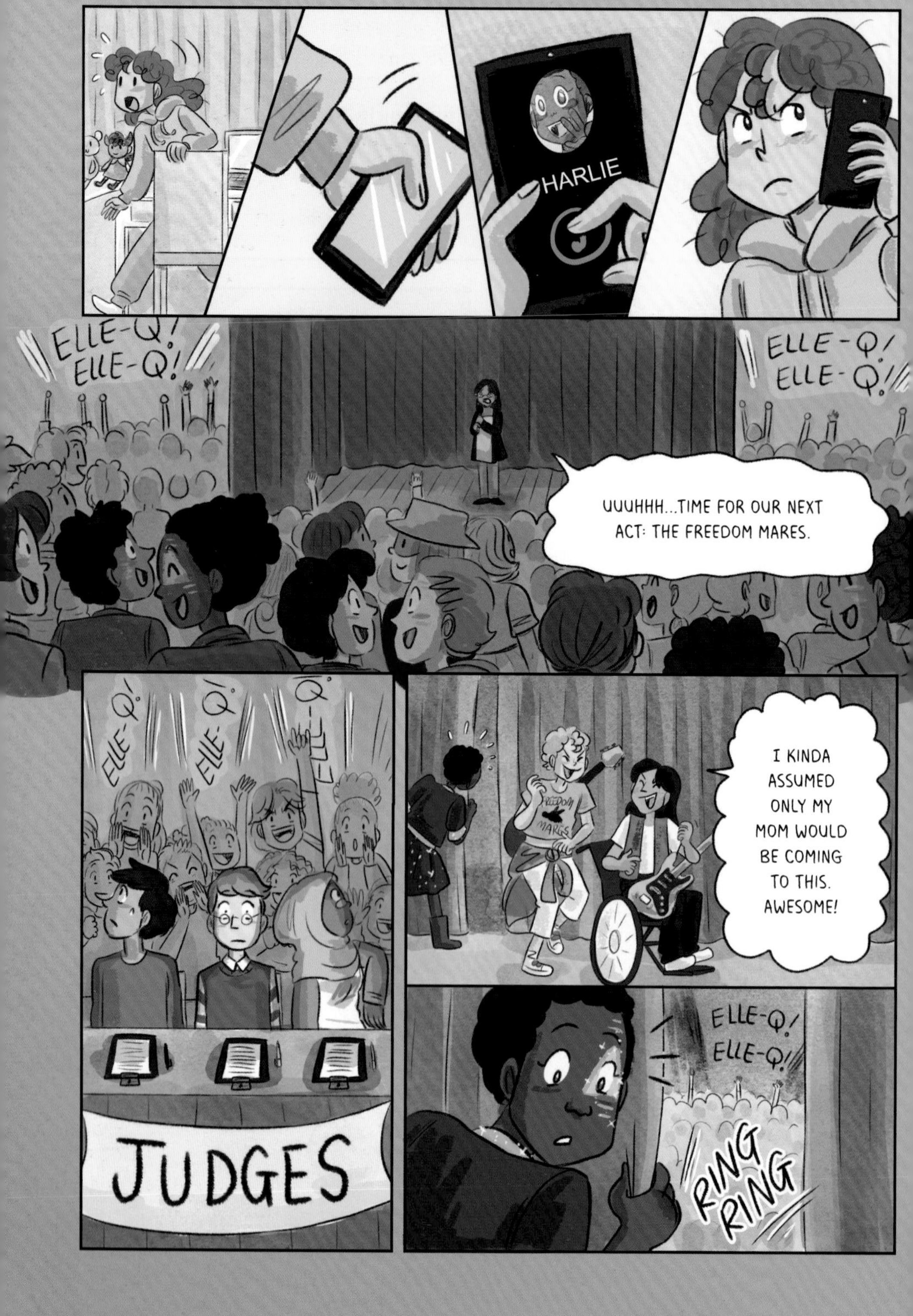
HARLIE
ELLE-Q! ELLE-Q!
ELLE-Q! ELLE-Q!
UUUHHH...TIME FOR OUR NEXT ACT: THE FREEDOM MARES.
ELLE-Q! ELLE-Q! ELLE-Q!
JUDGES
I KINDA ASSUMED ONLY MY MOM WOULD BE COMING TO THIS. AWESOME!
ELLE-Q! ELLE-Q!
RING RING

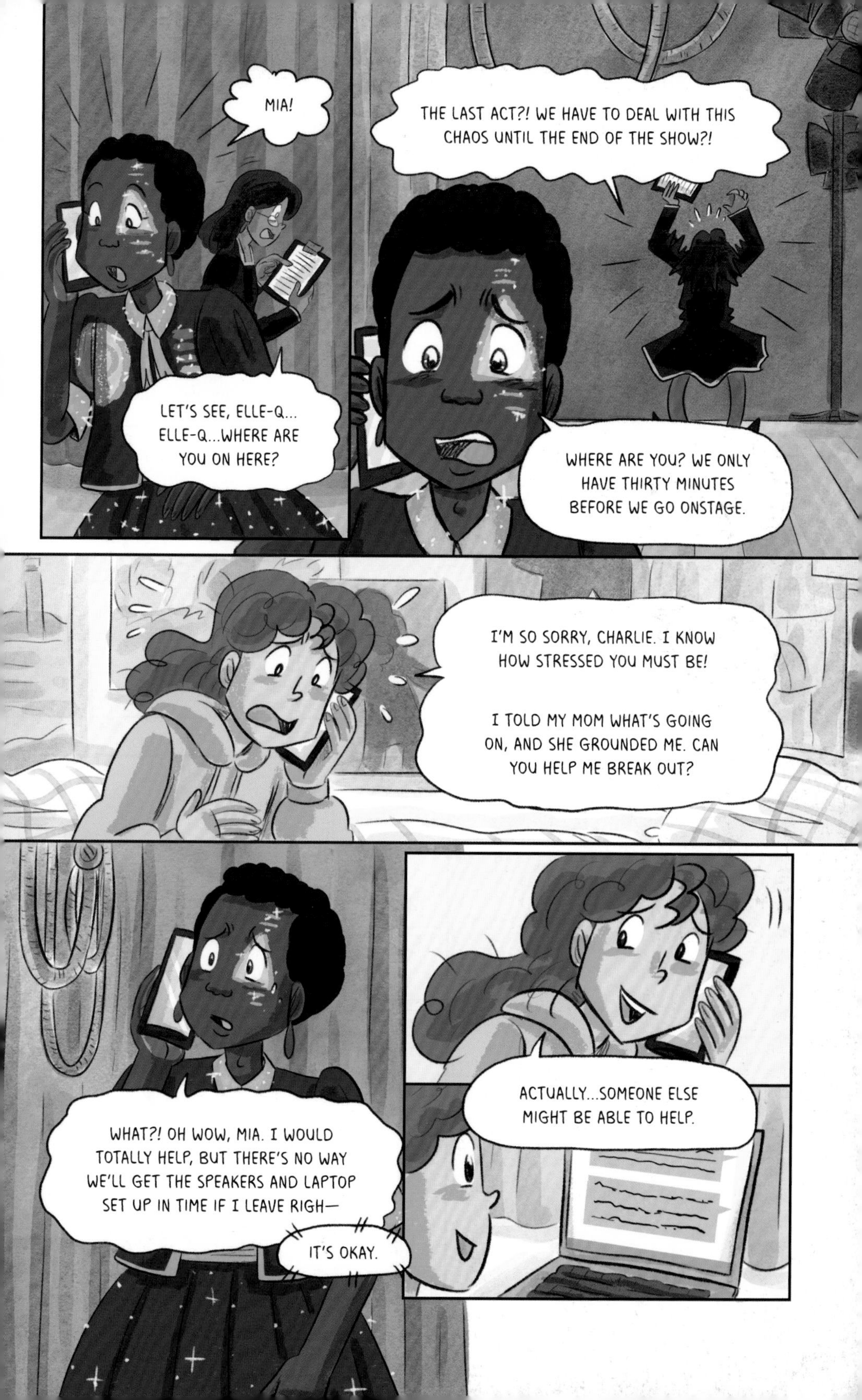
MIA!
LET'S SEE, ELLE-Q... ELLE-Q...WHERE ARE YOU ON HERE?
THE LAST ACT?! WE HAVE TO DEAL WITH THIS CHAOS UNTIL THE END OF THE SHOW?!
WHERE ARE YOU? WE ONLY HAVE THIRTY MINUTES BEFORE WE GO ONSTAGE.
I'M SO SORRY, CHARLIE. I KNOW HOW STRESSED YOU MUST BE!
I TOLD MY MOM WHAT'S GOING ON, AND SHE GROUNDED ME. CAN YOU HELP ME BREAK OUT?
WHAT?! OH WOW, MIA. I WOULD TOTALLY HELP, BUT THERE'S NO WAY WE'LL GET THE SPEAKERS AND LAPTOP SET UP IN TIME IF I LEAVE RIGH—
IT'S OKAY.
ACTUALLY...SOMEONE ELSE MIGHT BE ABLE TO HELP.

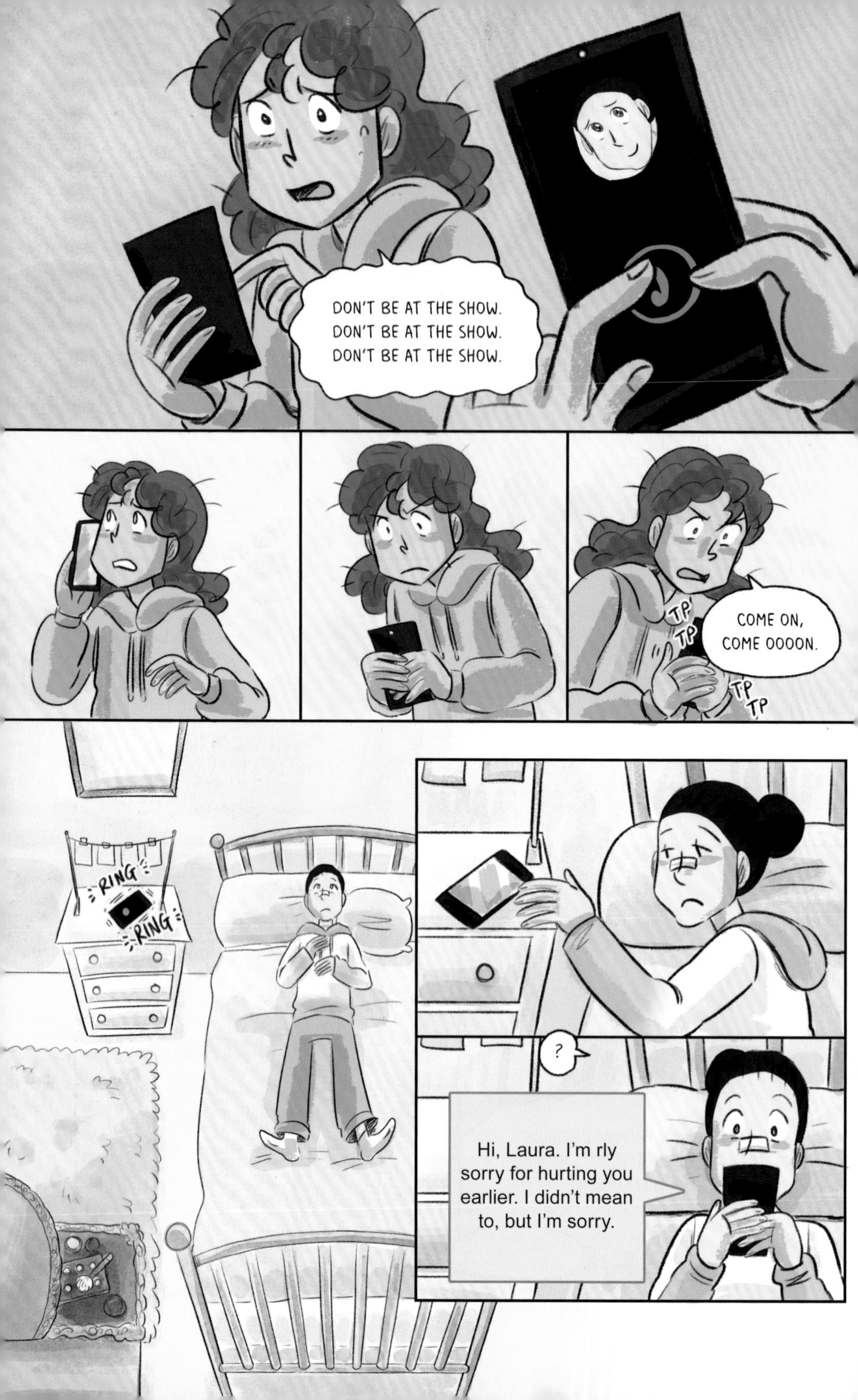
DON'T BE AT THE SHOW.
DON'T BE AT THE SHOW.
DON'T BE AT THE SHOW.
TP TP
COME ON,
COME OOOON.
TP TP
RING
RING
?
Hi, Laura. I'm rly sorry for hurting you earlier. I didn't mean to, but I'm sorry.

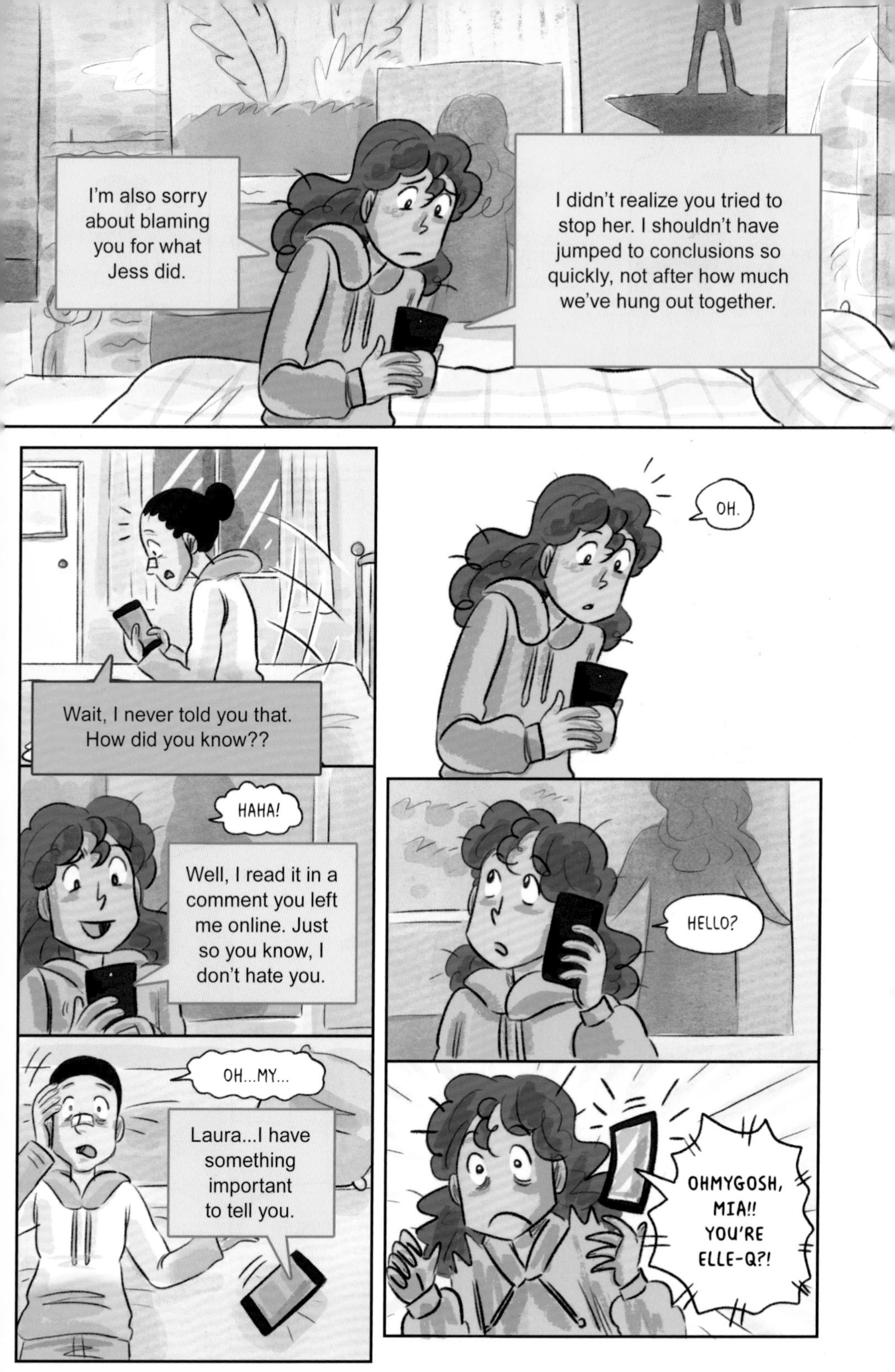
I'm also sorry about blaming you for what Jess did.
I didn't realize you tried to stop her. I shouldn't have jumped to conclusions so quickly, not after how much we've hung out together.
Wait, I never told you that. How did you know??
OH.
HAHA!
Well, I read it in a comment you left me online. Just so you know, I don't hate you.
HELLO?
OH...MY...
Laura...I have something important to tell you.
OHMYGOSH, MIA!! YOU'RE ELLE-Q?!

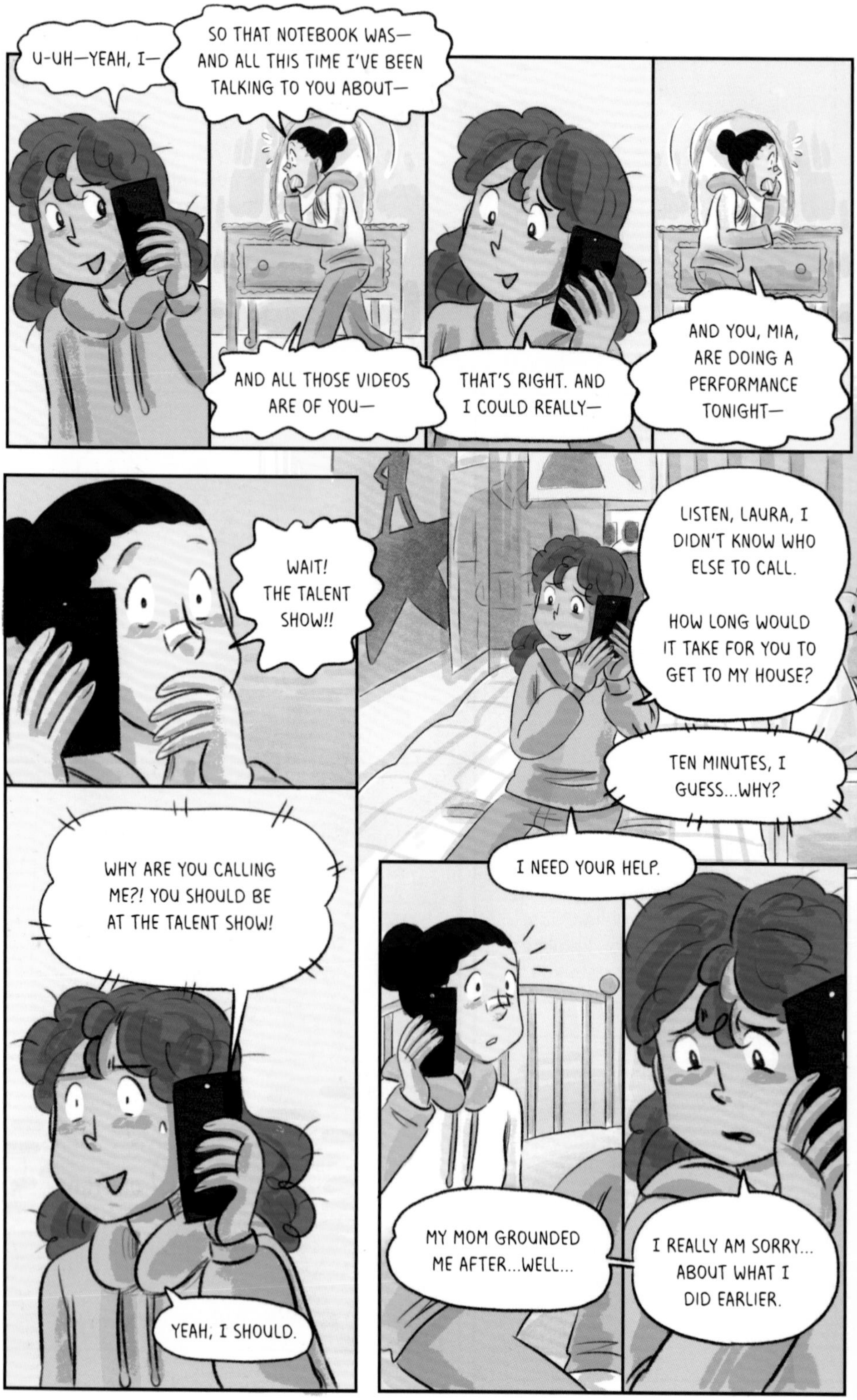
U-UH—YEAH, I—
SO THAT NOTEBOOK WAS— AND ALL THIS TIME I'VE BEEN TALKING TO YOU ABOUT—
AND ALL THOSE VIDEOS ARE OF YOU—
THAT'S RIGHT. AND I COULD REALLY—
AND YOU, MIA, ARE DOING A PERFORMANCE TONIGHT—
WAIT! THE TALENT SHOW!!
LISTEN, LAURA, I DIDN'T KNOW WHO ELSE TO CALL.
HOW LONG WOULD IT TAKE FOR YOU TO GET TO MY HOUSE?
TEN MINUTES, I GUESS...WHY?
I NEED YOUR HELP.
WHY ARE YOU CALLING ME?! YOU SHOULD BE AT THE TALENT SHOW!
YEAH, I SHOULD.
MY MOM GROUNDED ME AFTER...WELL...
I REALLY AM SORRY... ABOUT WHAT I DID EARLIER.

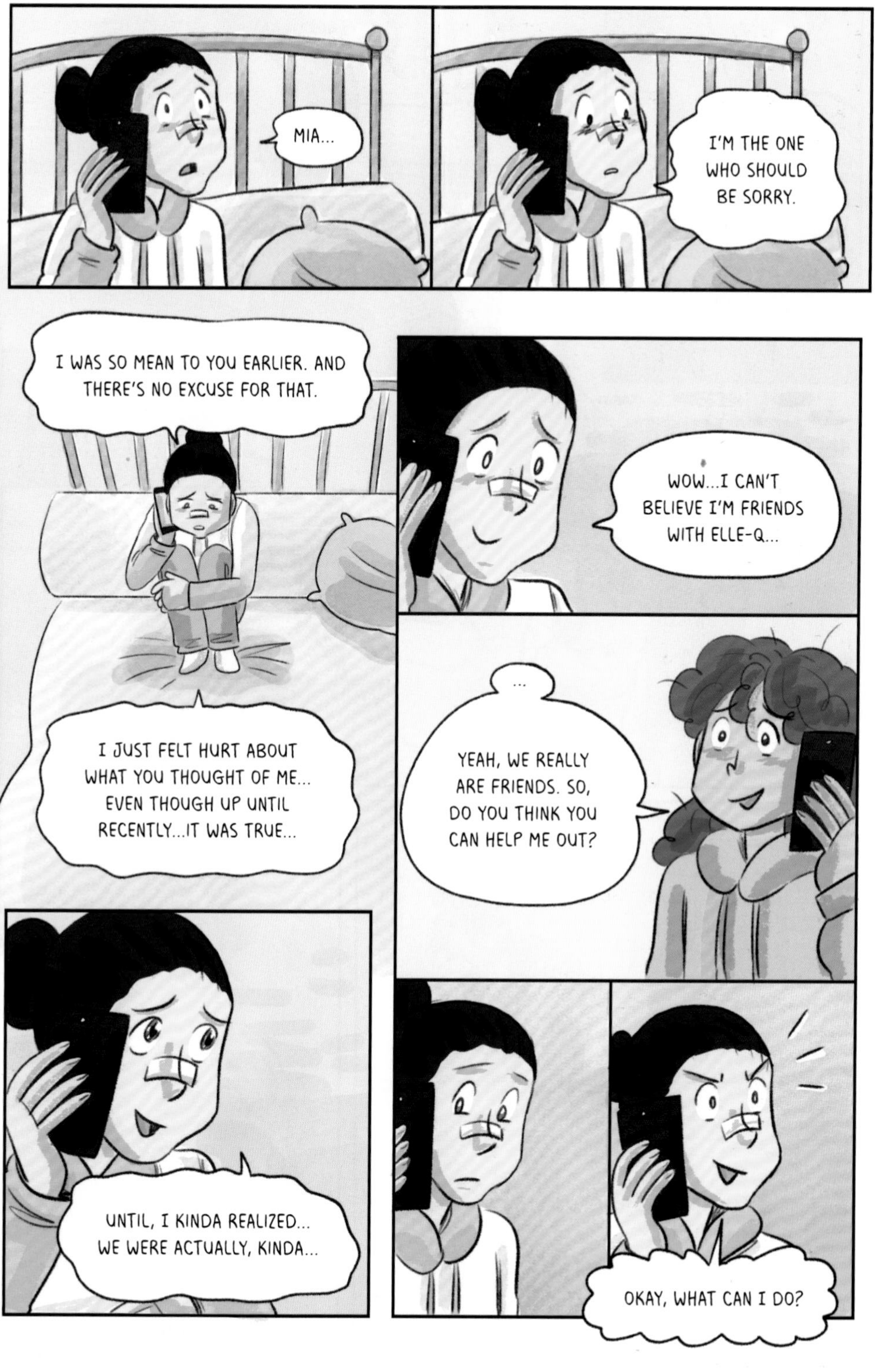
MIA...
I'M THE ONE WHO SHOULD BE SORRY.
I WAS SO MEAN TO YOU EARLIER. AND THERE'S NO EXCUSE FOR THAT.
I JUST FELT HURT ABOUT WHAT YOU THOUGHT OF ME... EVEN THOUGH UP UNTIL RECENTLY...IT WAS TRUE...
WOW...I CAN'T BELIEVE I'M FRIENDS WITH ELLE-Q...
...
YEAH, WE REALLY ARE FRIENDS. SO, DO YOU THINK YOU CAN HELP ME OUT?
UNTIL, I KINDA REALIZED... WE WERE ACTUALLY, KINDA...
OKAY, WHAT CAN I DO?

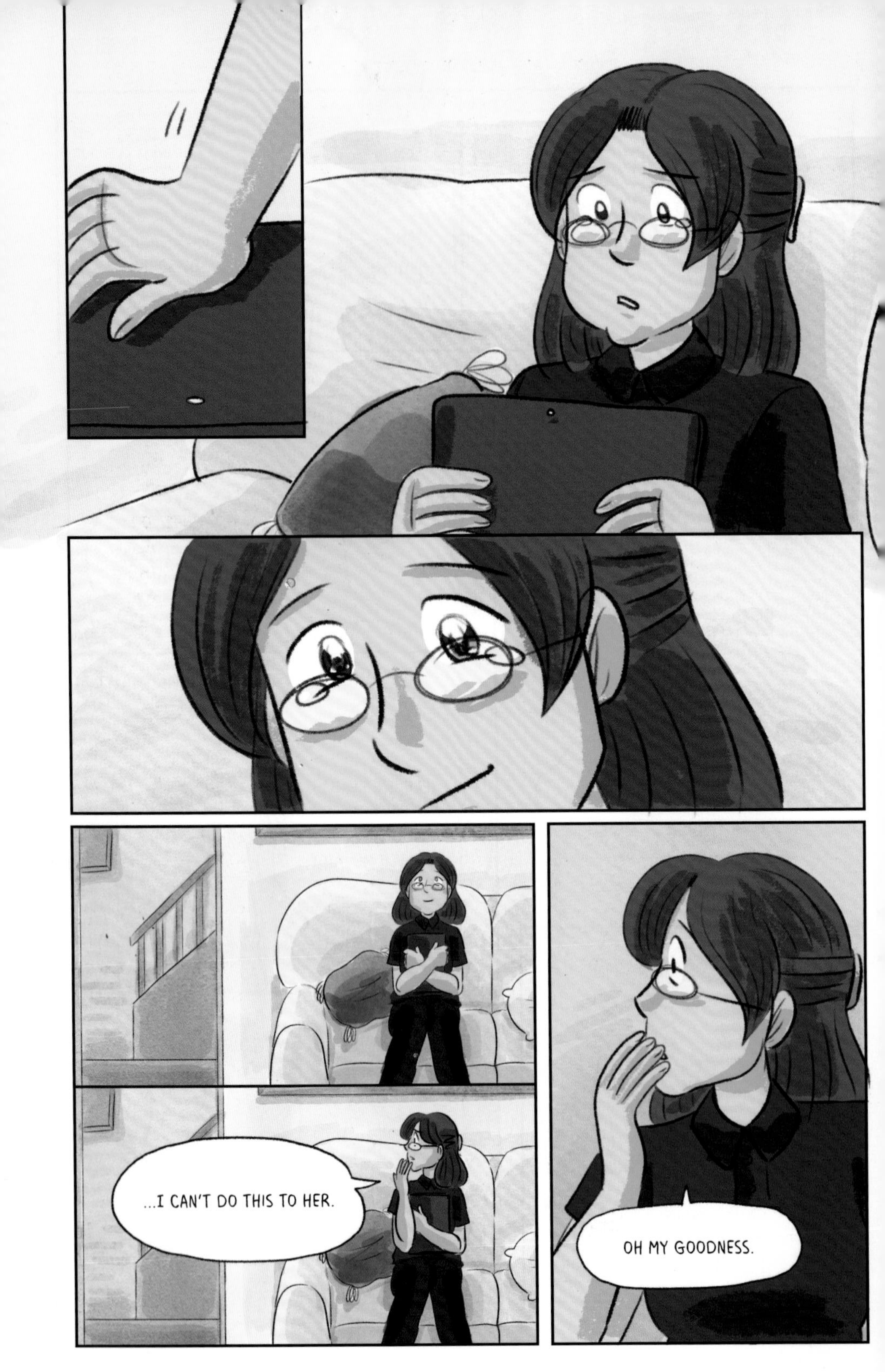
...I CAN'T DO THIS TO HER.
OH MY GOODNESS.

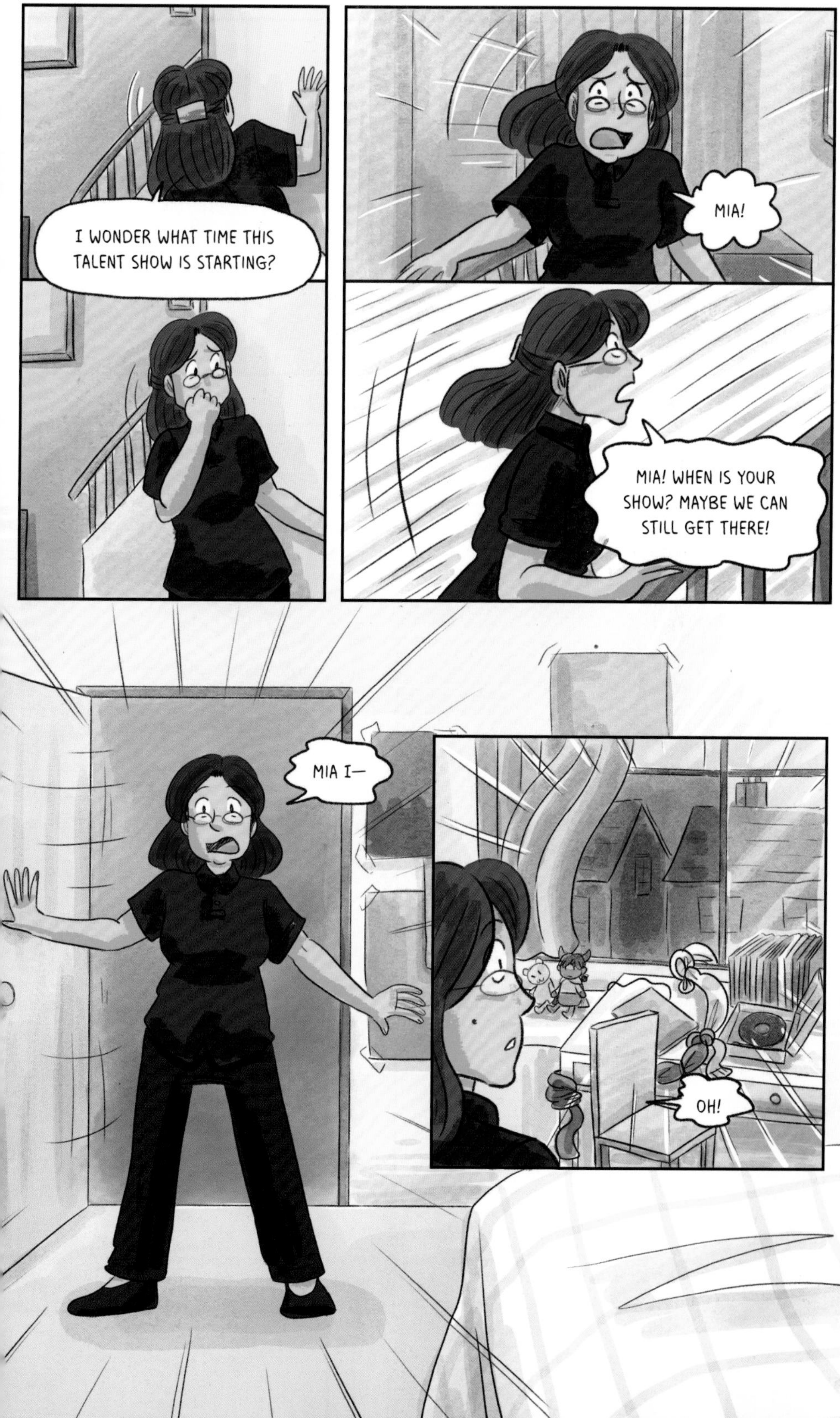
I WONDER WHAT TIME THIS TALENT SHOW IS STARTING?
MIA!
MIA! WHEN IS YOUR SHOW? MAYBE WE CAN STILL GET THERE!
MIA I—
OH!

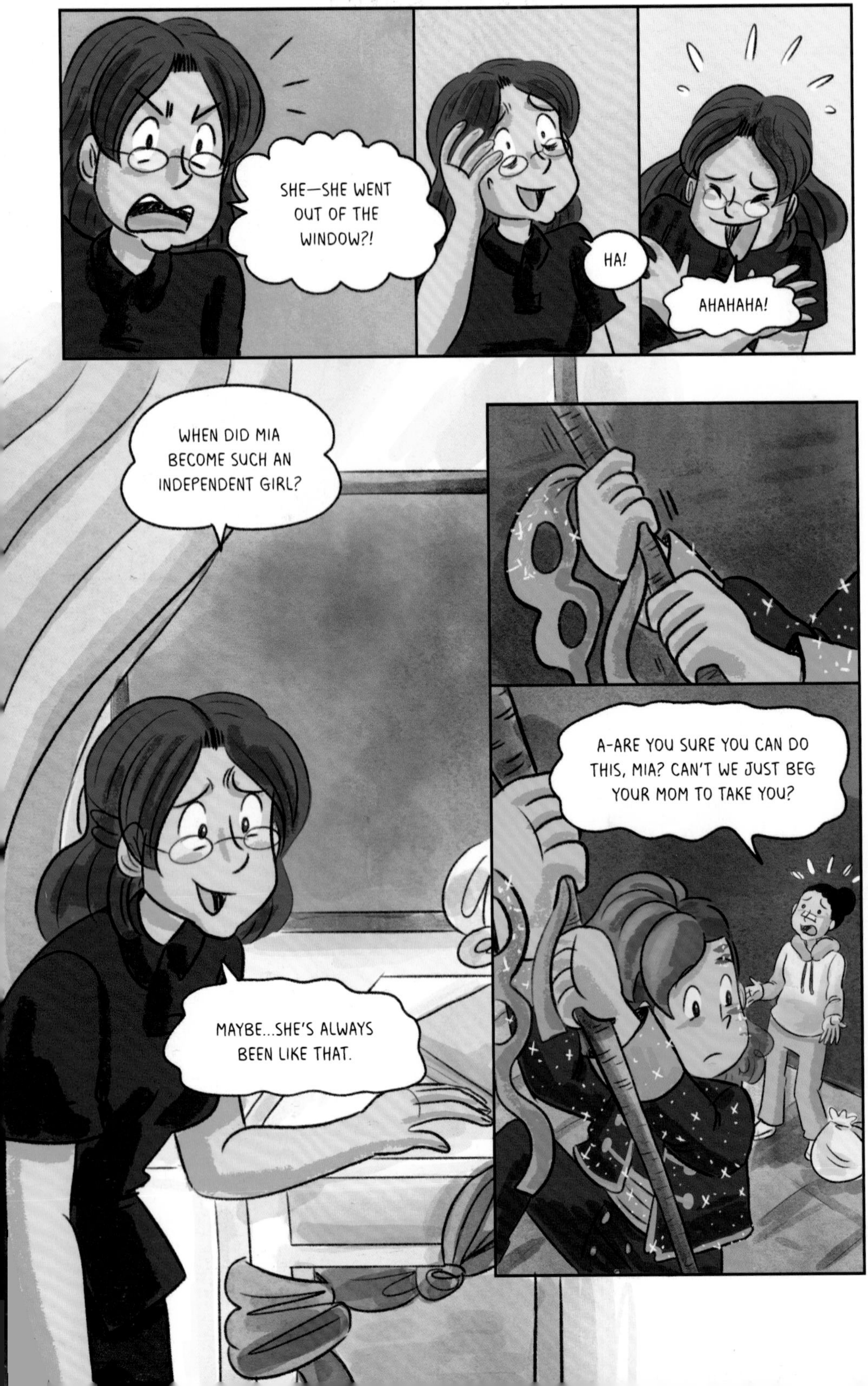
SHE—SHE WENT OUT OF THE WINDOW?!
HA!
AHAHAHA!
WHEN DID MIA BECOME SUCH AN INDEPENDENT GIRL?
MAYBE...SHE'S ALWAYS BEEN LIKE THAT.
A-ARE YOU SURE YOU CAN DO THIS, MIA? CAN'T WE JUST BEG YOUR MOM TO TAKE YOU?

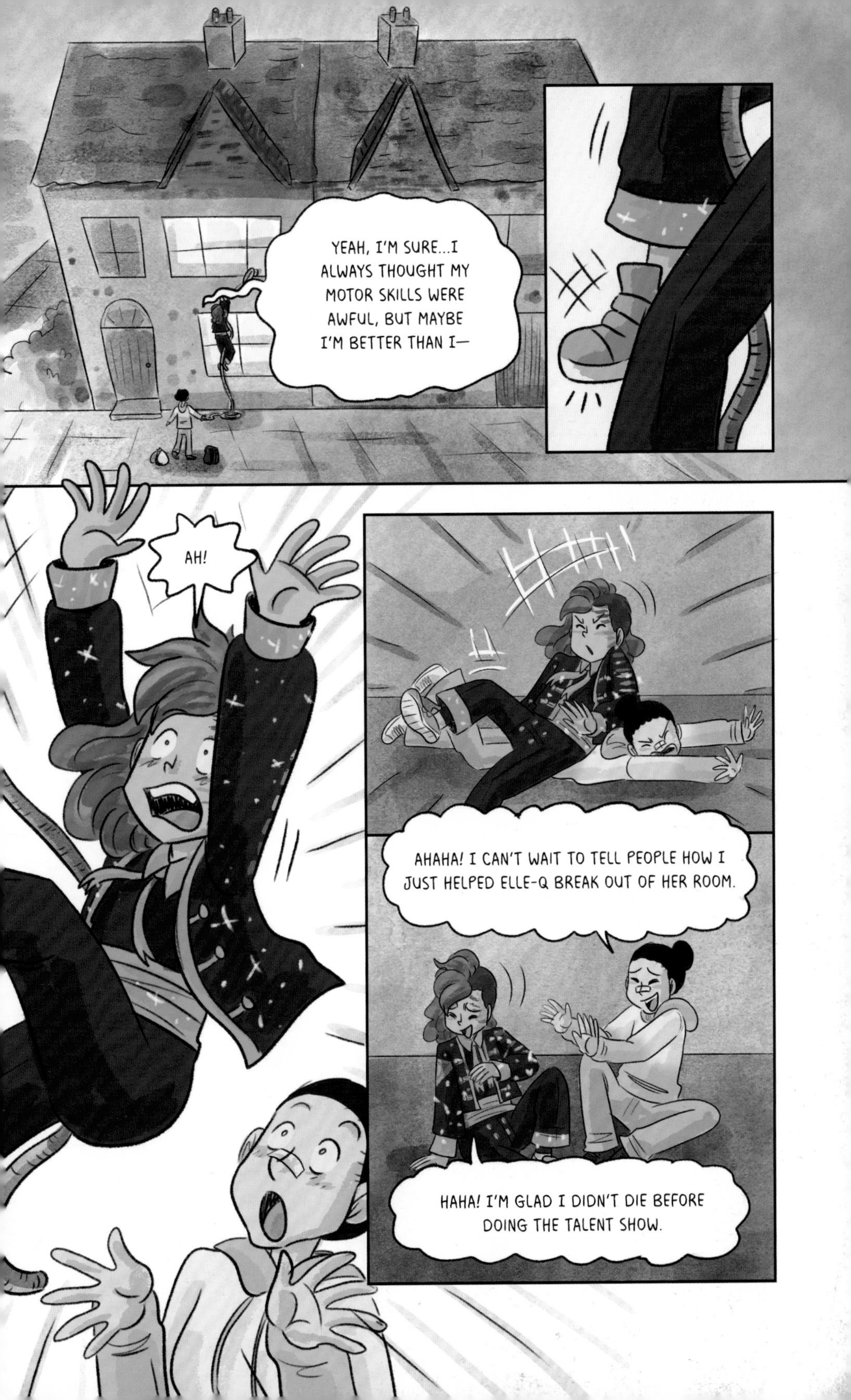
YEAH, I'M SURE...I ALWAYS THOUGHT MY MOTOR SKILLS WERE AWFUL, BUT MAYBE I'M BETTER THAN I—
AH!
AHAHA! I CAN'T WAIT TO TELL PEOPLE HOW I JUST HELPED ELLE-Q BREAK OUT OF HER ROOM.
HAHA! I'M GLAD I DIDN'T DIE BEFORE DOING THE TALENT SHOW.

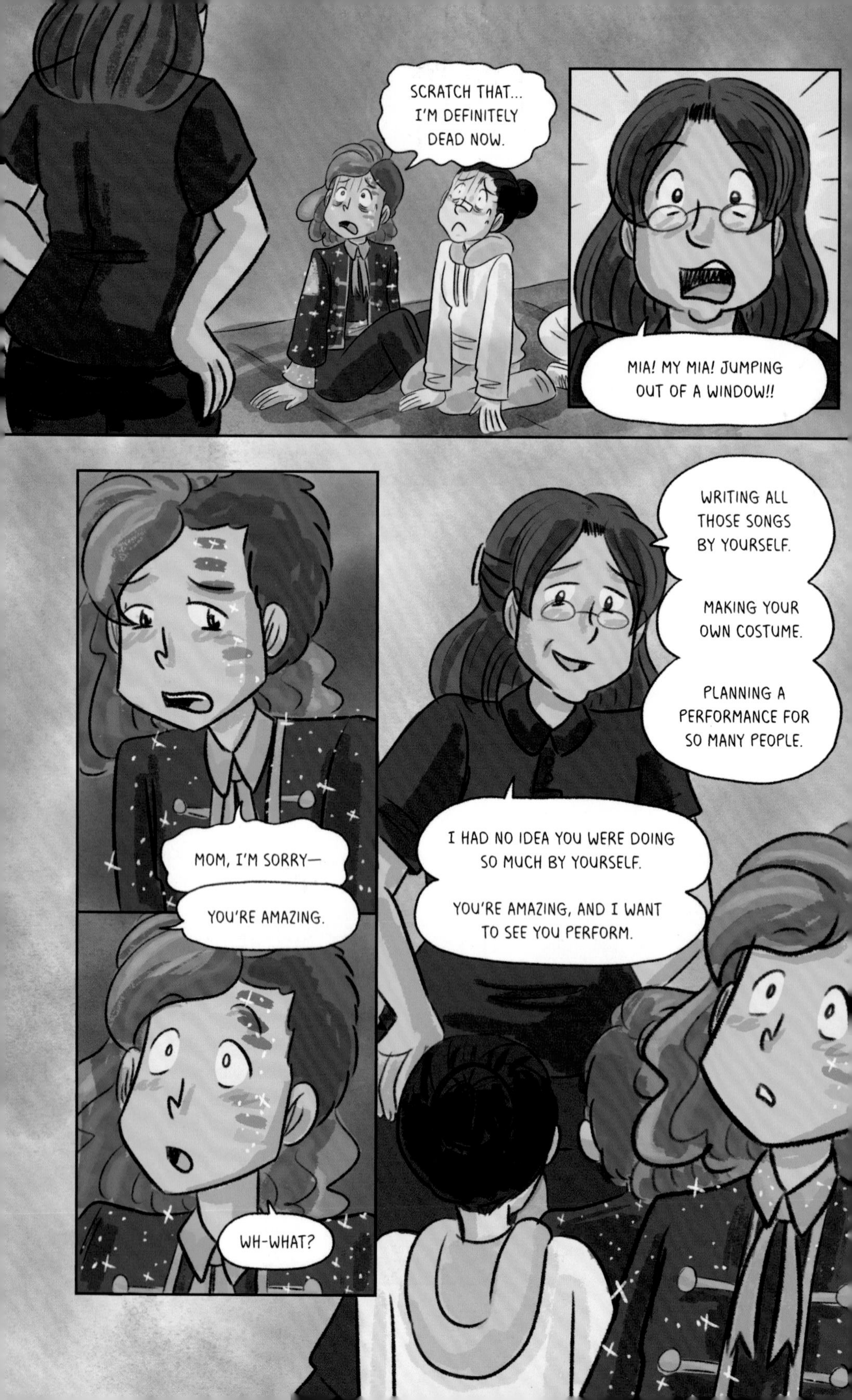
SCRATCH THAT... I'M DEFINITELY DEAD NOW.
MIA! MY MIA! JUMPING OUT OF A WINDOW!!
WRITING ALL THOSE SONGS BY YOURSELF.
MAKING YOUR OWN COSTUME.
PLANNING A PERFORMANCE FOR SO MANY PEOPLE.
MOM, I'M SORRY—
YOU'RE AMAZING.
I HAD NO IDEA YOU WERE DOING SO MUCH BY YOURSELF.
YOU'RE AMAZING, AND I WANT TO SEE YOU PERFORM.
WH-WHAT?

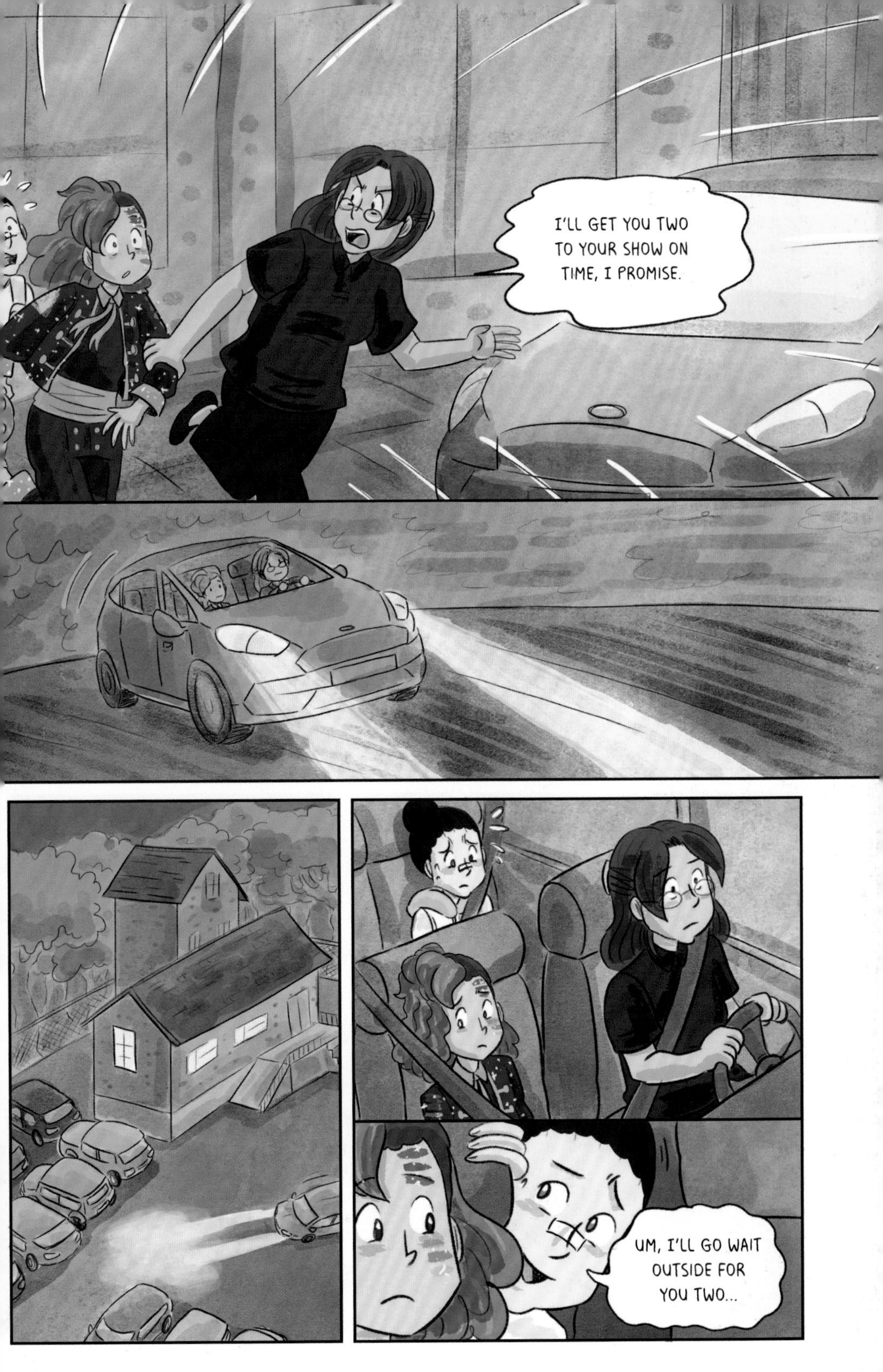
I'LL GET YOU TWO TO YOUR SHOW ON TIME, I PROMISE.
UM, I'LL GO WAIT OUTSIDE FOR YOU TWO...

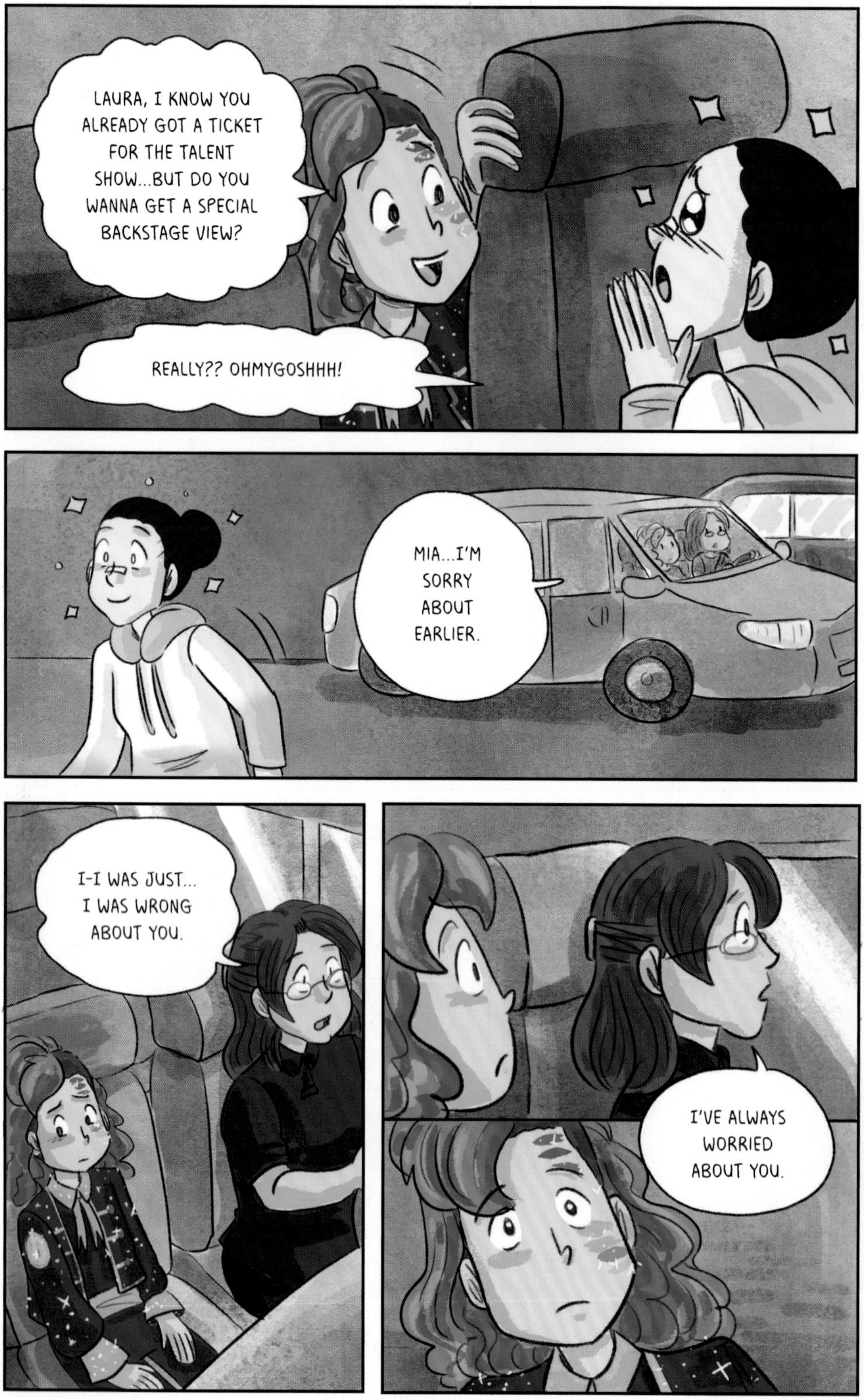
LAURA, I KNOW YOU ALREADY GOT A TICKET FOR THE TALENT SHOW...BUT DO YOU WANNA GET A SPECIAL BACKSTAGE VIEW?
REALLY?? OHMYGOSHHH!
MIA...I'M SORRY ABOUT EARLIER.
I-I WAS JUST... I WAS WRONG ABOUT YOU.
I'VE ALWAYS WORRIED ABOUT YOU.

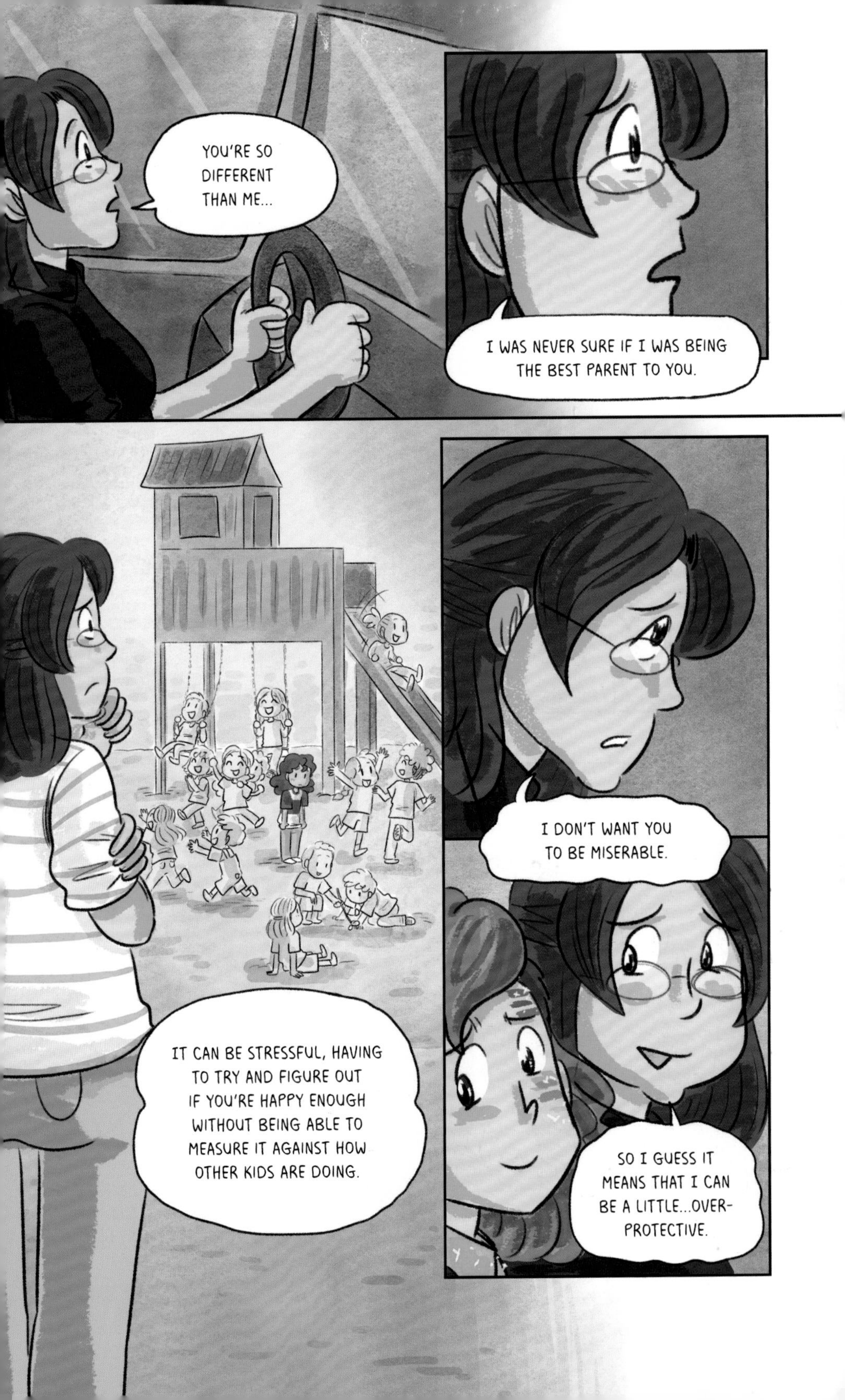
YOU'RE SO DIFFERENT THAN ME...
I WAS NEVER SURE IF I WAS BEING THE BEST PARENT TO YOU.
IT CAN BE STRESSFUL, HAVING TO TRY AND FIGURE OUT IF YOU'RE HAPPY ENOUGH WITHOUT BEING ABLE TO MEASURE IT AGAINST HOW OTHER KIDS ARE DOING.
I DON'T WANT YOU TO BE MISERABLE.
SO I GUESS IT MEANS THAT I CAN BE A LITTLE...OVER-PROTECTIVE.

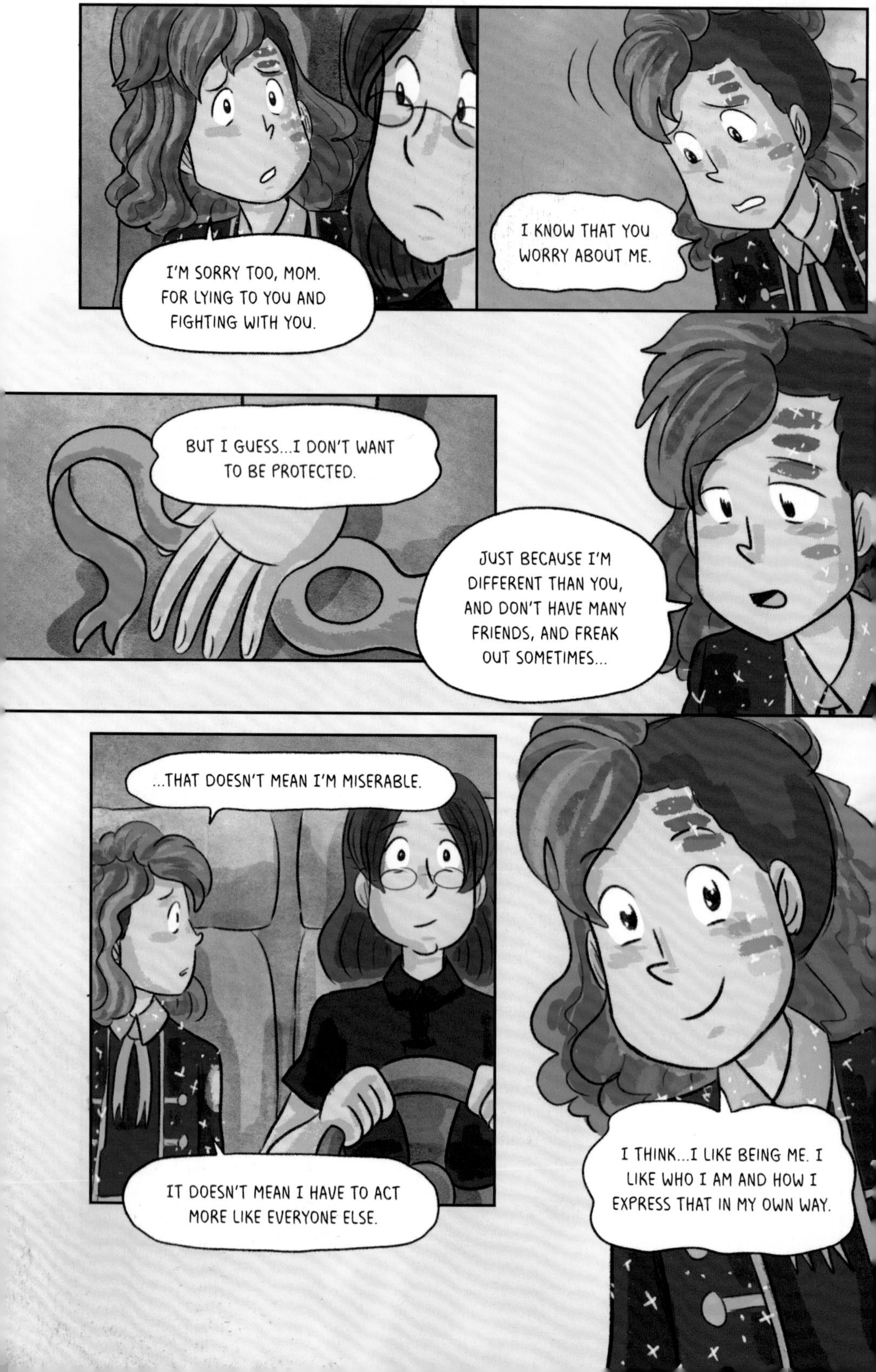
I'M SORRY TOO, MOM. FOR LYING TO YOU AND FIGHTING WITH YOU.
I KNOW THAT YOU WORRY ABOUT ME.
BUT I GUESS...I DON'T WANT TO BE PROTECTED.
JUST BECAUSE I'M DIFFERENT THAN YOU, AND DON'T HAVE MANY FRIENDS, AND FREAK OUT SOMETIMES...
...THAT DOESN'T MEAN I'M MISERABLE.
IT DOESN'T MEAN I HAVE TO ACT MORE LIKE EVERYONE ELSE.
I THINK...I LIKE BEING ME. I LIKE WHO I AM AND HOW I EXPRESS THAT IN MY OWN WAY.

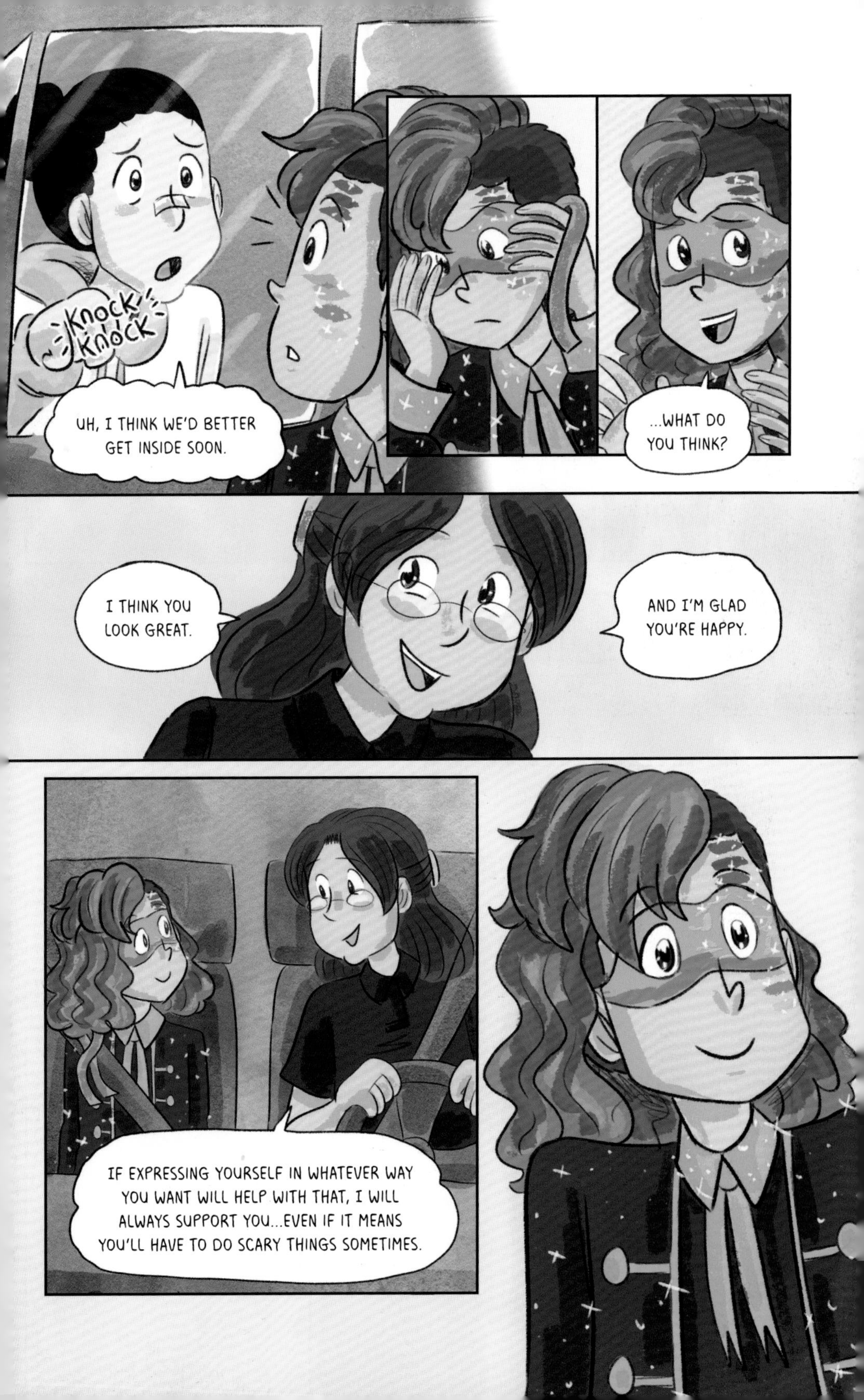
KNOCK KNOCK
UH, I THINK WE'D BETTER GET INSIDE SOON.
...WHAT DO YOU THINK?
I THINK YOU LOOK GREAT.
AND I'M GLAD YOU'RE HAPPY.
IF EXPRESSING YOURSELF IN WHATEVER WAY YOU WANT WILL HELP WITH THAT, I WILL ALWAYS SUPPORT YOU...EVEN IF IT MEANS YOU'LL HAVE TO DO SCARY THINGS SOMETIMES.

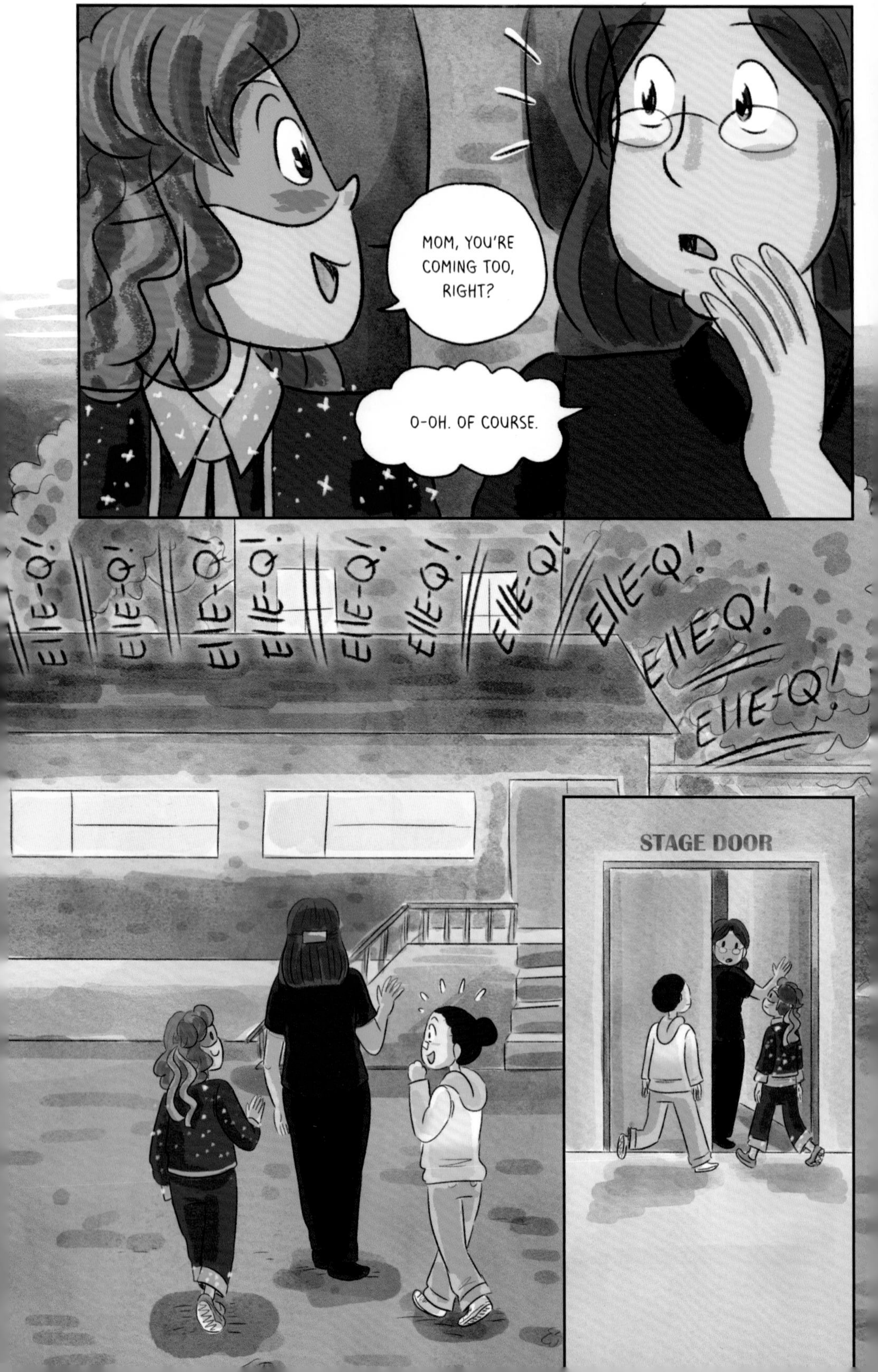
MOM, YOU'RE COMING TOO, RIGHT?
O-OH. OF COURSE.
ELLE-Q! ELLE-Q! ELLE-Q! ELLE-Q! ELLE-Q! ELLE-Q! ELLE-Q! ELLE-Q! ELLE-Q! ELLE-Q!
STAGE DOOR

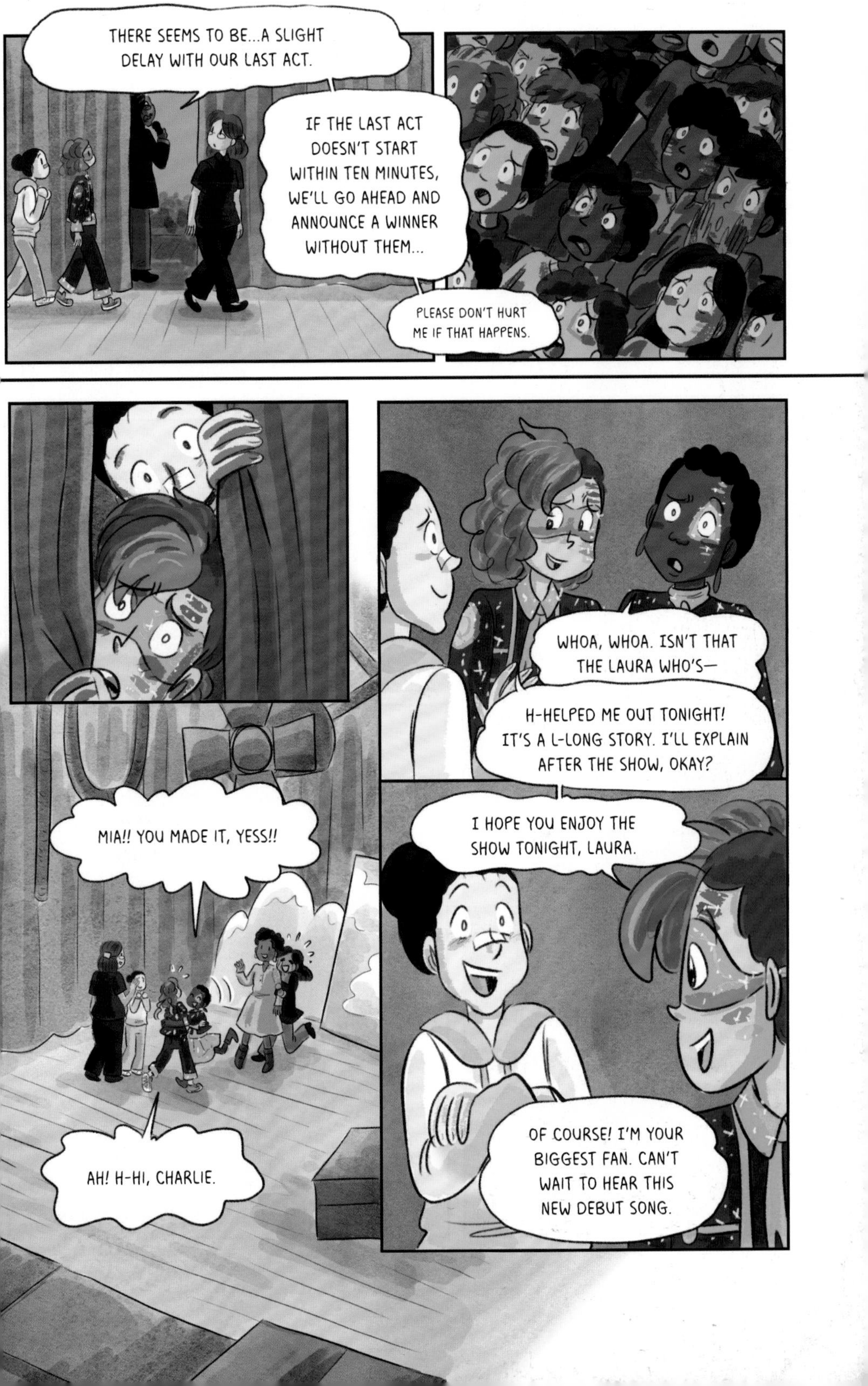
THERE SEEMS TO BE...A SLIGHT DELAY WITH OUR LAST ACT.
IF THE LAST ACT DOESN'T START WITHIN TEN MINUTES, WE'LL GO AHEAD AND ANNOUNCE A WINNER WITHOUT THEM...
PLEASE DON'T HURT ME IF THAT HAPPENS.
WHOA, WHOA. ISN'T THAT THE LAURA WHO'S—
H-HELPED ME OUT TONIGHT! IT'S A L-LONG STORY. I'LL EXPLAIN AFTER THE SHOW, OKAY?
MIA!! YOU MADE IT, YESS!!
AH! H-HI, CHARLIE.
I HOPE YOU ENJOY THE SHOW TONIGHT, LAURA.
OF COURSE! I'M YOUR BIGGEST FAN. CAN'T WAIT TO HEAR THIS NEW DEBUT SONG.

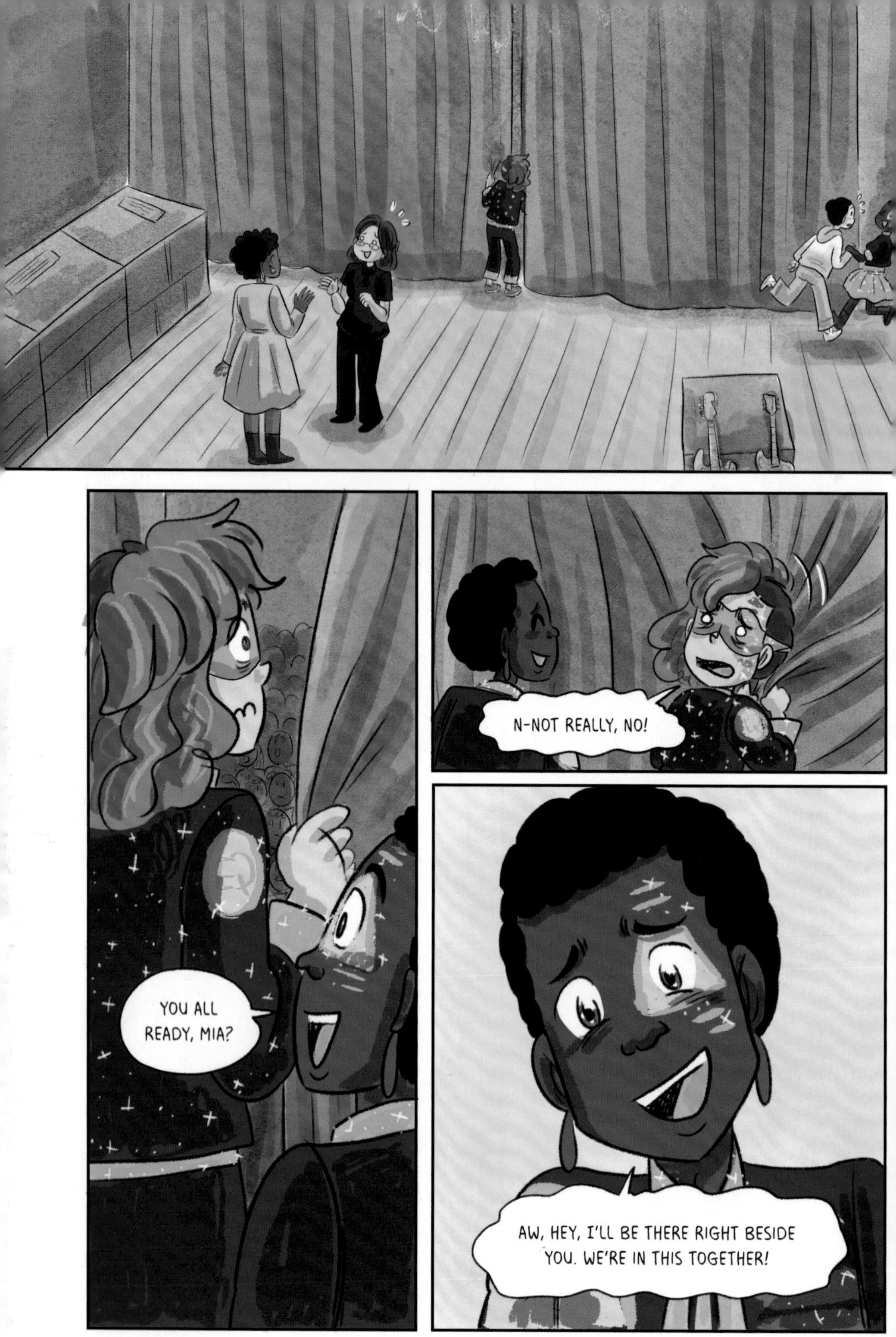
YOU ALL READY, MIA?
N-NOT REALLY, NO!
AW, HEY, I'LL BE THERE RIGHT BESIDE YOU. WE'RE IN THIS TOGETHER!

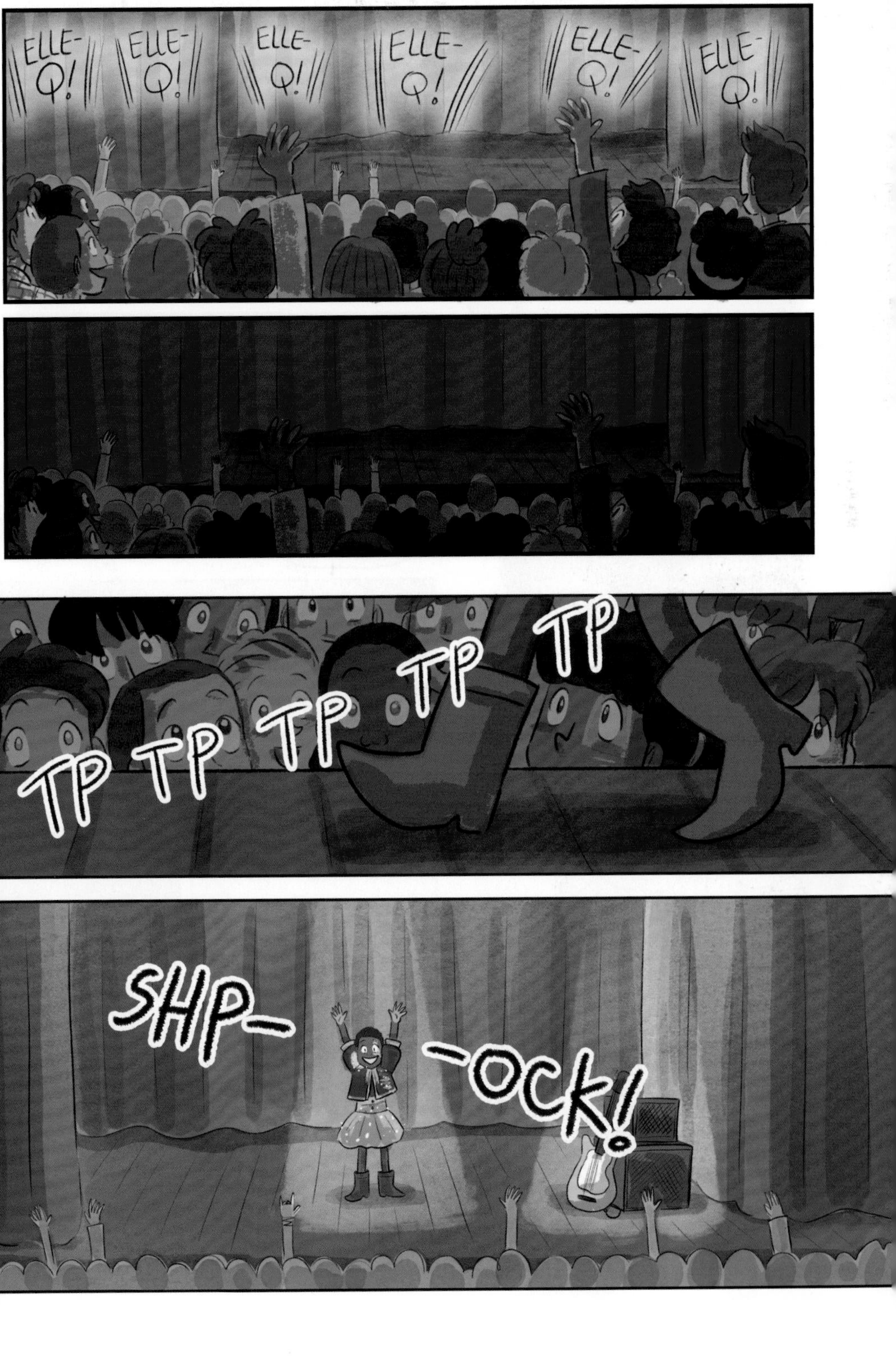
ELLE-Q!
ELLE-Q!
ELLE-Q!
ELLE-Q!
ELLE-Q!
ELLE-Q!
TP TP TP TP TP
SHP-
-OCK!

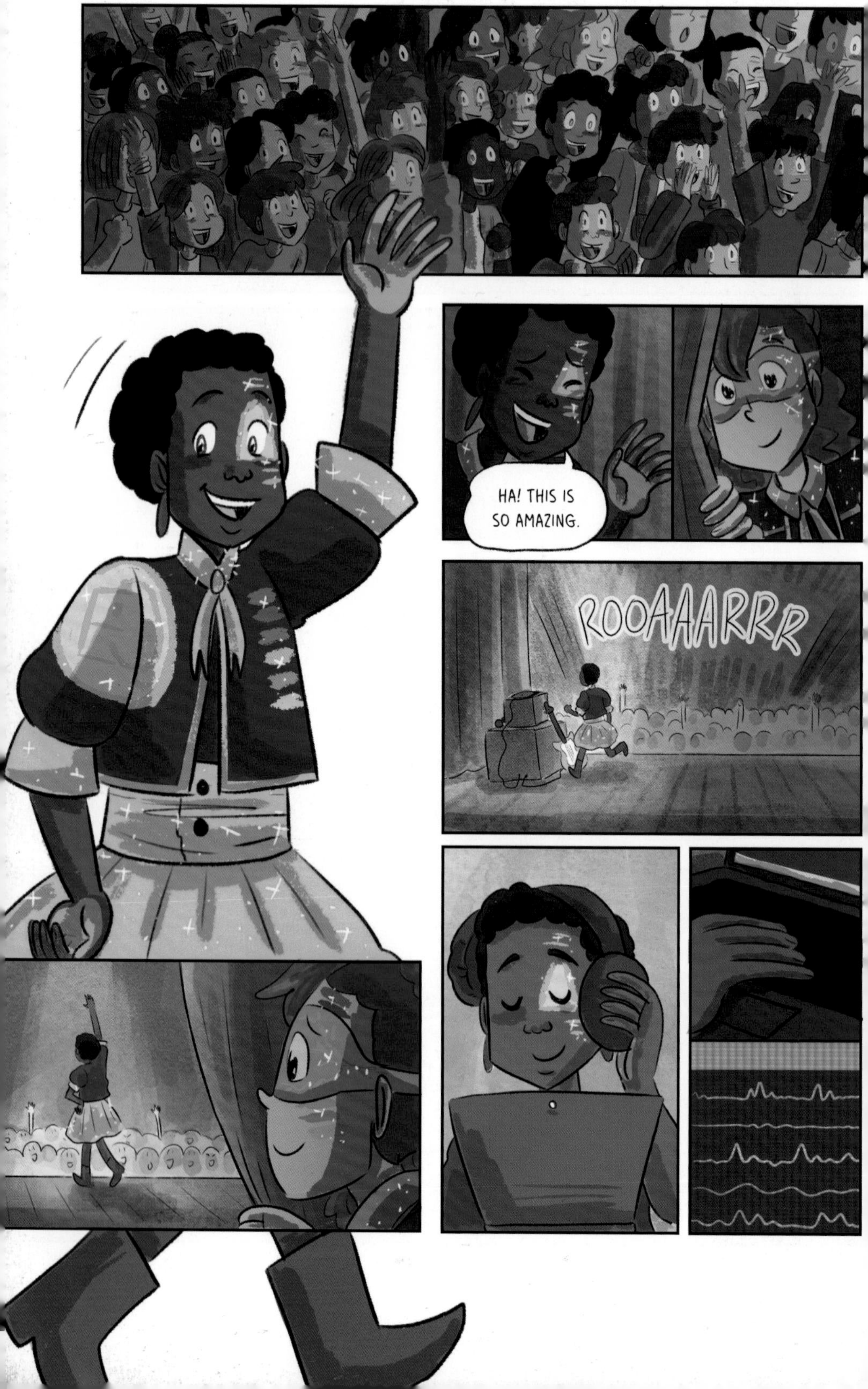
HA! THIS IS SO AMAZING.
ROOAAARRR

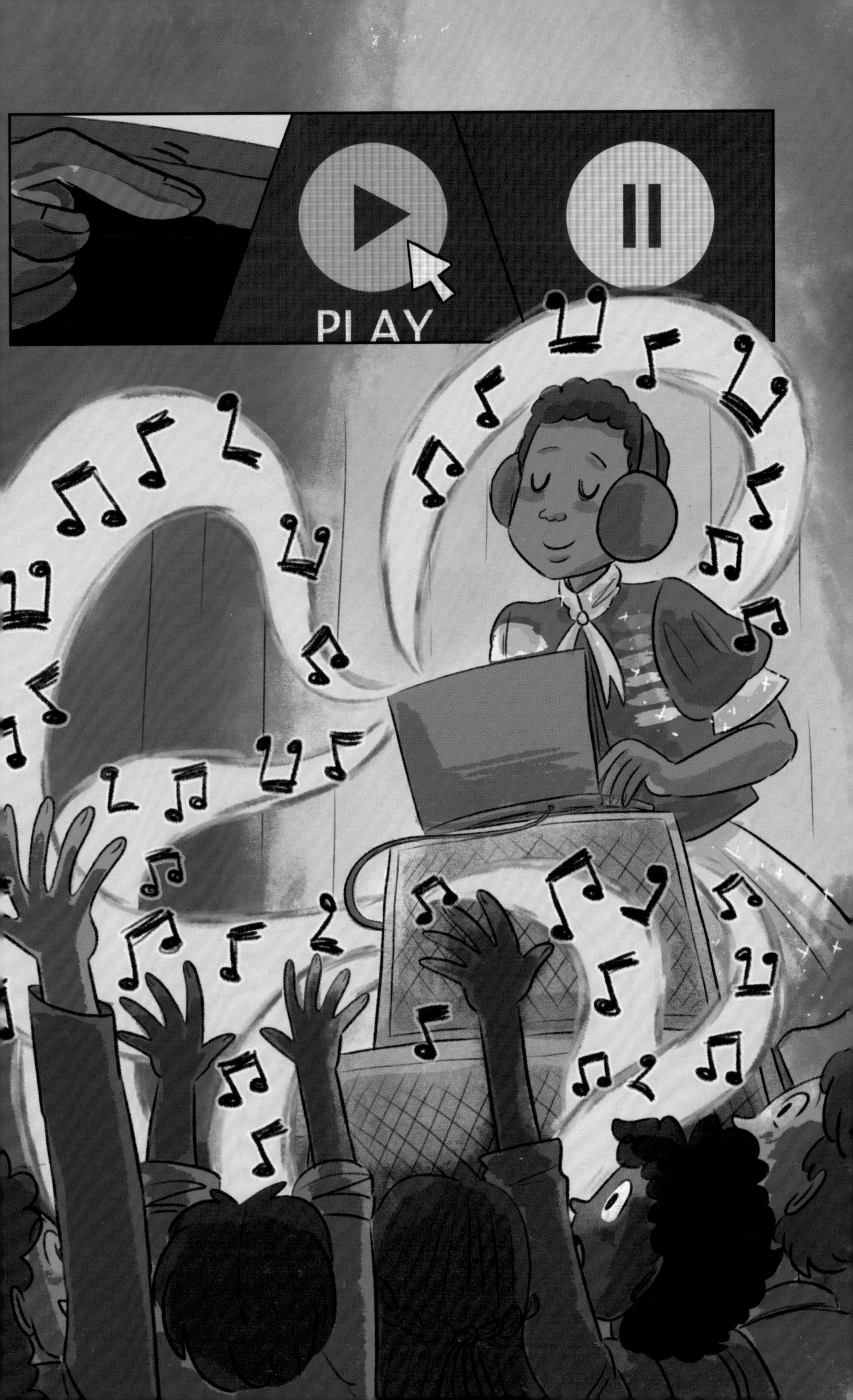
PLAY

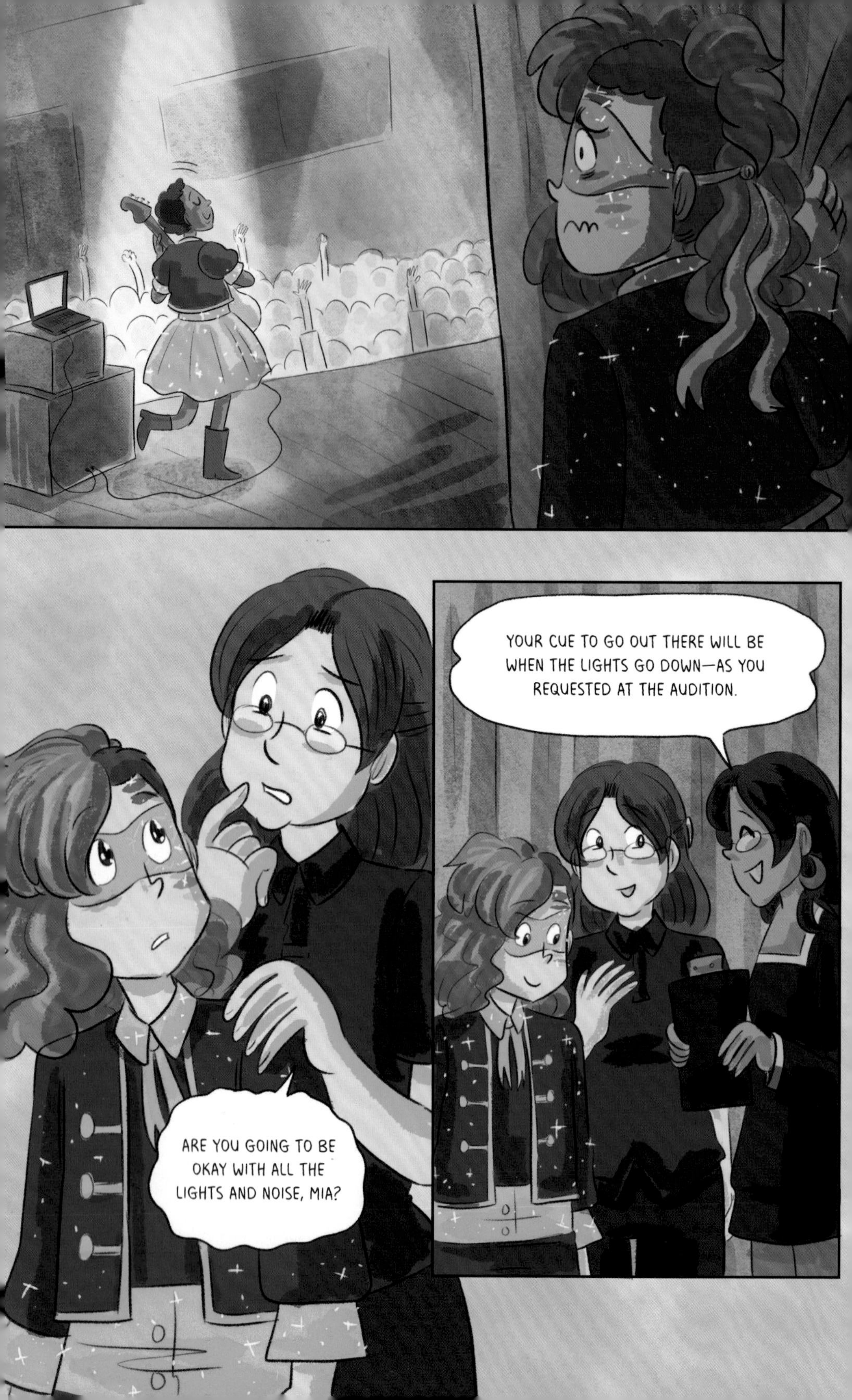
YOUR CUE TO GO OUT THERE WILL BE WHEN THE LIGHTS GO DOWN—AS YOU REQUESTED AT THE AUDITION.
ARE YOU GOING TO BE OKAY WITH ALL THE LIGHTS AND NOISE, MIA?

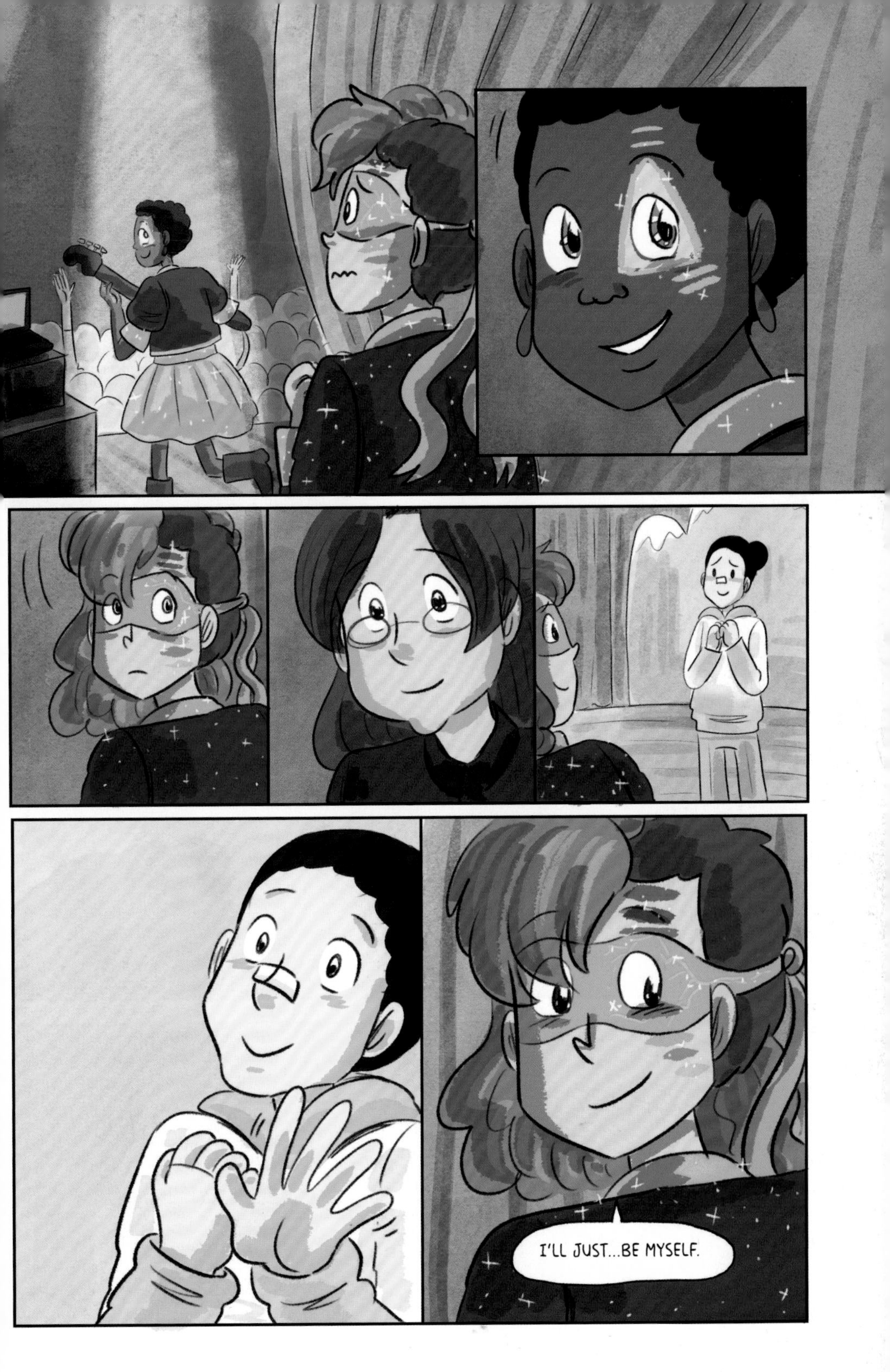
I'LL JUST...BE MYSELF.

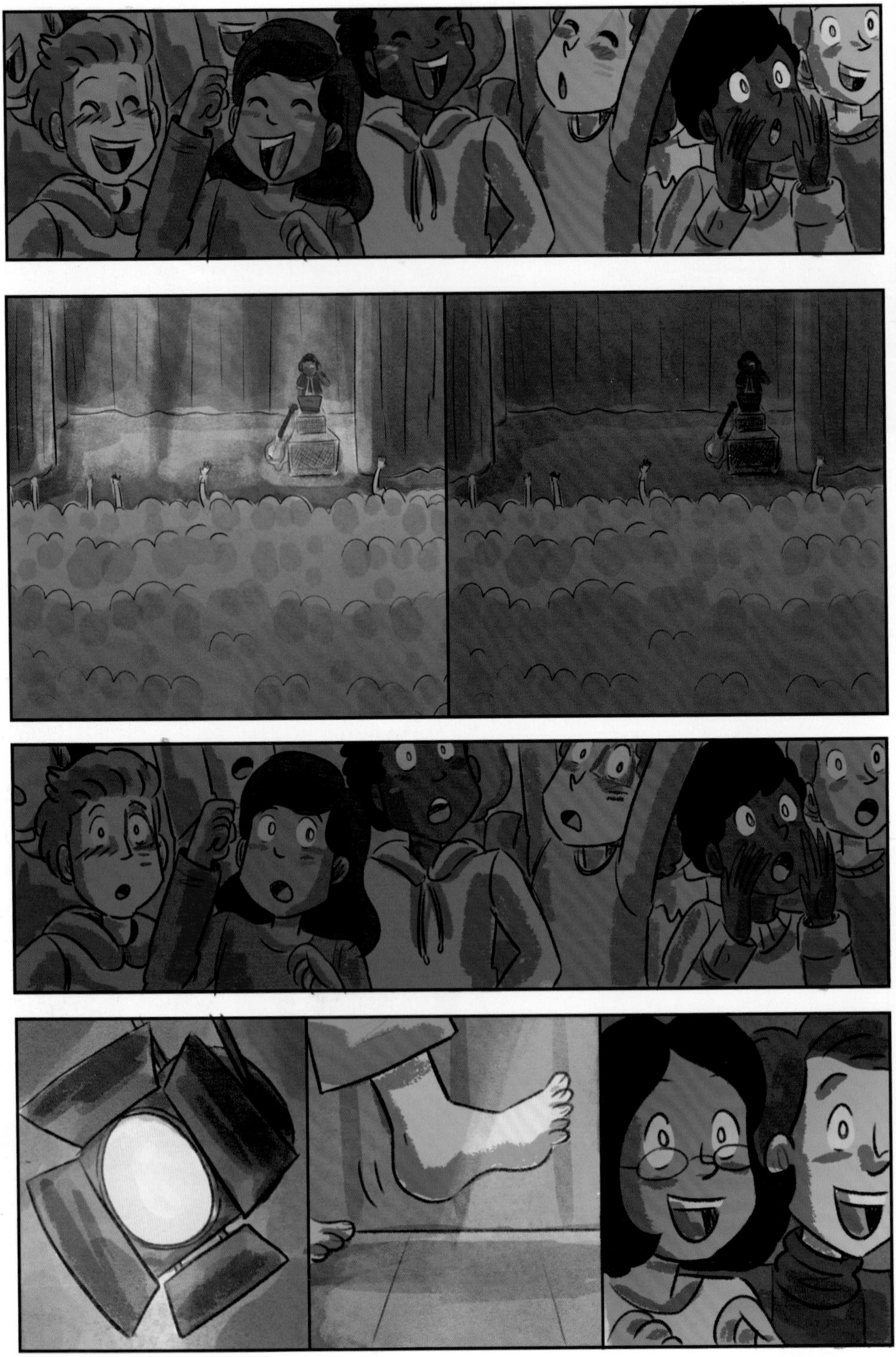

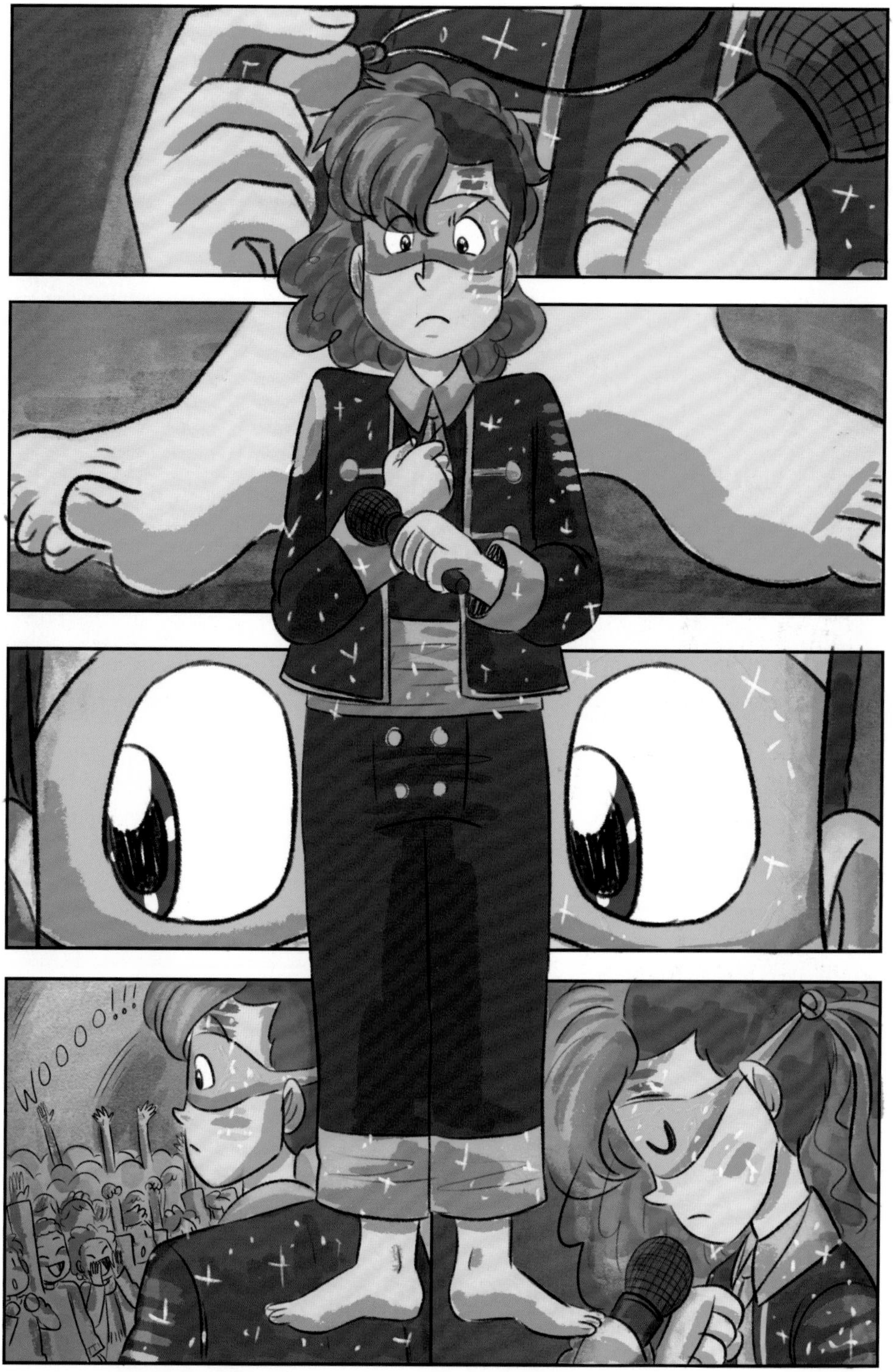
WOOOO!!!

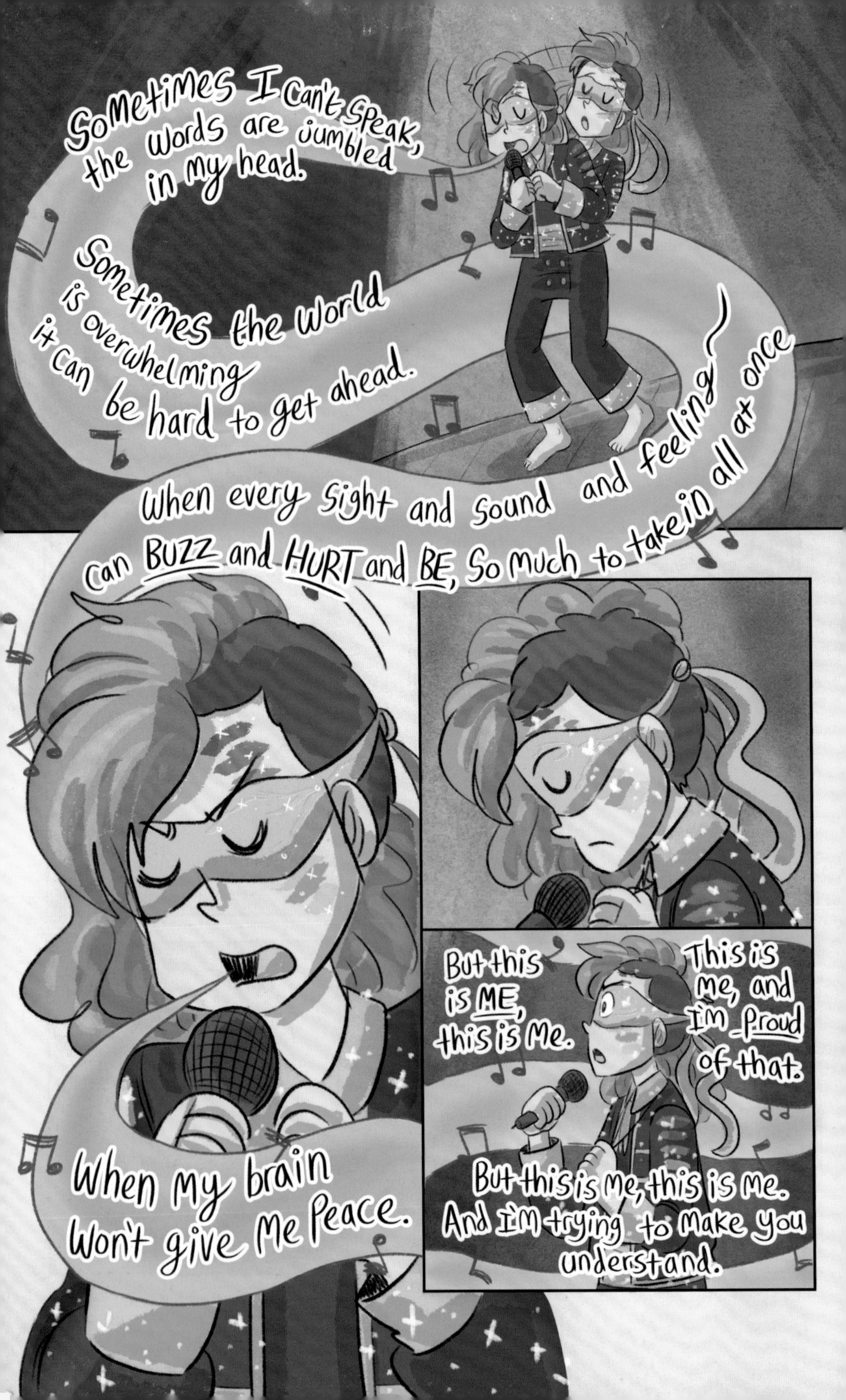
Sometimes I can't speak, the words are jumbled in my head.
Sometimes the world is overwhelming it can be hard to get ahead.
When every sight and sound and feeling~ can BUZZ and HURT and BE, so much to take in all at once
When my brain won't give me peace.
But this is ME, this is me.
This is me, and I'm proud of that.
But this is me, this is me. And I'm trying to make you understand.

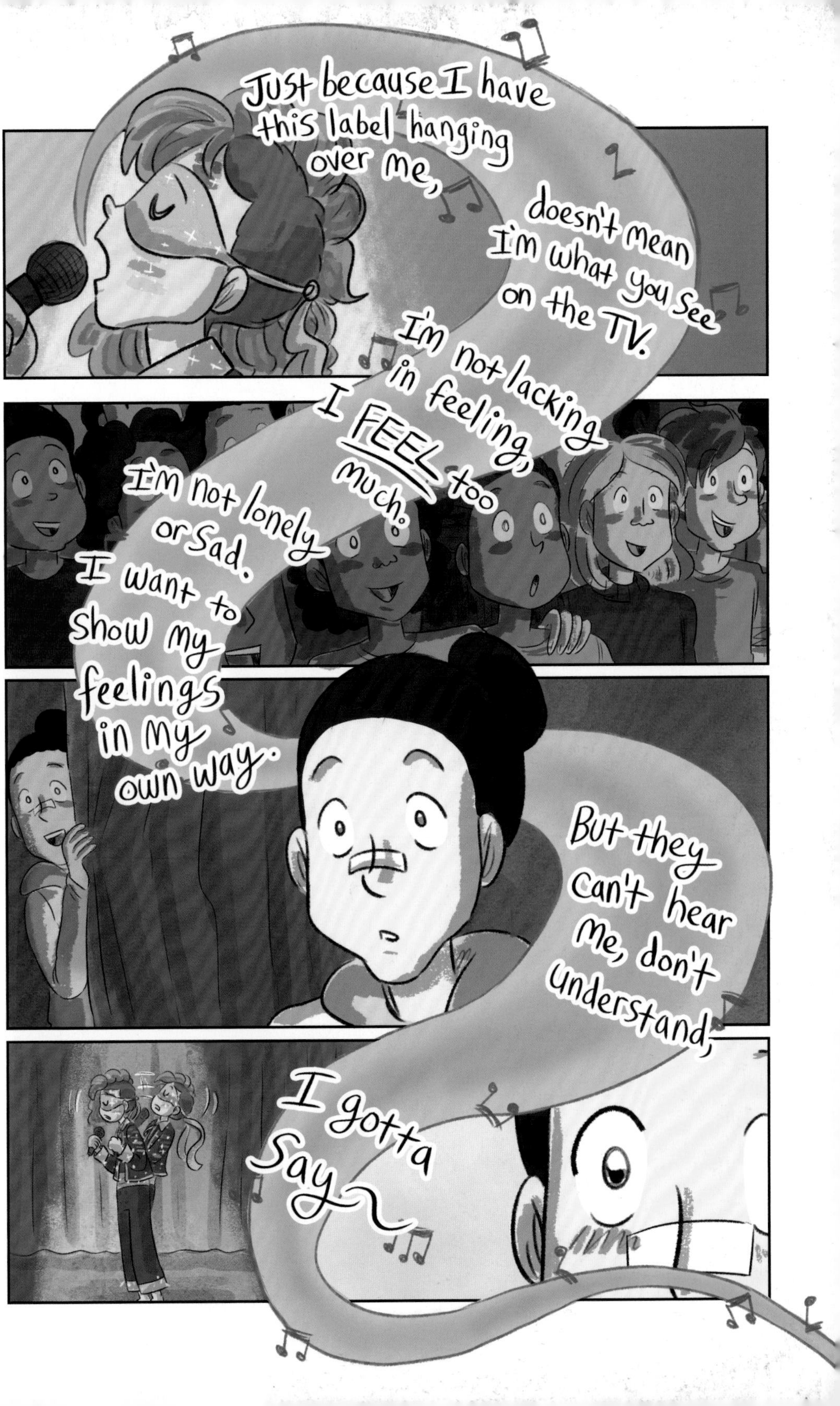
Just because I have this label hanging over me,
doesn't mean I'm what you see on the TV.
I'm not lacking in feeling, I FEEL too much.
I'm not lonely or sad. I want to show my feelings in my own way.
But they can't hear me, don't understand,
I gotta say~

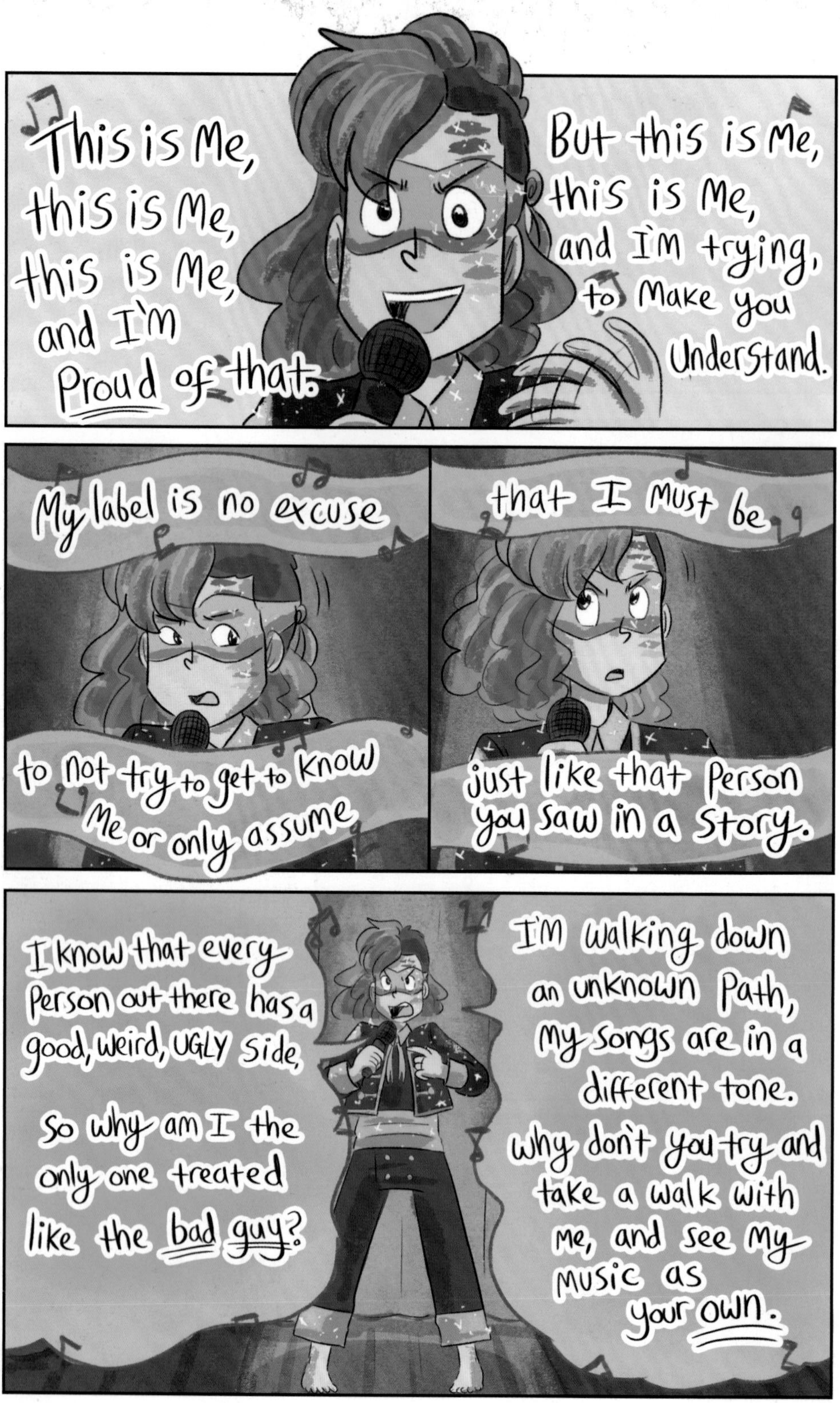
This is Me, this is Me, this is Me, and I'm Proud of that.
But this is Me, this is Me, and I'm trying, to Make you Understand.
My label is no excuse
to not try to get to know me or only assume
that I must be
just like that person you saw in a story.
I know that every person out there has a good, weird, UGLY side,
So why am I the only one treated like the bad guy?
I'm walking down an unknown path, my songs are in a different tone.
Why don't you try and take a walk with me, and see my music as your own.

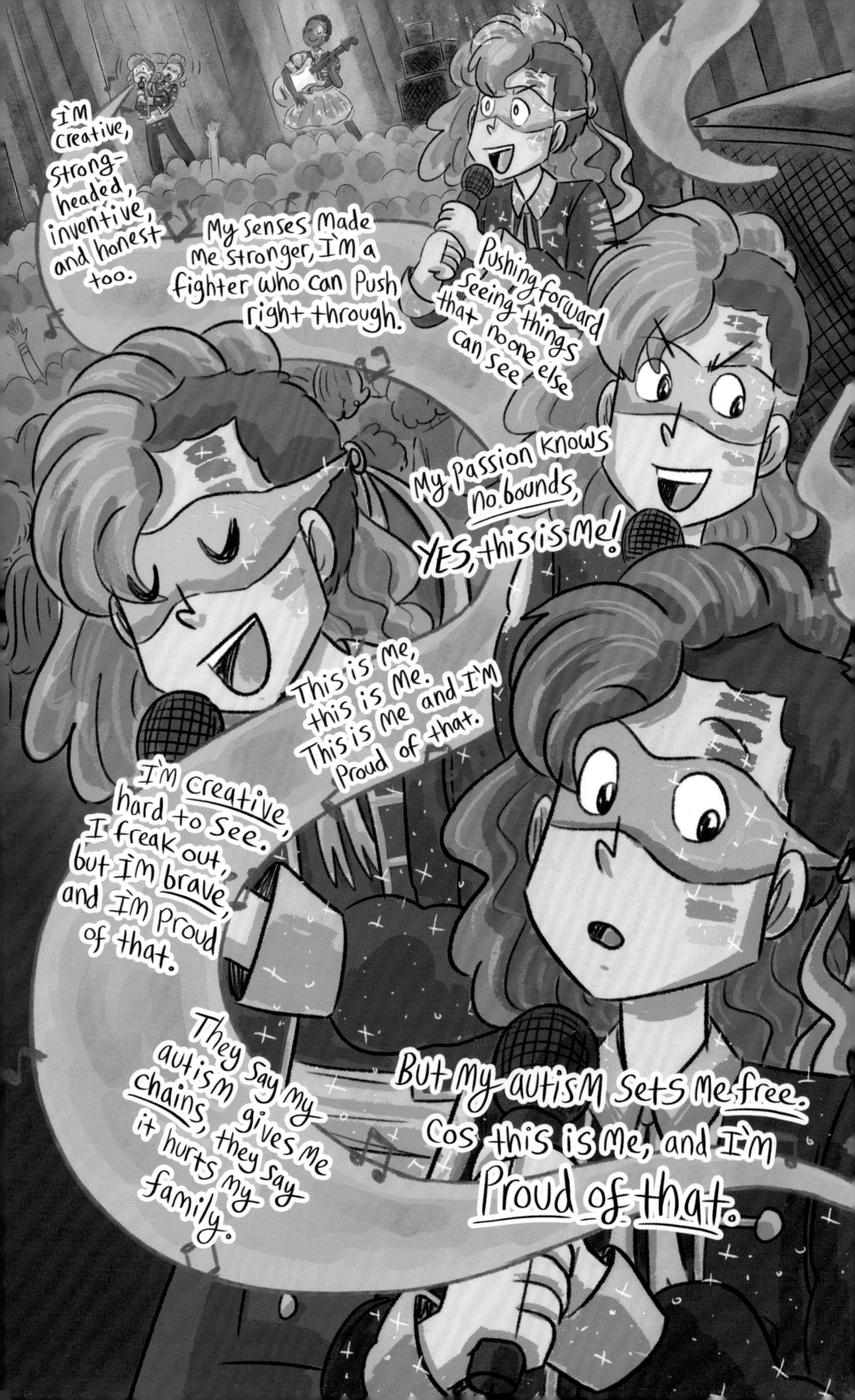

I'M creative, strong-headed, inventive, and honest too.
My senses made me stronger, I'm a fighter who can push right through.
Pushing forward seeing things that no one else can see
My passion knows no bounds, YES, this is me!
This is me, this is me. This is me and I'M proud of that.
I'M creative, hard to see. I freak out, but I'M brave, and I'M proud of that.
They say my autism gives me chains, they say it hurts my family.
But my autism sets me free. Cos this is me, and I'M proud of that.

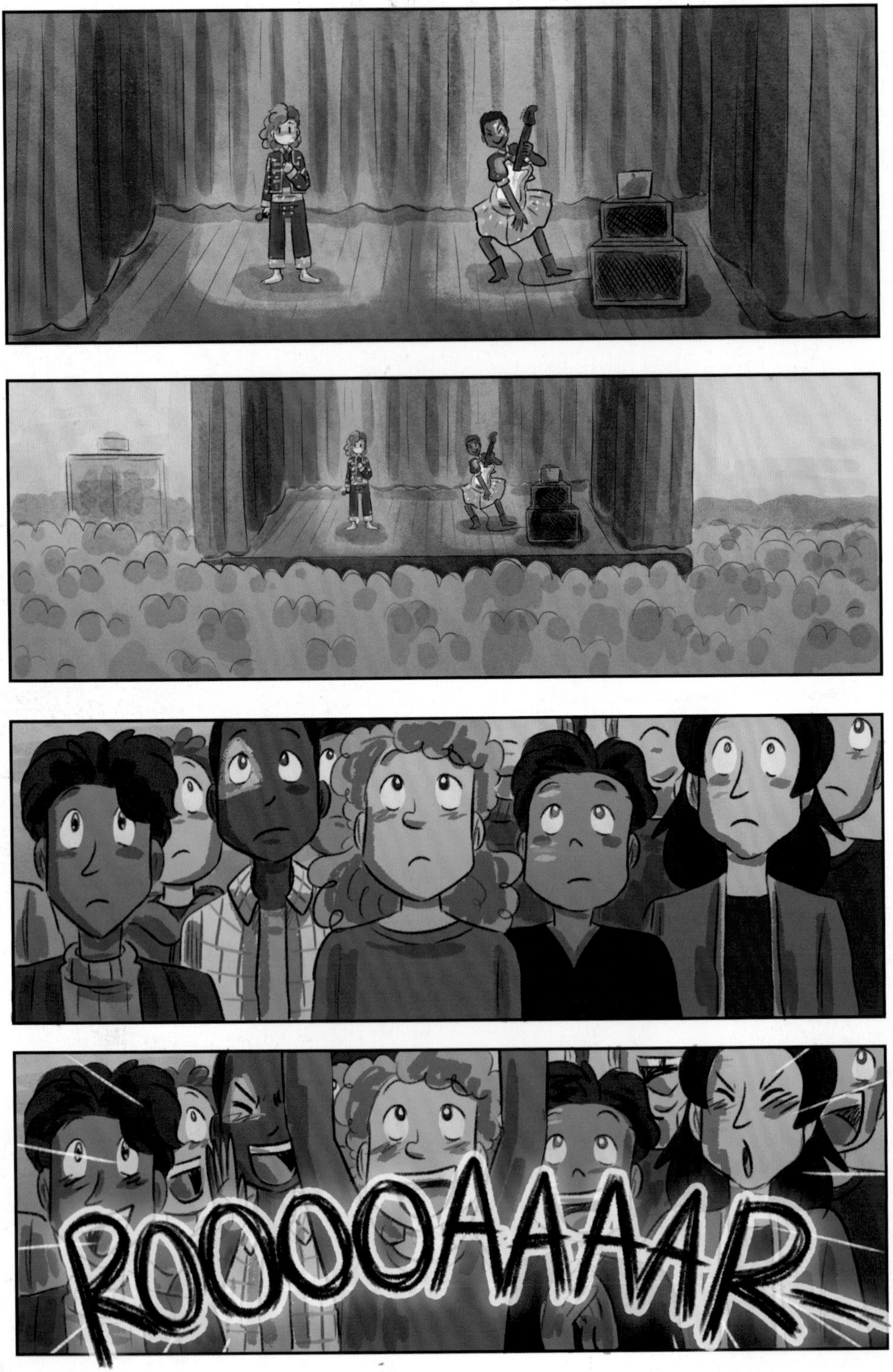
ROOOOAAAAR

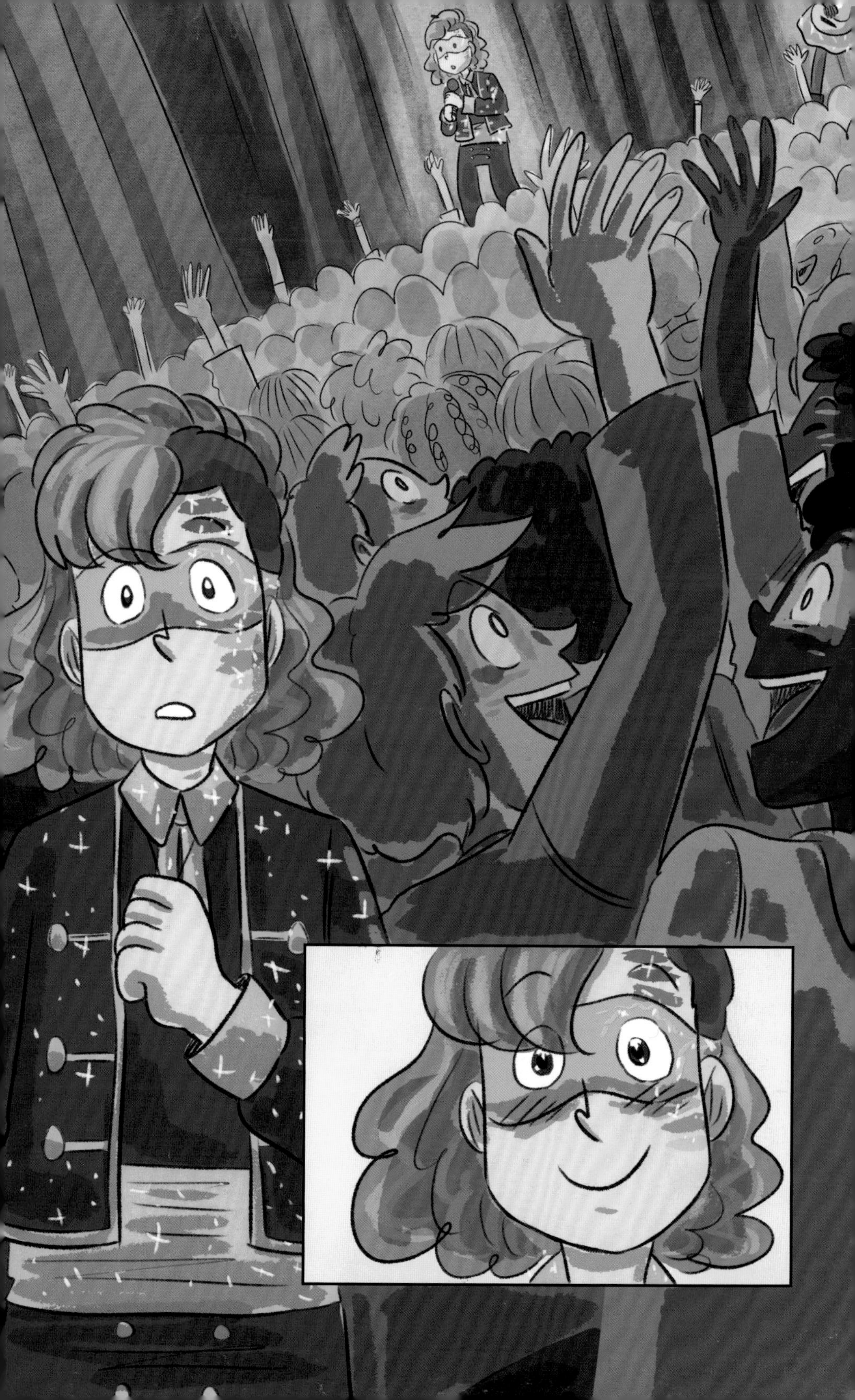

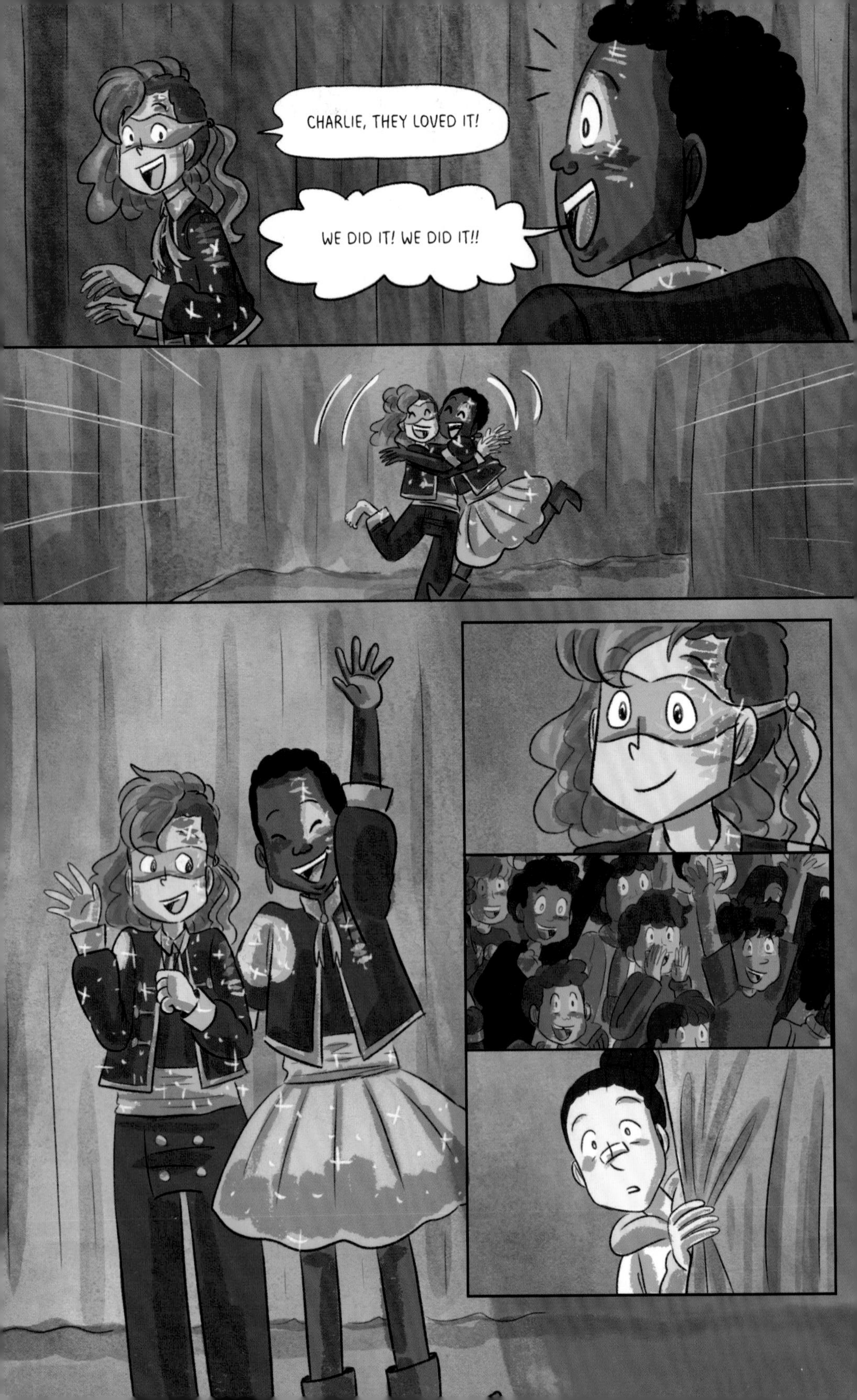
CHARLIE, THEY LOVED IT!
WE DID IT! WE DID IT!!

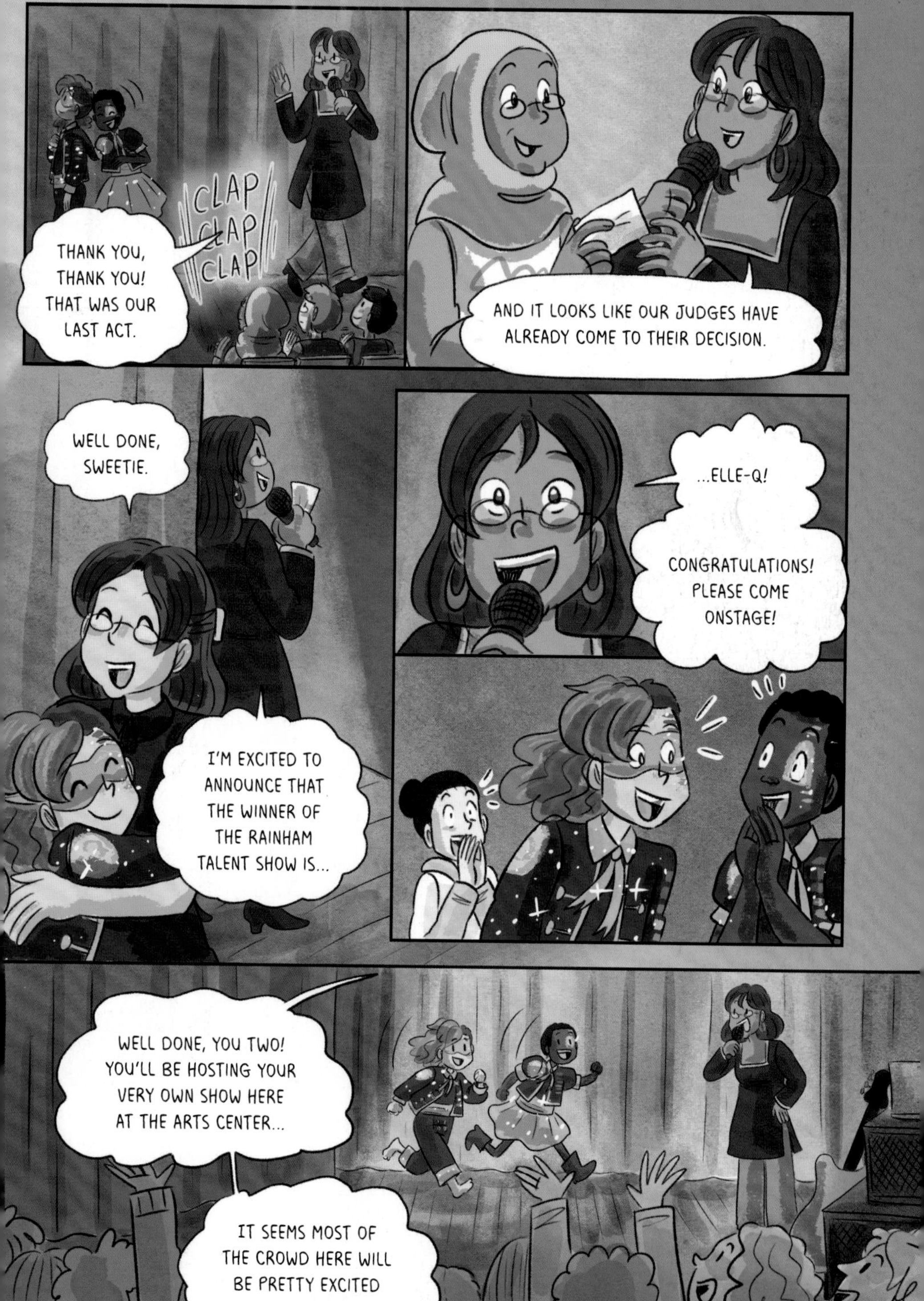
THANK YOU, THANK YOU! THAT WAS OUR LAST ACT.
CLAP CLAP CLAP
AND IT LOOKS LIKE OUR JUDGES HAVE ALREADY COME TO THEIR DECISION.
WELL DONE, SWEETIE.
I'M EXCITED TO ANNOUNCE THAT THE WINNER OF THE RAINHAM TALENT SHOW IS...
...ELLE-Q!
CONGRATULATIONS! PLEASE COME ONSTAGE!
WELL DONE, YOU TWO! YOU'LL BE HOSTING YOUR VERY OWN SHOW HERE AT THE ARTS CENTER...
IT SEEMS MOST OF THE CROWD HERE WILL BE PRETTY EXCITED ABOUT THAT!

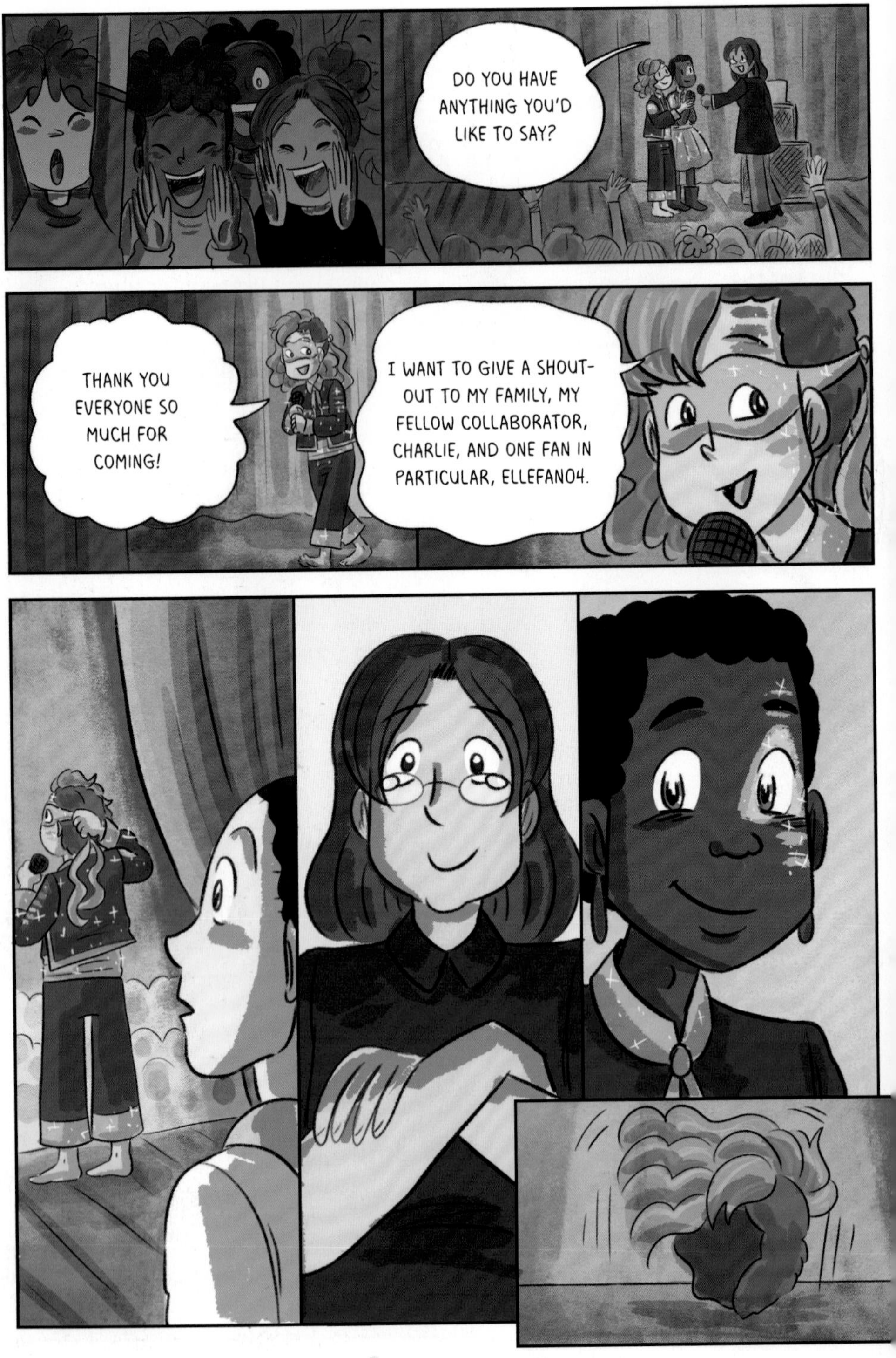
DO YOU HAVE ANYTHING YOU'D LIKE TO SAY?
THANK YOU EVERYONE SO MUCH FOR COMING!
I WANT TO GIVE A SHOUT-OUT TO MY FAMILY, MY FELLOW COLLABORATOR, CHARLIE, AND ONE FAN IN PARTICULAR, ELLEFAN04.

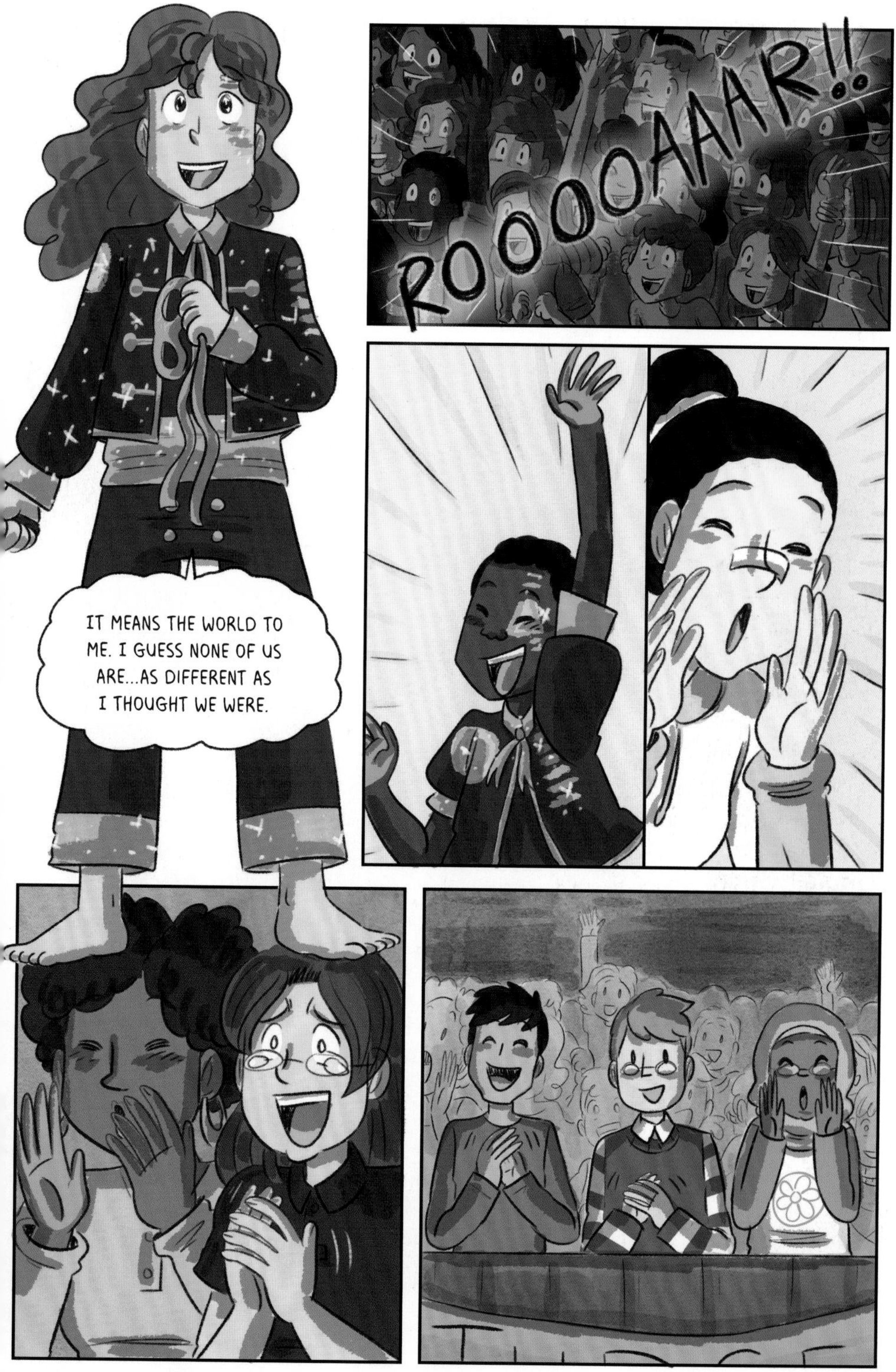
ROOOOAAAR!!
IT MEANS THE WORLD TO ME. I GUESS NONE OF US ARE...AS DIFFERENT AS I THOUGHT WE WERE.

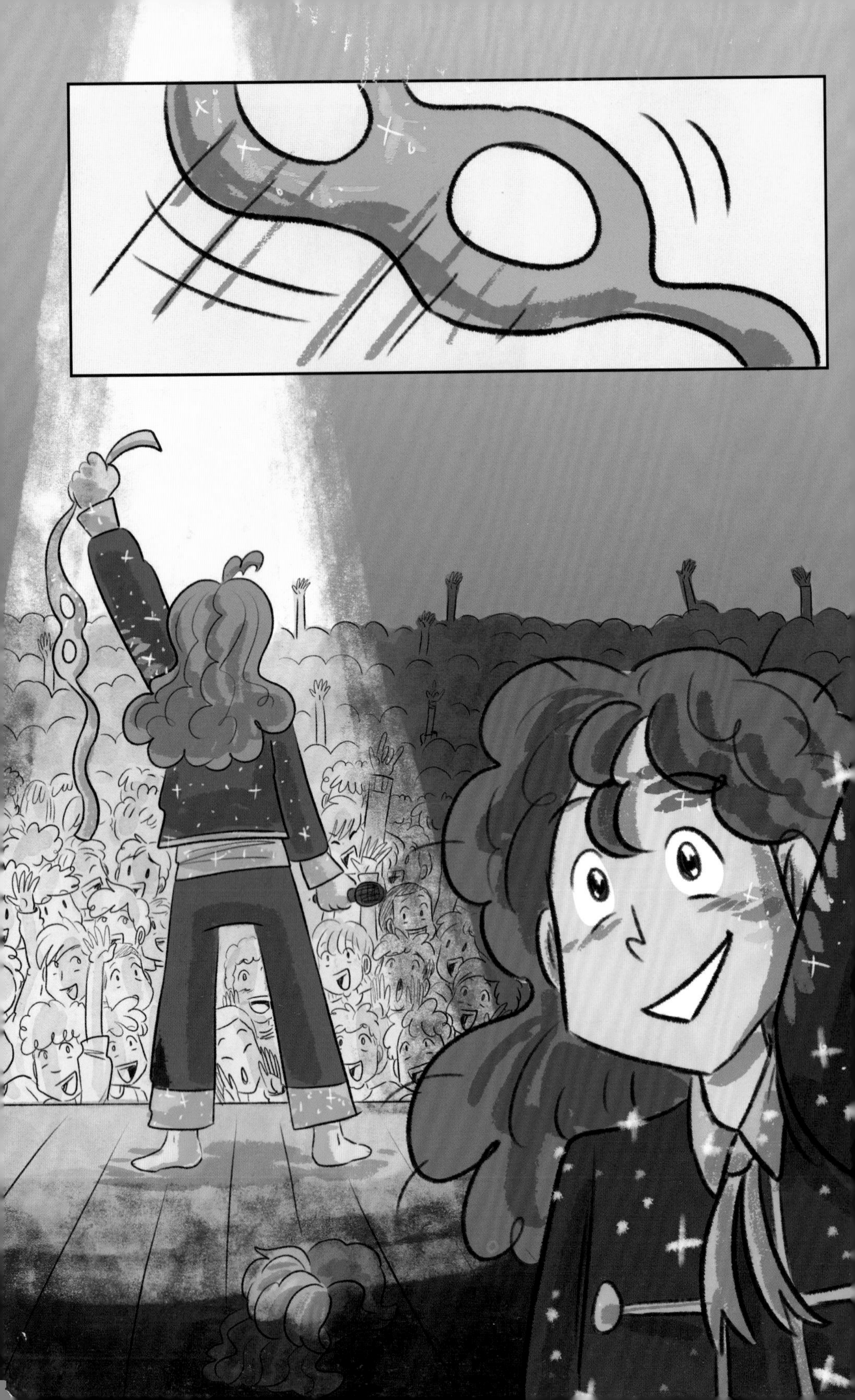